04/2017

READ HER ONCE
AND FALL IN LOVE

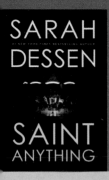

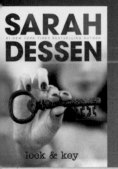

lock & key

along for the ride

this lullaby

just listen

that summer

keeping the moon

the truth
about forever

someone like you

Exposed . . .

"Ruby?"

Nate's voice was low, tentative. I swallowed, thinking how stupid I was, thinking that my mom might have actually come back, when I knew full well that everything she needed she'd taken with her. "I'll be done in a sec," I said to him, hating how my voice was shaking.

"Are you . . . ?" He paused. "Are you okay?"

I nodded, all business. "Yeah. I just have to grab something."

I heard him shift his weight, taking a step, although toward me or away, I wasn't sure, and not knowing this was enough to make me turn around. He was standing in the doorway to the kitchen, the front door open behind him, turning his head slowly, taking it all in. I felt a surge of shame; I'd been so stupid to bring him here. Like I, of all people, didn't know better than to lead a total stranger directly to the point where they could hurt me most, knowing how easily they'd be able to find their way back to it.

Novels by
SARAH DESSEN

SARAH DESSEN

lock and key

speak
An Imprint of Penguin Group (USA)

SPEAK
Published by the Penguin Group
Penguin Group (USA) LLC
375 Hudson Street
New York, New York 10014

USA * Canada * UK * Ireland * Australia
New Zealand * India * South Africa * China

penguin.com
A Penguin Random House Company

First published in the United States of America by Viking,
a division of Penguin Young Readers Group, 2008
Published by Speak, an imprint of Penguin Group (USA) Inc., 2009

THE LIBRARY OF CONGRESS HAS CATALOGED THE VIKING EDITION AS FOLLOWS:
Dessen, Sarah.
Lock and key / by Sarah Dessen.
p. cm.
Summary: When she is abandoned by her alcoholic mother, high school senior Ruby
winds up living with her sister Cora, whom she has not seen for ten years, where she learns
about Cora's new life, what makes a family, how to allow people to help her
when she needs it, and that she has something to offer to others as well.
ISBN 978-0-670-01088-2 (hardcover)
[1. Abandoned children—Fiction. 2. Self-actualization (Psychology)—Fiction.
3. Family—Fiction. 4. Child abuse—Fiction. 5. Emotional problems—Fiction.
6. Interpersonal relationships—Fiction.] I. Title.
Pz7.D455Lo 2008 [Fic]—dc22 2007025370

SPEAK ISBN 978-0-14-241472-9

*To Leigh Feldman, for seeing me through
this time, every time*

*and to Jay,
always waiting on the other side*

lock and key

Chapter One

"And finally," Jamie said as he pushed the door open, "we come to the main event. Your room."

I was braced for pink. Ruffles or quilting, or maybe even appliqué. Which was probably kind of unfair, but then again, I didn't know my sister anymore, much less her decorating style. With total strangers, it had always been my policy to expect the worst. Usually they—and those that you knew best, for that matter—did not disappoint.

Instead, the first thing I saw was green. A large, high window, on the other side of which were tall trees separating the huge backyard from that of the house that backed up to it. Everything was big about where my sister and her husband, Jamie, lived—from the homes to the cars to the stone fence you saw first thing when you pulled into the neighborhood itself, made up of boulders that looked too enormous to ever be moved. It was like Stonehenge, but suburban. So weird.

It was only as I thought this that I realized we were all still standing there in the hallway, backed up like a traffic jam. At some point Jamie, who had been leading this little tour, had stepped aside, leaving me in the doorway. Clearly, they wanted me to step in first. So I did.

The room was, yes, big, with cream-colored walls. There

were three other windows beneath the big one I'd first seen, although they each were covered with thin venetian blinds. To the right, I saw a double bed with a yellow comforter and matching pillows, a white blanket folded over the foot. There was a small desk, too, a chair tucked under it. The ceiling slanted on either side, meeting in a flat strip in the middle, where there was a square skylight, also covered with a venetian blind—a little square one, clearly custom made to fit. It was so matchy-matchy and odd that for a moment, I found myself just staring up at it, as if this was actually the weirdest thing about that day.

"So, you've got your own bathroom," Jamie said, stepping around me, his feet making soft thuds on the carpet, which was of course spotless. In fact, the whole room smelled like paint and new carpet, just like the rest of the house. I wondered how long ago they had moved in—a month, six months? "Right through this door. And the closet is in here, too. Weird, right? Ours is the same way. When we were building, Cora claimed it meant she would get ready faster. A theory that has yet to be proved out, I might add."

Then he smiled at me, and again I tried to force a smile back. Who was this odd creature, my brother-in-law—a term that seemed oddly fitting, considering the circumstances—in his mountain-bike T-shirt, jeans, and funky expensive sneakers, cracking jokes in an obvious effort to ease the tension of an incredibly awkward situation? I had no idea, other than he had to be the very last person I would have expected to end up with my sister, who was so uptight she wasn't even pretending to smile at his attempts. At least I was trying.

Not Cora. She was just standing in the doorway, barely over the threshold, arms crossed over her chest. She had on a sleeveless sweater—even though it was mid-October, the house was beyond cozy, almost hot—and I could see the definition of her biceps and triceps, every muscle seemingly tensed, the same way they had been when she'd walked into the meeting room at Poplar House two hours earlier. Then, too, it seemed like Jamie had done all the talking, both to Shayna, the head counselor, and to me while Cora remained quiet. Still, every now and again, I could feel her eyes on me, steady, as if she was studying my features, committing me to memory, or maybe just trying to figure out if there was any part of me she recognized at all.

So Cora had a husband, I'd thought, staring at them as we'd sat across from each other, Shayna shuffling papers between us. I wondered if they'd had a fancy wedding, with her in a big white dress, or if they'd just eloped after she'd told him she had no family to speak of. Left to her own devices, this was the story I was sure she preferred—that she'd just sprouted, all on her own, neither connected nor indebted to anyone else at all.

"Thermostat's out in the hallway if you need to adjust it," Jamie was saying now. "Personally, I like a bit of a chill to the air, but your sister prefers it to be sweltering. So even if you turn it down, she'll most likely jack it back up within moments."

Again he smiled, and I did the same. God, this was exhausting. I felt Cora shift in the doorway, but again she didn't say anything.

"Oh!" Jamie said, clapping his hands. "Almost forgot.

The best part." He walked over to the window in the center of the wall, reaching down beneath the blind. It wasn't until he was stepping back and it was opening that I realized it was, in fact, a door. Within moments, I smelled cold air. "Come check this out."

I fought the urge to look back at Cora again as I took a step, then one more, feeling my feet sink into the carpet, following him over the threshold onto a small balcony. He was standing by the railing, and I joined him, both of us looking down at the backyard. When I'd first seen it from the kitchen, I'd noticed just the basics: grass, a shed, the big patio with a grill at one end. Now, though, I could see there were rocks laid out in the grass in an oval shape, obviously deliberately, and again, I thought of Stonehenge. What was it with these rich people, a druid fixation?

"It's gonna be a pond," Jamie told me as if I'd said this out loud.

"A pond?" I said.

"Total ecosystem," he said. "Thirty-by-twenty and lined, all natural, with a waterfall. And fish. Cool, huh?"

Again, I felt him look at me, expectant. "Yeah," I said, because I was a guest here. "Sounds great."

He laughed. "Hear that, Cor? *She* doesn't think I'm crazy."

I looked down at the circle again, then back at my sister. She'd come into the room, although not that far, and still had her arms crossed over her chest as she stood there, watching us. For a moment, our eyes met, and I wondered how on earth I'd ended up here, the last place I knew either one of us wanted me to be. Then she opened her mouth to speak for the first time since we'd pulled up in the driveway and all this, whatever it was, began.

"It's cold," she said. "You should come inside."

*　　*　　*

Before one o'clock that afternoon, when she showed up to claim me, I hadn't seen my sister in ten years. I didn't know where she lived, what she was doing, or even who she was. I didn't care, either. There had been a time when Cora was part of my life, but that time was over, simple as that. Or so I'd thought, until the Honeycutts showed up one random Tuesday and everything changed.

The Honeycutts owned the little yellow farmhouse where my mom and I had been living for about a year. Before that, we'd had an apartment at the Lakeview Chalets, the run-down complex just behind the mall. There, we'd shared a one-bedroom, our only window looking out over the back entrance to the J&K Cafeteria, where there was always at least one employee in a hairnet sitting outside smoking, perched on an overturned milk crate. Running alongside the complex was a stream that you didn't even notice until there was a big rain and it rose, overflowing its nonexistent banks and flooding everything, which happened at least two or three times a year. Since we were on the top floor, we were spared the water itself, but the smell of the mildew from the lower apartments permeated everything, and God only knew what kind of mold was in the walls. Suffice to say I had a cold for two years straight. That was the first thing I noticed about the yellow house: I could breathe there.

It was different in other ways, too. Like the fact that

it was a *house*, and not an apartment in a complex or over someone's garage. I'd grown used to the sound of neighbors on the other side of a wall, but the yellow house sat in the center of a big field, framed by two oak trees. There was another house off to the left, but it was visible only by flashes of roof you glimpsed through the trees—for all intents and purposes, we were alone. Which was just the way we liked it.

My mom wasn't much of a people person. In certain situations—say, if you were buying, for instance—she could be very friendly. And if you put her within five hundred feet of a man who would treat her like shit, she'd find him and be making nice before you could stop her, and I knew, because I had tried. But interacting with the majority of the population (cashiers, school administrators, bosses, ex-boyfriends) was not something she engaged in unless absolutely necessary, and then, with great reluctance.

Which was why it was lucky that she had me. For as long as I could remember, I'd been the buffer system. The go-between, my mother's ambassador to the world. Whenever we pulled up at the store and she needed a Diet Coke but was too hungover to go in herself, or she spied a neighbor coming who wanted to complain about her late-night banging around *again*, or the Jehovah's Witnesses came to the door, it was always the same. "Ruby," she'd say, in her tired voice, pressing either her glass or her hand to her forehead. "Talk to the people, would you?"

And I would. I'd chat with the girl behind the counter as I waited for my change, nod as the neighbor again threatened to call the super, ignored the proffered literature as I firmly shut the door in the Jehovah's faces. I was the first line of defense, always ready with an explanation or a bit of spin. "She's at the bank right now," I'd tell the landlord, even as she snored on the couch on the other side of the half-closed door. "She's just outside, talking to a delivery," I'd assure her boss so he'd release her bags for the day to me, while she smoked a much-needed cigarette in the freight area and tried to calm her shaking hands. And finally, the biggest lie of all: "Of course she's still living here. She's just working a lot," which is what I'd told the sheriff that day when I'd been called out of fourth period and found him waiting for me. That time, though, all the spin in the world didn't work. I talked to the people, just like she'd always asked, but they weren't listening.

That first day, though, when my mom and I pulled up in front of the yellow house, things were okay. Sure, we'd left our apartment with the usual drama—owing back rent, the super lurking around watching us so carefully that we had to pack the car over a series of days, adding a few things each time we went to the store or to work. I'd gotten used to this, though, the same way I'd adjusted to us rarely if ever having a phone, and if we did, having it listed under another name. Ditto with my school paperwork, which my mom often filled out with a fake address, as she was convinced that creditors and old landlords would track us down that way. For a long time, I thought this was the way everyone lived. When I got old enough to realize otherwise, it was already a habit, and anything else would have felt strange.

Inside, the yellow house was sort of odd. The kitchen was the biggest room, and everything was lined up against one wall: cabinets, appliances, shelves. Against another wall was a huge propane heater, which in cold weather worked hard to heat the whole house, whooshing to life with a heavy sigh. The only bathroom was off the kitchen, poking out with no insulated walls—my mom said it must have been added on; there'd probably been an outhouse, initially—which made for some cold mornings until you got the hot water blasting and the steam heated things up. The living room was small, the walls covered with dark fake-wood paneling. Even at high noon, you needed a light on to see your hand in front of your face. My mother, of course, loved the dimness and usually pulled the shades shut, as well. I'd come home to find her on the couch, cigarette dangling from one hand, the glow from the TV flashing across her face in bursts. Outside, the sun might be shining, the entire world bright, but in our house, it could always be late night, my mother's favorite time of day.

In the old one-bedroom apartment, I was accustomed to sometimes being awoken from a dead sleep, her lips close to my ear as she asked me to move out onto the couch, please, honey. As I went, groggy and discombobulated, I'd do my best not to notice whoever slipped back in the door behind her. At the yellow house, though, I got my own room. It was small, with a tiny closet and only one window, as well as orange carpet and those same dark walls, but I had a door to shut, and it was all mine. It made me feel like we'd stay longer than a couple of months, that things would be better here. In the end, though, only one of these things turned out to be true.

I first met the Honeycutts three days after we moved in.

It was early afternoon, and we were getting ready to leave for work when a green pickup truck came up the driveway. A man was driving, a woman in the passenger seat beside him.

"Mom," I called out to my mother, who was in the bedroom getting dressed. "Someone's here."

She sighed, sounding annoyed. My mother was at her worst just before going to work, petulant like a child. "Who is it?"

"I don't know," I said, watching as the couple—he in jeans and a denim work shirt, she wearing slacks and a printed top—started to make their way to the house. "But they're about to knock on the door."

"Oh, Ruby." She sighed again. "Just talk to them, would you?"

The first thing I noticed about the Honeycutts was that they were instantly friendly, the kind of people my mother couldn't *stand*. They were both beaming when I opened the door, and when they saw me, they smiled even wider.

"Well, look at you!" the woman said as if I'd done something precious just by existing. She herself resembled a gnome, with her small features and halo of white curls, like something made to put on a shelf. "Hello there!"

I nodded, my standard response to all door knockers. Unnecessary verbals only encouraged them, or so I'd learned. "Can I help you?"

The man blinked. "Ronnie Honeycutt," he said, extending his hand. "This is my wife, Alice. And you are?"

I glanced in the direction of my mother's room. Although usually she banged around a lot while getting ready—

drawers slamming, grumbling to herself—now, of course, she was dead silent. Looking back at the couple, I decided they probably weren't Jehovah's but were definitely peddling something. "Sorry," I said, beginning my patented firm shut of the door, "but we're not—"

"Oh, honey, it's okay!" Alice said. She looked at her husband. "Stranger danger," she explained. "They teach it in school."

"Stranger what?" Ronnie said.

"We're your landlords," she told me. "We just dropped by to say hello and make sure you got moved in all right."

Landlords, I thought. That was even worse than Witnesses. Instinctively, I eased the door shut a bit more, wedging my foot against it. "We're fine," I told them.

"Is your mom around?" Ronnie asked as Alice shifted her weight, trying to see into the kitchen behind me.

I adjusted myself accordingly, blocking her view, before saying, "Actually, she's—"

"Right here," I heard my mother say, and then she was crossing the living room toward us, pulling her hair back with one hand. She had on jeans, her boots, and a white tank top, and despite the fact that she'd just woken up about twenty minutes earlier, I had to admit she looked pretty good. Once my mother had been a great beauty, and occasionally you could still get a glimpse of the girl she had been—if the light was right, or she'd had a decent night's sleep, or, like me, you were just wistful enough to look for it.

She smiled at me, then eased a hand over my shoulder as she came to the door and offered them her other one. "Ruby

Cooper," she said. "And this is my daughter. Her name's Ruby, as well."

"Well, isn't that something!" Alice Honeycutt said. "And she looks just like you."

"That's what they say," my mom replied, and I felt her hand move down the back of my head, smoothing my red hair, which we did have in common, although hers was now streaked with an early gray. We also shared our pale skin—the redhead curse or gift, depending on how you looked at it—as well as our tall, wiry frames. I'd been told more than once that from a distance, we could almost be identical, and although I knew this was meant as a compliment, I didn't always take it that way.

I knew that my mother's sudden reaching out for me was just an act, making nice for the landlords, in order to buy some bargaining time or leverage later. Still, though, I noticed how easy it was for me to fold into her hip, resting my head against her. Like some part of me I couldn't even control had been waiting for this chance all along and hadn't even known it.

"It's our standard practice to just drop by and check in on folks," Ronnie was saying now, as my mother idly twisted a piece of my hair through her fingers. "I know the rental agency handles the paperwork, but we like to say hello face-to-face."

"Well, that's awfully nice of you," my mom said. She dropped my hair, letting her hand fall onto the doorknob so casually you almost would think she wasn't aware of it, or the inch or so she shut it just after, narrowing even farther the space between us and them. "But as Ruby was saying, I'm actually going to work right now. So . . ."

"Oh, of course!" Alice said. "Well, you all just let us know if there's anything you need. Ronnie, give Ruby our number."

We all watched as he pulled a scrap of paper and a pen out of his shirt pocket, writing down the digits slowly. "Here you go," he said, handing it over. "Don't hesitate to call."

"Oh, I won't," my mom said. "Thanks so much."

After a few more pleasantries, the Honeycutts finally left the porch, Ronnie's arm locked around his wife's shoulders. He deposited her in the truck first, shutting the door securely behind her, before going around to get behind the wheel. Then he backed out of the driveway with the utmost caution, doing what I counted to be at least an eight-point turn to avoid driving on the grass.

By then, though, my mother had long left the door and returned to her room, discarding their number in an ashtray along the way. "'Hello face-to-face' my ass," she said as a drawer banged. "Checking up is more like it. Busybodies."

She was right, of course. The Honeycutts were always dropping by unexpectedly with some small, seemingly unnecessary domestic project: replacing the garden hose we never used, cutting back the crepe myrtles in the fall, or installing a birdbath in the front yard. They were over so much, I grew to recognize the distinct rattle of their truck muffler as it came up the driveway. As for my mom, her niceties had clearly ended with that first day. Thereafter, if they came to the door, she ignored their knocks, not even flinching when Alice's face appeared in the tiny crack the living-room window shade didn't cover, white and ghostly with the bright light behind it, peering in.

It was because the Honeycutts saw my mother so rarely that it took almost two months for them to realize she was gone. In fact, if the dryer hadn't busted, I believed they might have never found out, and I could have stayed in the yellow house all the way until the end. Sure, I was behind on the rent and the power was close to getting cut off. But I would have handled all that one way or another, just like I had everything else. The fact was, I was doing just fine on my own, or at least as well as I'd ever done with my mom. Which wasn't saying much, I know. Still, in a weird way, I was proud of myself. Like I'd finally proven that I didn't need her, either.

As it was, though, the dryer *did* die, with a pop and a burning smell, late one October night while I was making macaroni and cheese in the microwave. I had no option but to stretch a clothesline across the kitchen in front of the space heater I'd been using since the propane ran out, hang everything up—jeans, shirts, and socks—and hope for the best. The next morning, my stuff was barely dry, so I pulled on the least damp of it and left the rest, figuring I'd deal with it that evening when I got home from work. But then Ronnie and Alice showed up to replace some supposedly broken front-porch slats. When they saw the clothesline, they came inside, and then they found everything else.

It wasn't until the day they took me to Poplar House that I actually saw the report that the person from social services had filed that day. When Shayna, the director, read it out loud, it was clear to me that whoever had written it had embellished, for some reason needing to make it sound worse than it actually was.

Minor child is apparently living without running water or heat in rental home abandoned by parent. Kitchen area was found to be filthy and overrun with vermin. Heat is non-functioning. Evidence of drug and alcohol use was discovered. Minor child appears to have been living alone for some time.

First of all, I had running water. Just not in the kitchen, where the pipes had busted. This was why the dishes tended to pile up, as it was hard to truck in water from the bathroom just to wash a few plates. As for the "vermin," we'd always had roaches; they'd just grown a bit more in number with the lack of sink water, although I'd been spraying them on a regular basis. And I did have a heater; it just wasn't on. The drug and alcohol stuff—which I took to mean the bottles on the coffee table and the roach in one of the ashtrays—I couldn't exactly deny, but it hardly seemed grounds for uprooting a person from their entire life with no notice.

The entire time Shayna was reading the report aloud, her voice flat and toneless, I still thought that I could talk my way out of this. That if I explained myself correctly, with the proper detail and emphasis, they'd just let me go home. After all, I had only seven months before I turned eighteen, when all of this would be a moot point anyway. But the minute I opened my mouth to start in about topic one, the water thing, she stopped me.

"Ruby," she said, "where is your mother?"

It was only then that I began to realize what would later seem obvious. That it didn't matter what I said, how carefully I crafted my arguments, even if I used every tool of evasion and persuasion I'd mastered over the years. There was only one thing that really counted, now and always, and this was it.

"I don't know," I said. "She's just gone."

*　　*　　*

After the tour, the pond reveal, and a few more awkward moments, Jamie and Cora finally left me alone to go downstairs and start dinner. It was barely five thirty, but already it was getting dark outside, the last of the light sinking behind the trees. I imagined the phone ringing in the empty yellow house as Richard, my mother's boss at Commercial Courier, realized we were not just late but blowing off our shift. Later, the phone would probably ring again, followed by a car rolling up the drive, pausing by the front window. They'd wait for a few moments for me to come out, maybe even send someone to bang on the door. When I didn't, they'd turn around hastily, spitting out the Honeycutts' neat grass and the mud beneath it from behind their back wheels.

And then what? The night would pass, without me there, the house settling into itself in the dark and quiet. I wondered if the Honeycutts had already been in to clean things up, or if my clothes were still stretched across the kitchen, ghostlike. Sitting there, in this strange place, it was like I could feel the house pulling me back to it, a visceral tug on my heart, the same way that, in the early days of the fall, I'd hoped it would do to my mom. But she hadn't come back, either. And now, if she did, I wouldn't be there.

Thinking this, I felt my stomach clench, a sudden panic

settling over me, and stood up, walking to the balcony door and pushing it open, then stepping outside into the cold air. It was almost fully dark now, lights coming on in the nearby houses as people came home and settled in for the night in the places they called home. But standing there, with Cora's huge house rising up behind me and that vast yard beneath, I felt so small, as if to someone looking up I'd be unrecognizable, already lost.

Back inside, I opened up the duffel that had been delivered to me at Poplar House; Jamie had brought it up from the car. It was a cheap bag, some promo my mom had gotten through work, the last thing I would have used to pack up my worldly possessions, not that this was what was in it anyway. Instead, it was mostly clothes I never wore—the good stuff had all been on the clothesline—as well as a few textbooks, a hairbrush, and two packs of cotton underwear I'd never seen in my life, courtesy of the state. I tried to imagine some person I'd never met before going through my room, picking these things for me. How ballsy it was to just assume you could know, with one glance, the things another person could not live without. As if it was the same for everyone, that simple.

There was only one thing I really needed, and I knew enough to keep it close at all times. I reached up, running my finger down the thin silver chain around my neck until my fingers hit the familiar shape there at its center. All day long I'd been pressing it against my chest as I traced the outline I knew by heart: the rounded top, the smooth edge on one side, the series of jagged bumps on the other. The night before, as I'd stood in the bathroom at Poplar House, it had been all that was familiar, the one thing I focused on as I faced the mirror. I could not look at the dark hollows under my eyes, or the strange surroundings and how strange I felt in them. Instead, like now, I'd just lifted it up gently, reassured to see that the outline of that key remained on my skin, the one that fit the door to everything I'd left behind.

*   *   *

By the time Jamie called up the stairs that dinner was ready, I'd decided to leave that night. It just made sense—there was no need to contaminate their pristine home any further, or the pretty bed in my room. Once everyone was asleep, I'd just grab my stuff, slip out the back door, and be on a main road within a few minutes. The first pay phone I found, I'd call one of my friends to come get me. I knew I couldn't stay at the yellow house—it would be the obvious place anyone would come looking—but at least if I got there, I could pick through my stuff for the things I needed. I wasn't stupid. I knew things had already changed, irrevocably and totally. But at least I could walk through the rooms and say good-bye, as well as try to leave some message behind, in case anyone came looking for me.

Then it was just a matter of laying low. After a few days of searching and paperwork, Cora and Jamie would write me off as unsaveable, getting their brownie points for try-ing *and* escaping relatively unscathed. That was what most people wanted anyway.

Now, I walked into the bathroom, my hairbrush in hand. I knew I looked rough, the result of two pretty much sleepless nights and then this long day, but the lighting in the bathroom, clearly designed to be flattering, made me look better than I knew I actually did, which was unsettling. Mirrors, if nothing else, were supposed to be honest. I turned off the lights and brushed my hair in the dark.

Just before I left my room, I glanced down at my watch, noting the time: 5:45. If Cora and Jamie were asleep by, say, midnight at the latest, that meant I only had to endure six hours and fifteen minutes more. Knowing this gave me a sense of calm, of control, as well as the fortitude I needed to go downstairs to dinner and whatever else was waiting for me.

Even with this wary attitude, however, I could never have been prepared for what I found at the bottom of the stairs. There, in the dark entryway, just before the arch that led into the kitchen, I stepped in something wet. And, judging by the splash against my ankle, cold.

"Whoa," I said, drawing my foot back and looking around me. Whatever the liquid was had now spread, propelled by my shoe, and I froze, so as not to send it any farther. Barely a half hour in, and already I'd managed to violate Cora's perfect palace. I was looking around me, wondering what I could possibly find to wipe it up with—the tapestry on the nearby wall? something in the umbrella stand?—when the light clicked on over my head.

"Hey," Jamie said, wiping his hands on a dishtowel. "I thought I heard something. Come on in, we're just about—" Suddenly, he stopped talking, having spotted the puddle and my proximity to it. "Oh, shit," he said.

"I'm sorry," I told him.

"Quick," he said, cutting me off and tossing me the dishtowel. "Get it up, would you? Before she—"

I caught the towel and was about to bend over when I realized it was too late. Cora was now standing in the archway behind him, peering around his shoulder. "Jamie," she said, and he jumped, startled. "Is that—?"

"No," he said flatly. "It's not."

My sister, clearly not convinced, stepped around him and walked over for a closer look. "It is," she said, turning back to look at her husband, who had slunk back farther into the kitchen. "It's pee."

"Cor—"

"It's pee, *again*," she said, whirling around to face him. "Isn't this why we put in that dog door?"

Dog? I thought, although I supposed this was a relief, considering I'd been worried I was about to find out something really disturbing about my brother-in-law. "You have a dog?" I asked. Cora sighed in response.

"Mastery of a dog door takes time," Jamie told her, grabbing a roll of paper towels off a nearby counter and walking over to us. Cora stepped aside as he ripped off a few sheets, then squatted down, tossing them over the puddle and adjacent splashes. "You know that expression. You can't teach an old dog new tricks."

Cora shook her head, then walked back into the kitchen without further comment. Jamie, still down on the floor, ripped off a few more paper towels and then dabbed at my shoe, glancing up at me. "Sorry about that," he said. "It's an issue."

I nodded, not sure what to say to this. So I just folded the dishtowel and followed him into the kitchen, where he tossed the paper towels into a stainless-steel trash can. Cora was by the windows that looked out over the deck, setting the wide, white table there. I watched as she folded cloth napkins, setting one by each of three plates, before laying out silverware: fork, knife, spoon. There were also place-mats, water glasses, and a big glass pitcher with sliced lem-ons floating in it. Like the rest of the house, it looked like something out of a magazine, too perfect to even be real.

Just as I thought this, I heard a loud, rattling sound. It was like a noise your grandfather would make, once he passed out in his recliner after dinner, but it was com-ing from behind me, in the laundry room. When I turned around, I saw the dog.

Actually first, I saw everything else: the large bed, cov-ered in what looked like sheepskin, the pile of toys—plastic rings, fake newspapers, rope bones—and, most noticeable of all, a stuffed orange chicken, sitting upright. Only once I'd processed all these accoutrements did I actually make out the dog itself, which was small, black and white, and lying on its back, eyes closed and feet in the air, snoring. Loudly.

"That's Roscoe," Jamie said to me as he pulled open the fridge. "Normally, he'd be up and greeting you. But our dog walker came for the first time today, and I think it wore him out. In fact, that's probably why he had that accident in the foyer. He's exhausted."

"What would be *out* of the ordinary," Cora said, "is if he actually went outside."

From the laundry room, I heard Roscoe let out another loud snore. It sounded like his nasal passages were exploding.

"Let's just eat," Cora said. Then she pulled out a chair and sat down.

I waited for Jamie to take his place at the head of the table before claiming the other chair. It wasn't until I was seated and got a whiff of the pot of spaghetti sauce to my left that I realized I was starving. Jamie picked up Cora's plate, putting it over his own, then served her some spaghetti, sauce, and salad before passing it back to her. Then he gestured for mine, and did the same before filling his own plate. It was all so formal, and *normal*, that I felt strangely nervous, so much so that I found myself watching my sister, picking up my fork only when she did. Which was so weird, considering how long it had been since I'd taken any cues from Cora. Still, there had been a time when she had taught me everything, so maybe, like so much else, this was just instinct.

"So tomorrow," Jamie said, his voice loud and cheerful, "we're going to get you registered for school. Cora's got a meeting, so I'll be taking you over to my old stomping ground."

I glanced up. "I'm not going to Jackson?"

"Out of district," Cora replied, spearing a cucumber with her fork. "And even if we got an exception, the commute is too long."

"But it's mid-semester," I said. I had a flash of my locker, the bio project I'd just dropped off the week before, all of it, like my stuff in the yellow house, just abandoned. I swallowed, taking a breath. "I can't just leave everything."

"It's okay," Jamie said. "We'll get it all settled tomorrow."

"I don't mind a long bus ride," I said, ashamed at how tight my voice sounded, betraying the lump that had risen in my throat. So ridiculous that after everything that had happened, I was crying about *school*. "I can get up early, I'm used to it."

"Ruby." Cora leveled her eyes at me. "This is for the best. Perkins Day is an excellent school."

"Perkins Day?" I said. "Are you *serious*?"

"What's wrong with the Day?" Jamie asked.

"Everything," I told him. He looked surprised, then hurt. Great. Now I was alienating the one person who I actually had on my side in this house. "It's not a bad school," I told him. "It's just . . . I won't fit in with anyone there."

This was a massive understatement. For the last two years, I'd gone to Jackson High, the biggest high school in the county. Overcrowded, underfunded, and with half your classes in trailers, just surviving a year there was considered a badge of honor, especially if you were like me and did not exactly run with the most academic of crowds. After I'd moved around so much with my mom, Jackson was the first place I'd spent consecutive years in a long time, so even if it was a total shithole, it was still familiar. Unlike Perkins Day, the elite private school known for its lacrosse team, stellar SAT scores, and the fact that the student parking lot featured more luxury automobiles than a European car dealership. The only contact we ever had with Perkins Day kids was when they felt like slumming at parties. Even then, often their girls stayed in the car, engine running and radio on, cigarettes dangling out the window, too good to even come inside.

Just as I thought this, Jamie suddenly pushed his chair

back, jumping to his feet. "Roscoe!" he said. "Hold on! The dog door!"

But it was too late. Roscoe, having at some point roused himself from his bed, was already lifting his leg against the dishwasher. I tried to get a better look at him but only caught a fleeting glimpse before Jamie bolted across the floor, grabbing him in midstream, and then carried him, still dripping, and chucked him out the small flap at the bottom of the French doors facing us. Then he looked at Cora and, seeing her stony expression, stepped outside himself, the door falling shut with a click behind him.

Cora put a hand to her head, closing her eyes, and I wondered if I should say something. Before I could, though, she pushed back her chair and walked over to pick up the roll of paper towels, then disappeared behind the kitchen island, where I could hear her cleaning up what Roscoe had left behind.

I knew I should probably offer to help. But sitting alone at the table, I was still bent out of shape about the idea of me at Perkins Day. Like all it would take was dropping me in a fancy house and a fancy school and somehow I'd just be fixed, the same way Cora had clearly fixed herself when she'd left me and my mom behind all those years ago. But we were not the same, not then and especially not now.

I felt my stomach clench, and I reached up, pressing my fingers over the key around my neck. As I did so, I caught a glimpse of my watch, the overhead light glinting off the face, and felt myself relax. *Five hours, fifteen minutes*, I thought. Then I picked up my fork and finished my dinner.

*   *   *

Six hours and fifty long minutes later, I was beginning to worry that my brother-in-law—the Nicest Guy in the World and Lover of Incontinent Creatures—was also an insomniac. Figuring they were the early-to-bed types, I'd gone up to my room to "go to sleep" at nine thirty. Sure enough, I heard Cora come up about forty minutes later, padding past my bedroom to her own, which was at the opposite end of the floor. Her light cut off at eleven, at which point I started counting down, waiting for Jamie to join her. He didn't. In fact, if anything, there were more lights on downstairs now than there had been earlier, slanting across the backyard, even as the houses around us went dark, one by one.

Now I'd been sitting there for almost four hours. I didn't want to turn a light on, since I was supposed to be long asleep, so I'd spent the time lying on the bed, my hands clasped on my stomach, staring at the ceiling and wondering what the hell Jamie was doing. Truth be told, it wasn't that different from the nights a few weeks back, when the power had been cut off temporarily at the yellow house. At least there, though, I could smoke a bowl or drink a few beers to keep things interesting. Here, there was nothing but the dark, the heat cutting off and on at what—after timing them—I'd decided were random intervals, and coming up with possible explanations for the weird, shimmering light that was visible at the far end of the backyard. I was just narrowing it down to either aliens or some sort of celestial neo-suburban phenomenon when suddenly, the windows downstairs went dark. Finally, Jamie was coming to bed.

I sat up, brushing my hair back with my fingers, and

listened. Unlike the yellow house, which was so small and thin-walled you could hear someone rolling over in a bed two rooms away, Cora's palace was hard to monitor in terms of activity and movement. I walked over to my door, easing it open slightly. Distantly, I heard footsteps and a door opening and shutting. Perfect. He was in.

Reaching down, I grabbed my bag, then slowly drew the door open, stepping out into the hallway and sticking close to the wall until I got to the stairs. Downstairs in the foyer I got my first lucky break in days: the alarm wasn't set. Thank God.

I reached for the knob, then eased the door open, sliding my hand with the bag through first. I was just about to step over the threshold when I heard the whistling.

It was cheery, and a tune I recognized—some jingle from a commercial. Detergent, maybe. I looked around me, wondering what kind of company I would have on a subdivision street at one thirty in the morning. Soon enough, I got my answer.

"Good boy, Roscoe! Good boy!"

I froze. It was Jamie. Now I could see him, coming up the other side of the street with Roscoe, who had just lifted his leg on a mailbox, walking in front of him on a leash. *Shit*, I thought, wondering whether he was far enough away not to see if I bolted in the opposite direction, dodging the streetlights. After a quick calculation, I decided to go around the house instead.

I could hear him whistling again as I vaulted off the front steps, then ran through the grass, dodging a sprinkler spigot and heading for the backyard. There, I headed for that light I'd been studying earlier, now hoping that it *was* aliens, or some kind of black hole, anything to get me away.

Instead, I found a fence. I tossed my bag over and was wondering what my chances were of following, not to mention what I'd find there, when I heard a thwacking noise from behind me. When I turned around, I saw Roscoe emerging from his dog door.

At first, he was just sniffing the patio, his nose low to the ground, going in circles. But then he suddenly stopped, his nose in the air. *Uh-oh*, I thought. I was already reaching up, grabbing the top of the fence and scrambling to try and pull myself over, when he started yapping and shot like a bullet right toward me.

Say what you will about little dogs, but they can *move*. In mere seconds, he'd covered the huge yard between us and was at my feet, barking up at me as I dangled from the fence, my triceps and biceps already burning. "Shhh," I hissed at him, but of course this only made him bark more. Behind us, in the house, a light came on, and I could see Jamie in the kitchen window, looking out.

I tried to pull myself up farther, working to get more leverage. I managed to get one elbow over, hoisting myself up enough to see that the source of the light I'd been watching was not otherworldly at all, but a swimming pool. It was big and lit up and, I noticed, occupied, a figure cutting through the water doing laps.

Meanwhile, Roscoe was still yapping, and my bag was already in this strange person's yard, meaning I had little choice but to join it or risk being busted by Jamie. Straining,

I pulled myself up so I was hanging over the fence, and tried to throw a leg to the other side. No luck.

"Roscoe?" I heard Jamie call out from the patio. "Whatcha got there, boy?"

I turned my head, looking back at him, wondering if he could see me. I figured I had about five seconds, if Roscoe didn't shut up, before he headed out to see what his dog had treed. Or fenced. Another fifteen while he crossed the yard, then maybe a full minute before he'd put it all together.

"Hello?"

I was so busy doing all these calculations that I hadn't noticed that the person who'd been swimming laps had, at some point, stopped. Not only that, but he was now at the edge of the pool, looking up at me. It was hard to make out his features, but whoever it was was clearly male and sounded awfully friendly, considering the circumstances.

"Hi," I muttered back.

"Roscoe?" Jamie called out again, and this time, without even turning around, I could hear he was moving, coming closer. Unless I had a burst of superhuman strength or a black hole opened up and swallowed me whole, I needed a Plan B, and fast.

"Do you—?" the guy in the pool said, raising his voice to be heard over Roscoe, who was still barking.

"No," I told him as I relaxed my grip. His face disappeared as I slid down my side of the fence, landing on my feet with mere seconds to spare before Jamie ducked under the small row of trees at the edge of the yard and saw me.

"Ruby?" he said. "What are you doing out here?"

He looked so concerned that for a moment, I actually felt a pang of guilt. Like I'd let him down or something. Which was just ridiculous; we didn't even know each other. "Nothing," I said.

"Is everything okay?" He looked up at the fence, then back at me, as Roscoe, who'd finally shut up, sniffed around his feet, making snorting noises.

"Yeah," I said. I was making it a point to speak slowly. Calmly. Tone was everything. "I was just . . ."

Truth was, at that moment, I didn't know what I was planning to say. I was just hoping for some plausible excuse to pop out of my mouth, which, considering my luck so far, was admittedly kind of a long shot. Still, I was going to go for it. But before I could even open my mouth, there was a thunk from the other side of the fence, and a face appeared above us. It was the guy from the pool, who, in this better light, I could now see was about my age. His hair was blond and wet, and there was a towel around his neck.

"Jamie," he said. "Hey. What's up?"

Jamie looked up at him. "Hey," he replied. To me he said, "So . . . you met Nate?"

I shot a glance at the guy. *Oh, well,* I thought. *It's better than what I had planned.* "Yeah." I nodded. "I was just—"

"She came to tell me my music was too loud," the guy—Nate?—told Jamie. Unlike me, he didn't seem to be straining in the least, holding himself over the top of the fence. I wondered if he was standing on something. To me he added, "Sorry about that. I crank it up so I can hear it under the water."

"Right," I said. "I just . . . I couldn't sleep."

At my feet, Roscoe suddenly coughed, hacking up something. We all looked at him, and then Jamie said slowly, "Well . . . it's late. We've got an early day tomorrow, so . . ."

"Yeah. I should get to bed, too," Nate said, reaching down to pull up one edge of his towel and wiping it across his face. He had to be on a deck chair or something, I thought. No one has that kind of upper-body strength. "Nice meeting you, Ruby."

"You, too," I replied.

He waved at Jamie, then dropped out of sight. Jamie looked at me for a moment, as if still trying to decipher what had happened. I tried not to flinch as he continued to study my face, only relaxing once he'd slid his hands in his pockets and started across the lawn, Roscoe tagging along at his heels.

I'd just reached the line of trees, following him, when I heard a *"Pssst!"* from behind me. When I turned around, Nate had pushed open part of the fence and was passing my bag through. "Might need this," he said.

Like I was supposed to be grateful. *Unbelievable*, I thought as I walked over, picking up the bag.

"So what's it to?"

I glanced up at him. He had his hand on the gate and had pulled on a dark-colored T-shirt, and his hair was starting to dry now, sticking up slightly. In the flickering light from the nearby pool I could finally make out his face enough to see that he was kind of cute, but in a rich-boy way, all jocky and smooth edges, not my type at all. "What?" I said.

"The key." He pointed to my neck. "What's it to?"

Jamie was going into the house now, leaving the door open for me behind him. I reached up, twining my fingers around the chain hanging there. "Nothing," I told him.

I shifted my bag behind me, keeping it in my shadow as I headed across the lawn to the back door. *So close*, I thought. *A shorter fence, a fatter dog, and everything would be different*. But wasn't that always the way. It's never something huge that changes everything, but instead the tiniest of details, irrevocably tweaking the balance of the universe while you're busy focusing on the big picture.

When I got to the house, there was no sign of Jamie or Roscoe. Still, I figured it wasn't worth risking bringing my bag inside, and since the balcony was too high to toss it up, I decided to just stow it someplace and come back down for it in a couple of hours when the coast was clear. So I stuck it beside the grill, then slipped inside just as the shimmering lights from Nate's pool cut off, leaving everything dark between his house and ours.

I didn't see Jamie again as I climbed the stairs to my room. If I had, I wasn't sure what I would have said to him. Maybe he had fallen for my flimsy excuse, aided and abetted by a pool boy who happened to be in the right place at what, for me anyway, turned out to be the wrong time. It was possible he was just that gullible. Unlike my sister, who knew from disappearing and could spot a lie, even a good one, a mile off. She also probably would have happily provided the boost I needed up and over that fence, or at least pointed the way to the gate, if only to be rid of me once and for all.

I waited a full hour to slip back downstairs. When I eased open my door, though, there was my bag, sitting right there at my feet. It seemed impossible I hadn't heard Jamie leave it there, but he had. For some reason, seeing it made me feel the worst I had all day, ashamed in a way I couldn't even explain as I reached down, pulling it inside with me.

Chapter Two

My mom hated to work. Far from a model employee, she had never had a job, at least in my recollection, that she actually enjoyed. Instead, in our house, work was a four-letter word, the official end of good times, something to be dreaded and bitched about and, whenever possible, avoided.

Things might have been different if she was qualified for a glamorous occupation like travel agent or fashion designer. Instead, due to choices she'd made, as well as a few circumstances beyond her control, she'd always had low-level, minimum-wage, benefits-only-if-you're-really-lucky kinds of jobs: waitress, retail, telemarketer, temp. Which was why, when she got hired on at Commercial Courier, it seemed like such a good thing. Sure, it wasn't glamorous. But at least it was different.

Commercial Courier called itself an "all-purpose delivery service," but their primary business came from lost luggage. They had a small office at the airport where bags that had been routed to the wrong city or put onto the wrong plane would eventually end up, at which point one of their couriers would deliver them to their proper destination, whether it be a hotel or the bag owner's home.

Before Commercial, my mom had been working as a receptionist in an insurance office, a job she hated because it required the two things she hated above all else: getting up early and dealing with people. When her bosses let her go after six months, she'd spent a couple of weeks sleeping in and grumbling before finally hauling out the classifieds, where she spotted the ad for Commercial. DELIVERY DRIVERS NEEDED, it said. WORK INDEPENDENTLY, DAYS OR NIGHTS. She never would have called any job perfect, but just at a glance, it seemed pretty close. So she called and set up an interview. Two days later, she had a job.

Or, *we* did. The truth was, my mom was not a very good navigator. I'd suspected she was slightly dyslexic, as she was always mixing up her right and left, something that definitely would have been a problem for a job that relied almost entirely on following written driving directions. Luckily, though, her shift didn't start until five p.m., which meant that I could ride along with her, an arrangement that I'd assumed at first would only last for the initial few days, until she got the hang of things. Instead, we became coworkers, eight hours a day, five days a week, just her and me in her banged-up Subaru, reuniting people with their possessions.

Our night always started at the airport. Once the bags were stacked and packed in the car, she'd hand over the sheet of addresses and directions, and we'd set off, hitting the nearby hotels first before venturing farther to neighborhoods and individual homes.

People had one of two reactions when we arrived with their lost luggage. Either they were really happy and grateful, or chose to literally blame the messenger, taking out their ire at the entire airline industry on us. The best tactic, we learned, was empathy. "Don't I know it," my mom would say, holding her clipboard for the person's signature as they ranted on about having to buy new toiletries or clothes in a strange city. "It's an outrage." Usually, this was enough, since it was often more than the airlines had offered up, but occasionally someone would go above and beyond, being a total asshole, at which point my mom would just drop the bag at their feet, turn and walk back to the car, ignoring whatever they shouted after her. "It's karma," she'd say to me as we pulled away. "Watch. I bet we're here again before we know it."

Hotels were better, because we only had to deal with the bellmen or front-desk staff. They'd offer us some kind of perk for fitting them in early on our route, and we became regulars at all the hotel bars, grabbing a quick burger between deliveries.

By the end of the shift, the highways had usually cleared, and we were often the only car cresting silent hills in dark subdivisions. That late, people often didn't want to be bothered by us ringing the bell, so they'd leave a note on their front door asking us to drop the bag on the porch, or tell us, when we called to confirm the delivery, to just pop the trunk of their car and leave it in there. These were always the weirdest trips for me, when it was midnight or even later, and we pulled up to a dark house, trying to be quiet. Like a robbery in reverse, creeping around to leave something rather than take it.

Still, there was also was something reassuring about working for Commercial, almost hopeful. Like things that were lost could be found again. As we drove away, I always tried to imagine what it would be like to open your door to find something you had given up on. Maybe it had seen places you never had, been rerouted and passed through so many strange hands, but still somehow found its way back to you, all before the day even began.

*   *   *

I'd expected to sleep the same way I had at Poplar House— barely and badly—but instead woke with a start the next morning when Jamie knocked on my door, saying we'd be leaving in an hour. I'd been so out of it that at first I wasn't even sure where I was. Once I made out the skylight over my head, though, with its little venetian blind, it all came back to me: Cora's. My near-escape. And now, Perkins Day. Just three days earlier, I'd been managing as best I could at the yellow house, working for Commercial, and going to Jackson. Now, here, everything had changed again. But I was kind of getting used to that now.

When my mom first took off, I didn't think it was for good. I figured she was just out on one of her escapades, which usually lasted only as long as it took her to run out of money or welcome, a few days at most. The first couple of times she'd done this, I'd been so worried, then overwhelmingly relieved when she returned, peppering her with questions about where she'd been, which irritated her no end. "I just needed some space, okay?" she'd tell me, annoyed, before stalking off to her room to sleep—something that, by the looks of it, she hadn't done much of during the time she'd been gone.

It took me another couple of her disappearances—each a few days longer than the last—before I realized that this was exactly how I *shouldn't* react, making a big deal of it. Instead, I adopted a more blasé attitude, like I hadn't even really noticed she'd been gone. My mother had always been about independence—hers, mine, and ours. She was a lot of things, but clingy had never been one of them. By taking off, I decided, she was teaching me about taking care of myself. Only a weak person needed someone else around all the time. With every disappearance, she was proving herself stronger; it was up to me, in how I behaved, to do the same.

After two weeks with no word from her, though, I'd finally forced myself to go into her room and look through her stuff. Sure enough, her emergency stash—three hundred bucks in cash, last I'd checked—was gone, as were her saving-bonds certificates, her makeup, and, most telling, her bathing suit and favorite summer robe. Wherever she was headed, it was warm.

I had no idea when she'd really left, since we hadn't exactly been getting along. We hadn't exactly *not* been, either. But that fall, the hands-off approach we'd both cultivated had spilled over from just a few days here and there to all the time. Also, she'd stopped going to work—sleeping when I left for school in the morning, sleeping when I returned and headed out to Commercial, and usually out once I returned after all the deliveries were done—so it wasn't like we had a lot of chances to talk. Plus, the rare occasions she was home and awake, she wasn't alone.

Most times, when I saw her boyfriend Warner's beat-up old Cadillac in the driveway, I'd park and then walk around to my bedroom window, which I kept unlocked, and let myself in that way. It meant I had to brush my teeth with bottled water, and made washing my face out of the question, but these were small prices to pay to avoid Warner, who filled the house with pipe smoke and always seemed to be sweating out whatever he'd drunk the day before. He'd park himself on the couch, beer in hand, his eyes silently following me whenever I did have to cross in front of him. He'd never done anything I could point to specifically, but I believed this was due not to innocence but to lack of opportunity. I did not intend to provide him with one.

My mother, however, loved Warner, or so she said. They'd met at Halloran's, the small bar just down the street from the yellow house where she went sometimes to drink beer and sing karaoke. Unlike my mother's other boyfriends, Warner wasn't the meaty, rough-around-the-edges type. Instead, in his standard outfit of dark pants, cheap shirt, deck shoes, hat with captain's insignia, he looked like he'd just stepped off a boat, albeit not necessarily a nice one. I wasn't sure whether he had a nautical past and was pining for it, or was hoping for one still ahead. Either way, he liked to drink and seemed to have some money from somewhere, so for my mom he was perfect.

These days, when I thought about my mom, I sometimes pictured her on the water. Maybe she and Warner had gotten that old Cadillac all the way to Florida, like they'd always talked about doing, and were now on the deck of some boat, bobbing on the open sea. This was at least a prettier picture than the one I actually suspected, the little bit of denial I allowed myself. It wasn't like I had a lot of time for fantasies anyway.

When she left, it was mid-August, and I still had nine months before I turned eighteen and could live alone legally. I knew I had a challenge ahead of me. But I was a smart girl, and I thought I could handle it. My plan was to keep the job at Commercial until Robert, the owner, caught on to my mom's absence, at which point I'd have to find something else. As far as the bills went, because our names were identical I could access my mom's account for whatever paychecks—which were direct-deposited—I *was* able to earn. I figured I was good, at least for the time being. As long as I kept out of trouble at school, the one thing that I knew for sure would blow my cover, no one had to know anything was different.

And who knew? It could even have worked out if the dryer hadn't broken. But while my short-term plans might have changed, the long-term goal remained the same as it had been for as long as I could remember: to be free. No longer dependent or a dependent, subject to the whim or whimsy of my mother, the system, or anyone else, the albatross always weighing down someone's neck. It didn't really matter whether I served out the time at the yellow house or in Cora's world. Once I turned eighteen, I could cut myself off from everyone and finally get what I wanted, which was to be on my own, once and for all.

Now I did the best I could with my appearance, considering I was stuck with the same pair of jeans I'd had on for two days and a sweater I hadn't worn in years. Still, I thought, tugging down the hem of the sweater, which was about two sizes too small, it wasn't like I cared about impressing the people at Perkins Day. Even my best stuff would be their worst.

I grabbed my backpack off the bed, then started down the hall. Cora and Jamie's bedroom door was slightly ajar, and as I got closer, I could hear a soft, tinny beeping, too quiet to be an alarm clock but similar in sound and tone. As I passed, I glanced inside and saw my sister lying on her back, a thermometer poking out of her mouth. After a moment, she pulled it out, squinting at it as the beeping stopped.

I wondered if she was sick. Cora had always been like the canary in the coalmine, the first to catch anything. My mother said this was because she worried too much, that anxiety affected the immune system. She herself, she claimed, hadn't "had a cold in fifteen years," although I ventured to think this was because her own system was pickled rather than calm. At any rate, my memories of growing up with Cora were always colored with her various ailments: ear infections, allergies, tonsillitis, unexplained rashes and fevers. If my mother was right and it was stress related, I was sure I could blame myself for this latest malady, whatever it was.

Down in the kitchen, I found Jamie sitting at the island, a laptop open in front of him, a cell phone pressed to his ear. When he saw me, he smiled, then covered it with one hand. "Hey," he said. "I'll be off in a sec. There's cereal and stuff on the table—help yourself."

I glanced over, expecting to see a single box and some milk. Instead, there were several different boxes, most of them unopened, as well as a plate of muffins, a pitcher of orange juice, and a big glass bowl of fruit salad. "Coffee?" I asked, and he nodded, gesturing toward the opposite counter, where I saw a pot, some mugs laid out in front of it.

". . . yeah, but that's just the point," Jamie was saying as he cocked his head to one side, typing something on the keyboard. "If we're serious about considering this offer, we need to at least set some parameters for the negotiations. It's important."

I walked over to the coffeepot, picking up a mug and filling it. On Jamie's laptop, I could see the familiar front page of UMe.com, the networking site that it seemed like everyone from your favorite band to your grandmother had gotten on in the last year or so. I had a page myself, although due to the fact that I didn't have regular access to a computer, I hadn't checked it in a while.

"But that's just the point," Jamie said, clicking onto another page. "They say they want to preserve the integrity and the basic intention, but they've got corporate mindsets. Look, just talk to Glen, see what he says. No, not this morning, I've got something going. I'll be in by noon, though. Okay. Later."

There was a beep, and he put down the phone, picking up a muffin from beside him and taking a bite just as there was a *ping!* on the screen, the familiar sound of a new message in the UMe inbox. "You have a UMe page?" I asked him as I sat down at the table with my coffee. My sweater rode up again, and I gave it another tug.

He looked at me for a second. "Uh . . . yeah. I do." He nodded at my mug. "You're not eating?"

"I don't like breakfast," I told him.

"That's crazy talk." He pushed back his chair, walking over to grab two bowls out of a nearby cabinet, then stopped at the fridge, pulling it open and getting out some milk. "When I was a kid," he said, coming over and plopping everything onto the table beside me, "my mom fixed us eggs or pancakes every morning. With sausage or bacon, and toast. You gotta have it. It's brain food."

I looked at him over my coffee cup as he grabbed one of the cereal boxes, ripping it open and filling a bowl. Then he added milk, filling it practically to the top, and plopped it on a plate before adding a muffin and a heaping serving of fruit salad. I was about to say something about being impressed with his appetite when he pushed the whole thing across to me. "Oh, no," I said. "I can't—"

"You don't have to eat it all," he said, shaking cereal into his own bowl. "Just some. You'll need it, trust me."

I shot him a wary look, then put down my mug, picking up the spoon and taking a bite. Across the table, his own mouth full of muffin, he grinned at me. "Good, right?"

I nodded just as there was another *ping!* from the laptop, followed immediately by one more. Jamie didn't seem to notice, instead spearing a piece of pineapple with his fork. "So," he said, "big day today."

"I guess," I said, taking another bite of cereal. I hated to admit it, but now I was starving and had to work not to shovel the food in nonstop. I couldn't remember the last time I'd had breakfast.

"I know a new school is tough," he told me as there were

three more pings in quick succession. God, he was popular. "My dad was in the military. Eight schools in twelve years. It sucked. I was always the new kid."

"So how long did you go to Perkins Day?" I asked, figuring maybe a short stint would explain him actually liking it.

Ping. Ping. "I started as a junior. Best two years of my life."

"Really."

He raised an eyebrow at me, picking up a glass and helping himself to some orange juice. "You know," he said, "I understand it's not what you're used to. But it's also not as bad you think."

I withheld comment as four more messages hit his page, followed by a thwacking noise behind me. I turned around just in time to see Roscoe wriggling through his dog door.

"Hey, buddy," Jamie said to him as he trotted past us to his water bowl, "how's the outside world?"

Roscoe's only response was a prolonged period of slurping, his tags banging against the bowl. Now that I finally had a real chance to study him, I saw he was kind of cute, if you liked little dogs, which I did not. He had to be under twenty pounds, and was stocky, black with a white belly and feet, his ears poking straight up. Plus he had one of those pug noses, all smooshed up, which I supposed explained the adenoidal sounds I'd already come to see as his trademark. Once he was done drinking, he burped, then headed over toward us, stopping en route to lick up some stray muffin crumbs.

As I watched Roscoe, Jamie's laptop kept pinging: he had to have gotten at least twenty messages in the last five minutes. "Should you . . . check that or something?" I asked.

"Check what?"

"Your page," I said, nodding at the laptop. "You keep getting messages."

"Nah, it can wait." His face suddenly brightened. "Hey, sleepyhead! You're running late."

"Somebody kept hitting the snooze bar," my sister grumbled as she came in, hair wet and dressed in black pants and a white blouse, her feet bare.

"The same somebody," Jamie said, getting to his feet and meeting her at the island, "who was down here a full half hour ahead of you."

Cora rolled her eyes, kissing him on the cheek and pouring herself a cup of coffee. Then she bent down, mug in her hand, to pet Roscoe, who was circling her feet. "You guys should get going soon," she said. "There'll be traffic."

"Back roads," Jamie said confidently as I pushed back my chair, tugging down my sweater again before carrying my now empty bowl and plate to the sink. "I used to be able to get to the Day in ten minutes flat, including any necessary stoplights."

"That was ten years ago," Cora told him. "Times have changed."

"Not that much," he said.

His laptop pinged again, but Cora, like him, didn't seem to notice. Instead, she was watching me as I bent down, sliding my plate into the dishwasher. "Do you . . . ?" she said, then stopped. When I glanced up at her, she said, "Maybe you should borrow something of mine to wear."

"I'm fine," I said.

She bit her lip, looking right at the strip of exposed

stomach between the hem of my sweater and the buckle on my jeans I'd been trying to cover all morning. "Just come on," she said.

We climbed the stairs silently, her leading the way up and into her room, which was enormous, the walls a pale, cool blue. I was not surprised to see that it was neat as a pin, the bed made with pillows arranged so precisely you just knew there was a diagram in a nearby drawer somewhere. Like my room, there were also lots of windows and a sky-light, as well as a much bigger balcony that led down to a series of decks below.

Cora crossed the room, taking a sip from the mug in her hands as she headed into the bathroom. We went past the shower, double sinks, and sunken bath into a room beyond, which turned out not to be a room at all but a closet. A *huge* closet, with racks of clothes on two walls and floor-to-ceiling shelves on the other. From what I could tell, Jamie's things—jeans, a couple of suits, and lots of T-shirts and sneakers—took up a fraction of the space. The rest was all Cora's. I watched from the doorway as she walked over to one rack, pushing some stuff aside.

"You probably need a shirt and a sweater, right?" she said, studying a few cardigans. "You have a jacket, I'm as-suming."

"Cora."

She pulled out a sweater, examining it. "Yes?"

"Why am I here?"

Maybe it was the confined space, or this extended pe-riod without Jamie to buffer us. But whatever the reason, this question had just somehow emerged, as unexpected to me as I knew it was to her. Now that it was out, though, I was surprised how much I wanted to hear the answer.

She dropped her hand from the rack, then turned to face me. "Because you're a minor," she said, "and your mother abandoned you."

"I'm almost eighteen," I told her. "And I was doing just fine on my own."

"Fine," she repeated, her expression flat. Looking at her, I was reminded how really different we were, me a redhead with pale, freckled skin, such a contrast to her black hair and blue eyes. I was taller, with my mother's thin frame, while she was a couple of inches shorter and curvier. "You call that *fine?*"

"You don't know," I said. "You weren't there."

"I know what I read in the report," she replied. "I know what the social worker told me. Are you saying those accounts were inaccurate?"

"Yes," I said.

"So you weren't living without heat or water in a filthy house."

"Nope."

She narrowed her eyes at me. "Where's Mom, Ruby?"

I swallowed, then turned my head as I reached up, pressing the key around my neck into my skin. "I don't care," I said.

"Neither do I," she replied. "But the fact of the matter is, she's gone and you can't be by yourself. Does that answer your question?"

I didn't say anything, and she turned back to the clothes, pushing through them. "I told you, I don't need to borrow anything," I said. My voice sounded high and tight.

"Ruby, come on," she said, sounding tired. She pulled a black sweater off a hanger, tossing it over her shoulder before moving over to another shelf and grabbing a green T-shirt. Then she walked over, pushing them both at me as she passed. "And hurry. It takes at least fifteen minutes to get there."

Then she walked back through the bathroom, leaving me behind. For a moment, I just stood there, taking in the neat rows of clothes, how her shirts were all folded just so, stacked by color. As I looked down at the clothes she'd given me, I told myself I didn't care what the people at Perkins Day thought about me or my stupid sweater. Everything was just temporary anyway. Me being there, or here. Or anywhere, for that matter.

A moment later, though, when Jamie yelled up that it was time to go, I suddenly found myself pulling on Cora's T-shirt, which was clearly expensive and fit me perfectly, and then her sweater, soft and warm, over it. On my way downstairs, in clothes that weren't mine, to go to a school I'd never claim, I stopped and looked at myself in the bathroom mirror. You couldn't see the key around my neck: it hung too low under both collars. But if I leaned in close, I could make it out, buried deep beneath. Out of sight, hard to recognize, but still able to be found, even if I was the only one to ever look for it.

*   *   *

Cora was right. We got stuck in traffic. After hitting every red light between the house and Perkins Day, we finally pulled into the parking lot just as a bell was ringing.

All the visitor spaces were taken, so Jamie swung his car—a sporty little Audi with all-leather interior—into one in the student lot. I looked to my left—sure enough, parked there was a Mercedes sedan that looked brand-new. On our other side was another Audi, this one a bright red convertible.

My stomach, which had for most of the ride been pretty much working on rejecting my breakfast, now turned in on itself with an audible clench. According to the dashboard clock, it was 8:10, which meant that in a run-down classroom about twenty miles away, Mr. Barrett-Hahn, my homeroom teacher, was beginning his slow, flat-toned read of the day's announcements. This would be roundly ignored by my classmates, who five minutes from now would shuffle out, voices rising, to fight their way through a corridor designed for a student body a fraction the size of the current one to first period. I wondered if my English teacher, Ms. Valhalla—she of the high-waisted jeans and endless array of oversized polo shirts—knew what had happened to me, or if she just assumed I'd dropped out, like a fair amount of her students did during the course of a year. We'd been just about to start *Wuthering Heights*, a novel she'd promised would be a vast improvement over *David Copperfield*, which she'd dragged us through like a death march for the last few weeks. I'd been wondering if this was just talk or the truth. Now I'd never know.

"Ready to face the firing squad?"

I jumped, suddenly jerked back to the present and Jamie, who'd pulled his keys from the ignition and was now just sitting there expectantly, hand on the door handle.

"Oops. Bad choice of words," he said. "Sorry."

He pushed his door open and, feeling my stomach twist again, I forced myself to do the same. As soon as I stepped out of the car, I heard another bell sound.

"Office is this way," Jamie said as we started walking along the line of cars. He pointed to a covered walkway to our right, beyond which was a big green space, more buildings visible on the other side. "That's the quad," he said. "Classrooms are all around it. Auditorium and gym are those two big buildings you see over there. And the caf is here, closest to us. Or at least it used to be. It's been a while since I had a sloppy joe here."

We stepped up on a curb, heading toward a long, flat building with a bunch of windows. I'd just followed him, ducking under an overhang, when I heard a familiar *rat-a-tat-tat* sound. At first, I couldn't place it, but then I turned and saw an old model Toyota bumping into the parking lot, engine backfiring. My mom's car did the same thing, usually at stoplights or when I was trying to quietly drop a bag off at someone's house late at night.

The Toyota, which was white with a sagging bumper, zoomed past us, brake lights flashing as it entered the student parking lot and whipped into a space. I heard a door slam and then footsteps slapping across the pavement. A moment later, a black girl with long braids emerged, running, a backpack over one shoulder. She had a cell phone pressed to one ear and seemed to be carrying on a spirited conversation, even as she jumped the curb, went under the covered walkway, and began to sprint across the green.

"Ah, tardiness. Brings back memories," Jamie said.

"I thought you could get here in ten minutes."

"I could. But there were usually only five until the bell."

As we reached the front entrance and he pulled the glass door open for me, I was aware not of the stale mix of mildew and disinfectant Jackson was famous for but a clean, fresh-paint smell. It was actually very similar to Cora's house, which was a little unsettling.

"Mr. Hunter!" A man in a suit was standing just inside. As soon as he saw us, he strode right over, extending his hand. "The prodigal student returns home. How's life in the big leagues?"

"Big," Jamie said, smiling. They shook hands. "Mr. Thackray, this is my sister-in-law, Ruby Cooper. Ruby, this is Principal Thackray."

"Nice to meet you," Mr. Thackray said. His hand was large and cool, totally enveloping mine. "Welcome to Perkins Day."

I nodded, noting that my mouth had gone bone-dry. My experience with principals—and teachers and landlords and policemen—being as it was, this wasn't surprising. Even without a transgression, that same fight-or-flight instinct set in.

"Let's go ahead and get you settled in, shall we?" Mr. Thackray said, leading the way down the hallway and around the corner to a large office. Inside, he took a seat behind a big wooden desk, while Jamie and I sat in the two chairs opposite. Through the window behind him, I could see a huge expanse of soccer fields lined with bleachers. There was a guy on a riding mower driving slowly down one side, his breath visible in the cold air.

Mr. Thackray turned around, looking out the window, as well. "Looks good, doesn't it? All we're missing is a plaque honoring our generous benefactor."

"No need for that," Jamie said, running a hand through his hair. He sat back, crossing one leg over the other. In his sneakers, jeans, and zip-up hoodie, he didn't look ten years out of high school. Two or three, sure. But not ten.

"Can you believe this guy?" Mr. Thackray said to me, shaking his head. "Donates an entirely new soccer complex and won't even let us give him credit."

I looked at Jamie. "You did that?"

"It's not that big a deal," he said, looking embarrassed.

"Yes, it is," Mr. Thackray said. "Which is why I wish you'd reconsider and let us make your involvement public. Plus, it's a great story. Our students waste more time on UMe.com than any other site, and its owner donates some of the proceeds from that procrastination back into education. It's priceless!"

"Soccer," Jamie said, "isn't exactly education."

"Sports are crucial to student development," Mr. Thackray said. "It counts."

I turned my head, looking at my brother-in-law, suddenly remembering all those pings in his UMe inbox. *You could say that*, he'd said, when I'd asked if he had a page. Clearly, this was an understatement.

". . . grab a few forms, and we'll get a schedule set up for you," Mr. Thackray was saying. "Sound good?"

I realized, a beat too late, he'd been talking to me. "Yeah," I said. Then I swallowed. "I mean, yes."

He nodded, pushing back his chair and getting to his

feet. As he left the room, Jamie sat back, examining the tread of one sneaker. Outside, the guy on the mower had finished one side of the field and was now moving slowly up the other.

"Do you . . . ?" I said to Jamie. He glanced up at me. "You own UMe?"

He let his foot drop. "Well . . . not exactly. It's me and a few other guys."

"But he said you were the owner," I pointed out.

Jamie sighed. "I started it up originally," he said. "When I was just out of college. But now I'm in more of an overseeing position."

I just looked at him.

"CEO," he admitted. "Which is really just a big word, or a really small acronym, actually, for overseer."

"I can't believe Cora didn't tell me," I said.

"Ah, you know Cora." He smiled. "Unless you work eighty hours a week saving the world like she does, she's tough to impress."

I looked out at the guy on the mower again, watching as he puttered past. "Cora saves the world?"

"She tries to," he said. "Hasn't she told you about her work? Down at the public defender's office?"

I shook my head. In fact, I hadn't even known Cora had gone to law school until the day before, when the social worker at Poplar House had asked her what she did for a living. The last I knew, she'd been about to graduate from college, and that was five years ago. And we only knew that because, somehow, an announcement of the ceremony had made its way to us. It was on thick paper, a card with her name on it tucked inside. I remembered studying the envelope, wondering why it had turned up after all this time with no contact. When I'd asked my mom, she'd just shrugged, saying the school sent them out automatically. Which made sense, since by then, Cora had made it clear she wanted no part of us in her new life, and we'd been more than happy to oblige.

"Well," Jamie said as a palpable awkwardness settled over us, and I wondered what exactly he knew about our family, if perhaps my very existence had come as a surprise. Talk about baggage. "I guess you two have a lot of catching up to do, huh?"

I looked down at my hands, not saying anything. A moment later, Mr. Thackray walked back in, a sheaf of papers in his hand, and started talking about transcripts and credit hours, and this exchange was quickly forgotten. Later, though, I wished I had spoken up, or at least tried to explain that once I knew Cora better than anyone. But that was a long time ago, back when she wasn't trying to save the whole world. Only me.

*　　*　　*

When I was a kid, my mom used to sing to me. It was always at bedtime, when she'd come in to say good night. She'd sit on the edge of my bed, brushing my hair back with her fingers, her breath sweet smelling (a "civilized glass" or two of wine was her norm then) as she kissed my forehead and told me she'd see me in the morning. When she tried to leave, I'd protest, and beg for a song. Usually, if she wasn't in too bad a mood, she'd oblige.

Back then, I'd thought my mother made up all the songs

she sang to me, which was why it was so weird the first time I heard one of them on the radio. It was like discovering that some part of you wasn't yours at all, and it made me wonder what else I couldn't claim. But that was later. At the time, there were only the songs, and they were still all ours, no one else's.

My mother's songs fell into three categories: love songs, sad songs, or sad love songs. Not for her the uplifting ending. Instead, I fell asleep to "Frankie and Johnny" and a love affair gone very wrong, "Don't Think Twice It's All Right" and a bad breakup, and "Wasted Time" and someone looking back, full of regret. But it was "Angel from Montgomery," the Bonnie Raitt version, that made me think of her most, then and now.

It had everything my mother liked in a song—heartbreak, disillusionment, and death—all told in the voice of an old woman, now alone, looking back over all the things she'd had and lost. Not that I knew this; to me they were just words set to a pretty melody and sung by a voice I loved. It was only later, when I'd lie in a different bed, hearing her sing late into the night through the wall, that they kept me awake worrying. Funny how a beautiful song could tell such an ugly story. It seemed unfair, like a trick.

If you asked her, my mother would say that nothing in her life turned out the way she planned it. She was *supposed* to go to college and then marry her high-school sweetheart, Ronald Brown, the tailback for the football team, but his parents decided they were getting too serious and made him break up with her, right before Christmas of her junior year. Heartbroken, she'd allowed her friends to drag her to a party where she knew absolutely no one and ended up stuck talking to a guy who was in his freshman year at Middletown Tech, studying to be an engineer. In a kitchen cluttered with beer bottles, he'd talked to her about suspension bridges and skyscrapers, "the miracle of buildings," all of which bored her to tears. Which never explained, at least to me, why she ended up agreeing to go out with him, then sleeping with him, thereby producing my sister, who was born nine months later.

So at eighteen, while her classmates graduated, my mom was at home with an infant daughter and a new husband. Still, if the photo albums are any indication, those early years weren't so bad. There are tons of pictures of Cora: in a sunsuit, holding a shovel, riding a tricycle up a front walk. My parents appear as well, although not as often, and rarely together. Every once in a while, though, there's a shot of them—my mom looking young and gorgeous with her long red hair and pale skin, my dad, dark-haired with those bright blue eyes, his arm thrown over her shoulder or around her waist.

Because there was a ten-year gap between Cora and me, I'd always wondered if I was a mistake, or maybe a last-gasp attempt to save a marriage that was already going downhill. Whatever the reason, my dad left when I was five and my sister fifteen. We were living in an actual house in an actual neighborhood then, and we came home from the pool one afternoon to find my mom sitting on the couch, glass in hand. By themselves, neither of these things were noteworthy. Back then, she didn't work, and while she usually waited until my dad got home to pour herself a drink, occasionally she started without him. The thing that we did notice, though, right off, was that there was music playing, and my mom was singing along. For the first time, it wasn't soothing or pretty to me. Instead, I felt nervous, unsettled, as if the cumulative weight of all those sad songs was hitting me at once. From then on, her singing was always a bad sign.

I had vague memories of seeing my dad after the divorce. He'd take us for breakfast on the weekends or a dinner during the week. He never came inside or up to the door to get us, instead just pulling up to the mailbox and sitting there behind the wheel, looking straight ahead. As if he was waiting not for us but for anyone, like a stranger could have slid in beside him and it would have been fine. Maybe it was because of this distance that whenever I tried to remember him now, it was hard to picture him. There were a couple of memories, like of him reading to me, and watching him grilling steaks on the patio. But even with these few things, it was as if even when he was around, he was already distant, a kind of ghost.

I don't remember how or why the visits ceased. I couldn't recall an argument or incident. It was like they happened, and then they didn't. In sixth grade, due to a family-tree project, I went through a period where the mystery of his disappearance was all I could think about, and eventually I did manage to get out of my mom that he'd moved out of state, to Illinois. He'd kept in touch for a little while, but after remarrying and a couple of changes of address he'd vanished, leaving no way for her to collect child support, or any support. Beyond that, whenever I bugged her about it, she made it clear it was not a subject she wanted to discuss. With my mom, when someone was gone, they were gone. She didn't waste another minute thinking about them, and neither should you.

When my dad left, my mom slowly began to withdraw from my daily routine—waking me up in the morning, getting me ready for school, walking me to the bus stop, telling me to brush my teeth—and Cora stepped in to take her place. This, too, was never decided officially or announced. It just happened, the same way my mom just happened to start sleeping more and smiling less and singing late at night, her voice wavering and haunting and always finding a way to reach my ears, even when I rolled myself against the wall tight and tried to think of something, anything else.

Cora became my one constant, the single thing I could depend on to be there and to remain relatively unchanged, day in and day out. At night in our shared room, I'd often have to lie awake listening to her breathing for a long time before I could fall asleep myself.

"Shhh," I remembered her saying as we stood in our nightgowns in our bedroom. She'd press her ear against the door, and I'd watch her face, cautious, as she listened to my mom moving around downstairs. From what she heard—a lighter clicking open, then shut, cubes rattling in a glass, the phone being picked up or put down—she always gauged whether it was safe for us to venture out to brush our teeth or eat something when my mom had forgotten about dinner. If my mom was sleeping, Cora would hold my hand as we tiptoed past her to the kitchen. There I'd hold an old acrylic tray while she quickly piled it with cereal and milk—or, my favorite, English-muffin pizzas she made in the toaster oven, moving stealthily around the kitchen as my mother's breath rose and fell in the next room. When things went well, we'd get back upstairs without her stirring. When they didn't, she'd jerk awake, sitting up with creases on her face, her voice thick as she said, "What are you two doing?"

"It's okay," Cora would say. "We're just getting something to eat."

Sometimes, if she'd been out deeply enough, this was enough. More often, though, I'd hear the couch springs squeak, her feet hitting the hardwood floor, and it was then that Cora always stopped whatever she was in the midst of—sandwich making, picking through my mom's purse for lunch money, pushing the wine bottle, open and sweaty, farther back on the counter—and do the one thing I associated with her more than anything else. As my mother approached, annoyed and usually spoiling for a fight, my sister would always step in front of me. Back then, she was at least a head taller, and I remembered this so well, the sudden shift in my perspective, the view going from something scary to something not. Of course, I knew my mother was still coming toward me, but it was always Cora I kept my eyes on: her dark hair, the sharp angles of her shoulder blades, the way, when things were really bad, she'd reach her hand back to find mine, closing her fingers around it. Then she'd just stand there, as my mother appeared, ready to take the brunt of whatever came next, like the bow of a boat crashing right into a huge wave and breaking it into nothing but water.

Because of this, it was Cora who got the bulk of the stinging slaps, the two-hand pushes that sent her stumbling backward, the sudden, rough tugs on the arm that left red twisty welts and, later, bruises in the shape of fingertips. The transgressions were always hard to understand, and therefore even more difficult to avoid: we were up when we shouldn't have been, we were making too much noise, we provided the wrong answers to questions that seemed to have no right ones. When it was over, my mother would shake her head and leave us, returning to the couch or her bedroom, and I'd always look at Cora, waiting for her to decide what we should do next. More often than not, she'd just leave the room herself, wiping her eyes, and I'd fall in behind her, not talking but sticking very close, feeling safer if she was not just between me and my mom, but between me and the world in general.

Later, I'd develop my own system for dealing with my mom, learning to gauge her mood by the number of glasses or bottles already on the table when I came home, or the inflection in her tone when she said the two syllables that made up my name. I took a few knocks as well, although this became more rare when I hit middle school. But it was always the singing that was the greatest indicator, the one thing that made me hesitate outside a door frame, hanging back from the light. As beautiful as her voice sounded, working its way along the melodies I knew by heart, I knew there was a potential ugliness underneath.

By then, Cora was gone. A great student, she'd spent high school working shifts at Exclamation Taco! for college money and studying nonstop, to better her chances of receiving any one of the several scholarships she'd applied for. My sister was nothing if not driven and had always balanced the chaos that was our lives with a strict personal focus on order and organization. While the rest of the house was constantly dusty and in disarray, Cora's side of our shared room was neat as a pin, everything folded and in its place. Her books were alphabetized, her shoes lined up in a row, her bed always made, the pillow at a perfect right angle to the wall. Sometimes, sitting on my own bed, I'd look across and be amazed at the contrast: it was like a before-and-after shot, or a reverse mirror image, the best becoming the worst, and back again.

In the end, she received a partial scholarship to the U, the state university one town over, and applied for student loans to cover the rest. During the spring and summer of senior year, after she'd gotten her acceptance, there was a weird shift in the house. I could feel it. My sister, who'd spent most of the last year avoiding my mother entirely— going from school to work to bed and back again—suddenly seemed to loosen up, grow lighter. People came to pick her up on weekend nights, their voices rising up to our open windows as she got into their cars and sped away. Girls with easy, friendly voices called asking for Cora, who'd then take the phone into the bathroom where, even through the door, I could hear her voice sounded different speaking back to them.

Meanwhile my mother grew quieter, not saying anything as Cora brought home boxes to pack for school or cleaned out her side of the room. Instead, she just sat on the side porch during those long summer twilights, smoking

cigarettes and staring off into the side yard. We never talked
about Cora leaving, but as the day grew closer, that shift in
the air was more and more palpable, until it was as if I could
see my sister extracting herself from us, twisting loose and
breaking free, minute by minute. Sometimes at night, I'd
wake up with a start, looking over at her sleeping form
across the room and feel reassured only fleetingly, knowing
that the day would come soon when there would be nothing
there at all.

The day she moved out, I woke up with a sore throat. It
was a Saturday morning, and I helped her carry her boxes
and a couple of suitcases downstairs. My mother stayed in
the kitchen, chain-smoking and silent, not watching as we
carted out my sister's few possessions, loading them into
the trunk of a Jetta that belonged to a girl named Leslie
whom I'd never met before that day and never saw again.

"Well," Cora had said, when she pushed the hatchback
shut, "I guess that's everything."

I looked up at the house, where I could see my mom
through the front window, moving through the kitchen to
the den, then back again. And even with everything that had
happened, I remember thinking that of course she wouldn't
let Cora just go with no good-bye. But as the time passed,
she got no closer to the door or to us, and after a while, even
when I looked hard, I couldn't see her at all.

Cora, for her part, was just standing there, staring up
at the house, her hands in her pockets, and I wondered if
she was waiting, too. But then she dropped her hands, letting out a breath. "I'll be back in a sec," she said, and Leslie

nodded. Then we both watched her slowly go up the walk and into the house.

She didn't stay long—maybe a minute, or even two. And when she came out, her face looked no different. "I'll call you tonight," she said to me. Then she stepped forward, pulling me into a tight hug. I remembered thinking, as she drove away, that my throat was so sore I'd surely be totally sick within hours. But I wasn't. By the next morning it was gone.

Cora called that first night, as promised, and the following weekend, checking in and asking how I was doing. Both times I could hear chatter in the background, voices and music, as she reported that she liked her roommate and her classes, that everything was going well. When she asked how I was, I wanted to tell her how much I missed her, and that my mom had been drinking a lot since she'd left. Since we'd hardly discussed this aloud face-to-face, though, bringing it up over the phone seemed impossible.

She never asked to speak to my mother, and my mom never once picked up when she called. It was as if their relationship had been a business arrangement, bound by contract, and now that contract had expired. At least that was the way I looked at it, until we moved a few weeks later and my sister stopped calling altogether. Then I realized that deep down in the fine print, my name had been on it as well.

For a long time, I blamed myself for Cora cutting ties with us. Maybe because I hadn't told her I wanted to keep in touch, she didn't know or something. Then I thought that maybe she couldn't find our new number. But whenever I asked my mom about this, she just sighed, shaking her head. "She's got her own life now, she doesn't need us anymore," she explained, reaching out to ruffle my hair. "It's just you and me now, baby. Just you and me."

Looking back, it seemed like it should have been harder to lose someone, or have them lose you, especially when they were in the same state, only a few towns over. It would have been so easy to drive to the U and find her dorm, walk up to her door, and announce ourselves. Instead, as the time passed and it became clear Cora wanted nothing to do with me and my mother, it made sense to wipe our hands of her, as well. This, like the alliance between me and my sister all those years ago, was never officially decided. It just happened.

It wasn't like it was so shocking, anyway. My sister had made a break for it, gotten over the wall and escaped. It was what we both wanted. Which was why I understood, even appreciated, why she didn't want to return for a day or even an hour. It wasn't worth the risk.

There were so many times during those years, though, as we moved from one house to another, that I would find myself thinking about my sister. Usually it was late at night, when I couldn't sleep, and I'd try to picture her in her dorm room forty-odd miles and a world away. I wondered if she was happy, what it was like out there. And if maybe, just maybe, she ever thought of me.

Chapter Three

"Ruby, welcome. Come join us, there's a free seat right over here."

I could feel everyone in the room watching me as I followed the outstretched finger of the teacher, a slight, blonde woman who looked barely out of college, to the end of a long table where there was an empty chair.

According to my new schedule, this was Literature in Practice with an M. Conyers. Back at Jackson, the classes all had basic names: English, Geometry, World History. If you weren't one of the few golden children, anointed early for the AP–Ivy League fast track, you made your choices with the minimal and usually disinterested help of one of the three guidance counselors allotted for the entire class. Here, though, Mr. Thackray had spent a full hour consulting my transcript, reading descriptions aloud from the thick course catalog, and conferring with me about my interests and goals. Maybe it was for Jamie's benefit—he was super donor, after all—but somehow, I doubted it. Clearly, they did things differently here.

Once I sat down, I read over my list of classes, separated into neat blocks—Intro to Calculus, Global Cultures and Practices, Drawing: Life and Form—twice, figuring that would give people adequate time to stare at me before moving on to something else. Sure enough, by the time I lifted my head a couple of minutes later to turn my attention to the teacher, a cursory check revealed everyone else was pretty much doing the same.

"As you know," she was saying, walking over to a table in front of a large dry-erase board and hopping up onto it, "we'll be doing several assignments over the course of the rest of the year. You'll have your research project on the novel of your choosing, and we'll also be reading a series of memoirs and oral histories."

I took a minute, now that I felt a bit more comfortable, to look around the room. It was large, with three big windows on one side that looked out onto the common green, some new-looking computers in the back of the room, and instead of desks, a series of tables, arranged in three rows. The class itself was small—twelve or fourteen people, tops. To my left, there was a girl with long, strawberry-blonde hair, twisted into one of those effortlessly perfect knots, a pencil sticking through it. She was pretty, in that cheerleader/student-council president/future nuclear physicist kind of way, and sitting with her posture ramrod straight, a Jump Java cup centered on the table in front of her. To my right, there was a huge backpack—about fourteen key chains hanging off of it—that was blocking my view of whoever was on the other side.

Ms. Conyers hopped off her desk and walked around it, pulling out a drawer. With her jeans, simple oxford shirt, and red clogs, she looked about twelve, which I figured had to make it difficult to keep control in her classroom. Then again, this didn't seem like an especially challenging group.

Even the row of guys at the back table—pumped-up jock types, slumped over or leaning back in their chairs—looked more sleepy than rowdy.

"So today," she said, shutting the desk drawer, "you're going to begin your own oral history project. Although it isn't exactly a history, as much as a compilation."

She started walking down the aisle between the tables, and I saw now she had a small plastic bowl in her hand, which she offered to a heavyset girl with a ponytail. The girl reached in, pulling out a slip of paper, and Ms. Conyers told her to read what was on it out loud. The girl squinted at it. "Advice," she said.

"Advice," Ms. Conyers repeated, moving on to the next person, a guy in glasses, holding out the bowl to him. "What is advice?"

No one said anything for a moment, during which time she kept distributing slips of paper, one person at a time. Finally the blonde to my left said, "Wisdom. Given by others."

"Good, Heather," Ms. Conyers said to her, holding the bowl out to a skinny girl in a turtleneck. "What's another definition?"

Silence. More people had their slips now, and a slight murmur became audible as they began to discuss them. Finally a guy in the back said in a flat voice, "The last thing you want to get from some people."

"Nice," Ms. Conyers said. By now, she'd gotten to me, and smiled as I reached into the bowl, grabbing the first slip I touched. I pulled it back, not opening it as she moved past the huge backpack to whoever was on the other side. "What else?"

"Sometimes," the girl who'd picked the word said, "you go looking for it when you can't make a decision on your own."

"Exactly," Ms. Conyers said, moving down the row of boys in the back. As she passed one—a guy with shaggy hair who was slumped over his books, his eyes closed—she nudged him, and he jerked to attention, looking around until she pointed at the bowl and he reached in for a slip. "So for instance, if I was going to give Jake here some advice, it would be what?"

"Get a haircut," someone said, and everyone laughed.

"Or," Ms. Conyers said, "get a good night's sleep, because napping in class is *not* cool."

"Sorry," Jake mumbled, and his buddy, sitting beside him in a Butter Biscuit baseball hat, punched him in the arm.

"The point," Ms. Conyers continued, "is that no word has one specific definition. Maybe in the dictionary, but not in real life. So the purpose of this exercise will be to take your word and figure out what it means. Not just to you but to the people around you: your friends, your family, coworkers, teammates. In the end, by compiling their responses, you'll have your own understanding of the term, in all its myriad meanings."

Everyone was talking now, so I looked down at my slip, slowly unfolding it. FAMILY, it said, in simple block print. *Great*, I thought. *The last thing I have, or care about. This must be—*

"Some kind of *joke*," I heard someone say. I glanced over, just as the backpack suddenly slid to one side. "What'd you get?"

I blinked, surprised to see the girl with the braids from

the parking lot who'd been running and talking on her cell phone. Up close, I could see she had deep green eyes, and her nose was pierced, a single diamond stud. She pushed the backpack onto the floor, where it landed with a loud *thunk*, then turned her attention back to me. "Hello?" she said. "Do you speak?"

"Family," I told her, then pushed the slip toward her, as if she might need visual confirmation. She glanced at it and sighed. "What about you?"

"Money," she said, her voice flat. She rolled her eyes. "Of course the one person in this whole place who doesn't have it has to write about it. It would just be too *easy* for everyone else."

She said this loudly enough that Ms. Conyers, who was making her way back to her desk, looked over. "What's the matter, Olivia? Don't like your term?"

"Oh, I like the term," the girl said. "Just not the assignment."

Ms. Conyers smiled, hardly bothered, and moved on, while Olivia crumpled up her slip, stuffing it in her pocket. "You want to trade?" I asked her.

She looked over at my FAMILY again. "Nah," she said, sounding tired. "That I know too much about."

Lucky you, I thought as Ms. Conyers reassumed her position on her desk, a slim book in her hands. "Moving on," she said, "to our reading selection for today. Who wants to start us off on last night's reading of *David Copperfield*?"

Thirty minutes later, after what felt like some major literary déjà-vu, the bell finally rang, everyone suddenly pushing back chairs, gathering up their stuff, and talking at once. As I reached down, grabbing my own backpack off the floor, I couldn't help but notice that, like me, it looked out of place here—all ratty and old, still stuffed with notebooks full of what was now, in this setting, mostly useless information. I'd known that morning I should probably toss everything out, but instead I'd just brought it all with me, even though it meant flipping past endless pages of notes on *David Copperfield* to take even more of the same. Now, I slid the FAMILY slip inside my notebook, then let the cover fall shut.

"You went to Jackson?"

I looked up at Olivia, who was now standing beside the table, cell phone in hand, having just hoisted her own huge backpack over one shoulder. At first, I was confused, wondering if my cheap bag made my past that obvious, but then I remembered the JACKSON SPIRIT! sticker on my notebook, which had been slapped there by some overexcited member of the pep club during study hall. "Uh, yeah," I told her. "I do. I mean . . . I did."

"Until when?"

"A couple of days ago."

She cocked her head to the side, studying my face while processing this information. In the meantime, distantly through the receiver end of her phone, I heard another phone ringing, a call she'd clearly made but had not yet completed. "Me, too," she said, pointing at the coat she had on, which now that I looked more closely, was a Jackson letter jacket.

"Really," I said.

She nodded. "Up until last year. You don't look familiar,

though." Distantly, I heard a click. *"Hello?"* someone said, and she put her phone to her ear.

"It's a big place."

"No kidding." She looked at me for a minute longer, even as whoever was on the other end of the line kept saying hello. "It's a lot different from here."

"Seems like it." I shoved my notebook into my bag.

"Oh, you have *no* idea. You want some advice?"

As it turned out, this was a rhetorical question.

"Don't trust the natives," Olivia said. Then she smiled, like this was a joke, or maybe not, before putting her phone to her ear, our conversation clearly over as she began another one and turned toward the door. "Laney. Hey. What's up? Just between classes. . . . Yeah, no kidding. Well, obviously can't sit around waiting for you to call *me*. . . ."

I pulled my bag over my shoulder, following her out to the hallway, which was now bustling and busy, although at the same time hardly crowded, at least in terms of what I was used to. No one was bumping me, either by accident or on purpose, and if anyone did grab my ass, it would be pretty easy to figure out who it was. According to my schedule, I had Spanish in Conversation next, which was in building C. I figured that since this was my one day I could claim ignorance on all counts, there was no point in rushing, so I took my time as I walked along, following the crowd outside.

Just past the door, on the edge of the quad, there was a huge U-shaped sculpture made of some kind of chrome that caught the sunlight winking off it in little sparks and making everything seem really bright. Because of this effect, it was kind of hard at first to make out the people grouped around it, some sitting, some standing, which was why, when I first heard my name, I had no idea where it was coming from.

"Ruby!"

I stopped, turning around. As my eyes adjusted, I could see the people at the sculpture and immediately identified them as the same kind of crowd that, at Jackson, hung out on the low wall just outside the main office: the see-and-be-seens, the top of the food chain, the group that you didn't join without an express invitation. Not my kind of people. And while it was kind of unfortunate that the one person I knew outside of Perkins Day was one of them, it wasn't all that surprising, either.

Nate was standing on the edge of the green; when he saw me spot him, he lifted a hand, smiling. "So," he said as a short guy wearing a baseball hat skittered between us. "Attempted any great escapes lately?"

I glanced at him, then at his friends—which included the blonde Jump Java girl from my English class, I now noticed—who were talking amongst themselves a few feet behind him. *Ha-ha*, I thought. Moments ago, I'd been invisible, or as invisible as you can be when you're the lone new person at a school where everyone has probably known each other since birth. Now, though, I was suddenly aware that people were staring at me—and not just Nate's assembled friends, either. Even the people passing us were glancing over, and I wondered how many people had already heard this story, or would before day's end. "Funny," I said, and turned away from him.

"I'm only kidding around," he called out. I ignored this,

continuing on. A moment later he jogged up beside me, planting himself in my path. "Hey," he said. "Sorry. I was just . . . it was just a joke."

I just looked at him. In broad daylight, he looked even more like a jock than the night before—in jeans, a T-shirt with collared shirt over it, rope necklace around his neck, and thick flip-flops on his feet, even though it was way past beach season. His hair, as I'd noticed last night, was that white kind of blond, like he'd spent the summer in the sun, his eyes a bright blue. *Too perfect*, I thought. The truth was, if this was the first time I'd laid eyes on him, I might have felt a little bad about discounting him as a thick jock with a narrow mind-set and an even tinier IQ. As this was our second meeting, though, it was a little easier.

"Let me make it up to you," he said, nodding at my schedule, which I still had in my hand. "You need directions?"

"Nope," I said, pulling my bag higher up on my shoulder.

I expected him to look surprised—I couldn't imagine he got turned down much for anything—but instead he just shrugged. "All right," he said. "I guess I'll just see you around. Or tomorrow morning, anyway."

There was a burst of laughter from beside me as two girls sharing a pair of earphones attached to an iPod brushed past. "What's happening tomorrow morning?"

Nate raised his eyebrows. "The carpool," he said, like I was supposed to have any idea what he was talking about. "Jamie said you needed a ride to school."

"With you?"

He stepped back, putting a hand over his chest. "Careful,"

he said, all serious. "You're going to hurt my feelings."

I just looked at him. "I don't need a ride."

"Jamie seems to think you do."

"I don't."

"Suit yourself," he said, shrugging again. Mr. Easygoing. "I'll come by around seven thirty. If you don't come out, I'll move on. No biggie."

No biggie, I thought. *Who talks like that?* He flashed me another million-dollar smile and turned to leave, sliding his hands into his pockets as he loped back, casual as ever, to his crop of well-manicured friends.

The first warning bell rang just as started toward what I hoped—but was in no way sure—was Building C. *Don't trust the natives*, Olivia had told me, but I was already a step ahead of her: I didn't trust anyone. Not for directions, not for rides, and not for advice, either. Sure, it sucked to be lost, but I'd long ago realized I preferred it to depending on anyone else to get me where I needed to go. That was the thing about being alone, in theory or in principle. Whatever happened—good, bad, or anywhere in between—it was always, if nothing else, all your own.

* * *

After school, I was supposed to take a bus home. Instead, I walked out of Perkins Day's stone gates and a half mile down the road to the Quik Zip, where I bought myself a Zip Coke, then settled inside the phone booth. I held the sticky receiver away from my ear as I dropped in a few coins, then dialed a number I knew by heart.

"Hello?"

"Hey, it's me," I said. Then, too late, I added, "Ruby."

I listened as Marshall took in a breath, then let it out. "Ah," he said finally. "Mystery solved."

"I was a mystery?" I asked.

"You were something," he replied. "You okay?"

This was unexpected, as was the lump that rose up in my throat as I heard it. I swallowed, then said, "Yeah. I'm fine."

Marshall was eighteen and had graduated from Jackson the year before, although we hadn't known each other until he moved in with Rogerson, the guy who sold all my friends their pot. At first, Marshall didn't make much of an impression—just a tall, skinny guy who was always passing through or in the kitchen when we went over there to get bags. I'd never even talked to him until one day I went over by myself and Rogerson wasn't around, so it was just the two of us.

Rogerson was all business and little conversation. You knocked, you came in, got what you needed, and got out. I was expecting pretty much the same with Marshall, and at first he didn't disappoint, barely speaking as I followed him to the living room and watched him measure out the bag. I paid him and was just about to get to my feet when he reached over to a nearby cabinet, pulling open a drawer and taking out a small ceramic bowl. "You want some?" he asked.

"Sure," I replied, and then he handed it over, along with a lighter. I could feel him watching me, his dark eyes narrowed, as I lit it, took some in, and passed it back.

The pot was good, better than the stuff we bought, and I felt it almost instantly, the room and my brain slowly taking on a heavy, rolling haze. Suddenly, everything seemed that much more fascinating, from the pattern on the couch beneath me to Marshall himself, sitting back in his chair, his hands folded behind his head. After a few minutes, I realized we'd stopped passing the bowl back and forth and were just sitting there in silence, for how long I had no idea.

"You know what we need," he said suddenly, his voice low and flat.

"What's that?" My own tongue felt thick, my entire mouth dry.

"Slurpees," he said. "Come on."

I'd been afraid he would ask me to drive, which was completely out of the question, but instead, once outside, he led the way down a path that cut across a nearby field dotted with power lines, emerging a block down from a convenience store. We didn't talk the entire way there, or when we were in the store itself. It was not until we were leaving, in fact, each of us sucking away at our Slurpees—which were cold and sweet and perfect—that he finally spoke.

"Good stuff," he said, glancing over at me.

I nodded. "It's *fantastic.*"

Hearing this, he smiled, which was unnerving simply because it was something I'd never seen before. Even stranger, as we started back across the path, he reached behind him, grabbing my hand, and then held it, walking a little bit ahead, the whole way home. I will never forget that, my Slurpee cold on my teeth and Marshall's palm warm against mine as we walked in the late-afternoon sunshine, those power lines rising up and casting long shadows all around us.

When he stopped walking and kissed me a few minutes later, it was like time had stopped, with the air, my heart, and the world all so still. And it was this I remembered every other time I was with Marshall. Maybe it was the setting, us alone in that field, or because it was the first time. I didn't know yet that this was all either of us was capable of: moments together that were great but also fleeting.

Marshall was not my boyfriend. On the other hand, he wasn't just a friend either. Instead, our relationship was elastic, stretching between those two extremes depending on who else was around, how much either of us had had to drink, and other varying factors. This was exactly what I wanted, as commitments had never really been my thing. And it wasn't like it was hard, either. The only trick was never giving more than you were willing to lose. With Marshall and me, it was like a game called I Could Care Less. I talked to a guy at a party; he disappeared with some girl at the next one. He didn't return my calls; I'd stay away for a while, making him wonder what I was up to. And so on.

We'd been doing this for so long that really, it came naturally. But now, I was so surprised by how nice it was to hear his voice, something familiar in all this newness, that I found myself breaking my own rule, offering up more than I'd planned.

"Yeah, so, I've just been, you know, dealing with some family stuff," I said, easing back against the booth wall behind me. "I moved in with my sister, and—"

"Hang on a sec, okay?" he said, and then I heard his hand cover the receiver, muffling it. Then he was saying something, his words impossible to make out before I heard him come back on. "Sorry," he said, then coughed. "What were you saying?"

And just like that, it was over. Even missing him was fleeting, like everything else.

"Nothing," I told him. "I should go. I'll catch up with you later, okay?"

"Yeah. See you around."

I hung up, leaving my hand on the receiver as I reached into my pocket, pulling out some more change. Then I took a breath and put it back to my ear, dropped in a few coins, and called someone I knew would be more than happy to talk.

"Ruby?" Peyton said as soon as she heard my voice. "Oh my God. What *happened* to you?"

"Well," I said.

But she was already continuing, her voice coming out in a gush. "I mean, I was waiting for you in the courtyard, just like always, and you never showed up! So I'm like, she must be mad at me or something, but then Aaron said the cops had pulled you out of class, and nobody knew why. And then I went by your house, and it was all dark, and—"

"Everything's fine," I said, cutting her off more out of a time concern than rudeness. Peyton was always summarizing, even when you knew the story as well as she did. "It's just a family thing. I'm staying with my sister for a while."

"Well," she said, "it's all *anyone* is talking about, just so you know. You should hear the rumors."

"Yeah?"

"It's terrible!" she said, sounding truly aghast. "They have you doing everything from committing murder to teen prostitution."

"I've been gone for two days," I said.

"Of course, I've been sticking up for you," she added quickly. "I told them there was no way you'd ever sleep with guys for money. I mean, come on."

This was typical Peyton. Defending my honor vigorously, while not realizing that she was implying that I might be capable of murder. "Well," I said, "I appreciate it."

"No problem." I could hear voices behind her; from the sound of it, she was at the clearing a ways down from school, where we always hung out after final bell. "So, like, what's the real story, though? Is it your mom?"

"Something like that," I told her. "Like I said, it's not a big deal."

Peyton was my closest friend at Jackson, but like everyone else, she had no idea my mom had taken off. She'd actually never even met her, which was no accident; as a rule, I preferred to keep my private life just that, private. This was especially important with someone like Peyton, whose family was pretty much perfect. Rich and functional, they lived in a big house in the Arbors, where up until the year before, she'd been the ideal daughter, pulling straight As and lettering in field hockey. During the summer, though, she'd started dating my friend Aaron, who was a harmless but dedicated pothead. In the fall, she'd gotten busted with a joint at school and was asked to leave St. Micheline's, the Catholic school she'd been attending. Her parents, of course, were none too pleased, and hoped Peyton's new-found rebellion was a just a phase that would end when she and Aaron broke up. After a few weeks, they did, but by that point, she and I were already friends.

Peyton was, in a word, cute. Short and curvy, she was

also incredibly naive, which was alternately annoying and endearing. Sometimes I felt more like a big sister to her than a friend—I was always having to rescue her from weird guys at parties, or hold her head when she puked, or explain again how to work the various expensive electronics her parents were always buying her—but she was fun to hang out with, had a car, and never complained about having to come all the way out to pick me up, even though it was on the way to nowhere. Or back.

"So the thing is," I said to her now, "I need a favor."

"Name it," she replied.

"I'm over here by Perkins Day, and I need a ride," I told her. "Can you come get me?"

"At Perkins Day?"

"Near there. Just down the street."

There was a pause, during which time I heard laughter behind her. "God, Ruby . . . I wish I could. But I'm supposed to be home in an hour."

"It's not that far," I said.

"I know. But you know how my mom's been lately." Since the last time Peyton had come home smelling like beer, her parents had instituted a strict accountability program involving constant tracking, elaborate sniff tests, and surprise room searches. "Hey, did you try Marshall? I bet he can—"

"No," I said, shaking my head. Peyton had never quite gotten Marshall's and my arrangement; an incurable romantic, to her, every story was a love story. "It's fine, don't worry about it."

There was another pause, and again, I could hear what

was happening around her: laughter, someone's radio playing, a car engine starting up. It was true what I'd said: it wasn't that far from there to here, only fifteen miles or so. But at that moment, it suddenly seemed like a long way.

"You sure?" she asked. "Because I could ask someone here."

I swallowed, leaning back against the side of the booth. On the opposite side, above the phone, someone had written WHERE DO YOU SLEEP? in thick black marker. Scratched underneath, less legibly, was a reply: WITH YOUR MAMA. I reached up, rubbing my face with my hand. It wasn't like I'd expected anyone to come rescue me, anyway. "Nah," I said. "That's all right. I'll figure out something."

"All right," she said. A car horn beeped in the background. "Give me your sister's number, though. I'll call you tonight, we can catch up."

"I'm still getting settled," I told her. "I'll give you a call in a few days."

"Okay," she said easily. "And hey, Ruby."

"What?"

"I'm glad you're not a hooker or a murderer."

"Yeah," I said. "Me, too."

I hung up the phone, then stepped out of the booth to finish off my Coke and contemplate my next move. The parking lot, which had been mostly empty when I first got there, had filled up with Perkins Day students. Clearly, this was some sort of off-site hangout, with people sitting on the hoods and bumpers of their expensive cars, slumming at the Quick Zip. Scanning the crowd, I spotted Nate off to the right, arms crossed over his chest, leaning against the driver's-side door of a black SUV. A dark-haired girl in a ponytail and a cropped blue jacket was with him, telling some story and gesturing wildly, the Zip Coke in her hand waving back and forth as she spoke. Nate, of course, was smiling as he listened, the epitome of the Nicest Guy in the World.

Then something occurred to me. I glanced at my watch. It was just before four, which meant I had a little over an hour before I'd be late enough for anyone to notice. It was enough time to do what I had to do, if I got going soon. All I needed was a little help, and if I worked things right, maybe I wouldn't even have to ask for it.

As I hitched my backpack over my shoulder and started toward the road, I made it a point not to look at the Perkins Day contingent, even as I passed right in front of them. Instead, I just kept my focus forward, on the big intersection that lay ahead. It was a long walk home, and even farther to where I really needed to be, making this a serious gamble, especially considering how I'd acted earlier. But part of being nice was forgiveness—or so I'd heard—so I rolled the dice anyway.

Two blocks down the road, I heard a car horn, then an engine slowing behind me. I waited until the second beep before arranging my face to look surprised, and turned around. Sure enough, there was Nate.

"Let me guess," he said. He was leaning across the passenger seat, one hand on the wheel, looking up at me. "You don't need a ride."

"Nope," I told him. "Thanks, though."

"This is a major road," he pointed out. "There's not even a sidewalk."

"Who are you, the safety monitor?"

He made a face at me. "So you'd prefer to just walk the six miles home."

"It's not six miles," I said.

"You're right. It's six point two," he replied as a red Ford beeped angrily behind him, then zoomed past. "I run it every Friday. So I know."

"Why are you so hell-bent on driving me somewhere?" I asked.

"I'm chivalrous," he said.

Yeah, right, I thought. *That's one word for it.* "Chivalry's dead."

"And you will be, too, if you keep walking along here." He sighed. "Get in."

And it was just that easy.

※　※　※

Inside, Nate's car was dark, the interior immaculate, and still smelled new. Even so, there was an air freshener hanging from the rearview. The logo on it said REST ASSURED EXECUTIVE SERVICES: WE WORRY SO YOU DON'T HAVE TO.

"It's my dad's company," he explained when he saw me looking at it. "We work to make life simpler in these complicated times."

I raised my eyebrows. "That sounds like something right off a brochure."

"Because it is," he said. "But I have to say it if anybody asks what we do."

"And what if they want an actual answer?"

"Then," he said, glancing behind him as he switched lanes, "I tell them we do everything from picking up mail to

walking dogs to getting your dry-cleaning to frosting cupcakes for your kid's school party."

I considered this. "Doesn't sound as good."

"I know. Hence the rule."

I sat back in my seat, looking out the window at the
buildings and cars blurring past. Okay, fine. So he wasn't
terrible company. Still, I wasn't here to make friends.

"So look," he said, "about earlier, and that joke I made."

"It's fine," I told him. "Don't worry about it."

He glanced over at me. "What were you doing, though?
I mean, on the fence. If you don't mind my asking."

I did mind. I was also pretty much at his mercy at this
point, so I said, "Wasn't it obvious?"

"Yeah, I suppose it was," he said. "I think I was just, you
know, surprised."

"At what?"

"I don't know." He shrugged. "Just seems like most people would be trying to break *into* that house, not escape it.
Considering how cool Cora and Jamie are, I mean."

"Well," I said. "I guess I'm not most people."

I felt him look at me as I turned my head, looking out
the window again. My knowledge of this part of town was
fairly limited, but from what I could tell, we were getting
close to Wildflower Ridge, Jamie and Cora's neighborhood,
which meant it was time to change the subject. "So anyway," I said, shooting for casual, "I do appreciate the ride."

"No problem," he said. "It's not like we aren't going to
the same place."

"Actually . . ." I paused, then waited for him to look over

at me. When he did, I said, "If you could just drop me off by a bus stop, that'd be great."

"Bus stop?" he said. "Where are you going?"

"Oh, just to a friend's house. I have to pick something up."

We were coming up to a big intersection now. Nate slowed, easing up behind a VW bug with a flower appliqué on the back bumper. "Well," he said, "where is it?"

"Oh, it's kind of far," I said quickly. "Believe me, you don't want to have to go there."

The light changed, and traffic started moving forward. *This is it*, I thought. *Either he takes the bait, or he doesn't*. It was four fifteen.

"Yeah, but the bus will take you ages," he said after a moment.

"Look, I'll be fine," I said, shaking my head. "Just drop me off up here, by the mall."

The thing about negotiations, not to mention manipulation, is you can't go too far in any direction. Refusing once is good, twice usually okay, but a third is risky. You never know when the other person will just stop playing and you end up with nothing.

I felt him glance over at me again, and I made a point of acting like I didn't notice, couldn't see him wavering. *Come on*, I thought. *Come on.*

"Really, it's cool," he said finally, as the entrance to the highway appeared over the next hill. "Just tell me where to go."

*   *   *

"Man," Nate said as he bumped up the driveway to the yellow house, avoiding holes and a sizable stack of water-logged newspapers. Up ahead, I could already see my mom's Subaru, parked just where I'd left it, gas needle on empty, that last day Peyton had picked me up for school. "Who lives here again?"

"Just this girl I know," I said.

As far as I was concerned, this entire endeavor would be quick and painless. Get in, get what I needed, and get out, hopefully with as little explanation as necessary. Then Nate would take me back to Cora's, and this would all be over. Simple as that.

But then, just as we passed the bedroom window, I saw the curtain move.

It was very quick, so quick I wondered if I'd seen anything at all—just a shift of the fabric an inch to the left, then back again. The exact way it would have to for someone to peer out and yet still not be seen.

I wasn't sure what I'd been expecting to find here. Maybe the Honeycutts, in the midst of some project. Or the house empty, cleaned out as if we'd never been here at all. This possibility, though, had never crossed my mind.

Which was why Nate hadn't even finished parking when I pushed open my door and got out. "Hey. Do you want—?" I heard him call after me, but I ignored him, instead taking the steps two at time and arriving at the front door breathless, my fingers already fumbling for the key around my neck. Once I put it in the lock, the knob, familiar in my hand, turned with a soft click. And then I was in.

"Mom?" I called out, my voice bouncing off all the hard surfaces back at me. I walked into the kitchen, where I could see the clothesline was still strung from one wall to the other, my jeans and shirts now stiff and mildewy as I pushed past them. "Hello?"

In the living room, there was a row of beer bottles on the coffee table, and the blanket we usually kept folded over one arm of the sofa was instead balled into one corner. I felt my heart jump. I would have folded it back. Wouldn't I?

I kept moving, pushing open my bedroom door and flicking on the single bulb overhead. This did look just like I'd left it, save for my closet door being left open, I assumed by whoever packed up the clothes that had been brought to me at Poplar House. I turned, crossing back into the living room and walking over to the other bedroom door, which was shut. Then I put my hand on the knob and closed my eyes.

It wasn't like making a wish or trying to dream something into being real. But in that moment, I tried to remember all the times I'd come home and walked to this same door, easing it open to see my mom curled up in her bed, hair spilling over the pillowcase, already reaching a hand to shield her eyes from the light behind me. This image was so clear in my mind that when I first pushed open the door, I was almost sure I did see a glimpse of red, some bit of movement, and my heart jumped into my throat, betraying in one instant all the emotions I'd denied to myself and everyone else in the last week. Then, though, just as quickly, something shifted. The objects and room itself fell into place: bed, dark walls . . . and that window, where I now remembered the bit of broken pane, half–taped up, where a breeze still could inch in, ruffling the curtain. I'd been mistaken. But even so, I stayed where I was, as if by doing so the room would, in the next moment, suddenly be anything but empty.

"Ruby?"

Nate's voice was low, tentative. I swallowed, thinking how stupid I was, thinking that my mom might have actually come back, when I knew full well that everything she needed she'd taken with her. "I'll be done in a sec," I said to him, hating how my voice was shaking.

"Are you . . . ?" He paused. "Are you okay?"

I nodded, all business. "Yeah. I just have to grab something."

I heard him shift his weight, taking a step, although toward me or away, I wasn't sure, and not knowing this was enough to make me turn around. He was standing in the doorway to the kitchen, the front door open behind him, turning his head slowly, taking it all in. I felt a surge of shame; I'd been so stupid to bring him here. Like I, of all people, didn't know better than to lead a total stranger directly to the point where they could hurt me most, knowing how easily they'd be able to find their way back to it.

"This place," Nate said, looking at the bottles on the table, a lone cobweb stretching across the room between us, "it's, like—"

Suddenly there was a gust of wind outside, and a few leaves blew in the open door, skittering in across the kitchen floor. I felt so shaken, unsettled, that my voice was sharp as I said, "Just wait in the car. All right?"

He looked at me for a second. "Yeah," he said. "Sure thing." Then he stepped outside, pulling the door shut behind him.

Stop it, I told myself, feeling tears pricking my eyes, so stupid. I looked around the room, trying to clear my head and concentrate on what I should take with me, but everything was blurring, and I felt a sob work its way up my throat. I put my hand over my mouth, my shoulders shaking, and forced my feet to move.

Think, think, I kept saying in my head as I walked back to the kitchen and began pulling stuff off the clothesline. Everything was stiff and smelly, and the more I took down the more I could see of the rest of the kitchen: the pots and pans piled in the sink, the buckets I'd used to collect water from the bathroom, the clothesline, now sagging over my head. *I was doing just fine*, I'd told Cora, and at the time, I'd believed it. But now, standing there with my stiff clothes in my arms, the smell of rotting food filling my nostrils, I wasn't so sure anymore.

I reached up, wiping my eyes, and looked back out at Nate, who was sitting behind the wheel of his car, a cell phone to his ear. God only knew what he was thinking. I looked down at my clothes, knowing I couldn't bring them with me, even though they, the few things in the next room, and that beat-up, broken-down Subaru were all I really had. As I dropped them onto the table, I told myself I'd come back for them and everything else, just as soon as I got settled. It was such an easy promise to make. So easy that I could almost imagine another person saying the same thing to themselves as they walked out that door, believing it, too. Almost.

* * *

I was not looking forward to the ride home, as God only knew what Nate would say to me, or how I would dodge the questions he would inevitably ask. So I decided, as I locked the door behind me, to go with a route I knew well: complete and total denial. I'd act like nothing out of the ordinary had happened, as if this trip was exactly what I had expected it to be. If I was convincing enough, he'd have no choice but to see it the same way.

I was all casual as I walked back to the car, playing my part. When I got in, though, I realized it wasn't even necessary. He still had the phone clamped to his ear and didn't even glance at me as he shifted into reverse, backing away from the house.

While he was distracted, I took one last look at that window into my mom's room. Talk about denial; even from a distance and in motion, I could tell there was no one inside. There's something just obvious about emptiness, even when you try to convince yourself otherwise.

"It's not a problem," Nate said suddenly, and I glanced over at him. He had his eyes on the road, his mouth a thin line as he listened to whoever was speaking. "Look, I can be there in ten minutes. Maybe even less than that. Then I'll just grab it from her, and—"

Whoever it was cut him off, their voice rising enough that I could hear it, though not make out specific words. Nate reached up, rubbing a hand over his face. "I'll be there in ten minutes," he said, hitting the gas as we turned back onto the main road. "No . . ." He trailed off. "I just had to run this errand for school. Yeah. Yes. Okay."

He flipped the phone shut, dropping it with a clank into the console between our seats. "Problem?" I said.

"Nah," he said. "Just my dad. He's a little . . . controlling about the business."

"You forgot to frost some cupcakes?"

He glanced over at me, as if surprised I was capable of humor. "Something like that," he said. "I have to make a stop on the way home. If you don't mind."

"It's your car," I said with a shrug.

As we merged onto the highway, the phone rang again. Nate grabbed it, glancing at the display, then flipped it open. "Hello? Yes. I'm on the way. On the highway. Ten minutes. Sure. Okay. Bye."

This time, he didn't put the phone down, instead just keeping it in his hand. After a moment, he said, "It's just the two of us, you know. Living together, working together. It can get . . . kind of intense."

"I know," I said.

Maybe it was because my mother was on my mind, but this came out before I even realized it, an unconscious, immediate reaction. It was also the last thing I wanted to be talking about, especially with Nate, but of course then he said, "Yeah?"

I shrugged. "I used to work with my mom. I mean, for a while anyway."

"Really?" I nodded. "What'd you do?"

"Delivered lost luggage for the airlines."

He raised his eyebrows, either surprised or impressed. "People really do that?"

"What, you think they just get teleported to you or something?"

"No," he said slowly, shooting me a look. "I just mean . . . it's one of those things you know gets done. You just don't actually think of someone doing it."

"Well," I said, "I am that someone. Or was, anyway."

We were taking an exit now, circling around to a stoplight. As we pulled up to it, Nate said, "So what happened?"

"With what?"

"The luggage delivery. Why did you quit?"

This time, I knew enough not to answer, only evade. "Just moved on," I said. "That's all."

Thankfully, he did not pursue this further, instead just putting on his blinker and turning into the front entrance of the Vista Mall, a sprawling complex of stores and restaurants. The parking lot was packed as we zipped down a row of cars, then another before pulling up behind an old green Chevy Tahoe. The back door was open, revealing an extremely cluttered backseat piled with boxes and milk crates, which were in turn filled with various envelopes and packing materials. A woman with red hair coiled into a messy bun wearing a fuzzy pink sweater and holding a to-go coffee cup in one hand was bent over them, her back to us.

Nate rolled down his window. "Harriet," he called out.

She didn't hear him as she picked up a crate, shoving it farther back. An empty coffee cup popped out and started to roll away, but she grabbed it, stuffing it in another box.

"Harriet," Nate repeated. Again, no answer as she bent deeper over a crate.

"You're going to have to be louder," I told him as he was barely speaking above a normal tone of voice.

"I know," he said. Then he took a breath, wincing slightly, and put his hand on the horn.

He only did it once, and it was quick: *beep!* Still, the woman literally jumped in the air. Completely vertical, feet off the ground, coffee spilling out of the cup backward, splattering the pavement. Then she whirled around, her free hand to her chest, and goggled at us.

"Sorry," Nate called out. "But you weren't—"

"What are you doing?" she asked him. "Are you *trying* to give me a nervous attack?"

"No." He pushed open his door, quickly climbing out and walking over to her. "Here, let me get that. It's these three? Or the crates, too?"

"All of them," the woman—Harriet?—said, clearly still flustered as she leaned against the Tahoe's bumper, flapping a hand in front of her face. As Nate began to load the boxes into the back of his car, I noticed she was rather pretty, and had on a chunky silver necklace with matching earrings, as well as several rings. "He knows I'm a nervous person," she said to me, gesturing at Nate with her cup. "And yet he beeps. He *beeps*!"

"It was an accident," Nate told her, returning for the last box. "I'm sorry."

Harriet sighed, leaning back against the bumper again and closing her eyes. "No," she said, "it's me. I'm just under this massive deadline, and I'm way behind, and I just knew I wasn't going to get to the shipping place before they closed—"

"—which is why you have us," Nate finished for her, shutting his own back door with a bang. "I'm taking them over right now. No worries."

"They all need to go Ground, not Next Day," she told him. "I can't afford Next Day."

"I know."

"And be sure you get the tracking information, because they're promised by the end of the week, and there's been bad weather out West. . . ."

"Done," Nate told her, pulling his door open.

Harriet considered this as she stood there clutching her coffee cup. "Did you drop off that stuff at the cleaners yesterday?"

"Ready on Thursday," Nate told her.

"What about the bank deposit?" she asked.

"Dad did it this morning. Receipt is in the envelope in your mailbox."

"Did he remember to—"

"—lock it back? Yes. The key is where you said to leave it. Anything else?"

Harriet drew in a breath, as if about to ask another question, then slowly let it out. "No," she said slowly. "At least not right at this moment."

Nate slid behind the wheel. "I'll e-mail you all the tracking info as soon as I get home. Okay?"

"All right," she said, although she sounded uncertain as he cranked the engine. "Thanks."

"No problem. Call if you need us."

She nodded but was still standing by her bumper, gripping her cup and looking uncertain, as we pulled away. I waited until we'd turned onto the main road again before saying, "That's resting assured?"

"No," Nate said, his voice tired. "That's Harriet."

By the time we pulled up to Cora's, it was five thirty. Only a little over an hour had passed since he'd picked me up, and yet it felt like so much longer. As I gathered up my stuff, pushing the door open, his phone rang again; he glanced at the display, then back at me. "Dad's getting nervous," he said. "I better go. I'll see you tomorrow morning?"

I looked over at him, again taking in his solid good looks and friendly expression. Fine, so he was a nice guy, and maybe not entirely the dim jock that I'd pegged him as at first glance. Plus, he had helped me out, not once but twice, and maybe to him this meant my previous feelings about a carpool would no longer be an issue. But I could not so easily forget Peyton earlier on the other end of that pay-phone line, how quickly she had turned me down at the one moment I'd really needed her.

"Thanks for the ride," I said.

Nate nodded, flipping his phone open, and I shut the door between us. I wasn't sure whether he had noticed I hadn't answered his question, or if he'd even care. Either way, by the time I was halfway down the walk, he was gone.

*   *   *

Earlier that morning, after we'd set up my schedule, Jamie headed off to work and Mr. Thackray started to walk me off to my English class. We were about halfway there when I suddenly heard Jamie calling after us.

"Hold up!"

I turned around, looking down the hallway, which was rapidly filling with people streaming out of their first class, and spotted him bobbing through the crowd. When he reached us, slightly out of breath, he smiled and held his hand out to me, gesturing for me to do the same.

My first instinct was to hesitate, wondering what else he could possibly offer me. But when I opened up my hand, palm flat, and he dropped a key into it, it seemed ridiculous to have expected anything else.

"In case you beat us home," he said. "Have a good day!"

At the time, I'd nodded, closing my hand around the key and slipping it into my pocket, where I'd totally forgotten about it until now, as I walked up to the front door of the house and pulled it out. It was small and on a single silver fob, with the words WILDFLOWER RIDGE engraved on the other side. Weird how it had been there all day, and I hadn't even felt it or noticed. The one around my neck I was always aware of, both its weight and presence, but maybe that was because it was closer to me, where it couldn't be missed.

Cora's door swung open almost soundlessly, revealing the big, airy foyer. Like at the yellow house, everything was still and quiet, but in a different way. Not untouched or forgotten, but more expectant. As if even a house knew the difference between someone simply stepping out for while and being gone for good.

I shut the door behind me. From the foyer, I could see

into the living room, where the sun was already beginning to sink in the sky, disappearing behind the trees, casting that special kind of warm light you only get right before sunset.

I was still just standing there watching this, when I heard a tippity-tapping noise coming from my left. I glanced over; it was Roscoe, making his way through the kitchen. When he saw me, his ears perked up straight on his head. Then he sat down and just stared at me.

I stayed where I was, wondering if he was going to start barking at me again, which after starting a new school and breaking into my old house was going to be the last thing I could take today. Thankfully, he didn't. Instead, he just began to lick himself, loudly. I figured this signaled it was safe to continue on to the kitchen, which I did, giving him a wide berth as I passed.

On the island, there was a sticky note, and even though it had been years since I'd seen it, I immediately recognized my sister's super neat handwriting, each letter so perfect you had to wonder if she'd done a rough draft first. *J*, it said, *Lasagna is in the fridge, put it in (350) as soon as you get home. See you by seven at the latest. Love, me.*

I picked the note up off the counter, reading it again. If nothing else, this made it clear to me that my sister had, in fact, finally gotten everything she wanted. Not just the things that made up the life she'd no doubt dreamed of—the house, the job, the security—all those nights in our shared room, but someone to share it with. To come home to and have dinner with, to leave a note for. Such simple, stupid things, and yet in the end, they were the true proof of a real life.

Which was why, after she'd worked so hard to get here, it had to really suck to suddenly have me drop back in at the very moment she'd started to think she'd left the old life behind for good. *Oh, well,* I thought. The least I could do was put in the lasagna.

I walked over to the oven and preheated it, then found the pan in the fridge and put it on the counter. I was pulling off the Saran wrap when I felt something against my leg. Looking down, I saw Roscoe had at some point crossed the room and was now sitting between my feet, looking up at me.

My first thought was that he had peed on the floor and was waiting for me to yell at him. But then I realized he was shaking, bouncing back and forth slightly from one of my ankles to the other. "What?" I asked him, and in response he burrowed down farther, pressing himself more tightly against me. All the while, he kept his big bug eyes on me, as if pleading, but for what, I had no idea.

Great, I thought. Just what I needed: the dog dies on my watch, thereby officially cementing my status as a complete blight on the household. I sighed, then stepped carefully around Roscoe to the phone, picking it up and dialing Jamie's cell-phone number, which was at the top of a list posted nearby. Before I was even done, Roscoe had shuffled across the floor, resituating himself at my feet, the shaking now going at full force. I kept my eyes on him as the phone rang twice, and then, thankfully, Jamie picked up.

"Something's wrong with the dog," I reported.

"Ruby?" he said. "Is that you?"

"Yes." I swallowed, looking down at Roscoe again, who in turn scooted closer, pressing his face into my calf. "I'm sorry to bother you, but he's just acting really . . . sick. Or something. I didn't know what to do."

"Sick? Is he throwing up?"

"No."

"Does he have the runs?"

I made a face. "No," I said. "At least, I don't think so. I just came home and Cora had left this note about the lasagna, so I put it in and—"

"Oh," he said slowly. "Okay. It's all right, you can relax. He's not sick."

"He's not?"

"Nope. He's just scared."

"Of lasagna?"

"Of the oven." He sighed. "We don't really understand it. I think it may have something to do with this incident involving some Tater Tots and the smoke detector."

I looked down at Roscoe, who was still in full-on tremulous mode. You had to wonder how such a thing affected a little dog like that—it couldn't be good for his nervous system. "So," I said as he stared up at me, clearly terrified, "how do you make it stop?"

"You can't," he said. "He'll do it the entire time the oven's on. Sometimes he goes and hides under a bed or the sofa. The best thing is to just act normal. If he drives you too crazy, just shut him in the laundry room."

"Oh," I said as the dog rearranged himself, wedging himself between my shoe and the cabinet behind me. "Okay."

"Look, I'm breaking up," he said, "but I'll be home soon. Just—"

There was a buzz, and then he was gone, dropping off

altogether. I hung up, replacing the phone carefully on its base. I wasn't sure what "soon" meant, but I hoped it meant he was only a few blocks away, as I was not much of an animal person. Still, looking down at Roscoe trembling against my leg, it seemed kind of mean to just shut him up in a small space, considering the state he was in.

"Just relax, okay?" I said, untangling myself from around him and walking to the foyer to my bag. For a moment he stayed where he was, but then he started to follow me. The last thing I wanted was any kind of company, so I started up the stairs at a quick clip, hoping he'd get the message and stay behind. Surprisingly, it worked; when I got to the top of the stairs and looked down, he was still in the foyer. Staring up at me looking pitiful, but still there.

Up in my room, I washed my face, then slid Cora's sweater off and lay back across the bed. I don't know how long I was there, staring out the windows at the last of the sunset, before Roscoe came into the room. He was moving slowly, almost sideways, like a crab. When he saw that I'd noticed him, his ears went flat on his head, as if he was expecting to be ejected but couldn't help taking a shot anyway.

For a moment, we just looked at each other. Then, tentatively, he came closer, then a bit closer still, until finally he was wedged between my feet, with the bed behind him. When he started shaking again, his tags jingling softly, I rolled my eyes. I wanted to tell him to cut it out, that we all had our problems, that I was the last person he should come looking to for solace. But instead, I surprised myself by saying none of this as I sat up, reaching a hand down to his head. The moment I touched him, he was still.

Chapter Four

At first, it just a rumbling, punctuated by the occasional shout: the kind of thing that you're aware of, distantly, and yet can still manage to ignore. Right as my clock flipped over to 8:00, though, the real noise began.

I sat up in bed, startled, as the room suddenly filled with the clanking of metal hitting rock. It wasn't until I got up and went out on my balcony and saw the backhoe that it all started to make sense.

"Jamie!"

I glanced to my right, where I could see my sister, in her pajamas, standing on her own balcony. She was clutching the railing, looking down at her husband, who was on the back lawn looking entirely too awake, a mug of coffee in his hands and Roscoe at his feet. When he looked up and saw her, he grinned. "Great, right?" he said. "You can really visualize it now!"

Most of Cora's response to this was lost in the ensuing din as the backhoe dug once more into the lawn, scooping up more earth from within Jamie's circle of rocks and swinging to the side to dump it on the already sizable pile there. As it moved back, gears grinding, to go in again, I just caught the end, when she was saying, ". . . Saturday morning, when some people might want to *sleep.*"

"Honey, it's the pond, though," Jamie replied, as if he had heard every word. "We talked about this. Remember?"

Cora just looked at him, running a hand through her hair, which was sticking up on one side. Then, without further comment, she went inside. Jamie watched her go, his face quizzical. "Hey!" he shouted when he saw me. The backhoe dug down again, with an even louder clank. "Pretty cool, don't you think? If we're lucky, we'll have it lined by tonight."

I nodded, watching as the machine dumped another load of dirt onto the pile. Jamie was right, you could really picture it now: there was a big difference between a theoretical pond and a huge hole in the ground. Still, it was hard to imagine what he wanted—a total ecosystem, a real body of water, with fish and everything—seeming at home in the middle of such a flat, square yard. Even with the best landscaping, it would still look as if it had fallen from the sky.

Back inside, I flopped back into bed, although sleeping was clearly no longer an option. Hard to believe that the previous Saturday, I'd been at the yellow house, waking up on the couch with our old moldy afghan curled around me. Fast-forward a week, and here I was at Cora's. My basic needs were certainly being met—running water, heat, food—but it was still strange to be here. Everything felt so temporary, including me, that I hadn't even unpacked yet—my bag was still right by the bed, where I was living out of it like I was on a vacation, about to check out at any moment. Sure, it meant the little bit of stuff I had was that much more wrinkled, but rolling over every morning and seeing all my worldly possessions right there beside me made me feel somewhat in control of my situation. Which I needed, considering that everything else seemed completely out of my hands.

*   *   *

"The bus?" Jamie said that first night, when he mentioned Nate picking me up and I told him I'd prefer alternate transportation. "Are you serious?"

"There isn't a Perkins Day bus in the morning," Cora said from across the table. "They only run in the afternoon, to accommodate after-school activities."

"Then I'll take the city bus," I said.

"And go to all that trouble?" Jamie asked. "Nate's going to Perkins anyway. And he offered."

"He was just being nice," I said. "He doesn't really want to drive me."

"Of course he does," Jamie said, grabbing another roll from the basket between us. "He's a prince. And we're chipping in for gas. It's all taken care of."

"The bus is fine," I said again.

Cora, across the table, narrowed her eyes at me. "What's really going on here?" she asked. "You don't like Nate or something?"

I picked up my fork, spearing a piece of asparagus. "Look," I said, trying to keep my voice cool, collected, "it just seems like a big hassle. If I ride the bus, I can leave when I want, and not be at the mercy of someone else."

"No, you'll be at the mercy of the bus schedule, which is *much* worse," Jamie said. He thought for a second. "Maybe we should just get you a car. Then you can drive yourself."

"We're not buying another car," Cora said flatly.

"She's seventeen," Jamie pointed out. "She'll need to go places."

"Then she'll ride the bus. Or ride with Nate. Or borrow yours."

"Mine?"

Cora just looked at him, then turned her attention to me. "If you want to do the bus, fine. But if it makes you late, you have to do the carpool. All right?"

I nodded. Then, after dinner, I went online and printed out four different bus schedules, circling the ones I could catch from the closest stop and still make first bell. Sure, it meant getting up earlier and walking a few blocks. But it would be worth it.

Or so I thought, until I accidentally hit the snooze bar a few extra times the next morning and didn't get downstairs until 7:20. I was planning to grab a muffin and hit the road, running if necessary, but of course Cora was waiting for me.

"First bell in thirty minutes," she said, not looking up from the paper, which she had spread out in front of her. She licked a finger, turning a page. "There's no way."

So ten minutes later, I was out by the mailbox cursing myself, muffin in hand, when Nate pulled up. "Hey," he said, reaching across to push the door open. "You changed your mind."

That was just the thing, though. I hadn't. If anything, I was more determined than ever to not make friends, and this just made it harder. Still, it wasn't like I had a choice, so I got in, easing the door shut behind me and putting my muffin in my lap.

"No eating in the car."

The voice was flat, toneless, and came from behind me. As I slowly turned my head, I saw the source: a short kid wearing a peacoat and some serious orthodontia, sitting in the backseat with a book open in his lap.

"What?" I said.

He leaned forward, his braces—and attached headgear—catching the sunlight coming through the windshield. His hair was sticking up. "No eating in the car," he repeated, robotlike. Then he pointed at my muffin. "It's a rule."

I looked at Nate, then back at the kid. "Who are you?"

"Who are *you*?"

"This is Ruby," Nate said.

"Is she your new girlfriend?" the kid asked.

"No," Nate and I said in unison. I felt my face flush.

The kid sat back. "Then no eating. Girlfriends are the only exception to carpool rules."

"Gervais, pipe down," Nate said.

Gervais picked up his book, flipping a page. I looked at Nate, who was now pulling out onto the main road, and said, "So . . . where do you take him? The middle school?"

"Wrong," Gervais said. His voice was very nasal and annoying, like a goose honking.

"He's a senior," Nate told me.

"A senior?"

"What are you, deaf?" Gervais asked.

Nate shot him a look in the rearview. "Gervais is accelerated," he said, changing lanes. "He goes to Perkins in the morning, and afternoons he takes classes at the U."

"Oh," I said. I glanced back at Gervais again, but he ignored me, now immersed in his book, which was big and thick, clearly a text of some kind. "So . . . do you pick up anyone else?"

"We used to pick up Heather," Gervais said, his eyes still on his book, "when she and Nate were together. She got to eat in the car. Pop-Tarts, usually. Blueberry flavor."

Beside me, Nate cleared his throat, glancing out the window.

"But then, a couple of weeks ago," Gervais continued in the same flat monotone, turning a page, "she dumped Nate. It was big news. He didn't even see it coming."

I looked at Nate, who exhaled loudly. We drove on for another block, and then he said, "No. We don't pick up anyone else."

Thankfully, this was it for conversation. When we pulled into the parking lot five minutes later, Gervais scrambled out first, hoisting his huge backpack over his skinny shoulders and taking off toward the green without a word to either of us.

I'd planned to follow him, also going my own way, but before I could, Nate fell into step beside me. It was clear this just came so easily to him, our continuing companionship assumed without question. I had no idea what that must be like.

"So look," he said, "about Gervais."

"He's charming," I told him.

"That's one word for it. Really, though, he's not—"

He trailed off suddenly, as a green BMW whizzed past us, going down a couple of rows and whipping into a space. A moment later, the driver's-side door opened, and the blonde from my English class—in a white cable sweater, sunglasses parked on her head—emerged, pulling an over-stuffed tote bag behind her. She bumped the door shut with her hip, then started toward the main building, fluffing her hair with her fingers as she walked. Nate watched her for a moment, then coughed, stuffing his hands in his pockets.

"Really what?" I said.

"What's that?" he asked.

Ahead of us, the blonde—who I had now figured out was the infamous, blueberry Pop-Tart–eating Heather—was crossing to a locker, dropping her bag at her feet. "Nothing," I said. "See you around."

"Yeah," he replied, nodding, clearly distracted as I quickened my pace, finally able to put some space between us. "See you."

He was still watching her as I walked away. Which was kind of pathetic but also not my problem, especially since from now on I'd be sticking to my original plan and catching the bus, and everything would be fine.

Or so I thought until the next day, when I again overslept, missing my bus window entirely. At first, I was completely annoyed with myself, but then, in the shower, I decided that maybe it wasn't so bad. After all, the ride was a short one. At least distance-wise.

"What kind of shampoo is that?" Gervais demanded from the backseat as soon as I got in the car, my hair still damp.

I turned back and looked at him. "I don't know," I said. "Why?"

"It stinks," he told me. "You smell like trees."

"Trees?"

"Gervais," Nate said. "Watch it."

"I'm just saying," Gervais grumbled, flopping back against the seat. I turned around, fixing my gaze on him. For a moment, he stared back, insolent, his eyes seemingly huge behind his glasses. But as I kept on, steady, unwavering, he finally caved and turned to stare out the window. *Twelve-year-olds*, I thought. *So easy to break.*

When I turned back to face forward, Nate was watching me. "What?" I said.

"Nothing," he replied. "Just admiring your technique."

At school, Gervais did his normal scramble-and-disappearing act, and again Nate walked with me across the parking lot. This time, I was not only aware of him beside me—which was still just so odd, frankly—but also the ensuing reactions from the people gathered around their cars, or ahead of us at the lockers: stares, raised eyebrows, entirely too much attention. It was unsettling, not to mention distracting.

When I'd started at Perkins, I'd instinctively gone into New School Mode, a system I'd perfected over the years when my mom and I were always moving. Simply put, it was this: come in quietly, fly under the radar, get in and out each day with as little interaction as possible. Because Perkins Day was so small, though, I was realizing it was inevitable that I'd attract some attention, just because I was new. Add in the fact that someone had figured out my connection to Jamie—"Hey, UMe!" someone had yelled as I walked in the hall a couple of days earlier—and staying anonymous was that much more difficult.

Nate deciding we were friends, though, made it almost

impossible. Even by my second day, I'd figured out he was one of the most popular guys at Perkins, which made me interesting (at least to these people, anyway) simply by standing next to him. Maybe some girls would have liked this, but I was not one of them.

Now, I looked over at him, annoyed, as a group of cheerleaders standing in a huddle by a shiny VW tittered in our wake. He didn't notice, too busy watching that same green BMW, which was parked a couple of rows over. I could see Heather behind the wheel, her Jump Java cup in one hand. Jake Bristol, the sleeper from my English class, was leaning in to talk to her, his arms resting on her open window.

This was not my problem. And yet, as with Gervais, when I saw bad behavior, I just couldn't help myself. Plus, if he was going to insist on walking with me, he almost deserved it.

"You know," I said to him. "Pining isn't attractive. On anyone."

He glanced over at me. "What?"

I nodded at Heather and Jake, who were still talking. "The worst thing you can do if you miss or need someone," I said, "is let them know it."

"I don't miss her," he said.

Yeah, right. "Okay," I replied, shrugging. "All I'm saying is that even if you do want her back, you should act like you don't. No one likes someone who's all weak and pitiful and needy. It's basic relationship 101."

"Relationship 101," he repeated, skeptical. "And this is a course you teach?"

"It's only advice," I told him. "Ignore it if you want."

Really, I assumed he'd do just that. The next morning, though, as he again fell into step beside me—clearly, this was a habit now—and we began crossing the parking lot, Heather's car once again came into view. Even I noticed it, and her, by now. But Nate, I saw, did not. Or at least didn't act like it. Instead, he glanced over at me and then just kept walking.

As the week went on—and my losses to the snooze bar continued—I found myself succumbing to the carpool and, subsequently, our walk together into school itself, audience and all. Resistance was futile, and Nate and I were becoming friends, or something like it. At least as far as he was concerned.

Which was just crazy, because we had absolutely nothing in common. Here I was, a loner to the core, burnout personified, with a train wreck of a home life. And in the other corner? Nate, the good son, popular guy, and all around nice, wholesome boy. Not to mention—as I found out over the next week—student body vice president, homecoming king, community liaison, champion volunteerer. His name just kept coming up, in event after event listed in the flat monotone of the guy who delivered the announcements each morning over the intercom. Going to the senior class trip fund-raiser? Contact Nate Cross. Pitching in to help with the annual campus cleanup? Talk to Nate. Need a study buddy for upcoming midterms? Nate Cross is your man.

He was not my man, however, although as the week—not to mention the staring I'd first noticed in the parking lot—continued, it was clear some people wanted to think otherwise. It was obvious Heather and Nate's breakup had been huge news, at least judging by the fact that weeks later, I was still hearing about their relationship: how they'd dated since he'd moved from Arizona freshman year, been junior prom king and queen, had plans to go off to the U for college in the fall together. For all these facts, though, the cause of their breakup remained unclear. Without even trying, I'd heard so many different theories—He cheated with some girl at the beach! She wanted to date other guys!—that it was obvious no one really knew the truth.

Still, it did explain why they were all so interested in me. The hot popular guy starts showing up with new girl at school, right on the heels of breakup with longtime love. It's the next chapter, or so it seems, so of course people would make their assumptions. And in another school, or another town, this was probably the case. But not here.

As for Perkins Day itself, it *was* a total culture shift, with everything from the teachers (who actually seemed happy to be there) to the library (big, with all working, state-of-the-art computers) to the cafeteria (with salad bar and smoothie station) completely different from what I'd been used to. Also, the small class size made slacking off pretty much a non-option, and as a result, I was getting my ass kicked academically. I'd never been the perfect student by a long shot, but at Jackson I'd still managed to pull solid Bs, even with working nights and my quasi-extracurricular activities. Now, without transportation or friends to distract me, I had all the time in the world to study, and yet I was still struggling, big-time. I kept telling myself it didn't matter, that I'd probably only be there until I could raise the money to take off, so there wasn't any real point in killing myself to keep up. But then, I'd find myself sitting in my room with nothing to do, and pull out the books and get to work, if only for the distraction.

The mentality at Perkins was different, as well. For instance, at Jackson at lunch, due to the cramped cafeteria, lack of coveted picnic tables, and general angst, there was always some kind of drama going on. Fistfights, yelling, little scuffles breaking out and settling down just as quickly, lasting hardly long enough for you to turn your head and notice them. At Perkins, everyone coexisted peacefully in the caf and on the green, and the most heated anything ever got was when someone at the HELP table got a little too fired up about some issue and it burst into a full-fledged debate, but even those were usually civil.

The HELP table itself was another thing I just didn't get. Every day at lunch, just as the period began, some group would set up shop at one of the tables right by the caf entrance, hanging up a sign and laying out brochures to rally support for whatever cause they were promoting. So far, in the time I'd been there, I'd seen everything from people collecting signatures for famine relief to asking for spare change to buy a new flat-screen TV for the local children's hospital. Every day there was something new, some other cause that needed our help and attention RIGHT NOW so PLEASE SIGN UP or GIVE or LEND A HAND—IT'S THE LEAST YOU CAN DO!

It wasn't like I was a cruel or heartless person. I believed in charity as much as anyone else. But after everything I'd been through the last few months, I just couldn't wrap my mind around reaching out to others. My mother had taught me too well to look out for number one, and right now, in this strange world, this seemed smarter than ever. Still, every time I passed the HELP table, taking in that day's cause—Upcoming AIDS walk! Buy a cookie, it benefits early literacy! Save the Animals!—I felt strangely unsettled by all this want, not to mention the assumed and steady outpouring of help in return, which seemed to come as instinctively to the people here as keeping to myself did to me.

One person who clearly was a giver was Heather Wainwright, who always seemed to be at the HELP table, regardless of the cause. I'd seen her lecturing a group of girls with smoothies on the plight of the Tibetans, selling cupcakes for cancer research, and signing up volunteers to help clean up the stretch of highway Perkins Day sponsored, and she seemed equally passionate about all of them. This was yet another reason, at least in my mind, that whatever rumors were circulating about Nate and me couldn't have been more off the mark. Clearly, I wasn't his type, by a long shot.

Of course, if I had wanted to make friends with people more like me, I could have. The burnout contingent at Perkins Day was less scruffy than their Jackson counterparts but still easily recognizable, hanging out by the far end of the quad near the art building in a spot everyone called the Smokestack. At Jackson, the stoners and the art freaks were two distinct groups, but at Perkins, they had comingled, either because of the reduced population or the fact that there was safety in numbers. So alongside the guys in the rumpled Phish T-shirts, Hackey-sacking in their flip-flops, you also had girls in dresses from the vintage shop and combat boots, sporting multicolored hair and tattoos. The population of the Smokestack usually showed up about halfway through lunch, trickling in from the path that led to the lower soccer fields, which were farthest away from the rest of the school. Once they arrived, they could be seen furtively trading Visine bottles and scarfing down food from the vending machine, stoner behavior so classic and obvious I was continually surprised the administration didn't swoop in and bust them en masse.

It would have been so easy to walk over and join them, but even after a few lunches spent with only my sandwich, I still hadn't done so. Maybe because I wouldn't be there long, anyway—it wasn't like there was much point in making friends. Or maybe it was something else. Like the fact that I had a second chance now, an opportunity, whether I'd first welcomed it or not, to do things differently. It seemed stupid to not at least try to take it. It wasn't like the old way had been working for me so well, anyway.

Still, there was one person at Perkins Day that, if pressed, I could imagine hanging out with. Maybe because she was the only one less interested in making friends than I was.

By now, I'd figured out a few things about Olivia Davis, my seatmate and fellow Jackson survivor. Number one: she was *always* on the phone. The minute the bell rang, she had it out and open, quick as a gunslinger, one finger already dialing. She kept it clamped to her ear as she walked between classes and all through lunch, which she also spent alone, eating a sandwich she brought from home and talking the entire time. From the few snippets I overheard before our class started and just after it ended, she was mostly talking to friends, although occasionally she'd affect an annoyed, flat tone that screamed parental conversation. Usually, though, she was all noisy chatter, discussing the same things, in fact, that I heard from everyone else in the hallways or around me in my classrooms—school, parties, stress—except that her conversations were one-sided, her voice the only one I could hear.

It was also clear that Olivia was at Perkins Day under protest, and a vocal one at that. I had strong opinions about our classmates and their lifestyles but kept these thoughts to myself. Olivia practiced no such discretion.

"Yeah, right," she'd say under her breath as Heather Wainwright began a long analysis of the symbolism of poverty in *David Copperfield*. "Like *you* know from poverty. In your BMW and million-dollar mansion."

"Ah, yes," she'd murmur as one of the back-row jocks, prodded by Ms. Conyers to contribute, equated his experience not making starter with a character's struggle, "tell us about your pain. We're *riveted*."

Sometimes she didn't say anything but still made her point by sighing loudly, shaking her head, and throwing why-me-Lord? looks up at the ceiling. At first, her tortuous endurance of second period was funny to me, but after a while, it got kind of annoying, not to mention distracting. Finally, on Friday, after she'd literally tossed her hands up as one of our classmates struggled to define "blue collar," I couldn't help myself.

"If you hate this place so much," I said, "why are you here?"

She turned her head slowly, as if seeing me for the first time. "Excuse me?" she said.

I shrugged. "It's not like it's cheap. Seems like a waste of money is all I'm saying."

Olivia adjusted herself in her seat, as if perhaps a change of position might help her to understand why the hell I was talking to her. "I'm sorry," she said, "but do we know each other?"

"It's just a question," I said.

Ms. Conyers, up at the front of the room, was saying something about the status quo. I flipped a few pages in my notebook, feeling Olivia watching me. After a moment, I looked up and met her gaze, letting her know she didn't intimidate me.

"Why are *you* here?" she asked.

"No choice in the matter," I told her.

"Me neither," she replied. I nodded. This was enough, as far as I was concerned. But then she continued. "I was doing just fine at Jackson. It was my dad that wanted me here and made me apply for a scholarship. Better education, better teachers. Better class of friends, all that. You happy now?"

"Never said I wasn't," I told her. "You're the one moaning and groaning over there."

Olivia raised her eyebrows. Clearly, I'd surprised her, and I had a feeling this wasn't so easy to do. "What's your name again?"

"Ruby," I told her. "Ruby Cooper."

"Huh," she said, like this answered some other question, as well. The next time I saw her, though, in the quad between classes, she didn't just brush by, ignoring me in favor of whoever was talking in her ear. She didn't speak to me, either. But I did get a moment of eye contact, some acknowledgment, although of what I wasn't sure, and still couldn't say.

*   *   *

Now, lying on my bed Saturday morning, I heard a crash from outside, followed by more beeping. I got up and walked to the window, looking down at the yard. The hole was even bigger now, the red clay and exposed rock a marked contrast to the even green grass on either side of it. Jamie was still on the patio with the dog, although now he had his hands in his pockets and was rocking back on his heels as he watched the machine dig down again. It was hard to remember what the yard had looked like even twelve hours before, undisturbed and pristine. Like it takes so little not only to change something, but to make you forget the way it once was, as well.

Downstairs in the kitchen, the noise was even louder, vibrations rattling the glass in the French doors. I could see that Cora, now dressed, her hair damp from the shower, had joined Jamie outside. He was explaining something to her, gesturing expansively as she nodded, looking less than enthusiastic.

I got myself some cereal, figuring if I didn't, someone would give me another breakfast lecture, then picked up a section of the newspaper from the island. I was on my way to sit down when there was a bang behind me and Roscoe popped through the dog door.

When he saw me, his ears perked up and he pattered over, sniffing around my feet. I stepped over him, walking to the table, but of course he followed me, the way he'd taken to doing ever since the night of the lasagna trauma. Despite my best efforts to dissuade him, the dog liked me.

"You know," Jamie had said the day before, watching as Roscoe stared up at me with his big bug eyes during dinner, "it's pretty amazing, actually. He doesn't bond with just anyone."

"I'm not really a dog person," I said.

"Well, he's not just a dog," Jamie replied. "He's Roscoe."

This, however, was little comfort at times like this, when I just wanted to read my horoscope in peace and instead had to deal with Roscoe attending to his daily toilette—heavy on the slurping—at my feet. "Hey," I said, nudging him with the toe of my shoe. "Cut it out."

He looked up at me. One of his big eyes was running, which seemed to be a constant condition. After a moment, he went back to what he was doing.

"You're up," I heard Cora say from behind me as she came in the patio door. "Let me guess. Couldn't sleep."

"Something like that," I said.

She poured herself a cup of coffee, then walked over to the table. "Me," she said with a sigh as she sat down, dropping a hand to pat Roscoe's head, "I wanted a pool. Something we could swim in."

I glanced up at her, then out at the backhoe, which was swinging down into the hole. "Ponds are nice, though," I said. "You'll have fish."

She sighed. "So typical. He's already won you over."

I shrugged, turning a page. "I don't take sides."

I felt her look at me as I said this, her eyes staying on

me as I scanned the movie listings. Then she picked up her mug, taking another big sip, before saying, "So. I think we need to talk about a few things."

Just as she said this, the backhoe rattled to a stop, making everything suddenly seem very quiet. I folded the paper, pushing it aside. "Okay," I said. "Go ahead."

Cora looked down at her hands, twining her fingers through the handle of her cup. Then she raised her gaze, making a point of looking me straight in the eye as she said, "I think it's safe to say that this . . . situation was unexpected for both of us. It's going to take a bit of adjustment."

I took another bite of cereal, then looked at Roscoe, who was lying at Cora's feet now, his head propped up on his paws, legs spread out flat behind him like a frog. "Clearly," I said.

"The most important things," she continued, sitting back, "at least to Jamie and me, are to get you settled in here and at school. Routine is the first step to normalcy."

"I'm not a toddler," I told her. "I don't need a schedule."

"I'm just saying we should deal with one thing at a time," she said. "Obviously, it won't all run smoothly. But it's important to acknowledge that while we may make mistakes, in the long run, we may also learn from them."

I raised my eyebrows. Maybe I was still in survival mode, but this sounded awfully touchy-feely to me, like a direct quote from some book like *Handling Your Troubled Teen.* Turned out, I wasn't so far off.

"I also think," Cora continued, "that we should set you up to see a therapist. You're in a period of transition, and talking to someone can really—"

"No," I said.

She looked up at me. "No?"

"I don't need to talk to anyone," I told her. "I'm fine."

"Ruby," she said. "This isn't just me. Shayna at Poplar House really felt you would benefit from some discussion about your adjustment."

"Shayna at Poplar House knew me for thirty-six hours," I said. "She's hardly an expert. And sitting around talking about the past isn't going to change anything. There's no point to it."

Cora picked up her coffee cup, taking a sip. "Actually," she said, her voice stiff, "some people find therapy to be very helpful."

Some people, I thought, watching her as she took another slow sip. *Right.*

"All I'm saying," I said, "is that you don't need to go to a lot of trouble. Especially since this is temporary, and all."

"Temporary?" she asked. "How do you mean?"

I shrugged. "I'm eighteen in a few months."

"Meaning what?"

"Meaning I'm a legal adult," I told her. "I can live on my own."

She sat back. "Ah, yes," she said. "Because that was working out *so* well for you before."

"Look," I said as the backhoe started up again outside, startling Roscoe, who had nodded off, "you should be happy. You'll only be stuck with me for a little while and then I'll be out of your hair."

For a moment, she just blinked at me. Then she said, "To go where? Back to that house? Or will you get your own apartment, Ruby, with all the money at your disposal?"

I felt my face flush. "You don't—"

"Or maybe," she continued, loudly and dramatically, as if there was an audience there to appreciate it, "you'll just go and move back in with Mom, wherever she is. Because she probably has a great place with a cute guest room all set up and waiting for you. Is that your plan?"

The backhoe was rumbling again, scooping, digging deeper.

"You don't know anything about me," I said to her. "Not a thing."

"And whose fault is that?" she asked.

I opened my mouth, ready to answer this; it was a no-brainer, after all. Who had left and never returned? Stopped calling, stopped caring? Managed to forget, once she was free and past it, the life that she'd left behind, the one I'd still been living? But even as the words formed on my lips, I found myself staring at my sister, who was looking at me so defiantly that I found myself hesitating. Here, in the face of the one truth I knew by heart.

"Look," I said, taking another bite, "all I'm saying is that you shouldn't have to turn your whole life upside down. Or Jamie's, either. Go on as you were. It's not like I'm a baby you suddenly have to raise or something."

Her expression changed, the flat, angry look giving way to something else, something not exactly softer, but more distant. Like she was backing away, even while staying in the same place. She looked down at her coffee cup, then cleared her throat. "Right," she said curtly. "Of course not."

She pushed her chair up, getting to her feet, and I

watched her walk to the coffeemaker and pour herself another cup. A moment later, with her back still to me, she
said, "You will need some new clothes, though. At least a
few things."

"Oh," I said, looking down at my jeans, which I'd washed
twice in three days, and the faded T-shirt I'd worn my last
day at Jackson. "I'm okay."

Cora picked up her purse. "I've got an appointment this
morning, and Jamie has to be here," she said, taking out a
few bills and bringing them over to me. "But you can walk
to the new mall. There's a greenway path. He can show you
where it is."

"You don't have to—"

"Ruby. Please." Her voice was tired. "Just take it."

I looked at the money, then at her. "Okay," I said.
"Thanks."

She nodded but didn't say anything, instead just turning
around and walking out of the room, her purse under her
arm. Roscoe lifted his head, watching her go, then turned
his attention to me, watching as I unfolded the money. It
was two hundred bucks. *Not bad*, I thought. Still, I waited
another moment, until I was sure she'd gone upstairs, before pocketing it.

The door rattled beside me as Jamie came in, empty
coffee mug dangling from one finger. "Morning!" he said,
clearly on a pond high as he walked to the island, grabbing
a muffin out of the box on the table on his way. Roscoe
jumped up, following him. "So, did you guys get your shopping day all planned out? And FYI, there's no just browsing
with her. She *insists* on a plan of attack."

"We're not going shopping," I said.

"You aren't?" He turned around. "I thought that was the plan. Girls' day out, lunch and all that."

I shrugged. "She said she has an appointment."

"Oh." He looked at me for a moment. "So . . . where'd she go?"

"Upstairs, I think."

He nodded, then glanced back out at the backhoe, which was backing up—*beep beep*. Then he looked at me again before starting out of the room, and a moment later, I heard the steady thump of him climbing the stairs. Roscoe, who had followed him as far as the doorway, stopped, looking back at me.

"Go ahead," I told him. "Nothing to see here."

Of course, he didn't agree with this. Instead, as Cora's and Jamie's voices drifted down from upstairs—discussing me, I was sure—he came closer, tags jingling, and plopped down at my feet again. Funny how in a place this big, it was so hard to just be alone.

*　　*　　*

An hour and a half later, dressed and ready with Cora's money in my pocket, I headed outside to ask Jamie for directions to the shortcut to the mall. I found him at the far end of the yard, beyond the now sizable and deep hole, talking to a man by Nate's fence.

At first, I assumed it was one of the guys from the digging company, several of whom had been milling around ever since the backhoe had arrived. Once I got closer, though, it became apparent that whoever this guy was, he didn't drive machinery for a living.

He was tall, with salt-and-pepper gray hair and tanned skin, and had on faded jeans, leather loafers, and what I was pretty sure was a cashmere sweater, a pair of expensive-looking sunglasses tucked into his collar. As he and Jamie talked, he was spinning his car keys around one finger, then folding them into his palm, again and again. *Spin, clank, spin, clank.*

". . . figured you were digging to China," the man was saying as I came into earshot. "Or for oil, maybe."

"Nope, just putting in a pond," Jamie said.

"A pond?"

"Yeah." Jamie slid his hands into his pockets, glancing over at the hole again. "Organic to the landscaping and the neighborhood. No chemicals, all natural."

"Sounds expensive," the man said.

"Not really. I mean, the initial setup isn't cheap, but it's an investment. Over time, it'll really add to the yard."

"Well," the man said, flicking his keys again, "if you're looking for an investment, we should sit down and talk. I've got some things cooking that might interest you, really up-and-coming ideas. In fact—"

"Ruby, hey," Jamie said, cutting him off as he spotted me. He slid an arm over my shoulder, saying, "Blake, this is Ruby, Cora's sister. She's staying with us for a while. Ruby, this is Blake Cross. Nate's dad."

"Nice to meet you," Mr. Cross said, extending his hand. He had a firm handshake, the kind I imagined they must teach in business school: two pumps, with solid eye contact the entire time. "I was just trying to convince your brother-in-law it's a better thing to put money in a good idea than the ground. Don't you agree?"

"Um," I said as Jamie shot me a sympathetic smile. "I don't know."

"Of course you do! It's basic logic," Mr. Cross said. Then he laughed, flicking his keys again, and looked at Jamie, who was watching the backhoe again.

"So," I said to Jamie, "Cora said you could tell me how to get to the mall?"

"The mall?" Jamie asked. "Oh, the greenway. Sure. It's just down the street, to the right. Stones by the entrance."

"Can't miss it," Mr. Cross said. "Just look for all the people not from this neighborhood traipsing through."

"Blake," Jamie said, "it's a community greenway. It's open to everyone."

"Then why put it in a private, gated neighborhood?" Mr. Cross asked. "Look, I'm as community oriented as the next person. But there's a reason we chose to live here, right? Because it's exclusive. Open up a part of it to just anyone and you lose that."

"Not necessarily," Jamie said.

"Come on," Mr. Cross said. "I mean, what'd you spend on your place here?"

"You know," Jamie said, obviously uncomfortable, "that's not really—"

"A million—or close to it, right?" Mr. Cross continued, over him. Jamie sighed, looking over at the backhoe again. "And for that price, you should get what you want, whether it be a sense of security, like-minded neighbors, exclusivity—"

"Or a pond," I said, just as the backhoe banged down again, then began to back up with a series of beeps.

"What's that?" Mr. Cross asked, cupping a hand over his ear.

"Nothing," I said. Jamie looked over at me, smiling. "It was nice to meet you."

He nodded, then turned his attention back to Jamie as I said my good-byes and started across the yard. On my way, I stopped at the edge of the hole, looking down into it. It was deep, and wide across, much more substantial than what I'd pictured based on Jamie's description. A lot can change between planning something and actually doing it. But maybe all that really matters is that anything is different at all.

Chapter Five

Maybe it was my talk with Cora, or just the crazy week I'd had. Whatever the reason, once I got to the mall, I found myself heading to the bus stop. Two transfers and forty minutes later, I was at Marshall's.

He lived in Sandpiper Arms, an apartment complex just through the woods from Jackson that was best known for its cheap rent and the fact that its units were pre-furnished. They were also painted an array of pastel colors, candy pinks and sky blues, bright, shiny yellows. Marshall's was lime green, which wasn't so bad, except for some reason going there always made me want a Sprite.

When I first knocked on the door, nobody answered. After two more knocks, I was about to pull out my bus schedule and start plotting my ride home, but then the door swung open, and Rogerson peered out at me.

"Hey," I said. He blinked, then ran a hand through his thick dreadlock-like hair, squinting in the sun. "Is Marshall here?"

"Bedroom," he replied, dropping his hand from the door and shuffling back to his own room. I didn't know much about Rogerson, other than the pot thing and that he and Marshall worked together in the kitchen at Sopas, a Mexican joint in town. I'd heard rumors about him spending some time in jail—something about assault—but he wasn't the most talkative person and pretty much kept to himself, so who knew what was really true.

I stepped inside, shutting the door behind me. It took a minute for my eyes to adjust: Marshall and Rogerson, like my mother, preferred things dim. Maybe it was a late-shift thing, this aversion to daylight in general, and morning specifically. The room smelled like stale smoke as I moved forward, down the narrow hallway, passing the small kitchen, where pizza boxes and abandoned soda bottles crowded the island. In the living room, some guy was stretched out across the sofa, a pillow resting on his face: I could see a swath of belly, pale and ghostly, sticking out from under his T-shirt, which had ridden up slightly. Across the room, the TV was on, showing bass fishing on mute.

Marshall's door was closed, but not all the way. "Yeah?" he said, after I knocked.

"It's me," I replied. Then he coughed, which I took as permission to enter and pushed it open.

He was sitting at the pre-fab desk, shirtless, the window cracked open beside him, rolling a cigarette. His skin, freckled and pale, seemed to almost glow in the bit of light the window allowed, and, this being Marshall, you could clearly make out his collarbones and ribs. The boy was skinny, but unfortunately for me, I liked skinny boys.

"There she is," he said, turning to face me. "Long time no see."

I smiled, then cleared a space for myself across from him on the unmade bed and sat down. The room itself was a mess of clothes, shoes, and magazines, things strewn all over the place. One thing that stuck out was a box of candy, one of those samplers, on the bureau top, still wrapped in plastic. "What's that?" I asked. "You somebody's Valentine?"

He picked up the cigarette, sticking it into his mouth, and I instantly regretted asking this. It wasn't like I cared who else he saw, if anybody. "It's October."

"Could be belated," I said with a shrug.

"My mom sent it. You want to open it?" I shook my head, then watched as he sat back, exhaling smoke up into the air. "So what's going on?"

I shrugged. "Not much. I'm actually looking for Peyton. You seen her?"

"Not lately." A phone rang in the other room, then abruptly stopped. "But I've been working a lot, haven't been around much. I'm about to take off—have to work lunch today."

"Right," I said, nodding. I sat back, looking around me, as a silence fell over us. Suddenly I felt stupid for coming here, even with my lame excuse. "Well, I should go, too. I've got a ton of stuff to do."

"Yeah?" he said slowly, leaning forward, elbows on his knees, closer to me. "Like what?"

I shrugged, starting to push myself to my feet. "Nothing that would interest you."

"No?" he asked, stopping me by moving a little closer, his knees bumping mine. "Try me."

"Shopping," I said.

He raised his eyebrows. "No kidding," he said. "One week at Perkins Day and you're already fashion-conscious."

"How'd you know I was at Perkins Day?" I asked.

Marshall shrugged, pulling back a bit. "Someone was talking about it," he said.

"Really."

"Yeah." He looked at me for a moment, then slid his hands out, moving them up my thighs to my waist. Then he ducked his head down, resting it in my lap, and I smoothed my hands over his hair, running it through my fingers. As I felt him relax into me, another silence fell, but this one I was grateful for. After all, with me and Marshall, it had never been about words or conversation, where there was too much to be risked or lost. Here, though, in the quiet, pressed against each other, this felt familiar to me. And it was nice to let someone get close again, even if it was just for a little while.

It was only later, when I was curled up under his blankets, half asleep, that I was reminded of everything that had happened since the last time I'd been there. Marshall was getting ready for work, digging around for his belt, when he laid something cool on my shoulder. Reaching up, I found the key to Cora's house, still on its silver fob, which must have slipped out of my pocket at some point. "Better hang on to that," he said, his back to me as he bent over his shoes. "If you want to get home."

As I sat up, closing it in my hand, I wanted to tell him that Cora's house wasn't home, that I wasn't even sure what that word meant anymore. But I knew he didn't really care, and anyway he was already pulling on a Sopas T-shirt, getting ready to leave. So instead, I began collecting my own clothes, all business, just like him. I didn't necessarily have to get out first, but I wasn't about to be left behind.

*   *   *

I'd never been much of a shopper, mostly because, like sky-diving or playing polo, it wasn't really within my realm of possibility. Before my mom needed me for Commercial, I'd had a couple of jobs of my own—working at greasy fast-food joints, ringing up shampoo and paper towels at discount drugstores—but all that money I'd tried to put away. Even then I'd had a feeling that someday I would need it for something more than sweaters and lipsticks. Sure enough, once my mom had taken off, I'd pretty much cleared out my savings, and now I was back at zero, just when I needed money most.

Which was why it felt so stupid to even be buying clothes, especially with two hundred bucks I'd scored by doing absolutely nothing. On the flip side, though, I couldn't keep wearing the same four things forever. Plus, Cora was already pissed at me; making her think I'd just pocketed her money would only make things worse. So I forced myself through the narrow aisles of store after store, loud music blasting overhead as I scoured clearance racks for bargains.

It wasn't like I could have fit in at Perkins on my budget, even if I wanted to. Which, of course, I didn't. Still, in the time I'd been there, I'd noticed the irony in what all the girls were wearing, which was basically expensive clothes made to look cheap. Two-hundred-dollar jeans with rips and patches, Lanoler cashmere sweaters tied sloppily around their waists, high-end T-shirts specifically weathered and faded to look old and worn. My old stuff at the yellow house, mildew aside, would have been perfect; as it was, I was forced to buy not only new stuff but cheap new stuff, and the difference was obvious. Clearly, you had to spend a lot of money to properly look like you were slumming.

Still, after an hour and a half, I'd vastly increased my working wardrobe, buying two new pairs of jeans, a sweater, a hoodie, and some actual cheap T-shirts that, mercifully, were five for twenty bucks. Still, seeing my cash dwindle made me very nervous. In fact, I felt slightly sick as I started down the airy center of the mall toward the exit, which was probably why I noticed the HELP WANTED sign ahead right away. Stuck to the side of one of the many merchandise carts arranged to be unavoidable, it was like a beacon, pulling me toward it, step-by-step.

As I got closer, I saw it was on a jewelry stall, which appeared to be unmanned, although there were signs of someone having just left: a Jumbo Smoothie cup sweating with condensation was sitting on the register, and there was a stick of incense burning, the smoke wafting in long curlicues up toward the high, bright glass atrium-like ceiling above. The jewelry itself was basic but pretty, with rows and rows of silver-and-turquoise earrings, a large display of beaded necklaces, and several square boxes filled with rings of all sizes. I reached forward, drawing out a thick one with a red stone, holding it up in front of me and turning it in the light.

"Oh! Wait! Hello!"

I jumped, startled, then immediately put the ring back just as the redheaded woman from whom Nate had been picking up the boxes that day—Harriet—came bustling up, a Jump Java cup in one hand, out of breath but talking anyway.

"Sorry!" she gasped, planting it beside the smoothie cup on the register. "I've been trying to kick my caffeine habit—" here she paused, sucking in a big, and much needed, by the sound of it, breath—"by switching to smoothies. Healthy, right? But then the headache hit and I could feel myself crashing and I just had to run down for a fix." She took another big breath, now fanning her flushed face with one hand. "But I'm here now. Finally."

I just looked at her, not exactly sure what to say, especially considering she was still kind of wheezing. Now that I was seeing her up close, I figured she was in her mid-thirties, maybe a little older, although her freckles, hair, and outfit—low-slung jeans, suede clogs, and Namaste T-shirt—made it hard to pinpoint exactly.

"Wait," she said, putting her coffee on the register and pointing at me, a bunch of bangles sliding down her hand. "Do I know you? Have you bought stuff here before?"

I shook my head. "I was with Nate the other day," I said. "When he came to pick up those things from you."

She snapped her fingers, the bangles clanging again. "Right. With the beeping. God! I'm still recovering from that."

I smiled, then looked down at the display again. "Do you make all this yourself?"

"Yep, I'm a one-woman operation. To my detriment, at times." She hopped up on a stool by the register, picking up her coffee again. "I just made those ones with the red stones, on the second row. People think redheads can't wear red, but they're wrong. One of the first fallacies of my life. And I believed it for *years*. Sad, right?"

I glanced over at her, wondering if she'd been able to tell from a distance that this, in fact, was the one I'd been looking at. I nodded, peering down at it again.

"I love *your* necklace," she said suddenly. When I glanced over to see her leaning forward slightly, studying it, instinctively my hand rose to touch it.

"It's just a key," I said.

"Maybe." She took another sip of her coffee. "But it's the contrast that's interesting. Hard copper key, paired with such a delicate chain. You'd think it would be awkward or bulky. But it's not. It works."

I looked down at my necklace, remembering the day that—fed up with always losing my house key in a pocket or my backpack—I'd gone looking for a chain thin enough to thread through the top hole but still strong enough to hold it. At the time, I hadn't been thinking about anything but managing to keep it close to me, although now, looking in one of the mirrors opposite, I could see what she was talking about. It was kind of pretty and unusual, after all.

"Excuse me," a guy with a beard and sandals standing behind a nearby vitamin kiosk called out to her. "But is that a coffee you're drinking?"

Harriet widened her eyes at me. "No," she called out over her shoulder cheerily. "It's herbal tea."

"Are you lying?"

"Would I lie to you?"

"Yes," he said.

She sighed. "Fine, fine. It's coffee. But organic free-trade coffee."

"The bet," he said, "was to give up all caffeine. You owe me ten bucks."

"Fine. Add it to my tab," she replied. To me she added, "God, I *always* lose. You'd think I'd learn to stop betting."

I wasn't sure what to say to this, so I looked over the necklaces for another moment before saying, "So . . . are you still hiring?"

"No," she replied. "Sorry."

I glanced at the sign. "But—"

"Okay, *maybe* I am," she said. Behind her, the vitamin guy coughed loudly. She looked at him, then said reluctantly, "Yes. I'm hiring."

"All right," I said slowly.

"But the thing is," she said, picking up a nearby feather duster and busily running it across a display of bracelets, "I hardly have any hours to offer. And what I *can* give you is erratic, because you'd have to work around my schedule, which varies wildly. Some times I might need you a lot, others hardly at all."

"That's fine," I said.

She put the duster down, narrowing her eyes at me. "This is boring work," she warned me. "Lots of sitting in one place while everyone passes you by. It's like solitary confinement."

"It is not," Vitamin Guy said. "For God's sake."

"I can handle it," I told her as she shot him a look.

"It's like I said, I'm a one-woman operation," she added. "I just put up that sign. . . . I don't know why I put it up. I mean, I'm doing okay on my own."

There was pointed cough from the vitamin kiosk. She turned, looking at the guy there. "Do you need some water or something?"

"Nope," he replied. "*I'm* fine."

For a moment they just stared at each other, with me between them. Clearly, something was going on here, and my life was complicated enough. "You know, forget it," I said. "Thanks anyway."

I stepped back from the kiosk, hoisting my bags farther up my wrist. Just as I began to walk away, though, I heard another cough, followed by the loudest sigh yet.

"You have retail experience?" she called out.

I turned back. "Counter work," I said. "And I've cashiered."

"What was your last job?"

"I delivered lost luggage for the airlines."

She'd been about to fire off another question, but hearing this, she stopped, eyes widening. "Really."

I nodded, and she looked at me for a moment longer, during which time I wondered if I actually wanted to work for someone who seemed so reluctant to hire me. Before I could begin to consider this, though, she said, "Look, I'll be honest with you. I don't delegate well. So this might not work out."

"Okay," I said.

Still, I could feel her wavering. Like something balanced on the edge, that could go either way.

"Jesus," Vitamin Guy said finally. "Will you tell the girl yes already?"

"Fine," she said, throwing up her hands like she'd lost another bet, a big one. "We'll give it a try. But only a try."

"Sounds good," I told her. Vitamin Guy smiled at me.

She still looked wary, though, as she stuck out her hand. "I'm Harriet."

"Ruby," I said. And with that, I was hired.

*　　*　　*

Harriet was not lying. She was a total control freak, something that became more than clear over the next two hours, as she walked me through an in-depth orientation, followed by an intricate register tutorial. Only after I'd endured both of these things—as well as a pop quiz on what I'd learned—and had her shadow me while I waited on four separate customers did she finally decide to leave me alone while she went for another coffee.

"I'll just be right here," she said, pointing to the Jump Java outpost, which was less than five hundred feet away. "If you scream, I'll hear you."

"I won't scream," I assured her.

She hardly looked convinced, however, as she walked away, checking back on me twice before I stopped counting.

Once she was gone, I tried to both relax and remember everything I'd just been taught. I was busy dusting the displays when the vitamin guy walked over.

"So," he said. "Ready to quit yet?"

"She is a little intense," I agreed. "How do her other employees deal with it?"

"They don't," he said. "I mean, she doesn't have any others. Or she hasn't. You're the first."

This, I had to admit, explained a lot. "Really."

He nodded, solemn. "She's needed help forever, so this is a big step for her. Huge, in fact," he said. Then he reached into his pocket, pulling out a handful of small pill packs. "I'm Reggie, by the way. Want some free B-complexes?"

I eyed them, then shook my head. "Ruby. And um, no thanks."

"Suit yourself," he said. "Yo, Nate! How those shark-cartilage supplements treating you? Changed your life yet?"

I turned around. Sure enough, there was Nate, walking toward us, carrying a box in his hands. "Not yet," he said, shifting to slapping hands with Reggie. "But I only just started them."

"You got to keep them up, man," Reggie said. "Every day, twice a day. Those aches and pains will be gone. It's miraculous."

Nate nodded, then looked at me. "Hey," he said.

"Hi."

"She works for Harriet," Reggie said, nudging him.

"No way," Nate said, incredulous. "Harriet actually hired someone?"

"Why is that so surprising?" I said. "She had a HELP WANTED sign up."

"For the last six months," Nate said, putting his box down on the stool behind me.

"And tons of people have applied," Reggie added. "Of course she had a reason for rejecting every one of them. Too perky, bad haircut, possible allergies to the incense . . .'"

"She hired you, though," I said to Nate. "Right?"

"Only under duress," he replied, pulling some papers out of the box.

"Which is why," Reggie said, popping a B-complex, "it's so huge that she agreed to take you on."

"No kidding," Nate said. "It is pretty astounding. Maybe it's a redhead thing?"

"Like does speak to like," Reggie agreed. "Or perhaps our Harriet has finally realized how close she is to a stress-related breakdown. I mean, have you seen how much coffee she's been drinking?"

"I thought she switched to smoothies. You guys made a bet, right?"

"Already caved," Reggie said. "She owes me, like, a thousand bucks now."

"What are you guys doing?" Harriet demanded as she walked up, another large coffee in hand. "I finally hire someone and you're already distracting her?"

"I was just offering her some B-complexes," Reggie said. "I figured she'll need them."

"Funny," she grumbled, walking over to take the paper Nate was holding out to her.

"You know," he said to her as she scanned it, "personally, I think it's a great thing you finally admitted you needed help. It's the first step toward healing."

"I'm a small-business owner," she told him. "Working a lot is part of the job. Just ask your dad."

"I would," Nate said. "But I never see him. He's always working."

She just looked at him, then grabbed a pen from the register, signing the bottom of the paper and handing it back to him. "Do you want a check today, or can you bill me?"

"We can send a bill," he said, folding the paper and sliding it into his pocket. "Although you know my dad's pushing his new auto-draft feature these days."

"What's that?"

"We bill you, then take it directly out of your account. Draft it and forget it, no worries," Nate explained. "Want to sign up? I've got the forms in the car. It'll make your life even easier."

"No," Harriet said with a shudder. "I'm already nervous enough just letting you mail stuff."

Nate shot me a told-you-so look. "Well, just keep it in mind," he told her. "You need anything else right now?"

"Nothing you can help me with," Harriet replied, sighing. "I mean, I still have to teach Ruby so much. Like how to organize the displays, the setup and closing schedule, the right way to organize stock alphabetically by size and stone . . ."

"Well," Nate said, "I'm sure that's doable."

"Not to mention," she continued, "the process for the weekly changing of the padlock code on the cash box, alternating the incense so we don't run out of any one kind too quickly, and our emergency-response plan."

"Your what?" Reggie asked.

"Our emergency-response plan," Harriet said.

He just looked at her.

"What, you don't have a system in place as to how to react if there's a terrorist attack on the mall? Or a tornado?

What if you have to vacate the stall quickly and efficiently?"

Reggie, eyes wide, shook his head slowly. "Do you sleep at night?" he asked her.

"No," Harriet said. "Why?"

Nate stepped up beside me, his voice low in my ear. "Good luck," he said. "You're going to need it."

I nodded, and then he was gone, waving at Harriet and Reggie as he went. I turned back to the display, bracing myself for the terrorism-preparedness tutorial, but instead she picked up her coffee, taking another thoughtful sip. "So," she said, "you and Nate are friends?"

"Neighbors," I told her. She raised her eyebrows, and I added, "I mean, we just met this week. We ride to school together."

"Ah." She put the coffee back on the register. "He's a good kid. We joke around a lot, but I really like him."

I knew I was supposed to chime in here, agree with her that he was nice, say I liked him, too. But if anyone could understand why I didn't do this, I figured it had to be Harriet. She didn't delegate well in her professional life; I had the same reluctance, albeit more personal. Left to my own devices, I'd be a one-woman operation, as well. Unfortunately, though, with Nate the damage was already done. If I'd never tried to take off that first night, if I'd gotten a ride from someone else, we'd still really just be neighbors, with no ties to each other whatsoever. But now here I was, too far gone to be a stranger, not ready to be friends, the little acquaintance we had made still managing to be, somehow, too much.

✻   ✻   ✻

When I got back to Cora's house later that evening, the driveway was packed with cars and the front door was open, bright light spilling out onto the steps and down the walk. As I came closer, I could see people milling around in the kitchen, and there was music coming from the backyard.

I waited until the coast was clear before entering the foyer, easing the door shut behind me. Then, bags in hand, I quickly climbed the stairs, stopping only when I was at the top to look down on the scene below. The kitchen was full of people gathered around the island and table, the French doors thrown open as others milled back and forth from the backyard. There was food laid out on the counters, something that smelled great—my stomach grumbled, reminding me I'd skipped lunch—and several coolers filled with ice and drinks were lined up on the patio. Clearly, this wasn't an impromptu event, something decided at the last minute. Then again, me being here hadn't exactly been a part of Cora and Jamie's plan, either.

Just as I thought this, I heard voices from my right. Looking over, I saw Cora's bedroom door was open. Inside, two women, their backs to me, were gathered around the entrance to her bathroom. One was petite and blonde, wearing jeans and a sweatshirt, her hair in a ponytail. The other was taller, in a black dress and boots, a glass of red wine in one hand.

". . . okay, you know?" the blonde was saying. "You know the minute you stop thinking about it, it'll happen."

"Denise," the brunette said. She shook her head, taking a sip of her wine. "That's not helpful. You're making it sound like it's her fault or something."

"That's not what I meant!" Denise said. "All I'm saying is that you have plenty of time. I mean, it seems like just yesterday when we were all so *relieved* to get our periods when we were late. Remember?"

The brunette shot her a look. "The point is," she said, turning back to whoever they were speaking to, "that you're doing everything right: charting your cycle, taking your temperature, all that. So it's really frustrating when it doesn't happen when you want it to. But you've only just started this whole process, and there are a lot of ways to get pregnant these days. You know?"

I was moving away from the door, having realized this conversation was more than private, even before both women stepped back and I saw my sister walk out of her bathroom, nodding and wiping her eyes. Before she could see me, I flattened myself against the wall by the stairs, holding my breath as I tried to process this information. Cora wanted a *baby*? Clearly, her job and marital status weren't the only things that had changed in the years we'd been apart.

I could hear them still talking, their voices growing louder as they came toward the door. Just before they got to me, I pushed myself back up on the landing, as if I was just coming up the stairs, almost colliding with the blonde in the process.

"Oh!" She gasped, her hand flying up to her chest. "You scared me . . . I didn't see you there."

I glanced past them at Cora, who was watching me

with a guarded expression, as if wondering what, if any-thing, I'd heard. Closer up, I could see her eyes were red-rimmed, despite the makeup she'd clearly just reapplied in an effort to make it seem otherwise. "This is Ruby," she said. "My sister. Ruby, this is Denise and Charlotte."

"Hi," I said. They were both studying me intently, and I wondered how much of our story they'd actually been told.

"It's so nice to meet you!" Denise said, breaking into a big smile. "I can see the family resemblance, I have to say!"

Charlotte rolled her eyes. "Excuse Denise," she said to me. "She feels like she always has to say something, even when it's completely inane."

"How is that inane?" Denise asked.

"Because they don't look a thing alike?" Charlotte re-plied.

Denise looked at me again. "Maybe not hair color," she said. "Or complexion. But in the face, around the eyes . . . you can't see that?"

"No," Charlotte told her, taking another sip of her wine. After swallowing, she added, "No offense, of course."

"None taken," Cora said, steering them both out of the doorway and down the stairs. "Now go eat, you guys. Jamie bought enough barbecue to feed an army, and it's getting cold."

"You coming?" Charlotte asked her as Denise started down to the foyer, her ponytail bobbing with each step.

"In a minute."

Cora and I both stood there, watching them as they

made their way downstairs, already bickering about something else as they disappeared into the kitchen. "They were my suitemates in college," she said to me. "The first week I thought they hated each other. Turned out it was the opposite. They've been best friends since they were five."

"Really," I said, peering down into the kitchen, where I could now see Charlotte and Denise working their way through the crowd, saying hello as they went.

"You know what they say. Opposites attract."

I nodded, and for a moment we both just looked down at the party. I could see Jamie now, out in the backyard, standing by a stretch of darkness that I assumed was the pond.

"So," Cora said suddenly, "how was the mall?"

"Good," I said. Then, as it was clear she was waiting for more detail, I added, "I got some good stuff. And a job, actually."

"A job?"

I nodded. "At this jewelry place."

"Ruby, I don't know." She crossed her arms over her chest, leaning back against the rail behind her. "I think you should just be focusing on school for the time being."

"It's only fifteen hours a week, if that," I told her. "And I'm used to working."

"I'm sure you are," she said. "But Perkins Day is more rigorous, academically, than you're used to. I saw your transcripts. If you want to go to college, you really need to make your grades and your applications the number one priority."

College? I thought. "I can do both," I said.

"You don't have to, though. That's just the point." She shook her head. "When I was in high school, I was working thirty-hour weeks—I had no choice. You do."

"This isn't thirty hours," I said.

She narrowed her eyes at me, making it clear I just wasn't getting what she was saying. "Ruby, we want to do this for you, okay? You don't have to make things harder than they have to be just to prove a point."

I opened my mouth, ready to tell her that I'd never asked her to worry about my future, or make it her problem. That I was practically eighteen, as well as being completely capable of making my own decisions about what I could and could not handle. And that being in my life for less than a week didn't make her my mother or guardian, regardless of what it said on any piece of paper.

But just as I drew in a breath to say all this, I looked again at her red eyes and stopped myself. It had been a long day for both of us, and going further into this would only make it longer.

"Fine," I said. "We'll talk about it. Later, though. All right?"

Cora looked surprised. She clearly had not been expecting me to agree, even with provisions. "Fine," she said. She swallowed, then glanced back down at the party. "So, there's food downstairs, if you haven't eaten. Sorry I didn't mention the party before—everything's been kind of crazy."

"It's okay," I said.

She looked at me for another moment. "Right," she said slowly, finally. "Well, I should get back downstairs. Just . . . come down whenever."

I nodded, and then she stepped past me and started down the stairs. Halfway down, she looked back up at me, and I knew she was still wondering what exactly had precipitated this sudden acquiescence. I couldn't tell her, of course, what I'd overheard. It wasn't my business, then or now. But as I started to my room, I kept thinking about what Denise had said, and the resemblance she claimed to be able to see. Maybe my sister and I shared more than we thought. We were both waiting and wishing for something we couldn't completely control: I wanted to be alone, and she the total opposite. It was weird, really, to have something so contrary in common. But at least it was something.

X   X   X

". . . all I can say is, acupuncture works. What? No, it doesn't hurt. At all."

". . . so that was it. I decided that night, no more blind dates. I don't care if he *is* a doctor."

". . . only thirty thousand miles and the original warranty. I mean, it's such a steal!"

I'd been walking through the party for a little more than twenty minutes, nodding at people who nodded at me and picking at my second plate of barbecue, coleslaw, and potato salad. Even though Jamie and Cora's friends seemed nice enough, I was more than happy not to have to talk to anyone, until I heard one voice that cut through all the others.

"Roscoe!"

Jamie was standing at the back of the yard, past the far end of the pond, peering into the dark. As I walked over to him, I got my first up-close look at the pond, which I was

surprised to see was already filled with water, a hose dangling in from one side. In the dark it seemed even bigger,
and I couldn't tell how deep it was: it looked like it went
down forever.

"What's going on?" I asked when I reached him.

"Roscoe's vanished," he said. "He tends to do this. He's
not fond of crowds. It's not at the level of the smoke detector, but it's still a problem."

I looked into the dark, then slowly turned back to the
pond. "He can swim, right?"

Jamie's eyes widened. "Shit," he said. "I didn't even
think about that."

"I'm sure he's not in there," I told him, feeling bad for
even suggesting it as he walked to the pond's edge, peering
down into it, a worried look on his face. "In fact—"

Then we both heard it: a distinct yap, high-pitched and
definitely not obscured by water. It was coming from the
fence. "Thank God," Jamie said, turning back in that direction. "Roscoe! Here, boy!"

There was another series of barks, but no Roscoe. "Looks
like he might have to be brought in by force," Jamie said
with a sigh. "Let me just—"

"I'll get him," I said.

"You sure?"

"Yeah. Go back to the party."

He smiled at me. "All right. Thanks."

I nodded, then put my plate down by a nearby tree as he
walked away. Behind me, the party was still going strong,
but the voices and music diminished as I walked to the end
of the yard, toward the little clump of trees that ran along-

side the fence. Not even a week earlier, I'd been running across this same expanse, my thoughts only of getting away. Now, here I was, working to bring back the one thing that had stopped me. Stupid dog.

"Roscoe," I called out as I ducked under the first tree, leaves brushing across my head. "Roscoe!"

No reply. I stopped where I was, letting my eyes adjust to the sudden darkness, then turned back to look at the house. The pond, stretching in between, looked even more vast from here, the lights from the patio shimmering slightly in its surface. Nearer now, I heard another bark. This time it sounded more like a yelp, actually.

"Roscoe," I said, hoping he'd reply again, Marco Polo–style. When he didn't, I took a few more steps toward the fence, repeating his name. It wasn't until I reached it that I heard some frantic scratching from the other side. "Roscoe?"

When I heard him yap repeatedly, I quickened my pace, moving down to where I thought the gate was, running my hand down the fence. Finally, I felt a hinge, and a couple of feet later, a gap. Very small, almost tiny. But still big enough for a little dog, if he tried hard enough, to wriggle through.

When I crouched down, the first thing I saw was Mr. Cross, standing with his hands on his hips by the pool. "All right," he said, looking around him. "I know you're here, I saw what you did to the garbage. Get out and show yourself."

Uh-oh, I thought. Sure enough, I spotted Roscoe cowering behind a potted plant. Mr. Cross clearly hadn't yet seen him, though, as he turned, scanning the yard again. "You have to come out sometime," he said, bending down and looking under a nearby chaise lounge. "And when you do, you'll be sorry."

As if in response, Roscoe yelped, and Mr. Cross spun, spotting him instantly. "Hey," he said. "Get over here!"

Roscoe, though, was not as stupid as I thought. Rather than obeying this order, he took off like a shot, right toward the fence and me. Mr. Cross scrambled to grab him as he passed, missing once, then getting him by one back leg and slowly pulling him back.

"Not so fast," he said, his voice low, as Roscoe struggled to free himself, his tags clanking loudly. Mr. Cross yanked him closer, his hand closing tightly over the dog's narrow neck. "You and I, we have some—"

"Roscoe!"

I yelled so loudly, I surprised myself. But not as much as Mr. Cross, who immediately released the dog, then stood up and took a step back. Our eyes met as Roscoe darted toward me, wriggling through the fence and between my legs, and for a moment, we just looked at each other.

"Hi there," he called out, his voice all friendly-neighbor-like, now. "Sounds like quite a party over there."

I didn't say anything, just stepped back from the fence, putting more space between us.

"He gets into our garbage," he called out, shrugging in a what-can-you-do? kind of way. "Jamie and I have discussed it. It's a problem."

I knew I should respond in some way; I was just standing there like a zombie. But all I could see in my mind was his hand over Roscoe's neck, those fingers stretching.

"Just tell Jamie and Cora to try to keep him on that side, all right?" Mr. Cross said. Then he flashed me that same white-toothed smile. "Good fences make good neighbors, and all that."

Now I did nod, then stepped back, pulling the gate shut. The last glimpse I had of Mr. Cross was of him standing by the pool, hands in his pockets, smiling at me, his face rippled with the lights from beneath the water.

I turned to walk back to our yard, trying to process what I'd just seen and why exactly it had creeped me out so much. I still wasn't sure, even as I came up on Roscoe, who was sniffing along the edge of the pond. But I scooped him up under my arm and carried him the rest of the way, anyway.

*   *   *

As we got closer to the house, I heard the music. At first, it was just a guitar, strumming, but then another instrument came in, more melodic. "All right," someone said over the strumming. "Here's an old favorite."

I put Roscoe on the ground, then stepped closer to the assembled crowd. As a guy in a leather jacket standing in front of me shifted to the left, I saw it was Jamie who had spoken. He was sitting on one of the kitchen chairs, playing a guitar, a beer at his feet, a guy with a banjo nodding beside him as they went into an acoustic version of Led Zeppelin's "Misty Mountain Hop." His voice, I realized, was not bad, and his playing was actually pretty impressive. So strange how my brother-in-law kept surprising me: his incredible career, his passion for ponds, and now, this music. All things I might never have known had I found that gate the first night.

"Having fun?"

I turned around to see Denise, Cora's friend, standing beside me. "Yeah," I said. "It's a big party."

"They always are," she said cheerfully, taking a sip of the beer in her hand. "That's what happens when you're overwhelmingly social. You accumulate a lot of people."

"Jamie does seem kind of magnetic that way."

"Oh, I meant Cora," she replied as the song wrapped up, the crowd breaking into spontaneous applause. "But he is, too, you're right."

"Cora?" I asked.

She looked at me, clearly surprised. "Well . . . yeah," she said. "You know how she is. Total den-mother type, always taking someone under her wing. Drop her in a roomful of strangers, and she'll know everyone in ten minutes. Or less."

"Really," I said.

"Oh, yeah," she replied. "She's just really good with people, you know? Empathetic. I personally couldn't have survived my last breakup without her. Or any of my breakups, really."

I considered this as Denise took another sip of her beer, nodding to a guy in a baseball cap as he pushed past us. "I guess I don't really know that side of her," I said. "I mean, we've been out of touch for a while."

"I know," she said. Then she quickly added, "I mean, she talked about you a lot in college."

"She did?"

"Oh, yeah. Like, all the time," she said, emphatic. "She really—"

"Denise!" someone yelled, and she turned, looking over the shoulder of the guy beside us. "I need to get that number from you, remember?"

"Right," she said, then smiled at me apologetically. "One sec. I'll be right back. . . ."

I nodded as she walked away, wondering what she'd been about to say. Thinking this, I scanned the crowd until I spotted Cora standing just outside the kitchen door with Charlotte. She was smiling, looking much happier than the last time I'd seen her. At some point she'd pulled her hair back, making her look even younger, and she had on a soft-looking sweater, a glass of wine in her hand. Here I'd just assumed all these people were here because of Jamie, but of course my sister could have changed in the years we'd been apart. *She has her own life now,* my mom had told me again and again. This was it, and I wondered what that must be like, to actually get to start again, forget the world you knew before and leave everything behind. Maybe it had even been easy.

Easy. I had a flash of myself, just a week earlier, coming home from a long night at Commercial to the darkness of the yellow house. How much had I thought about it—my home or my school or anything from before—in the last few days? Not as much as I should have. All this time, I'd been so angry Cora had forgotten me, just wiped our shared slate clean, but now I was doing the same thing. Where *was* my mother? Was it really this easy, once you escaped, to just not care?

I suddenly felt tired, overwhelmed, everything that had happened in the last week hitting me at once. I stepped back from the crowd, slipping inside. As I climbed the stairs, I was glad for the enclosed space of my room, even if it, too, was temporary like everything else.

I just need to sleep, I told myself, kicking off my shoes and sinking down onto the bed. I closed my eyes, trying to shut out the singing, doing all I could to push myself into the darkness and stay there until morning.

When I woke up, I wasn't sure how long I'd been asleep, hours or just minutes. My mouth was dry, my arm cramped from where I'd been lying on it. As I rolled over, stretching out, my only thought was to go back to the dream I'd been having, which I couldn't remember, other than it had been good, in that distant, hopeful way unreal things can be. I was closing my eyes, trying to will myself back, when I heard some laughter and clapping from outside. The party was still going on.

When I went out onto my balcony, I saw the crowd had dwindled to about twenty people or so. The banjo player was gone, and just Jamie remained, plucking a few notes as people chatted around him.

"It's getting late," Charlotte, who'd put on a sweater over her dress, said. She stifled a yawn with her hand. "Some of us have to be up early tomorrow."

"It's Sunday," Denise, sitting beside her, said. "Who doesn't sleep in on Sunday?"

"One last song," Jamie said. He glanced around, looking behind him to a place I couldn't see from my vantage point. "What do you think?" he said. "One song?"

"Come on," Denise pleaded. "Just one."

Jamie smiled, then began to play. It was cold outside, at least to me, and I turned back to my room, feeling a yawn of my own rising up, ready to go back to bed. But then I realized there was something familiar about what he was playing; it was like it was tugging at some part of me, faint but persistent, a melody I thought was mine alone.

"'I am an old woman, named after my mother. . . .'"

The voice was strong and clear, and also familiar, but in a distant way. Similar to the one I knew, and yet different—prettier and not as harsh around the edges.

"'My old man is another child that's grown old. . . .'"

It was Cora. Cora, her voice pure and beautiful as it worked its way along the notes we'd both heard so many times, the song more than any other that made me think of my mother. I thought of how strange I'd felt earlier, thinking we'd both just forgotten everything. But this was scary, too, to be so suddenly connected, prompting a stream of memories—us in our nightgowns, her reaching out for me, listening to her breathing, steady and soothing, from across a dark room—rushing back too fast to stop.

I felt a lump rise in my throat, raw and throbbing, but even as the tears came I wasn't sure who I was crying for. Cora, my mom, or maybe, just me.

Chapter Six

I could not prove it scientifically. But I was pretty sure Gervais Miller was the most annoying person on the planet.

First, there was the voice. Flat and nasal with no inflection, it came from the backseat, offering up pronouncements and observations. "Your hair's matted in the back," he'd tell me, when I hadn't had adequate time with the blow-dryer. Or when I pulled a shirt last-minute from the laundry: "You stink like dryer sheets." Attempts to ignore him by pretending to study only resulted in a running commentary on my academic prowess, or lack thereof. "Intro to Calculus? What are you, stupid?" or "Is that a *B* on that paper?" And so on.

I wanted to punch him. Daily. But of course I couldn't, for two reasons. First, he was just a kid. Second, between his braces and his headgear, there was really no way to get at him and really make an impact. (The fact that I'd actually thought about it enough to draw this conclusion probably should have worried me. It did not.)

When it all got to be too much, I'd just turn around and shoot him the evil eye, which usually did the trick. He'd quiet down for the rest of the ride, maybe even the next day, as well. In time, though, his obnoxiousness would return, often even stronger than before.

In my more rational moments, I tried to feel empathy for Gervais. It had to be hard to be a prodigy, supersmart but so much younger than everyone else at school. Whenever I saw him in the halls, he was always alone, backpack over both shoulders, walking in his weird, leaning-forward way, as if powering up to head-butt someone in the chest.

Being a kid, though, Gervais also lacked maturity, which meant that he found things like burps and farts *hysterical*, and even funnier when they were his own. Put him in a small, enclosed space with two people every morning, and there was no end to the potential for hilarity. Suffice it to say, we always knew what he'd had for breakfast, and even though it was nearing winter, I often kept my window open, and Nate did the same.

On the Monday after Cora's party, though, when I got into the car at seven thirty, something just felt different. A moment later, I realized why: the backseat was empty.

"Where's Gervais?" I asked.

"Doctor's appointment," Nate said.

I nodded, then I settled into my seat to enjoy the ride. My relief must have been palpable, because a moment later Nate said, "You know, he's not so bad."

"Are you joking?" I asked him.

"I mean," he said, "I'll admit he's not the easiest person to be around."

"Please." I rolled my eyes. "He's *horrible*."

"Come on."

"He stinks," I said, holding up a finger. Then, adding another, I said, "And he's rude. And his burps could wake the dead. And if he says one more thing about my books or my classes I'm going to—"

It was at about this point that I realized Nate was looking at me like I was crazy. So I shut up, and we just drove in silence.

"You know," he said after a moment, "it's a shame you feel that way. Because I think he likes you."

I just looked at him. "Did you not hear him tell me I was fat the other day?"

"He didn't say you were *fat*," Nate replied. "He said you looked a little rotund."

"How is that different?"

"You know," he said, "I think you're forgetting Gervais is twelve."

"I assure you I am not."

"And," he continued, "boys at twelve aren't exactly slick with the ladies."

"'Slick with the ladies'?" I said. "Are *you* twelve?"

He switched lanes, then slowed for a light. "He teases you," he said slowly, as if I was stupid, "*because* he likes you."

"Gervais does not like me," I said, louder this time.

"Whatever." The light changed. "But he never talked to Heather when she rode with us."

"He didn't?"

"Nope. He just sat back there, passing gas, without comment."

"Nice," I said.

"It really was." Nate downshifted as we slowed for a red light. "All I'm saying is that maybe he just wants to be friends but doesn't exactly know how to do it. So he says you smell like trees or calls you rotund. That's what kids do."

I rolled my eyes, looking out the window. "Why," I said, "would Gervais want to be friends with me?"

"Why wouldn't he?"

"Because I'm not a friendly person?" I said.

"You're not?"

"Are you saying you think I am?"

"I wouldn't say you're unfriendly."

"I would," I said.

"Really."

I nodded.

"Huh. Interesting."

The light changed, and we moved forward.

"Interesting," I said, "meaning what?"

He shrugged, switching lanes. "Just that I don't see you that way. I mean, you're reserved, maybe. Guarded, definitely. But not unfriendly."

"Maybe you just don't know me," I said.

"Maybe," he agreed. "But unfriendly is usually one of those things you pick up on right away. You know, like B.O. There's no hiding it if it's there."

I considered this as we approached another light. "So when we met that first night," I said, "by the fence, you thought I was friendly?"

"I didn't think you weren't," he said.

"I wasn't very nice to you."

"You were jumping a fence. I didn't take it personally."

"I didn't even thank you for covering for me."

"So?"

"So I should have. Or at least not been such a bitch to you the next day."

Nate shrugged, putting on his blinker. "It's not a big deal."

"It is, though," I said. "You don't have to be so nice to everyone, you know."

"Ah," he said, "but that's the thing. I do. I'm compulsively friendly."

Of course he was. And I'd noticed it first thing that night by the fence, because it, too, was something you couldn't hide. Maybe I could have tried to explain myself more to Nate, that there was a reason I was this way, but he was already reaching forward, turning on the radio and flipping to WCOM, the local community station he listened to in the mornings. The DJ, some girl named Annabel, was announcing the time and temperature. Then she put on a song, something peppy with a bouncy beat. Nate turned it up, and we let it play all the way to school.

When we got out of the car, we walked together to the green, and then I peeled off to my locker, just like always, while he headed to the academic building. After I'd stuffed in a few books and taken out a couple of others, I shut the door, hoisting my bag back over my shoulder. Across the green, I could see Nate approaching his first-period class. Jake Bristol and two other guys were standing around outside. As he walked up, Jake reached out a hand for a high five, while the other two stepped back, waving him through. I was late myself, with other things to think about. But I stayed there and watched as Nate laughed and stepped

through the door, and they all fell in, following along behind him, before I turned and walked away.

* * *

"All right, people," Ms. Conyers said, clapping her hands.
"Let's get serious. You've got fifteen minutes. Start asking
questions."

The room got noisy, then noisier, as people left their seats
and began to move around the room, notebooks in hand.
After slogging my way through an extensive test on *David
Copperfield* (ten IDs, two essays), all I wanted to do was collapse. Instead, to get us started on our "oral definition" projects, we were supposed to interview our classmates, getting
their opinions on what our terms meant. This was good;
I figured I needed all the help I could get, considering the
way I defined my own family kept changing.

It had been almost two weeks since I'd come to Cora's,
and I was slowly getting adjusted. It wasn't like things were
perfect, but we had fallen into a routine, as well as an understanding. For my part, I'd accepted that leaving, at least
right now, was not in my best interest. So I'd unpacked my
bag, finally unloading my few possessions into the big, empty drawers and closet. I wasn't ready to spread out farther
into the house itself—I took my backpack upstairs with me
as soon as I came home and stood by the dryer as my clothes
finished, then folded them right away. It was a big place.
God only knew how much could get lost there.

It was weird to be living in such sudden largess, especially after the yellow house. Instead of stretching a pack
of pasta over a few days and scraping together change for

groceries, I had access to a fully packed pantry, as well as a freezer stocked with just about every entrée imaginable. And that wasn't even counting the "pocket money" Jamie was always trying to give me: twenty bucks for lunch here, another forty in case I needed school supplies there. Maybe someone else would have accepted all this easily, but I was still so wary, unsure of what would be expected of me in return, that at first I refused it. Over time, though, he wore me down and I gave in, although spending it was another matter entirely. I just felt better with it stashed away. After all, you never knew when something, or everything, might change.

Cora had compromised, as well. After much discussion—and some helpful lobbying from Jamie—it was decided I could work for Harriet through the holidays, at which point we'd "reconvene on the subject" and "evaluate its impact on my grades and school performance." As part of the deal, I also had to agree to attend at least one therapy session, an idea I was not at all crazy about. I needed the money, though, so I'd bitten my tongue and acquiesced. Then we'd reached across the kitchen island, shaking on it, her hand small and cool, her strong grip surprising me more than it probably should have.

I'd been thinking about my mother a lot, even more than when she'd first left, which was weird. Like it took a while to really miss her, or let myself do so. Sometimes at night, I dreamed about her; afterward, I always woke up with the feeling that she'd just passed through the room, convinced I could smell lingering smoke or her perfume in the air. Other times, when I was half asleep, I was sure I could feel her sitting on the side of my bed, one hand stroking my hair, the way she'd sometimes done late at night or early in the morning. Back then, I'd always been irritated, wishing she'd go to sleep herself or leave me alone. Now, even when my conscious mind told me it was just a dream, I remained still, wanting it to last.

When I woke up, I always tried to keep this image in my head, but it never stayed. Instead, there was only how she'd looked the last time I'd seen her, the day before she'd left. I'd come home from school to find her both awake and alone, for once. By then, things hadn't been good for a while, and I'd expected her to look bleary, the way she always did after a few beers, or sad or annoyed. But instead, as she turned her head, her expression had been one of surprise, and I remembered thinking maybe she'd forgotten about me, or hadn't been expecting me to return. Like it was me who was leaving, and I just didn't know it yet.

In daylight, I was more factual, wondering if she'd made it to Florida, or if she was still with Warner. Mostly, though, I wondered if she had tried to call the yellow house, made any effort to try and locate me. I wasn't sure I even wanted to talk to her or see her, nor did I know if I ever would. But it was important to simply be sought, even if you didn't ever want to be found.

What is family? I'd written in my notebook that first day, and as I opened it up now I saw the rest of the page was blank, except for the definition I'd gotten from the dictionary: *a set of relations, esp. parents and children.* Eight words, and one was an abbreviation. If only it was really that easy.

Now Ms. Conyers called out for everyone to get to work,

so I turned to Olivia, figuring I'd hit her up first. She hardly looked like she was in the mood for conversation, though, sitting slumped in her chair. Her eyes were red, a tissue clutched in one hand as she pulled the Jackson High letter jacket she always wore more tightly around herself.

"Remember," Ms. Conyers was saying, "you're not just asking what your term means literally, but what it means to the person you're speaking with. Don't be afraid to get personal."

Considering Olivia was hardly open on a *good* day, I decided maybe I should take a different tack. My only other option, though, was Heather Wainwright, on my other side, who was also looking around for someone to talk to, and I wasn't sure I wanted to go there.

"Well? Are we doing this or not?"

I turned back to Olivia. She was still sitting facing forward, as if she hadn't spoken at all. "Oh," I said, then shot a pointed look at the tissue in her hand. In response, she crumpled it up smaller, tucking it down deeper between her fingers. "All right. What does family mean to you?"

She sighed, reaching up to rub her nose. All around us, I could hear people chattering, but she was silent. Finally she said, "Do you know Micah Sullivan?"

"Who?"

"Micah Sullivan," she repeated. "Senior? On the football team? Hangs out with Rob Dufresne?"

It wasn't until I'd heard this last name that I realized she was talking about Jackson. Rob Dufresne had sat across from me in bio sophomore year. "Micah," I said, trying to think. Already, my classmates at Jackson were a big blur, their faces all running together. "Is he really short?"

"No," she snapped. I shrugged, picking up my pen. Then she said, "Okay, so he's not as *tall* as some people."

"Drives a blue truck?"

Now she looked at me. "Yeah," she said slowly. "That's him."

"I know of him."

"Did you ever see him with a girl? At school?"

I thought for another moment, but all I could see was Rob Dufresne going dead pale as we contemplated our frog dissection. "Not that I remember," I said. "But like you said, it's a big place."

She considered this for a moment. Then, turning to face me, she said, "So you never saw him all over some field-hockey player, a blonde with a tattoo on her lower back. Minda or Marcy or something like that?"

I shook my head. She looked at me for a long moment, as if not sure whether to trust me, then faced forward again, pulling her jacket more tightly around her. "Family," she announced. "They're the people in your life you don't get to pick. The ones that are given to you, as opposed to those you get to choose."

Since my mind was still on Micah and the field-hockey player, I had to scramble to write this down. "Okay," I said. "What else?"

"You're bound to them by blood," she continued, her voice flat. "Which, you know, gives you that much more in common. Diseases, genetics, hair, and eye color. It's like, they're part of your blueprint. If something's wrong with you, you can usually trace it back to them."

I nodded and kept writing.

"But," she said, "even though you're stuck with them, at the same time, they're also stuck with you. So that's why they always get the front rows at christenings and funerals. Because they're the ones that are there, you know, from the beginning to the end. Like it or not."

Like it or not, I wrote. Then I looked at these words and all the others I'd scribbled down. It wasn't much. But it was a start. "Okay," I said. "Let's do yours."

Just then, though, the bell rang, triggering the usual cacophony of chairs being banged around, backpacks zipping, and voices rising. Ms. Conyers was saying something about having at least four definitions by the next day, not that I could really hear her over all the noise. Olivia had already grabbed her phone, flipping it open and calling someone on speed dial. As I put my notebook away, I watched her stuff the tissue in her pocket, then run a hand over her braids as she got to her feet.

"It's Melissa," I told her as she turned to walk away.

She stopped, then looked at me, slowly lowering her phone from her ear. "What?"

"The blonde with the back tattoo. Her name is Melissa West," I said, picking up my bag. "She's a sophomore, a total skank. And she plays soccer, not field hockey."

People were moving past us now, en route to the door, but Olivia stayed where she was, not even seeming to notice as Heather Wainwright passed by, glancing at her red eyes before moving on.

"Melissa West," she repeated.

I nodded.

"Thanks."

"You're welcome," I told her. Then she put her phone back to her ear slowly, and walked away.

* * *

When I came out of school that afternoon after final bell, Jamie was waiting for me.

He was leaning against his car, which was parked right outside the main entrance, his arms folded over his chest. As soon as I saw him, I stopped walking, hanging back as people streamed past me on either side, talking and laughing. Maybe I was just being paranoid, but the last time someone had showed up unexpectedly for me at school, it hadn't been to deliver good news.

In fact, it wasn't until after I'd begun to mentally list the various offenses for which I *could* be busted that I realized there really weren't any. All I'd done lately was go to school, go to work, and study. I hadn't even been out on a weekend night. Still, I stayed where I was, hesitant out of force of habit or something else, until the crowd cleared and he spotted me.

"Hey," he called out, raising his hand. I waved back, then pulled my bag more tightly over my shoulder as I started toward him. "You working today?"

I shook my head. "No."

"Good. I need to talk to you about something."

He stepped away from the car, pulling the passenger door open for me. Once in, I forced myself to take a breath as I watched him round the front bumper, then get in and join me. He didn't crank the engine, though, just sat there instead.

Suddenly, it hit me. He was going to tell me I had to leave. Of course. The very minute I allowed myself to relax, they would decide they'd had enough of me. Even worse, as I thought this, I felt my breath catch, suddenly realizing how much I didn't want it to happen.

"The thing is . . ." Jamie said, and now I could hear my heart in my ears. "It's about college."

This last word—*college*—landed in my ears with a clunk. It was like he'd said *Minnesota* or *fried chicken*, that unexpected. "College," I repeated.

"You are a senior," he said as I sat there, still blinking, trying to decide if I should be relieved or more nervous. "And while you haven't exactly had the best semester—not your fault, of course—you did take the SATs last year, and your scores weren't bad. I was just in talking to the guidance office. Even though it's already November, they think that if we really hustle, we can still make the application deadlines."

"You went to the guidance office?" I asked.

"Yeah," he said. I must have looked surprised, because then he added, "I know, I know. This is more Cora's department. But she's in court all week, and besides, we decided that maybe . . ."

I glanced over at him as he trailed off, leaving this unfinished. "You decided maybe what?"

He looked embarrassed. "That it was better for me to bring this up with you. You know, since Cor was kind of tough on you about your job at first, and the therapy thing. She's tired of being the bad guy."

An image of a cartoon character twirling a mustache as

they tied someone to the train tracks immediately popped into my head. "Look," I said, "school isn't really part of my plans."

"Why not?"

I probably should have had an answer to this, but the truth was that I'd never actually been asked it before. Everyone else assumed the same thing that I had from day one: girls like me just didn't go further than high school, if they even got that far. "It's just . . ." I said, stalling. "It's not really been a priority."

Jamie nodded slowly. "It's not too late, though."

"I think it is."

"But if it isn't?" he asked. "Look, Ruby. I get that this is your choice. But the thing is, the spring is a long way away. A lot could change between now and then. Even your mind."

I didn't say anything. The student parking lot was almost empty now, except for a couple of girls with field-hockey sticks and duffel bags sitting on the curb.

"How's this," he said. "Just make a deal with me and agree to apply. That way, you're not ruling anything out. Come spring, you still decide what happens next. You just have more options."

"You're assuming I'll get in somewhere. That's a big assumption."

"I've seen your transcripts. You're not a bad student."

"I'm no brain, either."

"Neither was I," he said. "In fact, in the interest of full disclosure, I'll tell you I wasn't into the idea of higher education, either. After high school, I wanted to take my guitar and move to New York to play in coffeehouses and get a record deal."

"You did?"

"Yup." He smiled, running his hand over the steering wheel. "However, my parents weren't having it. I was going to college, like it or not. So I ended up at the U, planning to leave as soon as I could. The first class I took was coding for computers."

"And the rest is history," I said.

"Nah." He shook his head. "The rest is now."

I eased my grip on my bag, letting it rest on the floorboard between my feet. The truth was, I liked Jamie. So much that I wished I could just be honest with him and say the real reason that even applying scared me: it was one more connection at a time when I wanted to be doing the total opposite. Yes, I'd decided to stay here as long as I had to, but only because really, I'd had no choice. If I went to college—at least this way, with him and Cora backing me— I'd be in debt, both literally and figuratively, at the one time when all I wanted was to be free and clear, owing no one anything at all.

Sitting there, though, I knew I couldn't tell him this. So instead, I said, "So I guess you never have regrets. Wish you'd gone to New York, like you wanted."

Jamie sat back, leaning his head on the seat behind him. "Sometimes I do. Like on a day like today, when I'm dealing with this new advertising campaign, which is making me nuts. Or when everyone in the office is whining and I think my head's going to explode. But it's only in moments. And anyway, if I hadn't gone to the U, I wouldn't have met your sister. So that would have changed everything."

"Right," I said. "How did you guys meet, anyway?"

"Talk about being the bad guy." He chuckled, looking down at the steering wheel, then explained, "She doesn't exactly come across that well in the story."

I had to admit I was intrigued now. "Why not?"

"Because she yelled at me," he said flatly. I raised my eyebrows. "Okay, she'd say she didn't yell, that she was just being assertive. But her voice *was* raised. That's indisputable."

"Why was she yelling at you?"

"Because I was playing guitar outside on the dorm steps one night. Cor's not exactly pleasant when you get between her and her sleep, you know?" I actually didn't but nodded, anyway. "So there I was, first week of classes freshman year, strumming away on a nice late summer night, and suddenly this girl just opens up her window and lets me have it."

"Really."

"Oh, yeah. She just went ballistic. Kept saying it was so inconsiderate, keeping people up with my noise. That's what she called it. Noise. I mean, here I was, thinking I was an artiste, you know?" He laughed again, shaking his head.

I said, "You're awfully good-natured about it, considering."

"Yeah, well," he said. "That was just that first night. I didn't know her yet."

I didn't say anything, instead just looked down at my backpack strap, running it through my fingers.

"My point is," Jamie continued, "not everything's perfect, especially at the beginning. And it's all right to have a little bit of regret every once in a while. It's when you feel it all the time and can't do anything about it . . . that's when you get into trouble."

Over on the curb, the girls with the field-hockey sticks were laughing at something, their voices muffled by my window. "Like," I said, "say, not applying to college, and then wishing you had?"

He smiled. "Okay, fine. So subtlety is not my strong suit. Do we have a deal or what?"

"This isn't a deal," I pointed out. "It's just me agreeing to what you want."

"Not true," he replied. "You get something in return."

"Right," I said. "A chance. An opportunity I wouldn't have otherwise."

"And something else, too."

"What's that?"

"Just wait," he said, reaching forward to crank the engine. "You'll see."

*   *   *

"A fish?" I said. "Are you serious?"

"Totally!" Jamie grinned. "What more could you want?"

I figured it was best not to answer this, and instead turned my attention back to the round tank between us, which was filled with white koi swimming back and forth. In rows all around us were more tanks, also filled with fish I'd never heard of before: comets, shubunkin, mosquito fish, as well as many other colors of koi, some solid, some speckled with black or red.

"I'm going to go find someone to test my water, make sure it's all balanced," he said, pulling a small plastic container out of his jacket pocket. "Take your time, all right? Pick a good one."

A good one, I thought, looking back down at the fish in the tank beneath me. Like you could tell with a glance, somehow judge their temperament or hardiness. I'd never had a fish—or any pet, for that matter—but from what I'd heard they could die at the drop of a hat, even when kept in a safe, clean tank. Who knew what could happen outside, in a pond open to the elements and everything else?

"Do you need help with the fish?"

I turned around, prepared to say no, only to be startled to see Heather Wainwright standing behind me. She had on jeans and a DONOVAN LANDSCAPING T-shirt, a sweater tied around her waist, and seemed equally surprised by the sight of me.

"Hey," she said. "It's Ruby, right?"

"Yeah. I'm, um, just looking."

"That's cool." She stepped up to the tank, next to me, dropping a hand down into the water: as she did so, the fish immediately swam toward her, circling her fingers. She glanced up at me and said, "They get crazy when they think you're going to feed them. They're like begging dogs, practically."

"Really."

"Yep." She pulled her hand out and wiped it on her jeans. I had to admit, I was surprised to see she worked at a place like this. For some reason, I would have pegged her as the retail type, more at home in a mall. No, I realized a beat later. That was me. Weird. "The goldfish aren't quite as aggressive. But the koi are prettier. So it's a tradeoff."

"My brother-in-law just built a pond," I told her as she bent down and adjusted a valve on the side of the tank. "He's obsessed with it."

"They are pretty awesome," she said. "How big did he go?"

"Big." I glanced over at the greenhouses, where Jamie had headed. "He should be back soon. I'm supposed to be picking a fish."

"Just one?"

"It's my personal fish," I told her, and she laughed. Never in a million years would I have imagined myself here, by a fish tank, with Heather Wainwright. Then again, I wasn't supposed to be here with anyone, period. What I'd noticed, though, was that more and more lately, when I tried to picture where I *did* belong, I couldn't. At first, it had been easy to place myself in my former life, sitting at a desk at Jackson, or in my old bedroom. But now it was like I was already losing my old life at the yellow house, without this one feeling real, either. I was just stuck somewhere in the middle, vague and undefined.

"So you're friends with Nate," Heather said after a moment, adjusting the valve again. "Right?"

I glanced over at her. The whole school had noticed, or so it seemed; it only made sense she would have, as well. "We're neighbors," I told her. "My sister lives behind him."

She reached up to tuck a stray piece of hair behind her ear. "I guess you've heard we used to go out," she said.

"Yeah?" I said.

She nodded. "We broke up this fall. It was big news for a while there." She sighed, touching her hand to the water again. "Then Rachel Webster got pregnant. Which I wasn't happy about, of course. But it did make people stop talking about us, at least for a little while."

"Perkins Day is a small school," I said.

"Tell me about it." She sat back, wiping her hand on her jeans, then looked over at me. "So . . . how's he doing these days?"

"Nate?" I asked.

She nodded.

"I don't know," I said. "Fine, I guess. Like I said, we're not that close."

She considered this as we both watched the fish circling, first one way, then another. "Yeah," she said finally. "He's hard to know, I guess."

This hadn't been what I meant, actually, not at all. If anything, in my mind, Nate was too easy to read, all part of that friendly thing. But saying this seemed odd at that moment, so I just stayed quiet.

"Anyway," Heather continued a beat later, "I just . . . I'm glad you and Nate are friends. He's a really good guy."

I had to admit this was not what I was expecting—it wasn't exactly ex-girlfriend behavior. Then again, she was the queen of compassion, if her time logged at the HELP table was any indication. Of course Nate would fall in love with a *nice* girl. What else did I expect?

"Nate has a lot of friends," I told her now. "I doubt one more makes that much of a difference."

Heather studied my face for a moment. "Maybe not," she said finally. "But you never know, right?"

What? I thought, but then I felt a hand clap my shoulder; Jamie was behind me. "So the water's good," he said. "You find the perfect one yet?"

"How do you even pick?" I asked Heather.

"Just go on instinct," she replied. "Whichever one speaks to you."

Jamie nodded sagely. "There you go," he said to me. "Let the fish speak."

"There's also the issue of who runs from the net," Heather added. "That often makes the decision for you."

In the end, it was a mix of both these things—me pointing and Heather swooping in—that got me my fish. I went with a small white koi, which looked panicked as I held it in its plastic bag, circling again and again as Jamie picked out a total of twenty shubunkins and comets. He also got several more koi, although no other white ones, so I could always find mine in the crowd.

"What are you going to name it?" he asked me as Heather shot oxygen from a canister into the bags for the ride home.

"Let's just see if it survives first," I said.

"Of course it will," he replied as if there was no question.

Heather rang us up, then carried the bags out to the car, where she carefully arranged them in a series of cardboard boxes in the backseat.

"You will need to acclimate them slowly," she explained as the fish swam around and around in their bags, their faces popping up, then disappearing. "Put the bags in the water for about fifteen minutes so they can get adjusted to the temperature. Then open the bags and let a little bit of your pond water in to mix with what they're in. Give it another fifteen minutes or so, and then you can let them go."

"So the key is to ease them into it," Jamie said.

"It's a big shock to their systems, leaving the tank," Heather replied, shutting the back door. "But they usually do fine in the end. It's herons and waterbirds you really need to worry about. One swoop, and they can do some serious damage."

"Thanks for all your help," Jamie told her as he slid back behind the wheel.

"No problem," she said. "See you at school, Ruby."

"Yeah," I said. "See you."

As Jamie began backing out, he glanced over at me. "Friend of yours?"

"No," I said. "We just have a class together."

He nodded, not saying anything else as we pulled out into traffic. It was rush hour, and we didn't talk as we hit mostly red lights heading toward home. Because my fish was alone, in a small bag, I was holding it in my lap, and I could feel it darting from one side to the other. *It's a big shock to their systems*, Heather had said. I lifted the bag up to eye level, looking at my fish again. Who knew if it—or anything—would survive the week, or even the night.

Still, when we got back to Cora's, I went with Jamie to the backyard, then crouched by the pond, easing my bag into it and watching it bob there for those fifteen minutes before letting in that little bit of water, just as I was told. When I finally went to release the koi, it was almost totally dark outside. But even so, I could see my fish, white and bright, as it made its way past the opening into the vast body of water that lay beyond. I expected it to hesitate, or even turn back, but it didn't. It just swam, quick enough to blur, before diving down to the bottom, out of sight.

*　　*　　*

When Jamie first called up the stairs to me, I was sure I'd heard wrong.

"Ruby! One of your friends is here to see you!"

Instinctively, I looked at the clock—it was 5:45, on a random Tuesday—then out the window over at Nate's house. His pool lights were on, and I wondered if he'd come over for some reason. But surely, Jamie would've identified him by name.

"Okay," I replied, pushing my chair back and walking out into the hallway. "But who is—?"

By then, though, I'd already looked down into the foyer and gotten the answer as I spotted Peyton, who was standing there patting Roscoe as Jamie looked on. When she glanced up and saw me, her face broke into a wide smile. "Hey!" she said, with her trademark enthusiasm. "I found you!"

I nodded. I knew I should have been happy to see her— as unlike Nate or Heather, she actually *was* my friend—but instead I felt strangely uneasy. After all, I'd never even in- vited her into the yellow house, always providing excuses about my mom needing her sleep or it being a bad time— keeping the personal, well, personal. But now here she was, already in.

"Hey," I said when I reached the foyer. "What's going on?"

"Are you surprised?" she asked, giggling. "You would

not believe what I went through to track you down. I was like Nancy Drew or something!"

Beside her, Jamie smiled, and I forced myself to do the same, even as I noticed two things: that she reeked of smoke and that her eyes were awfully red, her mascara pooled beneath them. Peyton had always been bad with Visine, and clearly this had not changed. Plus, even though she was dressed as cute as ever—hair pulled back into two low ponytails, wearing jeans and red shirt with an apple on it, a sweater tied loosely around her waist—she had always been the kind of person who, when high, looked it, despite her best efforts. "How did you find me?" I asked her.

"Well," she said, holding her hands, palms facing out and up to set the scene, "it was like this. You'd told me you were living in Wildflower Ridge, so—"

"I did?" I asked, trying to think back.

"Sure. On the phone that day, remember?" she said. "So I figure, it can't be that big of a neighborhood, right? But then, of course, I get over here and it's freaking *huge*."

I glanced at Jamie, who was following this story, a mild smile on his face. Clueless, or so I hoped.

"Anyway," Peyton continued, "I'm driving around, getting myself totally lost, and then I finally just pull over on the side of the road, giving up. And right then, then I see this, like, totally hot guy walking a dog down the sidewalk. So I rolled down my window and asked him if he knew you."

Even before she continued, I had a feeling what was coming next.

"And he did!" she said, clapping her hands. "So he pointed me this way. Very nice guy, by the way. His name was—"

"Nate," I finished for her.

"Yeah!" She laughed again, too loudly, and I got another whiff of smoke, even stronger this time. Like I hadn't spent ages teaching her about the masking ability of breath mints. "And here I am. It all worked out in the end."

"Clearly," I said, just as I heard the door that led from the garage to the kitchen open then shut.

"Hello?" Cora called out. Roscoe, ears perked, trotted toward the sound of her voice. "Where is everybody?"

"We're in here," Jamie replied. A moment later, she appeared in the entrance to the foyer in her work clothes, the mail in one hand. "This is Ruby's friend Peyton. This is Cora."

"You're Ruby's sister?" Peyton asked. "That's so cool!"

Cora gave her the once-over—subtly, I noticed—then extended her hand. "Nice to meet you."

"You, too," Peyton replied, pumping it eagerly. "Really nice."

My sister was smiling politely. Her expression barely changed, only enough to make it more than clear to me that she had seen—and probably smelled—what Jamie had not. Like Peyton's mom, she didn't miss much. "Well," she said. "I guess we should think about dinner?"

"Right," Jamie said. "Peyton, can you stay?"

"Oh," Peyton said, "actually—"

"She can't," I finished for her. "So, um, I'm going to go ahead and give her the tour, if that's all right."

"Sure, sure," Jamie said. Beside him, Cora was studying Peyton, her eyes narrowed, as I nodded for her to follow me into the kitchen. "Be sure to show her the pond!"

"Pond?" Peyton said, but by then I was already tugging her onto the deck, the door swinging shut behind us. I waited until we were a few feet away from the house before stopping and turning to face her.

"What are you *doing*?" I asked.

She raised her eyebrows. "What do you mean?"

"Peyton, you're blinded. And my sister could totally tell."

"Oh, she could not," she said easily, waving her hand. "I used Visine."

I rolled my eyes, not even bothering to address this. "You shouldn't have come here."

For a moment, she looked hurt, then pouty. "And you should have called me," she replied. "You said you were going to. Remember?"

Cora and Jamie were by the island in the kitchen now, looking out at us. "I'm still getting settled in," I told her, but she turned, ignoring this as she walked over to the pond. In her ponytails and in profile, she looked like a little kid. "Look, this is complicated, okay?"

"For me, too," she said, peering down into the water. As I stepped up beside her I saw it was too dark to see anything, but you could hear the pump going, the distant waterfall. "I mean, a lot's happened since you left, Ruby."

I glanced back inside. Jamie was gone, but Cora remained, and she was looking right at me. "Like what?"

Peyton glanced over at me, then shrugged. "I just . . ."

she said softly. "I wanted to talk to you. That's all."

"About what?"

She took in a breath, then let it out just as Roscoe popped through the dog door and began to trot toward us. "Nothing," she said, turning back to the water. "I mean, I miss you. We used to hang out every day, and then you just disappear. It's weird."

"I know," I said. "And believe me, I'd go back to the way things were in a minute if I could. But it's just not an option. This is my life now. At least for a little while."

She considered this as she looked at the pond, then turned slightly, taking in the house rising up behind us. "It is different," she said.

"Yeah," I agreed. "It is."

In the end, Peyton stayed for less than an hour, just long enough to get a tour, catch me up on the latest Jackson gossip, and turn down two more invitations to stay for dinner from Jamie, who seemed beside himself with the fact that I actually had a real, live friend. Cora, however, had a different take, or so I found out later, when I was folding clothes and looked up to see her standing in my bedroom doorway.

"So," she said, "tell me about Peyton."

I focused on pairing up socks as I said, "Not much to tell."

"Have you two been friends a long time?"

I shrugged. "A year or so. Why?"

"No reason." She leaned against the doorjamb, watching as I moved on to jeans. "She just seemed . . . sort of scattered, I guess. Not exactly your type."

It was tempting to point out that Cora herself wasn't exactly in a position to claim to know me that well. But I held my tongue, still folding.

"Anyway," she continued, "in the future, though, if you could let us know when you were having people over, I'd appreciate it."

Like I'd had so many people showing up—all one of them!—that this was suddenly a problem. "I didn't know she was coming," I told her. "I forgot she even knew where I was staying."

She nodded. "Well, just keep it in mind. For next time."

Next time, I thought. *Whatever.* "Sure," I said aloud.

I kept folding, waiting for her to say something else. To go further, insinuating more, pulling me into an argument I didn't deserve, much less want to have. But instead, she just stepped back out of the doorway and started down the hall to her own room. A moment later, she called out for me to sleep well, and I responded in kind, these nicer last words delivered like an afterthought to find themselves, somewhere, in the space between us.

Chapter Seven

Usually I worked for Harriet from three thirty till seven, during which time she was supposed to take off to eat a late lunch and run errands. Invariably, however, she ended up sticking around for most of my shift, her purse in hand as she fretted and puttered, unable to actually leave.

"I'm sorry," she'd say, reaching past me to adjust a necklace display I'd already straightened twice. "It's just . . . I like things a certain way, you know?"

I knew. Harriet had built her business from the ground up, starting straight out of art school, and the process had been difficult, involving struggle, the occasional compromise of artistic integrity, and a near brush with bankruptcy. Still, she'd soldiered on, just her against the world. Which was why, I figured, it was so hard for her to adjust to the fact that now there were two of us.

Still, sometimes her neurosis was so annoying—following along behind me, checking and redoing each thing I did, taking over every task so I sometimes spent entire shifts doing nothing at all—that I wondered why she'd bothered to hire me. One day, when she had literally let me do nothing but dust for hours, I finally asked her.

"Truth?" she said. I nodded. "I'm overwhelmed. My orders are backed up, I'm constantly behind in my books, and

I'm completely exhausted. If it wasn't for caffeine, I'd be dead right now."

"Then let me help you."

"I'm *trying*." She took a sip from her ever-present coffee cup. "But it's hard. Like I said, I've always been a one-woman operation. That way, I'm responsible for everything, good and bad. And I'm afraid if I relinquish any control . . ."

I waited for her to finish. When she didn't, I said, "You'll lose everything."

Her eyes widened. "Yes!" she said. "How did you know?"

Like I was going to go there. "Lucky guess," I said instead.

"This business is the only thing I've ever had that was all mine," she said. "I'm scared to death something will happen to it."

"Yeah," I said as she took another gulp of coffee, "but accepting help doesn't have to mean giving up control."

It occurred to me, saying this, that I should take my own advice. Thinking back over the last few weeks, however—staying at Cora's, my college deal with Jamie—I realized maybe I already had.

Harriet was so obsessed with her business that, from what I could tell, she had no personal life whatsoever. During the day, she worked at the kiosk; at night, she went straight home, where she stayed up into the early hours making more pieces. Maybe this was how she wanted it. But there were clearly others who would welcome a change.

Like Reggie from Vitamin Me, for example. When he was going for food, he always stopped to see if she needed anything. If things were slow, he'd drift over to the open space between our two stalls to shoot the breeze. When

Harriet said she was tired, he instantly offered up B-complexes; if she sneezed, he was like a quick draw with the echinacea. One day after he'd brought her an herbal tea and some ginkgo biloba—she'd been complaining she couldn't remember anything anymore—she said, "He's just so nice. I don't know why he goes to so much trouble."

"Because he likes you," I said.

She jerked her head, surprised, and looked at me. "What?"

"He likes you," I repeated. To me, this was a no-brainer, as obvious as daylight. "You know that."

"Reggie?" she'd said, her surprised tone making it clear she did not. "No, no. We're just friends."

"The man gave you ginkgo," I pointed out. "Friends don't do that."

"Of course they do."

"Harriet, come on."

"I don't even know what you're talking about. I mean, we're friends, but the idea of something more is just . . ." she said, continuing to thumb through the receipts. Then, suddenly, she looked up at me, then over at Reggie, who was helping some woman with some protein powder. "Oh my God. Do you really think?"

"Yes," I said flatly, eyeing the ginkgo, which he'd piled neatly on the register with a note. Signed with a smiley face. "I do."

"Well, that's just ridiculous," she said, her face flushing.

"Why? Reggie's nice."

"I don't have time for a relationship," she said, picking up her coffee and taking a gulp. The ginkgo she now eyed warily, like it was a time bomb, not a supplement. "It's almost Christmas. That's my busiest time of the year."

"It doesn't have to be one or the other."

"There's just no way," she said flatly, shaking her head.

"Why not?"

"Because it won't work." She banged open the register drawer, sliding in the receipts. "Right now, I can only focus on myself and this business. Everything else is a distraction."

I was about to tell her this didn't have to be true, necessarily. That she and Reggie already had a relationship: they were friends, and she could just see how it went from there. But really, I had to respect where she was coming from, even if in this case I didn't agree with it. After all, I'd been determined to be a one-woman operation, as well, although lately this had been harder than you'd think. I'd found this out firsthand a few days earlier, when I was in the kitchen with Cora, minding my own business, and suddenly found myself swept up in Jamie's holiday plans.

"Wait," Cora said, looking down at the shirt on the table in front of her. "What is this for again?"

"Our Christmas card!" Jamie said, reaching into the bag he was holding to pull out another shirt—also a denim button-up, identical to hers—and handing it to me. "Remember how I said I wanted to do a photo this year?"

"You want us to wear matching shirts?" Cora asked as he took out yet one more, holding it up against his chest. "Seriously?"

"Yeah," Jamie said. "It's gonna be great. Oh, and wait. I forgot the best part!"

He turned, jogging out of the room into the foyer.

Cora and I just stared at each other across the table.

"Matching shirts?" I said.

"Don't panic," she said, although her own expression was hardly calm. She looked down at her shirt again. "At least, not yet."

"Check it out," Jamie said, coming back into the room. He had something behind his back, which he now presented to us, with a flourish. "For Roscoe!"

It was—yes—a denim shirt. Dog sized. With a red bow tie sewn on. Maybe I should have been grateful mine didn't have one of these, but frankly, at that moment, I was too horrified.

"Jamie," Cora said as he bent down beneath the table. I could hear banging around, along with some snuffling, as I assumed he attempted to wrangle Roscoe, who'd been dead asleep, into his outfit. "I'm all for a Christmas card. But do you really think we need to match?"

"In my family, we *always* wore matching outfits," he said, his voice muffled from the underside of the table. "My mom used to make sweaters for all of us in the same colors. Then we'd pose, you know, by the stairs or the fireplace or whatever, for our card. So this is a continuation of the tradition."

I looked at Cora. *"Do something,"* I mouthed, and she nodded, holding up her hand.

"You know," she said as Jamie finally emerged from the table holding Roscoe, who looked none too happy and was already gnawing at the bow tie, "I just wonder if maybe a regular shot would work. Or maybe just one of Roscoe?"

Jamie's face fell. "You don't want to do a card with all of us?"

"Well," she said, glancing at me, "I just . . . I guess it's just not something we're used to. Me and Ruby, I mean. Things were different at our house. You know."

This, of course, was the understatement of the century. I had a few memories of Christmas when my parents were still together, but when my dad left, he pretty much took my mom's yuletide spirit with him. After that, I'd learned to dread the holidays. There was always too much drinking, not enough money, and with school out I was stuck with my mom, and only my mom, for weeks on end. No one was happier to see the New Year come than I was.

"But," Jamie said now, looking down at Roscoe, who had completely spit-soaked the bow tie and had now moved on to chewing the shirt's sleeve, "that's one reason I really wanted to do this."

"What is?"

"You," he said. "For you. I mean, and Ruby, too, of course. Because, you know, you missed out all those years."

I turned to Cora again, waiting for her to go to bat for us once more. Instead, she was just looking at her husband, and I could have sworn she was tearing up. Shit.

"You know what?" she said as Roscoe coughed up some bow tie. "You're absolutely right."

"What?" I said.

"It'll be fun," she told me. "And you look good in blue."

This was little comfort, though, a week later, when I found myself posing by the pond, Roscoe perched in my lap, as Jamie fiddled with his tripod and self-timer. Cora, beside me in her shirt, kept shooting me apologetic looks, which I was studiously ignoring. "You have to understand," she said under her breath as Roscoe tried to lick my face. "He's just like this. The house, and the security, this whole life. . . . He's always wanted to give me what I didn't have. It's really sweet, actually."

"Here we go!" Jamie said, running over to take his place on Cora's other side. "Get ready. One, two . . ."

At three, the camera clicked, then clicked again. Never in a million years I thought, when I saw the pictures later, stacked up next to their blank envelopes on the island. HAPPY HOLIDAYS FROM THE HUNTERS! it said, and looking at the shot, you could almost think I was one of them. Blue shirt and all.

I wasn't the only one being forced out of my comfort zone. About a week later, I was at my locker before first bell when I felt someone step up beside me. I turned, assuming it was Nate—the only person I ever really talked to at school on a regular basis—but was surprised to see Olivia Davis standing there instead.

"You were right," she said. No hello or how are you. Then again, she didn't have her phone to her ear, either, so maybe this was progress.

"About what?"

She bit her lip, looking off to the side for a moment as a couple of soccer players blew past, talking loudly. "Her name is Melissa. The girl my boyfriend was cheating with."

"Oh," I said. I shut my locker door slowly. "Right."

"It's been going on for weeks, and nobody told me," she

continued, sounding disgusted. "All the friends I have there, and everyone I talk to regularly . . . yet somehow, it just doesn't come up. I mean, come on."

I wasn't sure what to say to this. "I'm sorry," I told her. "That sucks."

Olivia shrugged, still looking across the hallway. "It's fine. Better I know than not, right?"

"Definitely," I agreed.

"Anyway," she said, her tone suddenly brisk, all business, "I just wanted to say, you know, thanks. For the tip."

"No problem."

Her phone rang, the sound already familiar to me, trilling from her pocket. She pulled it out, glancing at it, but didn't open it. "I don't like owing people things," she told me. "So you just let me know how we get even here, all right?"

"You don't owe me anything," I said as her phone rang again. "I just gave you a name."

"Still. It counts." Her phone rang once more, and now she did flip it open, putting it to her ear. "One sec," she said, then covered the receiver. "Anyway, keep it in mind."

I nodded, and then she was turning, walking away, already into her next conversation. So Olivia didn't like owing people. Neither did I. In fact, I didn't like people period, unless they gave me a reason to think otherwise. Or at least, that was the way I had been, not so long ago. But lately, I was beginning to think it was not just my setting that had changed.

Later that week, Nate and I were getting out of the car before school, Gervais having already taken off at his usual breakneck pace. By this point, we weren't attracting as much attention—there was another Rachel Webster, I supposed, providing grist for the gossip mill—although we still got a few looks. "So anyway," he was telling me, "then I said that I thought maybe, just maybe, she could hire me and my dad to get her house in order. I mean, you should see it. There's stuff piled up all over the place—mail and newspapers and laundry. God. *Piles* of laundry."

"Harriet?" I said. "Really? She's so organized at work."

"That's work, though," he replied. "I mean—"

"Nate!"

He stopped walking and turned to look over at a nearby red truck, a guy in a leather jacket and sunglasses standing next to it. "Robbie," he said. "What's up?"

"You tell me," the guy called back. "Coach said you've quit the team for good now. And you had that U scholarship in the bag, man. What gives?"

Nate glanced at me, then pulled his bag farther up his shoulder. "I'm just too busy," he said as the guy came closer. "You know how it is."

"Yeah, but come on," the guy replied. "We need you! Where's your senior loyalty?"

I heard Nate say something but couldn't make it out as I kept walking. This clearly had nothing to do with me. I was about halfway to the green when I glanced behind me. Already, Nate was backing away from the guy in the leather jacket, their conversation wrapping up.

I only had a short walk left to the green. The same one I would have been taking alone, all this time, if left to my own devices. But as I stepped up onto the curb, I had a flash of Olivia, her reluctant expression as she stood by my locker, wanting to be square, not owing me or anyone anything. It was a weird feeling, knowing you were indebted, if not connected. Even stranger, though, was being aware of this, not liking it, and yet still finding yourself digging in deeper, anyway. Like, for instance, consciously slowing your steps so it still looked accidental for someone to catch up from behind, a little out of breath, and walk with you the rest of the way.

*   *   *

The picture was of a group of people standing on a wide front porch. By their appearance—sideburns and loud prints on the men, printed flowy dresses and long hair on the women—I guessed it was taken sometime in the seventies. In the back, people were standing in haphazard rows; in the front, children were plopped down, sitting cross-legged. One boy had his tongue sticking out, while two little girls in front wore flowers in their hair. In the center, there was a girl in a white dress sitting in a chair, two elderly women on each side of her.

There had to be fifty people in all, some resembling each other, others looking like no one else around them. While a few were staring right into the camera with fixed smiles on their faces, others were laughing, looking off to one side or the other or at each other, as if not even aware a picture was being taken. It was easy to imagine the photographer giving up on trying to get the shot and instead just snapping the shutter, hoping for the best.

I'd found the photo on the island when I came downstairs, and I picked it up, carrying it over to the table to look at while I ate my breakfast. By the time Jamie came down twenty minutes later, I should have long moved on to the paper and my horoscope, but I was still studying it.

"Ah," he said, heading straight to the coffeemaker. "You found the ad. What do you think?"

"This is an ad?" I asked. "For what?"

He walked over to the island. "Actually," he said, digging around under some papers, "that's not the ad. This is."

He slid another piece of paper in front of me. At the top was the picture I'd been looking at, with the words IT'S ABOUT FAMILY in thick typewriter-style block print beneath it. Below that was another picture, taken in the present day, of a bunch of twenty-somethings gathered on what looked like the end zone of a football field. They were in T-shirts and jeans, some with arms around each other, others with hands lifted in the air, clearly celebrating something. IT'S ABOUT FRIENDS, it said underneath. Finally, a third picture, which was of a computer screen, filled with tiny square shots of smiling faces. Looking more closely, I could see they were same ones as in the other pictures, cut out and cropped down, then lined up end to end. Underneath, it said, IT'S ABOUT CONNECTING: UME.COM.

"The idea," Jamie explained over my shoulder, "is that while life is getting so individualistic—we all have our own phones, our own e-mail accounts, our own everything—we continue to use those things to reach out to each other. Friends, family . . . they're all part of communities we make and depend on. And UMe helps you do that."

"Wow," I said.

"Thousands spent on an advertising agency," he said,

reaching for the cereal box between us, "hours wasted in endless meetings, and a major print run about to drop any minute. And all you can say is 'wow'?"

"It's better than 'it sucks,'" Cora said, entering the kitchen with Roscoe at her heels. "Right?"

"Your sister," Jamie told me in a low voice, "does not like the campaign."

"I never said that," Cora told him, pulling the fridge open and taking out a container of waffles as Roscoe headed my way, sniffing the floor. "I only said that I thought your family might not like being featured, circa nineteen seventy-six, in magazines and bus shelters nationwide."

I looked back at the top picture, then at Jamie. "This is your family?"

"Yep," he said.

"And that's not even all of them," Cora added, sticking some waffles into the toaster oven. "Can you even believe that? They're not a family. They're a tribe."

"My grandmother was one of six children," Jamie explained.

"Ah," I said.

"You should have seen it when we got married," Cora said. "I felt like I'd crashed my own wedding. I didn't know *anybody.*"

It took a beat for the awkwardness following this statement to hit, but when it did, we all felt it. Jamie glanced up at me, but I focused on finishing the bite of cereal I'd just taken, chewing carefully as Cora flushed and turned her attention to the toaster oven. Maybe it would have been easier to actually *acknowledge* the weirdness that was our estrangement and the fact that my mom and I hadn't even known Cora had gotten married, much less been invited to the wedding. But of course, we didn't. Instead we just sat there, until suddenly the smoke detector went off, breaking the silence.

"Shit," Jamie said, jumping up as ear-piercing beeping filled the room. Immediately I looked at Roscoe, whose ears had gone flat on his head. "What's burning?"

"It's this stupid toaster oven," Cora said, pulling it open and waving her hand back and forth in front of it. "It always does this. Roscoe, honey, it's okay—"

But it was too late. The dog was already bolting out of the room, in full flight mode, the way he'd taken to doing the last week or so. For some reason, Roscoe's appliance anxiety had been increasing, spurred on not only by the oven but anything in the kitchen that beeped or had the potential to do so. The smoke detector, though, remained his biggest fear. Which, I figured, meant that right about now he was probably up in my bathroom closet, his favorite hiding place of late, shaking among my shoes and waiting for the danger to pass.

Jamie grabbed the broom, reaching it up to hit the detector's reset button, and finally the beeping stopped. As he got down and came back to the table, Cora followed him, sliding into a chair with her waffle, which she then nibbled at halfheartedly.

"It may be time to call a professional," she said after a moment.

"I'm not putting the dog on antidepressants," Jamie told her, picking up the paper and scanning the front page. "I don't care how relaxed Denise's dachshund is now."

"Lola is a Maltese," Cora said, "and it wouldn't neces-sarily mean that. Maybe there's some training we can do, something that will help him."

"We can't keep coddling him, though," Jamie said. "You know what the books say. Every time you pick him up or soothe him when he's freaking out like that, you're reinforc-ing the behavior."

"So you'd prefer we just stand by and let him be trau-matized?"

"Of course not," Jamie said.

Cora put down her waffle, wiping her mouth with a napkin. "Then I just think that there's got to be a way to acknowledge his fear and at the same time—"

"Cora." Jamie put down the paper. "He's a dog, not a child. This isn't a self-esteem issue. It's Pavlovian. Okay?"

Cora just looked at him for a moment. Then she pushed back her chair, getting to her feet, and walked to the island, dropping her plate into the sink with a loud clank.

As she left the room, Jamie sighed, running a hand over his face as I pulled the family picture back toward me. Again, I found myself studying it: the varied faces, some smiling, some not, the gentle regalness of the elderly women, who were staring right into the camera. Across the table, Jamie was just sitting there, looking out at the pond.

"I do like the ad, you know," I said to him finally. "It's cool."

"Thanks," he said, distracted.

"Are you in this picture?" I asked him.

He glanced over at it as he pushed his chair out and got

to his feet. "Nah. Before my time. I didn't come along for a few more years. That's my mom, though, in the white dress. It was her wedding day."

As he left the room, I looked down at the picture again, and at the girl in the center, noticing how serene and happy she looked surrounded by all those people. I couldn't imagine what it would be like to be one of so many, to have not just parents and siblings but cousins and aunts and uncles, an entire tribe to claim as your own. Maybe you would feel lost in the crowd. Or sheltered by it. Whatever the case, one thing was for sure: like it or not, you'd never be alone.

* * *

Fifteen minutes later I was standing in the warmth of the foyer, waiting for Nate to pull up at the mailbox, when the phone rang.

"Cora?" the caller said, skipping a hello.

"No," I said. "This is—"

"Oh, Ruby, hi!" The voice was a woman's, entirely perky. "It's Denise, Cora's old roommate—from the party?"

"Right. Hi," I said, turning my head as Cora came down the stairs, briefcase in her hand.

"So how's life?" Denise asked. "School okay? It's gotta be a big adjustment, starting at a new place. But Cora did say it's not the first time you've switched schools. Personally, I lived in the same place my whole entire life, which is really not much better, actually, because—"

"Here's Cora," I said, holding the phone out as she got to the bottom step.

"Hello?" Cora said as she took it from me. "Oh, hey.

Yeah. At nine." She reached up, tucking a piece of hair be-hind her ear. "I will."

I walked over to the window by the door, looking for Nate. He was usually right on time, and when he wasn't, it was often because Gervais—who had trouble waking up in the morning and was often dragged to the car by his mother—held things up.

"No, I'm all right," Cora was saying. She'd gone down the hallway, but only a few steps. "Things are just kind of tense. I'll call you after, okay? Thanks for remembering. Yeah. Bye."

There was a beep as she hung up. When I glanced back at her, she said, "Look. About earlier, and what I said about the wedding. . . . I didn't mean to make you feel uncom-fortable."

"It's fine," I said just as the phone rang again. She looked down at it, then answered.

"Charlotte, hey. Can I call you back? I'm kind of in the middle of—Yeah. Nine a.m. Well, hopefully." She nodded. "I know. Positivity. I'll let you know how it goes. Okay. Bye."

This time, as she hung up, she sighed, then sat down on the bottom step, laying the phone beside her. When she saw me watching her she said, "I have a doctor's appointment this morning."

"Oh," I said. "Is everything—are you all right?"

"I don't know," she replied. Then she quickly added, "I mean, I'm fine, health-wise. I'm not sick or anything."

I nodded, not sure what to say.

"It's just . . ." She smoothed her skirt with both hands.

"We've been trying to get pregnant for a while, and it's just not happening. So we're meeting with a specialist."

"Oh," I said again.

"It's all right," she said quickly. "Lots of people have problems like this. I just thought you should know, in case you ever have to take a message from a doctor's office or something. I didn't want you to worry."

I nodded, turning back to the window. This would be a great time for Nate to show up, I thought. But of course he didn't. Stupid Gervais. And then I heard Cora draw in a breath.

"And like I was saying, about earlier," she said. "About the wedding. I just . . . I didn't want you to feel like I was . . ."

"It's fine," I said again.

". . . still mad about that. Because I'm not."

It took me a moment to process this, like the sentence fell apart between us and I had to string the words back together. "Mad?" I said finally. "About what?"

"You and Mom not coming," she said. She sighed. "Look, we don't have to talk about this. It's ancient history. But this morning, when I said that thing about the wedding, you just looked so uncomfortable, and I knew you probably felt bad. So I thought maybe it would be better to just clear the air. Like I said, I'm not mad anymore."

"You didn't invite us to your wedding," I said.

Now she looked surprised. "Yes," she said slowly. "I did."

"Well, then the invitation must have gotten lost in the mail, because—"

"I brought it to Mom, Ruby," she said.

"No, you didn't." I swallowed, taking a breath. "You . . . you haven't seen Mom in years."

"That's not true," she said simply, as if I'd told her the wrong time, something that innocuous. "I brought the invitation to her personally, at the place she was working at the time. I wanted you there."

Cars were passing by the mailbox, and I knew any moment one of them would be Nate's, and I'd have to leave. But right then, I couldn't even move. I was flattened against the window, as if someone had knocked the wind out of me. "No," I said again. "You disappeared. You went to college, and you were gone. We never heard from you."

She looked down at her skirt. Then, quietly, she said, "That's not true."

"It is. I was there." But even to me, I sounded unsure, at the one time I wanted—needed—to be absolutely positive. "If you'd ever tried to reach us—"

"Of *course* I tried to reach you," she said. "I mean, the time I spent tracking you down alone was—"

Suddenly, she stopped talking. Mid-sentence, mid-breath. In the silence that followed, a red BMW drove past, then a blue minivan. Normal people, off to their normal lives. "Wait," she said after a moment. "You do know about all that, don't you? You have to. There's no way she could have—"

"I have to go," I said, but when I reached down for the doorknob and twisted it, I heard her get to her feet and come up behind me.

"Ruby, look at me," she said, but I stayed where I was,

facing the small crack in the door, feeling cold air coming through. "All I wanted was to find you. The entire time I was in college, and after. . . . I was trying to get you out of there."

Now, of course, Nate did pull up to the curb. Perfect timing. "You left that day, for school," I said, turning to face her. "You never came back. You didn't call or write or show up for holidays—"

"Is that what you really think?" she demanded.

"That's what I know."

"Well, you're wrong," she said. "Think about it. All those moves, all those houses. A different school every time. The jobs she could never hold, the phone that was rarely hooked up, and then never in her real name. Did you ever wonder why she put down fake addresses on all your school stuff? Do you think that was some kind of accident? Do you have any idea how hard she made it for me to find you?"

"You didn't try," I said, and now my voice was cracking, loud and shaky, rising up into the huge space above us.

"I did," Cora said. Distantly, from outside, I heard a beep: Nate, getting impatient. "For years I did. Even when she told me to stop, that you wanted nothing to do with me. Even when you ignored my letters and messages—"

My throat was dry, hard, as I tried to swallow.

"—I still kept coming back, reaching out, all the way up to the wedding. She swore she would give you the invitation, give you the choice to come or not. By that time I had threatened to get the courts involved so I could see you, which was the last thing she wanted, so she promised me. She *promised* me, Ruby. But she couldn't do it. She upped and moved you away again instead. She was so afraid of be-ing alone, of you leaving, too, that she never gave you the chance. Until this year, when she knew that you'd be turn-ing eighteen, and you could, and most likely would. So what did she do?"

"Stop it," I said.

"*She left you,*" she finished. "Left you alone, in that filthy house, before you could do the same to her."

I felt something rising in my throat—a sob, a scream—and bit it back, tears filling my eyes, and I hated myself for crying, showing any weakness here. "You don't know what you're talking about," I said.

"I do, though." And now her voice was soft. Sad. Like she felt sorry for me, which was the most shameful thing of all. "That's the thing. I do."

Nate beeped again, louder and longer this time. "I have to go," I said, yanking the door open.

"Wait," Cora said. "Don't just—"

But I ran outside, pulling the door shut behind me. I didn't want to talk anymore. I didn't want anything, except a moment of peace and quiet to be alone and try to fig-ure what exactly had just happened. All those years there were so many things I couldn't rely on, but this, the story of what had happened to my family, had always been a given, understood. Now, though, I wasn't so sure. What do you do when you only have two people in your life, neither of whom you've ever been able to fully trust, and yet you have to believe one of them?

I heard the door open again. "Ruby," Cora called out. "Just wait a second. We can't leave it like this."

But this, too, wasn't true. Leaving was easy. It was everything else that was so damned hard.

*　*　*

I'd only just gotten my door shut and seat belt on when it started.

"What's wrong with *you*? You look like crap."

I ignored Gervais, instead keeping my eyes fixed straight ahead. Still, I could feel Nate looking at me, concerned, so I said, "I'm fine. Let's just go." It took him another moment, but then he was finally hitting the gas and we were pulling away.

For the first few blocks, I just tried to breathe. *It's not true*, I kept thinking, and yet in the next beat it was all coming back: those moves and new schools, and the paperwork we always fudged—addresses, phone—because of bad landlords or creditors. The phones that were never hooked up, that graduation announcement my mom had said was just sent out automatically. *Just you and me, baby. Just you and me.*

I swallowed, keeping my eyes on the back of the bus in front of us, which was covered with an ad reading IT'S A FESTIVAL OF SALADS! I narrowed my focus to just these five words, holding them in the center of my vision, even as there was a loud, ripping burp from behind me.

"Gervais." Nate hit his window button. As it went down he said, "What did we just spend a half hour talking about with your mom?"

"I don't know," Gervais replied, giggling.

"Then let me refresh your memory," Nate said. "The burping and farting and rudeness stops right now. Or else."

"Or else what?"

We pulled up to a red light, and Nate turned around, then leaned back between our seats. Suddenly, he was so close to me that even in my distracted state I couldn't help but breathe in the scent of the USWIM sweatshirt he had on: a mix of clean and chlorine, the smell of water. "Or else," he said, his voice sounding very un-Nate-like, stern and serious, "you go back to riding with the McClellans."

"No way!" Gervais said. "The McClellans are *first-graders*. Plus, I'd have to walk from the lower school."

Nate shrugged. "So get up earlier."

"I'm *not* getting up earlier," Gervais squawked. "It's already too early!"

"Then quit being such a pain in the ass," Nate told him, turning back around as the light changed.

A moment later I felt Nate glance at me. I knew he was probably expecting a thank-you, since he'd clearly gone to Mrs. Miller that morning to talk about Gervais because of what I'd said, trying to make things better. But I was so tired, suddenly, of being everyone's charity case. I never asked anyone to help me. If you felt compelled to anyway, that was your problem, not mine.

When we pulled into the lot five minutes later, for the first time I beat Gervais out of the car, pushing my door open before we were even at a full stop. I was already a row of cars away when Nate yelled after me. "Ruby," he said. "Wait up."

But I didn't, not this time. I just kept going, walking faster. By the time I reached the green, the first bell hadn't yet rung, and people were everywhere, pressing on all sides.

When I saw the door to the bathroom, I just headed straight for it.

Inside, there were girls at the sinks checking their make-up and talking on the phone, but the stalls were all empty as I walked past them, sliding into the one by the wall and locking the door. Then I leaned against it, closing my eyes.

All those years I'd given up Cora for lost, hated her for leaving me. What if I had been wrong? What if, somehow, my mother had managed to keep her away, the only other person I'd ever had? And if she had, why?

She left you, Cora had said, and it was these three words, then and now, that I heard most clearly of all, slicing through the roaring in my head like someone speaking right into my ear. I didn't want this to make sense, for her to be right in any way. But even I could not deny the logic of it. My mother had been abandoned by a husband and one daughter; she'd had enough of being left. So she'd done what she had to do to make sure it didn't happen again. And this, above all else, I could understand. It was the same thing I'd been planning to do myself.

The bell rang overhead, and the bathroom slowly cleared out, the door banging open and shut as people headed off to class. Then, finally, it was quiet, the hallways empty, the only sound the flapping of the flag out on the green, which I could hear from the high half-open windows that ran along the nearby wall.

When I was sure I was alone, I left the stall and walked over to the sinks, dropping my bag at my feet. In the mirror overhead, I realized Gervais had been right: I looked terrible, my face blotchy and red. I reached down, watching my fingers as they picked up the key at my neck, then closed themselves tightly around it.

"I told you, I had to get a pass and sign out," I heard a voice say suddenly from outside. "Because this place is like a prison, okay? Look, just hold tight. I'll be there as soon as I can."

I looked outside, just in time to see Olivia passing by, phone to her ear, walking down the breezeway to the parking lot. As soon as I saw her take her keys out of her backpack, I grabbed my bag and bolted.

I caught up with her by a row of lockers just as she was folding her phone into her back pocket. "Hey," I called out, my voice bouncing off the empty corridor all around us. "Where are you going?"

When she turned around and saw me, her expression was wary, at best. Then again, with my blotchy face, not to mention being completely out of breath, I couldn't exactly blame her. "I have to go pick up my cousin. Why?"

I came closer, taking a breath. "I need a ride."

"Where?"

"Anywhere."

She raised her eyebrows. "I'm going to Jackson, then home. Nowhere else. I have to be back here by third."

"That's fine," I told her. "Perfect, in fact."

"You have a pass?"

I shook my head.

"So you want me to just take you off campus anyway, risking my ass, even though it's totally against the rules."

"Yes," I said.

She shook her head, no deal.

"But we'll be square," I added. "You won't owe me any-more."

"This is way more than what I owe you," she said. She studied my face for a moment, and I stood there, waiting for her verdict. She was right, this was probably stupid of me. But I was tired of playing it smart. Tired of everything.

"All right," she said finally. "But I'm not taking you from here. Get yourself to the Quik Zip, and I'll pick you up."

"Done," I told her, pulling my bag over my shoulder. "See you there."

Chapter Eight

When I slid into Olivia's front seat ten minutes later, my foot immediately hit something, then crunched it flat. Looking down, I saw it was a popcorn tub, the kind you buy at the movies, and it wasn't alone: there were at least four more rolling across the floorboards.

"I work at the Vista Ten," she explained, her engine puttering as she switched into reverse. "It pays crap, but we get all the free popcorn we can eat."

"Right," I said. Now that I thought of it, that did explain the butter smell.

We pulled out onto the main road, then merged into traffic and headed for the highway. I'd spent so much time riding with Jamie and Nate that I'd almost forgotten what it was like to be in a regular car, i.e., one that was not new and loaded with every possible gadget and extra. Olivia's Toyota was battered, the fabric of the seats nubby, with several stains visible, and there was one of those prisms hanging on a cord dangling from the rearview. It reminded me of my mother's Subaru, the thought of which gave me a pang I quickly pushed away, focusing instead on the entrance to the highway, rising up in the distance.

"So what's the deal?" Olivia asked as we merged into traffic, her muffler rattling.

"With what?"

"You."

"No deal," I said, sitting back and propping my feet on the dashboard.

She eyed my feet pointedly. I dropped them back down again. "So you just decided to cut school for the hell of it," she said.

"Pretty much."

We were getting closer, passing another exit. The one to Jackson was next. "You know," she said, "you can't just show up and hang out on campus. They're not as organized as Perkins, but they *will* kick you off."

"I'm not going to campus," I told her.

When we came over the hill five minutes later and Jackson came into view—big, sprawling, trailers lined up behind—I felt myself relax. After so many weeks of being out of place, it was nice to finally see something familiar. Olivia pulled up in front, where there was a row of faded plastic benches. Sitting on the last one was a heavyset black girl with short hair and glasses. When she saw us, she slowly got to her feet and began to shuffle in our direction.

"Oh, look at this," Olivia said loudly, rolling down her window. "Seems like *someone* should have listened to someone else who said maybe running a mile wasn't such a smart idea."

"It's not because of the running," the girl grumbled, pulling open the back door and sliding gingerly onto the seat. "I think I have the flu."

"All the books say you should start slow," Olivia continued. "But not you. You have to sprint the first day."

"Just shut up and give me some Advil, would you please?"

Olivia rolled her eyes, then reached across me and popped the glove compartment. She pulled out a bottle of pills, then chucked it over her shoulder. "This is Laney, by the way," Olivia said, banging the glove compartment shut again. "She thinks she can run a marathon."

"It's a five-K," Laney said. "And some support would be nice."

"I'm supportive," Olivia told her, turning around in her seat. "I support you so much that I'm the only one telling you this isn't a good idea. That maybe, just maybe, you could hurt yourself."

Laney just looked at her as she downed two Advils, then popped the cap back on. "Pain is part of running," she said. "That's why it's an endurance sport."

"You don't know anything about endurance!" Olivia turned to me. "One night she sees that crazy woman Kiki Sparks in one of those infomercials, talking about caterpillars and butterflies and potential and setting fitness goals. Next think you know, she thinks she's Lance Armstrong."

"Lance Armstrong is a cyclist," Laney pointed out, wincing as she shifted her weight. "That's not even a valid analogy."

Olivia harrumphed but withheld further comment as we pulled forward out of the turnaround. As she put on her blinker to turn left, I said, "Do you mind going the other way? It's not far."

"There's nothing up there but woods," she said.

"It'll only take a minute."

I saw her glance back at Laney in the rearview, but then

she was turning, slowly, the engine chugging as we headed up the hill. The parking lots gave way to more parking lots, which then turned into scrub brush. About half a mile later, I told her to slow down.

"This is good," I said as we came up on the clearing. Sure enough, there were two cars parked there, and I could see Aaron, Peyton's ex—a chubby guy with a baby face he tried to counter by dressing in all black and scowling a lot—sitting on one of them, smoking a cigarette. "Thanks for the ride."

Olivia looked over at them, then back at me. "You want to get out here?"

"Yeah," I said.

She was clearly skeptical. "How are you planning to get back?"

"I'll find a way," I said. I got out of the car and picked up my bag. She was still watching me, so I added, "Look, don't worry."

"I'm not worried," she said. "I don't even know you."

Still, she kept her eyes on me while Laney opened the back door and slid out slowly, taking her time as she made her way into the front seat. As she pulled the door shut, Olivia said, "You know, I can take you home, if you want. I mean, I'm missing third by now, anyway, thanks to Laney."

I shook my head. "No, I'm good. I'll see you at school, okay?"

She nodded slowly as I patted the roof of the car, then turned around and headed for the clearing. Aaron squinted at me, then sat up straighter. "Hey, Ruby," he called out as I approached. "Welcome back."

"Thanks," I said, hopping up on the hood beside him. Olivia had stayed where I left her, watching me from behind the wheel, but now she moved forward, turning around in the dead end, her engine put-putting. The prism hanging from her rearview caught the light for a moment, throwing sparks, and then she was sliding past, over the hill and out of sight. "It's good to be here."

*   *   *

I'd actually come looking for Peyton, who had a free second period and often skipped third to boot, spending both at the clearing. But Aaron, whose schedule was flexible due to a recent expulsion, claimed he hadn't seen her, so I settled in to wait. That had been a couple of hours ago.

"Hey."

I felt something nudge my foot. Then again, harder. When I opened my eyes, Aaron was holding out a joint, the tip smoldering. I tried to focus on it, but it kept blurring, slightly to one side, then the other. "I'm okay," I said.

"Oh, yeah," he said flatly, putting it to his own lips and taking a big drag. In his black shirt and jeans, his white skin seemed so pale, almost glowing. "You're just fine."

I leaned back, then felt my head bonk hard against something behind me. Turning slightly, I saw thick treads, sloping metal, and I could smell rubber. It took me another minute, though, to realize I was sitting against a car. There was grass beneath me and trees all around; looking up, I could see a bright blue sky. I was still at the clearing, although how I got on the ground I wasn't exactly sure.

This was because I was also drunk, the result of the pint of vodka we'd shared soon after I'd arrived. That I remembered at least partially—him pulling out the bottle from his pocket, along with a couple of orange-juice cartons someone had nicked from the cafeteria during breakfast. We'd poured some of each into an empty Zip cup, then shook them up, cocktail style, and toasted each other in his front seat, the radio blasting. And repeat, until the orange juice was gone. Then we'd switched to straight shots, each burning a little less as they went down.

"Damn," he'd said, wiping his mouth as he passed the bottle back to me. The wind had been blowing, all the trees swaying, and everything felt distant and close all at once, just right. "Since when are you such a lush, Cooper?"

"Always," I remembered telling him. "It's in my genes."

Now he took another deep drag, sputtering slightly as he held it in. My head felt heavy, fluid, as he exhaled, the smoke blowing across me. I closed my eyes, trying to lose myself in it. That morning, all I'd wanted was to feel oblivious, block out everything I'd heard about my mom from Cora. And for a while, sitting with him and singing along to the radio, I had. Now, though, I could feel it hovering again, crouching just out of sight.

"Hey," I said, forcing my eyes open and turning my head. "Let me get a hit off that."

He held it out. As I took it, my fingers fumbled and it fell to the ground between us, disappearing into the grass. "Shit," I said, digging around until I felt heat—pricking, sudden—against my skin. As I came up with it, I had to concentrate on guiding it to my mouth slowly, easing my lips around it before pulling in a big drag.

The smoke was thick, sinking down into my lungs, and

feeling it I sat back again, my head hitting the fender behind me. God, this was good. Just floating and distant, every worry receding like a wave rushing out and then pulling
back, wiping the sand clean behind it. I had a flash of myself,
walking through these same woods not so long ago, feeling
this same way: loose and easy, everything still ahead. Then
I hadn't been alone, either. I'd been with Marshall.

Marshall. I opened my eyes, squinting down at my watch
until it came into focus. That was what I needed right now—
just any kind of closeness, even if it was only for a little
while. Sandpiper Arms was only a short walk from here, via
a path through the woods; we'd done it tons of times.

"Where you going?" Aaron asked, his voice heavy as I
pushed myself to my feet, stumbling slightly before regain-
ing my footing. "I thought we were hanging out."

"I'll be back," I told him, and started for the path.

By the time I reached the bottom of Marshall's stairs, I
felt slightly more coherent, although I was sweating from the
walk, and I could feel a headache setting in. I took a moment
to smooth down my hair and make myself slightly more
presentable, then pushed on up to the door and knocked
hard. A moment later, the door creaked open, and Rogerson
peered out at me.

"Hey," I said. My voice sounded low, liquidy. "Is Marshall
home?"

"Uh," he replied, looking over his shoulder. "I don't
know."

"It's cool if he's not," I told him. "I can wait in his room."

He looked at me for a long moment, during which I felt
myself sway, slightly. Then he stepped aside.

The apartment was dark, as usual, as I moved down the hallway to the living room. "You know," Rogerson said from behind me, his voice flat, "he probably won't be back for a while."

But at that point, I didn't care. All I wanted was to collapse onto the bed, pulling the sheets around me, and sleep, finally able to block out everything that had happened since I'd woken up in my own room that morning. Just to be someplace safe, someplace I knew, with someone, anyone, familiar nearby.

When I pushed open the door, the first thing I saw was that Whitman's sampler. It caught my eye even before I recognized Peyton, who was sitting beside it, a chocolate in her hand. I watched, frozen, as she reached it out to Marshall, who was lying beside her, hands folded over his chest, and dropped it into his open mouth. This was just the simplest gesture, taking mere seconds, but at the same time there was something so intimate about it—the way his lips closed over her fingers, how she giggled, her cheeks pink, before drawing them back—that I felt sick, even before Marshall turned his head and saw me.

I don't know what I was expecting him to do or say, if anything. To be surprised, or sorry, or even sad. In the end, though, his expression said it all: I Could Care Less.

"Oh, *shit*," Peyton gasped. "Ruby, I'm so—"

"Oh my God," I said, stumbling backward out of the door frame. I put my hand to my mouth as I turned, bumping the wall as I ran back down the hallway to the front door. Vaguely, I could hear her calling after me, but I ignored this as I burst out into the daylight again, gripping the banister as I ran down to the parking lot.

"Ruby, wait," Peyton was yelling, her own steps loud on the stairs as she followed me. "Jesus! Just let me explain!"

"Explain?" I said, whirling to face her. "How in the world do you explain this?"

She stopped by the banister, hand to her heart, to catch her breath. "I tried to tell you," she gasped. "That night, at your house. But it was so hard, and then you kept saying how things had changed, anyway, so—"

Suddenly, something clicked in my brain, and I had a flash of her that night, in the foyer with Roscoe and Jamie, then of Marshall handing me back my key that last time I'd seen him. *You told me you lived in Wildflower Ridge,* she'd said, but I was sure I hadn't. I was right. He had.

"That's why you came over?" I asked. "To tell me you were sleeping with my boyfriend?"

"You never called him that!" she shot back, pointing at me. "Not even once. You just said you had a *thing,* an *arrangement.* I thought I was being nice, wanting to tell you."

"I don't need you to be nice to me," I snapped.

"Of course you don't," she replied. At the top of the stairs, I could see Rogerson just past the open door, looking down at us. We were making a scene, the last thing he wanted. "You don't need anything. Not a boyfriend, not a friend. You were always so clear about that. And that's what you got. So why are you surprised now?"

I just stood there, looking at her. My head was spinning, my mouth dry, and all I could think about was that I wanted to go someplace safe, someplace I could be alone and okay, and that this was impossible. My old life had changed and my new one was still in progress, altering by the second. There was nothing, *nothing* to depend on. And why *was* I surprised?

I walked away from her, back to the path, but as I entered the woods I was having trouble keeping on it, roots catching my feet, branches scratching me from all sides. I was so tired—of this day, of everything—even as it all came rushing back: Cora's face in the foyer that morning, Olivia's prism glinting in the sun, stepping into the familiar dimness of the apartment, so sure of what I was there for.

As I stumbled again, I started to catch myself, then stopped, instead just letting my body go limp, hitting knees first, then elbows, in the leaves. Up ahead, I could see the edge of the clearing, and Aaron looking at me, but it suddenly felt right, even perfect, to be alone. So as I lay back on the ground, the sky already spinning above me, I tried to focus again on the idea of that wave I'd thought of earlier, wiping everything clean, blue and big and wide enough to suck me in. Maybe it was a wish, or a dream. Either way, it was so real that at some point, I could actually feel it. Like a presence coming closer, with arms that closed around me, lifting me up with a scent that filled my senses: clean and pure, a touch of chlorine. The smell of water.

* * *

The first thing I saw when I opened my eyes was Roscoe.

He was sitting on the empty seat beside me, right in front of the steering wheel, facing forward, panting. As I tried to focus, I suddenly smelled dog breath—ugh—and my stomach twisted. *Shit*, I thought, bolting forward, my hand fumbling for the door handle. Just in time, though,

I saw the Double Burger bag positioned between my feet. I'd only barely grabbed it and put it to my lips before I was puking up something hot and burning that I could feel all the way to my ears.

My hands were shaking as I eased the bag onto the floor, then sat back, my heart thumping in my chest. I was freezing, even though I was now wearing a USWIM sweatshirt that looked awfully familiar. Looking outside, I saw we were parked in some kind of strip mall—I could see a dry-cleaner and a video store—and I had no idea how I'd gotten here. In fact the only thing familiar, other than the dog, was the air freshener hanging from the rearview, which said: WE WORRY SO YOU DON'T HAVE TO.

Oh my God, I thought as these things all suddenly collided. I looked down at the sweatshirt again, breathing in that water smell, distant and close all at once. Nate.

Suddenly, Roscoe let out a yap, which was amplified by the small space around us. He leaped up on the driver's-side window, nails tap-tapping, his nub of a tail wriggling around wildly. I was wondering whether I was going to puke again when I heard a pop and felt a rush of fresh air from behind me.

Immediately, Roscoe bounded into the backseat, his tags jingling. It took me considerably longer to turn myself around—God, my head was pounding—and focus enough to see Nate, at the back of his car, easing in a pile of dry-cleaning. When he looked up and saw me, he said, "Hey, you're conscious. Good."

Good? I thought, but then he was slamming the back door shut (ouch) before walking around to pull open the driver's-side door and get in behind the wheel. As he slid his keys into the ignition, he glanced over at the bag at my feet. "How you doing there? Need another one yet?"

"Another one?" I said. My voice was dry, almost cracking on the words. "This . . . this isn't the first?"

He shot me a sympathetic look. "No," he said. "It isn't."

As if to punctuate this, my stomach rolled threateningly as he began to back out of the space. I tried to calm it, as Roscoe climbed up between our two seats, sticking his head forward and closing his eyes while Nate rolled down his window, letting in some fresh air.

"What time is it?" I asked, trying to keep my voice level, if only to control the nausea.

"Almost five," Nate replied.

"Are you serious?"

"What time did you think it was?"

Honestly, I didn't even know. I'd lost track of time on the walk back to the clearing when everything went fluid. "What—?" I said, then stopped, realizing I wasn't even sure what I was about to ask. Or even where to begin. "What is Roscoe doing here?"

Nate glanced back at the dog, who was still riding high, his ears blowing back in the wind. "He had a four o'clock vet appointment," he said. "Cora and Jamie both had to work, so they hired me to take him. When I went to pick him up and you weren't at home, I figured I'd better go looking for you."

"Oh," I said. I looked at Roscoe, who immediately took this as an invitation to start licking my face. I pushed him away, moving closer to the window. "But how did you—?"

"Olivia," he said. I blinked, a flash of her driving away popping into my head. "That's her name, right? The girl with the braids?"

I nodded slowly, still trying to piece this together. "You know Olivia?"

"No," he said. "She just came up to me before fourth period and said she'd left you in the woods—at your request, she was very clear on that—and thought I should know."

"Why would you need to know?"

He shrugged. "I guess she thought you might need a friend."

Hearing this, I felt my face flush, suddenly embarrassed. Like I was so desperate and needing to be rescued that people— strangers—were actually convening to discuss it. My worst nightmare. "I was with my friends," I said. "Actually."

"Yeah?" he asked, glancing over at me. "Well, then, they must be the invisible kind. Because when I got there, you were alone."

What? I thought. That couldn't be true. Aaron had been right there in the clearing, and he'd seen me lie down. Now that I thought about it, though, it had been midday then; it was late afternoon now. If Nate was telling the truth, how long had I been there, alone and passed out? *Are you surprised?* I heard Peyton say again in my head, and a shiver ran over me. I wrapped my arms around myself, looking out the window. The buildings were blurring past, but I tried to find just one I could recognize, as if I could somehow locate myself that way.

"Look," Nate said, "what happened today is over. It doesn't matter, okay? We'll get you home, and everything will be fine."

Hearing this, I felt my eyes well up unexpectedly with hot tears. It was bad to be embarrassed, hard to be ashamed. But pitied? That was the worst of all. Of course Nate would think this could all be so easily resolved. It was how things happened in his world, where he was a friendly guy and worried so you didn't have to as he went about living his life of helpful errands and good deeds. Unlike me, so dirty and used up and broken. I had a flash of Marshall looking over his shoulder at me, and my head pounded harder.

"Hey," Nate said now, as if he could hear me thinking this, slipping further and further down this slope. "It's okay."

"It's not," I said, keeping my eyes fixed on the window. "You couldn't even understand."

"Try me."

"No." I swallowed, pulling my arms tighter around myself. "It's not your problem."

"Ruby, come on. We're friends."

"Stop saying that," I said.

"Why?"

"Because it's not true," I said, now turning to face him. "We don't even know each other. You just live behind me and give me a ride to school. Why do you think that makes us somehow something?"

"Fine," he said, holding up his hands. "We're not friends."

And now I was a bitch. We rode in silence for a block, Roscoe panting between us. "Look," I said, "I appreciate what you did. What you've done. But the thing is . . . my life isn't like yours, okay? I'm messed up."

"Everybody's messed up," he said quietly.

"Not like me," I told him. I thought of Olivia in English class, throwing up her hands: *Tell us about your pain. We're riveted!* "Do you even know why I came to live with Cora and Jamie?"

He glanced over at me. "No," he said.

"Because my mom abandoned me." My voice felt tight, but I took a breath and kept going. "A couple of months ago, she packed up and took off while I was at school. I was living alone for weeks until my landlords busted me and turned me in to social services. Who then called Cora, who I hadn't seen in ten years, since *she* took off for school and never contacted me again."

"I'm sorry." This response was automatic, so easy.

"That's not why I'm telling you." I sighed, shaking my head. "Do you remember that house I brought you to that day? It wasn't a friend's. It was—"

"Yours," he finished for me. "I know."

I looked over at him, surprised. "You knew?"

"You had the key around your neck," he said quietly, glancing at it. "It was kind of obvious."

I blinked, feeling ashamed all over again. Here at least I thought I'd managed to hide something from Nate that day, kept a part of me a secret, at least until I was ready to reveal it. But I'd been wide open, exposed, all along.

We were coming up on Wildflower Ridge now, and as Nate began to slow down, Roscoe jumped onto my seat, clambering across me to press his muzzle against the window. Without thinking, I reached up to deposit him back where he'd come from, but as soon as I touched him he sank backward, settling into my lap as if this was the most natural thing in the world. For one of us, anyway.

When Nate pulled up in front of Cora's, I could see the kitchen lights were on, and both her and Jamie's cars were in the driveway, even though it was early for either of them to be home, much less both. Not a good sign. I reached up, smoothing my hair out of my face, and tried to ready myself before pushing open the door.

"You can tell them he got his shots and the vet said everything's fine," Nate said, reaching into the backseat for Roscoe's leash. Seeing it, the dog leaped up again, moving closer, and he clipped it on his collar. "And if they want to pursue behavioral training for the anxiety thing, she has a couple of names she can give them."

"Right," I said. He handed the leash to me, and I took it, picking up my bag with the other hand as I slowly slid out of the car. Roscoe, of course, followed with total eagerness, stretching the leash taut as he pulled me to the house. "Thanks."

Nate nodded, not saying anything, and I shut the door. Just as I started up the walk, though, I heard the whirring of a window lowering. When I turned around, he said, "Hey, and for what it's worth? Friends don't leave you alone in the woods. Friends are the ones who come and take you out."

I just looked at him. At my feet, Roscoe was straining at his leash, wanting to go home.

"At least," Nate said, "that's been my experience. I'll see you, okay?"

I nodded, and then his window slid back up, and he was pulling away.

As I watched him go, Roscoe was still tugging, trying to pull me closer to the house. My instinct was to do the total opposite, even though by now I'd left, and been left, enough times to know that neither of them was good, or easy, or even preferable. Still, it wasn't until we started up the walk to those waiting bright lights that I realized this— coming back—was the hardest of all.

*   *   *

"Where the hell have you been?"

It was Cora I was braced for, Cora I was expecting to be waiting when I pushed open the door. Instead, the first thing I saw was Jamie. And he was *pissed*.

"Jamie," I heard Cora say. She was at the end of the hall, standing in the doorway to the kitchen. Roscoe, who had bolted the minute I dropped his leash, was already circling her feet, sniffling wildly. "At least let her get inside."

"Do you have any idea how worried we've been?" Jamie demanded.

"I'm sorry," I said.

"Do you even *care*?" he said.

I looked down the hallway at my sister, who had picked Roscoe up and was now watching me. Her eyes were red, a tissue in her hand, and as I realized she, like Jamie, was still in the clothes she'd had on that morning, I suddenly remembered their doctor's appointment.

"Are you *drunk?*" Jamie said. I looked at the mirror by the stairs, finally seeing myself: I looked terrible—in Nate's baggy sweatshirt—and clearly, I stank of booze and who knew what else. I looked tired and faded and so familiar, suddenly, that I had to turn away, sinking down onto the bottom stair behind me. "This is what you do, after we take you in, put you in a great school, give you everything you need? You just run off and get *wasted?*"

I shook my head, a lump rising in my throat. It had been such a long, terrible day that it felt like years ago, entire lifetimes, since I'd been in this same place arguing with Cora that morning.

"We gave you the benefit of the doubt," Jamie was saying. "We gave you *everything*. And this is how you thank us?"

"Jamie," Cora said again, louder this time. "Stop it."

"We don't need this," he said, coming closer. I pulled my knees to my chest, trying to make myself smaller. I deserved this, I knew it, and I just wanted it to be over. "Your sister, who *fought* to bring you here, even when you were stupid and resisted? *She* doesn't need this."

I felt tears fill my eyes, blurring everything again, and this time I was glad, grateful for it. But even so, I covered my face with my hand, just to make sure.

"I mean," Jamie continued, his voice bouncing off the walls, rising up to the high ceiling above us, "what kind of person just takes off, disappears, no phone call, not even caring that someone might be wondering where they are? Who *does* that?"

In the silence following this, no one said a word. But I knew the answer.

More than anyone in that room, I was aware of exactly the sort of person who did such a thing. What I hadn't realized until that very moment, though, was that it wasn't just my mother who was guilty of all these offenses. I'd told myself that everything I'd done in the weeks before and since she left was to make sure I would never be like her. But it was too late. All I had to do was look at the way I'd reacted to what Cora had told me that morning—taking off, getting wasted, letting myself be left alone in a strange place—to know I already was.

It was almost a relief, this specific truth. I wanted to say it out loud—to him, to Cora, to Nate, to everyone—so they would know not to keep trying to save me or make me better somehow. What was the point, when the pattern was already repeating? It was too late.

But as I dropped my hand from my eyes to say this to Jamie, I realized I couldn't see him anymore. My view was blocked by my sister, who had moved to stand between us, one hand stretched out behind her, toward me. Seeing her, I remembered a thousand nights in another house: the two of us together, another part of a pattern, just one I'd thought had long ago been broken, never to be repeated.

Perhaps I was just like my mother. But looking up at Cora's hand, I had to wonder whether it was possible that this wasn't already decided for me, and if maybe, just maybe, this was my one last chance to try and prove it. There was no way to know. There never is. But I reached out and took it anyway.

Chapter Nine

When I came down the next morning, Jamie was out by the pond. From the kitchen, I could see his breath coming out in puffs as he crouched by its edge, his coffee mug on the ground by his feet. It was what he did every morning, rain or shine, even when it was freezing, the grass still shiny with frost all around him. Just a few minutes spent checking on the state of the small world he'd created, making sure it had all made it through to another day.

It was getting colder now, and the fish were staying low. Pretty soon, they'd disappear entirely beneath the leaves and rocks on the bottom to endure the long winter. "You don't take them in?" I'd asked him, when he'd first mentioned this.

Jamie shook his head. "It's more natural this way," he explained. "When the water freezes, they go deep, and stay there until the spring."

"They don't die?"

"Hope not," he said, adjusting a clump of lilies. "Ideally, they just kind of . . . go dormant. They can't handle the cold, so they don't try. And then when it warms up, they'll get active again."

At the time, this had seemed so strange to me, as well as yet another reason not to get attached to my fish. Now, though, I could see the appeal of just disappearing, then laying low and waiting until the environment was more friendly to emerge. If only that was an option for me.

"He's not going to come to you," Cora said now from where she was sitting at the island, flipping through a magazine. The clothes I'd been wearing the night before were already washed and folded on the island beside her, one thing easily fixed. "If you want to talk to him, you have to take the first step."

"I can't," I said, remembering how angry he'd been the night before. "He hates me."

"No," she said, turning a page. "He's just disappointed in you."

I looked back out at Jamie, who was now leaning over the waterfall, examining the rocks. "With him, that seems even worse."

She looked up, giving me a sympathetic smile. "I know."

The first thing I'd done when I woke up that morning—after acknowledging my pounding, relentless headache—was try to piece together the events from the day before. My argument with Cora I remembered, as well as my ride to school and to Jackson. Once I got to the clearing, though, it got fuzzy.

Certain things, however, were crystal clear. Like how strange it was not only to see Jamie angry, but to see him angry at me. Or catching that glimpse of my mother's face, distorted with mine, staring back from the mirror. And finally how, after I took her hand, Cora led me silently up the stairs to my room, where she'd stripped off my clothes and stood outside the shower while I numbly washed my hair and myself, before helping me into my pajamas and my bed. I'd wanted to say something to her, but every time I tried she just shook her head. The last thing I recalled before falling asleep was her sitting on the edge of my mattress, a dark form with the light coming in the window behind her. How long she stayed, I had no idea, although I vaguely remembered opening my eyes more than once and being surprised to find her still there.

Now the door behind me opened, and Jamie came in, Roscoe tagging along at his feet. I looked up at him, but he brushed past, not making eye contact, to put his mug in the sink. "So," Cora said slowly, "I think maybe we all should—"

"I've got to go into the office," he said, grabbing his phone and keys off the counter. "I told John I'd meet him to go over those changes to the campaign."

"Jamie," she said, looking over at me.

"I'll see you later," he said, then kissed the top of her head and left the room, Roscoe following. A moment later, I heard the front door shut behind him.

I swallowed, looking outside again. From anyone else, this would be hardly an insult, if even noticeable. But even I knew Jamie well enough to understand it as the serious snub it was.

Cora came over, sliding into the chair opposite mine. "Hey," she said, keeping her eyes on me until I finally turned to face her. "It's okay. You guys will work this out. He's just hurt right now."

"I didn't mean to hurt him," I said as a lump rose in my throat. I was suddenly embarrassed, although whether by the fact I was crying, or crying in front of Cora was hard to say.

"I know." She reached over, sliding her hand onto mine. "But you have to understand, this is all new to him. In his family, everyone talks about everything. People don't take off; they don't come home drunk. He's not like us."

Like us. Funny how up until recently—like maybe even the night before—I hadn't been convinced there was an us here at all. So maybe things *could* change. "I'm sorry," I said to her. "I really am."

She nodded, then sat back, dropping her hand. "I appreciate that. But the fact is, we did trust you, and you betrayed that trust. So there have to be some consequences."

Here it comes, I thought. I sat back, picking up my water bottle, and braced myself.

"First," she began, "no going out on weeknights. Weekends, only for work, for the foreseeable future. We strongly considered making you give up your job, but we've decided to let you keep it through the holidays, with the provision that we revisit the issue in January. If we find out that you skipped school again, the job goes. No discussion."

"All right," I said. It wasn't like I was in any position to argue.

Cora swallowed, then looked at me for a long moment. "I know a lot happened yesterday. It was emotional for both of us. But you doing drugs or drinking . . . that's unacceptable. It's a violation of the agreement we arranged so you could come here, and if the courts ever found out, you'd have to go back to Poplar House. It *cannot* happen again."

I had a flash of the one night I'd stayed there: the scratchy pajamas, the narrow bed, the house director reading over the sheriff's report while I sat in front of her, silent. I swallowed, then said, "It's not going to."

"This is serious, Ruby," she said. "I mean, when I saw you come in like that last night, I just . . ."

"I know," I said.

". . . it's too familiar," she finished. Then she looked at me, hard. "For both of us. You're better than that. You know it."

"It was stupid of me," I said. "I just . . . When you told me that about Mom, I just kind of freaked."

She looked down at the salt shaker between us, sliding it sideways, then back again. "Look, the bottom line is, she lied to both of us. Which shouldn't really be all that surprising. That said, though, I wish I could have made it easier for you, Ruby. I really do. There's a lot I'd do different, given the chance."

I didn't want to ask. Luckily, I didn't have to.

"I've thought about it so much since I left, how I could have tried harder to keep in touch," she said, smoothing back a few curls with her hand. "Maybe I could have found a way to take you with me, rent an apartment or something."

"Cora. You were only eighteen."

"I know. But I also knew Mom was unstable, even then. And things only got worse," she said. "I shouldn't have trusted her to let you get in touch with me, either. There were steps I could have taken, things I could have done. I mean, now, at work, I deal every day with these kids from messed-up families, and I'm so much better equipped to handle it. To handle taking care of you, too. But if I'd only known then—"

"Stop," I said. "It's over. Done. It doesn't matter now."

She bit her lip. "I want to believe that," she said. "I really do."

I looked at my sister, remembering how I'd always followed her around so much as a kid, clinging to her more and more as my mom pulled away. What a weird feeling to find myself back here, dependent on her again. Just as I thought this, something occurred to me. "Cora?"

"Yeah?"

"Do you remember that day you left for school?"

She nodded.

"Before you left, you went back in and spoke to Mom. What did you say to her?"

She exhaled, sitting back in her chair. "Wow," she said. "I haven't thought about that in years."

I wasn't sure why I'd asked her this, or if it was even important. "She never mentioned it," I said. "I just always wondered."

Cora was quiet for a moment, and I wondered if she was even going to answer me at all. But then she said, "I told her that if I found out she ever hit you, I would call the police. And that I was coming back for you as soon as I could, to get you out of there." She reached up, tucking a piece of hair behind her ear. "I believed that, Ruby. I really did. I wanted to take care of you."

"It's all right," I told her.

"It's not," she continued, over me. "But now, here, I have the chance to make up for it. Late, yes, but I do. I know you don't want to be here, and that it's far from ideal, but . . . I want to help you. But you have to let me. Okay?"

This sounded so passive, so easy, although I knew it wasn't. As I thought this, though, I had a flash of Peyton again, standing at the bottom of that stairway. *Why are you surprised?* she'd said, and for all the wrongness of the situation, I knew she was right. You get what you give, but also what you're willing to take. The night before, I'd offered up my hand. Now, if I held on, there was no telling what it was possible to receive in return.

For a moment we just sat there, the quiet of the kitchen all around us. Finally I said, "Do you think Mom's okay?"

"I don't know," she replied. And then, more softly, "I hope so."

Maybe to anyone else, her saying this would have seemed strange. But to me, it made perfect sense, as this was the pull of my mother: then, now, always. For all the coldness, her bad behavior, the slights and outright abuse, we were still tied to her. It was like those songs I'd heard as a child, each so familiar, and all mine. When I got older and realized the words were sad, the stories tragic, it didn't make me love them any less. By then, they were already part of me, woven into my consciousness and memory. I couldn't cut them away any more easily than I could my mother herself. And neither could Cora. This was what we had in common—what made us this us.

After outlining the last few terms of my punishment (mandatory checking-in after school, agreeing to therapy, at least for a little while), Cora squeezed my shoulder, then left the room, Roscoe rousing himself from where he'd been

planted in the doorway to follow her upstairs. I sat in the
quiet of the kitchen for a moment, then I went out to the
pond.

The fish were down deep, but after crouching over the
water for a few minutes, I could make out my white one,
circling by some moss-covered rocks. I'd just pushed myself to my feet when I heard the bang of a door slamming.
When I turned, expecting to see Cora, no one was there,
and I realized the sound had come from Nate's house. Sure
enough, a moment later I saw a blond head bob past on the
other side of the fence, then disappear.

Like the night before, when I'd been poised with Roscoe
at the top of the walk, my first instinct was to go back inside. Avoid, deny, at least while it was still an option. But
Nate had taken me out of those woods. For my own twisted
reasons, I might not have wanted to believe this made us
friends. But now, if nothing else, we were something.

I went inside, picked up his sweatshirt from the counter, then took in a breath and started across the grass to
the fence. The gate was slightly ajar, and I could see Nate
through the open door to the nearby pool house, leaning
over a table. I slid through the gate, then walked around the
pool to come up behind him. He was opening up a stack of
small bags, then lining them up one by one.

"Let me guess," I said. "They're for cupcakes."

He jumped, startled, then turned around. "You're not far
off, actually," he said when he saw me. "They're gift bags."

I stepped in behind him, then walked around to the
other side of the table. The room itself, meant to be some
kind of cabana, was mostly empty and clearly used for the

business; a rack on wheels held a bunch of dry-cleaning, and I recognized some of Harriet's milk-crate storage system piled against a wall. There was also a full box of WE WORRY SO YOU DON'T HAVE TO air fresheners by the door, giving the room a piney scent that bordered on medicinal.

I watched quietly as Nate continued to open bags until the entire table was covered. Then he reached beneath it for a box and began pulling plastic-wrapped objects out of it, dropping one in each bag. *Clunk, clunk, clunk.*

"So," I said as he worked his way down the line, "about yesterday."

"You look like you feel better."

"Define better."

"Well," he said, glancing at me, "you're upright. And conscious."

"Kind of sad when that's an improvement," I said.

"But it is an improvement," he replied. "Right?"

I made a face. Positivity anytime was hard for me to take, but in the morning with a hangover, almost impossible. "So," I said, holding out the sweatshirt, "I wanted to bring this back to you. I figured you were probably missing it."

"Thanks," he said, taking it and laying it on a chair behind him. "It is my favorite."

"It does have that feel," I replied. "Well worn and all that."

"True," he said, going back to the bags. "But it also reflects my personal life philosophy."

I looked at the sweatshirt again. "'You swim' is a philosophy?"

He shrugged. "Better than 'you sink,' right?"

Hard to argue with that. "I guess."

"Plus there's the fact," he said, "that wearing that sweatshirt is the closest I might get to the U now."

"I thought you had a scholarship," I said, remembering the guy who'd called out to him in the parking lot.

"I did," he said, going back to dropping things into the bags. "But that was before I quit swim team. Now I've got to get in strictly on my grades, which frankly are not as good as my swimming."

I considered this as he moved down the next row, still adding things to the bags. "So why did you quit?"

"I don't know." He shrugged. "I was really into it when I lived in Arizona, but here . . . it just wasn't that fun anymore. Plus my dad needed me for the business."

"Still, seems like a big decision, giving it up entirely," I said.

"Not really," he replied. He reached down, picking up another box. "So, was it bad when you came in last night?"

"Yeah," I said, somewhat surprised by the sudden change in subject. "Jamie was really pissed off."

"Jamie was?"

"I know. It was bizarre." I swallowed, taking a breath. "Anyway, I just wanted to say . . . that I appreciate what you did. Even if, you know, it didn't seem like it at the time."

"You weren't exactly grateful," he agreed. *Clunk, clunk, clunk.*

"I was a bitch. And I'm sorry." I said this quickly, probably too quickly, and felt him look up at me again. *So embarrassing*, I thought, redirecting my attention to the bag in front of me. "What are you putting in there, anyway?"

"Little chocolate houses," he replied.

"What?"

"Yeah," he said, tossing one to me. "See for yourself. You can keep it, if you want."

Sure enough, it was a tiny house. There were even windows and a door. "Kind of strange, isn't it?" I said.

"Not really. This client's a builder. I think they're for some open house or something."

I slid the house into my pocket as he dropped the box, which was now almost empty, and pulled out another one, which was full of brochures, a picture of a woman's smiling face taking up most of the front. QUEEN HOMES, it said. LET US BUILD YOUR CASTLE! Nate started sliding one into each bag, working his way down the line. After watching him for a moment, I reached across, taking a handful myself and starting on the ones closest to me.

"You know," he said, after we'd worked in silence for a moment, "I wasn't trying to embarrass you by showing up yesterday. I just thought you might need help."

"Clearly, I did," I said, glad to have the bags to concentrate on. There was something soothing, orderly, to dropping in the brochures, each in its place. "If you hadn't come, who knows what would have happened."

Nate didn't speculate as to this, which I had to admit I appreciated. Instead, he said, "Can I ask you something?"

I looked up at him, then slid another brochure in. "Sure."

"What was it really like, living on your own?"

I'd assumed this would be a question about yesterday, like why I'd done it, or a request for further explanation of my twisted theories on friendship. This, however, was completely unexpected. Which was probably why I answered it honestly. "It wasn't bad at first," I said. "In fact, it was kind of a relief. Living with my mom had never been easy, especially at the end."

He nodded, then dropped the box onto the floor and pulled out another one, this one filled with magnets emblazoned with the Queen Homes logo. He held it out to me and I took a handful, then began working my way up the line. "But then," I said, "it got harder. I was having trouble keeping up with bills, and the power kept getting turned off. . . ." I was wondering if I should go on, but when I glanced up, he was watching me intently, so I continued. "I don't know. There was more to it than I thought, I guess."

"That's true for a lot of things," he said.

I looked up at him again. "Yeah," I said, watching him continue to drop in magnets, one by one. "It is."

"Nate!" I heard a voice call from outside. Over his shoulder, I could see his dad, standing in the door to the main house, his phone to his ear. "Do you have those bags ready yet?"

"Yeah," he called over his shoulder, reaching down to pull out another box. "Just one sec."

"They need them now," Mr. Cross said. "We told them ten at the latest. Let's move!"

Nate reached into the new box, which was full of individually wrapped votive candles in all different colors, and began distributing them at warp speed. I grabbed a handful, doing the same. "Thanks," he said as we raced through the rows. "We're kind of under the gun here."

"No problem," I told him. "And anyway, I owe you."

"You don't," he said.

"Come on. You saved my ass yesterday. Literally."

"Well," he said, dropping in one last candle, "then you'll get me back."

"How?"

"Somehow," he said, looking at me. "We've got time, right?"

"Nate!" Mr. Cross called out, his tone clearly disputing this. "What the hell are you doing in there?"

"I'm coming," Nate said, picking up the empty boxes and beginning to stack the bags into them. I reached to help, but he shook his head. "It's cool, I've got it. Thanks, anyway."

"You sure?"

"*Nate!*"

He glanced over his shoulder at his dad, still standing in the doorway, then at me. "Yeah. I'm good. Thanks again for your help."

I nodded, then stepped back from the table as he shoved the last of the bags into a box, stacking it onto the other one. As he headed for the door, I fell in behind him. "Finally," Mr. Cross said as we came out onto the patio. "I mean, how hard is it—" He stopped, suddenly, seeing me. "Oh," he said, his face and tone softening. "I didn't realize you had company."

"This is Ruby," Nate said, bringing the box over to him.

"Of course," Mr. Cross said, smiling at me. I tried to reciprocate, even though I suddenly felt uneasy, remembering that night I'd seen him in this same place with Roscoe. "How's that brother-in-law of yours doing? There's some buzz he might be going public soon with his company. Any truth to that?"

"Um," I said. "I don't know."

"We should go," Nate said to him. "If they want us there by ten."

"Right." Still, Mr. Cross stayed where he was, smiling at me, as I started around the pool to the gate. I could see Nate behind him in the house. He was watching me as well, but when I raised my hand to wave, he stepped down a hallway, out of sight. "Take care," Mr. Cross said, raising his hand to me. He thought I'd been waving at him. "Don't be a stranger."

I nodded, still feeling unsettled as I got to the fence and pushed my way through. Crossing the yard, I remembered the house Nate had given me, and reached down to pull it out and look at it again. It was so perfect, pristine, wrapped away in plastic and tied with a pretty bow. But there was something so eerie about it, as well—although what, I couldn't say—that I found myself putting it away again.

*   *   *

"Okay," I said, uncapping my pen. "What does family mean to you?"

"Not speaking," Harriet replied instantly.

"Not speaking?" Reggie said.

"Yeah."

He was just staring at her.

"What? What were you going to say?"

"I don't know," he said. "Comfort, maybe? History? The beginning of life?"

"Well, that's you," she told him. "For me, family means the silent treatment. At any given moment, someone is always not speaking to someone else."

"Really," I said.

"We're passive-aggressive people," she explained, taking a sip of her coffee. "Silence is our weapon of choice. Right now, for instance, I'm not speaking to two of my sisters and one brother."

"How many kids are in your family?" I asked.

"Seven total."

"That," Reggie said, "is just plain sad."

"Tell me about it," Harriet said. "I never got enough time in the bathroom."

"I meant the silence thing," Reggie told her.

"Oh." Harriet hopped up on the stool by the register, crossing her legs. "Well, maybe so. But it certainly cuts down the phone bill."

He shot her a disapproving look. "That is not funny. Communication is crucial."

"Maybe at your house," she replied. "At mine, silence is golden. And common."

"To me," Reggie said, picking up a bottle of Vitamin A and moving it thoughtfully from one hand to the other, "family is, like, the wellspring of human energy. The place where all life begins."

Harriet studied him over her coffee cup. "What do your parents do, again?"

"My father sells insurance. Mom teaches first grade."

"So suburban!"

"Isn't it, though?" He smiled. "I'm the black sheep, believe it or not."

"Me, too!" Harriet said. "I was supposed to go to med school. My dad's a surgeon. When I dropped out to do the jewelry-design thing, they freaked. Didn't speak to me for months."

"That must have been awful," he said.

She considered this. "Not really. I think it was kind of good for me, actually. My family is so big, and everyone always has an opinion, whether you want to hear it or not. I'd never done anything all on my own before, without their help or input. It was liberating."

Liberating, I wrote down. Reggie said, "You know, this explains a *lot*."

No kidding, I thought.

"What's that supposed to mean?" Harriet asked.

"Nothing," he told her. "So what makes you give up the silent treatment? When do you decide to talk again?"

Harriet considered this as she took a sip of coffee. "Huh," she said. "I guess when someone else does something worse. Then you need people on your side, so you make up with one person, just as you're getting pissed off at another."

"So it's an endless cycle," I said.

"I guess." She took another sip. "Coming together, falling apart. Isn't that what families are all about?"

"No," Reggie says. "Only yours."

They both burst out laughing, as if this was the funniest thing ever. I looked down at my notebook, where all I had written was *not speaking, comfort, wellspring,* and *liberating*. This project was going to take a while.

"Incoming," Harriet said suddenly, nodding toward a guy and girl my age who were approaching, deep in conversation.

". . . wrong with a Persian cat sweatshirt?" said the guy, who was sort of chubby, with what looked like a home-done haircut.

"Nothing, if she's eighty-seven and her name is Nana," the girl replied. She had long curly hair, held back at the nape of her neck, and was wearing cowboy boots, a bright red dress, and a cropped puffy parka with mittens hanging from the cuffs. "I mean, think about it. What kind of message are you trying to send here?"

"I don't know," the guy said as they got closer. "I mean, I like her, so . . ."

"Then you don't buy her a sweatshirt," the girl said flatly. "You buy her jewelry. Come on."

I put down the feather duster I was holding, standing up straighter as they came up to the cart, the girl already eyeing the rows of thin silver hoops on display. "Hi," I said to the guy, who, up close, looked even younger and dorkier. His T-shirt—which said ARMAGEDDON EXPO '06: ARE YOU READY FOR THE END?—didn't help matters. "Can I help you?"

"We need something that screams romance," the girl said, plucking a ring out and quickly examining it before putting it back. As she leaned into the row of lights overhead, I noticed that her face was dotted with faint scars. "A ring is too serious, I think. But earrings don't say enough."

"Earrings don't say anything," the guy mumbled, sniffing the incense. He sneezed, then added, "They're inani-mate objects."

"And you are hopeless," she told him, moving down to the necklaces. "What about yours?"

Startled, I glanced back at the girl, who was looking right at me. "What?"

She nodded at my neck. "Your necklace. Do you sell those here?"

"Um," I said, my hand reaching up to it, "not really. But we do have some similar chains, and charms that you can—"

"I like the idea of the key, though," the girl said, coming around the cart. "It's different. And you can read it so many ways."

"You want me to give her a key?" the guy asked.

"I want you to give her a *possibility*," she told him, look-ing at my necklace again. "And that's what a key represents. An open door, a chance. You know?"

I'd never really thought about my key this way. But in the interest of a sale, I said, "Well, yeah. Absolutely. I mean, you could buy a chain here, then get a key to put on it."

"Exactly!" the girl said, pointing a finger at the nearby KEY-OSK, which sold keys and key accessories of all kinds. "It's perfect."

"You'll want a somewhat thick one," I told her. "But not too thick. You need it to be strong and delicate at the same time."

The girl nodded. "That's it," she said. "Just what I had in mind."

Ten minutes and fifteen dollars later, I watched them as they walked away, bag in hand, over to the KEY-OSK cart, where the girl explained what she wanted. I watched the saleswoman as she pulled out a small collection of keys, sliding them across for them to examine.

"Nice job," Harriet said, coming up beside me. "You salvaged the sale, even if we didn't have exactly what she was looking for."

"It was her idea," I said. "I just went with it."

"Still. It worked, right?"

I glanced over again at KEY-OSK, where the girl in the parka was picking up a small key as her friend and the saleswoman looked on. People were passing between us, hustling and bustling, but still I craned my neck, watching with Harriet as she slid it over the clasp, carefully, then down onto our chain. It dangled there for a second, spinning slightly, before she closed her hand around it, making it disappear.

*   *   *

I'd just stepped off the greenway, later that afternoon, when I saw the bird.

At first, it was just a shadow, passing overhead, temporarily blotting out the light. Only when it cleared the trees and reached the open sky did I see it in full. It was *huge*, long and gray, with an immense wingspan, so big it seemed impossible for it to be airborne.

For a moment, I just stood there, watching its shadow move down the street. It was only when I started walking again that it hit me.

It's herons and waterbirds you really need to worry about, Heather had said. *One swoop, and they can do some serious damage.*

No way, I thought, but at the same time I found myself picking up the pace as Cora's house came into view, breaking into a jog, then a run. It was cold out—the air was stinging my lungs, and I knew I had to look crazy, but I kept going, my breath ragged in my chest as I cut across the neighbor's lawn, then alongside Cora's garage to the side yard.

The bird was impossible to miss, standing in the shallow end, its wings slightly raised as if it had only just landed there. Distantly, I realized that it was beautiful, caught with the sun setting in the distance, its elegant form reflected in the pond's surface. But then it dipped its massive beak down into the water.

"Stop!" I yelled, my voice carrying and carrying far. "Stop it!"

The bird jerked, its wings spreading out a little farther, so it looked like it was hovering. But it stayed where it was.

For a long moment, nothing happened. The bird stood there, wings outstretched, with me only a short distance away, my heart thumping in my ears. I could hear cars passing on the street, a door slamming somewhere a few yards over. But all around us, it was nothing but still.

At any moment, I knew the bird could reach down and pluck up a fish, maybe even my fish. For all I knew I was already too late to save anything.

"Get out!" I screamed, louder this time, as I moved closer. "Now! *Get out now!*"

At first, it didn't move. But then, almost imperceptibly at first, it began to lift up, then a little farther, and farther still. I was so close to it as it moved over me, its enormous wings spread out, pumping higher and higher into the night sky, so amazing and surreal, like something you could only imagine. And maybe I would have thought it was only a dream, if Jamie hadn't seen it, too.

I didn't even realize he was standing right behind me, his hands in his pockets, and his face upturned, until I turned to watch as the bird soared over us, still rising.

"It was a heron," I told him, forgetting our silence. I was gasping, my breath uneven. "It was in the pond."

He nodded. "I know."

I swallowed, crossing my arms over my chest. My heart was still pounding, so hard I wondered if he could hear it. "I'm sorry for what I did," I said. "I'm so, so sorry."

For a moment, he was quiet. "Okay," he said finally. Then he reached a hand up, resting it on my shoulder, and together, we watched the bird soar over the roofline into the sky.

Chapter Ten

"You want buttered, or not?"

"Either is fine," I said.

Olivia eyed me over the counter, then walked over to the butter dispenser, sticking the bag of popcorn she was holding underneath it and giving it a couple of quick smacks with her hand. "Then you are officially my favorite kind of customer," she said. "As well as unlike ninety-nine percent of the moviegoing population."

"Really."

"Most people," she said, turning the bag and shaking it slightly, then adding a bit more, "have very strong views on their butter preference. Some want none—the popcorn must be dry, or they freak out. Others want it sopping to the point they can feel it through the bag."

I made a face. "Yuck."

She shrugged. "I don't judge. Unless you're one of those totally anal-retentive types that wants it in specific layers, which takes ages. Then I hate you."

I smiled, taking the popcorn as she slid it across to me. "Thanks," I said, reaching for my wallet. "What do I—?"

"Don't worry about it," she said, waving me off.

"You sure?"

"If you'd asked for butter layers, I would have charged you. But that was easy. Come on."

She came out from behind the counter, and I followed her across the lobby of the Vista 10—which was mostly empty except for some kids playing video games by the restrooms—to the box office door. She pulled it open, ducking inside, then flipped the sign in the window to OPEN before clearing a bunch of papers from a nearby stool for me to sit down. "You sure?" I said, glancing around. "Your boss won't mind?"

"My dad's the manager," she said. "Plus I'm working Saturday morning, the kiddie shift, against my will. The girl who was supposed to be here flaked out on him. I can do what I want."

"The kiddie—?" I began, then stopped when I saw a woman approaching with about five elementary school–aged children, some running ahead in front, others dragging along behind. One kid had a handheld video game and wasn't even looking where he was going, yet still managed to navigate the curb without tripping, which was kind of impressive. The woman, who appeared to be in her mid-forties and was wearing a long green sweater and carrying a huge purse, stopped in front of the window, squinting up.

"Mom," one of the kids, a girl with ponytails, said, tugging on her arm. "I want Smarties."

"No candy," the woman murmured, still staring up at the movie listings.

"But you promised!" the girl said, her voice verging on a whine. One of the other kids, a younger boy, was now on her other side, tugging as well. I watched the woman reach out to him absently, brushing her hand over the top of his head as he latched himself around her leg.

"Yes!" the kid with the handheld yelled, jumping up and down. "I made level five with the cherries!"

Olivia shot me a look, then pushed down the button by her microphone, leaning into it. "Can I help you?" she asked.

"Yes," the woman said, still staring up, "I need . . . five children and one adult for *Pretzel Dog Two.*"

Olivia punched this into her register. "That'll be thirty-six dollars."

"Thirty-six?" the woman said, finally looking at us. The girl was tugging her arm again. "With the child's price? Are you sure?"

"Yes."

"Well, that's crazy. It's just a movie!"

"Don't I know it," Olivia told her, hitting the ticket button a few times. She put her hand on the tickets as the woman reached into her huge purse, digging around for a few minutes before finally coming up with two twenties. Then Olivia slid them across, along with her change. "Enjoy the show."

The woman grumbled, hoisting her bag up her shoulder, then moved into the theater, the kids trailing along behind her. Olivia sighed, sitting back and stretching her arms over her head as two minivans pulled into the lot in front of us in quick succession.

"Don't I know it," I said, remembering my mom with

her clipboard, on so many front stoops. "My mom used to say that."

"Empathy works," Olivia replied. "And it's not like she's wrong. I mean, it *is* expensive. But we make the bulk of our money on concessions, and she's sneaking in food for all those rug rats. So it all comes out even, really."

I looked over my shoulder back into the lobby, where the woman was now leading her brood to a theater. "You think?"

"Did you see that purse? Please." She reached over, taking a piece of popcorn from my bag, which I hadn't even touched. Apparently she'd noticed, next saying, "What? Too much butter?"

I shook my head, looking down at it. "No, it's fine."

"I was about to say. Don't get picky on me now."

The minivans were deboarding now, people emptying car seats and sliding open back doors. Olivia sighed, checking her watch. "I didn't really come here for the popcorn," I said. "I wanted . . . I just wanted to thank you."

"You already did," she said.

"No," I corrected her, "I *tried*—twice—but you wouldn't let me. Which, frankly, I just don't understand."

She reached for the popcorn again, taking out a handful. "Honestly," she said as another pack of parents and kids approached, "it's not that complicated. You did something for me, I did something for you. We're even. Let it go already."

This was easier said than done, though, something I considered as she sold a bunch of tickets, endured more kvetching about the prices, and directed one woman with a very unhappy toddler in the direction of the bathroom. By the time things had calmed down, fifteen minutes had passed, and I'd worked my way halfway through the popcorn bag.

"Look," I said, "all I'm saying is that I just . . . I want you to know I'm not like that."

"Like what?" she said, arranging some bills in the register.

"Like someone who ditches school to get drunk. I was just having a really bad day, and—"

"Ruby." Her voice was sharp, getting my attention. "You don't have to explain, okay? I get it."

"You do?"

"Switching schools totally sucked for me," she said, sitting back in her chair. "I missed everything about my life at Jackson. I still do—so much so that even now, after a year, I haven't really bothered to get settled at Perkins. I don't even have any friends there."

"Me neither," I said.

"Yes, you do," she said. "You have Nate Cross."

"We're not really friends," I told her.

She raised her eyebrows. "The boy drove fifteen miles to pick you up out of the woods."

"Only because you told him to," I said.

"No," she said pointedly. "All I did was let him know where you were."

"Same thing."

"Actually, it isn't," she said, reaching over and taking another piece of popcorn. "There's a big difference between information and action. I gave him the facts, mostly because I felt responsible about leaving you there with that loser in the first place. But going there? That was all him. So I hope you were sufficiently grateful."

"I wasn't," I said quietly.

"No?" She seemed genuinely surprised. "Well . . ." she said, drawing the word out. "Why not?"

I looked down at my popcorn, already feeling that butter-and-salt hangover beginning to hit. "I'm not very good at accepting help," I said. "It's an issue."

"I can understand that," she said.

"Yeah?"

She shrugged. "It's not the easiest thing for me, either, especially when I think I don't need it."

"Exactly."

"But," she continued, not letting me off the hook, "you *were* passed out in the woods. I mean, you clearly needed help, so you're lucky he realized it, even if you didn't."

There was a big crowd approaching now, lots of kids and parents. We could see them coming at us from across the parking lot like a wide, very disorganized wave.

"I want to try to make it up to him," I said to Olivia. "To change, you know? But it's not so easy to do."

"Yeah," she said, taking another handful of popcorn and tossing it into her mouth as the crowd closed in. "Don't I know it."

*   *   *

Everyone has their weak spot. The one thing that, despite your best efforts, will always bring you to your knees, regardless of how strong you are otherwise. For some people, it's love. Others, money or alcohol. Mine was even worse: calculus.

I was convinced it was the reason I would not go to college. Not my checkered background, or that I was getting my applications together months after everyone else, or even the fact that up until recently, I hadn't even been sure I wanted to go at all. Instead, in my mind, it would all come down to one class and its respective rules and theorems, dragging down my GPA and me with it.

I always started studying with the best of intentions, telling myself that today just might be the day it all fell into place, and everything would be different. More often than not, though, after a couple of pages of practice problems, I'd find myself spiraling into an all-out depression. When it was really bad, I'd put my head down on my book and contemplate alternate options for my future.

"Whoa," I heard a voice say. It was muffled slightly by my hair, and my arm, which I locked around my head in an effort to keep my brain from seeping out. "You okay?"

I lifted myself up, expecting to see Jamie. Instead, it was Nate, standing in the kitchen doorway, a stack of dry-cleaning over one shoulder. Roscoe was at his feet, sniffing excitedly.

"No," I told him as he turned and walked out to the foyer, opening the closet there. With Jamie hard at work on the new ad campaign, and Cora backlogged in cases, they'd been outsourcing more and more of their errands to Rest Assured, although this Saturday morning was the first time Nate had shown up when I was home. Now I heard some banging around as he hung up the cleaning. "I was just thinking about my future."

"That bad, huh?" he said, crouching down to pet Roscoe, who leaped up, licking his face.

"Only if I fail calculus," I said. "Which seems increasingly likely."

"Nonsense." He stood up, wiping his hands on his jeans, and came over, leaning against the counter. "How could that happen, when you personally know the best calc tutor in town?"

"You?" I raised my eyebrows. "Really?"

"Oh God, no," he said, shuddering. "I'm good at a lot of things, but not that. I barely passed myself."

"You did pass, though."

"Yeah. But only because of Gervais."

Immediately, he popped into my head, small and foul smelling. "No thanks," I said. "I'm not that desperate."

"Didn't look that way when I came in." He walked over, pulling out a chair and sitting down opposite me, then drew my book over to him, flipping a page and wincing at it. "God, just looking at this stuff freaks me out. I mean, how basic is the power rule? And yet why can I still not understand it?"

I just looked at him. "The what?"

He shot me a look. "You need Gervais," he said, pushing the book at me. "And quickly."

"That is just what I *don't* need," I said, sitting back and pulling my leg to my chest. "Can you imagine actually asking Gervais for a favor? Not to mention owing him anything. He'd make my life a living hell."

"Oh, right," Nate said, nodding. "I forgot. You have that thing."

"What thing?"

"The indebtedness thing," he said. "You have to be self-sufficient, can't stand owing anyone. Right?"

"Well," I said. Put that way, it didn't sound like something you wanted to agree to, necessarily. "If you mean that I don't like being dependent on people, then yes. That is true."

"But," he said, reaching down to pat Roscoe, who had settled at his feet, "you *do* owe me."

Again, this did not seem to be something I wanted to second, at least not immediately. "What's your point?"

He shrugged. "Only that, you know, I have a lot of errands to run today. Tons of cupcakes to ice."

"And . . ."

"And I could use a little help," he said. "If you felt like, you know, paying me back."

"Do these errands involve Gervais?" I asked.

"No."

I thought for a second. "Okay," I said, shutting my book. "I'm in."

*　　*　　*

"Now," he said, as I followed him up the front steps of a small brick house that had a flag with a watermelon flying off the front, "before we go in, I should warn you about the smell."

"The smell?" I asked, but then he was unlocking the door and pushing it open, transforming this from a question to an all-out exclamation. *Oh my God*, I thought as the odor hit me from all sides. It was like a fog; even as you walked right through it, it just kept going.

"Don't worry," Nate said over his shoulder, continuing through the living room, past a couch covered with a brightly colored quilt to a sunny kitchen area beyond. "You get used to it after a minute or two. Soon, you won't even notice it."

"What *is* it?"

Then, though, as I waited in the entryway—Nate had disappeared into the kitchen—I got my answer. It started with just an odd feeling, which escalated to creepy as I realized I was being watched.

As soon as I spotted the cat on the stairs—a fat tabby, with green eyes—observing me with a bored expression, I noticed the gray one under the coatrack to my right, followed by a black one curled up on the back of the couch and a long-haired white one stretched out across the Oriental rug in front of it. They were everywhere.

I found Nate on an enclosed back porch where five carriers were lined up on a table. Each one had a Polaroid of a cat taped to it, a name written in clean block lettering beneath: RAZZY. CESAR. BLU. MARGIE. LYLE.

"So this is a shelter or something?" I asked.

"Sabrina takes in cats that can't get placed," he said, picking up two of the carriers and carrying them into the living room. "You know, ones that are sick or older. The unwanted and abandoned, as it were." He grabbed one of the Polaroids, of a thin gray cat—RAZZY, apparently—then glanced around the room. "You see this guy anywhere?"

We both looked around the room, where there were several cats but no gray ones. "Better hit upstairs," Nate said. "Can you look around for the others? Just go by the pictures on the carriers."

He left the room, jogging up the stairs. A moment later, I heard him whistling, the ceiling creaking as he moved around above. I looked at the row of carriers and the Polaroids attached, then spotted one of them, a black cat with yellow eyes—LYLE—watching me from a nearby chair. As I picked up the carrier, the picture flipped up, exposing a Post-it that was stuck to the back.

Lyle will be getting a checkup and blood drawn to monitor how he's responding to the cancer drugs. If Dr. Loomis feels they are not making a difference, please tell him to call me on my cell phone to discuss if there is further action to take, or whether I should just focus on keeping him comfortable.

"Poor guy," I said, positioning the carrier in front of him, the door open. "Hop in, okay?"

He didn't. Even worse, when I went to nudge him forward, he reached out, swiping at me, his claws scraping across my skin.

I dropped the carrier, which hit the floor, the open door banging against it. Looking down at my hand, I could already see the scratches, beads of blood rising up in places. "You little shit," I said. He just stared back at me, as if he'd never moved at all.

"Oh, man," Nate said, coming around the corner carrying two cats, one under each arm. "You went after Lyle?"

"You said to get them," I told him.

"I said to *look*," he said. "Not try to wrangle. Especially that one—he's trouble. Let me see."

He reached over, taking my hand and peering down at it to examine the scratches. His palm was warm against the underside of my wrist, and as he leaned over it I could see the range of color in his hair falling across his forehead, which went from white blond to a more yellow, all the way to almost brown.

"Sorry," he said. "I should have warned you."

"I'm okay. It's just a little scrape."

He glanced up at me, and I felt my face flush, suddenly even more aware of how close we were to each other. Over his shoulder, Lyle was watching, the pupils of his yellow eyes widening, then narrowing again.

In the end, it took Nate a full twenty minutes to get Lyle in the carrier and to the car, where I was waiting with the others. When he finally slid behind the wheel, I saw his hands were covered with scratches.

"I hope you get combat pay," I said as he started the engine.

"I don't scar, at least," he replied. "And anyway, you can't really blame the guy. It's not like he's ever been given a reason to like the vet."

I just looked at him as we pulled away from the curb. From behind us, someone was already yowling. "You know," I said, "I just can't get behind that kind of attitude."

Nate raised his eyebrows, amused. "You can't what?"

"The whole positive spin—the "oh, it's not the cat's fault

he mauled me" thing. I mean, how do you do that?"

"What's the alternative?" he asked. "Hating all crea-tures?"

"No," I said, shooting him a look. "But you don't have to give everyone the benefit of the doubt."

"You don't have to assume the worst about everyone, either. The world isn't always out to get you."

"In your opinion," I added.

"Look," he said, "the point is there's no way to be a hun-dred percent sure about anyone or anything. So you're left with a choice. Either hope for the best, or just expect the worst."

"If you expect the worst, you're never disappointed," I pointed out.

"Yeah, but who lives like that?"

I shrugged. "People who don't get mauled by psycho cats."

"Ah, but you *did*," he said, pointing at me. "So clearly, you aren't that kind of person. Even if you want to be."

After the group vet appointment—during which Lyle scratched the vet, the vet tech, and some poor woman minding her own business in the waiting room—we went back to Sabrina's and re-released the cats to their natural habitat. From there, we hit the dry-cleaners (where we col-lected tons of suits and dress shirts), the pharmacy (shock-ing how many people were taking antidepressants, not that I was judging), and One World—the organic grocery store—where we picked up a special order of a wheat-, eggs-, and gluten-free cake, the top of which read HAPPY FORTIETH, MARLA!

"Forty years without wheat or eggs?" I said as we carried it up the front steps of a big house with columns in the front. "That's got to suck."

"She doesn't eat meat, either," he told me, pulling out a ring of keys and flipping through them. When he found the one he was looking for, he stuck it in the lock, pushing the door open. "Or anything processed. Even her shampoo is organic."

"You buy her shampoo?"

"We buy everything. She's always traveling. Kitchen's this way."

I followed him through the house, which was huge and immensely cluttered. There was mail piled on the island, recycling stacked by the back door, and the light on the answering machine was blinking nonstop, the way it does when the memory is packed.

"You know," I said, "for someone so strict about her diet, I'd expect her to be more anal about her house."

"She used to be, before the divorce," Nate said, taking the cake from me and sliding it into the fridge. "Since then, it's gone kind of downhill."

"That explains the Xanax," I said as he took a bottle out of the pharmacy bag, sticking it on the counter.

"You think?"

I turned to the fridge, a portion of which was covered with pictures of various Hollywood actresses dressed in bikinis. On a piece of paper above them, in black marker, was written THINK BEFORE YOU SNACK! "Yes," I said. "She must be really intense."

"Probably is," Nate said, glancing over at the fridge. "I've never met her."

"Really?"

"Sure," he said. "That's kind of the whole point of the business. They don't have to meet us. If we're doing our job right, their stuff just gets done."

"Still," I said, "you have to admit, you're privy to a lot. I mean, look at how much we know about her just from this kitchen."

"Maybe. But you can't really *know* anyone just from their house or their stuff. It's just a tiny part of who they are." He grabbed his keys off the counter. "Come on. We've got four more places to hit before we can quit for the day."

I had to admit it was hard work, or at least harder than it looked. In a way, though, I liked it. Maybe because it reminded me of Commercial, driving up to houses and leaving things, although in this case we got to go inside, and often picked things up, as well. Plus there was something interesting about these little glimpses you got into people's lives: their coat closet, their garage, what cartoons they had on their fridge. Like no matter how different everyone seemed, there were some things that everyone had in common.

Our last stop was a high-rise apartment building with a clean, sleek lobby. As I followed Nate across it, carrying the last of the dry-cleaning, I could hear both our footsteps, amplified all around us.

"So what's the story here?" I asked him as we got into the elevator. I pulled the dry-cleaning tag where I could see it. "Who's P. Collins?"

"A mystery," he said.

"Yeah? How so?"

"You'll see."

On the seventh floor, we stepped out into a long hall lined with identical doors. Nate walked down about half-way, then pulled out his keys and opened the door in front of him. "Go ahead," he said.

When I stepped in, the first thing I was aware of was the stillness. Not just a sense of something being empty, but almost hollow, even though the apartment was fully furnished with sleek, contemporary furniture. In fact, it looked like something out of a magazine, that perfect.

"Wow," I said as Nate took the cleaning from me, disappearing into a bedroom that was off to the right. I walked over to a row of windows that looked out over the entire town, and for miles farther; it was like being on top of the world. "This is amazing."

"It is," he said, coming back into the room. "Which is why it's so weird that whoever it belongs to is never here."

"They must be," I said. "They have dry-cleaning."

"That's the only thing, though," he said. "And it's just a duvet cover. We pick it up about every month or so."

I walked into the kitchen, looking around. The fridge was bare, the counters spotless except for one bottle cap, turned upside down. "Aha," I said. "They drink root beer."

"That's mine," Nate said. "I left it there last time as an experiment, just to see if anyone moved it or threw it away."

"And it's still here?"

"Weird, right?" He walked back over to the windows, pulling open a glass door. Immediately I could smell fresh air blowing in. "I figure it's got to be a rental, or some company-owned kind of deal. For visiting executives or something."

I went into the living room, scanning a low bookcase by the couch. There were a few novels, a guide to traveling in Mexico, a couple of architectural-design books. "I don't know," I said. "I bet someone lives here."

"Well, if they do, I feel for them," he said, leaning into the open door. "They don't even have any pictures up."

"Pictures?"

"You know, of family or friends. Some proof of a life, you know?"

I thought of my own room back at Cora's—the blank walls, how I'd only barely unpacked. What would someone think, coming in and seeing my stuff? A few clothes, some books. Not much to go on.

Nate had gone outside, and was now on the small terrace, looking out into the distance. When I came to stand next to him, he looked down at my hand, still crisscrossed with scratches. "Oh, I totally forgot," he said, reaching into his pocket and pulling out a small tube. "I got something at One World for that."

BOYD'S BALM, it said in red letters. As he uncapped it, I said, "What is this, exactly?"

"It's like natural Neosporin," he explained. When I gave him a doubtful look, he added, "Marla swears by it."

"Oh, well. Then by all means." He gestured for me to stick out my hand. When I did, he squeezed some on, then began to rub it in, carefully. It burned a bit at first, then turned cold, but not in a bad way. Again, with us so close to each other, my first instinct was to pull back, like I had before. But instead, I made myself stay where I was and relax as his hand moved over mine.

"Done," he said after a moment, when it was all rubbed in. "You'll be healed by tomorrow."

"That's optimistic."

"Well, you can expect your hand to fall off, if you want," he said. "But personally, I just can't subscribe to that way of thinking."

I smiled despite myself. Looking up at his face, the sun just behind him, I thought of that first night, when he'd leaned over the fence. Then it had been impossible to make out his features, but here, all was clear, in the bright light of day. He wasn't really at all what I'd assumed or expected, and I wondered if I'd surprised him, too.

Later, after he dropped me off, I came in to find Cora at the stove, peering down into a big pot as she stirred something. "Hey," she called out as Roscoe ran to greet me, jumping up. "I didn't think you were working today."

"I wasn't," I said.

"Then where were you?"

"Everywhere," I said, yawning. She looked up at me, quizzical, and I wondered why I didn't just tell her the truth. But there was something about that day that I wanted to keep to myself, if just for a little while longer. "Do you need help with dinner?"

"Nah, I'm good. We'll be eating in about a half hour, though, okay?"

I nodded, then headed up to my room. After dropping my bag onto the floor, I went out onto my balcony, looking across the yard and the pond to Nate's house. Sure enough, a minute later I saw him carrying some things into the pool house, still working.

Back inside, I kicked off my shoes and climbed onto the bed, stretching out and closing my eyes. I was just about to drift off when I heard a jingle of tags and looked over to see Roscoe in the doorway to my room. *Cora must have turned on the oven*, I thought, waiting for him to move past me to my closet, where he normally huddled until the danger had passed. Instead, he came to the side of the bed, then sat down, peering up at me.

I looked at him for a second, then sighed. "All right," I said, patting the bed. "Come on."

He didn't hesitate, instantly leaping up, then doing a couple of quick spins before settling down beside me, his head resting on my stomach. As I began to pet him, I looked down at the scratches Lyle had given me, smoothing my fingers across them and feeling the slight rises there as I remembered Nate doing the same. I kept doing this, in fact, for the rest of the night—during dinner, before bed—tracing them the way I once had the key around my neck, as if I needed to memorize them. And maybe I did, because Nate was right: By the next morning, they were gone.

Chapter Eleven

"All I'm saying," Olivia said, picking up her smoothie and taking a sip, "is that to the casual observer, it looks like something is going on."

"Well, the casual observer is mistaken," I said. "And even if there was, it wouldn't be anyone's business, anyway."

"Oh, right. Because *so* many people are interested. All one of me."

"You're asking, aren't you?"

She made a face at me, then picked up her phone, opening it and hitting a few buttons. The truth was, Olivia and I had never officially become friends. But clearly, somewhere between that ride and the day in the box office, it had happened. There was no other explanation for why she now felt so completely comfortable getting into my personal life.

"Nothing is going on with me and Nate," I said to her, for the second time since we'd sat down for lunch. This was something else I never would have expected, us eating together—much less being so used to it that I barely noticed as she reached over, pinching a chip out of my bag. "We're just friends."

"A little while ago," she said, popping the chip into her mouth, "you weren't even willing to admit to that."

"So?"

"So," she said as the phone suddenly rang, "who knows what you'll be copping to a week or two from now? You might be engaged before you're willing to admit it."

"We are not," I said firmly, "going to be engaged. Jesus."

"Never say never," she said with a shrug. Her phone rang again. "Anything's possible."

"Do you even see him here?"

"No," she said. "But I do see him over at the sculpture, *looking* over here."

I turned my head. Sure enough, Nate was behind us, talking to Jake Bristol. When he saw us watching him, he waved. I did the same, then turned back to Olivia, who was regarding me expressionlessly, her phone still ringing.

"Are you going to answer that?" I asked.

"Am I allowed to?"

"Are you saying I make the rules now?"

"No," she said flatly. "But I certainly don't want to be rude and inconsiderate, carrying on two conversations at once." This was, in fact, exactly what I'd said, when I got sick of her constantly interrupting me to take calls. Which, now that I thought of it, was very friend-like as well, in its own way. "Unless, of course, you feel differently now?"

"Just make it stop ringing, please," I said.

She sighed, as if it was just such a hardship, then flipped open her phone, putting it to her ear. "Hey. No, just eating lunch with Ruby. What? Yes, she did say that," she said, eyeing me. "I don't know, she's fickle. I'm not even trying to understand."

I rolled my eyes, then looked over my shoulder at Nate again. He was still talking to Jake and didn't see me this time, but as I scanned the rest of the courtyard, I did spot someone staring right at me. Gervais.

He was alone, sitting at the base of a tree, his backpack beside him, a milk carton in one hand. He was also chewing slowly, while keeping his eyes steady on me. Which was kind of creepy, I had to admit. Then again, Gervais had been acting sort of strange lately. Or stranger.

By this point, I'd gotten so used to his annoying car behavior that I hardly even noticed it anymore. In fact, as Nate and I had gotten closer, Gervais had almost become an afterthought. Which was probably why, at least at first, I didn't realize when he suddenly began to change. But Nate did.

"How can you not have noticed he's combing his hair now?" he'd asked me a couple of mornings earlier, after Gervais had already taken off and we were walking across the parking lot. "*And* he's lost the headgear?"

"Because unlike some people," I said, "I don't spend a lot of time looking at Gervais?"

"Still, it's kind of hard to miss," he replied. "He looks like a totally different person."

"*Looks* being the operative word."

"He smells better, too," Nate added. "He's cut down considerably on the toxic emissions."

"Why are we talking about this again?" I asked him.

"I don't know," he said, shrugging. "When someone starts to change, and it's obvious, it's sort of natural to wonder why. Right?"

I wasn't wondering about Gervais, though. In fact, even if he got a total makeover and suddenly smelled like petunias,

I couldn't have cared less. Now, though, as I looked across the green at him, I had to admit that Nate was right—he did look different. The hair was combed, not to mention less greasy, and without the headgear his face looked completely changed. When he saw me looking at him, he flinched, then immediately ducked his head, sucking down the rest of his carton of milk. *So weird*, I thought.

". . . no, I don't," Olivia was saying now as she took another sip of her smoothie. "Because shoes are not going to make you run faster, Laney. That's all hype. What? Well, of course they're going to tell you that. They get paid on commission!"

"Who does?" Nate said, sliding onto the bench beside me. Olivia, listening to Laney, raised her eyebrows at me.

"No idea," I told him. "As you'll notice, she's not talking to me. She's on the phone."

"Ah, right," he said. "You know, that's really kind of rude."

"Isn't it?"

Olivia ignored us, picking up my chip bag and helping herself again. Then she offered it to Nate, who took a handful out, popping them into his mouth. "Those are mine," I pointed out.

"Yeah?" Nate said. "They're good."

He smiled, then bumped me with his knee. Across the table, Olivia was still talking to Laney about shoes, her voice shifting in and out of lecture mode. Sitting there with them, it was almost hard to remember when I first came to Perkins, so determined to be a one-woman operation to the end. But that was the thing about taking help and giving it, or so I was learning: there was no such thing as really getting even. Instead, this connection, once opened, remained ongoing over time.

*   *   *

At noon on Thanksgiving Day I was positioned in the foyer, ready to perform my assigned duty as door-opener and coat-taker. Just as the first car slowed and began to park in front of the house, though, I realized there was a hole in my sweater.

I took the stairs two at a time to my room, heading into the bathroom to my closet. When I pulled the door open, I jumped, startled. Cora was inside, sitting on the floor with Roscoe in her lap.

"Don't say it," she said, putting a hand up. "I know this looks crazy."

"What are you doing?"

She sighed. "I just needed to take a time-out. A few deep breaths. A moment for myself."

"In my closet," I said, clarifying.

"I came to get Roscoe. You know how he gets when the oven is on." She shot me a look. "But then, once I was in here, I began to understand why he likes it so much. It's very soothing, actually."

For the first time, Cora and Jamie were hosting Thanksgiving dinner, which meant that within moments, we'd be invaded by no less than fifteen Hunters. Personally, I was kind of curious to meet this extended tribe, but Cora, like Roscoe, was a nervous wreck.

"You were the one who suggested it," Jamie had said to her the week before as she sat at the kitchen table in full stress mode, surrounded by cookbooks and copies of

Cooking Light. "I never would have asked you to do this."

"I was just being polite!" she said. "I didn't think your mother would actually take me up on it."

"They want to see the house."

"Then they should come for drinks. Or appetizers. Or dessert. Something simple. Not on a major holiday, when I'm expected to provide a full meal!"

"All you have to do is the turkey and the desserts," Jamie told her. "They're bringing everything else."

Cora glared at him. "The turkey," she said, her voice flat, "is the center of the whole thing. If I screw it up, the entire holiday is ruined."

"Oh, that's not true," Jamie said. Then he looked at me, but I stayed quiet, knowing better than to get involved in this. "It's a turkey. How hard can it be?"

This question had been answered the night before, when Cora went to pick up the bird she'd ordered, which weighed twenty-two pounds. It took all three of us just to get it inside, and then it wouldn't even fit in the fridge.

"Disaster," Cora announced once we'd wrestled it onto the island. "Complete and total disaster."

"It's going to be fine," Jamie told her, confident as always. "Just relax."

Eventually, he had managed to get it into the fridge, although it meant removing just about everything else. As a result, the countertops were lined not only with all the stuff Cora had bought for the meal, but also all the condiments, breads, and cans of soda and bottled water— everything that didn't absolutely have to be refrigerated. Luckily, we'd been able to arrange to use Nate's oven for overflow—he and his dad were going to be gone all day, getting double time from clients who needed things done for their own dinners—as nothing else could fit in ours while the turkey was cooking. Still, all of this had only made Cora more crabby, to the point that I'd finally taken a loaf of bread, some peanut butter, and jelly into the enormous dining room, where I could fix myself sandwiches and eat in peace.

"You know," Jamie had said the night before, as Cora rattled around the kitchen beyond the doorway, "I think this is actually going to be a really good thing for us."

I looked at my sister, who was standing by the stove, examining a slotted spoon as if not exactly sure what to do with it. "Yeah?"

He nodded. "This is just what this house needs—a real holiday. It gives a place a sense of fullness, of family, you know?" He sighed, almost wistful. "And anyway, I've always loved Thanksgiving. Even before it was our anniversary."

"Wait," I said. "You guys got married on Thanksgiving?"

He shook his head. "June tenth. But we got together on Turkey Day. It was our first anniversary, you know, before the wedding one. It was, like, our first real date."

"Who dates on a major holiday?"

"Well, it wasn't exactly planned," he said, pulling the bread toward him and taking out a few slices. "I was supposed to go home for Thanksgiving that year. I was pumped for it, because, you know, I'm all about an eating holiday."

"Right," I said, taking a bite of my own sandwich.

"But then," he continued, "the night before, I ate some weird squid at this sushi place and got food poisoning. Seriously bad news. I was up sick all night, and the next day I was completely incapacitated. So I had to stay in the dorm, alone, for Thanksgiving. Isn't that the saddest thing you ever heard?"

"No?" I said.

"Of course it is!" He sighed. "So there I am, dehydrated, miserable. I went to take a shower and felt so weak I had to stop and rest on the way back in the hallway. I'm sitting there, fading in and out of consciousness, and then the door across from me opens up, and there's the girl that yelled at me the first week of classes. Alone for the holiday, too, fixing English-muffin pizzas in a contraband toaster oven."

I looked in at my sister, who was now consulting a cookbook, her finger marking the page, and suddenly remembered those same pizzas—English muffin, some cheap spaghetti sauce, cheese—that she'd made for me, hundreds of times.

He picked up the knife out of the jelly jar. "At first, she looked alarmed—I was kind of green, apparently. So she asked me if I was okay, and when I said I wasn't sure, she came out and felt my forehead, and she told me to come in and lie down in her room. Then she walked over to the only open convenience store—which was, like, miles away—bought me a six-pack of Gatorade, and came back and shared her pizzas with me."

"Wow," I said.

"I know." He shook his head, flipping a piece of bread over. "We spent the whole weekend together in her room, watching movies and eating toasted things. She took care of me. It was the best Thanksgiving of my life."

I glanced back at Cora again, remembering what Denise

had said about her that night at the party. Funny how it was so hard to picture my sister as a caretaker, considering that had been what she was to me, once. And now again.

"Which is not to say," Jamie added, "that other Thanksgivings can't be equally good, or even better in their own way. That's why I'm excited about this year. I mean, I love this house, but it's never totally felt like home to me. But tomorrow, when everyone's here, gathered around the table, and reading their thankful lists, it will."

I was listening to this, but still thinking about Cora and those pizzas so intently that I didn't really hear the last part. At least intially. "Thankful lists?"

"Sure," he said, pulling another piece of bread out and bringing the peanut butter closer to him. "Oh, that's right. You guys didn't do those, either, did you?"

"Um, no," I said. "I don't even know what that is."

"Just what it sounds like," he said, scooping out a glop of peanut butter and putting it on his bread. "You make a list of everything you're thankful for. For Thanksgiving. And then you share it with everyone over dinner. It's great!"

"Is this optional?" I asked.

"What?" He put down the knife with a clank. "You don't want to do it?"

"I just don't know . . . I'm not sure what I'd say," I said. He looked so surprised I wondered if he was hurt, so I added, "Off the top of my head, I mean."

"Well, that's the great thing, though," he said, going back to spreading the peanut butter. "You don't have to do it at the moment. You can write up your list whenever you want."

I nodded, as if this was actually my one hesitation. "Right."

"Don't worry," he said. "You'll do great. I know it."

You had to admire Jamie's optimism. For him, anything was possible: a pond in the middle of the suburbs, a wayward sister-in-law going to college, a house becoming a home, and thankful lists for everyone. Sure, there was no guarantee any of these things would actually happen as he envisioned. But maybe that wasn't the point. It was the planning that counted, whether it ever came to fruition or not.

Now, as Cora and I sat in the closet, we heard the doorbell ring downstairs. Roscoe perked up his ears, then yelped, the sound bouncing around the small space.

"That's me," I said, pulling off my sweater and grabbing another one off a nearby hanger. "I'll just—"

I felt a hand clamp around my leg, jerking me off balance. "Let Jamie get it," she said. "Just hang out here with me for a second. Okay?"

"You want me to get in there?"

"No." She reached over to rub Roscoe's ears before adding, more quietly, "I mean, only if you want to."

I crouched down, and she scooted over as I crawled in, moving aside my boots so I could sit down.

"See?" she said. "It's nice in here."

"Okay," I told her. "I will say it. You're acting crazy."

"Can you blame me?" She leaned back with a thud against the wall. "Any minute now, the house will be crawling with people who are expecting the perfect family Thanksgiving. And who's in charge? Me, the last person who is equipped to produce it."

"That's not true," I said.

"How do you figure? I've never done Thanksgiving before."

"You made pizzas that year, for Jamie," I pointed out.

"What, you mean back in college?" she asked.

I nodded.

"Okay, that is so *not* the same thing."

"It was a meal, and it counts," I told her. "Plus, he said it was the best Thanksgiving of his life."

She smiled, leaning her head back and looking up at the clothes. "Well, that's Jamie, though. If it was just him, I wouldn't be worried. But we're talking about his entire family here. They make me nervous."

"Why?"

"Because they're all just so well adjusted," she said, shuddering. "It makes our family look like a pack of wolves."

I just looked at her. "Cora. It's one day."

"It's Thanksgiving."

"Which is," I said, "just one day."

She pulled Roscoe closer to her. "And that's not even including the whole baby thing. These people are so fertile, it's ridiculous. You just know they're all wondering why we've been married five years and haven't yet delivered another member into the tribe."

"I'm sure that's not true," I said. "And even if it is, it's none of their business, and you're fully entitled to tell them so if they start in on you."

"They won't," she said glumly. "They're too nice. That's what so unsettling about all this. They all get along, they love me, they'll eat the turkey even if it's charred *and* raw.

No one's going to be drunk and passed out in the sweet potatoes."

"Mom never passed out in food," I said.

"That you remember."

I rolled my eyes. We hadn't talked about my mom much since the day Cora had laid down my punishment, but she also wasn't as taboo a topic as before. It wasn't like we agreed wholeheartedly now on our shared, or unshared, past. But at the same time, we weren't split into opposing camps—her attacking, me defending—either.

"I'm just saying," she said, "it's a lot of pressure, being part of something like this."

"Like what?"

"A real family," she said. "On the one hand, a big dinner and everyone at the table is the kind of thing I always wanted. But at the same time, I just feel . . . out of place, I guess."

"It's your house," I pointed out.

"True." She sighed again. "Maybe I'm just being hormonal. This medication I'm taking might be good for my ovaries, but it's making me crazy."

I made a face. Being privy to the reproductive drama was one thing, but specific details, in all honesty, made me kind of queasy. A few days before, I'd gone light-headed when she'd only just mentioned the word *uterus*.

The doorbell rang again. The promise of visitors clearly won out over the fear of the oven, as Roscoe wriggled loose, taking off and disappearing around the corner.

"Traitor," Cora muttered.

"Okay. Enough." I got out of the closet, brushing myself

off, then turned around to face her. "This is happening. So you need to go downstairs, face your fears, and make the best of it, and everything will be okay."

She narrowed her eyes at me. "When did you suddenly become so positive?"

"Just get out of there."

A sigh, and then she emerged, getting to her feet and adjusting her skirt. I shut the closet door, and for a moment we both stood there, in front of the full-length mirror, staring at our reflections. Finally I said, "Remember Thanksgiving at our house?"

"No," she said softly. "Not really."

"Me neither," I said. "Let's go."

*   *   *

It wasn't so much that I was positive. I just wasn't fully subscribing to such a negative way of thinking anymore.

That morning, when Cora had been in serious food-prep freak-out mode—covered in flour, occasionally bursting into tears, waving a spoon at anyone who came too close—all I'd wanted was a reason to escape the house. Luckily, I got a good one.

"Hey," Nate said from the kitchen as I eased in through his sliding-glass door, carrying the four pies stacked on two cookie sheets. "For me? You shouldn't have."

"If you even as much as nip off a piece of crust," I warned him, carrying them carefully to the stove, "Cora will eviscerate you. With an eggbeater, most likely."

"Wow," he said, recoiling slightly. "That's graphic."

"Consider yourself warned." I put the pies down. "Okay to go ahead and preheat?"

"Sure. It's all yours."

I pushed the proper buttons to set the oven, then turned and leaned against it, watching him as he flipped through a thick stack of papers, jotting notes here and there. "Big day, huh?"

"Huge," he said, glancing up at me. "Half our clients are out of town and need their houses or animals checked on, the other half have relatives visiting and need twice as much stuff done as usual. Plus there are those who ordered their entire dinners and want them delivered."

"Sounds crazy," I said.

"It isn't," he replied, jotting something else down. "It just requires military precision."

"Nate?" I heard his dad call out from down a hallway. "What time is the Chambells' pickup?"

"Eleven," Nate said. "I'm leaving in ten minutes."

"Make it five. You don't know how backed up they'll be. Do you have all the keys you need?"

"Yes." Nate reached over to a drawer by the sink, pulling out a key ring and dropping it on the island, where it landed with a clank.

"Double-check," Mr. Cross said. "I don't want to have to come back here if you end up stuck somewhere."

Nate nodded, making another note as a door slammed shut in another part of the house.

"He sounds stressed," I said.

"It's his first big holiday since we started the business," he said. "He signed up a lot of new people just for today. But he'll relax once we get out there and start getting things done."

Maybe this was true. Still, I could hear Mr. Cross muttering to himself in the distance, the noise not unlike that
my own mother would make, banging around before she
reluctantly headed off to work. "So when, in the midst of all
this, do *you* get to eat Thanksgiving dinner?"

"We don't," he said. "Unless hitting the drive-through at
Double Burger with someone else's turkey and potatoes in
the backseat counts."

"That," I said, "is just plain sad."

"I'm not much for holidays," he said with a shrug.

"Really."

He raised his eyebrows. "Why is that surprising?"

"I don't know," I said. "I guess I just expected someone
who was, you know, so friendly and social to be a big fan of
the whole family-gathering thing. I mean, Jamie is."

"Yeah?"

I nodded. "In fact, I'm supposed to be making up my
thankful list as we speak."

"Your what?"

"Exactly," I said, pointing at him. "Apparently, it's a list
of the things you're thankful for, to be read aloud at dinner.
Which is something we never did. Ever."

He flipped through the pages again. "Neither did we. I
mean, back when we *were* a we."

I could hear Mr. Cross talking now, his voice bouncing down the hall. He sounded much more cheerful than
before, and I figured he had to be talking to a customer.
"When did your parents split, anyway?"

Nate nodded, picking up the key ring and flipping
through it. "When I was ten. You?"

"Five," I said as the oven beeped behind me. Instantly, I thought of Roscoe, huddling in my closet. "My dad's pretty much been out of the picture ever since."

"My mom lives in Phoenix," he said, sliding a key off the ring. "I moved out there with her after the divorce. But then she got remarried and had my stepsisters, and it was too much to handle."

"What was?"

"Me," he said. "I was in middle school, mouthing off, a pain in her ass, and she just wanted to do the baby thing. So year before last, she kicked me out and sent me back here." I must have looked surprised, because he said, "What? You're not the only one with a checkered past, you know."

"I just never imagined you checkered," I told him. Which was a massive understatement, actually. "Not even close."

"I hide it well," he said easily. Then he smiled at me. "Don't you need to put in those pies?"

"Oh. Right."

I turned around, opening the oven and sliding them onto the rack, side by side. As I stood back up, he said, "So what's on your thankful list?"

"I haven't exactly gotten it down yet," I said, easing the oven shut. "Though, actually, you being checkered might make the top five."

"Really," he said.

"Oh, yeah. I thought I was the only misfit in the neighborhood."

"Not by a long shot." He leaned back against the counter behind him, crossing his arms over his chest. "What else?"

"Well," I said slowly, picking up the key he'd taken off

the ring, "to be honest, I have a lot to choose from. A lot of good things have happened since I came here."

"I believe it," he said.

"Like," I said slowly, "I'm very thankful for heat and running water these days."

"As we should all be."

"And I've been really lucky with the people I've met," I said. "I mean, Cora and Jamie, of course, for taking me in. Harriet, for giving me my job. And Olivia, for helping me out that day, and just, you know, being a friend."

He narrowed his eyes at me. "Uh-huh."

"And," I continued, shifting the key in my hand, "there's always Gervais."

"Gervais," he repeated, his voice flat.

"He's almost totally stopped burping. I mean, it's like a miracle. And if I can't be thankful for that, what can I be thankful for?"

"Gee," Nate said, cocking his head to the side, "I don't know."

"There *might* be something else," I said slowly, turning the key in my palm, end over end. "But it's escaping me right now."

He stepped closer to me, his arm brushing, then staying against mine as he reached out, taking the key from my palm and sliding it back onto the table. "Well," he said, "maybe it'll come to you later."

"Maybe," I said.

"Nate?" Mr. Cross called out. He was closer now, and Nate immediately stepped back, putting space between us just before he stuck his head around the corner. He glanced at me, giving a curt nod instead of a hello, then said, "What happened to five minutes?"

"I'm leaving right now," Nate told him.

"Then let's go," Mr. Cross said, ducking back out. A nearby door slammed and I heard his car start up, the engine rumbling.

"I better hit it," Nate said, grabbing up the stack of papers and the key ring. "Enjoy your dinner."

"You, too," I said. He squeezed my shoulder as he passed behind me, quickening his steps as he headed out into the hallway. Then the door banged behind him, and the house was quiet.

I checked on the pies again, then washed my hands and left the kitchen, turning off the light behind me. As I walked to the door that led out onto the patio, I saw another one at the end of the hallway. It was open just enough to make out a bed, the same USWIM sweatshirt Nate had lent me that day folded on top of it.

I don't know what I was expecting, as it wasn't like I'd been in a lot of guys' rooms. A mess, maybe. Some pinup in a bikini on the wall. Perhaps a shot of Heather in a frame, a mirror lined with ticket stubs and sports ribbons, stacks of CDs and magazines. Instead, as I pushed the door open, I saw none of these things. In fact, even full of furniture, it felt . . . empty.

There was a bed, made, and a bureau with a bowlful of change on it, as well as a couple of root beer bottle caps. His backpack was thrown over the chair of a nearby desk, where a laptop was plugged in, the battery light blinking. But there were no framed pictures, and none of the bits and pieces I'd expected, like Marla's fridge collage, or even Sabrina's tons of cats. If anything, it looked more like the last apartment he'd taken me to, almost sterile, with few if any clues as to who slept, lived, and breathed there.

I stood looking for a moment, surprised, before backing out and returning the door to exactly how it had been. All the way back home, though, I kept thinking about his room, trying to figure out what it was about it that was so unsettling. It wasn't until I got back to Cora's that I realized the reason: it looked just like mine. Hardly lived in, barely touched. Like it, too, belonged to someone who had just gotten there and still wasn't sure how long they'd be sticking around.

                    *   *   *

"Can I have your attention, please. Hello?"

At first, the plinking noise was barely audible. But as people began to quiet down, and then quieted those around them, it became louder, until finally it was all you could hear.

"Thanks," Jamie said, putting down the fork he'd been using to tap his wineglass. "First, I want to thank all of you for coming. It means a lot to us to have you here for our first holiday meal in our new place."

"Hear, hear!" someone in the back said, and there was a pattering of applause. The Hunters were effusive people, or so I'd noticed while letting them in and taking their coats. His mom, Elinor, was soft-spoken with a kind face; his dad, Roger, had grabbed me in a big hug, ruffling my hair like I was ten. All three of his sisters shared Jamie's dark coloring and outspokenness, whether it was about the pond (which they admired, loudly) or the recent elections (about which they disagreed, also loudly, albeit good-naturedly). And then there were children, and brothers-in-law, various uncles and cousins—so many names and relationships to remember that I'd already decided to give up trying and was just smiling a lot, hoping that compensated. It would have to.

"And now that we have you here," Jamie continued, "there's something else we'd like to share with you."

Standing at the entrance to the foyer, I was behind him, with the perfect view of his audience as he said this. The response was two-pronged: first, hopeful expressions—raised eyebrows, mouths falling open, hands to chests—followed by everyone looking at Cora at once. *Oh, shit,* I thought.

My sister turned pink instantly, then pointedly took a sip from the wineglass in her hand before forcing a smile. By then, Jamie had realized his mistake.

"It's about UMe," he said quickly, and everyone slowly directed their attention back to him. "Our new advertising campaign. It rolls out officially tomorrow, all over the country. But you get to see it here first."

Jamie reached behind a chair, pulling out a square piece of cardboard with the ad I'd seen blown up on it. I looked at Cora again, but she'd disappeared into the kitchen, her glass abandoned on a bookcase.

"I hope you like it," Jamie said, holding the picture up in front of him. "And, um, won't want to sue."

I slipped through the foyer, missing the Hunters' initial reactions, although I did hear some gasps and shrieks, followed by more applause, as I entered the kitchen where

Cora was sliding rolls into the oven, her back to me. She didn't turn around as she said, "Told you."

I glanced behind me, wondering how on earth she could have known for sure it was me. "He felt horrible," I said. "You could tell."

"I know." She shut the oven, tossing a potholder onto the island. From the living room, I could hear people talking over one another, their voices excited. Cora glanced over at the noise. "Sounds like they like it."

"Did he really think they wouldn't?"

She shrugged. "People are weird about family stuff, you know?"

"Really?" I said as I slid onto a stool by the island. "I wouldn't know a thing about that."

"Me either," she agreed. "Our family is perfect."

We both laughed at this, although not nearly loudly enough to drown out the merriment from the next room. Then Cora turned back to the oven, peering in through the glass door. "So," I said, "speaking of family. What does it mean to you?"

She looked at me over her shoulder, one eyebrow raised. "Why do you ask?"

"It's a project for school. I'm supposed to ask everybody."

"Oh." Then she was quiet for a moment, her back still to me. "What are people saying?"

"So far, different things," I told her. "I haven't made a lot of headway, to be honest."

She moved down to the stove, lifting up a lid on a pot and examining the contents. "Well, I'm sure my definition is probably similar to yours. It would have to be, right?"

"I guess," I said. "But then again, you have another family now."

We both looked into the living room. From my angle, I could see Jamie had put the blown-up ad on the coffee table, and everyone else was gathered around. "I guess I do," she said. "But maybe that's part of it, you know? That you're not supposed to have just one."

"Meaning what?"

"Well," she said, adjusting a pot lid, "I have my family of origin, which is you and Mom. And then Jamie's family, my family of marriage. And hopefully, I'll have another family, as well. Our family, that we make. Me and Jamie."

Now I felt bad, bringing this up so soon after Jamie's gaffe. "You will," I said.

She turned around, crossing her arms over her chest. "I hope so. But that's just the thing, right? Family isn't something that's supposed to be static or set. People marry in, divorce out. They're born, they die. It's always evolving, turning into something else. Even that picture of Jamie's family was only the true representation for that one day. By the next, something had probably changed. It had to."

In the living room, I heard a burst of laughter. "That's a good definition," I said.

"Yeah?"

I nodded. "The best yet."

Later, when the kitchen had filled up with people looking for more wine, and children chasing Roscoe, I looked across all the chaos at Cora, thinking that of course you would assume our definitions would be similar, since we had come from the same place. But this wasn't actually true.

We all have one idea of what the color blue is, but pressed to describe it specifically, there are so many ways: the ocean, lapis lazuli, the sky, someone's eyes. Our definitions were as different as we were ourselves.

I looked into the living room, where Jamie's mom was now alone on the couch, the ad spread out on the table in front of her. When I joined her, she immediately scooted over, and for a moment we both studied the ad in silence.

"Must be kind of weird," I said finally. "Knowing this is going to be out there for the whole world to see."

"I suppose." She smiled. Of all of them, to me she looked the most like Jamie. "At the same time, I doubt anyone would recognize me. It was a long time ago."

I looked down at the picture, finding her in the center in her white dress. "Who were these women?" I asked, pointing at the elderly women on each side of her.

"Ah." She leaned forward, a little closer. "My great-aunts. That's Carol on the far left, and Jeannette, next to her. Then Alice on my other side."

"Was this at your house?"

"My parents'. In Cape Cod," she said. "It's so funny. I look at all those children in the front row, and they're all parents themselves now. And all my aunts have passed, of course. But everyone still looks so familiar, even as they were then. Like it was just yesterday."

"You have a big family," I told her.

"True," she agreed. "And there are times I've wished otherwise, if only because the more people you have, the more likely someone won't get along with someone else. The potential for conflict is always there."

"That happens in small families, too, though," I said.

"Yes," she said, looking at me. "It certainly does."

"Do you know who all these people are, still?" I asked.

"Oh, yes," she said. "Every one."

We were both quiet for a moment, looking at all those faces. Then Elinor said, "Want me to prove it?"

I looked up at her. "Yeah," I said. "Sure."

She smiled, pulling the photo a little closer, and I wondered if I should ask her, too, the question for my project, get her definition. But as she ran a finger slowly across the faces, identifying each one, it occurred to me that maybe this was her answer. All those names, strung together like beads on a chain. Coming together, splitting apart, but still and always, a family.

*　　*　　*

Despite Cora's concerns, when dinner did hit a snag, it wasn't her fault. It was mine.

"Hey," Jamie said as we cleared the table, having told Cora to stay put and relax. "Where are the pies?"

"Whoops," I said. With all the time in the closet, not to mention the chaos of turkey for eighteen, I'd forgotten all about the ones over at Nate's.

"Whoops," Jamie repeated. "As in, whoops the dog ate them?"

"No," I said. "They're still next door."

"Oh." He glanced into the dining room, biting his lip. "Well, we've got cookies and cake, too. I wonder if—"

"She'll notice," I said, answering this question for him. "I'll go get them."

It had been bustling and noisy at our house for so long

that I was actually looking forward to the quiet of Nate's house. When I stepped inside, all I could hear was the whirring of the heating system and my own footsteps.

Luckily, I'd set the timer, so the pies weren't burned, although they were not exactly warm, either. I was just starting to arrange them back on the cookie sheets when I heard a thud from the other side of the wall.

It was solid and sudden, something hitting hard, and startled me enough that I dropped one of the pies onto the stove, where it hit a burner, rattling loudly. Then there was a crash, followed by the sound of muffled voices. Someone was in the garage.

I put down the pies, then stepped out into the hallway, listening again. I could still hear someone talking as I moved to the doorway that led to the garage, sliding my hand around the knob and carefully pulling it open. The first thing I saw was Nate.

He was squatting down next to a utility shelf that by the looks of it had been leaning against the garage wall up until very recently. Now, though, it was lying sideways across the concrete floor, with what I assumed were its contents—a couple of paint cans, some car-cleaning supplies, and a glass bowl, now broken—spilled all around it. Just as I moved forward to see if he needed help, I realized he wasn't alone.

". . . *specifically* said you should check the keys before you left," Mr. Cross was saying. I heard him before I saw him, now coming into view, his phone clamped to his ear, one hand covering the receiver. "One thing. *One thing* I ask you to be sure of, and you can't even get that right. Do you even know how much this could cost me? The Chambells are half our business in a good week, easily. Jesus!"

"I'm sorry," Nate said, his head ducked down as he grabbed the paint cans, stacking them. "I'll just get it now and go straight there."

"It's too late," Mr. Cross said, snapping his phone shut. "You screwed up. *Again*. And now I'm going to have to deal with this personally if we're going to have any hope of saving the account, which will put us even more behind."

"You don't. I'll talk to them," Nate told him. "I'll tell them it was my fault—"

Mr. Cross shook his head. "No," he said, his voice clenched. "Because that, Nate, is admitting incompetence. It's bad enough I can't count on you to get a single goddamned thing right, *ever*, but I'll be damned if I'm going to have you blabbing about it to the clients like you're proud of it."

"I'm not," Nate said, his voice low.

"You're not what?" Mr. Cross demanded, stepping closer and kicking a bottle of Windex for emphasis. It hit the nearby lawnmower with a bang as he said, louder, "*Not what*, Nate?"

I watched as Nate, still hurriedly picking things up, drew in a breath. I felt so bad for him, and somehow guilty for being there. Like this was bad enough without me witnessing it. His voice was even quieter, hard to make out, as he said, "Not proud of it."

Mr. Cross just stared at him for a moment. Then he shook his head and said, "You know what? You just disgust me. I can't even look at your face right now."

He turned, then crossed the garage toward me, and I quickly moved down the hallway, ducking into a bathroom.

There, in the dark, I leaned back against the sink, listening to my own heart beat, hard, as he moved around the kitchen, banging drawers open and shut. Finally, after what seemed like forever, I heard him leave. I waited a full minute or two after hearing a car pull away before I emerged, and even then I was still shaken.

The kitchen looked the same, hardly touched, my pies right where I'd left them. Past the patio and over the fence, Cora's house, too, was unchanged, the lights all bright downstairs. I knew they were waiting for the pies and for me, and for a moment I wished I could just go and join them, stepping out of this house, and what had just happened here, entirely. At one time, this might have even come naturally. But now, I opened the garage door and went to find Nate.

He was down on the floor, picking up glass shards and tossing them into a nearby trash can, and I just stood there and watched him for a second. Then I took my hand off the door behind me, letting it drop shut.

Immediately, he looked up at me. "Hey," he said, his voice casual. *I hide it well*, I heard him say in my head. "What happened to dinner? You decide to go AWOL rather than do your thankful list?"

"No," I said. "I, um, forgot about the pies, so I had to come get them. I didn't think anyone was here."

Just like that, his face changed, and I knew he knew— either by this last sentence, or the look on my face—that I'd been there. "Oh," he said, this one word flat, toneless. "Right."

I came closer and, after a moment, bent down beside him

and started to pick up pieces of glass. The air felt strange all around me, like just after or before a thunderstorm when the very ions have been shifted, resettled. I knew that feeling. I hadn't experienced it in a while, but I knew it.

"So," I said carefully, my voice low, "what just happened here?"

"Nothing." Now he glanced at me, but only for a second. "It's fine."

"That looked like more than nothing."

"It's just my dad blowing off steam. No big deal. The shelf took the brunt of it."

I swallowed, taking in a breath. Out on the street, beyond the open garage door, an older couple in windsuits walked by, arms swinging in tandem. "So . . . does he do that a lot?"

"Pull down shelves?" he asked, brushing his hands off over the trash can.

"Talk to you like that."

"Nah," he said.

I watched him as he stood, shaking his hair out of his face. "You know," I said slowly, "my mom used to slap us around sometimes. When we were younger. Cora more than me, but I still caught it occasionally."

"Yeah?" He wasn't looking at me.

"You never knew when to expect it. I hated that."

Nate was quiet for a moment. Then he said, "Look, my dad's just . . . he's got a temper. Always has. He blows up, he throws stuff. It's all hot air."

"Has he ever hit you, though?"

He shrugged. "A couple of times when he's really lost it. It's rare, though."

I watched as he reached down, picking up the shelf and pushing it back up against the wall. "Still," I said, "it sounds like he's awfully hard on you. That stuff about you disgusting him—"

"Please," he replied, stacking the paint cans on the bottom shelf. "That's nothing. You should have heard him at my swim meets. He was the only parent to get banned from the deck entirely, for life. Not that it stopped him. He just yelled from behind the fence."

I thought back to that day in the parking lot, the guy who had called after him. "Is that why you quit?"

"One reason." He picked up the Windex. "Look, like I said, it's no big deal. I'm fine."

Fine. I'd thought the same thing. "Does your mom know about this?"

"She's aware that he's a disciplinarian," he said, drawing out this last word in such a way that it was clear he'd heard it a lot, said in a certain way. "She tends to be a bit selective in how she processes information. And anyway, in her mind, when she sent me back here, that was just what I needed."

"Nobody needs that," I said.

"Maybe not. But it's what I've got."

He headed for the door, pulling it open. I followed him inside, watching as he went to the island, picking up the key that I'd been holding earlier. I could remember so clearly turning it in my palm, the way he'd taken it from me—putting it back on the island but not on the ring—and suddenly

I felt culpable, even more a part of this than I already was.

"You could tell someone, you know," I said as he slid it into his pocket. "Even if he's not always hitting you, it's not right."

"What, and get put into social services? Or shipped off to live with my mom, who doesn't want me there? No thanks."

"So you have thought about it," I said.

"Heather did. A lot," he said, reaching up to rub his face. "It freaked her out. But she just didn't understand. My mom kicked me out, and at least he took me in. It's not like I have a lot of options here."

I thought of Heather, that day at the pond place. *I'm glad you and Nate are friends*, she'd said. "She was worried about you," I said.

"I'm fine." I couldn't help notice each time he said this. "At this point, I've only got six months until graduation. After that, I'm coaching a swim camp up north, and as long as I get into school somewhere, I'm gone."

"Gone," I repeated.

"Yeah," he said. "To college, or wherever. Anyplace but here."

"Free and clear."

"Exactly." He looked up at me, and I thought of us standing in this same spot earlier as he took that key from my hand. I'd felt so close to something then—something that, back at the yellow house or even in my first days at Cora's, I never would have imagined. "I mean, you stayed with your mom, stuck it out even though it was bad. You understand, right?"

I did. But it was more than that. Sure, being free and clear had been just what I'd wanted, so recently that it should have been easy to agree with it. But if it was still true, I wouldn't have even been there. I'd have left when I'd had the chance earlier, staying out of this, of everything.

But I hadn't. Because I wasn't the same girl who'd run to that fence the first night, thinking only of jumping over it and getting away. Somewhere, something had changed.

I could have stood there and told him this, and more. Like how glad I was, now, that the Honeycutts had turned me in, because in doing so they'd brought me here to Cora and Jamie and all the things I was thankful for, including him. And how even when you felt like you had no options or didn't need anyone, you could be wrong. But after all he'd just told me, to say this seemed foolish, if not impossible. Six months wasn't that long. And I'd been left behind enough.

You understand, right? he'd said. There was only one answer.

"Yeah," I said. "Of course I do."

Chapter Twelve

"There you are! Thank God!"

It was the day after Thanksgiving, the biggest shopping day of the year, and the mall was opening at six a.m. for door-buster specials. Harriet, however, insisted I had to be there at five thirty to get ready. This seemed a little extreme to me, but still I'd managed to rouse myself in the dark and stumble into the shower, then pour myself a big cup of coffee, which I sucked down as I walked along the greenway, a flashlight in my other hand. When I got to the mall itself, people were already lined up outside the main entrance, bundled up in parkas, waiting.

Inside, all the stores I passed were bustling—employees loading up stock, chattering excitedly—everyone in serious preparation mode, bracing for the crowds. When I got to Harriet's kiosk, it was clear she had already been there for a while: there were two Jump Java cups already on the register, a third clamped in her hand. Needless to say, she was pumped.

"Hurry, hurry," she called out to me now, waving her arms back and forth as if she could move me closer faster, by sheer force of will. "We don't have much time!"

Slightly alarmed, I looked over at Reggie, who was sitting at the Vitamin Me kiosk, a cup with a tea bag poking out of it in one hand. He took a sleepy sip, waving at me as I passed.

"You had to be here early, too?" I asked him. I couldn't imagine someone actually wanting some shark cartilage for Christmas.

He shrugged. "I don't mind it. I kind of like the bustle."

Then he smiled and looked at Harriet, who was maniacally lighting another incense stick. *Yeah*, I thought. *The bustle.*

"Okay," Harriet said, pulling me to stand next to her in front of the cart as she took another gulp of coffee. "Let's do a check and double check. We've got the low-dollar stuff on the bottom, higher on the top. Rings by the register for impulse buyers, incense burning for ambience, plenty of ones in the register. Do you remember the disaster plan?"

"Grab the cashbox and the precious gems, do a headcount, proceed to the food court exit," I recited.

"Good," she said with a curt nod. "I don't think we'll need it, but on a day like this you never know."

I glanced over at Reggie, who just shook his head, stifling a yawn.

"You know," Harriet continued, studying the kiosk, "as I'm looking at this now, I think maybe we should switch the earrings and bracelets. They don't look right. In fact—"

"Harriet. They're great. We're ready," I told her.

She sighed. "I don't know," she said. "I still feel like I'm missing something."

"Could it be, maybe, the true meaning of the holiday season?" Reggie called out from his kiosk. "In which we focus on goodwill and peace on earth, and not on making as much money as possible?"

"No," Harriet said. Then she snapped her fingers, the sound loud, right by my ear. "Hold on!" she said. "I can't believe I almost forgot."

She bent down beneath the register, pulling out the plastic bin where she kept all her stock. As she picked through the dozens of small plastic bags, finally pulling one out and opening it, I looked at my watch. It was 5:51. When I looked back at Harriet, she was fastening a clasp around her neck, her back to me.

"Okay," she said. "I made these a couple of weeks back, just fooling around, but now I'm wondering if I should put them out. What do you think?"

When she turned around, the first thing I saw was the key. It was silver and delicate, dotted with red stones, and hung from a braided silver chain around her neck. Instantly, I was aware of my own key, which was bulkier and not nearly as beautiful. But even so, seeing this one, I understood why I'd gotten so many comments on it. There was something striking about a single key. It was like a question waiting to be answered, a whole missing a half. Useless on its own, needing something else to be truly defined.

Harriet raised her eyebrows. "Well?"

"It's—"

"You hate it, don't you," she decided, before I could even finish. "You think it's tacky and derivative."

"It's not," I said quickly. "It's beautiful. Really striking."

"Yeah?" She turned to the mirror, reaching up to touch

the key, running her finger over it. "It kind of is, isn't it? Unique, at any rate. You think they'll sell?"

"You made more?"

She nodded, reaching into the box again. As she laid more bags out on the counter, I counted at least twenty, none of them the same: some keys were smaller, some bigger, some plain, others covered in gemstones. "I got inspired," she explained as I examined them one by one. "It was kind of manic, actually."

"You should definitely put them out," I told her. "Like, right now."

In record time, we'd slapped on price tags and organized a display. I was just putting the last necklace on the rack when the clock hit six and the doors opened. At first, the sound was distant, but then, like a wave, it got louder and louder as people spilled into sight, filling the long, wide corridor between us. "It's on," Harriet said. "Here we go."

We sold the first key necklace twenty minutes later, the second, a half hour after that. If I hadn't been there to see it myself, I never would have believed it, but every single customer who came by paused to look at them. Not everyone bought, but clearly they drew people's attention. Over and over again.

The day passed in a blur of people, noise, and the Christmas music overhead, which I only heard in bits and pieces, whenever the din briefly died down. Harriet kept drinking coffee, the key necklaces kept selling, and my feet began to ache, my voice getting hoarse from talking. The zinc lozenges Reggie offered up around one o'clock helped, but not much.

Still, I was grateful for the day and the chaos, if only because it kept my mind off what had happened the day before with Nate. All that evening, after I'd taken the pies back and watched them get devoured, then helped Cora load the dishwasher before collapsing onto my bed, I'd kept going over and over it in my head. It was all so unsettling: not only what I'd seen and heard, but how I'd responded afterward.

I never would have thought of myself as someone who would want to help or save anybody. In fact, this was the one thing that bugged me so much about Nate in the first place. And yet, I was surprised, even disappointed, that at that crucial moment—*You understand, right?*—I'd been so quick to step back and let the issue drop, when, as his friend, I should have come closer. It wasn't just unsettling, even. It was shameful.

At three o'clock, the crowds were still thick, and despite the lozenges, I'd almost totally lost my voice. "Go," Harriet said, taking a sip of her umpteenth coffee. "You've done more than enough for one day."

"Are you sure?" I asked.

"Yes," she replied, smiling at a young woman in a long red coat who was buying one of the last key necklaces. She handed over the bag, then watched the woman disappear into the crowd. "That's fifteen we've sold today," she said, shaking her head. "Can you even believe it? I'm going to have to go home and stay up all night making more. Not that I'm complaining, of course."

"I told you," I said. "They're beautiful."

"Well, I have you to thank for them. Yours was the

inspiration." She picked up one trimmed with green stones. "In fact, you should take one. It's the least I can do."

"Oh, no. You don't have to."

"I want to." She gestured at the rack. "Or I can make you one special, if you prefer."

I looked at them, then down at my own necklace. "Maybe later," I said. "I'm good for now."

Outside, the air was crisp, cool, and as I headed toward the greenway and home, I reached up, running my hand over my own necklace. The truth was, lately I'd been thinking about taking it off. It seemed kind of ridiculous to be carrying around a key to a house that was no longer mine. And anyway, it wasn't like I could go back, even if I wanted to. More than once, I'd even gone so far as to reach up to undo the clasp before stopping myself.

On that first night, when Nate and I had met, he had asked me, *What's it to?* and I'd told him, nothing. In truth, though, then and now, the key wasn't just to that lock at the yellow house. It was to me, and the life I'd had before. Maybe I'd even begun to forget it a bit over the last few weeks, and this was why it was easier to imagine myself without it. But now, after what had happened the night before, I was thinking maybe having a reminder wasn't such a bad idea. So for now, it would stay where it was.

* * *

After everything that had happened on Thanksgiving, I'd thought things might be a little awkward for the ride on the first day back at school. And they were. Just not in the way I was expecting.

"Hey," Nate said as I slid into the front seat. "How's it going?"

He was smiling, looking the same as always. Like nothing out of the ordinary had happened. But then to him, I supposed that it hadn't. "Good," I said, fastening my seat belt. "You?"

"Miserable," he announced cheerfully. "I've got two papers and a presentation due today. I was up until two last night."

"Really," I said, although actually, I knew this, as I'd been awake until about the same time, and I could see the lights from his room—two small squares, off to the right—breaking up the dark that stretched between our two houses. "I've got a calculus test that I have to pass. Which means, almost certainly, that I won't."

As soon as I said this, I expected Gervais to chime in from the backseat, agreeing with this, as it was the perfect setup to slam me. When I turned around, though, he was just sitting there, quiet and unobtrusive, the same way he had been for the last couple of weeks. As if to compensate for his silence, though, I was seeing him more and more. At least once a week, I caught him watching me at lunch, the way he had that one day, and whenever I passed him in the hallways he was always giving me these looks I couldn't figure out.

"What?" he said now, as I realized I was still looking strangely at him.

"Nothing," I replied, and turned back.

Nate reached for the radio, cranking it up, and then we

were turning out into traffic. Everything actually felt okay, wholly unchanged, and I realized maybe I'd overreacted, thinking they would have. The bottom line was, I knew something I hadn't the week before, and we were friends— at least for another six months or so. I didn't have to get all wrought up about what was going on with his dad; I'd never wanted anyone to get involved with me and my domestic drama. Maybe what we had now, in the end, was best—to be close but not too close, the perfect middle ground.

Half a block from school, Nate pulled into the Quik Zip for gas. As he got out to pump it, I sat back in my seat, opening the calc book in my lap. About half a page in, though, I heard a noise from behind me.

By this point, I was well acquainted with Gervais's various percussions, but this wasn't one I was used to. It was more like an intake, a sudden drawing in of breath. The first one I ignored; the second, barely noted. By the third, though, I was starting to think he might be having an attack of some sort, so I turned around.

"What are you doing?" I asked him.

"Nothing," he said, instantly defensive. But then, he did it again. "The thing is—"

He was interrupted by Nate opening his door and sliding back behind the wheel. "Why is it," he said to me, "that whenever I'm in a hurry I always get the slowest gas pump in the world?"

I glanced at Gervais, who had hurriedly gone back to his book, his head ducked down. "Probably the same reason you hit every red light when you're late."

"And lose your keys," he added, cranking the engine.

"Maybe it's the universe conspiring against you."

"I have had a run of bad luck lately," he agreed.

"Yeah?"

He glanced over at me. "Well, maybe not all bad."

Hearing this, I had a flash of us in the kitchen that day, his hand brushing against mine as he reached for the key lying in my palm. As Nate turned back to the road, I suddenly did feel awkward, in just the way I'd thought I would. Talk about bad luck. Maybe this wouldn't be so easy after all.

*   *   *

For me, December was all about work. Working for Harriet, working on my applications, working on calculus. And when I wasn't doing any of these things, I was tagging along with Nate on his job.

Logically, I knew the only way to stay in that middle ground with Nate was to let space build up between us. But it wasn't so easy to stop something once it had started, or so I was learning. One day you were all about protecting yourself and keeping things simple. The next thing you know, you're buying macaroons.

"Belgian macaroons," Nate corrected me, pulling two boxes off the shelf. "That's key."

"Why?"

"Because a macaroon you can buy anywhere," he replied. "But these, you can only find here at Spice and Thyme, which means they are gourmet and expensive, and therefore suitable for corporate gift-giving."

I looked down at the box in my hand. "Twelve bucks is a lot for ten macaroons," I said. Nate raised his eyebrows. "*Belgian* macaroons, I mean."

"Not to Scotch Design Inc.," he said, continuing to add boxes to the cart between us. "In fact, this is the very low end of their holiday buying. Just wait until we get to the nut-and-cheese-straw towers. *That's* impressive."

I glanced at my watch. "I might not make it there. My break is only a half hour. If I'm even a minute late, Harriet starts to have palpitations."

"Maybe," he said, adding a final box, "you should buy her some Belgian macaroons. For ten bucks, they might cure her of that entirely."

"I somehow doubt the solution is that easy. Or inexpensive."

Nate moved back to the head of the cart, nudging it forward past the chocolates into the jelly-bean section. Spice and Thyme was one of those huge gourmet food stores designed to feel small and cozy, with narrow aisles, dim lighting, and stuff stacked up everywhere you turned. Personally, it made me feel claustrophobic, especially during Christmas, when it was twice as crowded as usual. Nate, however, hardly seemed bothered, deftly maneuvering his cart around a group of senior citizens studying the jelly beans before taking the corner to boxed shortbreads.

"I don't know," he said, glancing at the list in his hand before beginning to pull down tins decorated with the face of a brawny Scotsman playing a bagpipe. "I think that what Harriet needs might be simpler than she thinks."

"Total organization of her house, courtesy of Rest Assured?" I asked.

"No," he said. "Reggie."

"Ah," I said as the senior citizens passed us again, squeezing by the cart. "So you noticed, too."

"Please." He rolled his eyes. "It's kind of flagrant. What does she think all that ginkgo's about?"

"That's what I said," I told him. "But when I suggested it to her, she was shocked by the idea. *Shocked.*"

"Really," he said, pulling the cart forward again. "Then she must be more distracted than we even realize. Which, honestly, I'm not quite sure is possible."

We jerked to a stop suddenly, narrowly missing a collision with two women pushing a cart entirely full of wine. After some dirty looks and a lot of clanking, they claimed their right of way and moved on. I said, "She said she was too busy for a relationship."

"Everyone's busy," Nate said.

"I know. I think she's really just scared."

He glanced over at me. "Scared? Of Reggie? What, she thinks he might force her to give up caffeine for real or something?"

"No," I said.

"Of what, then?" he asked.

I paused, only just now realizing that the subject was hitting a little close to home. "You know, getting hurt. Putting herself out there, opening up to someone."

"Yeah," he said, adding some cheese straws to the cart, "but risk is just part of relationships. Sometimes they work, sometimes they don't."

I picked up a box of cheese straws, examining it. "Yeah," I said. "But it's not all about chance, either."

"Meaning what?" he asked, taking the box from me and adding it to the rest.

"Just that, if you know ahead of time that there might an issue that dooms everything—like, say, you're incredibly controlling and independent, like Harriet—maybe it's better to acknowledge that and not waste your time. Or someone else's."

I looked over at Nate, who I now realized was watching me. He said, "So being independent dooms relationships? Since when?"

"That was just one example," I said. "It can be anything."

He gave me a weird look, which was kind of annoying, considering he'd brought this up in the first place. And anyway, what did he want me to do, just come out and admit it would never work between us because it was too hard to care about anyone, much less someone I had to worry about? It was time to get back to the theoretical, and quickly. "All I'm saying is that Harriet won't even trust me with the cashbox. So maybe it's a lot to ask for her to give over her whole life to someone."

"I don't think Reggie wants her life," Nate said, nudging the cart forward again. "Just a date."

"Still," I said, "one can lead to the other. And maybe, to her, that's too much risk."

I felt him look at me again, but I made a point of checking my watch. It was almost time to go. "Yeah," he said. "Maybe."

Ten minutes later—and one minute late—I arrived back at Harriet's, where, true to form, she was waiting for me. "Am I glad to see you," she said. "I was starting to get nervous. I think we're about to have a big rush. I can just kind of feel it."

I looked down the middle of the mall, which was busy but not packed, and then the other way at the food court, which looked much the same. "Well, I'm here now," I said, sticking my purse in the cabinet under the register. As I did, I remembered the thing I'd bought for her, pulling it out. "Here," I said, tossing it over. "For you."

"Really?" She caught it, then turned the box in her hand. "Macaroons! I love these."

"They're Belgian," I said.

"All right," she replied, tearing them open. "Even better."

* * *

"Come on, Laney! Pick up the pace!"

I looked at Olivia, then in the direction she was yelling, the distant end of the mall parking lot. All I could see were a few cars and a Double Burger wrapper being kicked around by the breeze. "What are you doing, again?"

"Don't even ask," she told me. This was the same thing she'd said when I'd come across her, ten minutes earlier, sitting on the curb outside the Vista 10 box office on this unseasonably warm Saturday, a book open in her lap. "All I can say is it's not my choice."

"Not your—" I said, but then this sentence, and my concentration, were interrupted by a *thump-thump* noise. This time when I turned, I saw Laney, wearing a purple tracksuit, rounding the distant corner of Meyer's Department Store at a very slow jog, headed our way.

"Finally," Olivia said, pulling a digital kitchen timer out from beneath her book and getting to her feet. "You're going to have to go faster than that if you want me to sit out here for another lap!" she yelled, cupping her hands around her mouth. "You understand?"

Laney ignored her, or just didn't hear, keeping her gaze straight as she kept on, *thump-thump, thump-thump.* As she got closer I saw her expression was serious, her face flushed, although she did give me a nod as she passed.

Olivia consulted the stopwatch. "Eight minutes," she called out as Laney continued on toward the other end of the mall. "That's a sixteen-minute mile. Also known as *slow.*"

"Still training for the five-K, huh?" I asked as a mall security guard rolled by, glancing at us.

"Oh, she's beyond training now," Olivia replied, sitting down on the curb again and setting the timer beside her. "She's focused, living and breathing the run. And yes, that *is* a direct quote."

"You're supportive," I said.

"No, I'm realistic," she replied. "She's been training for two months now, and her times aren't improving. At all. If she insists on doing this, she's just going to embarrass herself."

"Still," I said, looking at Laney again, who was still plodding along. "You have to admit, it's kind of impressive."

Olivia harrumphed. "What is? Total denial?"

"Total commitment," I said. "You know, the idea of discovering something that, for all intents and purposes, goes against your abilities, and yet still deciding to do it anyway. That takes guts, you know?"

She considered this as the security guard passed by, going the other way. "If she's so gutsy, though, why is it that she usually quits at about the two-mile mark, then calls me to come pick her up?"

"She does that?" I asked.

"Only about every other time. Oh, wait. Is that not supportive, though?"

I sat back, ignoring this, planting my hands on the pavement behind me. It wasn't like I was some expert on the meaning of being supportive. Was it being loyal even against your better judgment? Or, like Olivia, was it making your displeasure known from the start, even when someone didn't want to hear it? I'd been thinking about this more and more since Nate's and my discussion at Spice and Thyme. Maybe he was someone who lived in the moment, easily able to compartmentalize one part of his life from another. But to me, the Nate I was spending more and more time with was still the same one who was going home to a bad situation with his dad and who planned to get out as soon as he could—both of these were reasons I should have kept away, or at least kept my distance. Yet if anything, I kept moving closer, which just made no sense at all.

Now, I looked over at Olivia, who was squinting into the distance, the timer still counting down in her lap. "Do you remember," I asked, "how you said that when you first came from Jackson, it was hard for you, and that's why you never bothered to talk to anyone or make friends?"

"Yeah," she said, sounding a bit wary. "Why?"

"So why did you, then?" I asked, looking at her. "I mean, with me. What changed?"

She considered this as a minivan drove by, pulling up on the other side of the box office. "I don't know," she said. "I guess it was just that we had something in common."

"Jackson."

"Yeah, that. But also, not being like everyone else at Perkins. You know, having some part that's different, and yet shared. I mean, with me it's my family, my economic standing. You, well, you're a lush and a delinquent—"

"Hey," I said. "That was just one day."

"I know, I'm just kidding," she said, waving me off with her hand. "But neither of us exactly fit the mold there."

"Right."

She sat back, brushing her braids away from her face. "My point is, there are a lot of people in the world. No one ever sees everything the same way you do; it just doesn't happen. So when you find one person who gets a couple of things, especially if they're important ones . . . you might as well hold on to them. You know?"

I looked down at the stopwatch sitting on the curb between us. "Nicely put," I said. "And all in less than two minutes."

"Conciseness is underrated," she said easily. Then she looked over my shoulder, suddenly raising her hand to wave to someone behind me. When I turned, I was surprised to see Gervais, in his peacoat standing in front of the box office. Seeing me, his face flushed, and he hurriedly grabbed his ticket from under the glass and darted inside.

"You know Gervais?" I asked her.

"Who, extra salt, double–lic whip? Sure. He's a regular." I just looked at her. "That's his concession order," she explained. "Large popcorn, no butter, extra salt, and two packs of licorice whips. He hits at least one movie a week. The boy likes film. How do you know him?"

"We ride to school together," I said. So Gervais had a life outside of carpool. It wasn't like it should have been surprising, but for some reason, it was.

Just then, I heard a buzzing: her phone. She pulled it out of her pocket, looked at the screen, then sighed. Laney. "I'd say I told you so," she said. "But it's not like I get any satisfaction from this."

I watched as she flipped it open, hitting the TALK button and saying she'd be there in a minute. Then she picked up her book and got to her feet, brushing herself off. "Still," I said, "you have to get something, though."

"From what? "

"From this." I gestured around me. "I mean, you are out here timing her. So you can't be totally opposed to what she's doing."

"No, I am." She pulled her keys out of her pocket, shoving the book under her arm. "But I'm also a sucker. Clearly."

"You are not," I said.

"Well, then, I don't know the reason," she said. "Other than she's my cousin, and she asked, so I'm here. I try not to go deeper than that. I'll see you around, okay?"

I nodded, and then she was walking away, across the lot to her car. Watching her, I kept thinking of what she'd said earlier about having things in common, and then of Nate and me in his garage on Thanksgiving, when I'd told him about my mom and our history. Clearly, sharing something could take you a long way, or at least to a different place than you'd planned. Like a friendship or a family, or even just alone on a curb on a Saturday, trying to get your bearings as best you can.

* * *

It wasn't just me that was feeling out of sorts. Even the weather was weird.

"You have to admit," Harriet said, shaking her head as we stepped out into the employee parking lot later that night, "this is very strange. When has it ever been seventy-seven degrees a week before Christmas?"

"It's global warming," Reggie told her. "The ice caps are melting."

"I was thinking more along the lines of the apocalypse," she said.

He sighed. "Of course you were."

"Seriously, though, who wants to Christmas-shop when it feels like summer?" she asked as we started across the lot. "This *cannot* be good for sales."

"Do you ever think about anything but business?" Reggie said.

"The apocalypse," she told him. "And occasionally coffee."

"You know," he said, "I'm aware that you're kidding, but that's still really—"

"Good night," I called out as I peeled off toward the greenway. They both waved, still bickering. This, however, was not strange in the least; it was the way I always left them.

Often, Harriet gave me a ride home, as she hated me taking the greenway in the dark, but as the weather had grown oddly warm I'd been insisting on walking instead, just to make the most of the unseasonable weather while it lasted. On my way back to Cora's, I passed several bicyclists, two runners, and a pack of kids on scooters, all with the same idea. Weirdest of all, though, was what I saw at home when I walked in the front door: Jamie, at the bottom of the stairs, wearing his bathing suit and swim fins, a towel thrown over his shoulder. It might not have been a sign of the apocalypse, but it seemed pretty close.

At first, it was clear that I'd surprised him: he jumped, flustered, before quickly recovering and striking a casual pose. "Hey," he said, like he hung out in swimgear in the foyer every day. "How was work?"

"What are you—?" I began, then stopped as Cora appeared at the top of the stairs, a pair of shorts pulled over her own suit.

"Oh," she said, stopping suddenly, her face flushing. "Hi."

"Hi," I said slowly. "What's going on?"

They exchanged a guilty look. Then Cora sighed and said, "We're going pool jumping."

"You're what?"

"It's seventy-five degrees! In December!" Jamie said. "We have to. We can't help ourselves."

I looked up at my sister again. "It is pretty nice out," she said.

"But the neighborhood pool doesn't even have water in it," I said.

"That's why we're going to Blake's," Jamie told me. "You want to come?"

"You're sneaking into Nate's pool?"

Cora bit her lip as Jamie said, "Well, technically, it's not really sneaking. I mean, we're neighbors. And it's right there, heated, with nobody using it."

"Do you have permission?" I asked.

He looked up at Cora, who squirmed on the step. "No," she said. "But I saw Blake earlier and he said he and Nate were taking off for an overnight business thing. So . . ."

". . . you're just going to jump their fence and their pool," I finished for her.

Silence. Then Jamie said, "It's seventy-five degrees! In December! Do you know what this means?"

"The apocalypse?" I asked.

"What?" he said. "No. God. Why would you—"

"She's right, you know," Cora said, coming down the stairs. "We're not exactly setting a good example."

"It was your idea," Jamie pointed out. Cora flushed again. "Your sister," he said to me, "is a serious pool jumper. In college, she was always the first to go over the fence."

"Really," I said, turning to look at her.

"Well," she replied, as if about to justify this. Then she just said, "You know, it's seventy-five degrees. In December."

Jamie grabbed her hand, grinning. "That's my girl," he said, then pointed at me. "You coming?"

"I don't have a bathing suit," I told him.

"In my closet, bottom right-hand drawer," Cora said. "Help yourself."

I just shook my head, incredulous, as they started through the kitchen. Cora was laughing, Jamie's flippers slapping the floor, and then they were outside, the door swinging shut behind them.

I wasn't going to go and certainly didn't plan to swim. But after sitting on my bed in the quiet for a few moments, I did go find a suit of Cora's, pull on some sweatpants over it, and head downstairs, crossing the yard to where I could hear splashing just beyond the fence.

"There she is," Jamie said as I slipped through. He was in the shallow end, next to Roscoe, who was on the deck, barking excitedly, while Cora was underwater, swimming down deep, her hair streaming out behind her. "Couldn't resist, huh?"

"I don't think I'm coming in," I said, walking over and sitting down on the edge, my knees pulled to my chest. "I'll just watch."

"Ah, that's no fun," he said. Then, with Roscoe still barking, he dove under, disappearing. As he swam the length of the pool, the dog ran alongside, following him.

I looked over at Cora, who was now bobbing in the deep end, brushing her hair back from her face. "You know," I said, "I never would have figured you for a lawbreaker."

She made a face at me. "It's not exactly a felony. And besides, Blake owes us."

"Really? Why?" I asked, but she didn't hear me, or chose not to answer, instead diving under again to join Jamie, who was circling along the bottom.

As they emerged a moment later, laughing and splashing each other, I kicked off my shoes, then rolled up my sweatpants and dunked my feet in the water. It was warm, even more so than the air, and I leaned back on my palms, turning my face up to the sky. I hadn't been swimming since the last time we'd lived in a complex with a pool, around ninth grade. In the summer, I would spend hours there, staying in until my mom had to come get me when dark was falling.

Jamie and Cora stayed in for about a half hour, dunking each other and playing Marco Polo. By the time they climbed out, it was past ten, and even Roscoe—who'd been barking nonstop—was exhausted. "See," Jamie said as they toweled off, "one dip, no harm done."

"It is nice," I agreed, moving my feet through the water.

"You coming back with us?" Cora asked as they walked behind me, heading for the fence.

"In a minute. I think I'll hang out a little while longer."

"Might as well make the most of it," Jamie said as Roscoe trotted behind him. "After all, it won't be like this forever."

Then they were gone, through the fence, where I could hear their voices fading as they crossed the yard. I waited until it had been quiet for a few minutes before slipping off my sweatpants. Then, with one last quick look around me to make sure I was alone, I jumped in.

It was startling, at first, being back in a pool after so long not swimming. Just as quickly, though, all the instinct came back, and before I knew it I was moving steadily to the other side, the water filling my ears. I don't know how many laps I'd done, back and forth, only that I had hit such a rhythm that at first, I didn't even notice when a light clicked on in the house. By the time the second one came on, it was too late.

I froze, sinking down below the pool's edge, as a figure

moved through the now-bright living room. After it crossed back once, then again, I heard a door slide open. *Shit*, I thought, then panicked, taking a deep breath and submerging myself.

Which, as it turned out, was not the smartest move, as became apparent when I looked up through the shifting blue water above to see Nate staring down at me. By that time, my lungs were about to explode, so I had no choice but to show myself.

"Well, well," he said as I sputtered to the surface. "What's this all about?"

I swam to the edge, just to do something, then ran a hand over my face. "Um," I said. "Actually—"

"Cora and Jamie were pool jumping, huh?" he said. I just looked at him, confused, until he pulled one flipper, then another, from behind his back. "They're not exactly slick about it," he said, dropping them on the deck beside his feet. "These were right there on that chair. Last time they left a swimming noodle."

"Oh," I said. "Yeah. I guess we're busted."

"No big deal." He crouched down by me, dipping his hand in the water. "It's good someone's getting some use out of this thing. My dad's always complaining about how much it costs to heat it."

"You don't swim at all anymore?"

"Not really," he said.

"You must miss it, though."

He shrugged. "Sometimes. It was a good escape. Until, you know, it wasn't."

I thought of what he'd said, about his dad getting banned but still yelling from the fence. "You should come in," I said. "It's really warm."

"Nah, I'm okay." He sat on a nearby chair. "You go ahead, though."

I bobbed there for a second, neither of us talking. Finally I said, "So I thought you were out of town on a business thing."

"Change of plans," he said. "It was decided I should come home early."

"Decided," I repeated.

He looked up, then gave me a tired smile. "It's been a long day, let's just say that."

I'll bet, I thought. Out loud, I said, "All the more reason to take a dip. I mean, it's December. Seventy-five degrees. You know you want to."

I honestly didn't think he'd agree with this; I was just talking. But then he nodded slowly, and pushed himself to his feet. "All right," he said. "I'll be back in a sec."

As he disappeared inside, it occurred to me that maybe this was not the smartest idea. After all, I was trying to keep my distance and now, with this invitation, had narrowed the space we were in considerably. Before I could figure out how to change this, though—or even if I wanted to—he was coming back outside, now in trunks, and walking across the patio. Needless to say, this was distracting. That first night, I hadn't really seen him shirtless, and now I could focus on little else. All the more reason, I realized, to backtrack, but before I could he was stretching his arms overhead and diving in, hitting the water with barely a splash and disappearing below.

You swim, I thought, having a flash of that sweatshirt as he came to the surface, then closer toward me with a breast-stroke that looked effortless. When he emerged, shaking his head and sending droplets flying, I said, "Nice form."

"Thanks," he said, bobbing in front of me. "Years of training."

Suddenly, I was so aware of how close we were to each other, with only the water between us. I looked down: beneath the surface my skin looked so pale, almost blue, my necklace lying across it. When I glanced up again, he was looking at it, too, and after meeting my gaze for a second he reached over, catching it in one hand to lie flat on his palm.

"How many of those key necklaces do you think Harriet has sold since Thanksgiving?" he asked.

"I don't know," I said. "A lot."

"I saw a girl at Jump Java today wearing one. It was so weird."

"I'll be sure to tell Harriet you said that," I said. "She'll be overjoyed."

"I don't mean it like that." He turned his palm, letting the key fall loose, and it slowly floated back down to rest against me again. "It's just that I associate them with you, and this one. You know? It was the first thing I noticed about you that night we met."

"Even before I was jumping the fence?"

"Okay." He smiled. "Maybe the second."

All around us, the neighborhood was quiet, the sky

spread out wide and sprinkled with stars overhead. I could feel him right there in front of me, and I thought of what Jamie had said earlier: *It won't be like this forever.* That was true, and also the reason I should have climbed out right then, as well as why I knew I would stay.

He was still watching me, both of us bobbing, and I could feel the water around me, pressing in, pulling back. Then, slowly, Nate was moving closer, leaning in, and despite all I'd told myself, and all I wanted to believe I was and wasn't capable of, I stayed where I was as he kissed me. His lips were warm, his skin wet, and when he drew back, I felt myself shiver, unaccustomed to anyone being so close, and yet still not ready for him to pull away.

"Are you cold?" he asked.

I was about to shake my head, say it wasn't that at all, but before I could, I felt his hand close over mine. "Don't worry," he said, "it's warmer the deeper you go." Then, to prove it, he went under, and I took a deep breath, the biggest I could, and let him pull me down with him.

*   *   *

I already knew Jamie liked holidays. There were the matching blue shirts, for one thing, not to mention the thankful lists. But even armed with this knowledge, I still was not fully prepared for how he approached Christmas.

"Just stand still, okay?" Cora said, making a face as she stuffed the pillow farther up under his jacket. "Stop wriggling around."

"I can't," Jamie replied. "This long underwear is a lot itchier than I thought it would be."

"I told you to just wear your boxer shorts."

"Santa doesn't wear boxers!" he said, his voice rising slightly as she yanked the wide black belt of his costume tight over the pillow, holding it in place. "If I'm going to do this, I want to be authentic about it."

"I seriously doubt," Cora said, pushing herself to her feet, "that the Santa police do an underwear check. Now where's your beard?"

"On the bed," he told her. Then he saw me. "Hey, Ruby! So what do you think? Pretty great, right?"

This wasn't exactly the first word that had come to mind at seeing him in a full-on Santa outfit: red suit, black boots, and big white wig, which to me looked itchier than any underwear could ever be. But in the interest of family, I decided to play along.

"Yeah," I agreed as Cora reached over his head, fastening his beard. "Are you going to a party or something?"

"No," he said. Cora stepped back, hands on her hips, examining her work. "It's Christmas Eve."

"Right," I said slowly. "So this is for . . ."

"Walking around the neighborhood!" he finished for me. I just looked at Cora, who simply shook her head. "My dad always dressed up like Santa on Christmas Eve," he explained. "It was a family tradition."

"Which we did not have a lot of," Cora added. "And Jamie knows that, which is why he's made it a personal mission to make up for it now."

Jamie looked from her to me, then back at her again. Even in the full costume, wig and all, he still looked so boyish, like *Santa: The Early Days*. "I know, it's a little over the top," he said. "It's just . . . we always made a big deal of Christmas at my house. I guess it's kind of rubbed off on me."

Even without the Santa outfit, this was an understatement. All month long, Jamie had thrown himself into getting ready for Christmas: stringing up an elaborate light show out front, putting Advent calendars in practically every room, dragging home the biggest tree he could find, which we then decorated with a mix of brand-new ornaments and homemade ones from Hunter holidays past. Between all this and working at the mall, I'd frankly been over the holidays weeks ago. But as with most things involving Jamie, I'd gone along anyway, allowing myself to be dragged to the neighborhood tree-lighting ceremony, watching the Charlie Brown Christmas special over and over again, even holding Roscoe down while Jamie outfitted him in an elaborate harness of jingle bells.

"Here," he said now, reaching behind him to the bed to pick up a red elf's hat. "For you."

"Me?"

"Yeah. So we'll match, when we go out."

I looked at Cora again, but this time she avoided my eyes, busily putting away her blusher, which she'd used to give Jamie his festive red cheeks. "Where," I said slowly, "are we going?"

"To hand out gifts in the neighborhood," he said, like this was obvious. "They're all in the foyer, ready to go. Come on!"

He brushed past me, his own hat in hand, and bounded down the stairs, his boots thumping on the carpet. I narrowed my eyes at Cora until she finally turned to face me.

"I'm sorry," she said, looking like she meant it. "But I did it last year."

And that was how I ended up out in Wildflower Ridge, at eight o'clock on Christmas Eve, with Jamie in his Santa suit, and Roscoe in his jingle bells, spreading good cheer. Or, looking at it another way, walking in the cold—which had returned with a vengeance—and interrupting people from their own family celebrations while scaring the occasional motorist.

After the first couple of houses, we worked out a system: I rang the bell, then let Jamie stay front and center, hanging back with Roscoe until the door was opened, and pitching in when needed to help hand out the gifts, which were mostly stuffed animals and boxes of mini candy canes. Aside from a few weird looks—and some people who were clearly home but chose to ignore us—people seemed happy to see us, especially the kids, and after about an hour and three blocks, our stuff was mostly gone.

"We've got enough for maybe two more stops," Jamie said as we stood on the corner by Nate's house, having paused for Roscoe, bells jingling, to relieve himself against a mailbox. "So which ones do you think? You want to take something to Nate?"

I looked over at the Cross house, dark except for a couple of lights in the back. "I don't know," I said. "He might not be your target audience. Maybe we should go a little younger."

"I'll do that," he said, reaching into his almost-empty sack. "But you go ahead and bring him some candy canes. I'll meet you back here. All right?"

"Okay," I said, handing over Roscoe's leash. He took it,

then tossed his sack over his shoulder—the Santa police would have approved—and started across the street to a house with brightly lit snowflakes on either side of the front steps.

I slid the box of candy canes in my pocket, then headed up Nate's walk, taking a deep breath of cool air. The truth was, I'd thought about getting him a Christmas gift. I had even picked out more than one before stopping myself, not sure even after that night in the pool that I was ready or able to make such a grand gesture. But in the days since, I'd also realized that with Nate, everything just came so easily, as easily as letting him take my hand and pull me beneath the surface. Maybe it was impossible for someone to share everything with you, but I was beginning to think what we had was enough. And anyway, it was Christmas, a time above all for hope, or so I'd been told. He'd given me so much, and now, here, I was finally ready to reciprocate. So I stepped up to the door and rang the bell.

The moment he opened the door, I knew something was wrong. It was just the look on his face—surprised, even alarmed—followed immediately by the way he eased the door a bit more shut, the same move I'd once mastered with the Jehovah's and landlords. "Ruby," he said, his voice low. "Hey. What are you doing here?"

Right that moment, I heard his dad: loud, bellowing, barely muffled from behind a nearby wall. I swallowed, then said, "Jamie was just handing out stuff, for Christmas—"

"It's not a good time," he said as there was a bang, or a thud, discernible. "I'll call you a little later, okay?"

"Are you all right?" I asked him.

"I'm fine."

"Nate—"

"I am. But I've got to go," he said, easing the door closed a bit more. I could barely see him now. "I'll talk to you tomorrow."

I didn't get a chance to answer this, as the door was already shutting with an audible click. I just stood there, my mouth dry, wondering what I should do. *I'm fine*, he'd said. I reached out, putting my hand on the knob and turning it. Here I was, finally ready to let him in, and it was me locked out.

"Hey!" Jamie called from behind me. I turned. He and Roscoe were across the street, coming closer. "Are they there?"

Say something, I thought, but even as I tried to form the words, any words, I remembered that day in the garage, how he'd asked me to keep this quiet. *You understand*. Did I want to be the Honeycutts, stepping in and ruining everything, even if I thought it was for the best? Jamie was coming up the walk, Roscoe pulling ahead. I had to decide, now.

"They're not home," I said, stepping off the porch. The box of candy canes was still in my pocket, and I slid my fingers in, cupping them around it. It felt almost like a hand, resting in mine. "Let's just go."

Chapter Thirteen

I was up until way late, but not waiting for Santa. Instead, I lay on my bed, watching the lights from Nate's pool dance across the trees, the same way I had that first night. More than once, I thought about sneaking over again to find him and see if he was okay. But then I'd remember him shutting the door in my face, the click of the latch catching, and stay where I was.

The next morning, I got a new backpack, some CDs, a few books, and a laptop. Cora got her period.

"I'm fine, I'm fine," she sputtered when, shortly after we'd opened gifts, I found her sitting on her bed, crying. "Really."

"Honey." Jamie came over, sitting beside her and sliding his arm over her shoulder. "It's okay."

"I know." Her voice was still choked as she reached up, wiping her eyes with the back of her hand. "It's just, I really had a feeling it had happened this month. Which I know is so stupid . . ."

"You're not stupid," Jamie said softly, smoothing a hand over her head.

". . . but I just started thinking how great it would be to find out today and be able to tell you guys, and how it would be the best gift ever—" She drew in a long, shaky breath, her eyes welling up again. "But it didn't happen. I'm not pregnant. Again."

"Cora."

"I know," she said, waving her hand. "It's Christmas, we have a wonderful life, roof over our head, things so many people want. But I want this. And no matter what I do, I can't get it. It just . . ." She trailed off, wiping her eyes again. This time, Jamie didn't say anything.

"Sucks," I finished for her.

"Yeah," she said, looking up at me. "It *sucks*."

I felt so helpless, the way I always did when I saw Cora upset about the baby issue. It was the one thing that could take her from zero to emotional in less than five minutes, the single tender spot in her substantial personal armor. The previous month she'd finally agreed to a little pharmaceutical help, via an ovulation drug, which made her hot and emotional, liable to be sweating or weeping or both at any given moment. Not a good mix, especially during the holidays. And now, it was all for nothing. It did suck.

"We'll just try again," Jamie was saying now. "It was just the first month. Maybe the second time will be the charm."

Cora nodded, but I could see she was hardly convinced as she reached up, running her finger over the gift I'd given her that morning: one of Harriet's key necklaces, a silver one lined with red stones. I'd been strangely nervous as she opened the box, worried she wouldn't like it, but the minute she slid it out into her hand, her eyes widening, I knew I'd scored. "It's beautiful," she said, looking up at me. "It's like yours!"

"Kind of," I said. "But not completely."

"I love it," she told me, reaching up immediately to put it on. She brushed her hair over her shoulders. "What do you think? Does it look good?"

It had, and did now, as she rested her head on Jamie's shoulder, curling into him. She still had one hand around the key. The necklace looked different on her than on me, but you could see some similarities. You just had to know where to look.

Just then, the doorbell rang. Roscoe, who'd been snoozing at the foot of the bed, perked up his ears and let out a yap. "Was that the door?" Jamie asked.

"It was," Cora said as Roscoe hopped down, bolting from the room. A moment later, we heard him barking from the foyer as the bell sounded again. "Who would show up on Christmas?"

"I'll find out," I said, although as I quickly got up, heading for the stairs, I was hoping I already knew. The bell rang again when I was halfway down, then once more as I approached the door. When I got to the door and looked through the peephole, though, Nate wasn't there. Nobody was. Then it chimed again—so weird—so I just opened it.

It was Gervais. Too short for the peephole, he was standing on the front step, in his glasses, peacoat, and scarf, with what looked like a brand-new scooter parked on the walk behind him. "Hi," he said.

I just looked at him. "Hey," I said slowly. "What are you—?"

"I have a proposition for you," he said, all business. "Can I come in?"

"Um," I said. Behind me, Roscoe had stopped barking but was still trying to nudge past me. "We're kind of busy, actually—"

"I know." He reached up, adjusting his glasses. "This will only take a minute."

I still didn't really want to let him in. But in the spirit of the holiday, I stepped aside. "Shouldn't you be with your family?" I asked as he shut the door behind him.

"We finished Christmas hours ago," he told me. "My dad already took down the tree."

"Oh." Now we were just standing there, together, in the foyer. "Well," I said, "we're still kind of doing things, so—"

"Do you think you'll be prepared for your next big calculus exam?"

I just looked at him. "What?"

"Your next exam. It's in March and counts for half your grade, right?"

"How do you know that?"

"Will you be prepared for it?"

Upstairs, I heard Cora laughing. A good sign. "Define prepared," I said.

"Scoring a ninety or higher."

"No," I said. Which was, sadly, the truth. Even with all my studying and preparation, calculus was still the one thing that could take me from zero to panicked in less than thirty seconds.

"Then you should let me help you," Gervais said.

"Help me?"

"I'm very good at calculus," he explained, pushing up his glasses. "Not only doing it, but explaining it. I'm tutoring two people in my class at the U right now. And that's college-level calc, not that easy-schmeezy kind you're doing."

Easy-schmeezy, I thought. He hadn't changed entirely. "You know," I said, "that's a very nice offer. But I think I'll be okay."

"It's not an offer," he said. "It's a proposition."

Suddenly, I had a flash of him in the car that day, drawing in his breath. Plus the staring at lunch in the green, and the weird way he'd acted at the Vista 10. *Oh, God*, I thought, finally getting it. Nate was right. He *liked* me. This was just what I needed. "You know," I said, reaching behind him for the door, "you're a nice kid, Gervais, but—"

"It's about Olivia," he said.

I stopped, mid-sentence, not sure I was hearing him right. "What?"

He coughed. Then blushed. "Olivia Davis," he said. "You're friends with her, aren't you?"

"Yes," I said slowly. "Why?"

"Because," he said. He coughed again. "I, um, like her. Kind of."

"You like *Olivia*?"

"Not like that," he said quickly. "I just . . ."

I waited. It seemed like a long time passed.

". . . I want to be her friend," he finished.

This was kind of sweet, I had to admit. Also surprising. Which brought me to my next question. "Why?"

"Because," he said as if it was simple, obvious. When it became clear this was not the case, he added, "She talks to me."

"She talks to you," I repeated.

He nodded. "Like, at the theater. And when she sees me in the hall at school, she always says hello. Nobody else does that. Plus, she likes the same movies I do."

I looked down at him, standing there before me in his heavy coat and glasses. Sure, he was annoying, but it did have to be hard for him. No matter how smart you were, there was a lot you couldn't learn from books. "Then just be friends with her," I said. "You don't need me for that."

"I do, though," he said. "I can't just go up and talk to her. But if I was, you know, helping you with your calculus at lunch or something, then I could just hang out with you guys."

"Gervais," I said slowly. "I think that's really sweet—"

"Don't say no," he pleaded.

"—but it's also deceptive."

He shook his head, adamant. "It's not, though! I don't like her that way. I just want to be friends."

"Still, it would be like I'm setting her up. And friends don't do that."

Never in a million years would I have thought I would be offering up a primer on friendship, much less to Gervais Miller. Even less likely? That I would feel sorry for him after I did so. But as he regarded me glumly, then stepped back to the door, I did.

"All right," he said, his voice flat. Defeated. "I understand."

I watched him as he turned the knob, pulling the door open. Once again, I found myself torn as to what to do, but this time, the stakes weren't so high. Maybe I couldn't do anything for Nate. But I could help someone.

"How about this," I said. He turned back to me slowly. "I'll hire you."

"Hire me?"

"As a tutor. I pay what everyone else pays, you do what you do. If it just so happens we meet during lunch and Olivia is there, then so be it. But she is not part of the deal. Understood?"

He nodded vigorously, his glasses bobbing slightly. "Yes."

"All right then," I said. "Merry Christmas."

"Merry Christmas," he replied, stepping outside and starting down the stairs. Halfway there, he turned back to me. "Oh. I'm twenty dollars an hour, by the way. For the tutoring."

Of course he was. I said, "Am I going to pass calculus?"

"It's guaranteed," he replied. "My method is proven."

I nodded, and then he continued down the steps, grabbing his helmet from his scooter and pulling it on. Maybe this was a big mistake, one among many. But sometimes, we all need a little help, whether we want to admit it or not.

*　　*　　*

"Come in, come in," Jamie said as yet another group came bustling in, their chatter rising up to the high ceiling of the foyer. "Welcome! Drinks are in the back, and there's tons of food. Here, let me take your coat. . . ."

I leaned back against the doorjamb of the laundry room, where I'd been hiding out with Roscoe ever since Jamie and Cora's post-Christmas, pre–New Year holiday open house began. Officially, it was my job to keep the ice bucket full and make sure the music was audible, but other than doing this on a most perfunctory level, I wasn't exactly mingling.

Now, though, as Jamie, with his arms full of coats, glanced around him, I knew I should show myself and offer to help him stow them upstairs. Instead, I slid down into a sitting position, my back to the dryer, nudging the door shut with my foot. Roscoe, who'd been exiled here for his own mental well-being, immediately hopped up from his bed and came over to join me.

It had been two days since Christmas, and I hadn't seen or talked to Nate. Once, this would have seemed impossible, considering our very proximity—not to mention how often we crossed paths, intentionally or otherwise. Maybe it was just that school was out, we weren't riding together, and we were both busy with our respective jobs, where things hadn't slowed down, even after Christmas. But even so, I had the distinct feeling he was avoiding me.

This was surprising, but even more shocking was the fact that it was bothering me so much. After all, this was what I'd wanted once—more space between us, less connection. Now that I had it, though, I felt more worried about him than ever.

Just then, the door opened. "One second, I just have to grab another roll of—" Cora was halfway inside, still talking to someone over her shoulder, when she stopped in mid-stride and sentence, seeing me and Roscoe on the floor. "Hey," she said slowly. "What's going on?"

"Nothing," I said. She shut the door as Roscoe got up, wagging his tail. "Just taking a breather."

"But not in the closet," she said.

"This was closer."

She reached over the washing machine, pulling down a

roll of paper towels. "Already a spill on the carpet," she said, tearing them open. "Happens every year."

"Sounds like it's going well otherwise, though," I said as some people passed by in the hallway outside, their voices bouncing off the walls.

"It is." She turned back to me, the towels in her arms. "You should come out, have some food. It's not that bad, I promise."

"I'm a little low on cheer," I told her.

She smiled. "You've been a real trooper, I have to say. Christmas with Jamie is like an endurance trial. My first year I almost had a total breakdown."

"It's just weird," I said. "I mean, last year . . ." I trailed off, realizing I didn't even remember what I'd done last year for the holidays. I had a vague recollection of delivering luggage, maybe a company party at Commercial. But like everything else from my old life, this was distant, faded. "I'm just tired, I guess."

"Just make an appearance," she said. "Then you can come back here, or hit the closet for the rest of the day. All right?"

I looked up at her, dubious, as she extended her hand to me. But then I let her pull me to my feet and followed her out into the hallway. Two steps later, as we entered the kitchen, we were ambushed.

"Cora! Hello!" I jumped, startled, as a petite woman in a flowing, all-white ensemble, her dark hair pulled back at her neck, suddenly appeared in front of us, a wineglass in one hand. "Happy holidays!"

"Happy holidays," Cora replied, leaning forward to

accept a kiss—and a shadow of a lipstick stain—on her cheek. "Barbara, this is my sister, Ruby. Ruby, this is Barbara Starr."

"You have a sister?" Barbara asked. She was wearing several multicolored beaded necklaces that swayed and clacked across her chest each time she moved, as she did now, turning to face me. "Why, I had no idea!"

"Ruby just came to live with us this year," Cora explained. To me, she said, "Barbara is an author. Best-selling, I might add."

"Oh, stop," Barbara replied, waving her hand. "You'll embarrass me."

"She was one of my very first clients," Cora added. "When I was working in a family law practice, just out of school."

"Really," I said.

"I got divorced," Barbara explained, taking a sip of her wine. "Which is never fun. But because of your sister, it was the *best* divorce I've ever had. And that's really saying something."

I looked at Cora, who shook her head almost imperceptibly, making it clear I should not ask what exactly this meant. Instead, she said, "Well, we should probably go check on the food, so . . ."

"Everything is just wonderful. I love the holidays!" Barbara said, sighing. Then she smiled at me and said, "Is the rest of your family here, as well? I'd just love to meet your mother."

"Um," I said, "actually—"

"We're not really in touch with our mom these days,"

Cora told her. "But we *are* lucky to have so many great friends like you here today. Would you like some more wine?"

"Oh," Barbara said, looking at her glass, then at us. "Well, yes. That would be lovely."

Cora eased the glass from her hand—still smiling, smiling—then passed it off to me, touching the small of my back with her other hand. As I took this cue, moving forward, I looked back at her. Barbara was talking again, her hands fluttering as she made some point, but my sister, even as she nodded, was watching me. Awfully smooth, I thought. But then again, she'd been away from my mom a lot longer than I had. Practice does make perfect, or close to it.

Glass in hand, I made my way through the crowd, which had grown considerably since the last time I'd checked the ice and music. Jamie was still in the foyer, answering the door and taking coats, when I finally reached the bar area to get the white wine.

"Macaroons!" I heard him say suddenly. "You shouldn't have."

I turned around. Sure enough, there was Nate, in jeans and a blue collared shirt, his hands in his pockets. His dad was beside him, shrugging off his jacket and smiling as Jamie admired his offering. "They're Belgian," Mr. Cross said. "*Very* expensive."

"I'll bet," Jamie replied, clapping Nate on the shoulder. "Now, let me get you a drink. What's your poison, Blake? We've got beer, Scotch, wine . . ."

He gestured toward the bar, and as they all turned, Nate's eyes met mine. Mr. Cross lifted a hand, waving at

me, but I just picked up the glass, quickly folding myself
back into the crowd.

When I returned to the spot where I'd left Cora and
Barbara, however, they were both gone, a couple of Jamie's
UMe.com employees—easily identified by their so-nerdy-
they're-cool glasses, expensive jeans, and vintage T-shirts—
in their place, jabbering about Macs. I turned slowly, scanning the crowd for Barbara. Instead, I came face-to-face
with Nate.

"Hey," he said. "Merry Christmas."

I swallowed, then took in a breath. "Merry Christmas."

There was a pause, which then stretched to an awkward
pause, even as someone laughed behind us.

"So I brought you a present," he said, reaching behind
him and pulling out a wrapped parcel from his back pocket.

"Let me guess," I said. "Macaroons."

"No," he replied, making a face as he held it out to me.
"Open it up."

I looked down at the gift, which was wrapped in red
paper decorated with little Christmas trees, and thought of
myself standing at his door that night, my own small offering in hand. "You know," I said, nodding to the glass of wine
I was still holding, "I should probably—"

"Never delay opening a gift," Nate said, reaching to take
the glass from me, putting it on a nearby counter. "Especially one that's already belated."

Emptyhanded, I had no choice but to take it from him,
turning it over in my hands and running a finger under the
tape. Two women passed by us, chattering excitedly, their

heels clacking, as it fell open to reveal a T-shirt. On the front, in that same familiar block lettering: USWIM.

"Your personal philosophy," I said.

"Well," he said, "I looked for one that said 'If you expect the worst you'll never be disappointed,' but they were all out."

"I'll bet." I looked up at him. "This is really nice. Thank you."

"No problem." He leaned back against the wall behind him, smiling at me, and I had a flash of us in the pool together, how he'd grabbed my hand and pulled me under. The memory was so close, I could see every bit of it. But just as clearly, there was the other night, how his face had looked, retreating through the crack in that door. Two opposite images, one easing me closer, another pushing away. "So," he said, "how was your Christmas?"

"How was yours?" I replied, and while I didn't mean for there to be an edge in my voice, even I could hear it. So could he. His face immediately changed, the smile not disappearing, but seeming to stretch more thin. I cleared my throat, then looked down at the shirt again. "I mean, you had to expect I'd ask."

Nate nodded, glancing across the kitchen to the living room, where I could see his dad was talking to a stout woman in a red Christmas sweater. "It was fine," he said. "A little stressful, as you saw."

"A little?" I asked.

"It's not a big deal, okay?"

"Sure seemed that way."

"Well, it wasn't. And it's ancient history."

"It was three days ago," I pointed out.

"So the holidays suck. That's not exactly a news flash, is it?" He ducked his head, a shock of hair falling across his face as the same women passed back by in a cloud of perfumed hand soap, leaving the powder room. When they were gone, he said, "Look, I'm sorry I couldn't talk to you that night. But I'm here now. And I brought a gift. That's got to count for something, right?"

I looked back down at the shirt. *You swim*, I thought. Like he'd said, it was better than sinking. Maybe this was just part of staying afloat. "I don't have anything for you, though."

"Not even Belgian macaroons?"

I shook my head.

"That's all right. They're actually pretty overrated."

"Really."

He nodded, glancing over across the party again, then reached down, sliding his hand around my free one and tugging me a bit down the hallway, around the corner. There, out of sight, he leaned against the wall, gently looping his arms around my waist and pulling me closer. "Okay," he said, his voice low. "Let's try this again. Merry Christmas, Ruby."

I looked up at him, taking in the line of his chin, his eyes and long lashes, the way his fingers were already brushing a bit of my hair off my face, entwining themselves in the strands there. So nearby now, after the distance before. But he was here.

"Merry Christmas," I said, and it was this closeness I tried to concentrate on—not that it might be fleeting, a feeling I knew too well—as he leaned down and put his lips to mine, kissing me, as around the corner the party went on without us, noisy and continuous and completely unaware.

* * *

"Cora," I said as we pulled up outside the mall, "we really don't have to do this."

"We do," she replied, cutting the engine. "Like I said, desperate times call for desperate measures."

"That's just my point, though," I said as she pushed open her door to climb out and I reluctantly did the same. "I'm not desperate."

She just looked at me as I came around the back of the car, then hoisted her purse over one shoulder. "First," she said, "I gave you money for clothes. You bought four things."

"Seven, actually," I pointed out.

"Then," she continued, ignoring this, "for Christmas, I gave you gift cards, with which you bought nothing."

"I don't need anything!"

"And so really, you have given me no choice but to take you shopping by force." She sighed, then reached up, dropping her sunglasses down from their perch on her head to cover her eyes. "Do you even realize how happy the average teenage girl would be in your shoes? I have a credit card. We're at the mall. I want to buy you things. It's like adolescent nirvana."

"Well," I said as we passed two moms pushing strollers, "I guess I'm not the average teenage girl."

She looked over at me as we approached the entrance. "Of course you're not," she said more quietly. "Look, I know this is kind of weird for you. But we have the money, and it's something Jamie and I want to do."

"It's not weird," I told her. "Just unnecessary."

"You know," she said as the automatic doors to Esther Prine, the upscale department store, slid open in front of us, "it's okay to accept things from people. It doesn't make you weak or helpless, even if that is how Mom felt about it."

This was a bit too reminiscent of the ground I'd been forced to cover during my first (and hopefully only) therapy session a few weeks earlier, so instead of responding, I stepped inside. As always, I was temporarily blinded by the gleaming white tile of the store, as well as the polished-to-a-high-sheen jewelry cases. To our left, a guy in a tuxedo was playing Pachelbel by the escalators. It was always kind of odd to be talking about my mother, anyway, but in this setting, it bordered on surreal.

"It's not about Mom," I said as Cora gestured for me to follow her up to the next floor. "Or not just about her. It's a big change. I'm not used to . . . We didn't have much these last few years."

"I know," she replied. "But that's just what I'm saying. In some ways, that was a choice, too. There were things Mom could have done to make things easier for you and for herself."

"Like get in touch with you," I said.

"Yes." She cleared her throat, looking out over cosmetics as we rose up higher, then higher. "But it goes even further back than that. Like with Dad, and the money he tried to give her. But she was so stubborn and angry, she wouldn't take it."

"Wait," I said as we finally reached the top, and she stepped off into Juniors. "I thought Dad never gave her any money. That he dodged her for child support, just disappeared."

Cora shook her head. "Maybe he did later, once he moved to Illinois. But those early years, right after he moved out? He tried to do the right thing. I remember."

Maybe this shouldn't have surprised me. After all, by now I knew my mom had kept so much secret, tweaking her history and my own. Cora was not what I'd been led to believe, so why would my father be, either? Thinking this, though, something else occurred to me. Something that also didn't belong in the polished world of Esther Prine, and yet I had to bring it in, anyway.

"Cora," I said as she drifted over to a table of sweaters, running her hand over them, "do you know where Dad is?"

In the pause that followed, I saw my entire life changing again, twisted and shifting and different. But then she turned around to face me. "No," she said softly as a salesgirl drifted past, pushing a rack of flimsy dresses. "I've thought about looking for him, though, many times. Mostly because Jamie's been really insistent about it, how easy it would be. But I guess I'm sort of afraid still."

I nodded. This, if nothing else, I could understand. There were so many levels to the unknown, from safe to dangerous to outright nebulous, scariest of all.

"You never know, though," she said. "Maybe we can do it together. Strength in numbers and all that."

"Maybe," I said.

She smiled at me, a bit tentatively, then looked back

at the sweaters. "Okay, now—down to business. We're not leaving here until you have at least two new outfits. And a jacket. And new shoes."

"Cora."

"No arguments." She hoisted her purse over her shoulder, then pushed on into Juniors, disappearing between two racks of jeans. After a moment, all I could see was her head bobbing in and out of the displays, her expression caught in the occasional mirror, focused and determined. At first, I stayed where I was, out in the open aisle as the salegirl passed by once more, smiling at me. But then I looked for Cora again and couldn't spot her right away, which was enough to make me force myself forward, in after her.

Chapter Fourteen

"Wow," Nate said. "You look great."

This was exactly the kind of reaction I'd been hoping to avoid, especially considering Cora had assured me repeatedly that my new clothes did not necessarily look that, well, new. Apparently she was wrong.

"It's just a jacket," I told him, pulling my seat belt over my shoulder. As I did so, I glanced at Gervais, who was studying me, as well. "What?"

"Nothing," he said, shrinking back a little bit in his seat.

I sighed, shaking my head, then looked over at Nate, who was just sitting behind the wheel, a half smile on his face. "So what's the occasion for the makeover? Got a hot date for Valentine's or something?"

"Nope," I said, and he laughed, shifting into gear and pulling away from the curb. As we came up to the stop sign at the end of the street, though, he reached over, squeezing my knee, and kept his hand there as we turned onto the next street.

It was February now, which meant Nate and I had been doing whatever it was we were doing—dating, making out, spending most of our free time together—for over a month. And I had to admit, I was happy about it, at least most of the time. But regardless of how well we were getting to know each other, there was always the issue with his dad, the one part of himself he still held back and kept from me. It was only a single thing, but somehow it counted for a lot. Like even when things were as good as they could be, they could only be good enough.

Such as Valentine's Day, which was less than twenty-four hours away. Normally, I'd be happy to have a boyfriend (or something close to it) on the very day you're made to be *very* aware when you don't. But even as Nate hinted at his big plans for us—which, by the sound of it, were secret, detailed, and still in development—I couldn't completely just relax and enjoy it. Rest Assured had run a special promotion for gift baskets and flower delivery for its customers, and the response had been overwhelming. As a result, they were booked fully for that day, just like on Thanksgiving, and I'd not forgotten how that had turned out.

"It's going to be fine," Nate had assured me the night before, out by the pond, when I'd brought this up. We'd taken to meeting there sometimes in the evening, between our respective homework and work schedules, if only for a few moments. "I'll do deliveries all afternoon, be done by seven. Plenty of time for what I have in mind."

"Which is what?" I asked.

"You'll see." He reached over, brushing my hair back from my face. Behind him I could see the lights from the pool flickering over the fence, and even as he leaned in, kissing my temple, I was distracted, knowing that he was supposed to be over there, assembling gift baskets and that any moment his dad might wander out and find him gone. This must have been obvious, as after a moment he pulled back. "What's wrong?"

"Nothing."

"You look worried."

"I'm not."

"Look," he said, his expression serious, "if this is about my gift . . . just relax. I'm not expecting anything phenomenal. Just, you know, super great."

I just looked at him, regretting once again that in a moment of weakness a few days earlier, I'd confessed to Olivia—who then had of course told Nate—that I was stressing about finding the right thing for him for Valentine's. Her loyalty aside, though, the truth was that having dropped the ball at Christmas, it seemed especially important to deliver something good here, if not phenomenal.

"It's not about your gift," I told him.

"Then what is it?"

I shrugged, then looked past him again, over at the pool house. After a moment, he turned and glanced that way as well, then back at me, finally getting it. "It's fine, okay? I'm off the clock," he said. "All yours."

But that was just the thing. Even in these moments—sitting by the pond with his leg linked around mine, or riding in the car with his hand on my knee—I never felt like I had all of Nate, just enough to make me realize what was missing. Even stranger was that with anyone else I'd ever been with—especially Marshall—what I was given, as well as what I gave, had always been partial, and yet that had still been plenty.

Now, we pulled into the Perkins lot, and Gervais jumped

out, bolting for the building as always. As soon as the door shut behind him, Nate leaned across the console between us and kissed me. "You do look great," he said. "So what made you finally break down and spend those gift cards?"

"I didn't. Cora ambushed me and took me to Esther Prine. I was powerless to resist."

"Most girls I know would consider that wish fullfill-ment, not torture."

I sat back, shaking my head. "Why does everyone keep saying that? Who says just because I'm a girl I'm hardwired to want to spent a hundred and eighty bucks on jeans?"

Nate pulled away, holding up his hands. "Whoa there," he said. "Just making an observation."

"Well, don't." I looked down at my lap and those ex-pensive jeans, not to mention the shoes I had on with them (suede, not on sale) and my jacket (soft leather, some la-bel I'd never even heard of). Who was this person in these fancy clothes, at this expensive school, with a for-all-in-tents-and-purposes boyfriend who she was actually worried wasn't opening up to her enough emotionally? It was like I'd been brainwashed or something.

Nate was still watching me, not saying anything. "Sorry," I said finally. "It's just . . . I don't know. Everything feels overwhelming right now, for some reason."

"Overwhelming," he repeated.

It was times like these that I knew I should just come clean and tell him that I worried about him. Having the courage to do that was the part of me *I* was still holding back. And I was always aware of it, even as, like now, I did it once again.

"Plus," I said, sliding my knee so it rested against his, "there's this issue of your gift."

"My gift," he repeated, raising an eyebrow.

"It's just so all-encompassing," I said with a sigh, shaking my head. "Huge. And detailed . . . I mean, the flow charts and spread sheets alone are out of control."

"Yeah?" he said.

"I'll be lucky if I get it all in place by tonight, to be honest."

"Huh." He considered this. "Well. I have to admit, I'm intrigued."

"You should be."

He smiled, then reached over, running a hand over my jacket. "This is pretty cool," he said. "What's the inside look like?"

"The inside . . ." I said, just as he slid his hand over my shoulder, easing off one sleeve. "Ah, right. Well, it's equally impressive."

"Yeah? Let me see." He nudged it off over the other shoulder, and I shook my head. "You know, it is. This sweater is pretty nice, too. Who makes it?"

"No idea," I said.

I felt his hand go around my waist, then smoothly move up my back to the tag. "Lanoler," he read slowly, ducking his head down so his lips were on my collarbone. "Seems well made. Although it's hard to tell. Maybe if I just—"

I glanced outside the car, where people were walking past to the green, coffees in hand, backpacks over shoulders. "Nate," I said. "It's almost first bell."

"You're so conscientious," he said, his voice muffled by

my sweater, which he was still trying to ease off. "When did that happen?"

I sighed, then looked at the dashboard clock. We had five minutes before we'd be officially late. Not all the time we wanted, but maybe this, too, was too much to ask for. "Okay," I told him as he worked his way back around my neck, his lips moving up to my ear. "I'm all yours."

*   *   *

When I got home that afternoon, I saw Jamie seated at the island with his laptop. As he heard me approach, he quickly leaped up, grabbing a nearby loaf of bread and holding it in front of him as if struck by a sudden desire to make a sandwich.

I raised my eyebrows. "What are you doing?"

He exhaled loudly. "I thought you were Cora," he said, tossing the bread down. "Whew! You scared me. I've worked too hard on this for her to find out about it now."

As he sat back down, I saw that the island was covered with piles of CDs, some in their cases, others scattered all over the place. "So this is your Valentine's Day gift?"

"One of them," he said, opening a case and taking out a disk. "It'll be, like, the third or fourth wave."

"Wave?"

"That's my V-day technique," he explained, sliding the disk into the side of his laptop. I heard a whirring, then some clicks, and the screen flickered. "Multiple gifts, given in order of escalating greatness, over the entire day. So, you know, you begin with flowers, then move to chocolates, maybe some balloons. This'll come after that, but before the gourmet dinner. I'm still tweaking the order."

"Right," I said glumly, sitting down across from him and picking up a Bob Dylan CD.

He glanced over at me. "What's wrong? Don't tell me you don't like Valentine's Day. *Everyone* likes Valentine's Day."

I considered disputing this, but as he'd said the same thing about Thanksgiving, Christmas, and New Year's, I figured it wasn't worth the argument. "I'm just kind of stuck," I said. "I need to get something for someone. . . ."

"Nate," he said, hitting a couple of buttons on the laptop. I looked up at him. "Ruby, come on. We're not that *dense*, you know. Plus half the house does look out at the pond, even at night."

I bit my lip, turning the CD case in my hands. "Anyway," I said, "I want it to be, like, this great gift. But I can't come up with anything."

"Because you're overthinking it," he said. "The best gifts come from the heart, not a store."

"This from the man who buys in waves."

"I'm not buying this," he pointed out, nodding at the laptop. "I mean, I bought the CDs, yeah. But the idea is from the heart."

"And what's the idea?"

"All the songs Cora loves to sing, in one place," he said, sounding pleased with himself. "It wasn't easy, let me tell you. I wrote up a list, then found them online or at the record store. For the really obscure ones, I had to enlist this guy one of my employees knows from his Anger Management class who's some kind of music freak. But now I finally have them all. 'Wasted Time,' 'Frankie and Johnny,' 'Don't Think Twice, It's All Right' . . ."

"'Angel from Montgomery,'" I said quietly.

"Exactly!" He grinned. "Hey, you can probably help me, now that I think of it. Just take a look at the list, and see if I'm missing anything."

He pushed a piece of paper across to me, and I glanced down at it, reading over the familiar titles of the songs my mom had always sung to me, listed in block print. "No," I said finally. "This is pretty much all of them."

"Great." He hit another button, taking out the CD and putting it on the counter as I pushed out my chair, getting to my feet. "Where you headed?"

"Shopping," I said, pulling my bag over my shoulder. "I have to find something phenomenal."

"You will," he replied. "Just remember: the heart! Start there, and you can't go wrong."

I remained unconvinced, however, especially once I got to the mall, where there were hearts everywhere: shaped into balloons and cookies, personalized on T-shirts, filled with chocolate and held by fuzzy teddy bears. But even after going into a dozen stores, I still couldn't find anything for Nate.

"Personally," Harriet said as I slumped onto her stool an hour later for a much-needed rest, "I think this holiday is a total crock, completely manufactured by the greeting-card companies. If you really love someone, you should show it every day, not just one."

"And yet," Reggie said, from his kiosk, "you are not averse to running a two-for-one Valentine's Day special on bracelets and assorted rings."

"Of course not!" she said. "I'm a businesswoman. As

long as the holiday exists, I might as well profit from it."

Reggie rolled his eyes and went back to stacking daily multis. "I just want to get something good," I said. "Something that *means* something."

"Just try to forget about it for a while," she replied, adjusting a rack of pendants. "Then, out of nowhere, the perfect gift will just come to you."

I looked at my watch. "I have about twenty-six hours. Not exactly a lot of time for inspiration to strike."

"Oh." She took a sip of her coffee. "Well, then I'd get him some of those macaroons you bought me at Christmas. Those you can't go wrong with."

In the end, though, it didn't come to that, although what I did end up with was almost as pathetic: a gift card to PLUG, the music store. It wasn't phenomenal, not even decent, and as I left the mall feeling thoroughly defeated, all I could hope was that Harriet was right, and I'd come up with something better in the short time I had remaining.

The next morning, though, this still hadn't happened, a fact made even more obvious when I came down for breakfast and walked right into Jamie's first wave. Four dozen roses in varying colors were arranged in vases all around the kitchen, each tied with a big white bow. Cora was at the counter, reading the card off of one of them, her face flushed, as I helped myself to coffee.

"He *always* overdoes it on Valentine's," she said, although she looked kind of choked up as she tucked the card into her purse. "The first year we were married, he got me a new car."

"Really," I said.

"Yep. Totally overwhelmed me." She sighed, picking up her mug. "It was so sweet, but I felt terrible. All I'd gotten him was a gift card."

I swallowed. "I have to go."

What I needed, I decided as I headed down the walkway to Nate's car ten minutes later, was to just stop thinking about Valentine's Day altogether. Which seemed easy, at least until I opened the car door and found myself face-to-face with a huge basketful of candy and flowers.

"Sorry," Nate said from somewhere behind the tiny balloons that were poking out of the top of it. "We're a little cramped in here. Do you mind holding that in your lap?"

I picked up the basket, then slid into the seat, pulling the door shut behind me. The instant it was closed, the smell of roses was overpowering, and as I shifted in my seat I saw why: the entire back was piled with baskets of assorted sizes, stacked three deep. "Where's Gervais?" I asked.

"I'm here," I heard a muffled voice say. A huge bunch of baby's breath shifted to one side, revealing his face. "And I think I'm having an allergic reaction."

"Just hang in there for a few more minutes," Nate told him, opening his window as we pulled away from the curb. His phone rang, rattling the console, and I peered around the flowers in my lap to look at him as he grabbed it, putting it to his ear. "Yeah," he said, slowing for the next light. "I'm on my way to school right now, so in ten or so I'll start down the list. Lakeview first, then over to the office complex. Right. Okay. Bye."

"You're not going to school today?" I asked as he hung up.

"Duty calls," he said, shutting his phone. "My dad got

a little overambitious with the response to the special, so we're pretty booked. We'll be lucky to get it all done, even with the two of us going all day."

"Really," I said quietly.

"Don't worry," he said as his phone rang again. "I'll be done in plenty of time for our thing tonight."

But this wasn't what I was worried about, and I wondered if he knew it. It was hard to tell, since he was talking to his dad again as he pulled up in front of Perkins Day, and Gervais and I extracted ourselves to disembark. As he headed off, sneezing, I put the basket I'd been holding back on the seat, then stood by the open door, waiting for Nate to hang up. Even as he did, he was already shifting back into gear, moving on.

"I gotta go," he said to me, over the flowers. "But I'll see you tonight, okay? Seven, at the pond. Don't be late."

I nodded and shut the door. He already had his phone back to his ear as he pulled into traffic. As he drove off, all I could see were a bunch of heart-shaped balloons in the back window, bobbing and swaying, first to one side, then back again.

* * *

Jamie and Cora were out for dinner—in the midst of a wave, no doubt—so I was alone, sitting at the kitchen table, my stupid gift card in hand, when the clock over the stove flipped to seven o'clock.

I stood up, sliding it into my pocket, then ran a hand through my hair as I stepped out onto the patio, Roscoe rousing himself from his dog bed to follow along behind me. Outside, the air was cold, the lights from Nate's pool and house visible over the fence.

Call it a bad feeling. Or just the logical conclusion to an unavoidable situation. But I think I knew, even before that first fifteen minutes passed with no sign of him, that he wasn't just late, something was wrong. Before my fingers—even jammed into the pockets of my new jacket—began to get numb, before Roscoe abandoned me for the warmth of the house, before another set of lights came up from the opposite side, lighting up the trees briefly before cutting off and leaving me in darkness again. It was eight fifteen when I saw Cora appear in the patio doorway, cupping a hand over her eyes. A moment later, she stuck her head out.

"Are you okay?" she said. "It's freezing out there."

"How was dinner?" I asked her.

"Fantastic." She glanced behind her at Jamie, who was walking into the kitchen with one of those leftover containers shaped into a swan. "You should hear this CD he made for me. It's—"

"I'll be in soon," I told her. "Just a couple more minutes."

She nodded slowly. "Okay," she said. "Don't wait too long, though."

But I already had. And not just that hour and fifteen minutes, but every moment that had passed since Thanksgiving, when I should have told Nate I couldn't just stand by and worry about him. Instead, though, I had let months pass, pushing down my better instincts, and now, sitting out in the February chill, I was getting exactly what I deserved.

When I finally went inside, I tried to distract myself

with homework and TV, but instead I kept looking over at Nate's house, and his window, which I could see clearly from my own. Behind the shade, I could see a figure moving back and forth. After a little while, it stopped, suddenly so still that I wondered if it was really anyone at all.

It was over an hour later when the phone rang. Cora and Jamie were downstairs, eating wave-two chocolates out of the box and listening to her CD, their voices and the music drifting up to me. I didn't even look at the caller ID, lying back on my bed instead, but then Jamie was calling my name. I looked at the receiver for a minute, then hit the TALK button. "Hello?"

"I know you're probably pissed," Nate said. "But meet me outside, okay?"

I didn't say anything, not that it mattered. He'd hung up, the dial tone already buzzing in my ear.

Billie Holiday was playing as I went downstairs and back outside, retracing my steps across the grass, which felt stiff and ungiving beneath my feet. This time, I didn't sit, instead crossing my arms over my chest as Nate emerged from the shadows. He had one hand behind his back, a smile on his face.

"Okay," he said, before he'd even gotten to me, "I know that me being over two hours late was not *exactly* the surprise you were expecting. But today was crazy, I just now got home, and I'll make it up to you. I promise."

We were in the swath of darkness between the lights from his house and those of Cora's, so it was hard to make out all the details of his face. But even so, I could tell there was something off: a nervous quality, something almost jittery. "You've been home," I told him. "I saw your light was on."

"Yeah, but we had stuff to do," he said easily, although now he was slowing his steps. "I had to put things away, get the accounts all settled. And then, you know, I had to wrap this."

He pulled his hand out from behind his back, extending a small box to me, tied with a simple bow. "Nate," I said.

"Go ahead," he told me. "It won't make it all better. But it might help a little bit."

I took the box but didn't open it. Instead, I sat down on the bench, holding it between my knees, and a moment later he came and sat down beside me. Now closer, I could see his neck was flushed, the skin pink around his collar. "I know you've been home for a couple of hours," I said quietly. "What was going on over there?"

He slid one leg over the bench, turning to face me. "Nothing. Hey, we've got two hours left of Valentine's Day. So just open your gift, and let's make the most of it."

"I don't want a gift," I said, and my voice sounded harsher than I meant it to. "I want you to tell me what happened to you tonight."

"I got held up dealing with my dad," he replied. "That's all."

"That's all," I repeated.

"What else do you want me to say?"

"Do you understand how worried I've been about you? How I've sat over here all night, looking at your house, wondering if you're okay?"

"I'm fine," he said. "I'm here now. With you, on Valentine's Day, which is the only place I've wanted to be all day. And now that I *am* here, I can think of a million things I'd rather talk about than my dad."

I shook my head, looking out over the water.

"Like," he continued, putting his hands on either side of me, "my gift, for instance. Word on the street is that it's phenomenal."

"It's not," I said flatly. "It's a gift card, and it sucks."

He sat back slightly, studying my face. "Okay," he said slowly. "So maybe we shouldn't talk."

With this, I could feel him moving closer, and then his lips were on my ear, moving down my neck. Normally, this was enough to push everything away, at least temporarily, the sudden and indisputable closeness that made all other distance irrelevant. Tonight, though, was different. "Stop," I said, pulling back and raising my hands between us. "Okay? Just stop."

"What's wrong?"

"What's wrong?" I repeated. "Look, you can't just come here and tell me everything's fine and kiss me and just expect me to go along with it."

"So," he said slowly, "you're saying you don't want me to kiss you."

"I'm saying you can't have it both ways," I told him. "You can't act like you care about someone but not let them care about you."

"I'm not doing that."

"You are, though," I said. He looked away, shaking his head. "Look, when we first met, you practically made a practice of saving my ass. That night at the fence, coming to pick me up at Jackson—"

"That was different."

"Why? Because it was me, not you?" I asked. "What, you think just because you help people and make their lives easier that you're somehow better and don't need help yourself?"

"I don't."

"So it's just fine that your dad yells at you and pushes you around."

"What happens between me and my dad is private," he said. "It's a family thing."

"So was my living alone in that place you called a slum," I told him. "Are you saying you would have left me there if I had told you to? Or in the clearing that day?"

Nate immediately started to say something in response to this, then let out a breath instead.

Finally, I thought. *I'm getting through.*

"I don't understand," he said, "why these two things always have to be connected."

"What two things?" I said.

"Me and my dad, and me and everyone else." He shook his head. "They're not the same thing. Not even close."

It was that word—*always*—that did it, nudging a memory loose in my brain. Me and Heather, that day over the fish. *You never know*, she'd said, when I'd told her one more friend would hardly make a difference. The sad way he looked at her, all those mornings walking to the green, so many rumors, and maybe none of them true. "So that's why you and Heather broke up," I said slowly. "It wasn't that she couldn't take what was happening. It was not being able to help you."

Nate looked down at his hands, not saying anything. Here I'd thought Heather and I were so different. But we, too, had something in common, all along.

"Just tell someone what's going on," I said. "Your mom, or—"

"I can't," he said. "There's no point. Don't you understand that?"

This was the same thing he'd asked me, all those weeks ago, and I'd told him yes. But now, here, we differed. Nate might not have thought that whatever was happening with his dad affected anything else, but I knew, deep in my heart, that this wasn't true. My mother, wherever she was, still lingered with me: in the way I carried myself, the things that scared me, and the way I'd reacted the last time I'd been faced with this question. Which was why this time, my answer had to be no.

But first, I lifted my hand, putting it on his chest, right over where I'd noticed his skin was flushed earlier. He closed his eyes, leaning into my palm, and I could feel him, warm, as I slowly pushed his shirt aside. Again, call it a bad feeling, a hunch, or whatever—but there, on his shoulder, the skin was not just pink but red and discolored, a broad bruise just beginning to rise. "Oh, Jesus," I said, my voice catching. "Nate."

He moved closer, covering my hand with his, squeezing it, and then he was kissing me again, sudden and intense, as if trying to push down these words and everything that had prompted them. It was so hungry and so good that I was almost able to forget all that had led up to it. But not quite.

"No," I said, pulling back. He stayed where he was, his mouth inches from mine, but I shook my head. "I can't."

"Ruby," he said. Even as I heard this, though, breaking my heart, I could see his shirt, still pushed aside, the reason undeniable.

"Only if you let me help you," I said. "You have to let me in."

He pulled back, shaking his head. Over his shoulder, I could see the lights of the pool flickering—otherworldy, alien. "And if I don't?" he said.

I swallowed, hard. "Then no," I told him. "Then go."

For a moment, I thought he wouldn't. That this, finally, more than all the words, would be what changed his mind. But then he was pushing himself to his feet, his shirt sliding back, space now between us, everything reverting to how it had been before. *You don't have to make it so hard,* I wanted to say, but there was a time I hadn't believed this, either. Who was I to tell anyone how to be saved? Only the girl who had tried every way not to be.

"Nate," I called out, but he was already walking away, his head ducked, back toward the trees. I sat there, watching him as he folded into them, disappearing.

A lump rose in my throat as I stood up. The gift he'd brought was still on the bench, and I picked it up, examining the rose-colored paper, the neatly tied bow. So pretty on the surface, it almost didn't matter what was inside.

When I went back in the house, I tried to keep my face

composed, thinking only of getting up to my room, where I could be alone. But just as I started up the stairs, Cora came out of the living room, where her CD was still playing—Janis Joplin now—the chocolate box in her hands. "Hey, do you want—?" she said, then stopped suddenly. "Are you all right?"

I started to say yes, of course, but before I could, my eyes filled with tears. As I turned to the wall and sucked down a breath, trying to steady myself, I felt her come closer. "Hey," she said, smoothing my hair gently off my shoulder. "What's wrong?"

I swallowed, reaching up to wipe my eyes. "Nothing."

"Tell me."

Two words, said so easily. But even as I thought this, I heard myself doing it. "I just don't know," I said, my voice sounding bumpy, not like mine, "how you help someone who doesn't want your help. What do you do when you can't do anything?"

She was quiet for a moment, and in that silence I was bracing myself, knowing the next question would be harder, pulling me deeper. "Oh, Ruby," she said instead, "I know. I know it's hard."

More tears were coming now, my vision blurring. "I—"

"I should have known this CD would remind you of all that," she said. "Of course it would—that was stupid of me. But Mom's not your responsibility anymore, okay? We can't do anything for her. So we have to take care of each other, all right?"

My mother. Of course she would think that was what

I was talking about. What else could there be? What other loss would I ever face comparable to it? None. None at all.

Cora was behind me, still talking. Through my tears, I could hear her saying it was all going to be okay, and I knew she believed this. But I was sure of something, too: it's a lot easier to be lost than found. It's the reason we're always searching, and rarely discovered—so many locks, not enough keys.

Chapter Fifteen

"So as you can see," Harriet said, moving down the kiosk with a wave of her hand, "I work mostly in silver, using gemstones as accents. Occasionally I've done things with gold, but I find it's less inspiring to me."

"Right," the reporter replied, scribbling this down as her photographer, a tall guy with a mustache, repositioned one of the key necklaces on the rack before taking another shot. "And how long have you been in business at this location?"

"Six years." As the woman wrote this down, Harriet, a nervous expression on her face, glanced over at Vitamin Me, where I was standing with Reggie. I flashed her a thumbs-up, and she nodded, then turned back to the reporter.

"She's doing great," Reggie said, continuing work on his pyramid of omega-3 bottles, the centerpiece of his GET FISH, GET FIT display. "I don't know why she was so nervous."

"Because she's Harriet," I told him. "She always nervous."

He sighed, adding another bottle to the stack. "It's the caffeine. If she'd give it up, her whole life would change. I'm convinced of it."

The truth was, Harriet's life *was* changing, though coffee had nothing to do with it. Instead, it was the KeyChains—as she'd taken to calling them since Christmas—which were now outselling everything else we carried, sparking some-what of a local phenomenon. Suddenly we had shoppers coming from several towns over, seeking them out, not to mention multiple phone calls from people in other states, asking if we did mail order (yes) or had a Web site (in the works, up any day). When she wasn't fielding calls or requests, Harriet was busy making more keys, adding shapes and sizes and different gems, as well as experimenting with expanding the line to bracelets and rings. The more she made, the more she sold. These days, it seemed like every girl at my school was wearing one, which was kind of weird, to say the least.

This reporter was from the style section of the local paper, and Harriet had been getting ready all week, making new pieces and working both of us overtime to make sure the kiosk looked perfect. Now, Reggie and I watched as—at the reporter's prompting—she posed beside it, a KeyChain studded with rhinestones around her neck, smiling for the camera.

"Look at her," I said. "She's a superstar."

"That she is," Reggie replied, adding another bottle to his stack. "But it's not because she's suddenly famous. Harriet's always been special."

He said this so easily, so matter-of-factly, that it kind of broke my heart. "You know," I said to him as he opened another box, "you could tell her that. How you feel, I mean."

"Oh, I have," he replied.

"You have? When?"

"Over Christmas." He picked up a bottle of shark-cartilage capsules, examining it, then set it aside. "We went down to Garfield's one night after closing, for drinks. I had a couple of margaritas, and the next thing I knew . . . it was all out."

"And?"

"Total bust," he said, sighing. "She said she's not in a relationship place right now."

"A relationship place?" I repeated.

"That's what she said." He emptied the box, folding it. "The KeyChains are selling so well, she's got to focus on her career, maybe expanding to her own store someday. Eye on the ball, and all that."

"Reggie," I said softly. "That sucks."

"It's okay," he replied. "I've known Harriet a long time. She's not much for attachments."

I looked over at Harriet again. She was laughing, her face flushed, as the photographer took another picture. "She doesn't know what she's missing."

"That's very nice of you to say," Reggie replied, as if I'd complimented his shirt. "But sometimes, we just have to be happy with what people can offer us. Even if it's not what we want, at least it's something. You know?"

I nodded, even though it was exactly what I didn't believe, at least not since Nate and I had argued on Valentine's Day. The space I'd once claimed to want between us was now not just present, but vast. Whatever it was we'd had—something, nothing, anything—it was over.

As a result, so was my involvement in the carpool, which I'd decided to opt out of after a couple of very silent and very awkward rides. In the end, I'd dug out my old bus schedules, set my alarm, and decided to take advantage of the fact that my calculus teacher, Ms. Gooden, was an early bird who offered hands-on help before first bell. Then I asked Gervais to pass this information along to Nate, which he did. If Nate was surprised, he didn't show it. But then again, he wasn't letting on much these days, to me or anyone.

I still had the gift he'd given me, if only because I couldn't figure out a way to return it that wasn't totally awkward. So it sat, wrapped and bow intact, on my dresser, until I finally stuffed it into a drawer. You would think it would bother me, not knowing what was inside, but it didn't, really. Maybe I'd just figured out there were some things you were better off not knowing.

As for Nate himself, from what I could tell, he was always working. Like most seniors in spring semester—i.e., those who hadn't transferred from other schools with not-so-great grades they desperately needed to keep up in order to have any chance at college acceptance—he had a pretty light schedule, as well as a lot of leeway for activities. While most people spent this time lolling on the green between classes or taking long coffee runs to Jump Java, whenever I saw Nate, either in the neighborhood or at school, he seemed to be in constant motion, often loaded down with boxes, his phone pressed to his ear as he moved to and from his car. I figured Rest Assured had to be picking up, business-wise, although his work seemed even more ironic to me than ever. All that helping, saving, taking care. As if these were the only two options, when you had that kind of home life: either caring about yourself and no one else, like I had, or only about the rest of the world, as he did now.

I'd been thinking about this lately every time I passed

the HELP table, where Heather Wainwright was set up as usual, accepting donations or petition signatures. Ever since Thanksgiving, I'd sort of held it against her that she'd broken up with Nate, thinking she'd abandoned him, but now, for obvious reasons, I was seeing things differently. So much so that more than once, I'd found myself pausing and taking a moment to look over whatever cause she was lobbying for. Usually, she was busy talking to other people and just smiled at me, telling me to let her know if I had any questions. One day, though, as I perused some literature about saving the coastline, it was just the two of us.

"It's a good cause," she said as I flipped past some pages illustrating various stages of sand erosion. "We can't just take our beaches for granted."

"Right," I said. "I guess not."

She sat back, twirling a pen in her hand. Finally, after a moment, she said, "So . . . how's Nate doing?"

I shut the brochure. "I wouldn't really know," I said. "We're kind of on the outs these days."

"Oh," she said. "Sorry."

"No, it's okay," I said. "It's just . . . it got hard. You know?"

I wasn't expecting her to respond to this, really. But then she put her pen down. "His dad," she said, clarifying. I nodded, and she smiled sadly, shaking her head. "Well, I hate to tell you, but if you think keeping your distance makes it easier not to worry . . . it doesn't. Not really."

"Yeah," I said, looking down at the brochure again. "I'm kind of getting that."

"For me, the worst was just watching him change, you know?" She sighed, brushing her hair back from her face.

"Like with quitting swim team. That was his entire world. But in the end, he gave it up, because of this."

"He gave you up, too," I said. "Right?"

"Yeah." She sighed. "I guess so."

Across the green, there was a sudden burst of laughter, and we both looked in its direction. As it ended, she said, "Look, for what it's worth, I think I could have tried harder. To stick by him, or force the issue. I kind of wish I had."

"You do?"

"I think he would have done it for me," she said. "And that's been the hardest part of all of this, really. That maybe I failed him, or myself, somehow. You know?"

I nodded. "Yeah," I said. "I do."

"So," a dark-haired girl with a ponytail said to Heather, sliding into the empty seat beside her. "I just spent, like, a half hour working on Mr. Thackray, and he's finally agreed to let us plug our fund-raiser again this afternoon during announcements. I'm thinking we should write some new copy, though, to really make an impact, like . . ."

I started to move down the table, our conversation clearly over. "Take care, Ruby," Heather called after me.

"You, too," I told her. As she turned back to the girl, who was still talking, I reached into my pocket, pulling out the few dollars' change from my lunch and stuffing it into the SAVE OUR BEACHES! jar. It wasn't much, in the grand scheme of things. But it made me feel somewhat better, nonetheless.

Also slightly encouraging was the fact that while I hadn't been of help to Nate, I didn't have to look far to find someone who *had* benefited from my actions. Not now that Gervais was front and center, at my picnic table, every weekday from 12:05 to 1:15.

"Again," he said to me, pointing at the book with his pencil, "remember the power rule. It's the key to everything you're trying to do here."

I sighed, trying to clear my head. The truth was, Gervais was a good tutor. Already, I understood tons more than I had before he'd begun working with me, stuff even my early-morning help sessions couldn't make sense of. But there were still distractions. Initially, it had been me worrying about how he'd interact with Olivia, whether he'd act so goopy or lovesick she'd immediately suspect something, and rightfully blame me. As it turned out, though, this wasn't an issue at all. If anything, I was a third wheel now.

"The power rule," Olivia recited, flipping her phone open. "The derivative of any given variable (x) to the exponent (n) is equal to product of the exponent and the variable to the (n–1) power."

I just looked at her. "Exactly right," Gervais said, beaming. "See? Olivia gets it."

Of course she did. Olivia was apparently a whiz at calculus, something she had neglected to mention the entire time we'd been sharing our lunch hour. Now that Gervais had joined us, though, they were in math heaven. That is, when they weren't talking about one of the other myriad, inexplicable things they had in common, including but not limited to a love of movies, the pros and cons of various college majors, and, of course, picking on me.

"What exactly is going on with you two?" I'd asked her

recently after one of Gervais's visits, which I had spent alternately struggling with the power rule and sitting by, open-mouthed, as they riffed on the minute details of a recent sci-fi blockbuster, down to the extra scenes after the credits.

"What do you mean?" she asked. We were crossing the green. "He's a nice kid."

"Look, I have to be honest," I told her. "He likes you."

"I know."

She said this so simply, so matter-of-factly, that I almost stopped walking. "You know?"

"Sure. I mean, it's kind of obvious, right?" she said. "He was always hanging around the theater when I was working. Not exactly slick."

"He wants to be friends with you," I told her. "He asked me to help him do it."

"Did you?"

"No," I said. "But I did tell him he could help me with my calculus at lunch. And that you might, you know, be there."

I kind of spit this last part out, as I was already bracing myself for her reaction. To my surprise, though, she seemed hardly bothered. "Like I said," she said with a shrug, "he's a nice kid. And it's got to be tough for him here, you know?"

Ah, I thought, remembering back to what she'd said to me about having things in common. Who knew Gervais would count, too? "Yeah," I said. "I guess you're right."

"Plus," she continued, "he knows nothing is going to happen between us."

"Are you *sure* he knows that?"

Now she stopped walking, narrowing her eyes at me. "What?" she said. "Do you think I'm not capable of being clear?"

I shook my head. "No. You are."

"That's right." She started walking again. "We both know the limits of this relationship. It's understood. And as long as we're both comfortable with that, nobody gets hurt. It's basic."

Basic, I thought. *Just like the power rule.*

Calculus aside, I had surprised myself by not only keeping up my end of the deal I'd made with Jamie but actually feeling slightly confident as I sent off my applications back at the end of January. Because of ongoing worries about my GPA, I'd done all I could to strengthen the rest of my material, from my essays to my recommendations. In the end, I'd applied to three schools: the U, Cora's alma mater and one town over; a smaller, more artsy college in the mountains called Slater-Kearns; and one long shot, Defriese University, in D.C. According to Mrs. Pureza, my guidance counselor, all three were known to take a second look at "unique" students like myself. Which meant I might actually have a chance, a thought that at times scared the hell out of me. I'd been looking ahead to the future for so long, practically my entire life. Now that it was close, though, I found myself hesitant, not so sure I was ready.

There was still a lot of the year to go, though, which I reminded myself was a good thing whenever I surveyed what I had done so far on my English project. One day, in a burst of organization I'd hoped would lead to inspiration, I'd spread out everything I had on the desk in my room: stacks of notes, Post-its with quotes stuck up on the wall above, the books I'd used as research—pages marked—piled on either side. Lately, after dinner or when I wasn't working, I'd sit down and go through it bit by bit waiting for that spark.

So far, no luck. In fact, the only thing that ever made me feel somewhat close was the picture of Jamie's family, which I'd taken from the kitchen and tacked up on the wall, right at eye level. I'd spent hours, it felt like, sitting there looking over each individual face, as if one of them might suddenly have what I was searching for. *What is family?* For me, right then, it was one person who'd left me, and two I would have to leave soon. Maybe this was an answer. But it wasn't the right one. Of that, I was sure.

Now, I heard Harriet call my name, jerking me back to the mall, and the present. When I looked up, she was waving me over to the kiosk, where she was standing with the reporter.

"This is my assistant, Ruby Cooper," she said to the reporter as I walked up. "She had on that necklace the day I hired her, and it was my inspiration."

As both the photographer and the reporter immediately turned their attention to my key, I fought not to reach up and cover it, digging my hands into my pockets instead. "Interesting," the reporter said, making a note on her pad. "And what was *your* inspiration, Ruby? What compelled you to start wearing your key like that?"

Talk about being put on the spot. "I . . . I don't know," I said. "I guess I just got tired of always losing it."

The reporter wrote this down, then glanced at the photographer, who was still snapping some shots of the necklaces. "I think that ought to do it," she said to Harriet. "Thanks for your time."

"Thank you," Harriet said. When they'd walked away, she whirled around to face me. "Oh my God. I was a nervous wreck. You think I did all right?"

"You were great," I told her.

"Better than," Reggie added. "Cool as a cuke."

Harriet sat down on her stool, wiping a hand over her face. "They said it will probably run on Sunday, which would be huge. Can you imagine if this gives us an even bigger boost? I can barely keep up with orders as it is."

This was typical Harriet. Even the good stuff meant worrying. "You'll do fine," Reggie said. "You have good help."

"Oh, I know," Harriet said, smiling at me. "It's just . . . a little overwhelming, is all. But I guess I can get Rest Assured to do more, too. Blake's been pushing me to do that anyway. You know, shipping, handling some of the Web site stuff, all that. . . ."

"Just try to enjoy this right now," Reggie told her. "It's a good thing."

I could understand where Harriet was coming from, though. Whenever something great happens, you're always kind of poised for the universe to correct itself. Good begets bad, something lost leads to found, and on and on. But even knowing this, I was surprised when I came home later that afternoon to find Cora and Jamie sitting at the kitchen table, the phone between them. As they both turned to look at me, right away I knew something was wrong.

"Ruby," Cora said. Her voice was soft. Sad. "It's about Mom."

* * *

My mother was not in Florida. She was not on a boat with Warner or soaking up sun or waiting tables in a beachside pancake joint. She was in a rehab clinic, where she'd ended up two weeks earlier after being found unconscious by a maid in the hotel where she'd been living in Tennessee.

At first, I was sure she was dead. So sure, in fact, that as Cora began to explain all this, I felt like my own heart stopped, only beating again once these few words—*hotel, unconscious, rehab, Tennessee*—unscrambled themselves in my mind. When she was done, the only thing I could say was, "She's okay?"

Cora glanced at Jamie, then back at me. "She's in treatment," she said. "She has a long way to go. But yes, she's okay."

It should have made me feel better now that I knew where she was, that she was safe. At the same time, the thought of her in a hospital, locked up, gave me a weird, shaky feeling in my stomach, and I made myself take in a breath. "Was she alone?" I asked.

"What?" Cora said.

"When they found her. Was she alone?"

She nodded. "Was . . . Should someone have been with her?"

Yes, I thought. *Me.* I felt a lump rise up in my throat, sudden and throbbing. "No," I said. "I mean, she had a boyfriend when she left."

She and Jamie exchanged another look, and I had a flash of the last time I'd come back to find them waiting for me in this same place. Then, I'd caught a glimpse of myself in the mirror and seen my mother, or at least some part of her—bedraggled, half-drunk, messed up. But at least someone had been expecting me. No one was picking up my mom from the side of the road, getting her home safe. It was probably only coincidence—a maid's schedule, one room, one day—that got her found in time.

And now she was found, no longer lost. Like a bag I'd given up for good suddenly reappearing in the middle of the night on my doorstep, packed for a journey I'd long ago forgotten. It was odd, considering I'd gotten accustomed to her being nowhere and anywhere, to finally know where my mother was. An exact location, pinpointed. Like she'd crossed over from my imagination, where I'd created a million lives for her, back into this one.

"So what . . ." I said, then swallowed. "What happens now?"

"Well," Cora replied, "the initial treatment program is ninety days. After that, she has some decisions to make. Ideally, she'd stay on, in some kind of supported environment. But it's really up to her."

"Did you talk to her?" I asked.

She shook her head. "No."

"Then how did you hear?"

"From her last landlords. The hospital couldn't find anyone to contact, so they ran a records search, their name came up, and they called us." She turned to Jamie. "What was their name? Huntington?"

"Honeycutt," I said. Already they'd popped into my head, Alice with her elfin looks, Ronnie in his sensible plaid. *Stranger danger!* she'd said that first day, but how weird that they were now the ones that led me back not only to Cora but to my mother, as well.

I felt my face get hot; suddenly, it was all too much. I looked around me, trying to calm down, but all I could see was this clean, lovely foyer, in this perfect neighborhood, all the things that had risen up in my mother's absence, settling into the space made when she left.

"Ruby," Jamie said. "It's all right, okay? Nothing's going to change. In fact, Cora wasn't even sure we should tell you, but—"

I looked at my sister, still seated, the phone in her hands. "But we did," she said, keeping her eyes steady on me. "That said, you have no obligation to her. You need to know that. What happens next with you and Mom, or even if anything does, is up to you."

As it turned out, though, this wasn't exactly true. We soon found out that the rehab place where my mother was staying—and which Cora and Jamie were paying for, although I didn't learn that until later—had a strong policy of patient-focused treatment. Simply put, this meant no outside contact with family or friends, at least not initially. No phone calls. No e-mails. If we sent letters, they'd be kept until a date to be decided later. "It's for the best," Cora told me, after explaining this. "If she's going to do this, she needs to do it on her own."

At that point, we didn't even know if my mom would stay in the program at all, as she hadn't exactly gone willingly. Once they resuscitated her at the hospital, the police found some outstanding bad-check warrants, so she'd had to choose: rehab or jail. I would have had more faith if she'd gone of her own accord. But at least she was there.

Nothing's going to change, Jamie had said that day, but I'd known even then this wasn't true. My mother had always been the point that I calibrated myself against. In knowing where she was, I could always locate myself, as well. These months she'd been gone, I felt like I'd been floating, loose and boundaryless, but now that I knew where she was, I kept waiting for a kind of certainty to kick in. It didn't. Instead, I was more unsure than ever, stuck between this new life and the one I'd left behind.

The fact that this had all happened so soon after Nate and I had fallen out of touch seemed ironic, to say the least. At the same time, though, I was beginning to wonder if this was just how it was supposed to be for me, like perhaps I wasn't capable of having that many people in my life at any one time. My mom turned up, Nate walked away, one door opening as another clicked shut.

As the days passed, I tried to forget about my mom, the way I'd managed to do before, but it was harder now. This was partly because she wasn't lost anymore, but there was also the fact that everywhere I went—school, work, just walking down the street—I saw people wearing Harriet's KeyChains, each one sparkling and pretty, a visible reminder of this, my new life. But the original was there as well—more jaded and rudimentary, functional rather than romantic. It fit not just the yellow house but another door, deep within my own heart. One that had been locked so tight for so long that I was afraid to even try it for fear of what might be on the other side.

Chapter Sixteen

"So basically," Olivia said, "you dig a hole and fill it with water, then throw in some fish."

"No," I said. "First, you have to install a pump system and a skimmer. And bring in rocks and plants, and do something to guard it against birds, who want to eat the fish. And that's not even counting all the water treatments and algae prevention."

She considered this as she leaned forward, peering down into the pond. "Well," she said, "to me, that seems like a lot of trouble. Especially for something you can't even swim in."

Olivia and I were taking a study break from working on our English projects, ostensibly so I could introduce to her to Jamie, who'd been out puttering around the pond, the way he always did on Saturday mornings. When we'd come out, though, he'd been called over to the fence by Mr. Cross, and now, fifteen minutes later, they were still deep in discussion. Judging by the way Jamie kept inching closer to us, bit by bit—as well as the fact that Nate's dad seemed to be doing all the talking—I had a feeling he was trying to extricate himself, although he'd had little luck thus far.

"Then again," Olivia said, sitting back down on the bench, "with a spread like this, you could have a pond *and* a pool, if you wanted."

"True," I agreed. "But it might be overkill."

"Not in this neighborhood," she said. "I mean, honestly. Did you see those boulders when you come in? What is this supposed to be, Stonehenge?"

I smiled. Over by the fence, Jamie took another step backward, nodding in that all-right-then-see-you-later kind of way. Mr. Cross, not getting the hint—or maybe just choosing not to—came closer, bridging the gap again.

"You know, he looks familiar," Olivia said, nodding toward them.

"That's Nate's dad," I told her.

"No, I meant your brother-in-law. I swear, I've seen him somewhere."

"He donated some soccer fields to Perkins," I told her.

"Maybe that's it," she said. Still, she kept her eyes on them as she said, "So Nate lives right there, huh?"

"I told you we were neighbors."

"Yeah, but I didn't realize he was right behind you, only a few feet away. Must make this stalemate—or breakup— you two are in the midst of that much harder."

"It's not a stalemate," I told her. "Or a breakup."

"So you just went from basically hanging out constantly, pretty much on the verge of dating, to not speaking and totally ignoring each other for no reason," she said. "Yeah. *That* makes sense."

"Do we have to talk about this?" I asked as Jamie took another definitive step backward from Mr. Cross, lifting his hand. Mr. Cross was still talking, although this time he stayed where he was.

"You know," Olivia said, "it's pretty rare to find someone

you actually *like* to be with in this world. There are a lot of annoying people out there."

"Really?"

She made a face at me. "My point is, clearly you two had something. So maybe you should think about going to a little trouble to work this out, whatever it is."

"Look," I said, "you said yourself that relationships only work when there's an understanding about the limits. We didn't have that. So now we don't have a relationship."

She considered this for a moment. "Nice," she said. "I especially like how you explained that without actually telling me anything."

"The bottom line is that I just get where you're coming from now, okay?" I said. "You don't want to waste your time on anything or anyone you don't believe in, and neither do I."

"You think that's how I am?" she asked.

"Are you saying it's not?"

Jamie was crossing the yard to us, finally free. He lifted a hand, waving hello. "I'm not saying anything," Olivia replied, leaning back again and shaking her head. "Nothing at all."

"Ladies," Jamie said, ever the happy host as he came up to the bench. "Enjoying the pond?"

"It's very nice," Olivia said politely. "I like the skimmer."

I just looked at her, but Jamie, of course, beamed. "Jamie, this is my friend Olivia," I said.

"Nice to meet you," he said, sticking out his hand.

They shook, and then he crouched down at the edge of the pond, reaching his hand down into the water. As he scooped some up, letting it run over his fingers, Olivia suddenly gasped. "Oh my God. I know where I know you from!" she said. "You're the UMe guy!"

Jamie looked at her, then at me. "Um," he said. "Yeah. I guess I am."

"You recognize him from UMe?" I asked.

"Hello, he's only on the new sign-in page, which I see, like, ten million times a day," she said. She shook her head, clearly still in shock. "Man, I can't believe this. And Ruby never even said anything."

"Well, you know," Jamie said, pushing himself back to his feet, "Ruby is not easily impressed."

Unlike Olivia, who now, as I watched, incredulous, began to actually gush. "Your site," she said to Jamie, putting a hand to her chest, "saved my *life* when I had to switch schools."

"Yeah?" Jamie said, obviously pleased.

"Totally. I spent every lunch in the library on my UMe page messaging with my old friends. And, of course, all night, too." She sighed, wistful. "It was, like, my only connection with them."

"You still had your phone," I pointed out.

"I can check my page on that, too!" To Jamie she said, "Nice application, by the way. Very user friendly."

"You think? We've had some complaints."

"Oh, please." Olivia flipped her hand. "It's easy. Now, the friends system? *That* needs work. I hate it."

"You do?" Jamie said. "Why?"

"Well," she said, "for starters, there's no way to search through them easily. So if you have a lot, and you want to reorganize, you have to just keep scrolling, which takes forever."

I thought of my own UMe.com page, untouched all these months. "How many friends do you have, anyway?" I asked her.

"A couple of thousand," she replied. I just looked at her. "What? Online, I'm popular."

"Obviously," I said.

Later, when Olivia had gone—taking with her a promotional UMe.Com messenger bag packed with UMe.com stickers and T-shirts—I found Jamie in the kitchen, marinating some chicken for dinner. As I came in, the phone began to ring: I went to grab it, but after glancing at the caller ID, he shook his head. "Just let the voice mail get it."

I looked at the display screen, which said CROSS, BLAKE. "You're screening Mr. Cross?"

"Yeah," he said with a sigh, dribbling some olive oil over the chicken and shaking the pan slightly. "I don't want to. But he's being really persistent about this investment thing, so . . ."

"What investment thing?"

He glanced up at me, as if not sure whether or not he wanted to expound on this. Then he said, "Well, you know. Blake's kind of a wheeler-dealer. He's always got some grand plan in the works."

I thought of Mr. Cross that morning, practically stalking Jamie in the yard. "And he wants to do a deal with you?"

"Sort of," he said, going over to the cabinet above the stove and opening it, then rummaging through the contents.

After a minute, he pulled out a tall bottle of vinegar. "He says he wants to expand his business and is looking for silent partners, but really I think he's just short on cash, like last time."

I watched him add a splash of vinegar, then bend down and sniff the chicken before adding more. "So this has happened before."

He nodded, capping the bottle. "Last year, a few months after we moved in. We had him over, you know, for a neighborly drink, and we got to talking. Next thing I know, I'm getting the whole epic saga about his hard financial luck—none of which was his fault, of course—and how he was about to turn it all around with this new venture. Which turned out to be the errand-running thing."

Roscoe came out of the laundry room, where he'd been enjoying one of his many daily naps. Seeing us, he yawned, then headed for the dog door, vaulting himself through it, and it shut with a *thwack* behind him.

"Did you see that?" Jamie said, smiling. "Change is possible!"

I nodded. "It is impressive."

We both watched Roscoe go out into the yard and lift his leg against a tree, relieving himself. Never had a simple act resulted in such pride. "Anyway," Jamie said, "in the end I gave him a check, bought in a bit to the business. It wasn't that much, really, but when your sister found out, she hit the roof."

"Cora did?"

"Oh, yeah," he said. "She's been off him from the start, for some reason. She claims it's because he always talks about money, but my uncle Ronald does that, too, and him she loves. So go figure."

I didn't have to, though. In fact, I was pretty sure I knew exactly why Cora didn't like Mr. Cross, even if she herself couldn't put her finger on it.

"Anyway," Jamie said, "now Blake's scrambling again, I guess. He's been hounding me about this new billing idea and the money ever since Thanksgiving, when I asked him about borrowing his oven. I keep putting him off, but man, he's tenacious. I guess he figures since I'm a sucker, he can pull me in again."

I had a flash of Olivia on the curb, using this same word. "You're not a sucker. You're just nice. You give people the benefit of the doubt."

"Usually to my detriment," he said as the phone rang again. We both looked at it: CROSS, BLAKE. The message light was already beeping. "However," he continued, "other times, people even surpass my expectations. Like you, for instance."

"Does this mean you're going to give me a check?" I asked.

"No," he said flatly. I smiled. "But I am proud of you, Ruby. You've come a long way."

Later, up in my room, I kept thinking about this, the idea of distance and accomplishment. The further you go, the more you have to be proud of. At the same time, in order to come a long way, you have to be behind to begin with. In the end, though, maybe it's not how you reach a place that matters. Just that you get there at all.

* * *

Middle-school girls, I had learned, moved in packs. If you saw them coming, the best thing to do was step aside and save yourself.

"Look, you guys! These are the ones I was telling you about!" a brown-haired girl wearing all pink, clearly the leader of this particular group, said as they swarmed the kiosk, going straight for the KeyChains. "Oh my God. My brother's girlfriend has this one, with the pink stones. Isn't it great?"

"I like the diamond one," a chubby blonde in what looked like leather pants said. "It's the prettiest."

"That's not a diamond," the girl in pink told her as their two friends—twins, by the look of their matching red hair and similar features—moved down to the bracelets. "Otherwise, it would be, like, a million dollars."

"It's diamonelle," Harriet corrected her, "and very reasonably priced at twenty-five."

"Personally," the brunette said, draping the pink-stoned one across her V-necked sweater, "I like the plain silver. It's classic, befitting my new, more streamlined, eco-chic look."

"Eco-chic?" I said.

"Environmentally friendly," the girl explained. "Green? You know, natural metals, non-conflict stones, minimal but with big impact? All the celebrities are doing it. Don't you read *Vogue*?"

"No," I told her.

She shrugged, taking off the necklace, then moved down the kiosk to her friends, who were now gathered around the rings, quickly dismantling the display I'd just spent a good twenty minutes organizing. "You would think," I said to Harriet as we watched them take rings on and off, "that they could at least try to put them back. Or pretend to."

"Oh, let them make a mess," she said. "It's not that big a deal cleaning it up."

"Says the person who doesn't have to do it."

She raised her eyebrows at me, walking over to take her coffee off the register. "Okay," she said slowly. "You're in a bad mood. What gives?"

"I'm sorry," I said as the girls finally moved on, leaving rings scattered across the counter behind them. I went over and began to put them away. "I think I'm just stressed or something."

"Well, it kind of makes sense," Harriet said, coming over to join me. She put an onyx ring back in place, a red one beside it. "You're in your final semester, waiting to hear about college, the future is wide open. But that doesn't necessarily have to get you all bent out of shape. You could look at it as, you know, a great opportunity to embrace stepping out of your comfort zone."

I stopped what I was doing, narrowing my eyes at her as she filled out another row of rings, calm as you please. "Excuse me?" I said.

"What?"

I just looked at her, waiting for her to catch the irony. She didn't. "Harriet," I said finally, "how long did you have that HELP WANTED sign up before you hired me?"

"Ah," she said, pointing at me, "but I *did* hire you, right?"

"And how long did it take you to leave me alone here, to run the kiosk myself?"

"Okay, so I was hesitant," she admitted. "However, I

think you'll agree that I now leave you fairly often with little trepidation."

I considered pointing out that the *fairly* and *little* spoke volumes. Instead I said, "What about Reggie?"

She wiped her hands on her pants, then moved down to the KeyChains, adjusting the pink one on the rack. "What about him?"

"He told me what happened at Christmas," I said. "What was it you said? That you weren't in a 'relationship place'? Is that anywhere near your comfort zone?"

"Reggie is my friend," she said, straightening a clasp. "If we took things further and it didn't work out, it would change everything."

"But you don't know it won't work out."

"I don't know it *will*, either."

"And that's reason enough to not even try," I said. She ignored me, moving down to the rings. "You didn't know that hiring me would work out. But you did it anyway. And if you hadn't—"

"—I'd be enjoying a quiet moment at my kiosk right now, without being analyzed," she said. "Wouldn't that be nice!"

"—you never would have made the KeyChains and seen them be so successful," I finished. "Or been able to enjoy my company, and this conversation, right now."

She made a face at me, then walked back over and hopped up on her stool, opening up the laptop she'd recently bought to keep up with her Web site stuff. "Look. I know in a perfect, utterly romantic world, I'd go out with

Reggie and we'd live happily ever after," she said, hitting the power button. "But sometimes you just have to follow your instincts, and mine say this would not be a good thing for me. All right?"

I nodded. Really, considering everything I'd just gone through, Harriet was someone I should be trying to emulate, not convince otherwise.

I moved back to the rings, reorganizing them the way I had originally, in order of size and color. I was just doing another quick pass with the duster when I heard Harriet say, "Huh. This is weird."

"What is?"

"I'm just checking into my account, and my balance is kind of off," she said. "I know I had a couple of debits out, but not for this much."

"Maybe the site's just delayed," I said.

"I knew I shouldn't have signed on for this new system with Blake. I just feel better when I sign every check myself, you know?" She sighed, then picked up her phone and dialed. After a moment, she closed it. "Voice mail. Of course. Do you know Nate's number, offhand?"

I shook my head. "No. I don't."

"Well, when you see him, tell him I need to talk to him. Like, soon. Okay?"

I wanted to tell her I wouldn't be seeing him, much less delivering messages. But she was already back on the computer, scrolling down.

Harriet wasn't the only one not resting assured, or so I found out when I got home and found Cora in the foyer, wiping up the floor with a paper towel. Roscoe, who usually could not be prevented from greeting me with a full body attack, was conspicuously absent.

"No way," I said, dropping my bag on the floor. "He's mastered the dog door."

"We lock it when we're not here," she told me, pushing herself to her feet. "Which is usually no problem, but someone didn't bother to show up to walk him today."

"Really?" I said. "Are you sure? Nate's usually really dependable."

"Well, not today," she replied. "Clearly."

It was weird. So much so that I wondered if maybe Nate had taken off or something, as that seemed to be the only explanation for him just blowing off things he usually did like clockwork. That night, though, his lights were on, just like always, as were the ones in the pool. It was only when I really looked closely, around midnight, that I saw something out of the ordinary: a figure cutting through the water. Moving back and forth, with steady strokes, dark against all that blue light. I watched him for a long time, but even when I finally turned out the light, he was still swimming.

Chapter Seventeen

That weekend, there was only one thing I should have been thinking about: calculus. The test that pretty much would decide the entire fate of both my GPA and my future was on Monday, and according to Gervais—whose method was proven—it was time to shift into what he called "Zen mode."

"I'm sorry?" I'd said the day before, Friday, when he'd announced this.

"It's part of my technique," he explained, taking a sip of his chocolate milk, one of two he drank each lunch period. "First, we did an overview of everything you were supposed to learn so far this year. Then, we homed in on your weaknesses therein, pinpointing and attacking them one by one. Now, we move into Zen mode."

"Meaning what?" I asked.

"Admitting that you are powerless over your fate, on this test and otherwise. You have to throw out everything that you've learned."

I just looked at him. Olivia, who was checking her UMe page on her phone, said, "Actually, that is a very basic part of Eastern cinema tradition. The warrior, once taught, must now, in the face of his greatest challenge, rely wholly on instinct."

"Why have I spent weeks studying if I'm now supposed to forget everything I've learned?" I said. "That's the stupidest thing I've ever heard."

Olivia shrugged. "The man says his method is proven."

Man? I thought.

Gervais said, "The idea isn't to forget everything. It's that by now, you should know all this well enough that you don't *have* to actively think about it. You see a problem, you know the solution. It's instinct."

I looked down at the practice sheet he'd given me, problems lined up across it. As usual, with just one glance I felt my heart sink, my brain going fuzzy around the edges. If this was my instinct talking, I didn't want to hear what it was saying.

"Zen mode," Gervais said. "Clear your head, accept the uncertainty, and the solutions appear. Just trust me."

I was not convinced, and even less so when he presented me with his instructions for my last weekend of studying. (Which, incidentally, were bullet-pointed and divided into headings and subheadings. The kid was nothing if not professional.) Saturday morning, I was supposed to do a final overview, followed in the afternoon by a short series of problems he'd selected that covered the formulas I had most trouble with. Sunday, the last full day before the test, I wasn't supposed to study at all. Which seemed, frankly, insane. Then again, if the goal was to forget everything by Monday morning, this did seem like the way to do it.

Early the next morning, I sat down on my bed and started my overview, trying to focus. More and more, though, I found myself distracted, thinking about Nate, as I had been pretty much nonstop—occasional calculus obsessions aside—since I'd seen him swimming a couple of nights earlier. In the end, both Harriet and Cora had heard from Mr. Cross, who was wildly apologetic, crediting Harriet's account and offering Cora a free week's worth of walks to compensate. But in the days since, whenever I'd seen Nate across the green or in the halls at school, I couldn't help but notice a change in him. Like even with the distance between us, something about him—in his face or the way he carried himself—was suddenly familiar in a way I hadn't felt before, although how, exactly, I couldn't say.

After two hours of studying, I felt so overwhelmed that I decided to take a break and quickly run over to get my paycheck from Harriet. As soon as I stepped off the greenway, I saw people everywhere—lined up on the curb that ran alongside the mall, gathered in the parking lot, crowded at the base of a stage set up by the movie theater.

"Welcome to the Vista Five-K!" a voice boomed from the stage as I worked my way toward the main entrance, stepping around kids and dogs and more runners stretching and chatting and jogging in place. "If you're participating in the race, please make your way to the start line. Ten minutes to start!"

The crowd shifted as people headed toward the banner— VISTA 5K: RUN FOR YOUR LIFE!—strung between the parking lot and the mall entrance. Following them, I kept an eye out for Olivia but didn't see her—just runners of all shapes and sizes, some in high-tech lycra bodysuits, others in gym shorts and ratty T-shirts.

Inside the mall, it was much quieter, with few shoppers

moving between stores. I could still hear the announcer's voice from outside, along with the booming bass of the music they were playing, even as I walked from the entrance down to the kiosk courtyard, where I found Harriet and Reggie standing at Vitamin Me.

"I'm not doing the fish oil," she was saying as I walked up. "I'm firm on that."

"Omega-threes are crucial!" Reggie told her. "It's like a wonder drug."

"I didn't agree to wonder drugs. I agreed to take a few things, on a trial basis. Nobody said anything about fish."

"Fine." Reggie picked up a bottle, shaking some capsules into a plastic bag. "But you're taking the zinc and the B-twelve. Those are deal breakers."

Harriet shook her head, taking another sip of coffee. Then she saw me. "I thought you might turn up," she said. "Forget vitamins. Money is crucial."

Reggie sighed. "That kind of attitude," he said, "is *precisely* why you need more omega-threes."

Harriet ignored this as she walked over to her register, popping it open and taking out my check. "Here," she said, handing it over to me. "Oh, and there's a little something extra in there for you, as well."

Sure enough, the amount was about three hundred bucks more than I was expecting. "Harriet," I said. "What is this?"

"Profit-sharing," she said, then added, "And a thank-you for all the work you've put in over the last months."

"You didn't have to do this," I said.

"I know. But I got to thinking the other day, after we

had that talk. You were right. The KeyChains, all that. I couldn't have done it without you. Literally."

"That's not why I said that," I told her.

"I know. But it made me think. About a lot of things."

She looked over at Reggie, who was still adding things to her bag. Now that I thought of it, she had been awfully receptive to that zinc. And what was that about a few things, on a trial basis? "Wait," I said, wagging my finger between his kiosk and ours. "What's going on here?"

"Absolutely nothing," she replied, shutting the register.

I raised my eyebrows.

"Fine. If you must know, we just had drinks last night after work, and he convinced me to try a few samples."

"Really."

"Okay, maybe there was a dinner invitation, too," she added.

"Harriet!" I said. "You changed your mind."

She sighed. Over at Vitamin Me, Reggie was folding the top of her bag over neatly, working the crease with his fingers. "I didn't mean to," she said. "Initially, I just went to tell him the same thing I said to you. That I was worried about it not working out, and what that would do to our friendship."

"And?"

"And," she said, sighing, "he said he totally understood, we had another drink, and I said yes to dinner anyway."

"What about the vitamins?"

"I don't know." She flipped her hand at me. "These things happen."

"Yeah," I said, looking over at Reggie again. He'd been

so patient, and eventually he, too, got what he wanted. Or at least a chance at it. "Don't I know it."

By the time I went to the bank, ran a couple of errands, and then doubled back around to the greenway, the Vista 5K was pretty much over. A few runners were still milling around, sipping paper cups of Gatorade, but the assembled crowd had thinned considerably, which was why I immediately spotted Olivia. She was leaning forward on the curb, looking down the mall at the few runners left that were slowly approaching the finish line.

"No Laney yet?" I asked.

She shook her head, not even turning to look at me. "I figure she's dropped out, but she has her phone. She should have called me."

"Thanks to everyone who came out for the Vista Five-K!" a man with a microphone bellowed from the grandstand. "Join us next year, when we'll run for our lives again!"

"She's probably collapsed somewhere," Olivia said. "God, I *knew* this was going to happen. I'll see you, okay?"

She was about halfway across the street when I looked down the mall again and saw something. Just a tiny figure at first, way off in the distance.

"Olivia," I called out, pointing. "Look."

She turned, her eyes following my finger. It was still hard to be sure, so for a moment we just stood there, watching together, as Laney came into sight. She was going so slowly, before finally coming to a complete stop, bending over with her hands on her knees. "Oh, man," Olivia said finally. "It's her."

I turned around, looking at the man on the stage, who

had put down his microphone and was talking to some woman with a clipboard. Nearby, another woman in a Vista 5K T-shirt was climbing a stepladder to the clock, reaching up behind it.

"Wait," I called out to her. "Someone's still coming."

The woman looked down at me, then squinted into the distance. "Sorry," she said. "The race is over."

Olivia, ignoring this, stepped forward, raising her hands to her mouth. "Laney!" she yelled. "You're almost done. Don't quit now!"

Her voice was raw, strained. I thought of that first day I'd found her here with her stopwatch, and all the complaining about the race since. Olivia was a lot of things. But I should have known a sucker wasn't one of them.

"Come on!" she yelled. She started clapping her hands, hard, the sound sharp and single in the quiet. "Let's go, Laney!" she yelled, her voice rising up over all of us. *"Come on!"*

Everyone was staring as she jumped up and down in the middle of the road, her claps echoing off the building behind us. Watching her, I thought of Harriet, doubtfully eyeing those vitamins as Reggie dropped them into the bag, one by one, and then of me with Nate on the bench by the pond the last time we'd been together. *And if I don't?* he'd asked, and I'd thought there could be only one answer, in that one moment. But now, I was beginning to wonder if you didn't always have to choose between turning away for good or rushing in deeper. In the moments that it really counts, maybe it's enough—more than enough, even—just to be there. Laney must have thought so. Because right then, she started running again.

When she finally finished a few minutes later, it was hard to tell if she was even aware that the crowds had thinned, the clock was off, and the announcer didn't even call her time. But I do know that it was Olivia she turned to look for first, Olivia she threw her arms around and hugged tight, as that banner flapped overhead. Watching them, I thought again of how we can't expect everybody to be there for us, all at once. So it's a lucky thing that really, all you need is someone.

* * *

Back home, I sat down with my calculus notes, determined to study, but within moments my mind wandered past the numbers and figures and across the room to the picture of Jamie's family, still up on the wall over my desk. It was the weirdest thing—I'd studied it a thousand times, in this same place, the same way. But suddenly, all at once, it just made sense.

What is family? They were the people who claimed you. In good, in bad, in parts or in whole, they were the ones who showed up, who stayed in there, regardless. It wasn't just about blood relations or shared chromosomes, but something wider, bigger. Cora was right—we had many families over time. Our family of origin, the family we created, as well as the groups you moved through while all of this was happening: friends, lovers, sometimes even strangers. None of them were perfect, and we couldn't expect them to be. You couldn't make any one person your world. The trick was to take what each could give you and build a world from it.

So my true family was not just my mom, lost or found;

my dad, gone from the start; and Cora, the only one who had really been there all along. It was Jamie, who took me in without question and gave me a future I once couldn't even imagine; Olivia, who did question, but also gave me answers; Harriet, who, like me, believed she needed no one and discovered otherwise. And then there was Nate.

Nate, who was a friend to me before I even knew what a friend was. Who picked me up, literally, over and over again, and never asked for anything in return except for my word and my understanding. I'd given him one but not the other, because at the time I thought I couldn't, and then proved myself right by doing exactly as my mother had, hurting to prevent from being hurt myself. Needing was so easy: it came naturally, like breathing. Being needed by someone else, though, that was the hard part. But as with giving help and accepting it, we had to do both to be made complete—like links overlapping to form a chain, or a lock finding the right key.

I pushed out my chair, and headed downstairs, through the kitchen and out into the yard. I knew this was crazy, but suddenly it seemed so crucial that I somehow tell Nate I was sorry, reach out to him and let him know that I was here.

When I got to the gate, I pulled it open, then peered in, looking for him. But it was Mr. Cross I saw a moment later, walking quickly through the living room, his phone to his ear. Immediately I stepped back, around the fence, hiding as he slid open the glass door and came out onto the patio.

"I told you, I've been out of town all day," he was saying as he crossed by the pool, over to the garage. "He was supposed to be doing pickups and check-ins. Did he come by and get the cleaning today?" He paused, letting out a breath. "Fine. I'll keep looking for him. If you see him, tell him I want him home. Now. Understood?"

As he went back inside, all I could hear, other than my breathing, was the bubbling of the nearby pump, pushing the water in and out, in and out. I thought of Nate swimming laps that night, his dark shadow moving beneath the trees, how long it had been since I'd seen him alone in the pool.

Mr. Cross was inside now, still looking as his pace quickened, moving faster, back and forth. Watching him, I had a flash of Nate at school the last time I'd seen him, suddenly realizing why his expression—distant, distracted—had been so familiar. It was the same one on my mother's face the last time I'd seen her, when I walked into a room and she turned, surprised.

And this was why, as Mr. Cross called his name again, I knew his searching was useless. There's just something obvious about emptiness, even when you try to convince yourself otherwise. Nate was gone.

Chapter Eighteen

"Here," Jamie said. "For luck."

I watched him as he slid his car keys across the table toward me. "Really?" I said. "Are you sure?"

"Positive," he replied. "It's a big day. You shouldn't have to start it on the bus."

"Wow," I said, slipping them into my pocket. "Thanks."

He sat down across from me, pouring himself his usual heaping bowl of cereal, which he then drowned with milk. "So," he said, "what's your state of mind. Confident? Nervous? Zen?"

I made a face at him. "I'm fine," I told him. "I just want to get it over with."

His phone, which was on vibrate, suddenly buzzed, skipping itself sideways across the table. Jamie glanced at the caller ID and groaned. "Jesus," he said, but answered anyway. Still, his voice was curt, not at all Jamie-like, as he said, "Yes?"

I pushed out my chair, taking my own bowl to the sink. As I passed him, I could hear a voice through the receiver, although the words were indistinguishable.

"Really," Jamie said, and now he sounded concerned. "When was the last time you saw him? Oh. Okay, hold on, I'll ask her." He moved the phone away from his ear. "Hey, have you talked to Nate lately? His dad's looking for him."

I knew it, I thought. Out loud, I said, "No."

"Did you see him this weekend?"

I shook my head. "Not since school on Friday."

"She hasn't seen him since Friday," Jamie repeated into the phone. "Yeah, absolutely. We'll definitely let you know if we do. Keep us posted, okay?"

I opened the dishwasher, concentrating on loading in my bowl and spoon as he hung up. "What's going on?" I asked.

"Nate's gone AWOL, apparently," he said. "Blake hasn't seen him since Friday night."

I stood up, shutting the dishwasher. "Has he called the police?"

"No," he said, taking a bite of cereal. "He thinks he probably just took off for the weekend with his friends— you know, senioritis or whatever. Can't have gone far, at any rate."

But I, of course, knew this wasn't necessarily true. You could get anywhere on foot, especially if you had money and time. And Nate hadn't had a fence to jump. He'd just walked out. Free and clear.

And I was too late. If I'd just gone over there that night I'd seen him swimming, or talked to him on Friday at school, maybe, just maybe, I might have been able to help. Now, even if I wanted to go after him, I didn't know where to start. He could be anywhere.

It was weirder than I'd expected, driving myself to school after so many long months of being dependent on someone else. Under any other circumstances, I probably would have enjoyed it, but instead it felt almost strange to be sitting in traffic in the quiet of Jamie's Audi, other cars on all sides of me. At one light, I glanced over to see a woman in a minivan looking at me, and I wondered if to her I was just a spoiled teenage girl in an expensive car, a backpack on the seat beside her, blinker on to turn in to an exclusive school. This was unnerving for some reason, so much so that I found myself staring back at her, hard, until she turned away.

Once at school, I started across the green, taking a deep breath and trying to clear my head. Because of my certainty that Nate had taken off—even before I knew it for sure— I'd actually ended up following Gervais's Zen-mode plan, if only because I'd been too distracted to study the night before. Now, though, calculus was the last thing on my mind, even as I approached my classroom and found him waiting outside the door for me.

"All right," he said. "Did you follow my pre-test instructions? Get at least eight hours sleep? Eat a protein-heavy breakfast?"

"Gervais," I said. "Not right now, okay?"

"Remember," he said, ignoring this, "take your time on the first sets, even if they seem easy. You need them to prime your brain, lay the groundwork for the harder stuff."

I nodded, not even bothering to respond this time.

"If you find yourself stumbling with the power rule, remember that acronym we talked about. And write it down on the test page, so you can have it right in front of you."

"I need to go," I said.

"And finally," he said as, inside, my teacher Ms. Gooden was picking up a stack of papers, shuffling them as she prepared to hand them out, "if you get stuck, just clear your head. Envision an empty room, and let your mind examine it. In time, you will find the answer."

He blurted out this last part, not very Zen at all, as he rushed to fit it in as the bell rang. Even in my distracted state, as I looked at him I realized I should be more grateful. Sure, we'd had a deal, and I had paid him his twenty bucks an hour when he invoiced me (which he did on a biweekly basis on preprinted letterhead, no joke). But showing up like this, for a last-minute primer? That was above the call of duty. Even for a multipronged, proven method like his.

"Thanks, Gervais," I said.

"Don't thank me," he replied. "Just go get that ninety. I don't want you messing up my success rate."

I nodded, then turned to go into my classroom, sliding into my seat. When I looked back out the door, he was still standing there, peering in at me. Jake Bristol, who was sitting beside me looking sleepy, leaned across the aisle, poking my shoulder. "What's up with you and Miller?" he asked. "You into jailbait or something?"

I just looked at him. Jerk. "No," I said. "We're friends."

Now, Ms. Gooden came down the aisle, smiling at me as she slid a test, facedown, onto the desk in front of me. She was tall and pretty, with blonde hair she wore long, twisting it back with a pencil when she got busy filling up the board with theorems. "Good luck," she said as I turned it over.

At first glance, I felt my heart sink, immediately overwhelmed. But then I remembered what Gervais had said, about taking my time and priming my brain, and picked up my pencil and began.

The first one was easy. The second, a little harder, but still manageable. It wasn't until I got to the bottom of the front page that I realized that somehow, I was actually doing this. Carefully moving from one to the next, following Gervais's advice, jotting the power rule down in the margin: *The derivative of any given variable (x) to the exponent (n) is equal to product of the exponent and the variable to the (n–1) power.* I could hear Olivia saying it in my head, just as I heard Gervais's voice again and again, telling me the next step, and then the one following, each time I found myself hesitating.

There were ten minutes left on the clock when I reached the last problem, and this one did give me pause, more than any of the others. Staring down at it, I could feel myself starting to panic, the worry rising up slowly from my gut, and this time, no voices were coming, no prompting to be heard. I glanced around me at the people on either side still scribbling, at Ms. Gooden, who was flipping through *Lucky* magazine, and finally at the clock, which let me know I had five minutes left. Then I closed my eyes.

An empty room, Gervais had said, and at first I tried to picture white walls, a wood floor, a generic anywhere. But as my mind began to settle, something else came slowly into view: a door swinging open, revealing a room I recognized. It wasn't one in the yellow house, though, or even Cora's, but instead one with high glass windows opposite, a bedroom to the side with a dry-cleaned duvet, sofas that had hardly been used. A room empty not in definition, but in feeling. And finally, as my mind's eye moved across all of these, I saw one last thing: a root-beer cap sitting square on a countertop, just where someone had left it to be found.

I opened my eyes, then looked back down at the one blank spot on my paper, the problem left unsolved. I still had three minutes as I quickly jotted down an answer, not thinking, just going on instinct. Then I brought my paper to the front of the room, handed it in, and pushed out the door onto the green, heading toward the parking lot. I could just barely hear the bell, distant and steady, as I drove away.

*　　*　　*

In a perfect world, I would have remembered not only where the apartment building was, what floor to take the elevator to, but also the exact number of the unit. Because this was my world, however, I found myself on the seventh floor, all those doors stretching out before me, and no idea where to begin. In the end, I walked halfway down the hallway and just started knocking.

If someone answered, I apologized. If they didn't, I moved on. At the sixth door, though, something else happened. No one opened it, but I heard a noise just inside. On instinct—call it Zen mode—I reached down and tried the knob. No key necessary. It swung right open.

The room was just as I'd pictured it earlier. Sofas undisturbed, counter clutter-free, the bottle cap just where it had been. The only difference was a USWIM sweatshirt hanging over the back of one of the island stools. I picked it up, putting it to my face as I breathed in the smell of

chlorine, of water. Of Nate. And then, with it still lingering, I looked outside and found him.

He was standing on the balcony, hands on the rail, his
back to me, even though it was cold, so cold I could feel the
air seeping through the glass as I came closer. I reached for
the door handle to pull it open, then stopped halfway, suddenly nervous. How do you even begin to return to someone, much less convince them to do the same for you? I had
no idea. More than ever, though, right then I had to believe
the answer would just come to me. So I pulled the door
open.

When Nate turned around, I could tell I'd startled him.
His face was surprised, only relaxing slightly when he saw it
was me. By then, I'd already noticed the marks on his cheek
and chin, red turning to blue. There comes a point when
things are undeniable and can't be hidden any longer. Even
from yourself.

"Ruby," he said. "What are you doing here?"

I opened my mouth to say something in response to
this. Anything, just a word, even if it wasn't the perfect one.
But as nothing came, I looked at the landscape spread out
behind him, wide and vast on either side. It wasn't empty,
not at all, but maybe this could inspire you as well, because
right then, I knew just what to say, or at least a good place
to start, even if only because it was what Cora had said to
me back when all this began.

"It's cold," I said, holding out my hand to him. "You
should come inside."

Chapter Nineteen

Nate did come in. Getting him to come back with me, though, was harder.

In fact, we'd sat on the couch in that apartment for more than two hours, going over everything that had happened, before he finally agreed to at least talk to someone. This part, at least, I didn't even have to think about. I'd picked up his phone and dialed a number, and by the time we got back to my house, Cora was already waiting.

They sat at the kitchen table, me hanging back against the island, as Nate told her everything. About how when he'd first moved back, living with his dad had been okay—occasionally, he had money problems and issues with creditors, but when he took out his stress on Nate it was infrequent. Since the fall, though, when Rest Assured began to struggle, things had been getting worse, culminating in the months since Christmas, when a bunch of loans had come due. Nate said he had always planned to stick it out, but after a particularly bad fight a few nights earlier—the end result of which were the bruises on his face—he'd had enough.

Cora was amazing that day. She did everything—from just listening, her face serious, to asking careful questions, to calling up her contacts at the social-services division to answer Nate's questions about what his options were. In the end, it was she who dialed his mom in Arizona, her voice calm and professional as she explained the situation, then nodded supportively as she handed the receiver over to Nate to do the rest.

By that night, a plane ticket was booked, a temporary living arrangement set. Nate would spend the rest of the school year in Arizona, followed by working the swim-camp job in Pennsylvania he'd already set up through the summer. Come fall, he'd head off to the U, where he'd recently gotten in early admission, albeit without his scholarship due to quitting swim team midyear. Still, it was his hope that the coach might be open to letting him try for alternate, or at least participate in practices. It wasn't exactly what he'd planned, but it was something.

Mr. Cross was not happy when he found out about all this. In fact, at first he insisted that Nate return home, threatening to get the police involved if he didn't. It wasn't until Cora informed him that Nate had more than enough cause to press charges against him that he acquiesced, although even then he made his displeasure known with repeated phone calls, as well as making it as difficult as he could for Nate to collect his stuff and move in with us for the few days before he left town.

I did my best to distract Nate from all this, dragging him to movies at the Vista 10 (where we got free popcorn and admission, thanks to Olivia), hanging out with Roscoe, and taking extended coffee trips to Jump Java. He didn't go back to Perkins, as Cora had arranged for him to finish the little bit of work he had left via correspondence or online, and every afternoon as I came up the front walk, I was nervous, calling out to him the minute I stepped in the door. I finally understood what Jamie and Cora had gone through with me those first few weeks, if only from the relief I felt every time I heard his voice responding.

All the while, though, I knew he soon wouldn't be there. But I never talked to him about this. He had enough to worry about, and what mattered most was that I was just there for him, however he needed me to be. Still, the morning of his flight, when I came downstairs to find him in the foyer, his bags at his feet, I felt that same twist in my stomach.

I wasn't the only one upset. Cora sniffled through the entire good-bye, hugging him repeatedly, a tissue clutched in her hand. "Now, I'll call you tonight, just to make sure you're getting settled in," she told him. "And don't worry about things on this end. It's all handled."

"Okay," Nate said. "Thanks again. For everything."

"Don't be a stranger, all right?" Jamie told him, giving him a bear hug and a back slap. "You're family now."

Family, I thought as we pulled out of the driveway. The neighborhood was still asleep, houses dark as we drove out past those big stone pillars, and I remembered how I'd felt, coming in all those months ago, with everything so new and different.

"Are you nervous?" I asked Nate as we pulled out onto the main road.

"Not really," he replied, sitting back. "It's all kind of surreal, actually."

"It'll hit you eventually," I told him. "Probably at the exact moment it's too late to come back."

He smiled. "But I am coming back," he said. "I just have to survive Arizona and my mother first."

"You think it'll be that bad?"

"I have no idea. It isn't like she chose for me to come there. She's only doing this because she has to."

I nodded, slowing for a light. "Well, you never know. She might surprise you," I said. He did not look convinced, so I added, "Either way, don't decide to pack it in the first night, or jump any fences. Give it a few days."

"Right," he said slowly, looking over at me. "Any other advice?"

I switched lanes, merging onto the highway. It was so early, we had all the lanes to ourselves. "Well," I said, "if there's some annoying neighbor who tries to make nice with you, don't be a total jerk to them."

"Because you might need them later," he said. "To take you out of the woods, or something."

"Exactly."

I felt him look at me but didn't say anything as we came up to the airport exit. As I took it, circling around, I could see a plane overhead—just a sliver of white, heading up, up, up.

At the terminal, even at this early hour, there were a fair amount of people, heading off, arriving home. The sun was coming up now, the sky streaked with pink overhead as we unloaded his stuff, piling it on the curb beside him. "All right," I said. "Got everything?"

"Think so," he said. "Thanks for the ride."

"Well, I did kind of owe you," I said, and he smiled. "But there is one more thing, actually."

"What's that?"

"Even if you do make tons of new friends," I told him, "try not to forget where you came from, okay?"

He looked down at me. "I seriously doubt that could happen."

"You'd be surprised," I told him. "New place, new life. It's not hard to do."

"I think," he said, "that I'll have plenty to remind me."

I hoped this was true. Even if it wasn't, all I could do was hand over what I could, with the hope of something in return. But of course, this was easier said than done. Ever since Christmas, I'd been trying to come up with the perfect gift for Nate, something phenomenal that might come close to all he'd given me. Once again, I thought I had nothing to offer. But then I looked down and realized I was wrong.

The clasp of my necklace was stubborn at first, and as I took the key to the yellow house off and put it into my pocket, I noticed how worn it was. Especially in comparison to the bright, shiny new one to Jamie and Cora's, which I slid onto the chain in its place. Then I took Nate's hand, turning it upward, and pressed the necklace, with Cora's key on it, into his palm.

"Well," I said, "just in case."

He nodded, wrapping his hand around the necklace, and my hand, as well. This time, I let my palm relax against his, feeling the warmth there and pressing back, before stepping in closer. Then I reached up, sliding my hand behind his neck and pulling him in for a kiss, closing that space between us once and for all.

In the weeks since, Nate and I had been in constant contact, both by phone and on UMe.com. My page, long inactive, was now not only up and running but full of extras, thanks to Olivia, who helped me set it up and tweaked it on a regular basis. So far, I'd only accrued a few friends—her, Nate, Gervais, as well as Jamie, who sent me more messages than anyone—although I had lots of photos, including a couple Nate had sent of him at his new job, lifeguarding at a pool near his mom's house. He was swimming every day now, working on his times and getting back into shape; he said it was slow progress, but he was seeing improvements, bit by bit. Sometimes at night in my room when I couldn't sleep, I imagined him in the pool, crossing its length again and again, stroke by even stroke.

In my favorite picture, though, he's not in the water but posing in front of a lifeguard stand. He's smiling, the sun bright behind him, and has a whistle around his neck. If you look really closely, you can see there's another, thinner chain behind, with something else dangling from it. It was hard to make it out, exactly. But I knew what it was.

Chapter Twenty

"Ruby? You about ready?"

I turned, looking over my shoulder at Cora, who was standing in the door to the kitchen, her purse over her shoulder. "Are we leaving?" I asked.

"As soon as Jamie finds the camcorder," she replied. "He's determined to capture every moment of this milestone."

"You have to document important family events!" I heard Jamie yell from somewhere behind her. "You'll thank me later."

Cora rolled her eyes. "Five minutes, whether he finds it or not. We don't want to be late. Okay?"

I nodded, and she ducked back inside, the door falling shut behind her, as I turned back to the pond. I'd been spending a lot of time out there lately, ever since the day a couple of months earlier when I'd come home from work to find her and Jamie huddled over something in the foyer.

"Jamie. Put it down."

"I'm not opening it. I'm just looking."

"Would you stop?"

I came up right behind them. "What are you guys doing?"

Cora jumped, startled. "Nothing," she said. "We were just—"

"You got a letter from the U," Jamie told me, holding up what I now saw was an envelope. "I brought it in about an hour ago. The anticipation has been *killing* us."

"It was killing Jamie," Cora said. "I was fine."

I walked over to where they were standing, taking the envelope from him. After all I'd heard and read about thick and thin letters, this one was, of course, neither. Not bulky, not slim, but right in the middle.

"It only takes a page to say no," Jamie told me as if I'd said this aloud. "It is only one word, after all."

"Jamie, for God's sake!" Cora swatted him. "Stop it."

I looked at the envelope again. "I'm going to take it outside," I said. "If that's okay."

Jamie opened his mouth to protest, but Cora put her hand over it. "That's fine," she said. "Good luck."

Then it was April. The grass had gone from that nubby, hard brown to a fresh green, and the trees were all budding, shedding pollen everywhere. A nice breeze was blowing as I walked out to the pond, the envelope dangling from my hand. I walked right up to the edge, where I could see my reflection, then tore it open.

I was just about to unfold the pages within when I saw something, out of the corner of my eye, moving quickly, so quickly I almost doubted it. I stepped closer, peering down into the murky depths, past the rocks and algae and budding irises, and there, sure enough, I saw a flash of white blurring past. There were others as well, gold and speckled and black, swimming low. But it was the white one, my fish, that I saw first. I took a deep breath and tore the letter open.

Dear Ms. Cooper, it began. *We are pleased to inform you . . .*

I turned around, looking back at the kitchen door where, unsurprisingly, Jamie and Cora were both standing, watching me. Jamie pushed it open, then stuck his head out. "Well?" he said.

"Good news," I said.

"Yeah?" Beside him, Cora put her hand to her mouth, her eyes widening.

I nodded. "And the fish are back. Come see."

Now, in mid-June, they were even more present, circling around the lilies and water grasses. Above them, in the water's surface, I could see my reflection: my hair loose, black gown, cap in one hand. Then a breeze blew across the yard, rustling the leaves overhead and sending everything rippling. Beside me, sitting on the grass, Roscoe closed his eyes.

As always, when I saw myself, it was weird to be without my necklace. Even now, I was still very aware of its absence, the sudden empty space where for so long I'd always seen something familiar. A few days earlier, though, I'd been digging through a drawer and come across the box Nate had given me for Valentine's Day. The next time we spoke, I mentioned this, and he told me to open it. When I did, I saw that once again he'd known what I needed, even before I did. Inside was a pair of key-shaped earrings—clearly Harriet's work—studded with red stones. I'd been wearing them every day since.

I looked across the yard, the trees swaying overhead, to Nate's house. I still called it that, a habit that I had yet to break, even though neither he nor his dad had lived there for a while. Mr. Cross had put it up for sale in May, just after a lawsuit was filed by several Rest Assured clients who had began to notice, and question, various discrepancies on their accounts. The last I'd heard, he was still in business, but just barely, and renting an apartment somewhere across town. The new owners of the house had small children and used the pool all the time. On warm afternoons, from my window, I could hear them laughing and splashing.

As for me, thanks to Gervais's method, I'd made a ninety-one on my calc test—guaranteeing my own spot at the U—and soon would be walking across the green at Perkins Day, taking my diploma from Mr. Thackray, officially a high-school graduate. In the lead up to the ceremony, I'd received endless paperwork and e-mails about getting tickets for family, and all the rules and regulations about how many we were allowed to reserve. In the end, I'd taken four, for Cora and Jamie, Reggie and Harriet. Not all family, but if there was one thing I'd learned over these last few months, it was that this was a flexible definition.

At least, that was the final thesis of my English project, which I'd handed in during the last week of classes. We'd each had to get up in front of the class and do a presentation that showcased our research and findings, and for mine, I'd brought in two pictures. The first was of Jamie's extended tribe, which I put up while I explained about the different definitions I'd gathered, and how they all related to one another. The second was more recent, from the eighteenth birthday party Cora had thrown me at the end of May. I'd told her not to make a fuss, but of course she'd ignored me, insisting that we had to do something, and that I should invite anyone I wanted to celebrate with me.

In the picture, we're all posing by the pond, one big group. I'm in the center, with Cora on one side, Olivia on the other. You can see Jamie, slightly blurred from running back into the shot after setting the timer on the camera—he's standing by Harriet, who is looking at me and smiling, and Reggie, who is of course looking at her. Next to them you can see Laney, smiling big, and then Gervais, the only one eating, a plate of cake in his hand. Like the first one, which I'd studied all these months, it is not a perfect picture, not even close. But in that moment, it was exactly what it was supposed to be.

It was also, like the one of Jamie's family, already changing, even if that day we hadn't known it yet. That came a couple of weeks later, when I was leaving for school one morning and found my sister sitting on her bed, crying.

"Cora?" I dropped my backpack, then came over to sit beside her. "What's wrong?"

She drew in a big, shuddering breath, shaking her head, clearly unable to answer. By then, though, I didn't need her to; I'd already seen the pregnancy-test box on the bedside table. "Oh, Cora," I said. "It's okay."

"I—I—" she said, sobbing through the words.

"What's going on?" Jamie, who had just come up the stairs, said as he came into the room. I nodded at the test box, and his face fell. "Oh," he said, taking a seat on her other side. "Honey. It's all right. We've got that appointment next week—we'll see what's going on—"

"I'm fine," Cora sputtered as I grabbed her some tissues. "I really am."

I reached over, taking her hand so I could put the tissues into it. She was still holding the test stick, so I took it from her as she drew in another breath. It wasn't until after I put it down on the bed beside me that I actually looked at it.

"Are you, though?" Jamie was saying, rubbing her shoulders. "Are you sure?"

I stared at the stick again, double-checking it. Then tripling. "Yeah," I said, holding it up, the plus sign more than clear as Cora dissolved in tears again. "She's positive."

She was also sick as a dog, morning and night, as well as so tired she couldn't stay up much past dinner. Not that I'd heard her complain, even once.

All of this had got me thinking, and a few days before my birthday, I'd sat down at my desk to write a letter, long overdue, to my own mother, who was still in rehab in Tennessee. I wasn't sure what I wanted to say, though, and after sitting there for a full hour, with nothing coming, I'd just photocopied my acceptance letter from the U and slid it inside the envelope. It wasn't closure, by any means, but it was progress. If nothing else, now we knew where to find each other, even if only time would tell if either of us would ever come looking.

"Got it! Let's go!" I heard Jamie yell from inside. Roscoe perked up his ears, and I watched him run, tags jingling, across the grass to the house.

It was only then, when I knew I was alone, at least for the moment, that I reached under my gown into the pocket of my dress. As I pulled out my key from the yellow house, which I'd kept on my bureau since the day Nate left, I traced the shape one last time before folding my hand tightly around it.

Behind me, Cora was calling again. My family was waiting. Looking down at the pond, all I could think was that it is an incredible thing, how a whole world can rise from what seems like nothing at all. I stepped closer to the edge, keeping my eyes on my reflection as I dropped the key into the water, where it landed with a splash. At first, the fish darted away, but as it began to sink they circled back, gathering around. Together, they followed it down, down, until it was gone.

Turn the page to read an excerpt from

SARAH DESSEN'S

SAINT
ANYTHING

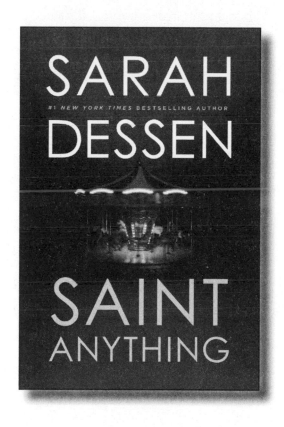

CHAPTER

"WOULD THE defendant please rise."

This wasn't an actual question, even though it sounded like one. I'd noticed that the first time we'd all been assembled here, in this way. Instead, it was a command, an order. The "please" was just for show.

My brother stood up. Beside me, my mom tensed, sucking in a breath. Like the way they tell you to inhale before an X-ray so they can see more, get it all. My father stared straight forward, as always, his face impossible to read.

The judge was talking again, but I couldn't seem to listen. Instead, I looked over to the tall windows, the trees blowing back and forth outside. It was early August; school started in three weeks. It felt like I had spent the entire summer in this very room, maybe in this same seat, but I knew that wasn't the case. Time just seemed to stop here. But maybe, for people like Peyton, that was exactly the point.

It was only when my mother gasped, bending forward to grab the bench in front of us, that I realized the sentence had been announced. I looked up at my brother. He'd been known for his fearlessness all the way back to when we were kids playing in the woods behind our house. But the day those older boys had challenged him to walk across that wide, gaping sinkhole on a skinny branch and he did it, his ears had been bright red. He was scared. Then and now.

There was a bang of the gavel, and we were dismissed. The attorneys turned to my brother, one leaning in close to speak while the other put a hand on his back. People were getting up, filing out, and I could feel their eyes on us as I swallowed hard and focused on my hands in my lap. Beside me, my mother was sobbing.

"Sydney?" Ames said. "You okay?"

I couldn't answer, so I just nodded.

"Let's go," my father said, getting to his feet. He took my mom's arm, then gestured for me to walk ahead of them, up to where the lawyers and Peyton were.

"I have to go to the ladies' room," I said.

My mom, her eyes red, just looked at me. As if this, after all that had happened, was the thing that she simply could not bear.

"It's okay," Ames said. "I'll take her."

My father nodded, clapping him on the shoulder as we passed. Out in the courthouse lobby, I could see people pushing the doors open, out into the light outside, and I wished more than anything that I was among them.

Ames put his arm around me as we walked. "I'll wait for you here," he said when we reached the ladies' room. "Okay?"

Inside, the light was bright, unforgiving, as I walked to the sinks and looked at myself in the mirror there. My face was pale, my eyes dark, flat, and empty.

A stall door behind me opened and a girl came out. She was about my height, but smaller, slighter. As she stepped up beside me, I saw she had blonde hair, plaited in a messy braid that hung over one shoulder, a few wisps framing her face, and she wore a summer dress, cowboy boots, and a denim jacket. I felt her look at me as I washed my hands once, then twice, before grabbing a towel and turning to the door.

I pushed it open, and there was Ames, directly across the hallway, leaning against the wall with his arms folded over his chest. When he saw me, he stood up taller, taking a step forward. I hesitated, stopping, and the girl, also leaving, bumped into my back.

"Oh! Sorry!" she said.

"No," I told her, turning around. "It was . . . my fault."

She looked at me for a second, then past my shoulder, at Ames. I watched her green eyes take him in, this stranger, for a long moment before turning her attention back to me. I had never seen her before. But with a single look at her face, I knew exactly what she was thinking.

You okay?

I was used to being invisible. People rarely saw me, and if they did, they never looked close. I wasn't shiny and charming like my brother, stunning and graceful like my mother, or smart and dynamic like my friends. That's the thing, though. You always think you want to be noticed. Until you are.

The girl was still watching me, waiting for an answer to the question she hadn't even said aloud. And maybe I would have answered it. But then I felt a hand on my elbow. Ames.

"Sydney? You ready?"

I didn't reply to this, either. Somehow we were heading toward the lobby, where my parents were now standing with the lawyers. As we walked, I kept glancing behind me, trying to see that girl, but could not in the shifting crowd of people pressing into the courtroom. Once we were clear of them, though, I looked back one last time and was surprised to find her right where I'd left her. Her eyes were still on me, like she'd never lost sight of me at all.

CHAPTER

2

～つ⌒

THE FIRST thing you saw when you walked into our house was a portrait of my brother. It hung directly across from the huge glass door, right above a wood credenza and the Chinese vase where my father stored his umbrellas. You'd be forgiven if you never noticed either of these things, though. Once you saw Peyton, you couldn't take your eyes off him.

Though we shared the same looks (dark hair, olive skin, brown, almost black, eyes) he somehow carried them totally differently. I was average, kind of cute. But Peyton—the second in our house, with my father Peyton the first—was gorgeous. I'd heard him compared to everything from movie idols of long before my time to fictional characters tromping across Scottish moors. I was pretty sure my brother was unaware as a child of the attention he received in supermarkets or post office lines. I wondered how it had felt when he'd suddenly understood the effect his looks had on people, women especially. Like discovering a superpower, both thrilling and daunting, all at once.

Before all that, though, he was just my brother. Three years older, blue King Combat sheets on his bed in contrast to my pink Fairy Foo ones. I basically worshipped him. How could I not? He was the king of Truth or Dare (he always went with the latter, naturally), the fastest runner in the neighborhood, and the only person I'd ever seen who could stand, balanced, on the handlebars of a rolling bicycle.

But his greatest talent, to me, was disappearing.

We played a lot of hide-and-seek as kids, and Peyton took it *seriously*. Ducking behind the first chair spotted in a room, or choosing the obvious broom closet? Those were for amateurs. My brother would fold himself beneath the cabinet under the bathroom sink, flatten completely under a bedspread, climb up the shower stall to spread across the ceiling, somehow holding himself there. Whenever I asked him for his secrets, he'd just smile. "You just have to find the invisible place," he told me. Only he could see it, though.

We practiced wrestling moves in front of cartoons on weekend mornings, fought over whom the dog loved more (just guess), and spent the hours after school we weren't in activities (soccer for him, gymnastics for me) exploring the undeveloped green space behind our neighborhood. This is how my brother still appears to me whenever I think of him: walking ahead of me on a crisp day, a stick in his hand, through the dappled fall colors of the woods. Even when I was nervous we'd get lost, Peyton never was. That fearlessness again. A flat landscape never appealed to him. He always needed something to push up against. When things got bad with Peyton, I always wished we were back there, still walking. Like we hadn't reached where we were going yet, and there was still a chance it might be somewhere else.

I was in sixth grade when things began to change. Until then, we had both been on the lower campus of Perkins Day, the private school we'd attended since kindergarten. That year, though, he moved to Upper School. Within a couple of weeks, he'd started hanging out with a bunch of juniors and seniors. They treated him like a mascot, daring him to do stupid stuff like lifting Popsicles from the cafeteria line or climbing into a car trunk to sneak off campus for lunch. This was when Peyton's legend began in earnest. He was bigger than life, bigger than *our* lives.

Meanwhile, when I didn't have gymnastics, I was now riding the bus home solo, then eating my snack alone at the kitchen island. I had my own friends, of course, but most of them were highly scheduled, never around on weekday afternoons due to various activities. This was typical of our neighborhood, the Arbors, where the average household could support any extracurricular activity from Mandarin lessons to Irish dancing and everything in between. Financially, my family was about average for the area. My father, who started his career in the military before going to law school, had made his money in corporate conflict resolution. He was the guy called when a company had a problem—threat of a lawsuit, serious issues between employees, questionable practices about to be brought to light—and needed it worked out. It was no wonder I grew up believing there was no problem my father couldn't solve. For much of my life, I'd never seen any proof otherwise.

If Dad was the general, my mom was the chief operating officer. Unlike some parents, who approached parenting as a tag-team sport, in our family the duties were very clearly divided. My father handled the bills, house, and yard upkeep, and my mom dealt with everything else. Julie Stanford was That Mother, the one who read every parenting book and stocked her minivan with enough snacks and sports equipment for every kid in the neighborhood. Like my dad, if my mom did something, she did it right. Which was why it was all the more surprising when, eventually, things went wrong anyway.

The trouble with Peyton started in the winter of his tenth grade year. One afternoon I was watching TV in the living room with a bowl of popcorn when the doorbell rang. When I looked outside, I saw a police car in the driveway.

"Mom?" I called upstairs. She was in her office, which was basically command central for our entire house. My dad called it the War Room. "Someone's here."

I don't know why I didn't tell her it was the police. It just seemed saying it might make it real, and I wasn't sure what was out there yet.

"Sydney, you are perfectly capable of answering the door," she replied, but sure enough, a beat later I heard her coming down the stairs.

I kept my eyes on the TV, where the characters from my favorite reality show, *Big New York*, were in the midst of yet another dinner party catfight. The Big franchise had been part of my afternoon ritual since Peyton had started high school, the guiltiest of guilty pleasures. Rich women being petty and pretty, I'd heard it described, and that summed it up. There were about six different shows—*Dallas, Los Angeles,* and *Chicago* among them—enough so that I could easily watch two every day to fill the time between when I got home and dinner. I was so involved in the show, it was like they were my friends, and I often found myself talking back to the TV as if they could hear me, or thinking about their issues and problems even when I wasn't watching. It was a weird kind of loneliness, feeling that some of my closest friends didn't actually know I existed. But without them, the house felt so empty, even with my mom there, which made *me* feel empty in a way I'd grown to dread the moment I stepped off the bus after school. My own life felt flat and sad too much of the time; it was reassuring, somehow, to lose myself in someone else's.

So I was watching Rosalie, the former actress, accuse Ayre, the model, of being a bully, when everything in our family's life shifted. One minute the door was shut and things were fine. The next, it was open and there was Peyton, a police officer beside him.

"Ma'am," the cop said as my mother stepped back, putting a hand to her chest. "Is this your son?"

This was what I would remember later. This one question, the answer a no-brainer, and yet still one my parents, and Mom especially, would grapple with from that point on. Starting that day, when Peyton got caught smoking pot in the Perkins Day parking lot with his friends, my brother began a transformation into someone we didn't always recognize. There would be other visits from the authorities, trips to the police station, and, eventually, court dates and rehab stays. But it was this first one that stayed in my mind, crisp in detail. The bowl of popcorn, warm in my lap. Rosalie's sharp voice. And my mom, stepping back to let my brother inside. As the cop led him down the hallway to the kitchen, my brother looked at me. His ears were bright red.

Because he hadn't had any pot on his person, Perkins Day decided to handle the infraction itself, with a suspension and volunteer hours doing tutoring at the Lower School. The story—especially the part about how Peyton was the only one who ran, forcing the cops to chase him down—made the rounds, with how far he'd gotten (a block, five, a mile) growing with each telling. My mom cried. My dad, furious, grounded him for a full month. Things didn't go back to the way they had been, though. Peyton came home and went to his room, staying there until dinner. He served his time, swore he'd learned his lesson. Three months later, he got busted for breaking and entering.

There's a weird thing that happens when something goes from a one-time thing to a habit. Like the problem is no longer just a temporary houseguest but has actually moved in.

After that, we fell into a routine. My brother accepted his punishment and my parents slowly relaxed, accepting as fact their various theories about why this would never happen again. Then Peyton would get busted—for drugs, shoplifting, reckless driving—and we'd all go back down the rabbit hole of charges, lawyers, court, and sentences.

After his first shoplifting arrest, when the cops found pot during his pat-down, Peyton went to rehab. He returned with a thirty-day chip on his key chain and interest in playing guitar thanks to his roommate at Evergreen Care Center. My parents paid for lessons and made plans to outfit part of the basement as a small studio so he could record his original compositions. The work was halfway done when the school found a small amount of pills in his locker.

He got suspended for three weeks, during which time he was supposed to be staying home, getting tutored and preparing for his court date. Two days before he was due to go back to school, I was awakened out of a deep sleep by the rumbling of the garage door opening. I looked out the window to see my dad's car backing onto our street. My clock said three fifteen a.m.

I got up and went out into the hallway, which was dark and quiet, then padded down the stairs. A light was on in the kitchen. There I found my mother, in her pajamas and a U sweatshirt, making a pot of coffee. When she saw me, she just shook her head.

"Go back to sleep," she told me. "I'll fill you in tomorrow."

By the next morning, my brother had been bailed out, charged yet again with breaking and entering, this time with added counts of trespassing and resisting arrest. The previous evening, after my parents had gone to bed, he'd snuck out of his room, walked up our road, then climbed the fence around the Villa, the biggest house in the Arbors. He found an unlocked window and wriggled through, then poked around for only a few minutes before the cops arrived, alerted by the silent alarm. When they came in, he bolted out the back door. They tackled him on the pool deck, leaving huge, bloody scrapes across his face. Amazingly, my mother seemed more upset about this than anything else.

"It just seems like we might have a case," she said to my dad later that morning. She was dressed now, all business: they had a meeting with Peyton's lawyer at nine a.m. sharp. "I mean, did you see those wounds? What about police brutality?"

"Julie, he was running from them," my dad replied in a tired voice.

"Yes, I understand that. But I also understand that he is still a minor, and force was not necessary. There was a *fence*. It's not like he was going anywhere."

But he was, I thought, although I knew better than to say this aloud. The more Peyton got into trouble, the more my mom seemed desperate to blame anyone and everyone else. The school was out to get him. The cops were too rough. But my brother was no innocent: all you had to do was look at the facts. Although sometimes, I felt like I was the only one who could see them.

By the next day at school, word had spread, and I was getting side-eyed all over the hallways. It was decided that Peyton would withdraw from Perkins Day and finish high school elsewhere, although opinions differed on whether it was the school or my parents who made this choice.

I was lucky to have my friends, who rallied around me, letting people know that I was not my brother, despite our shared looks and last name. Jenn, whom I'd known since our days at Trinity Church Preschool, was especially protective. Her dad had had his own tangles with the law, back in college.

"He was always honest about it, that it was just experimentation," she told me as we sat in the cafeteria at lunch. "He paid his debt to society, and now look, he's a CEO, totally successful. Peyton will be, too. This, too, shall pass."

Jenn always sounded like this, older than she was, mostly because her parents had had her in their forties and treated her like a little adult. She even looked like a grown-up, with her sensible haircut, glasses, and comfortable footwear. At times it was strange, like she'd skipped childhood altogether, even when she was in it. But now, I was reassured. I wanted to believe her. To believe anything.

Peyton received three months in jail and a fine. That was the first time we were all in court together. His lawyer, Sawyer Ambrose, whose ads were on bus stops all over town (NEED A LAWYER? CALL ON SAWYER!), maintained that it was crucial for the jury to see us sitting behind my brother like the loyal, tight family we were.

Also present was my brother's new best friend, a guy he'd met in the Narcotics Anonymous group he was required to attend. Ames was a year older than Peyton, tall with shaggy hair and a loping walk, and had gotten busted for dealing pot a year earlier. He'd served six months and stayed out of trouble ever since, setting the kind of example everyone agreed my brother needed. They drank a lot of coffee drinks together, played video games, and studied, Peyton with his books from the alternative school where he'd landed, Ames for the classes he was taking in hospitality management at Lakeview Tech. They planned that Peyton would do the same once he got his diploma, and together they'd go work at one resort or another. My mom loved this idea, and already had all the paperwork necessary to make it happen: it sat in its own labeled envelope on her desk. There was just the little matter of the jail thing to get out of the way first.

My brother ended up serving seven weeks at the county lockup. I was not permitted to see him, but my mother visited every time it was allowed. Meanwhile, Ames remained; it seemed like he was always parked at our kitchen table with a coffee drink, ducking out occasionally to the garage to smoke cigarettes, using a sand-bucket ashtray my mom (who abhorred the habit) put out there just for him. Sometimes he showed up with his girlfriend, Marla, a manicurist with blonde hair, big blue eyes, and a shyness so prevalent she rarely spoke. If you addressed her, she got super nervous, like a small dog too tightly wound and always shaking.

I knew Ames was a comfort to my mom. But something about him made me uneasy. Like how I'd catch him watching me over the rim of his coffee cup, following my movements with his dark eyes. Or how he always found a way to touch me—squeezing my shoulder, brushing against my arm—when he said hello. It wasn't like he'd ever done anything to me, so I felt like it had to be my problem. Plus, he had a girlfriend. All he wanted, he told me again and again, was to take care of me the way Peyton would.

"It was the one thing he asked me the day he went in," he told me soon after my brother was gone. We were in the kitchen, and my mom had stepped out to take a phone call, leaving us alone. "He said, 'Look out for Sydney, man. I'm counting on you.'"

I wasn't sure what to say to this. First of all, it didn't sound like Peyton, who'd barely given me the time of day in the months before he'd gone away. Plus, even before that, he'd never been the protective type. But Ames knew my brother well, and the truth was that I no longer did. So I had to take his word for it.

"Dessen weaves a sometimes funny, mostly emotional, and very satisfying story."   —*VOYA*

"Characterization and dialogue are expertly done."
                                                          —*Booklist*

AN ALA BEST BOOK FOR YOUNG ADULTS

The Paris Winter

By Imogen Robertson

Instruments of Darkness
Anatomy of Murder
Island of Bones
Circle of Shadows
The Paris Winter

The Paris Winter

IMOGEN
ROBERTSON

headline
review

First published in Great Britain in 2013
by HEADLINE REVIEW
An imprint of HEADLINE PUBLISHING GROUP

1

Cataloguing in Publication Data is available from the British Library

ISBN 978 0 7553 9011 3 (Hardback)
ISBN 978 0 7553 9012 0 (Trade paperback)

Typeset in Adobe Caslon by Avon DataSet Ltd,
Bidford-on-Avon, Warwickshire

Printed and bound in Great Britain by Clays Ltd, St Ives plc

Headline's policy is to use papers that are natural, renewable and recyclable
products and made from wood grown in sustainable forests. The logging and
manufacturing processes are expected to conform to the environmental
regulations of the country of origin.

HEADLINE PUBLISHING GROUP
An Hachette UK Company
338 Euston Road
London NW1 3BH

www.headline.co.uk
www.hachette.co.uk

Gran, Gillian and Hazel with love

Acknowledgements

The support of friends and family make the writing possible and letters, emails and so on from readers make it fun. Huge thanks to my agent Annette Green, my editor Flora Rees and all at Headline for their advice and support. Particular thanks to David Downie and Alison Harris for their expert help guiding us round Paris; to artists Caroline de Peyrecave and Claire Zakiewicz for talking to me about their training and careers; to Richard Campbell at Lucie Campbell in Bond Street for showing me diamonds; Hervé Guyot for sharing his collection of photographs of the Paris floods and to Ahren Warner and Susan Powell for their help with the research. Thank you also to my husband Ned who arranged so much of our wedding while I was in 1909. This book was originally inspired by my grandmothers and great-aunts who travelled independently in Europe in the first half of the twentieth century.

PROLOGUE

At the Académie Lafond oil on board 29.3 × 23.6 cm

This charming, loosely painted study shows a life-class in progress. The model is just visible on the left, but it is the students – bored, intent or nervous – who are the subjects of the painting. One seems to be blowing on her hands to warm them. Lafond began offering training to young artists, male and female, in 1875 and opened his first all-female atelier in 1890, seven years before women were admitted to the Académie des Beaux Arts. He managed his various studios in Paris with great success until his death in 1919. His students received a thorough training in oils and were encouraged to be both experimental and imaginative in their use of colour and in their composition.

The tonal range in this painting is narrow and the colours cold, the model almost invisible and the students placed almost haphazardly in the frame. In this way, the artist gives an impression of a snatched, unstaged moment on a chilly morning. Note the middle-class appearance of the women in the portrait. Lafond's fees for women were high, but his reputation was irreproachable.

Extract from the catalogue notes to the exhibition 'The Paris Winter: Anonymous Treasures from the de Civray Collection', Southwark Picture Gallery, London, 2010

Part One

Saturday, 20 November 1909, Paris

CHAPTER 1

*T*HE NEWS OF THE SUICIDE OF ROSE CHAMPION
reached her fellow students at the Académie Lafond on
a pale wintry morning a little before ten o'clock. The heat from the
black and clanking stove had not yet reached the far corners of the
studio, and the women on the outer reaches of the group had to
blow on their fingers to make them warm enough to work. Maud
Heighton was always one of the first to arrive each day and set up
her easel, which meant she could have taken her pick of places on
each Monday when the model for the week was chosen, but the
Englishwoman liked to sit on the far eastern side of the room. The
challenge of the narrow angle she had on the model throne and
whatever man, woman or child happened to occupy it seemed to
please her – and she returned to the spot week after week when
warmer ones, or those with an easier angle of view were available.

She was there that morning, silent and studious as ever, when
the news of Rose's death came tumbling up the stairs, so she was
among the first to hear it. It was unfortunate – shocking even –
that the news reached the female students so raw and sudden, but
even in the best-run establishments, such things do occur.

It was by chance the women painting in Passage des Panoramas
heard so quickly and so brutally of the tragedy. One of Lafond's

male students, a young romantic Englishman called John Edwards, lived in the room beside Rose Champion's in a shabby tenement hunkered off the Boulevard Clichy. It was an unpleasant building without gas or electricity, and with only one tap which all the inhabitants had to share. He knew his neighbour was a student in one of the all-female ateliers, but she was not pretty enough to attract his attention, not while the streets were full of French girls who made it their business to charm the male gaze; what's more, he assumed that as a woman she would have little of interest to say about art. When he took up his residence, though, he noticed that Rose kept herself and her threadbare wardrobe clean and approved of that, then thought no more about her. In the month they had been neighbours they had had one short conversation on the stairs about the teaching at Académie Lafond. It ended when he asked to see her work and Rose told him he wouldn't understand it. He had wished only to be polite and was offended by her refusal. They did not speak again.

The walls that divided their rooms were thin and he happened to be awake and waiting that morning for the matt-grey light of the Paris dawn to filter into the sky. It was the hour and the season when the city looked unsure of itself. In the full darkness, the clubs and cabarets shone like the jewels. The city then was a woman in evening dress certain of her beauty and endlessly fascinating. The air smelled of roasting chestnuts, and music spilled out of every café, humble or luxurious, into the streets. In the full light of day Paris was chic and confident. The polished shops were filled with colour and temptation and on every corner was a scene worth painting. It was modern without being vulgar, tasteful without being rigid or dull. A parade of elegant originality. Only in this hour, just before dawn on a winter's morning, did the city seem a little haggard, a little stale. The shutters were up and the cafés all closed or closing. The streets were almost empty – only the occasional man, purple in the face and stale with smoke and drink, hailing a cab in Place Pigalle, or the old women washing out the gutters with stiff-brushed brooms.

Sitting in the window with a blanket round his shoulders and his pipe clamped between his teeth, John Edwards was thinking about Matisse, his solid blocks of colour that at times seemed ugly, but with an ugliness more honest than beauty. He pictured himself making this argument to the poets and painters who gathered at *Le Lapin Agile* in Montmartre; he imagined them nodding seriously then telling their friends they had found an Englishman of talent and wisdom. They would introduce him to the most interesting art dealers in the city, the most advanced collectors and critics. He would write a manifesto . . .

He was enjoying the opening night of his first sensational solo show when he heard the sound of a chair overturning and the creak of a rope. There was no doubt where it came from. He dropped the blanket from his shoulders, ran into the corridor and started hammering at the door, calling her name, then rattling the handle. It was locked. By the time he put his shoulder to the door, the other residents of the house had emerged from their rooms and were watching, peering over the banister rails, their eyes dull with the new day. Finally the lock splintered and he tumbled into the room. She had hung a rope from one of the central beams. Her body still swung a little from side to side like a pendulum just before it stops completely. John had to scream in the face of the waiter who lived in the other room on this floor before he would help him get her down. It was too late. She was most likely dead even before he had begun shouting her name.

They laid her on the bed and one of the women went to phone the police from *Le Rat Mort* on Place Pigalle. He waited with the body until they arrived. The misery in the room pressed on him, as if Rose Champion had left a desperate ghost behind her to whisper in his ear about the hopeless vanity of his ambitions.

By the time the police arrived, John Edwards was not young or romantic any more. Once the gendarmes had been and the morgue van had taken away the body, he packed his trunk and left the building for good. He called at Académie Lafond to inform his professor what had happened and of his decision to leave Paris, but his master was not there and the rather off-hand way Mrs Lafond spoke to him irritated his already over-strung nerves. Rather than leave a note he simply told her what had happened, perhaps rather more graphically than necessary and without regard to the fact there was a servant in the room. The latter's shocked face haunted him as he prepared to return to his mother's comfortable house in Clapham and resume his career as a clerk at Howarth's Insurance Company in the City. There can be too much truth.

The servant in the room was the maid who tended to the ladies in the Passage des Panoramas atelier. She left the offices in Rue Vivienne before Mme Lafond could tell her to keep the news to herself and so it escaped, awkward and disturbing and stinking of misery.

Even though the women who studied at Académie Lafond paid twice the fees the men did, their studio accommodation was no more than adequate. The only light came from the glassed ceiling and the room was narrow and high, so that it seemed sometimes as if their models were posing at the bottom of a well. The stove was unpredictable and bad-tempered. Nevertheless it was worth paying the money to be able to study art. The rough manners of the male students meant that no middle-class woman could work in a mixed class – and sharing life models with male students caused ugliness. At the women-only studios a female could prepare for a career as an artist without sacrificing her dignity or reputation, and even if the professional artists who visited them did not spend as much time guiding their female students, at least they did come, so the modest women could make modest progress and their families could trust that although they were artists, their daughters were still reasonably sheltered. The suicide of a student put a dangerous question-mark over this respectability, and news of it would probably have been suppressed if it had been given privately. As it was, it spilled out of Lafond's office and made its way up the stairs and into the room where Maud Heighton and her fellow students were at work.

Maud, perched on a high stool with her palette hooked on her thumb, heard their teaching assistant exclaim and turned her head. Mademoiselle Claudette was making the sign of the cross over her thin chest. That done, she squeezed her almond-shaped eyes closed for a second, then helped the maid set down the kettle on the top of the stove. When it was safe, she placed a hand on the servant's shoulder.

Maud frowned, her attention snagged by that initial gasp. There was some memory attached to the sound. Then it came to her. It was just the noise her sister-in-law, Ida, had made on the morning of the fire. Her brother, James, had driven the car right up to Maud where she stood at the front of the fascinated crowd, her hair down and her face marked with soot. Ida had got out of the car without waiting for James to open the door for her, looked at the smoking ruins of the auctioneer's place of business and the house Maud and James had grown up in, and given just that same gasp.

Maud turned towards Mademoiselle Claudette the moment the older woman rested her hand on the maid's shoulder. The assistant was normally a woman of sharp, nervous movements, but this gesture was softly intimate. Maud wanted to click her fingers to stop the world, like a shutter in a camera, and fix what she saw: the neatly coiffed heads of the other young women turned away from their easels, the model ignored, all those eyes leading towards the two women standing close together by the stove. The finished painting formed in Maud's mind – a conversation piece entitled *News Arrives*. The shaft of light reaching them from above fell across Mademoiselle Claudette's back, while the maid's anxious face was in shadow. Was it possible to capture shock in paint, Maud wondered – that moment of realisation that today was not going to be as other days?

Mademoiselle Claudette ushered the maid out into the hallway then closed the door to the studio behind them. The semi-sacred atmosphere of concentration still hung over the women, keeping them silent, but no one put brush to canvas again. They paused like mermaids just below the water, waiting for one of their number to be the first to break the surface, into the uncertain air.

'Rose Champion is dead!' Francesca blurted out. It was done. A flurry of exclamations ran around the room. The high walls echoed with taps and clicks as palettes were put aside, brushes set down and the women looked at the plump Prussian girl who had spoken. Her eyes were damp and her full bottom lip shook. The high collar on her blouse made her look like a champagne bottle about to burst. 'The maid said she killed herself. She was found hanged in her room this morning. Oh Lord, have mercy on us! Poor Rose!' She looked about her. 'When did we see her last?'

'Not since summer, I think,' a blonde, narrow-hipped girl answered, one of the Americans whose French accent remained

unapologetically Yankee. 'She didn't come back this year, did she?'
There was general agreement. 'Did anyone see her about since
then?'

'I saw her,' Maud said at last, remembering even as she spoke.
She felt the eyes of the women swing towards her, she who spoke
so rarely. 'She was in the Tuileries Gardens sketching Monsieur
Pol with his sparrows.' The other women nodded. Pol was one of
the sights of Paris, ready to be admired just outside the Louvre in
his straw boater, whistling to the birds, and calling to them by
name. 'It was a month ago perhaps. She was thinner, but . . . just
as she always was.'

One of the students had begun to make the tea and the boiling
water splashed a little. The girl cursed in her own language, then
with a sigh put down the kettle and produced a coin from her
pocket to pay her fine. Claudette used the money to buy the little
cakes and pastries the women ate during their morning breaks.
When funds were low they fined each other for inelegant phrasing.
In the Paris art world, Lafond's girls were said to paint like
Academicians and speak like duchesses.

'Poor Rose,' Francesca said more softly. The women sighed and
shook their heads.

The room was filling with cigarette smoke and murmured
conversation. '*La pauvre, la pauvre . . .*' echoed round the studio
like a communal prayer.

Maud looked to see if any painting of Miss Champion's
remained on the walls. Perhaps once a month during his twice-
weekly visits to his students, M. Lafond would nod at one of the
women's paintings and say, 'Pop it up, dear.' It was a great honour.
Francesca had cried when Lafond had selected one of her pictures.
He had not yet selected any work of Maud's. She had submitted
successfully to the official Paris Salon early this year – the head and

shoulders oil portrait of a fellow student – but even if the Academicians approved of her worked, careful style and thought it worthy of exhibition in the Grand Palais, Lafond did not think she had produced anything fresh enough for his draughty attic classroom.

Maud had written to her brother and sister-in-law about having the painting in the exhibition. Even in the north-east of England they had heard of the Paris Salon, but the reaction had not been what she had hoped for. If James had sounded proud or impressed, she might have asked him for a loan and used the money to spend the summer in Fontainebleau and recover her health out of the heat and dust of the capital. All the other women she worked with seemed to have funds to do so. Instead he had asked if a sale were likely, reminding her that she still owed him ten pounds. Her little half-brother Albert though had sent her a cartoon of a great crowd of men in hats grouped round a painting and shouting *Hurrah!* There had been no sale. Her portrait hung high on the walls, and surrounded by so many similar works, it went unnoticed.

There *was* a canvas from Rose Champion. It showed the Place Pigalle in early-morning light. The human figures were sketchy and indistinct, blurred by movement. One of the new double-decker motor-buses, identifiable only by its colours and bulk, rattled along the Boulevard Clichy. By the fountain a few rough female figures lounged – the models, mostly Italian, some French, who gathered there every morning waiting for work from the artists of Montmartre and Pigalle. They were scattered like leaves under the bare, late-autumn trees. Rose had lavished her attention on the light; the way it warmed the great pale stone buildings of Paris into honey tones; the regular power and mass of the hotels and apartment blocks, the purple and green shadows, the glint on the pitch-black metalwork around the balconies. The American was right, Rose had not returned to the studio after the summer, but the picture remained. M. Lafond must have bought it for himself. Maud felt as if someone were pressing her heart between their palms. The girl was dead and she was still jealous.

'She was ill,' the American said to Francesca. 'I called on her before I left for Brittany this summer. She said everything she had done was a failure and that there was . . .' she rubbed her fingertips together '. . . no money. I've never seen a woman so proud and so poor. Most girls are one or the other, don't you agree?'

'I saw her a week ago,' said an older woman, sitting near the model. Her shoulders were slumped forward. 'She was outside Kahnweiler's gallery. She seemed upset, but she wouldn't talk to me.'

Maud wondered if Rose had seen something in the wild angular pictures sold by Kahnweiler which she herself was trying to achieve but could not – whether that would have been enough to make her hang herself. Or was it hunger? More likely. Hunger squeezed the hope out of you. Maud held her hand out in front of her. It shook. I hate being poor, she thought. I hate being hungry. But I will survive. Another year and I shall be able to paint as I like and people will buy my work and I shall eat what I want and be warm. If I can just manage another winter.

She looked up, possessed by that strange feeling that someone was eavesdropping on her thoughts. Yvette, the model for the life-class that week, was watching her, her dressing-gown drawn carelessly up over her shoulders as she sat on the dais, tapping her cigarette ash out on the floor. She was a favourite in the studio, cheerfully complying when asked for a difficult pose, still and controlled while they worked but lively and happy to talk to them about other studios and artists in her breaks. Yvette was a little older than some of the girls, and occasionally Maud wondered what she thought of them all as she looked out from the dais with those wide blue eyes, what she observed while they tried to mimic the play of light across her naked shoulders, her high cheekbones. Now the model nodded slightly to Maud, then looked away. Her face, the angle of it, suggested deep and private thought.

Mademoiselle Claudette returned and soon realised that the news she had to give was already known. The facts she had to offer were simply a repeat of what Francesca had already overheard.

'Is there anyone here who knows anything of Miss Champion's people in England?'

'I believe she had an aunt in Sussex she lived with as a child,' Maud said into the silence that followed. 'But I have no idea of her address. Were there no letters?'

'We shall discover something, I hope. Very well.' The woman looked at her watch. 'It is ten to the hour. Let us return to work at ten minutes past. Monsieur Lafond asks me to tell you that in light of this unhappy event he will reserve the pleasure of seeing you until tomorrow.' There was a collective groan around the room. Mademoiselle Claudette ignored it, but frowned as she clicked the cover back onto her watch and turned to the tea-table.

'Does he fear a plague of suicides if he tells us we are miserable oafs today?' Francesca said, a little too loudly. The students began to stand, stretch, make their way to the pile of teacups and little plates of cakes.

'My darlings, good day! How are you all on this dismal morning? Why is everyone looking so *terribly* grim?' Tatiana Sergeyevna Koltsova made her entrance in a cloud of furs and fragrance. Maud smiled. It was a pleasure to look at her. For all that she was Russian, it seemed to Maud that Tanya was the real spirit of Paris, the place Maud had failed to become part of: bright, beautiful, modern, light. She would chat to Yvette or tease Lafond himself and they all seemed to think her charming. Not all the other women students liked her, no one with looks, talent and money will be short of enemies, but Tanya seemed blissfully ignorant of any animosity directed towards her.

Francesca straightened up from the tea-table where she had been leaning. 'Be gentle with us today, my sweet. There's been a death in the family.'

The Russian's kid glove flew up to cover her pretty little mouth. At the same moment she let her furs drop from her shoulders and her square old maid bundled forward to gather them in her arms before they could pool onto the paint-stained floor. Maud watched as Francesca lowered her voice and explained. The Russian was blinking away tears. That was the thing about Tanya. She could be genuinely moved by the sufferings of others even as she threw off her cape for her maid to catch. She arrived late every day and one could still smell on her the comfort of silk sheets, chocolate on her breath. Then she would paint, utterly absorbed, for two hours until the clock struck and the women began to pack away. She would shake herself and look about her smiling, her canvas glowing and alive with pure colour.

Yvette tied her dressing-gown round her then clambered down from the model throne on the dais and passed the table, dropping the stub of her cigarette on the floor and grabbing up a spiced cake in the same moment. As she chewed she put her hand on the Russian's elbow and led her away into a far corner of the room. The movement seemed to wake Maud. She stood and went over to the food and helped herself, trying not to move too urgently nor take too much. She ate as slowly as she could.

The Russian materialised at her side like a spirit while she was still licking her lips. 'Miss Heighton?' Maud was startled, but managed a 'Good morning'. She had never had any conversation with Tanya, only watched her from a distance as if she were on the other side of a glass panel. 'I know it is not the most pleasant day for walking, but will you take a little stroll with me after we pack away today? I have something particular to ask you.'

Maud said she would be pleased to do so. Tanya smiled at her, showing her sharp white teeth, then turned to find her place amidst the tight-packed forest of easels. Maud steered her own way back to her place on the other side of the room and stared at the canvas in front of her, wondering what the Russian could want with her. The model was once again taking her place on the raised platform. She glanced at Maud and winked. Maud smiled a little uncertainly and picked up her brush.

An atmosphere of quiet concentration began to fill the room once more – Rose Champion already, to some degree, forgotten. The food seemed to have woken Maud's hunger rather than suppressed it. She closed her eyes for a moment, waiting for the sting of it to pass, then set to work.

CHAPTER 2

'VLADIMIR! WE ARE READY FOR YOU!'

Maud thought Tanya would speak to her on the pavement where the covered arcade of Passage des Panoramas gave out onto the wide, tree-lined expanse of Boulevard Montmartre, but instead she put her arm through Maud's and waved her free hand at a smart blue motor which was waiting, its engine idling, under the winter skeleton of a plane tree. It rolled smoothly towards them and stopped precisely by the ladies. Maud noticed as the chauffeur hopped out of the machine and went to open the automobile's rear door for them that his livery matched the dark blue enamel of the car itself. Tanya's maid clambered into the front with the painting gear while Tanya herself ushered Maud into the back seat and said something in Russian to the driver. Maud heard the words *Parc Monceau* and the driver bowed before closing the door on them and returning to his seat.

'I hope you don't mind, Maud – by the way, may I call you Maud? Good. I need a little greenery after being shut up inside all morning. We shall run you to wherever you want to go later on.' The Russian pulled off her leather gloves and lay back with a sigh against the heavily upholstered seat. Maud made some polite reply and looked out of the window as the car pulled away into the stream of other motors, carriages and motor-buses. What did this princess want of her? Did she perhaps have a drawing pupil for her? Pupils were hard to come by in a city packed to its heaving gills with artists, but if she did, a few extra francs a month would make all the difference to Maud. She felt the curl of hope in her belly under the hunger.

Paris ate money. Paint and canvas ate money. Maud's training ate money. Paris yanked each copper from her hand and gave her back nothing but aching bones and loneliness. It was as if she had never quite arrived, as if she had stepped out of the grand frontage of the Gare du Nord, and Paris – the real Paris – had somehow retreated round the corner leaving all these open palms behind it. She was on the wrong side of the glass, pressed up against it, but trapped by her manners, her sober serious nature, behind this invisible divide. She spent her evenings alone in cheap lodgings reading and sketching in poor light. Her illness last winter – she had been feeding herself too little, been too wary of lighting the fire when the damp crawled off the river – had swallowed francs by the fistful. She must not get ill again, but she had even less money now. Sometimes she felt her stock of bravery had been all used up in getting here at all.

Even with winter closing in, the boulevard was full of activity – the shop girls in short skirts running errands with round candy-striped hatboxes dangling from their wrists, the women with their fashionable pinched-in jackets being ushered into restaurants by bowing waiters.

'Tell me,' Tanya said, 'did you know Miss Champion well? I thought, perhaps, you both being Englishwomen . . .'

Maud shook her head; her thoughts were loose and drifting and it took her a moment to recall where she was. She blinked and found herself looking into Tanya's large black eyes. She thought of

Rose, all sharp angles and anger. 'Not well at all. I found her rather . . . rather cruel, as a matter of fact.'

Tanya drew a small metal compact from her purse and examined her complexion, brushing away a little loose powder with her fingertip. Most women in Paris went into the world masked with heavy white foundation and their mouths coloured a false glistening red. Tanya's use of powder and paint was subtle by comparison, but brought up as she had been, Maud found it rather shocking and was embarrassed by her own unworldliness. She had thought herself rather wise in the ways of the world until she came to Paris. Every day that passed, she was in danger of thinking a little less of herself.

'I'm glad you say that,' Tanya said and snapped the compact shut again. 'Lord knows I am sorry anyone gets so desperate they hurt themselves, but she *was* terribly mean. I once asked her to comment on a study I was doing – it was my own fault really, I didn't want her opinion, it was simply I admired her and wanted her to praise me – and her advice was "stop painting".'

Maud laughed suddenly and covered her mouth.

Tanya grinned. 'I know! I said it was my own fault, but still – what a thing to say! She painted beautifully, I think, and in fairness she was not vain about it.'

'Yes, if one dared to say anything to her she looked as if she despised one,' Maud replied. 'She didn't think of any of us as artists at all. Perhaps she was right.'

'Nonsense,' Tanya said firmly and Maud blushed. 'There are some women at Lafond's who will do nothing more than paint nasty still lifes. There are others who are serious. You are serious, Maud. So am I. About my work at least.' The compact went back into the little embroidered bag over her arm. 'Now I shall be quiet for a minute and let you look out of the window.'

The sensation of being driven was very pleasant. Maud had been in her brother's motor a few times before, but she couldn't see why he liked it. The thing rattled your teeth and shook, and was forever making strange banging noises. This motor though was quite different; they seemed to float over the streets and the engine's regular fricatives made Maud think of contented pets. For the past few weeks, walking through the city between her classes and her lodgings had been a bleak necessity rather than a pleasure. The cold was bitter and Maud could not afford a coat thick enough to keep it from getting into her bones, and you needed money to rest in the pavement cafés, heated with braziers and defended from the winds with neat barriers of clipped box-hedge. Now though, Maud was snug behind the window seals of the motor-car, her legs covered with a rug lined in fur, and Paris unrolled in front of them like a cinema film.

The car argued its way through the traffic under the fifty-two Corinthian pillars and wide steps of the new Eglise de la Madeleine, then swung up Boulevard Malesherbes past the dome of Saint-Augustin. All movement and variety. Street-hawkers and boulevardiers, women dragging carts of vegetables or herring. The charming busy face of Paris a thousand miles away from Maud's draughty room in one of the back alleys around Place des Vosges, in a house just clinging to respectability, with its paper-thin sheets and the miserable collection of failed businessmen and poor widows who gathered around the landlady's table in the evening and tried to pretend her thin soups and stews were enough to sustain them.

Tanya grew quiet and let Maud enjoy the view until they reached Parc Monceau and the motor-car came to a gentle halt near the colonnade. Tanya sprang out before the chauffeur had time to open the door for her. 'Actual trees! Don't you feel like a butterfly pinned up in a case in Paris sometimes?'

Maud followed her onto the path. 'A little, I suppose. Though butterflies in cases are meant to be looked at, and no one looks at me.'

'I wish I could go out and about without being watched sometimes,' Tanya said casually, then turned to her maid and said something in Russian. You could try being poor, Maud thought. The conversation with the maid became a long and passionate debate that ended with Tanya stamping her foot and the maid crossing her arms over her bosom and frowning. The chauffeur had returned to the car and stared straight ahead the whole time, his face immobile.

'My maid Sasha is convinced still water is unhealthy,' Tanya said, taking Maud's arm and flouncing with her towards the little lake. 'She swears if I get typhoid she will not nurse me! You would think I had said I was going to swim the length of the Seine before lunch rather than take a little walk with you.'

Tanya's indignation had made her eyes shine and she held her chin high. She reminded Maud suddenly of little Albert, six years old and always right, and always shocked at the gross stupidity and moral turpitude of his elders. 'She had care of you when you were a child, perhaps?'

'Yes, and I was a sickly infant. Now I must spend hours every day convincing her and my aunts that I am sickly no more. You are not too cold?'

'Not at all, Miss Koltsova.'

'Oh, I am Tanya. Call me that. I love to walk here. It is the most respectable park in Paris, so my old cats can't complain, even if Sasha does.'

'Old cats?'

'My two aunts who live with me and make sure I am kept *comme il faut*. Vera Sergeyevna can tell you the order in which any company should come in to dinner within five minutes of entering a draw-ing room – she is an expert in all forms of protocol – and Lila Ivanovna, my late mother's sister, is here to agree with everything she says. Papa would not let me come to Paris without them! Lord, the weeping I had to do to make him let me come at all. They are my guardian angels, apparently. Guardian gargoyles, they seem to me.' She paused and Maud wondered if she was about to tell her what she wanted to hear: about rich pupils who wanted long lessons in warm houses. Instead she went on, 'The best families in Paris send their nurses here with their little babies for their fresh air.'

Tanya walked on with a slight swaying step as if on the verge of breaking into a skip or a run; her long straight skirt swung and rippled round her. Maud began to think she had been wrong about the drawing lessons. Something like that could have been discussed while walking through Passage des Panoramas surely, and there was a nervous edge to Tanya's chatter. Well, she would ask event-ually. In the meantime Maud had never been to this park before, so she looked about her with pleasure and saw full, mature trees and pathways that wandered in curves; it made the Tuileries seem a desert.

The lake was edged with a semi-circle of Corinthian columns, not on the monumental scale of the Madeleine, but with the same classical decadence, narrow trunks topped with stylised foliage. Great swathes of ivy had been allowed to clamber over them in romantic festoons. It made Maud realise how ordered, how con-structed Paris in general could appear. The grand boulevards seemed like a demand for order, the tree roots ringed with gratings as if they might escape. Here nature was controlled with a lighter touch. A handful of smartly dressed women read novels on scattered metal chairs, their faces hidden by the swooping brims of their hats. Maud looked at them, the angles of their necks and hands, the physical body in the world. A formally dressed gentleman complete with silk top hat looked out over the surface of the lake and smoked his cigar, creating a personal fog-bank. A dozen *nourrices* in their high white muslin caps and long cloaks pushed prams along the gravel paths, nodding to one another like society beauties in the Bois de Boulogne.

'It is possible to see how rich the baby is by the quality of the cap and cloak of his nurse,' Tanya said, watching one young woman pass them with her little nose in the air. 'Look at those ribbons! The baby is either a prince or an American. Which here amounts to the same thing, of course. I am sure they are all shocking snobs, these girls.'

Maud wanted very much to say something light and clever in reply, but she was becoming tired and every woman here made her feel shabby and afraid. There was some trick of dress taught to every Frenchwoman in the cradle, it seemed. The *trottins* who fetched and carried for the dressmakers and milliners could be no richer than Maud, yet they seemed to know how to look neat and fresh. One of Lafond's male students told her that the French gendarmes said they always knew the nationality of a suicide pulled from the river by their clothes; the English girls were always badly dressed. Maud had not been sure what reaction the young man had been expecting, but he saw something in her face that had made him apologise and back away quickly.

'If I say something to you, will you try very hard not to take offence at it?' Tanya said.

Maud's heart sank. It did not sound like the opening of a conversation about drawing pupils, and if the Russian did say something offensive to her now she would have to leave at once, painfully hungry and further from home than she had been at the studio.

'I will try and take anything you say as it is meant,' she replied quietly.

'Very well, dear.' Tanya patted her arm. Maud glanced at her. Her face was shadowed by the brim of her hat, but one could still see the long clean line of her jaw. Her hair was beautifully black. She could not be more than twenty-two. 'I am a little worried about you, my dear Maud. You are looking too thin and too pale for a girl about to face a Paris winter. I am afraid you are spending money on colours you should be spending on food.' Maud felt herself blush and she straightened herself. Tanya was talking quickly, looking forward. 'There's no shame in it, naturally. The men behave as if poverty alone can make you a genius, but it is easier for them. So many girls come to Paris and find it rather more expensive than they had bargained for – it is Paris, after all. I am forever signing cheques to charitable foundations who are trying to get them back home before any greater harm comes to them!'

It was a sign of her hunger and the truth of what Tanya was saying that Maud's discreet good manners were not enough to stop her tongue. 'You wish to pay my fare home before I hang myself or take on a gentleman protector, Miss Koltsova?'

Tanya came to a sudden halt, and looked at Maud with wide and frightened eyes. 'Lord, is it that bad? I only thought you were beginning to look a bit unwell! You're not about to do either of those things, are you?'

'Certainly not, but—'

'I'm very glad to hear that! What a ghastly thought!' She looked so shocked that Maud suddenly laughed. One of the readers lifted her eyes briefly from her novel. Tanya gave a great sigh and hugged Maud's arm to her again. 'Oh, you mustn't tease me like that, I shall have nightmares.'

'I did not mean to tease you. I meant to tell you to mind your own business, but you rather cut me off.'

Tanya looked a little guilty. 'Yes, I suppose I did. I am sorry. Do you wish to tell me to mind my own business now?'

Maud shook her head. 'No, I find the wind has gone out of my sails rather. But I still have enough money to buy my fare home, so I need not apply to one of those charities you mention. I do not want to go home, Tanya. I find life here . . . difficult, I admit that, but I have so much more to learn and no chance of learning it back home. I'd have to live with my brother and he'd try to marry me to one of his chinless friends.'

'Urff, we have those in Russia too. When I marry, I shall choose a nice modern American. They are so beautifully clean.' She came to a halt and put her hand to her forehead. 'I have said things the wrong way about, then rattled off in the wrong direction. I had a terrible education, you know, and now I say what I think! That would never do in England, would it?'

'Certainly not,' Maud answered, thinking of her sister-in-law Ida, mistress of the pointed euphemism.

'Thank goodness I am in Paris where they see me as an eccentric and think it charming. My eldest aunt is far worse. She tells the women they all dress like prostitutes and she has become quite the social success as a result.' Tanya began walking again, pulling Maud alongside her. 'I think I might be able to help you, and I did not mean to suggest you should go home, but do you really think you have so much left to learn? I mean, the sort of things that are taught rather than found in oneself, through work. I think your painting terribly accomplished. Perhaps you just need to learn to trust yourself. Be a little more free. Don't you think that Manet and Degas have broken off our shackles? We must learn to stretch our limbs.'

Maud's head was beginning to swim rather and to concentrate on her answer took effort. 'Then I hope *that* can be taught, because I do not trust myself now. I think . . . I think if I could stay in Paris until next summer, then perhaps . . . But I cannot take charity, Miss Koltsova, however kindly meant. I would hate myself.'

It was as if Tanya had not heard her. 'Have you visited the Steins in Rue de Fleurus near the Luxembourg Gardens? Oh, I must take you there this evening then. Such paintings they have on their walls! All wildness and change and new ideas. There are no rules left, it seems. I think while those painters charge ahead like bulls, sweeping everything away before them, they make some space for us to paint as we like.'

'Tanya . . .'

The Russian paused again and blushed. 'I asked you to walk with me because I want to take you to see someone this afternoon. Her name is Miss Harris, and she has a house in Avenue de Wagram for English and American girls who find themselves destitute in Paris. Oh, don't bridle up again! She has a free registrar for work, and yes, I have contributed to her funds in the past. I am sure she might have something of use to you – English lessons or some such. You know, many ladies in Paris pay good money for a few hours' conversation a week. Now, you cannot be offended by that, can you? We shall go there at once.'

The idea of asking for help, even if it were just a recommendation from a charitable English lady, made Maud shrink away. Her pride flared up. She had got this far by her own efforts, why should she start becoming obliged to people now? What would her brother say, if he knew she was reduced to begging for a few hours' teaching English? If Tanya had asked her to teach some young relative or friend, then Maud could have felt the benefit of the extra francs and convinced herself that she, Maud, was the one granting the favour. To go and see this woman would be an open admission of failure. She felt as if all the activity in Parc Monceau had been frozen, as if everyone there, the ladies with their novels, the nurses with their pampered little charges, was staring at her to see if she would admit defeat. Whether by accident or design their conversation had carried them round the perimeter of the lake and they were once again beside Tanya's motor-car. The chauffeur had already stepped out and opened the door for them.

Maud generally ate no breakfast on studio days, trusting in the little spiced cakes to see her through to lunchtime when for a franc she might get an omelette, bread and vin ordinaire at one of the cafés near the studio. That would then sustain her till evening, or nearly sustain her. There was no way to squeeze more nourishment from her coin, that she knew by long trial. She should have eaten that meagre meal almost an hour ago and she could feel her hunger turning darker and more threatening. The idea of going anywhere, doing anything with her stomach aching and a feathery weakness beginning to spread through her limbs was impossible, yet resisting or telling Tanya the urgency of her hunger was likewise unthinkable. She let herself be guided back into the car and heard Tanya give another address then sat in the car with her eyes downcast.

CHAPTER 3

*T*HEIR DESTINATION WAS VERY CLOSE BY. TANYA took her arm as they got out of the car and Maud felt herself sway against her. Tanya took the pressure for affection and squeezed her arm happily in return. Maud looked around her. They were in front of a good-sized building. The façade showed the familiar restrained elegance of Haussmann's Paris. Classical, stately, like all the main avenues and boulevards, it gave no hint of the poverty or fear that might be hidden in the yards and alleys behind it. English manners in stone.

Tanya pulled Maud up to the door with her, then looked up and, shielding her eyes against the grey glare of the sky, waved. Maud followed her gaze and saw leaning over the balcony of the second floor a woman of perhaps sixty, bright-eyed, bundled up warmly in a long dark-green coat and waving vigorously back.

'Miss Harris!' Tanya called up even as she pulled on the bell. 'We have come to see you. Are we welcome?'

'Always, dear!' the lady shouted back cheerfully and the white head disappeared again as the front door opened. A maid, looking particularly fearsome in tightly fitting black and solid shoes, stood in front of them. Behind her was a black and white tiled floor and a steeply climbing staircase. Everything was clean and orderly. A woman dressed in a monkish style crossed the corridor with a pile of papers in her hand and somewhere in the house, Maud heard the trill of a telephone bell.

'Miss 'Arris is not at home,' the maid said, and began to close the door again. 'If you wish to register for work, use the back-door bell. The refuge is full and the times of the free dinner and Bible study are marked 'ere.' She pointed at a little box of pamphlets attached to a railing and fluttering damply in the cold breeze.

Tanya flushed and put her hand on the wood of the door. 'Nonsense, my girl. I have just seen Miss Harris on the balcony.'

'Miss 'Arris has been working since six this morning,' the maid said darkly and not moving an inch. 'Miss 'Arris is now taking the air. Miss 'Arris is not at home.'

The lady called down from the balcony again. 'Simone, do be reasonable. I swear I have been out here twenty minutes. I have had quite enough air! Do let the girls in and come and unlock the door so I can get back to my office.'

The maid stepped out into the street and called up angrily. 'Ten! Ten minutes only!'

'Simone . . .' The lady's voice had a hint of steel in it now. The maid threw up her hands.

'Very well! We shall let these women in, we shall let you work yourself to death and then we shall all starve in the gutter or go to be registered. Much better than letting these women wait or go to the side door – oh, much better!' Simone stood aside to let Maud and Tanya in, then slammed the street door hard enough to make the vase on the hall-table rattle. She thrust open a door to the right that led into a small office with a table and chairs and several filing cabinets, and took them through into another room of about the same size, with one large desk and a number of rather sentimental watercolours on the walls. Most seemed to involve children and dogs. Simone picked up two dining chairs and thumped them down in front of the desk then stared fiercely at Tanya. 'Ten minutes!' she hissed, her finger raised and pointed. 'Starve!' Feeling her point had been made, she sighed deeply and removed a large key from the pocket of her apron, nodded over it sadly then left them.

Tanya looked a little sheepish and normally Maud would have been amused, but keeping her wits about her was as much as she could manage. She took her seat, afraid she might faint. In a very few minutes Miss Harris joined them, pink in the face and unbuttoning her coat. She hung it rather carelessly on the coatstand by the door, closed the door behind her then smoothed her skirts and put out her hand to them both. Maud wavered a little as she stood again and had to grab onto the back of her chair. Though Miss Harris was shaking Tanya's hand with both her own, Maud thought her unsteadiness had not gone unnoticed. She shook hands with Miss Harris as Tanya introduced her and felt the quick appraising look from her small dark eyes.

'Sit down, dears! Sit down. My apologies for Simone. She always promises she will not lock me out then, hoop-la, as soon as my back is turned I find she has turned the key. She means well, of course.'

The woman settled herself behind the desk. There was a little heap of messages left in front of her and, on either side of her, paperwork was piled into towers that reached as high as her own head. She rifled through the messages with one hand, while reaching blindly behind her to pick up a speaking tube fastened to the wall. Still reading, she whistled down it and on hearing a grunt at the other end spoke. 'Beef tea and sandwiches, dear, quick as you can,' then she stoppered the tube and clipped it back into place. Her right hand now free, she picked up a pen and began to make notes in very small handwriting on the papers in front of her. For the first time since she had met Tanya, Maud noticed out of the corner of her eye that the Russian looked a little unsure of herself. Miss Harris said nothing more until the fearsome maid arrived with the tray and set it down on the desk, directly in front of Maud.

'I am very sorry to have disturbed you, Miss Harris,' Tanya said a little plaintively, 'when you wish to eat.'

'Don't be absurd, dear,' Miss Harris replied evenly. 'The food is for Miss Heighton.' She smiled at Maud, wrinkling her nose a little as she did. 'Eat up before you faint away, dear girl. Now, Tanya dear, to your left is yesterday's *Times*. I wish you would read to me the correspondence page while I finish these little notes and Miss Heighton gets her wind back.'

Tanya managed to pick up the newspaper while casting a look both shocked and a little offended at Maud. 'Maud, why did you not say you were hungry?'

'What did you expect her to say?' Miss Harris said sharply. 'I am afraid I have had more chance to see the signs of hunger in a girl than you have, Tanya. Now do read, if you can manage the English.'

'Naturally I can,' Tanya said, and while she read the various letters very carefully and in a clear voice Maud ate as slowly and steadily as she could. She could not remember the last time she had eaten good meat or bread that did not taste of chalk, and the beef tea seemed to enter her bloodstream like a drug, warming and comforting her. The room felt calm and secure as she ate everything that had been brought to her to the sound of Tanya's pretty Russian accent and the scratchings of Miss Harris's pen. When she had finished, she sat back with a sigh.

Miss Harris at once replaced the cap on her fountain pen with a businesslike click and then rang the little bell beside her. The door opened immediately and the young woman they had seen crossing the hall earlier entered. Her dress was very dark and severe in its cut. She stood very straight and unsmiling. Her hair was scraped back from her face and she wore little round eyeglasses. Tanya shuddered.

'Charlotte, dear, do take the tray away, and here . . .' Miss Harris piled her notes onto it next to Maud's crumbs, 'are the answers to the messages and notes from this morning.' She shook her head. 'I sometimes wish we had never thought to have a telephone installed. Is there anyone here for me, Charlotte?'

The severe young woman nodded. 'Two new girls and Mr Allardyce.'

Miss Harris waved her hand. 'Feed them and I will see them anon. The girls, I mean. I doubt Mr Allardyce would enjoy the beef tea.'

Charlotte did not smile. 'He is here to see if you have any unpleasant business for him this afternoon.'

'Certainly I shall. Well, you may send him in when I have finished with these ladies and look out the file on Miss Knight. I am sure he will help us there.'

Charlotte made a note in her little book then gathered up the tray and swept out of the room again while Miss Harris settled back in her chair. 'Dear Mr Allardyce! Such a useful young man. Miss Knight was forced to leave her luggage behind her in her last lodgings and her former landlord is being unreasonable about releasing it. When Charlotte went to demand it, I'm afraid she threatened him with hellfire and he laughed at her. Mr Allardyce will simply mention by name any number of officials he knows through his newspaper work and the landlord will be much more impressed.'

Miss Harris leaned forward and hunched her shoulders, speaking rather low. 'Of course, our mighty Creator is our first and final help, but Mr Allardyce's methods are certainly efficacious. He is himself an answer to a prayer. I asked God for some practical help, and the very next day Mr Allardyce appeared wishing to write something about our work for the American periodicals. I drummed him into service at once. I have no idea why anyone doubts the power of sincere prayer, I find it most reliable.' She blinked brightly as if God were a trusted tradesman. 'How is Yvette?'

'Quite well,' Tanya said without any hint of the surprise Maud felt. 'She sits for us at Passage des Panoramas this week.'

Maud's confusion must have shown on her face even if she did not manage to put it into words. Mrs Harris nodded briskly, setting a little gold cross at her neck bouncing, then gathered up another pile of papers from the tower next to her and began to go through them. 'Yvette is a soul close to God, though she would laugh at me for saying so. It was she who first encouraged Miss Koltsova to favour us with her charity.' Tanya snorted and Maud guessed that Yvette had phrased the suggestion a little more abruptly than that. 'I have no doubt it was Yvette who told Tanya to bring you to me today, Miss Heighton.' Tanya blushed a little.

'How did you come to meet her, Miss Harris?' Maud asked. It was wonderful to feel the physical effects of a good meal. She began to see the details in the room more clearly, the light glimmering on the brass bell at Miss Harris's elbow. The silver-framed photograph of Queen Alexandra hanging on the pale green wall.

'Yvette came to tell me an Italian with a nasty reputation was hiring out three young English girls as models from Place Pigalle. The oldest was twelve. Mr Allardyce and I went to see the gentleman and took the girls into our care. The Italian was most indignant. He had bought the three sisters from their parents for five pounds on Gray's Inn Road in London. They were all adopted by a most respectable family in North Wales in the end, and they still send me postcards occasionally – some of which are quite well-spelled. Now, I think you have had sufficient time to gather your wits, Miss Heighton. What do you want of me, children?'

Maud realised at last that all this chatter, the correspondence page of *The Times*, the praise of Mr Allardyce, had been undertaken solely to allow her to recover a little. She blushed and tried to answer but her tongue seemed to lock in her mouth. Tanya spoke for her.

'Miss Heighton needs a few hours' paid work a week to see her through the winter. Nothing that will interfere with her classes at Lafond's and she will still wish to study in the afternoons for part of the week at least. What do you have on your books that might be suitable? Someone requiring English lessons, perhaps?'

Miss Harris drew back a little. 'Oh my dear, I am afraid that Paris is awash with educated Englishmen and -women willing and eager to give lessons. All I have on my books at the moment are positions for governesses, shop girls and maidservants.'

Maud bit her lip. She had not wanted to come here, but having come only to find herself useless and unwanted was humiliating. She thought of an artist she sometimes saw on Boulevard Saint-Michel, his corduroy jacket buttoned up to the throat to hide his lack of a clean shirt, selling oil sketches of the Luxembourg Gardens in violent pure colours. He would be there all day, hunched by his stand, selling them for a couple of francs a time. A woman doing the same would be stared at and mocked by the crowd, and avoided by the curious tourists who were his few customers.

'There must be something,' Tanya insisted, almost affronted. 'Does no old lady need a companion in the afternoons?'

'All the old ladies in Paris have their lap-dogs and the Bois de Boulogne,' Miss Harris replied. Then she brightened suddenly like a lap-dog who has seen the shadow of a rabbit cross its vision, and began rummaging through the pile of papers to her right with more energy than care. 'Now there was something I noticed the other day – Charlotte put it to one side for some reason. Companion . . . companion . . .' Still pulling at the papers, she called out, 'Charlotte? Charlotte, dear!' The monkish female appeared behind them again and sighed at the tumble of papers. 'Yesterday or the day before? Companion?'

Maud thought the two women must have been working together for some time as this abbreviated communication seemed sufficient.

'Monsieur Christian Morel. A live-in companion for his younger sister, Miss Sylvie – a sickly young woman who wishes to spend her free hours sketching the Paris streets and must have some respectable person to accompany her. He asked for a lady with some knowledge of art.' She turned back a few pages in her little black notebook. 'Rue de Seine. Board and lodging. And a weekly stipend.'

Miss Harris beamed. 'Perfect then! Why, the dear Lord has managed everything once again.' If the Deity had been present, Miss Harris would have patted Him. 'Send Mr Morel a card, dear, to say a Miss Heighton will be calling to discuss the position on Monday afternoon.'

Maud found her tongue at last. 'But my classes . . . ?'

Miss Harris waved her hand. 'I'm sure the Lord has thought of *that*. You shall see. Give the ladies the address, Charlotte dear.' A look on Charlotte's pale round face seemed to give Miss Harris pause. 'What is it?'

'He smiled too much,' Charlotte said. She was frowning over her notebook as if she were afraid of being thought foolish. 'And he is offering too much money.'

Miss Harris folded her hands in front of her. 'Miss Heighton is a sensible young woman. She will not allow anything to occur that might reflect badly on herself or us, I am sure.'

The Dress oil on canvas 64 × 41 cm

In contrast to the painting of the life-class at the Académie Lafond, this painting contains no human subject at all. Instead, the focus falls on a luxurious pink evening gown hanging by a mirror in a white dressing room. The setting is opulent: note the gilding on the room's panelling, the chandelier just appearing at the top of frame, the amount of tissue paper and striped boxes on the floor around the mirror, and the glimmer of sequins on the dress itself. However, it is the emptiness that fascinates. Who will wear the dress that has been chosen? Any other painter might have made this scene one of feminine intimacy, yet despite the delicate colouring the image is cold and empty; the woman who should be the centre and focal-point of the scene has been removed and the image becomes one of hollow vanity and excess.

Extract from the catalogue notes to the exhibition 'The Paris Winter: Anonymous Treasures from the de Civray collection', Southwark Picture Gallery, London, 2010

CHAPTER 4

*T*HE DOOR SWUNG OPEN AND A RATHER SHORT, square woman looked up at them.

'On whose introduction are you here?'

Maud did not catch the name Tanya gave, but it seemed to satisfy their host. The woman smiled, shook their hands and their little party was ushered inside. They entered a large high room, white-washed to the ceiling, with various odds and ends of heavy-looking furniture pushed against the walls, which were filled with the most bizarre and confusing canvases Maud had ever seen.

Tanya put her arm through Maud's. 'Are you glad we have come?'

'I am.'

Maud's day had been so disorientating it seemed only right it should end here. Tanya had not wanted to release her when they left Miss Harris and invited her to spend the evening with her. Maud had agreed, was touched by Tanya's transparent delight, and within an hour was enfolded in the luxury of Tanya's house in Rue Chalgrin. Tanya ushered her up the wide curved staircase and into her bedroom. It was a massive room, exploding with white and gold, but before Maud could get her bearings she was being chivvied into the dressing room which was almost as large again.

Tanya's French maid was summoned and Maud was persuaded to try on any number of evening dresses. Tanya left her to telephone a couple of young men approved of by her aunts who would take them to the Steins' At Home and then out to supper. Maud was on the other side of the glass certainly, but if she liked it or not she was still too dizzy to say. She was wrapped in one expensive dress after another while Tanya skipped about with delight and kept offering her more food, mostly chocolate.

'The pink, Maud! There's no doubt. You must wear the pink.' Tanya was sprawled on the chaise longue in a long evening dress of gold with black beading which shimmered as she moved. Maud felt the maid's quick hands adjusting the dress that Tanya had picked out for her. Her arms felt bare and cold.

Tanya glanced at the maid then said in English, 'What did you think of that young man, Maud?'

She looked over her shoulder and the maid sighed. Tanya was unwrapping another chocolate, dropping its gold wrapper back into the box and staring up at the chandelier. 'The American? Mr Allardyce? I thought he seemed very pleasant.'

Tanya frowned. 'Just pleasant? You didn't think he was handsome?'

Maud smiled. 'Handsome too.' He *was* handsome, now she thought of it. They had met for a few moments in the hall as they were leaving the house in Avenue de Wagram, and even in the confusion of her feelings Maud had noticed how he had looked at Tanya. Could these things happen in such a way? They had never happened to her.

Tanya begin ferreting about in the chocolate box for another bon-bon, then as soon as she had found one, dropped it again. 'He has a nice voice, I think.'

The maid presented Maud with a pair of low-heeled shoes dyed to match the dress and Maud was just slipping them onto her feet when the door opened and a large woman in a wide purple dress thirty years out of fashion though crackling with newness swept into the room. She spoke to Tanya loudly and in Russian, and the tone did not sound happy. A smaller lady in a dress of a similar cut albeit in yellow silk appeared behind her. It was the second lady who noticed Maud first and murmured something to the woman in purple. The titan paused and Tanya spoke in French.

'My dear aunts, may I present Miss Maud Heighton? I have invited her this evening, and really it's very respectable – half of Paris goes to the Steins'.'

'Yes, but which half?' the woman in purple replied, her French rich and dark as Tanya's gold-wrapped chocolates.

'Maud, my aunts, Vera Sergeyevna and Lila Ivanovna.'

Maud curtsied neatly and Vera Sergeyevna lifted her lorgnette to watch her do so, then nodded slightly. 'And who might you be? I do not know you.'

She would have replied, but Tanya was too quick. 'Miss Heighton is a fellow student at the Académie.' Vera Sergeyevna's eyes widened. 'Mikhail Pavlovich Perov is taking us to the Steins' this evening,' Tanya continued in a rush. Vera's gaze shifted to her niece and her expression softened slightly, then she and Tanya had a short conversation in Russian after which the two older ladies departed rather more calmly. Vera only inclined her head to Maud as she left; the other woman smiled at her more warmly.

When they had gone Tanya collapsed back onto the sofa with a deep sigh. 'Thank goodness I spoke to Perov. They are forever badgering me to accept his invitations so they couldn't protest now.' She grinned up at Maud. 'I don't suppose you have a cousin who is a baronet, do you, darling?'

'No, I do not. Is that what you told them?'

Her dark eyes fluttered wide and innocent. 'Yes – and that you've just arrived in Paris and your luggage was lost. I had to, otherwise by tomorrow Vera would be writing to my father about my keeping low company, though it was Perov who saved us. Are you sure? I thought everyone in England had a cousin who's a baronet.'

'Not everyone, Tanya.'

'Ah well, I suppose you know best. Now what shall we do with your hair?'

The crowd in the Steins' atelier was almost as interesting as the paintings on the walls and, Maud found, far easier to look at. Tanya had told her what she knew of the place while they were dressing; a pair of Americans, a brother and sister called Leo and Gertrude Stein, amused themselves by purchasing the most extreme examples of the new art they could find in studios and from specialist dealers, then allowed anyone with an introduction to visit them and be appalled by it any Saturday evening at their home on Rue de Fleurus.

There were already a great number of people in the room when the girls and their escorts arrived, some clothed as they were in fashionable evening dress, others *à la bohème* in loose trousers and high jackets for the men, peasant skirts and blouses for the women, who hung on their arms and took the cigarettes from their mouths when they wished to smoke. Maud heard German, French, English and what she thought might be Hungarian running off the tongues around her. She tried to ignore them and looked instead at the pictures. These were the wild, animalistic paintings that had come snorting and stamping into the Salons in the last few years, the colours of nature made somehow blistering and violent, the figures simplified until they were more ideas of humans than their likenesses. There was a portrait of their host, her face flattened into planes as if she were carved. Maud stood with her arm through Tanya's, at last so lost in what she was looking at that she forgot to be self-conscious about her dress or the way in which Tanya's maid had arranged her hair for her.

The girls walked slowly round the room until without consulting one another they came to a stop in front of a painting of a pair of circus performers, a mother and father sitting with their baby, an ape squatting at their feet and looking up at them. There was something of the Nativity Scene about it, a sense of calm, the gentle warmth of the colouring. Maud felt almost as if she were intruding on them by looking at it so closely. The harlequin father of the little group wore a costume of the same pale pink as Maud's borrowed dress.

'We shall have to take it down now, I suppose,' a voice said beside her in English. Maud turned to find her host, Miss Stein, beside them, her strong plain face shining with a religious intensity. 'He is painting quite differently now. You can see the whole of the modern revolution in art between the canvas you are looking at now and that one over there.' She pointed to the image of a woman, but cut up into geometrical planes, straight-edged shapes and black curves, and lurching, animal-like towards the viewer, her face a crude mask. Tanya peered up at it, lifting her white throat so that the jewels on her neck sparkled, trying to see by the yellowish gas-light.

'When I look at that, I feel as if someone is very angry with me,' she said at last.

Miss Stein laughed, a single exclamation.

'I shall tell Pablo that, but it is the future. He and Matisse are the only painters in town.' Then she added more quietly, 'I'm afraid your men are getting bored, girls. Best take them away quickly before they say something stupid and one of the artists punches them. Happens once a month at least.' She turned to greet some new arrival and Tanya glanced over her shoulder. The two men whom she had telephoned to come with them were slouching against the desk in the centre of the room, apparently oblivious to the art. Mr Perov was examining his nails and Mr Lebedev was yawning widely. Tanya's eyes narrowed.

'Oh Lord. I suppose she is right and we must take them away before they become offensive.' She looked up again at the butchered figure on the wall. 'Is that the future, do you think? It seems very cruel.'

'I do not think it is mine, Tanya.'

The Russian girl nodded. 'Yes, I hope some people will always want pictures that resemble something in the real world. Not all Americans are like the Steins, are they? Some of them might even prefer the way I paint.'

Maud wondered if she was thinking of Mr Allardyce again. 'I am certain that is so, Tanya.' The Russian girl smiled very brightly and led Maud over to their lounging escorts.

The following morning Maud woke in her narrow room wondering if the previous day had been a dream. Not until she saw the dusky-pink evening gown with its heavy beading of ribbons and pearls could she believe it had happened at all. Rose Champion dead. Miss Harris. The strange pictures and then supper at Maxim's. The images came back to her as if refracted through glass, and the gypsy band she had heard there seemed still to be playing their insistent music inside her head. Champagne, cigar smoke and laughter. Everywhere Maud looked, men and women had been laughing, heads flung back and their throats open. They had reappeared in her dreams, braying like donkeys till they grew long furred ears to match. The two Russian gentlemen had ordered supper for them then amused themselves by abusing the paintings on display at the Steins' house.

'How do they ever expect anyone to buy such things?' Perov said, still apparently fascinated by the study of his fingernails. He had a thin sandy moustache that seemed to dribble past the corners of his mouth. 'I would rather have this glass of champagne than everything that was on those walls. And the people! At least here one sees human beings properly dressed.'

He tittered, then waved to one of the crisply attired waiters and asked for more champagne while Maud winced at the gaiety around her. There was such noise. Everyone seemed to be speaking unnaturally loudly and the women moved so much when they spoke, pushing their shoulders back even as they leaned forward and constantly lifted their hands to the level of their heads. Maud noticed that the sequins on their dresses glimmered as they did so, and the shaded electric lights caught the jewels in their hair and on their hands with shifting rainbows of colour. Perhaps that was why they were doing it. The walls were golden and the pillars marble and mirrored so that everyone was forced to see a dozen shattered images of themselves in the crowd.

The woman on the next table wore a spray of ostrich plumes in her hair, fastened at their base with a diamond the size of a sovereign.

'Fake,' Mr Lebedev said, leaning towards her. She wondered if he meant her, that he had seen through the flim-flam of Tanya and her maid to the prudish poor Englishwoman who was not related to any baronet. 'The diamonds,' he elaborated, and she realised he meant the jewel at which she had been staring. 'Most of them anyway. Half the people here are liars and frauds. All show.' He then sat back in his chair again. It was as much as he had said all evening.

She sipped her champagne slowly – it tasted acid – and watched as any number of patrons approached the tables and spoke either to Tanya or one of the two men. The noise was shocking and the smoke from her neighbour's cigar made her feel a little nauseous. There must be something else, she thought. Something between the hungry squalor in which she had been living and this. She saw great platters of expensive food and rich sauces slowly turning cold in front of the silk- and velvet-clad diners. After an hour she began to be afraid she might be ill. Only Tanya's insistence meant that their escorts agreed to take them home with anything like good grace. Her old clothes were handed to her in a bundle by the chauffeur as he walked her to the door of her lodging-house and saw her let into the building. Perhaps the Morels would offer somewhere she could be comfortable, between the sinuous insinuating richness of the café with its twisted ironwork that pressed like a fever dream and the coldness of her room; between the wild anarchy of the painters who sold to the Steins and the facile decorations of the Académies. It formed a sort of desperate hope as she lay in her bed that Sunday morning, sick with surfeit rather than with hunger but sick nonetheless, and staring at the pink dress.

After an hour she managed to get out of bed and dress and spent a little time with her sketchbook until it was time to have her lunch; she then left the boarding house to spend the rest of her Sunday in the Louvre. Monsieur Pol was there in the gardens as always with his birds, and she thought of Rose Champion as she stopped to watch him whistling his songs. The birds settled on his outstretched arms and shoulders and they chirruped insistently back to him. Sparrows pretending to be canaries. She closed her eyes and hoped for deliverance.

On the Monday morning Maud took rather longer than usual making herself ready before she left for Lafond's. She tried to make her dress as neat as possible and brushed and bound up her hair three times before she was content with what the ragged glass could show her. It did no good when she tried to tell herself to be calm; her imagination had begun to rage. What if M. Morel and his sickly sister did not like her? Might she seem too young? Perhaps a more matronly woman would be more suitable to be a companion for the sister. She thought of the elderly relatives – the 'cats' – who guarded Tanya. Perhaps she could say she was twenty-four rather than twenty-three. She smiled into the mirror. 'Delighted to meet you,' she said to herself then turned from the glass with a groan. She felt like a child about to be interviewed by a strict headmaster. And what if the Morels themselves were not quite right? What if they were vulgar or unpleasant? Rude or off-hand? She tried to decide what level of respectability or otherwise would be acceptable for her comfort, what would the shy small-town miss in her think? Perhaps he would smell of drink. Perhaps *she* would. The thoughts argued and twitched at her all the way to the Académie then through the first hour.

At the first break in their work she stayed at her easel, too nervous to eat and too distracted to exchange pleasantries with her fellow students. Tanya had yet to arrive. She studied the portrait in front of her and thought of those strange cut-up bodies at Miss

Stein's. It seemed to her they were about the painter not the subject, a painter trying to see everything at once and consume it, rather than know one thing and communicate that. She dipped her brush in linseed oil and then in the purple madder on the palette and with it began to thicken the shadows so that Yvette's pale skin would seem more fragile by contrast. When Yvette spoke to her she started.

'Miss Heighton? I was hoping you'd look a bit more cheery this morning. I passed by Miss Harris's yesterday afternoon and heard they might have something to suit.'

'Oh, good morning, Yvette.' Maud blinked and turned away from the painting, becoming aware of the continuing bustle and chatter around her. The model held her tatty silk dressing-gown around her, her weight all on one jutting hip and a cigarette in her hand. There was something childlike about her thin face, a quickness, those large eyes that seemed to draw everything in, shivering with an animal glee. More fox than cat. 'Yes, I am to go along and see a Monsieur Morel this afternoon with Miss Koltsova. Perhaps they won't like me.'

'They will. You know English is all the rage. Half the girls I know who normally make their money looking after kiddies can't get work at the moment, because every mother wants their little ones to learn "proper cockney". Any Frenchman would love to get his sister a real English miss as a companion.'

Yvette leaned forward to study the picture of her on Maud's easel and blew a long lungful of smoke over the depiction of her own naked skin. 'You're coming on, Miss Heighton.' She suddenly straightened and set her feet more widely apart, clasping her hands behind her back. The collar of her dressing-gown opened and Maud could see the bluish tint to her skin. 'Your tone sense improves, but watch your lines around the model's elbow, Miss

Heighton. Anatomy! Anatomy! Is Yvette a human or a horse? For that is the joint of a horse, not of a beautiful Frenchwoman.'

Maud laughed. It really was a very good impression of Lafond. She put out her hand. 'Call me Maud.' Yvette shook it and gave a little bow, still in the character of Lafond. 'I understand it was you who suggested Tanya take me to see Miss Harris. Thank you. If this Mr Morel and his sister like me, you'll have made my life a lot easier.'

Yvette wrinkled her nose. 'He'll like you, and Tanya will be able to tell you if it's a proper establishment for a lady like yourself. Her aunts have drilled that into her well enough, I think. It's being poor she doesn't understand. She sees in straight lines sometimes, and only looks for the pretty and charming. Not a bad way to be, but she assumes because she's well fed, everyone who speaks nicely is well fed too. She never thought what a difference a bit of respectable work might make to someone like you. And never noticed you were too proud and lonesome to go and look for it yourself.'

Maud looked down at her palette, the grain of the wood as familiar as her own hands. 'You seem to know us very well, Yvette.'

The model stretched her shoulders. 'I spend half my mornings up there watching you all, and I know how hard Paris can be.'

Maud frowned suddenly, realising. 'Yvette, did you try to help Rose?'

The model winced as if Maud had hurt her and twisted her body away slightly, looking tangled and upset. 'I told her about Miss Harris, but I mucked it all up and she just swore at me.'

'That's why you asked Tanya to speak to me? You didn't think I would swear at you, did you?'

'No, but . . .' She scratched her neck. 'I could see you admire Tanya and I thought to myself, if she spoke to you, it might do some good. Would you really have taken advice on how to live from someone like me?'

Maud tried to imagine what she would have done if Yvette had spoken to her. She would have been offended, certainly. 'I almost told Tanya to go to hell, so no, probably not,' she admitted. 'But I'll try not to be so stupid in future.'

Yvette gave her a small, tight smile. On the other side of the room Mademoiselle Claudette clapped her bony hands and the students began to return to their places. Yvette dropped her cigarette and wound her way back to the dais. Maud watched her go. She was still a young woman – not more than twenty-five, Maud guessed – but thin as a boy around the hips and shoulders, and there was a wary edge to her that Maud normally associated with much older women. A certain guardedness even when she was teasing. Perhaps not always. When, a little later, Lafond arrived and during his progress round the room told Maud to watch the structure of the upper arm, she glanced at Yvette. The model was biting on the material of the collar of her dressing-gown to hold back her giggles. Maud only managed to keep her own composure by looking down and fixing her attention on her teacher's shining black shoes.

CHAPTER 5

HRISTIAN MOREL WAS A HANDSOME MAN OF SOME
years past forty, judging by the lines around his eyes;
clean-shaven, though his dark hair reached to his shining white
collar. From the moment he opened the door to Tanya and Maud
he gave the impression it was he and his home that were on trial,
that he was campaigning for the privilege to have Maud with them.
Her nerves leaked away under his quick smile, his concern for their
comfort and air of sincere supplicant.

He began by apologising for the very beautiful apartment. He
had meant to stay at his club, but his cousin, with whom his sister
was supposed to lodge while he was away had become ill, so they
had little time to find somewhere suitable for them both in town.
Tanya sympathised, but to Maud the accommodation looked
palatial. The drawing room was narrow but long, with high
windows draped in lace that let in the winter light, and a fireplace
at each end of the room. Starburst mirrors hung above both. The
south end of the room was occupied by a chaise longue, a piano,
and a few armchairs upholstered in yellow; the other end was
dominated by a round, lace-covered dining-table and dresser. All
the light-coloured wood in the room was worked into long supple
lines; electric lamps were dotted around on the occasional tables.

Maud thought of the heavy dark furniture in her father's house; every piece of it had seemed hulking and angry. Here everything was cheerful but not overwhelming, comfortable without being oppressively rich. She was delighted.

'There is a maid's room,' Morel was saying, 'but we'd rather not have a servant live in. The house girl comes in every morning and prepares our lunch. In the evening we order up from the café on the corner.' He looked at Maud, gently questioning. 'They have a good chef. It's not the Café Anglais, but who can eat like that every night? We live simply and dine early. I hope that is acceptable, Miss Heighton?'

'Oh, quite,' Maud said politely. As Morel led them out into the main corridor, Tanya pinched Maud's arm. Maud turned and made her eyes wide. Tanya stifled a giggle. Morel had reached a door, the first in the corridor from the entrance to the apartment. He pushed it open gently with his fingertips.

'If Miss Heighton were willing to stay with us over the winter, this would be her room.' With a bow he invited her to walk in ahead of him; as she did so she was shocked by the pricking of tears in her eyes. Stupid to be so sentimental, but it was just as she had imagined her room in Paris *might* be when she had climbed onto the train in Alnwick two years ago. It was a large room. The bed was brass, wide and covered in white linen, the washstand was ash, the floor carpeted with thick rugs in red and brown. Soft shadows rested comfortably in the corners and draped themselves over the bed. Mr Morel was watching her anxiously.

'But I am so foolish, you cannot see a thing.' He crossed the room and opened the shutters. Light and air tumbled into the room and seemed to wake it; Maud felt it greet her as a friend. She went to the window and looked out. It gave onto a courtyard at the rear of the building where white-washed walls gathered the afternoon sun and flung it into the room. There was a lean-to by the entrance to the communal cellars and a girl was sitting on a rough stool outside it. She was plucking a chicken for the pot, her red apron a sudden splash of colour over the earth floor. Maud looked down on her, resting her hand on the windowsill.

'Naturally, this room is a little shaded in the mornings, but I understand you ladies work elsewhere in those hours.' He looked at his feet. 'Miss Harris explained to me you have lessons every morning, Miss Heighton. I wish you to know that would be no difficulty, no difficulty at all if you are content to live here. My sister keeps to her bed in the mornings.'

Maud realised they were waiting for a response from her. 'It is a lovely room,' she said. 'Absolutely lovely.'

Morel looked relieved, then started as he heard a clatter of cups from the drawing room. 'Ah, our tea. Let us go and refresh ourselves.'

Over tea, served in the English fashion, Tanya set about questioning Morel. Maud watched her surreptitiously. Yvette had been right about her willingness to sniff out any threat to Maud or her reputation. She was polite but thorough, smiling as she asked questions about the background of the Morel family and nodding as they were answered. Her aunt would have been proud of her.

Morel was born in 1867 in Luxeuil-les-Bains, the only son of a prosperous merchant in the town and his first wife. This lady had died in 1871 but Morel's father had eventually remarried and was blessed with a daughter in 1889, Sylvie. Morel spoke with the dignity and restraint of an Englishman when telling them of the carriage accident that killed their father and Sylvie's mother in the year 1904. Sylvie had been with her parents at the time and the injuries she had suffered had made her health delicate. She was easily tired even now. Morel had taken on her care and support. Then, having given the two young women the facts of the case, he moved the topic on and spoke of how impressed he had been by Miss Harris and her good works. He hoped Maud and Sylvie would speak English together. He wished to go to America in the spring, he informed them, to pursue some promising business opportunities, and wanted to take Sylvie with him. To have her English fluent and practised would make her life there much easier.

This gave Tanya the chance to enquire as to what his business was. He smiled and waved his hand. 'Moving money! Trains and planes and automobiles, the telegraph and now telephones. Money has to learn how to keep up in this modern age. But it is dull business in comparison with yours. Let us talk about you young artists instead.' He turned towards Maud. 'You are an artist, Miss Heighton? Tell me what your family think of you living so independently and so far away from them. Do your parents approve of your coming here?'

Maud put down her cup. 'My father was an auctioneer in the north of England, Mr Morel. He died three years ago. My mother died when I was twelve.'

'An orphan like my poor sister and me? But not alone in the world, I hope.'

'My elder brother James is a solicitor in Darlington. I have a younger brother too, only six years old, from my father's second marriage. He lives with James and his wife now.'

'Perfect woman!' he said, lifting his hands and looking upwards as if thanking heaven. 'You understand then the bond between Sylvie and myself.'

She thought of Albert, his round face always dirty and his wide blue eyes.

'I do.'

'And there is no better man to do business with in my opinion than an English solicitor,' Morel continued. He seemed more at ease now than when the girls had first arrived. He picked up his teacup again and arched one eyebrow. 'One always knows exactly what they are going to say. I think I can quite easily imagine what they are likely to say about a young woman living in Paris alone.' He frowned slightly. 'Or am I being unfair?'

Maud shook her head, trying not to smile. 'No, you are quite right. James thinks Paris a very dangerous place, and his wife thinks any city a mortal danger, and art only ladylike if taken in moderation. Perhaps they are right. However, they have little to say on the matter. My father's property was insured and the money divided equally between the three of us. It is not enough to provide an income, but enough to support me during my training until I can earn money of my own.'

She felt his eyes examine her threadbare cuffs, but he made no comment and when he found he was being watched, smiled at her warmly.

'Ah! You are one of the new women. Independent in thought and deed. Excellent.'

'Christian? We have visitors?' A woman's voice. They stood and turned towards it and Maud saw Sylvie Morel for the first time.

She was much lighter in colouring than her brother, with white-gold hair loosely tied up and pale skin. She leaned against the doorframe looking as if she had just stepped out of a Burne-Jones painting. Her afternoon dress of ivory silk suited her slim figure and had some suggestion of classical drapery about it. It was as if Canova's marble sculpture of *Psyche* in the Louvre had woken and dressed herself. Maud looked away, suddenly shy.

'My dear, we have woken you,' Morel said. 'I'm so sorry. Please, come and join us.' She approached slowly, not quite looking at either of them. 'This is Miss Koltsova. Miss Koltsova, my sister.'

'Delighted,' Tanya said, putting out her hand. Miss Morel took it with a smile and repeated the word, drawing it out as if she were enjoying the taste of it.

'And this is Miss Heighton,' Morel continued. 'I hope, if you think you might like each other, that Miss Heighton will spend this winter here as our guest.'

Mademoiselle Morel turned towards Maud and after a moment smiled with more warmth. Maud put out her hand and for a moment held Mademoiselle Morel's fingers between her own. They were dry and cool. 'I think I should like that,' Sylvie said. 'Will you come? It might be very dull for you, but we will do our best to make you welcome.'

'Then I shall come,' Maud said, and released her hand.

'Very good, come tomorrow if you can. I get so bored with Christian away all hours. Forgive me, I must go back to my room. This is not one of my good days.' She turned to go at once, then looked back over her shoulder. I wonder if she will model for me, Maud thought. One would have to thin the paint so as to create only a suggestion of colour. 'May I ask your first name?'

'Maud.'

'A proper English name, I am glad. *Queen rose of the rosebud garden of girls . . .*' she quoted in English, her accent giving a heavy new fragrance to the line.

'My mother was a great admirer of Lord Tennyson.'

'It suits you. My name is Sylvie.' She left them, her slippers whispering across the hardwood floor.

'Then it is settled!' Morel said, looking triumphant and relieved.

He hesitated as if to say something more, then looked uncertainly between his guests. Tanya at once put out her hand to him.

'There is a darling little bookshop on the corner I noticed as we came in. Would you think me terribly rude if I take the chance to have a look at what they have? I can see myself out. Maud, I'll be waiting for you when you are ready.'

Morel bowed over her hand and did not speak again until the door had clicked behind her. 'What a charming woman! Are you very good friends?'

Maud smiled. 'I hope so.'

He cleared his throat. 'I should like to offer you a consideration of five louis a week, Miss Heighton, as well as your board. Would that be acceptable?'

'You are too generous,' Maud replied sincerely. She lived on that amount a month.

'Do not be too quick to say so,' he said. 'Please, sit with me a moment more.'

Maud took her place in front of the cold teacups again. Morel reached into his pocket and produced a cigarette-case, blue enamel and decorated with a tiny circle of brilliants. He asked her permission with a raised eyebrow and she nodded her consent. She found she was holding onto her little purse quite tightly on her lap. The fear that something would deny her that room, this company elegantly balanced between champagne or gruel, reared up again. It was so comfortable here.

Morel lit his cigarette and then exhaled; the smoke curled upwards in the light. 'My sister . . . Sylvie . . .' He crossed and uncrossed his legs. 'This is a matter of some delicacy. My sister has a weakness that I know is tolerated in some parts of Paris, but I cannot condone it. I was not perhaps the guardian I should have been to her during these last few years, and she was introduced to bad influences in my absence. I hoped bringing Sylvie to Paris might break these connections with certain corrupting influences, but I find she cannot now manage yet without . . .' His voice trailed away and he scratched suddenly and hard at the underside of his chin.

Maud shook her head. 'I am so sorry, sir. I do not understand you.'

'Of course not. You know that laudanum can be of great help to those in pain?'

'Yes, I have heard it can do a great deal of good.'

'So it can, so it can, and properly administered under the care of a professional medical man it did help my sister a great deal. Then she was introduced by a "friend" into taking the drug in a vaporised form – that is, smoking it in the fashion they do in the East.'

Maud was startled. 'Opium?' she said faintly. All she knew of opium came from the cheap novels her step-mother had left lying around the house. The illustrations showed hovels in the bowels of London full of emaciated, corpse-like figures and sinister Chinamen rubbing their hands. It all seemed rather at odds with this elegant apartment and the beautiful girl. Though she was rather ghostly, a little lost in her own dreams.

'You are shocked, naturally. Perhaps I can reassure you. I purchase the poison for my sister and she has sworn to use it only in this apartment. She knows no one in Paris. You will not be dragged into any low or dangerous places, Miss Heighton, I assure you. No one visits us, no low company will offend you here. Though, I admit her use of the drug does make Sylvie very reluctant to leave the apartment in the evenings. I would be happy for you to go out from time to time if I were at home, but I am afraid you will find this a dull place. No parties, no visits to the theatres or cabarets. If the consideration I offered you perhaps seems a little high, let us say it is by way of compensation for robbing you of the delights of Paris to a great degree over the winter.'

Miss Charlotte's fears were explained away. Maud felt a sudden relief. Not only could she live here through the winter, she could be useful to the lovely girl and her concerned brother. She would distract Sylvie with sketching and English conversation and keep a watchful eye on her.

'Please, Mr Morel, I came to Paris to study art, not for the cabarets. I also know very few people in the city. You would be robbing me of nothing.' He looked greatly relieved. They made their arrangements for her belongings to be removed to Rue de Seine the next day.

Later in the afternoon Tanya and Maud walked arm-in-arm past the secondhand book stalls that lined the embankment opposite the solid square towers of Notre Dame. The sky had cleared slightly, and they were both a little giddy with their success. They drank in the cold air as if it were fresh water in the desert. It was strange for Maud. She had never made friends easily, having been isolated as a child and reserved throughout her youth. She wished that some of her old school fellows who had thought her such a strange girl, always sketching and never joining in with their gossip and whisperings, could see her now, in step with this glamorous Russian girl, strolling the Paris pavements as if they owned them. She felt as if her old tired skin was being shed and she, fascinating and original as Paris itself, had suddenly emerged at some moment between Miss Harris's beef tea and the handshake with Morel.

'My eyes, what a beauty! I declare I hate her,' Tanya said. And when Maud laughed at her: 'I do! We brunettes are expected to be fiery and clever and passionate all the time. It's exhausting. With her colouring, all Mademoiselle Sylvie has to do is recline on a day-bed and the world will drop to its knees in admiration. It is very, very unfair.'

'I shan't pity either of you for being rich and beautiful,' Maud said.

'Well, that's very cold-hearted of you.' Tanya dropped Maud's arm to pick up a volume of Baudelaire from the closest *bouquiniste*, but after reading a couple of lines, she made a face and replaced it. 'Oof, I am glad I am a painter. Poets are never cheerful – but not all writers are like that, are they? Mr Allardyce is a journalist.' Maud smiled at Tanya and she blushed. 'So your father, Mr Heighton, he was an auctioneer?'

'He was a drunk,' Maud said, surprising herself.

'Ah.'

'And his name was not Heighton, but Creely. Heighton was my mother's name before she married.'

'My dear Maud, you are full of surprises. Why did you change it?'

On the pavement behind Tanya an elderly man with long, well-groomed whiskers and a long black cloak was arguing over the price of a book with the stall-holder. Each bent forward from the waist and argued their point nose to nose. Behind him on the pavement and apparently waiting for him was a handsome young woman very fashionably dressed and leading a tiny dog. Her lips were painted a deep crimson and her figure drew glances from the cabmen driving by.

Maud looked too, as boldly as a born Parisian, and sketched them in her mind as she replied, 'It would not surprise you if you had met my father, or seen the shop. The name Creely reminds me of him and of that horrid place. I was delighted when it burned down. I was cheering on the flames. Everyone in the crowd thought I was distraught. Poor Miss Creely losing her father, and now this! But it was all I could do not to burst out laughing. It was a wonderful fire. They couldn't save a thing.'

The man in the long cloak concluded his negotiations and huffing into his moustache handed over a number of coins. The young lady took his arm and they set off again along the pavement. Her skirt hung so straight and narrow from her hips she could take only tiny rapid steps. Her stride seemed to match that of the toy dog that trotted beside her. The man with the book, she with her skirt and dog. Money was paid and collections formed, passions indulged. Maud felt wise and amused by the pageant, then there was an unexpected pang inside her – a distant warning of a storm coming. It was all too sudden, too perfect.

'Tanya, what do you think of them, truly?' she asked. 'Is this wise of me? Is there not something a little . . . strange about them?' She had said nothing to Tanya about the opium, and Morel seemed a gentleman indeed, a concerned brother and Sylvie so young. Drink was a worse addiction, surely? She thought of her father's sudden rages and repentance.

'They seem respectable enough to me. I would say it does not look as if you will have much fun, but judging by our night in Maxim's you will not mind that.'

Did Tanya sound a little hurt? The Russian girl had taken her in and dressed her and shown her a side of Paris she would not otherwise have seen. Maud felt ashamed. 'I do not mean to be ungrateful, Tanya.'

'Well, I certainly don't want you to be *grateful* either!' She bit her lip. 'Do you think, Maud, I can be a good painter but still enjoy my clothes and my evenings out?'

'I see no reason why not,' Maud said, surprised by her sudden vulnerability. 'I think you are a fine painter, Tanya. You cannot doubt it.'

'No,' but she did seem doubtful. 'It is hard to find the time to work when one must go to dressmakers every other day and change one's clothes three times in the course of an afternoon. My aunts feel it is a disgrace to my family to do less. When I have a family as well, how shall I find the time to paint? I do want a family.'

Maud did not know how to answer her. Tanya seemed to shimmer and dance through her life so, Maud could not see her as a woman with worries of her own.

Tanya shook herself a little and said firmly, 'Morel seems to have the proper respect for an Englishwoman's virtue. If he tries to force himself on you, come running to me. I shall send Vladimir after him.' She put her hand on Maud's sleeve. 'Wouldn't the comfort there do you a little good, Maud? If someone gives you a free horse, do not check the bridle.' Maud thought of that bright little room again and what Miss Harris had said about prayers being answered – but Maud had not asked God for anything for a very long time.

'Charlotte was right, he does smile a lot and he is offering a great deal of money.' Tanya had become brisk again. 'You can leave if you are unhappy. I shall be in Paris all winter and will not desert you. Always have the means to a graceful exit to hand – don't you think that is one of the best lessons we learn? I always have a gold sovereign sewn into my travelling dress. Actually half a dozen, so the line isn't spoiled.'

Maud considered. Mr Morel had offered her board, her own room and a weekly consideration that he called a trifle and that Maud called a fortune. She could simply wait and see how matters unfolded. The wind had been fierce yesterday evening, rattling her windows while she sketched her memories of the day, giving birth to new cold draughts, harbinger of the freezing depths of winter.

'Thank you, Tanya. Even if I only stayed there a week it would do me good. It has been difficult these last months.'

Tanya squeezed her arm again then looked up. 'Oh Lord, the rain is coming again, and I am expected back at the cathouse.' She turned and lifted her hand, and the dark blue motor materialised beside them. Vladimir and Sasha were staring out of the windscreen like dolls in a shop window. 'Can I give you a lift somewhere? No? Do you have an umbrella? Vladimir, do give Miss Heighton an umbrella, please, there's a dear. And that package.'

Tanya thrust a bundle tied in brown paper and string into her arms. 'It is only an old walking dress of mine, so don't say no. You cannot wear your working dress every afternoon while you shepherd that beauty round the streets.' Before she could thank Tanya or refuse it, the umbrella had been placed in her other hand and Tanya had scrambled up into the back seat. She leaned out of the window and took Maud by the hand.

'The angels have given you a gift, my dear. Embrace it! Now say you shall. I shan't let go of your hand until you do.'

She looked quite determined and Maud said, 'Very well, I shall!' Then as Tanya released her grip, Maud held on. 'Tanya, why have we not been friends before now?' The car was beginning to cause an obstruction in the road. A carter shouted and Vladimir yelled back something in Russian.

'Sweet, you always seemed so sober and serious, so contained, I've been quite terrified of you. Somehow I knew you weren't the type for Maxim's. Even if you did look charming in that dress.'

Maud let go of her hand and Tanya blew her a kiss as the car pulled away. Maud watched it retreat into the stream of taxicabs, omnibuses, carts and motor-cars heading along the quayside. It was a few moments before she remembered the umbrella and opened it to protect her and her package from the increasing pace of the rain. It had a tortoiseshell handle and bore the name of a shop in Rue de la Paix. Maud knew the place. She had walked past it shivering in the cold every day for a month when she lived off Rue de Lille, and each morning had wondered who could possibly be rich enough to spend such a vast number of francs on an umbrella. Now she held one over her head – an elegant, oiled-silk shield of money. She leaned her back against the wall, the wave of relief spreading over her so quick and full she would have fallen otherwise under its force.

CHAPTER 6

23 November 1909

*S*OMETIMES WE DO NOT REALISE HOW MUCH WE HAVE been suffering until that suffering is removed. On her first night in Rue de Seine, as Maud undressed she realised that her hands were shaking. She was a wrecked sailor crawling onto a sandbank and only then acknowledging the pain in her muscles. She wondered what would have happened to her if Yvette, Tanya, Miss Harris and the Morels had not intervened. The thought frightened her so much it hurt her.

Morel had been there when she arrived, to see her trunk stowed into her new room and to host her first lunch in the apartment. It was a pleasure he could not promise himself every day, he sighed. He asked if Maud was happy with the arrangements he had made for her comfort. The daily maid would leave luncheon for them. The ladies were then at liberty to do whatever they wished. Supper would be fetched for them, if they required it, at seven. He would join them when he could; but he expected to dine often at his club.

Sylvie was quiet but pleasant at that first lunch. She seemed content in a self-contained way. Her brother made all the conversation. He asked Maud a hundred questions about herself and gave every impression of finding the answers fascinating. There was nothing offensive about the questions or the way he asked them, but Maud found herself drawing away from him slightly as she gave her usual responses. Not lies, but truths that concealed some of the misery of her youth.

The food was excellent, though he had apologised for it as simple fare just as he had apologised for his palatial apartment. Maud had been subsisting on ten-sou omelettes in the worst of the respectable cafés, so to see game pie and *hâchis portugais* set out, with cheese on the sideboard for later and white wine dripping with chill . . . She had to be careful not to eat too quickly. She wondered if, under his flow of talk, Morel had noticed her hunger and was teasing her with his questions when she wanted to eat. She glanced at him. His expression was open and friendly.

'When did you discover you were an artist, Miss Heighton?' he asked, filling up her wine glass and piling more potatoes onto her plate.

'I am not an artist yet, I think. I am just trying to be a painter.'

He laughed. 'I shall remember that! But you are too modest. To come here as you have, leave home and family, suffer hardships to study here. That suggests a greater calling.'

She shook her head. 'My mother drew and painted. I think I began by copying her, and I never stopped. Drawing was simply what I did. She was my first teacher and when she could, she would take me to the galleries nearby, and find me books of reproductions.' The child's voice in her head whispered in awe, *some in colour*. She remembered the hours she had spent with those books curled up under her mother's dressing-table. She had had one with coloured plates from the Louvre and would study each one for an hour before she allowed herself to turn to the next. When she had first seen the originals in the museum the day she arrived in Paris, it had been like seeing much-loved, long-missed friends, but so much brighter and more alive. Her father had sold all of the art books to a London gentleman three months after her mother died. He had been disgusted by her distress when she found them gone. He had got five pounds for them, which was four pounds more than he had thought they were worth. She had been too busy crying to see the blow come that time.

She took a careful sip of her wine; it was fruit and acid on her tongue. 'All the best moments of my life have been bound up with painting. *That* is perhaps why I have come here, rather than some great calling, or particular talent.'

Morel nodded to himself, as if this confirmed some idea of his own, and then, by chatting to his silent sister about a letter he had received from home, let her eat in peace.

When Morel left them Maud felt suddenly embarrassed by this enforced intimacy with Sylvie. The maid cleared the table and Sylvie sat down at the pianoforte and picked out a few stray notes. Maud waited until the maid had said her farewells. They had spoken in French while her brother was present, but Maud was thinking of her duties now and switched to English.

'Perhaps you would like to show me your drawings, Sylvie? So I can see what instruction I might offer.'

Sylvie twisted round from the piano and sucked in her cheeks. 'I am afraid that you will think I am a great fool. I am not good, not at all. It is my brother's plan to keep me occupied. He will buy me opium when I show him sketchbooks filled with pictures of fruit. Is that not a strange,' she searched for the word, 'trade?'

Maud was shocked to hear her speak about the opium so plainly and wondered if there was some element of challenge in the confession. She said calmly, 'If you must do them, you might as well do them to the best of your ability, Sylvie.'

The young woman sighed, but with a nod left the piano and returned a few minutes later with a sketchbook covered in green; she sat down beside Maud on the sofa, holding it on her knees for a moment before handing it over. Maud opened the pages with an encouraging smile and looked at the drawings. They had been done in haste, certainly, but they proved that Sylvie could see what was in front of her and had some idea of how to hold a pencil.

'They are bad, is that not so?'

'Not at all. You just need a little guidance.' Maud pointed at the opened page, a drawing of the table in front of them with a lamp-stand on the centre of it. 'You see, you are drawing what you know is there, rather than what you see.' Sylvie touched the weave of the paper, apparently concentrating hard. 'You must avoid drawing outlines if you are to make progress, Sylvie. We see edges to things because of changes in light and tone, not because they have a line around them.' Sylvie nodded slowly, then slid the book back onto her own lap. Maud was afraid she had discouraged her. 'The best thing we could do is to go somewhere and try to draw something together.' She looked up and out of the window opposite, just as the wind threw a scatter of rain against the window like a handful of sand.

Sylvie laughed. 'The gods say no, Maud!' Then at once the light faded from her eyes and she yawned. 'I always rest for a little while after lunch. Perhaps in an hour you could knock at my door and we will go out then.'

'As you wish.' Maud was unsure. She had not thought in any depth about her relationship with Sylvie and what it might entail. Her considerations had centred solely on whether the position was respectable, followed by a happy vision of food, warmth and comfort; now she realised she was to some degree Sylvie's creature, though a polite fiction might be maintained.

'If you want to go out for a walk before then, Maud, you must do so. This is not a prison. Do as you would at your own house,' the girl went on. Maud felt she had been dismissed, but on balance was grateful for a little time on her own. She could think more about how to instruct Sylvie – look for interesting places where they might sit and draw when the weather was good.

Sylvie stood and with the sketchbook held loosely at her side, made to leave the room. On the threshold she paused and looked back.

'There is no need to come into my room, Maud. You may knock at the door and I shall join you here a little while later.'

Maud retreated to her room. There was an envelope on the bed with her name on it. She picked it up and her fingers brushed the cotton of the bedspread on their way to the thick paper. Comfort. The envelope held two fifty-franc notes and a message from M. Morel asking her to make use of the money for any little items she might need to make herself at home with them. He added that this was, of course, in addition to her weekly stipend. Maud sat suddenly on the bed and stared at the pink and blue notes, the paper smothered with engravings of anchors and cherubs. No Empress has ever felt their wealth as wide and inexhaustible as Maud did in that moment. She lifted her head: there was a faint sweet smell in the air, heavy and pungent, reaching into the room. She tucked the money away in the lid of her box of painting materials and left the apartment.

Funeral oil on canvas 64.8 × 76.3 cm

The narrow range of colours gives the suggestion of physical and spiritual chill to this picture, and the framing forces the viewer to be part of the scene rather than the observer. The grave is at our feet; the figures jostling the frame are at our shoulder. In the distance and on the right, a break in the cloud allows a glimmer of sunlight and warmth of colour into the scene, though whether this is hope, or a false dawn, we cannot say. None of the figures surrounding us at the graveside have noticed it; it is a beam of light offered only to the artist and now the viewer.

Extract from the catalogue notes to the exhibition 'The Paris Winter: Anonymous Treasures from the de Civray Collection', Southwark Picture Gallery, London, 2010

CHAPTER 7

*T*HE DAYS QUICKLY DEVELOPED A PATTERN. MAUD left the apartment every morning before M. Morel or his sister had woken; had her breakfast at a zinc by the entrance to Passage des Panoramas, and was ready to begin her day's work with an unfamiliar lightness and ease. The studio had become a more welcoming place now. Tanya had made a pet of her, and having decided that their figures were practically identical, had given her two more of her old dresses: a working dress of soft grey, and another walking dress that meant she needn't be ashamed of wandering the boulevards with Sylvie in the afternoons. The other women began to warm to her too. They teased her about her luck and when she laughed along and agreed with them, they liked her for it. The following week, when the dais was filled with another of their regular models, Maud realised she had no idea of the life Yvette lived when she was not in the studio with them. She asked Tanya about it as they drank tea.

'Oh, Yvette is a child of Montmartre, you know,' she said, waving her hand and almost knocking Francesca's cup from her hands. 'When she's not here she'll be with the other models at Place Pigalle. Old Degas has used her a fair amount in the past. And she normally has some boyfriend or other to keep her amused.

I envy her freedom, don't you?' Maud shook her head. 'Truly you don't?' Tanya seemed a little disconcerted. 'Am I being stupid? I know it must be hard to be poor, but it is hard to be as harried and pursued as I am. My aunts are giving a dinner next week and that means I must go to Rue Taitbout again this afternoon for a dress fitting when I would rather be working.' When Francesca almost choked on her tea, Tanya looked genuinely distressed. 'Oh, do not laugh at me.'

Maud offered her a pastry. 'Tanya, I promise I do not envy you either.'

The Russian appeared to be slightly mollified. 'You are very kind, Maud. Would you like to come to the dinner? I could lend you the dress again?'

'No, thank you. I do not think I can use the Morels' flat as if it were some sort of hotel. Sylvie does not go out, so neither can I. In the spring when they have left Paris I shall come and visit you whenever you wish.' At that moment, Maud realised that Mademoiselle Claudette was at their elbow waiting for an opportunity to speak.

'Ladies, I wished to tell you that the funeral of Rose Champion will be held tomorrow morning. Her aunt has arrived in Paris to see it done. I shall attend. If any of you wish it, we may leave from here together.'

'Monsieur Lafond . . . ?' Francesca asked and Claudette shook her head. They understood. Their master's income relied on his good reputation and his attendance at the burial might draw attention to the squalid nature of Miss Champion's death. Tanya spoke for them.

'We shall come.'

M. Lafond might not wish to attend the funeral himself, but he did provide Claudette with the fare for a taxi to take them there. It was a cold but clear day and the women found themselves drawing in great lungfuls of clean air, enjoying the contrast to the centre of the city until they remembered their business and became quiet.

Miss Champion's aunt and the priest were already waiting by the grave. There were no other mourners. The aunt introduced herself as Mrs Fuller and seemed distracted and exhausted as well as distressed by the death of her niece. Her hat, dark purple and heavy with black blooms, was rather crushed and her woollen skirt and jacket showed signs of travel. She peered at them short-sightedly and her hand, when Maud shook it, was damp and limp. The priest recited his lines mechanically, the grave-diggers began their work. As Maud made the proper remarks the damp grip tightened slightly.

'You are English? And an artist?' Mrs Fuller sounded hopeful.

'I am.'

'Oh, please tell me what is to be done with the paintings Rose left. There are only four of them. I have them in the taxicab, but I know my husband and my son will not like them. They are not cheerful. I prefer the paintings Rose did when she was little, though not many of them were cheerful either . . .' Her words trailed away and she came to a halt in the middle of her memories. 'She was always such a difficult child. I had always wanted a little girl, but she never liked me. Still, I cannot throw away her paintings. Oh, I hate to travel this time of year. Still a pretty day, but so many cars.' She pulled a handkerchief from her bag and blew her nose.

Maud was at a loss. Perhaps some dealer would take the paint-ings, though Rose's poverty suggested that she had not managed to sell very much work. Even if she could find someone who would take them, the idea of dragging the canvases from one shop to another then arranging for the money to be sent to England seemed a thankless task, and in any case she was engaged to spend her time with Sylvie.

'I shall buy them,' Tanya said. Mrs Fuller looked up at her in surprise then let her eyes travel over Tanya's fur-trimmed coat, her wide picture hat and the pearls in her ears.

'But you haven't even seen them,' she said suspiciously, her rumpled face lined like damp linen being wrung out.

'No matter. I know Miss Champion's work and thought highly of it. I shall take all four and pay you fifty francs for each of them.' Claudette rolled her eyes and even Francesca looked a little shocked. Mrs Fuller looked up at Maud, her tongue darting out of her mouth a little to moisten her lips.

'Is that a proper figure, Miss Heighton? After all, I hear that some paintings my husband says are the most terrible scribbles are sold for thousands, and poor Rose will paint no more now. Does that not make them worth rather more?'

Maud could see the attendants of the cemetery continuing to fill in Rose's grave behind them. She tried to speak evenly. 'Rose was a talented artist, Mrs Fuller, but entirely unknown here or in London. It is unlikely you would ever sell those canvases at all to anyone else, let alone for eight pounds each. Miss Koltsova's offer is extremely generous.'

'Is it now?' Mrs Fuller narrowed her eyes and looked sidelong at Tanya again, and even though it must be clear to her that she was understood, she said, 'Is the young lady Jewish?'

'I am not,' Tanya said. 'Though I fail to see what the significance is of that.'

Mrs Fuller smiled thinly. 'I am sure you are very clever with money at any rate. Still, I suppose I must believe it is a fair price.

Poor dear Rose, such a terrible loss to us all. Do you have the money with you? I have the cab waiting at the gates.'

Sylvie agreed to go with Maud to the Jardin du Luxembourg that afternoon as the day continued fine. They took their sketchbooks with them and found a seat near the grand octagonal pond at the front of the palace, where the children pushed their rented sailboats across the rippling waters. Maud suggested that Sylvie try to draw one of the ornamental urns, thinking the curve of its body and the mass of its high pediment might give her hand some useful practice, particularly as the long afternoon shadows fell across it and turned it into strong patterns of light and shade. Maud watched the children for a while, smiling at the fierce concentration of the sailors, the pressure of the wind on the hand-kerchief sails, and she listened to the scud of running footsteps on the gravel paths, the shrieks of laughter. Opposite them, tiny in front of the walls of the pale palace, a girl no more than six years old was playing with her diabolo, running the cylinder along the string, throwing and catching it again while her mother sat nearby, occasionally looking up from her sewing to applaud her daughter's efforts. Still, nothing caught her eye and Maud started to sketch what she had seen that morning, the clear day and the tiny band of mourners shivering around the grave. She began to tell Sylvie about the mean little funeral, and the greed of Miss Champion's aunt.

'But Maud, simply because you knew that her niece's pictures were worth very little, it does not mean that she did. And consider, are you English not taught from the date of your birth that every foreigner you meet is trying to take away your money? She was doing that which she was taught to do, and you cannot reproach people for that.' Sylvie swore softly under her breath. 'I shall never manage this. It looks like a plant pot.'

Maud leaned over and examined her work. 'Do not press so hard, or try to make such long strokes.' Sylvie tried again. 'Yes, that is better. I think you are too kind to Mrs Fuller. She was standing in front of her niece's grave and thinking of what profit it might bring her. How can that ever be proper?'

'Proper? Bah! So might anyone if they were not very attached to the person who died. And I think it would be a very easy mistake to make. Who knows what makes one painter rich and another poor?' She tapped her drawing with her pencil. 'What if I hold this up high and say it is the new art. Very rare and valuable. Give me two hundred francs for it.'

Maud looked at the rather misshapen drawing with its heavy lines. 'No one would believe you.'

Sylvie looked triumphant. 'But that is nothing to do with my poor picture. It is only because I haven't published a manifesto first. Everything that is worth money in the world is so because someone says very loudly, "This is beautiful and rare". Every piece of art is rare because a person has only so many hours to live, so many bits of art they can make. Now all you have to do is convince them the art is beautiful . . . or clever at least. I shall write an article for the newspaper proclaiming myself a genius then we can sell this,' she flicked the page with a smooth fingernail, 'for a hundred francs. The rare work of a genius.' She bent down and picked up a piece of gravel between her finger and thumb; it was a pale lilac. 'Now if there existed in the world only a very little of this, and a million tons of diamonds, this is what queens would wear in their crowns and we would put diamonds down on the walkways. Beautiful and rare. Beautiful because it is rare, or beautiful because we have been trained to think it rare. Then we can make it into money.'

Maud felt strangely sad at the idea. 'You make it sound like a trick.'

Sylvie shrugged. Whether it was because she was unhappy with her drawing or because she had not rested after lunch, her mood had become suddenly brittle.

'Come. Perhaps it is just I know too little of art. You must educate me. This place is full of art shops, books on art. Let us go at once.'

Maud began to put away her materials, sensing Sylvie's impatience, then allowed herself to be dragged down Rue de Tournon. The bookshop Sylvie happened upon was in Rue Saint-Sulpice, but though the impulse and the plan were hers, as soon as the two women entered the shop, it was clear she wished to be gone. The bookseller, a young man with a ready smile, obviously wanted only to help, but Sylvie made her purchases distractedly. Maud found a translation of Ruskin, and though she thought him a little old-fashioned, she offered it as a useful place for Sylvie to begin her reading.

'Very well, Maud. Whatever you wish,' Sylvie said briskly. She picked up two or three more of the volumes the bookseller had put in front of her on his polished counter, then handed them to him without more than a glance. 'And these.' Maud thought of her lost, loved books and wondered where they had ended up.

As he bound up the package, Sylvie tapped her foot and when she handed him her money, her fingers shook. Maud stayed silent and let herself be whisked out of the shop and back to Rue de Seine without comment. As soon as they were back in the apartment, Sylvie put the package into her hands. 'Open them if you wish.' She went into her room without another word.

Maud took the books into the living room and untied the paper wrapping. Her education in the history of art had been all at second hand until she came to Paris. It had been a wonder to see in life the images she had learned to know in hazy reproduction, as if the sun had suddenly appeared to drive off the mist on the dale and reveal the landscape below it. She removed her hat and gloves and sat at the table, but did not open the books. She thought instead of the strange ugly pictures that Tanya had bought from Mrs Fuller and what Sylvie had said about art. They had returned to Passage des Panoramas before examining Rose's pictures, and had done so in a sort of sorry silence. The palette of each was limited and muddy, purple lake and brown madder with sickly touches of citron to suggest sources of light weak and out of the frame. They were loosely painted, sketchy in places and oddly placed, flattened, the perspective lost and lurching. Where the eye expected to see most within the frame was a dingy absence of form; only at the edges of the whole did figures lurk, pressed down in the composition as if irrelevant, yet the only interest the artist offered. The gutters of Paris. A long table surrounded by gaunt and stooping figures, their grey fingers curled around wooden bowls. A woman leaning against one of the elegant lamp-posts, but crushed by the darkness around her. No street was as dark in the city of light as Rose had painted this one. When you looked long enough, that darkness seemed to seethe with half-realised faces, painted as a layer of darkness on a deeper dark.

Mademoiselle Claudette had touched the half-seen figure of the woman, feeling the thickness of the paint. 'I do not understand,' she said, and Maud realised she had tears in her eyes.

The American girl looked over her shoulder and shuddered. 'You've wasted your money.'

Tanya looked up sharply. 'I do not think I have. She was trying to do something . . .'

Francesca had hooked her palette over her thumb again and

taken her seat by the stove. 'I can respect the attempt, but I have not learned to paint to make the world miserable. I paint the world to celebrate it.' There was a murmur of agreement around the room.

Tanya bit her lip and set the painting down. Maud was not sure if she did so with respect or fear. 'What do you think, Maud? I think Rose might have been almost a genius. But some of this seems clumsy and Francesca is right – even if it is clever, it is still very ugly.'

Maud said nothing, only sighing and continuing to prepare her palette for the remaining hour of the morning. Rose's pictures crawled behind her eyes, insisting on overlaying themselves on her vision. *What can paint catch?* they said. *What can it make visible that is hidden? Are these pictures more true than your pretty women posed on a model throne with their lips a little reddened?*

At Rue de Seine, Maud smelled the heavy sweet scent in the hallway and went straight to her room, taking Ruskin with her for company. For a moment it seemed that she had carried Rose Champion's ghosts with her into the room. The deepening shadows seemed to be full of her whispering demons carrying darkness on their backs. Their breath smelled heavy and sweet. She turned on the electric light and opened the window, sat by it and let the cold air stream in until the demons were gone and the room was hers again. The fierceness of the light rather overwhelmed her, and only when she had wrapped a thin scarf round the shade could she read in comfort. Ruskin had no doubts or demons, it seemed. His heavy baroque sentences made her think of the rose window in Notre Dame, their thick colours hanging off his phrases like coronation robes.

Maud ate her supper alone in the drawing room that evening and was asleep in her room long before M. Morel returned home.

CHAPTER 8

*A*S THE DAYS PASSED THEIR WALKS GREW LONGER, then when they came home Sylvie began to look into the art books and ask Maud about what she found. Maud sketched her for the first time a week after she arrived. Heavy rain had kept them indoors, but Sylvie had not retreated to her own room and oblivion. Rather she stretched out on the chaise longue under a Lavery landscape and turned the pages of one of her books. Maud began her sketch and quickly became lost in it, not thinking of anything but the line on the paper until Sylvie asked in a strange, whining voice, 'Are you nearly finished, Maud?'

Maud looked at her, changing her way of seeing from the model to the girl.

'Almost. One moment more.'

Sylvie was staring at the clock behind Maud's shoulder. It might have been a little more than a moment, but the second that Maud put down her pencil, Sylvie scampered from the room leaving Maud wondering. She emerged for supper with her though, her manner vacant and gentle, her half-smile drifting over her lips – and though she ate very little, she did eat.

Maud's health improved. The rest from worry, the good food, the calm of life in Rue de Seine was making her a better artist. Her hand was steadier, her lines more confident; at the Académie her use of colour grew bolder and more her own. She could almost feel the shackles that Tanya had mentioned coming loose, their weight falling from her wrists, and when she walked through Paris between her classes and Rue de Seine she did so with her head up and watching. The shouts of the street-sellers accompanied her; the old woman with her cart of glistening blue and silver fish arranged in fans on a bed of green grass, the girl her own age with milk-white skin and cap, her cart piled with potatoes with thin gold skins and deep mounds of cabbage, all arranged and turned to face any passing customer with their folds of malachite green frothing round them like crumpled lace. Each seller sang their calls to the housewives of the *quartier* like birds, each with their own particular rhythm, rise and fall: *'les haricots verts, les pommes de terre'*, *'J'ai les poissons pour quinze sous'*. While the models were resting from their poses, Maud joined the women in conversation, no longer obsessed with the provisions laid out for them. She and Tanya looked through the old illustrated catalogues of exhibitions, comparing the lines of composition, the gauzy fantasies of the Symbolists or the strange bare spaces of André Sureda with his Turneresque pursuits of light through mist.

Some afternoons, Sylvie rebelled against sketching and demanded that they take a turn through the Jardin des Tuileries then along Rue Saint-Honoré so she could peer in at the windows. The displays were becoming more splendid by the hour as Christmas approached: sweet shops filled with great banked displays of pastel-coloured macaroons or truffles like scrunched scraps of silk peppered with flakes of gold; stationers, their windows heaving with reams of butter-coloured writing paper and glistening silver fountain pens; haberdashers plumed in an explosion of lace.

On one such expedition Sylvie claimed she was still not tired as they reached Place de la Madeleine, and despite the threatening weather insisted on turning down Rue Royale. It was a confusion of dark umbrellas as on the crowded pavements the shoppers of Paris protected themselves and their purchases from the sudden squalls of rain. The clanging of metal wheels against the stone cobbles seemed louder than usual, and Maud felt the strangeness of being on the wide streets of Paris with such a fragmented view. When she looked behind her, the towering colonnaded frontage of the church of the Madeleine appeared occasionally through the stormy sea of oiled silk like a fevered dream of Ancient Greek temples.

'Here.' Sylvie took her arm to lead her into the relative calm of a jeweller's shop halfway down the street. The interior was a different sort of dream, mirrors and wood painted white, gold and pale green, and carved in places to imitate drapery. The light from above was stained turquoise and pale yellow. The clerk stood behind a small circular station in the centre of the room, and at his back a mosaic peacock spread its wings over the wall.

Sylvie went at once to a case held up on narrow curving wooden legs that contained a single necklace of opaque glass. It looked as if it had been fashioned out of snow. There were three other women in the shop, all moving with the slow graciousness of wealth. They were as magnificent and polished as the shop itself. The clerk stepped out from behind the desk and approached Maud. His polite smile did not reach his eyes. 'Miss, is there anything I can show you?' Maud felt the expensive gaze of the other women settling on her, her black merino dress and the loose arrangement of her hair. She straightened her back and answered with a not-quite smile of her own: 'I doubt that, Monsieur. Your goods are a little too gaudy for my taste.'

The smile was fixed and he remained in a half-bow as if carved by the same snaking hand that had created his surroundings. 'And all so terribly expensive!' he said very quietly. 'A number of English ladies remark on it every day. I wonder why they come in at all.' He let his eyes travel over her poor dress and her unpowdered skin, pink from the cold. 'They do not seem to understand Paris fashions.'

Maud would have dearly liked to slap his face but she could not help seeing herself over his shoulder in one of the many mirrors. She looked like a country wife at court.

Sylvie left her contemplation of the frosted-glass necklace on display and glided across the mosaic floor towards them. 'I am sorry to keep you waiting, Maud dear,' she said, and then turned to the clerk. He took in the sable collar of her winter coat and bowed a little more deeply. 'Brooches, please, Monsieur. I need a little something to cheer me up now the weather has grown so dull. Will you oblige me with a selection?'

Maud waited by the door watching the people pass outside while Sylvie examined whatever Monsieur offered. The other women circulated, more came in or out and Maud observed them admiring themselves and examining each other until Sylvie was ready to leave. She and the clerk both had a vague air of disappointment clinging to them. It seemed they had concluded there was nothing quite right for her among the blue and gold and enamel. They shook hands with mutual expressions of esteem and regret then Sylvie took Maud's arm and led her back onto Rue Royale then down towards Place de la Concorde with her shoulders slightly drooping.

Maud was expecting her to suggest they returned home until they rounded the corner and found themselves outside the new

Hôtel de Crillon. At that point, Sylvie suddenly put her head back and laughed – a deep, throaty laugh Maud had never heard from her before and liked. She pulled Maud under the shelter of the colonnade. The afternoon shadows were lit by crystal chandeliers blazing inside the hotel dining room. She opened her palm and Maud saw sitting on her white glove a brooch the size of a hen's egg. It was an oval of turquoise enamel, edged in gold with lotus shapes in a darker blue fanned around it and a milk-white opal pendant on a single stripe of gold.

'Ha!' she said, grinning so her small white teeth showed. 'That will deal with the nasty little invert. How could he be so rude to my friend? He will have to work a month to pay them back for losing this.' She spoke in French and there was a vicious edge to her voice.

Maud looked around her, terrified. 'Sylvie, you did not *steal* this?'

The other girl slipped it into the deep pocket of her coat. 'Yes, I did, and I was very brilliant too. He won't know a thing about it for hours, the disgusting wretch.' She returned to English, sounding like herself again. 'Now, will we take some tea at Smith and Sons? You may read *The Times* while we drink Earl Grey and I shall imagine myself in London.'

She made to move, obviously delighted with herself. Maud put a hand out to detain her. 'Sylvie, you cannot steal. You must take it back at once.'

'I don't want to! Maud, I did it for you, after all. Now do come and have tea.'

'I shall have to tell your brother, Sylvie.'

'I do not care what you do as long as you come along now. I shall freeze to death if you keep me talking here a moment longer.'

She left Morel a polite note before she went to bed, and found him waiting for her the following morning in the living room. He wore a long dressing-gown of patterned silk and the remnants of evening dress. His face was a little grey in the lamplight and Maud realised he had not yet been to bed. She explained what had happened while standing in front of him in her working dress, ready to leave for the studio. She thought that if painted, the pair of them would appear as some sort of allegory of Dawn – she all upright industry and he jaded decadence.

Christian sighed deeply when he had heard her out. Then, to Maud's surprise, he shrugged. 'Rue Royale, you say? Very well, I shall call there today, explain the mistake and pay for the thing.' He looked up at her, a cautious smile on his face. 'I think you are shocked, Miss Heighton?'

'I'm afraid I am, sir.' She had her hands clasped in front of her. She felt like a governess.

'Then please accept my apology on Sylvie's behalf. I feared that as she started using less of the drug she might take these odd fits. You are doing her good.'

'The drug, sir?'

He looked up at her with his eyebrows raised. 'She has been spending more hours of the day with you than resting, I think. The hour when she starts to smoke is gradually being pushed back, and so a little more of Sylvie returns.'

'That may be so, but you cannot condone theft, Monsieur Morel!'

He looked amused, as if she had done something charming. 'Naturally I do not, but I do welcome her recovery. After all these years of her being only half-alive, caught in her dream and hardly seeing the world outside . . . Whatever the inconvenience, I delight in seeing her take interest in life again.'

With that Maud had to be satisfied and she left him to make her way to the Académie in distracted mood. Her work did not go well in the first hour, and she was still brooding about Sylvie's larceny when Tanya arrived. Perhaps that was why she did not notice the Russian's dangerous mood until the next rest period in their work. As they gathered round the stove complaining of the damp, Francesca said something to Tanya. She replied in a high cracked voice though Maud did not catch the words, and then fled out of the room, already in tears. Her maid Sasha sighed and began to pack up her knitting but seemed to be in no great hurry about it. Maud put down her cup.

'Francesca! What on earth did you say to her?'

The Czech was a little red in the face, but looked angry more than ashamed. 'Nothing! Only she's been sighing for the last hour about how hard her life is in Paris and how long her fitting took yesterday and I said perhaps she'd paint better if she spent more time working and less shopping. I know she's your friend, Maud, and there's no malice in her, but I couldn't think for her complaining.'

Mademoiselle Claudette was looking at her questioningly. 'I shall go,' Maud said. As she left the room and lifted her skirts a little to climb down the narrow stairs, she noticed that Tanya's maid had taken out her knitting again.

She found Tanya sheltering in the lobby of the Hôtel Chopin. She was collapsed in one of their deep leather armchairs and crying her eyes out. The man behind the desk looked relieved when Maud went across and sat down beside her.

'Tanya? My dear, what is the matter?'

Tanya sniffed and struggled with her handkerchief. 'Oh, nothing! How could anything be the matter?' She turned away from Maud so that all she could see was the quivering lace across her shoulders.

'Now Tanya, don't be foolish. Something has upset you, so do stop crying for a moment and tell me what it is or I shall fetch your maid. Have your aunts been unkind? Come now – I promise not to be angry with you for being rich and beautiful for at least half an hour.'

The crying slowed down a little. Maud lifted her hand and the nervous young man behind the desk hurried over and bent low to hear whatever she commanded. 'A little brandy and water for my friend.' He reversed away from them before standing up with a quick shimmering step to rush away and do her bidding. Maud wished Tanya had seen it. By the time he had returned with the brandy in a balloon glass the size of her head, on a silver tray perched on his fingertips, and made his obeisance, Tanya's crying had given way to the occasional damp sniff. She drank a little of the brandy, which made her sneeze like a cat.

'Now can you speak?' Maud asked. 'Is it your aunts?'

'Everyone says I am to marry Mikhail Pavlovich Perov,' Tanya said very quietly, and tucked her handkerchief back into her sleeve. 'He has written to my father to ask permission and my aunts are taking it as a settled thing. We were at supper at the house of one of their ghastly cronies last night and they were dropping hints to everyone there.'

Maud remembered. 'Oh, not that young man with the horrible laugh?'

'Yes,' she whispered. 'His father is very rich too – grain import like my father, so it would be a merger more than a marriage. Mikhail Pavlovich told my aunts it would suit him to continue living in Paris while he learns the business. Then in five years we will return to St Petersburg where I can show off my Parisian polish. He actually said that to them. They thought it was charming, though he laughs at them behind their backs, the dirty hypocrite.'

Maud remembered him staring at the dancers at Maxim's but not even pretending to look at the paintings at Miss Stein's house.

'You can't possibly marry him,' she said.

Tanya turned towards her with her eyes black and wide. 'No one has thought to ask *me*, Maud. What can *I* have to say? He is rich and I am rich and he will let me *shop* all I want. After all, that is all I am good for, is it not? Shopping and a way . . .' she waved her hand in the air, 'a way for men to give money to each other. I am not a woman at all. I am a saddlebag filled with gold.'

Maud laughed. Tanya looked down at her hands and the corners of her mouth twitched. 'I must marry someone though, Maud. And there are not many suitable men. My family are all so pleased.'

'Surely that cannot be enough?' Maud asked. 'There must be some liking, some affection?'

'I don't know. I must be taken care of. I have never had to look after myself, and perhaps it would not be so bad. There would be children, I suppose, and I think he would let me carry on with painting.'

'Tanya, don't say such a thing. Perhaps you should learn to look after yourself. But would your father cut you off for refusing to marry a man you didn't like?'

Tanya took the great balloon glass of brandy in her hands again. 'Perhaps not. Though I think he would if I decided to marry a man without money. He fears adventurers, of course – that is why my aunts are so often with me – but he thinks if I enjoy the wealth of the family I have a duty to add to it, rather than take it away.' She lifted the glass to her lips and took a smaller sip. 'How many happy marriages have you seen, Maud?'

Maud's mother had married a man in no way worthy of her and had suffered for it. Maud's step-mother had married thinking she was taking a step up in the world and found herself saddled with a self-pitying drunk. Though the times she had visited her son Albert, now in James and Ida's care, she had come with the drover she had married shortly after her first husband's funeral. The couple seemed affectionate and happy together, although of course, it was early days.

'See? You have nothing to say,' Tanya said, 'so if I cannot have a happy marriage perhaps it would be better to be rich than fall in love with someone who may seem rather wonderful but who would have to work every day, and expect me to work adding things up in notebooks and finding out where to buy cheap clothes. It would be boring and I would be bad at it, and even a very nice man might get impatient with me then.'

Maud watched her drink the rest of the brandy and wondered about the slightly wistful tone in her voice. Some remark of hers from another day crossed her mind. 'Tanya, have you seen much of Paul Allardyce?'

She blushed. 'My aunts were driving us in the Bois. They think the atmosphere in the studio is damaging my bloom. He came and spoke to us for a while and asked after you. I told you that.' Maud nodded. Tanya's attempt to be casual about seeing the handsome American again had been charming really, but Maud, too busy with learning about the Morels and settling into her life in Rue de Seine, had not pressed her about it. 'Then he happened to be at the Circus when we went the next night. And I have seen him once or twice at the theatre. He is a writer so he will never have any real money.'

'That is not what is important, Tanya.'

The other girl put her brandy glass down on the table and straightened her back. Her eyes were still a little red but she was in control of herself again. 'Would you have said that a few weeks ago, when you were still hungry, Maud?' She didn't wait for an answer. 'I think I might do one brave thing in my life, but to live without plenty of money, that would be doing a brave thing every day. Only a fool would think otherwise.' She stood up and smoothed the long folds of her dress then spoke to the clerk at the desk, her head tilted to one side and smiling. 'Thank you so much. I will send my maid down to pay the bill.' He whispered his delight in being of use and as she swept out of the door with her head high, Maud followed like a bruised shadow in her wake.

CHAPTER 9

The Drunk oil on prepared board 45.7 × 40.7 cm

The background is roughly sketched; in places the prepared board is left unpainted and the brushwork is light and loose as if the brush can hardly bear to create the face. Note the lowered brow and the blotched pink and white of the skin, the mouth slightly open and the eyes wide. Its raw power disturbs even now.

Extract from the catalogue notes to the exhibition 'The Paris Winter: Anonymous Treasures from the de Civray Collection', Southwark Picture Gallery, London, 2010

15 December 1909

The late-afternoon calm of the apartment in Rue de Seine was shaken by a hard and rapid knocking at the door. Maud closed her book and left her room, then hesitated in the corridor. They never had visitors and the waiter who brought their supper in the evening was not due to arrive for another hour at least. And he never struck the door so violently, rather announced himself with a tap and delivered their food with the gentleness of a ghost. Sylvie's door remained closed.

The thought that M. Morel might have had some accident decided her. Maud opened the door but instead of the concierge with an urgent message she found herself faced by an elderly woman. She held herself very straight but with her head jutted forward, her lips pursed tight, and she was frowning so hard her eyes seemed to have disappeared into their sockets. Her coat was threadbare, old-fashioned; her hair was coming loose from its pins and her hat was a little battered. Around her neck she wore a ragged fox fur, the thin head still attached and its black bead eyes glinting. The woman's expression was one of violent disgust, though in the twitch of her thin lips there was something of triumph.

'Where are they?' she demanded at once, peering round Maud into the apartment. 'Where are the devils? I have found them! I have run them to ground at last, the dirty monsters! Oh, the pretty little devils! How can they sleep so comfortable, knowing they have stolen every penny from a poor widow! Not that I was poor then. Oh no, I was rich when I met them – and hardly a bone to gnaw on now! All charity!'

The creature was obviously insane. 'Who are you and what do you want?' Maud said.

'I want nothing from *you*, you silly tart. I want Christian Gravot and his bitch childwife!'

Maud started to close the door. 'There is no one here by that name. Good day.'

The old woman was too quick for her, and put her hand round the doorframe. Maud could only close it now by slamming it on her fingers, and she did not have the courage to do that.

'Morel, then! That's what they call themselves.' She was very close now, but if Maud stepped back she was afraid the woman would push her way into the flat. She felt her heart thudding in her chest.

'They are not at home. Perhaps if you left your card.'

'Ha!' The woman reached into her bag, continuing to block the door with her shoulder, and pulled out a piece of card which she flung straight at Maud's face. Maud flinched away, covering her eyes, and it fell at her feet. The woman pushed the door fully open and loomed hideous as a witch towards her. Maud felt panic tightening on her throat. 'There. Do you think he'll call? Do you think he will visit me at my hotel? After all the letters and telegrams from me and nothing, nothing from him in six months?' She took a step forward again and stared about the apartment, at the flowers on the hall-table, the gleaming floors, the calm polished comfort of it all. 'Where is he? Where is he now? Tell me, or I shall smash up your pretty home – and don't think you can stop me. I will have what is owed.'

'Monsieur Morel is at his club – The Travellers in the Champs Elysées. If you have any business with him, go there.' Maud's voice was high, protesting. The woman smiled, seeing Maud afraid, and her own voice became soft and wheedling. She looked up at the girl through her thin pale lashes with lizard eyes.

'What of the bitch who used to hold my hand and call me Granny? Where's she? Where has she hidden my diamonds? Did she eat them? Did *he*? I will have what I am owed.' Maud could not help herself; she glanced towards Sylvie's door and the old woman saw it. She began to glide towards the door with her wrinkled hand outstretched. Maud tried to make herself step forward, but failed.

There was a shout on the stairs and the concierge appeared with her husband lumbering up behind her. The old woman left the door to Sylvie's room to face them.

'There's the old monster!' the concierge said, her thin chest heaving with indignation and red spots showing on her cheeks. 'Sorry, miss, but she got by me. Now will you leave the ladies in peace, or will Georges here have to pick you up and carry you?' She put a hand on the old woman's shoulder and was shaken off.

'Paid in advance, has he, dear? Paid with a bit extra for you to keep an eye out? Count your silver before he leaves. That's all.'

The concierge's husband hunched his shoulders. 'What are you thinking of, Granny, coming round and disturbing people? What sort of house do you think this is? Come on, out of here, you old baggage.'

The woman looked back at the door to Sylvie's room. Maud wondered if she was thinking of making a dash for it, forcing the door open and attacking the girl. Maud could see it in front of her: the horror of the struggle, the vase smashed, Sylvie's screams and the howls of the madwoman.

Georges took a small step forward and the old woman looked back at him and growled. 'All the same to me!' she said, sniffing and pulling her coat around her. 'I'll be off to the club then, now I know where to ferret him out. And I'll sing my songs there.' She turned on Maud then, her eyes small and angry. 'And you, you silly tart, if you've got a shred of decency left, you should put your coat on and clear off out of it right now.'

Maud said nothing, unable to speak or act in her own defence or to save Sylvie.

'Enough of that! Time to go,' Georges said, his voice rising, and the woman let herself be jostled away. Maud found she could move again and followed them on to the landing to see them go. The old woman kept turning to look at her as they went down the stairs, muttering to herself. In the hallway below, she burst out again: 'I shall have you, Christian Gravot! I shall have you in this world or the next, you monster!'

Maud turned back into the flat. The door to Sylvie's room was still closed; for a moment she considered knocking, but to what purpose? The card that the woman had thrown at her was still lying on the floor. Maud bent down to pick it up. It was a visiting card. *Madame Prideux, 4, Place Saint-Pierre, Luxeuil-les-Bains.* She carried it back into her room and stared at it while her heart slowed to its usual beat. The old lady had not seemed the type to have a visiting card. Perhaps she had found it on the street.

Maud sat in her usual seat by the window and took out her sketchbook, tucking the card between the back pages. She thought about what she had said to Tanya about being brave, about taking care of herself, and felt ashamed. She then pulled the pencil free of the book's spine. She had thought she was going to draw that hard angry face with the threadbare fox fur and its dead glass eyes staring up from under the woman's pointed chin, but instead she found herself drawing her father.

When Maud's mother was alive her father had been a ghost in her life, a brooding presence slouched in an armchair with the whisky bottle at his side, staring into the fire while her mother sewed or read to them. Maud thought her mother had been beautiful, though she had never been photographed and Maud's memories of her face were hazy and ill-defined. When she died, quietly and quickly when her illness could no longer be concealed, Maud and her father were strangers. She realised then how much of the work of Creely & Sons, the auctioneers business her father had inherited, her mother had been doing. As long as Maud could remember, when she came down for breakfast her mother was already at the table working at long columns of figures in black account books or writing letters with neat scratches of her fountain pen. Later in the mornings Maud would accompany her mother as she made her calls around the town, playing with the black and white cat at the grocer's while her mother placed her order for the boy to bring round in the afternoon, or sitting on a sofa quietly while her mother talked to her friends in their dark living rooms full of heavy furniture and loudly ticking clocks. She was told that she was a good child and given paper to draw on, then her mother's friends would tell her how clever she was. She revelled in being a good child, a quiet child, an obedient child, rewarded with praise and her mother's love. It never occurred to her she could be anything else.

She had no hope of taking her mother's place. She was far too young and had not been trained to it. A month after her mother's funeral she began to see the home she knew becoming neglected. Two maids left in quick succession and her father spent days now as well as his evenings in his armchair with the bottle at his elbow. She went for a fortnight without a bath and only realised it when she overheard the butcher's wife saying she needed to be washed. She became deeply ashamed and hid away from the town as much as she could. She was no longer a good child to be admired so she stayed at home, only occasionally going to the back of the grocer's to meet her old friend the cat. The grocer's wife would bring out biscuits and milk and look at her with troubled eyes.

Maud's father started coming home less, and when he did he stank of tobacco and beer. The latest maid never looked at her and fed her on bread and butter and the occasional herring. Maud wanted very much to sit in those rooms with the ticking clocks again with her hair brushed and be told she was a good girl. One night she put on the cleanest pinafore she owned and waited for her father to come home. He looked surprised when he saw her sitting on the stair. She stood up and went to stand in front of him and asked if they might have their old maid back because she needed to be bathed and did not want any more bread for her supper. He bent towards her, his breath wheezing in and out of his lungs as if he'd been running, and his face red. His nose was covered with little broken veins but the skin around his eyes was oddly white. He watched her for what seemed an age, then he pulled back his arm and slapped her hard across the face. It knocked her to the ground. She heard him go into the parlour and slam the door behind him. A week later she was struck because she cried over the sold art books. Another time because he heard her complaining to the maid about her food again.

Someone must have seen the bruises. The grocer's wife probably. Maud's elder brother James arrived two days after the last bruising. He had qualified as a solicitor the year before and was freshly established as a junior partner in a firm in Darlington. She saw him walking up the road from the station in his high white collar and brown waistcoat and did not recognise him until he turned up their garden path. He was nine years her senior and as much a stranger as her father. Doors opened and closed downstairs, and before long Maud could hear her father's voice buckled with rage. A few minutes later, James came into her room and told her to pack her things. She was to go to school in Darlington.

She still had to come home during the holidays. Before her first full year had passed, her father had married the barmaid from the local pub. She at least dealt better with his drunken rages than Maud had done, happy to strike back when he raised his hand. She had a child and made her husband work, rationing his drink and screaming at him to support his children. Maud remained in her own room sketching and reading. Her step-mother tried to be kind to her, but Maud shrank from her loud laugh and her teasing. Her step-mother thereafter confined her efforts to her husband

and child, though Maud was not struck again and was grateful.

For all her step-mother's efforts there was very little of the business left when her father died. He fell one day in the shop when Maud was at home for the Christmas holidays, and the first she knew of it was the jangle of the bell on the ambulance. He died three days later in hospital, and though her step-mother asked if she wished to go, Maud did not visit. She did not go back to school in Darlington but remained in Alnwick under her step-mother's care. After years of having little to do with each other, they developed a wary sort of mutual affection. Her father's will split his estate equally between his wife and surviving children, though other than the building itself, that amounted to only a few pounds. It was a shabby place, and her step-mother could find no one interested in taking it on.

Three months after the funeral, her step-mother left, saying only that she had met a drover from Newcastle she liked the look of and would be on her way. It seemed to Maud that she was miserable to leave her son, Albert, but James and Ida were married by that time and offered to bring him up as their own. Maud watched the woman decide, and having decided she acted. She took three pounds out of the savings account in her and Maud's name and said they were welcome to keep whatever the building fetched, she'd rather be shot of it. James invited Maud to join them in Darlington. She refused and for a month lived alone in the family home. Then came the fire, her share of the insurance money and Paris. She left many things in Alnwick, but more than anything she wanted to leave her father dead among the ashes. Now he appeared on the page in front of her in profile with his chin lifted.

The time unrolled and Maud was surprised when a far lighter knock came at the front door: it was the waiter from the corner café bringing them their supper. M. Morel arrived as he was bowing his way back out of the apartment.

CHAPTER 10

*I*T WAS NOT UNTIL AFTER THEY HAD FINISHED EATING that Maud mentioned the strange old woman who had visited, and apologised for giving the address of the club.

'I'm afraid she rather frightened me. I hope she didn't give any trouble.'

'Oh, it was you who sent her, was it? That was kind, I must say.' Morel pushed his plate away from him. Maud started to apologise, but he stopped her and said more seriously. 'Poor lady, no, you did quite right to give her the address. Though I am afraid I was not there when she called and she caused quite a row. The porters saw her off the premises and threatened her with the police. By the time I got back there, she was gone. I came here this evening to warn the concierge to keep an eye out for her. I hope she has decided to go home. Perhaps I should send a telegraph to her son and say she has been up to mischief before she does any worse.'

'Who was it, Christian? Maud, you didn't say anyone had called.' Sylvie had as usual eaten very little, just picking at her food.

'You were resting, Sylvie.' How deep must her dreams be, Maud thought, not to have heard that.

'It was poor Madame Prideux,' Morel said. His voice was solemn, like a clerk of the court reading a charge. He scraped at the lace tablecloth with his fingernail. Maud noticed how neatly trimmed and polished they were.

'Madame Prideux? Here in Paris?' Sylvie half-sat up, then dropped again into her chair and turned her head away. 'What an awful bore. I hate her. You must take the proper precautions, Christian. I have only just begun to explore, and now I fear I will see that foul crone round every corner. It could ruin everything. Did it cause a problem at the club? Did she tell the porters where she was staying?'

Morel looked across the table at her, his nails still making a little scratching noise on the lines of the cloth. 'They understood the lady was a little mad. Yes, she told them where she was staying, and you are right. I shall deal with it in the morning.'

Sylvie shook her head, all at once more animated and more present than she was normally at this time in the evening. Maud had not realised her dream-like state could be set aside so easily. 'No, I shan't be able to sleep. You had better go now.'

He sighed. 'If it will make you happy, Sylvie.'

'It is what should be done,' Sylvie replied simply. 'But first perhaps you should explain to Maud who she is.'

Morel folded his hands in front of him on the tablecloth. 'You spoke to her, Miss Heighton. What did she say to you?'

Maud felt deeply embarrassed. She could think of nothing but her own cowardice when the woman was reaching for Sylvie's door. The amount of money that Morel was paying her above her bed and board would entitle him to expect her to make some effort to protect his sister, but she had done nothing of use. She had let the old woman into the apartment, given up Morel's club at once when a lie would have served just as well, and then stood there without speech or action until the concierge arrived. 'She said many things. But you have no need to explain yourself to me. None at all.'

'She said we stole from her, I imagine. I can assure you she is a confused old woman and we did no such thing,' he said.

'Naturally, I did not for one moment believe it. The lady was obviously quite mad.'

'We are grateful for your confidence, Miss Heighton. You see, Sylvie, ladies of sense like Miss Heighton are aware that she is nothing more than a mad old woman to be pitied. We need say no more about it.'

Sylvie shook her head again. 'I think you had better tell her the whole story, Christian. The siege and the diamonds. Then she can understand why Madame Prideux is as mad as she is and not think me a coward for wishing to avoid her.'

Sylvie got up from the table and fetched her cigarette-case from the side-table. 'Let him tell you, Maud. Or I shall worry you will think him a fiend. I am sure she told you we are man and wife.' She settled back down, lit a cigarette and dropped the case on the table. Maud still found the sight of women smoking rather shocking and flinched. 'See, Christian? Maud is blushing. She did say so.' The enamel stripes on the case were of subtly different blues. French ultramarine, brilliant ultramarine, new blue.

'Perhaps you can tell her the story as you see fit, Sylvie, after I have left.' Morel's voice was a little clipped.

'Oh no, Christian. You tell it so much better than I do.' She tapped the ash off her cigarette and sat back in her chair watching him.

Maud put her hands together on her lap. 'If you do not wish to tell the story, sir, I am sure I do not wish to hear it.'

'Unfortunately, Miss Heighton, Sylvie wishes the story told and wants you to hear – and we must in all things be ruled by her.' He took a cigarette himself and leaned forward so Sylvie could light it, cupping her hand to protect the flame from an imaginary breeze.

Maud said nothing. Morel filled his glass. The apartment was particularly silent this evening. The slight creak in the chair, the rub of cloth on cloth as Morel settled himself was quite audible. 'Miss Heighton, do you know anything of the Siege of Paris? And the terrible week that followed the break-up of the Paris Commune?'

'A little.' The electric lamps around the room shed a dull orange glow about them; the smooth curves of the furniture seemed to shift a little in the light, like the vines of a forest floor caught in the act of growth. She recalled a hot summer's afternoon and her teacher reading from *Lessons of History*. In 1870 the Prussian army had defeated the French and for a year laid siege to the capital. The poor suffered the worst of it, but in the end even the rich who had not escaped in time were eating rats. Napoleon III fled and the new government made terms, but the militias formed for the defence of the city wanted something more for their sacrifices than the new government were offering. Suddenly France was at war with herself. For a little while the Paris Commune made its laws and decrees before the new French government sent in troops from Versailles and slaughtered them.

'Madame Prideux was born and has lived most of her life in our home town,' Morel said, 'but she was in Paris in 1871 with her husband and her young child – a boy of about four years of age. Her husband was a diamond polisher who worked on Rue de la Paix. It was possible if he was skilled and lucky that they could have had a respectable, even a comfortable life – but seeing those diamonds every day made him greedy. It became harder and harder for him to work with such priceless rarities and then take home only a few francs for his wife and child. The chaos in Paris seemed too good an opportunity to miss, and with the help of his friend who worked in the same establishment, he managed to steal half-a-dozen good-quality stones. He needed only to pay off his accomplice and meet his family before returning to his native soil with the means to buy a good-sized farm. His accomplice was a man named Christian Gravot.'

Morel drank slowly from his glass and Maud noticed him seeking out Sylvie's gaze. She smiled brightly at him and blew out a long thin stream of smoke from between her pale lips.

'This was just the time when the troops were beginning to pour through the streets. They were searching for the ring-leaders of the rebellion, but in truth anyone not obviously bourgeois who had remained in the city was regarded as guilty. A patrol approached him when he was in sight of the place where he had agreed to meet Gravot, and in a desperate attempt to conceal his crime and protect his plunder, he swallowed the stones. The patrol was not put off. Perhaps they had taken fire from that building. No doubt Prideux looked guilty and afraid, perhaps his hands were dirty and they took him for an arsonist. For whatever reason they shot him where he stood. Many others met the same fate. Often the bodies were buried in the roadways where they fell. There was no trial, no arrest and examination in those days.'

Maud remembered her history lessons. The bodies stacked in piles like wood ready for the fire. The stories of the burning of Paris when the Tuileries Palace was reduced to rubble and Notre Dame itself was threatened by the mob. She tried to imagine Paris in chaos: the fresh-washed streets she walked along every morning pooled with blood, the sound of soldiers marching, of men and women trying to build barricades across the wide streets, and gunfire, a man hauled off to be shot with a group of strangers against the shop windows where now rich women bought their silk gloves. The bodies rotting to nothingness under their satin slippers.

'How horrible,' she said.

'Oh, just wait,' Sylvie said, blowing out another smooth flow of smoke. 'It gets a great deal worse.'

'Oh!'

'What is it, Miss Heighton?'

'Only the old lady, Madame Prideux, said she wanted her diamonds. She asked if you'd swallowed them.'

Sylvie made a noise of disgust in her throat, and Morel's skin became a little grey. Maud tried to imagine that angry old woman, young and caught among the gunfire and flames.

'So the diamonds were lost?' she asked.

'I wish they had been. This is where, as Sylvie says, it gets worse. Madame Prideux was waiting for her husband nearby. He did not come at the appointed time and she could hear shots being fired so she went to find him at the place where he was supposed to meet his accomplice, Gravot. His plan too must have been to leave Paris at once as he had his pretty wife and their bundles with him. Madame Prideux saw them bent over a body in the street and ran towards them. She was just in time to see her husband's corpse being gutted for the diamonds he had swallowed. She threw herself on them, but Gravot's wife held her back. All she could do was watch.' Horror made Maud's skin crawl. 'It is terrible what people will do for a little wealth, Miss Heighton, terrible.'

Maud felt a touch on her arm. Sylvie had put out her cigarette and now drawn her chair close. She lowered her head onto Maud's shoulder. Without thinking, Maud put out her hand and Sylvie took it. Their hands lay loosely entwined on Maud's lap. Morel stubbed his cigarette out fiercely on the edge of his plate.

'Tell her what happened next,' Sylvie said.

'She went home, borrowed enough money from her family to open a grocery shop. Ran it for more than thirty years and told that story to her child every night for his bedtime story. I fear he did not turn out well.'

'Did she want revenge?'

His mouth twitched – a sad quick smile. 'No, Miss Heighton, she wanted the diamonds that they had cheated her of. She believed her husband's sacrifice should have made her a rich woman. Instead she spent her life scrimping for the basic necessities of existence while watching richer women come and go in her shop, and sacrificing any ounce of comfort to pay back the money she had borrowed. She was always a bitter woman with a sharp tongue. She would flatter her customers and spit acid when their backs were turned. Her son was no better. He was sent to the prison camps in Guiana in the end after he was caught stealing.'

'A harsh punishment,' Maud said quietly.

'He was caught stealing diamonds. A lot of them. I suspect he meant to give them to her.'

Maud squeezed her eyes shut for a moment, trying to think. 'But why does she believe *you* are Gravot, sir?'

'She is mad,' Sylvie said without lifting her head. 'It came on her slowly. I remember she was found once or twice on the street apparently unaware of where she was. Christian was away on business at that time, but when he returned, her mania fixed on him. There was some resemblance perhaps. I am not sure she understood that it all happened forty years ago. She began to call at our house. I tried to be kind, but it was a terrible strain.'

Maud looked down at her profile; the young woman's skin was golden in the lamplight. 'Is that why you came to Paris?'

Sylvie shook her head. 'No. Her son came home, claiming to be a reformed character. He took over the shop and kept her off the streets. She must have escaped him.'

Maud was silent for a while. Her father used to rant about

Quakers, claiming that the fact he was losing business to an auctioneer in Darlington who was of that faith was proof of a conspiracy against a good Methodist like himself. The conviction would grow on him as he talked, and when Maud and her step-mother could take no more and left the table to go to their separate pursuits, he could be heard continuing his monologue with only the walls for audience. Outside, a drunk was singing to his lady-friend, his slurred swooping songs punctuated by her laughter. 'What a terrible story.'

'I am sorry to tell it, sorry that Madame Rémy did not do a better job of protecting your peace, but perhaps Sylvie was right and it is best you know, having seen her.'

Sylvie moved and stretched; the fabric of her gown slipped down her arms, showing them smooth and glowing.

'You will take the proper steps, Christian?'

He stood, tucked his chair under the table and brushed down the sleeves of his coat. 'I will, at once. I shall telegraph. Her son must come and retrieve her. She shall not spoil Paris for us, Sylvie. I promise.' She kissed her fingertips to him. He came round the table to kiss his sister on her white forehead. Maud noticed there was more blue in his skin than usual. She looked up at him.

'I know it is a difficult story to tell,' she said, 'but you tell it beautifully. It almost reminds me to be sorry for her and her son again.'

'Then I suppose it is worthwhile. And now, dear ladies, I must leave you. I may be late back.'

CHAPTER 11

*M*AUD DID NOT ENJOY HER WALK TO THE ACADÉMIE as much as usual the following morning. The story haunted her and she found herself examining the smooth classical façades of the buildings for bullet-holes, or waiting for the dead to reach up through the pavement and grab her ankles. The sounds of the street seemed a little jangled and out of tune and she felt watched, persecuted. She was afraid of meeting Madame Prideux on the street, afraid of her withered hands and the acrid bite of her breath.

Sylvie showed no sign of nerves when they met at lunch. She chattered about how much her sketching and her English was improving under Maud's care and made a great show of serving Maud with the best pieces of meat from the stewpot and piling her plate with thick greens. Then, as soon as Maud had put down her fork, she was itching to be away, drumming her long fingers on the cover of her sketchbook while she waited for Maud to change. She did not lead Maud in the direction of one of their usual sketching spots in the Jardin du Luxembourg, however, but instead turned in the opposite direction towards the river. She wanted to walk along the Quai de la Tournelle and then cross the Seine at the Pont Sully. It was no hardship to Maud. Sylvie's mood, the sun and the clear cold breeze drove all the demons away. Paris became a romance again and the life of the riverside always pleased her eye, such was its variety. Barges loaded and unloaded gravel onto the lower embankment where young boys climbed the piles like conquerers then slid down their flanks in giggling heaps. The little steam-boats carrying the curious travellers for a penny an hour chugged between the piers, each papered in advertisements with letters two feet high and backed with burnt sienna orange or Prussian blue, while the floating white buildings of the public swimming baths looked down on them like duchesses watching a lively toddler at play.

Sylvie chattered while they walked, pointing out the men washing and trimming the poodles of the rich by the water and exclaiming on the brightness of the day. Three times Maud suggested finding a place where they might stop and sketch the broad views in front of them, the river heavy and placid rolling through all the noise and activity of the city, the houses on the Île St-Louis seeming to hang over and watch it as it passed, but Sylvie would not stop as yet.

'Have you visited Père Lachaise, Maud?' she said over her shoulder as they crossed the river a second time on to the right bank. Then when Maud shook her head, Sylvie took her arm and pulled her close to her side. 'Then we must go at once. Christian took me there before you came and I think you shall like it.'

'I have heard of it, of course,' Maud said. 'But are you sure you would like to go there now? Are you not tired?' She did not know the precise time, but she was sure that Sylvie would wish to return to her room in a little while.

Sylvie waved her hand. 'Not at all. I do not wish to go home at all. Shall we take the omnibus? It is only right to go there when the weather is good. Who knows when it might be so pretty again, and

there are many nice places to sit and we can rest and draw there.'
She was wearing a long winter coat that Maud had not seen before.
It was fawn in colour but there was something darker mixed into
the weave so it looked to Maud like the pelt of a lioness. Its collar
was of some glossy black fur.

'If you are sure, Sylvie.'

'Oh, quite sure,' she said, all but dragging Maud up Boulevard
Henri IV past the sudden stalls on the pavement selling children's
toys and bundles of mistletoe.

When they reached Père Lachaise Sylvie chose to rest on a bench
on Chemin Denon opposite the tomb of Chopin. She did not, she
said, feel any great sympathy for the man's music, but she
remembered liking the kneeling angel that guarded the tomb.
Maud wondered if she realised it looked quite like her. She had
lost the strange vivacity with which she had begun the trip but
made no complaint when Maud handed her her sketchbook and
suggested she try and copy the musician's profile, stamped on his
tomb. Maud herself, however, did not begin to draw at once. Her
eyes were still too full of the place, its peculiar gothic beauty.
The cemetery where they had buried Rose had been a flat and
dreary sort of a place. Rows of square low tombs without greenery
or flowers to cheer it. Père Lachaise was quite different. The hill
on which the cemetery was built was covered with a city of its own,
complete with avenues and squares, poor quarters and rich. There
were rows upon rows of tiny mausoleums about the height of a
man and with pitched roofs like sentry boxes, but their designs
were not uniform. Every one was marked out by some individual
feature – iron grilles, gothic touches at the roof-edge, a medallion

or carved quotation, and dotted among them were weeping angels, busts of generals, carved drapery.

On the Avenue des Acacias were a number of larger establishments, mausoleums built like Grecian temples with broad staircases leading from their porticoes to the damp cobbles of the avenue. The jumbled edges of the crowded monuments tricked the eye. The contrast of the stone with the trees that grew between them, the dank mossy shadows, the distances of the city below offered a puzzle for Maud to work out in her sketches. There was too much to take in; she had to select the details to find the peculiar mood of the place without making the viewer drunk. People walked along the paths in twos or threes with their guide books in their hands, visiting the tombs of the illustrious dead. They peered at the names, giving a sharp nod if they recognised it, as if the sight confirmed something they had always thought, then moving on to the next.

A young woman had followed them up the path, and as they sat down she stood in front of the composer's tomb with her head lowered as if she were waiting to perform. She had a white rose in her hand. Maud began to sketch her, then stopped. It was a storybook picture being offered to her: the beautiful girl with a rose in front of a tomb would be a classic Victorian *memento mori*. She might as well paint a faithful hound. She could imagine her father sneering at it at some house sale – the sentimentality of it. Instead she shifted her position on the bench so she could look past the tomb and down the path. Sylvie's silhouette, her chin tucked into her collar, became the edge of the picture, the path that reached away from them; that way, the eye could understand the confusion of statuary around them.

'What will you do when you have finished in Paris?' Sylvie said quietly, looking between the tomb and her page. 'Will you go and paint portraits of your town dignitaries and give drawing lessons?'

Maud smiled slightly but the idea seemed a good one. She pictured herself in rooms of her own where there was good light to work by. She had been seeing it through a haze of desperation in the past year. Now it reappeared in her mind's eye quite clearly. There were not many artists trained in Paris living in Darlington, but there was money there. James's business was flourishing and his occasional stiff letters were full of the names of influential people whom he had met. It would appeal to the vanity of the local officials to have someone trained on the continent to immortalise them, and the surrounding countryside was beautiful. She would then be able to spend time working for her own pleasure as well as theirs.

'Something of that sort,' she said.

'That does not sound like a good life. Stuck in some provincial backwater where there is nothing to see and nothing to do,' Sylvie said. Maud said nothing, only thought how Sylvie's English was improving. It was quite possible that tomorrow Sylvie would demand to know all about her home town, the landscape, the people, and sigh at how much she wanted to visit. There was a pause, and Maud noticed her companion had stopped in her work, and was simply staring at the angel and the girl with the rose.

'Madame Prideux is dead,' Sylvie said suddenly.

At first Maud did not quite understand her. 'Did you say dead, Sylvie?'

'I did. A traffic accident on the Champs Elysées last night. I suppose she was too distracted to see where she was going. My brother had not managed to send his telegram to her son before he heard. The porters were discussing it at the club. He told me to tell you. I am sorry she is dead, though I cannot think her life did anyone much good.'

Sylvie did not seem to feel that any more needed to be said and turned back to her sketch. Maud did not know what to feel; she should be sorry, shocked. Perhaps she *was* shocked at the suddenness of the news, but she was not sure she was sorry. Perhaps it was better to die quickly like that, rather than be confined in an asylum, or rotting away behind the walls of your home – and to her, Madame Prideux had seemed unimaginably old. However, even surrounded by tombs, the idea that a person could be in the world one moment, then disappear from it the next felt extraordinary. The glass eyes of Madame Prideux's fox fur seemed to glimmer at her for a moment from the shadows in the path. Again she wondered what she should have done the previous day, whether she could have found words to calm the old woman.

'Her family will be informed?'

'I imagine so. Christian will write to them perhaps. Are you sorry for her, Maud? She was a wicked old woman.' Sylvie was looking at her over her thick fur collar.

'I am sorry for anyone who is so lost. Her life seems tragic to me.'

Sylvie smiled. 'If it was tragic, perhaps it is better her life is now over.'

Maud could not think how to reply so returned thoughtfully to her work. The ghost of the old woman retreated and the world became once more a series of visual problems to be solved. She made her notes, ideas for the tints she might use to recreate this scene on canvas, the variegated greys and greens. At last she felt the familiar ache between her shoulderblades and sighed, placing her pencil on the pad and spreading her fingers wide. Sylvie was still sitting very quietly beside her, but there was some tension in her shoulders. Her right hand still held her pencil but it did not move. Her breathing was a little shallow.

'Sylvie? What is it? Have you been getting cold? You need only tell me.'

The girl started as if she had been sleeping, but didn't look at her. Instead she took out her cigarette-case, shook one free then lit it. Maud watched her, frowning. Her fingers were shaking.

'Maud, I think I've done something stupid.' Maud waited. 'I threw away my *chandu* last night. The opium.' Maud closed her sketchbook and slipped the pencil she had been using into the hollow of the spine. 'I was thinking of America. How nice it would be to be free of France, how much better it would be to go there with clear eyes. I thought . . . I felt I did not need it at the time. Now, I am afraid.'

Tears appeared in her eyes and she tried to blink them back, tilting her head so she looked into the empty grey sky above them.

Maud felt her heart go out to her, poor strange Sylvie who had tried to break free of her chains. Yesterday she had failed the Morels, today she would not. Maud began to think in small, practical steps. 'Are you in pain?' A quick nod. 'We must go home.'

Maud put away her book, helped Sylvie to her feet and threaded her arm through hers. Sylvie leaned on her as they walked quickly down the slope to the main gate, her head lowered. Her grip on Maud's arm spasmed. As they walked down the Avenue Principale, a gentleman with a face like a bulldog turned to stare at them, ignoring his companion who was trying to point out Rossini's empty tomb. Maud thought of how she might look with Sylvie's thin pale form hanging on her arm. As if she was stealing one of the ghosts away from the place, no doubt.

If the cab driver they found at the stand by the gates noticed that Sylvie was unwell, he said nothing. Sylvie lowered the blind and leaned into the corner of the carriage as they drove. Her breathing was quick and harsh and she pressed her hand to her stomach. It had come on her very quickly. Maud's first thought had been to telegram to Morel in his club as soon as they were safely back in Rue de Seine, but he might not be there – and even if he were, what could she say in such a message? She could hardly mention opium openly, and if she said Sylvie was ill he would certainly hurry back to Rue de Seine, but then he would have to go out again to buy whatever Sylvie needed. She was suffering so greatly now, Maud was very afraid of what her condition would be in a few hours. She felt she had not the authority to summon in a doctor, since that too would surely bring scandal, would be a betrayal of trust. A panicked English miss might call a doctor, but an experienced woman who could take care of herself in the world would be more circumspect.

'Sylvie, do I understand rightly? You do not wish to continue with this attempt to abandon the drug?'

'I cannot. It is too sudden. I was stupid.'

'And your brother has no supply in the apartment? I will happily force a lock on his bureau and explain later what has happened.'

Sylvie shook her head and sank further into the corner of the cab, closing her eyes. Maud thought of her father. When he was taken into hospital, the nurses had stopped him drinking. Maud's step-mother stood by Maud at the grave staring fiercely at the earth as it covered the coffin, Albert's little hand held tightly in her red fist. 'It was the cutting off the drink that killed him. Seen it before when a drinker gets taken in by these religious types. So keen to do you good, they'll kill you in a minute.'

Maud put her hand on Sylvie's knee and said quietly, 'Can I fetch it for you? Do you know where I should go?'

The girl did not look round or open her eyes, but Maud felt her shudder with relief. 'Oh Maud, will you? Thank you. I am sorry to be so much trouble.'

'I am happy to help you in any way, my dear.'

Sylvie half-laughed, half-gasped and brought her hand to her face. 'There is a little place in the Rue Croix des Petits Champs – it sells prints and ornaments from China. Ask the girl for "a box" – she'll know what you mean. Just wait till you are the only customer there.'

Maud didn't ask her any more, letting her rest in the shadows while the cab danced and dodged along the streets. Once back inside the building, Sylvie straightened up as they passed the concierge's door, but the effort came at a cost. Maud wondered if she would be able to get her to her room, but somehow they managed. In the safety of Sylvie's bedroom, she helped her undress, and when Sylvie was in her shift, Maud pulled back the covers so the sick girl could crawl into her bed. Maud fetched water then opened her purse. Sylvie saw her.

'Maud, no. Don't use your own money.' Sylvie rummaged in the single drawer of the bedside-table. 'Here, take this. Please – I insist.'

Rather than a coin or a note, Maud found she was holding a small brooch, a bar set with diamonds with a sapphire in the centre. 'I've no paper money to hand. Pawn it, please. Rue des Blancs Manteaux. I never wear it.'

Maud would have argued, but Sylvie had already turned away with a low groan. She decided she would do as she had been asked, pawn the jewel and buy the opium. The decision made her shiver with complicity. She was no longer the same as other women of her class and country. She dropped the brooch into her clasp bag and snapped it shut, then let herself out of the flat feeling like a woman of the world for the first time since she had come to Paris. The skies were growing dark and fat with rain.

Shop Interior oil on canvas 152.4 × 182.9 cm

A bravura riot of pure colour, but notice the presence of the shopkeeper in her dark tunic. She ignores the viewer, is a point of calm and control in the centre of this profusion of oriental luxury and excess. Chinese and Japanese art and artefacts were extremely fashionable throughout the Belle Époque and were a profound influence on artists from Manet to Pierre Bonnard.

Extract from the catalogue notes to the exhibition 'The Paris Winter: Anonymous Treasures from the de Civray Collection', Southwark Picture Gallery, London, 2010

CHAPTER 12

*T*HE SENSE THAT SHE WAS DOING SOMETHING difficult and dangerous for someone she cared about made Maud brave. She went to the government pawnbroker's shop prepared to meet any sort of insult or insolence but found in fact a clean and efficient office, and the people waiting with her did not seem desperate or ashamed. There were ladies in fashionable walking dress talking to each other with the same ease as if they had run into each other in the glove department in Printemps. Some men in worker's overalls sat with bundles of clothing between their knees, but several of them were comfortable enough in their surroundings to lean back on the benches with their flat caps over their eyes and sleep until it was their turn to magically transform their property into a few coins.

When Maud's number was called, the man behind the desk greeted her with a polite smile. He examined the brooch through a jeweller's loupe that left a crease in the skin below his eye when he removed it. He wrote for a few moments in a notebook and handed her one of the carbon copies, stamped and sealed, explaining that she should take it to the cashier. Then he put the brooch into a little labelled bag and shut it inside one of the drawers below his desk, wishing her a good day as he did so.

The shop on the corner of Rue Croix des Petits Champs was very different. The air was perfumed with sandalwood and every available inch of space was crammed with fancy goods decorated in strong colours. The ceiling was hung with opened parasols, all painted with birds of paradise and trailing greenery, and the shelves were packed with bowls, some painted with blue dragons chasing their tails, others in vivid red and green cloisonné work. There were dozens of little figurines, dragons and lions in blue enamel seated on plinths and showing their teeth, half-open ivory fans and black lacquer boxes inlaid with mother-of-pearl. A Chinese woman stood behind the counter at the back of the shop, her dark hair pulled back from her face and wearing a high-collared dark tunic. She was wrapping a scarlet bowl patterned with chrysanthemums for a gentleman with thick white whiskers. She used a great quantity of newspaper and chatted to him in fluent French while she worked. When the package was tied the gentleman left, touching the brim of his hat to Maud as he let himself out of the door, leaving the bell jangling behind him. The woman cleared away her paper and string and folded her hands, waiting till Maud approached.

'I was told to ask for a box,' Maud said, trying not to blush. The woman's expression did not alter. She lifted her hand and with her palm flat indicated the shelves surrounding them. 'There are many here, miss. Would you like one of these?'

Maud shook her head but said nothing.

'Very well.' The woman slid from her stool and went into the back of the shop, returning a little later with a box the size of Maud's clenched fist. It was decorated with a picture of a phoenix lifting its heavy body away from the dark brown of the wood. The woman named a price, about half what the pawn shop had given her for the brooch and Maud counted out the money. The phoenix disappeared into wrappings of newspaper and string, and though the woman did not chatter as she had done to the man with the white whiskers, she was perfectly calm and the pleasant smile never left her lips. Maud realised she had expected something sordid; that the shop would be dirty and half-empty – an obvious front for vice; that whoever served her would be skeletal and creeping. She looked back over her shoulder as she left. The shopkeeper had picked up some sewing from the basket beside her and did not look up. Maud hurried back towards the river and Rue de Seine through the courtyard of the Louvre feeling oddly diminished, the colours she had seen in the shop beating behind her eyes.

Sylvie's bedroom was large and rectangular with a polished brass bedstead draped in white linen, the twin of Maud's own. The bedside-table was piled with cheap editions of English novels, the only books Maud had seen in the apartment other than the ones she had brought into it herself. The shutters were closed but letting in the last light of the afternoon through the slats. Two small armchairs upholstered in malachite green, embroidered with pale yellow and pink silk, sat in front of the fire. Sylvie must have heard the door to the apartment open, for she was sitting up on the edge of the bed with her dressing-gown on when Maud tapped and opened the door.

'Did you get it?'

Maud nodded and reached into her bag for the phoenix box, but Sylvie had already stood up and padded round to the other side of the bed, her bare feet making no more noise than a cat's. She dropped to her knees and pulled a tray from under the pleated valance. The tray was narrow, perhaps eighteen inches long and richly enamelled in scarlet and a dark but powerful green; its geometric patterns were studded with white circles, each containing a Chinese character in black. Cloisonné work. On it was a lamp with a glass chimney, the base decorated to match the tray, and to one side of it lay a pipe – a tube about the length of a conductor's baton, but thicker, with a bowl in blue and white porcelain attached to its side which looked strangely like a door knob. The mouthpiece at the other end was ivory. On either side of the lamp were a number of small tools and boxes, all decorated with the same enamelwork. Maud was reminded of the luxurious dressing-cases for rich travellers that had occasionally passed through her father's sale room. Every convenience at hand.

'Fetch me a cushion,' Sylvie said. She was trying to light the lamp, but one match after another failed.

Maud placed the cushion beside her, put the phoenix box containing the drug on the tray and took the matches from Sylvie's hand. She bent over the little lamp to light it and fitted the glass cover over it again while Sylvie twisted the lid off the wooden box, lifted it to her face and inhaled deeply. Something in Maud told her she had crossed a line in her life, that the act of lighting the lamp for Sylvie was one of great significance, but what that significance was, she could not say. She felt worldly and wise again after the challenges of her shopping excursion.

Sylvie was lying down on the floor with the tray beside her. Maud curled her legs underneath her and watched while Sylvie pulled a twist of waxed paper from the box and teased it open. It held a dark brown, slightly oval ball which glistened in the lamplight. Maud watched fascinated as the girl prepared her pipe. A tiny morsel was separated from the greater mass of the ball then needled to the edge of the bowl and heated on the lamp. Sylvie then put her lips around the mouthpiece and inhaled; there was a slight fizz and crackle as the drug vaporised. Her body seemed to relax at once. She did not fall into a stupor, nor behave as if she had become instantly drunk; nor did she seem to see visions – all of which Maud had suspected might happen. There was just this loosening in her muscles and a slow cat-like smile.

Almost immediately, she lifted herself onto her elbow once more to prepare another pipe and inhaled it in the same way. Maud could hear the faintest bubbling sound as she drew in the smoke. She then set the pipe down and looked at Maud. The tray in front of her, iridescent in the lamplight, was a burst of prime colour. In the outer glow of the flame Sylvie had become a spirit of greys and pale purple shadows: the lilac silk of her dressing-gown with its cream trimming of antique lace, the girl herself, her blond hair falling around her face and large grey eyes. Maud had left her sketchbook here when she had first put Sylvie to bed. She reached for it and drew the pencil out of the spine.

'May I?'

'If you wish, Maud.'

She began to draw. It seemed no time at all before the knock at the door heralded the waiter and their evening meal.

Sylvie oil on paper, mounted on canvas 69.2 × 64.7 cm

A woman reclines in half-light with the paraphernalia of opium smoking laid out in front of her. This is a sensitive, intimate painting of what was seen at the time as a dangerous vice. The drapery around the room, the subject's dressing-gown and even her skin seem to be painted in shades of smoke.

Extract from the catalogue notes to the exhibition 'The Paris Winter: Anonymous Treasures from the de Civray Collection', Southwark Picture Gallery, London, 2010

The weather was becoming more and more unpredictable, and inclined to turn viciously cold without warning. Sylvie said it was too chilly to sketch outdoors so instead took Maud driving through the Bois de Bologne in a hired car or on shopping trips in the grand department stores. Maud saw Sylvie smoking on one more occasion, when she asked if she could paint rather than sketch her. There had been some discussion at the Académie about the advantages of producing a work in a single sitting, and Maud was keen to experiment.

They established themselves on the floor of Sylvie's room, Maud pinning her oil sketching paper to a deal board to support it then choosing her tints, squeezing each onto the palette in abstemious amounts, attaching the little tin cup with its reservoir of linseed oil to its edge, setting out her hog-hair and sable brushes. As she did so, Sylvie prepared her tray with a similar satisfaction, and Maud was aware that the ritual was important to them both. Then each settled to their addiction.

Time ceased to consist of one moment following another. Maud's hand travelled with a will of its own; she felt as if she were hardly present. Her body was obeying its training to observe and record without intervention. Each tint she required she could mix at once, and the sensuality of the process took over her senses. Moving the brush along the paper was like brushing soft skin with her fingertips. The long lines of the picture appeared beneath the gentle pressure of her brush, the shape of the dusky shadows behind Sylvie, the pattern of light through the shutters . . . She painted for two hours then slowly put down her brush; it rattled with the others in the jar and it sounded like applause. Sylvie seemed to have fallen into a half-doze and Maud left her, to clean her palette and brushes before the evening meal arrived.

Maud managed to persuade Sylvie to visit the Louvre once – but almost immediately, they ran into Francesca. Maud was very happy to see her out of the studio, and the two women began to talk about the painting in front of them for a few minutes until they realised that Sylvie had, rather pointedly, wandered away. It was clear she did not wish to be introduced. Maud did not know how to apologise for her.

'She is not used to company,' she said, rather awkwardly.

Francesca rolled her eyes. 'Tanya did say she was a bit of an odd fish. Beautiful, though.'

'I should go after her.'

'Of course, treasure. But you should also take my advice and get married. It's so much easier to be dependent on a man for one's bed and board. As long as my husband is fed and I tell him he's a handsome devil once a week, he's as good as a lamb. Now hurry along.'

Every time Maud suggested going to one of the museums after that, Sylvie accused her of wanting to see her artist friends and of being bored with her company. During one of his brief appearances in the flat, Maud mentioned this to Morel. He nodded and chewed his lip. 'I understand, Miss Heighton. Sylvie has never been fond of company or crowds. I can only say that your friendship and patience has improved her greatly. You would have to have seen the stupor in which she lived in the past to truly appreciate this. I only fear that our home will become tiresome to you. A healthy young woman like yourself should not be so confined.'

Maud protested. 'Please, Monsieur Morel! I am more than happy.'

He did not seem to believe her. 'I know what happened a few days ago, Miss Heighton. Sylvie would never have attempted to give up the drug without your example; even if that attempt failed, it gives me hope. But I must arrange some thank you fitting to your help for us. Let me think on it – a Christmas gift!'

Maud slept badly that night. It was the first time she had not enjoyed a full night's rest since she had arrived at Rue de Seine. She lay, uncomfortably awake, staring at the shadows on the ceiling, trying to account for it. She thought of the picture of Sylvie. She had stored it with her other sketches in oil in the lid of her painting box and she could feel it glowing there. The picture, and her ability to paint it, to bring it so close to what she saw in her own mind, excited her. It was a bold piece in the narrowness of its range of hues, shocking perhaps in its subject, but not vulgar the way she found some of Manet's nudes vulgar. There was none of the flat, blatant invitation of Olympia, or the contrived nudity of the Académie's bound Andromedas, fastened to a rock for the sea-beast or for the critics to examine the quality of her skin. Still, it was certainly true that the painting of Sylvie was sensual; frankly so.

Maud turned over in her bed, echoing the pose of the painting, wondering what her brother and sister-in-law would say if they saw the picture. She had nothing to be ashamed of, she told herself. Nothing – so why this creeping sense of shame as if she had lost something? She had absorbed in her youth an idea of herself that could not, it seemed, include pawn shops and opium lamps. They put her outside her class in a way that having a drunk as a father had not. He had never left the house without a collar and tie, and people would exchange a 'Good day' with him in the street though they crossed the road to avoid her step-mother.

Maud wondered why it had been so important to her to stay in lodgings that could be thought respectable even when she was starving, why she paid the fees at Lafond's to paint the nude with no men in the room. She felt as if she were on a tower of Notre

Dame looking down like one of the gargoyles at herself – herself as she had been, spinning in little circles in her sensible black working dress, as confined in her movements as a child's toy, when all around her, experiences and lives which she could not think of, could not admit to knowing, existed just out of sight.

Feeling suddenly vertiginous, she opened her eyes, sat up to pour a glass of water and went with it to the window. The gaslights shone ghostly in the thick dark and although she could not see the river, she could sense it, the mass of water between the embankments, pushing itself towards the eventual relief of the open waters of the English Channel.

Catching sight of herself in the glass, she toasted her reflection then set the glass down; as it clicked down she heard another click – of a latch in the hall. She stepped noiselessly across the floor in her bare feet and knelt down, peering through the keyhole like a butler in a peepshow film. Sylvie's door opposite was ajar and the light fell across the corridor for a moment before it was blocked by the shadow of a man emerging from the room; he turned to say something in a low voice and Maud saw it was Morel. His shirt was untucked, his braces hanging down from his waist. He was laughing a little, showing his white teeth. Sylvie appeared beside him, her body hidden by the angle of the door. She put a hand to his face and reached up to kiss him, her lips pressing his face just by his mouth. The warmth of their affection gave Maud a pang of jealousy. She thought of her mother, and wondered if she would ever be loved like that again. They said something more, too softly for Maud to hear, then Morel turned towards his own room and Sylvie quietly shut the door behind him.

CHAPTER 13

*W*HEN MAUD RETURNED TO THE APARTMENT THE following day and was shaking her umbrella off in the passageway, she heard the voice of M. Morel greeting her. He was beside her at once, helping her off with her damp coat.

'Mademoiselle Heighton! I am delighted to see you. Do come in. I hope you'll forgive my rudeness but we are already at table. I only had a moment to dash back from the club.'

Caught up in her coat and bag, Maud had no time to do more than assure him no apologies were needed before she was ushered through to the drawing room like a favoured guest rather than a girl who ate there every day. Sylvie was at the table looking far brighter than usual and dressed to go out.

'Maud, darling! Are you famished? It's boiled chicken for lunch again, I'm afraid, but they know we like it and their imagination seems to be running out. Christian has arranged his treat for us though.'

Morel pushed in her chair behind her and while Sylvie piled stew on her plate and fussed with cutting more bread, he leaned over Maud, his eyes wide.

'Now Miss Heighton, have you heard tell of the splendid, the refulgent Madame de Civray?'

'Naturally.' Everyone had. She was a French Countess though American by birth, and very rich. Rumour said she bought a great deal of art and said a great deal of stupid things about it which the painters all repeated to each other with great glee while they spent her money in the Montmartre cafés. Or so it was said at the Académie. Maud had never been near enough to a café in Montmartre to know what was said. Yvette was their only connection to the artists on the hill and all they knew of what was discussed there, they heard from her. She had told them her own story of the Countess too. She had been modelling for M. Degas one afternoon when the Countess arrived at his studio with her footman and her little yapping dogs.

'Well, Master was not best pleased to see her, but even he cannot drive a woman like her out once she has her foot in the door. "Am I disturbing you, *maestro*?" she says. "Yes, you are, Madame," he says, and looks as angry as all hell. "Well, honey, I'm only here to pick up a couple of little things for the smoking room," she says, and I promise you she picks up the first two canvases she can put her hands on and passes them to the footman. Then she draws out a wedge of notes the size of my fist and pops them on the table. All this time, old Degas is too angry to speak. Then she backs out of the room with, I promise you, her finger on her lips! As soon as the door closed he threw his palette so hard against it, it cracked. Then she was heard the next day in Galérie Georges saying she couldn't understand why people were so rude about him, because he was such a sweet old stick!'

Morel dropped down into the seat next to Sylvie, his arm still slung around the back of her chair. 'The Countess and I have friends in common. I begged a favour. You and Sylvie are invited to her home this afternoon – early, mind you – to see her paintings. She leaves for her husband's country estate for Christmas today.'

Maud didn't know what to say. Morel lowered his voice. 'You know, Miss Heighton, that Sylvie finds public places rather a strain on her nerves, but there you will be free to feast your eyes on pictures in privacy. Sylvie is more and more ready to brave the outside world, in this limited way. It isn't even a formal visit. Come, haven't I done well?'

Sylvie put out her hand and covered Maud's. 'It is all good, isn't it? I hate for you to be shut up here all the time. Christian tells me I have been selfish, and I agree.'

Maud looked at her and said, 'Not at all. You know I take such pleasure in your company.'

'No, I can be strange and cross and I know it. But we are hoping this might make up for your patience, and to thank you for your help.' She jumped to her feet. 'See? I am already dressed. Now say you'll come, Maud, do. Tell us how clever we have been, then eat quickly.'

Maud looked at her with pleasure. 'I'll be delighted, but you must let me change.'

'No need!' Sylvie said. 'She knows it is a poor friendless painter Christian wishes to see her collection. Spend the moments we have eating, Maud. Christian shall go and fetch a cab.'

Maud looked back at her plate. Sylvie was as brutal as a child sometimes.

Sylvie was unusually animated on the way to the Countess's house, and in spite of the crowds thronging the pavements, she made the cab stop twice in order to dart into one or other of the shops on Rue de Rivoli. Each time she made Maud wait in the cab and emerged with a number of parcels and boxes. 'Presents,' she mouthed as she returned. She stared out of the window at the passing streets with renewed excitement. 'How happy everyone looks! Perhaps this time next year I shall be well again. We will be in America by then. They understand business there. And now I speak English very well. You will come with us to Midnight Mass tomorrow, will you not? Did you go last year?'

Maud was becoming used to her whirring changes of subject. 'I was unwell. But there was a little party in the boarding house where I was staying, and the landlady brought me up some of the food.'

'How horrible it is to be unwell, particularly at Christmas when everyone else is so happy. This year you shall enjoy it more.'

'I'm sure I shall, Sylvie.' Maud had prepared her gifts. To her brothers and Ida she had sent French confectionery and picture books. For Yvette and Tanya she had made cards with portraits of them both. Morel was to have a tie from Charvet, and for Sylvie she had found a pretty fan in ivory, painted with peacock colours. They were all of them modest gifts, but she felt a certain pleasure in giving them.

'Oh, we are here!' Sylvie counted out coins from her purse for the cabman while Maud stepped out onto the pavement and looked up, amazed. The Countess's house on Place Saint-Georges was astonishing, a can-can dancer among a row of stately matrons. Four storeys high, each window surrounded by stone Graces and Muses, garlands, flourishing black ironwork – all exuberance. It was a frivolous, pretty building that seemed to be laughing sideways at the flat, self-important front of the Thiers Library opposite.

Sylvie appeared beside her. 'I hope the lady is not too like her house,' she said, 'or I may find her exhausting.'

The manservant took Sylvie's card and within moments his mistress was approaching with quick steps, her hands stretched out in front of her and a pair of yapping dogs dancing around her heels.

'Oh Miss Morel! Delighted! And this must be Miss Heighton, I think? I'm so pleased you could drop by and see me at such short notice.'

Maud had always liked the American accent. It sounded friendly to her, its easy musical swing so unlike the clipped English of glass and china she had learned at her mother's knee. The Countess was wearing a day gown of green silk rippling with pearls set into its lace bodice and sleeves. Maud waited for the familiar long contemptuous look her own clothes tended to draw in Paris, but none came. Instead the Countess shook hands very heartily and gave her an open smile. 'Now, I want to hear your opinion on something straight away. Then I shall be very rude and leave you to wander about as you see fit. I have to get the evening train for the Loire and there's not a thing packed. This way! You too, Miss Morel!'

'Are you going to be away long, Madame?' Sylvie asked as she trailed behind them, staring up at the high ceilings, the baroque mouldings and gilt and red velvet furnishings. It was like being in a private Versailles.

'Only a week, thank God. We are paying our winter visit to my husband's family. A whole château full of titles and unmarried aunts and not a chin between them.'

Maud smiled and the Countess winked at her. She thrust open a pair of doors off the hall then turned to face them as they waited in the corridor, her arms still wide and holding the doors apart, a firm but glorious guardian of the space beyond. 'Now, Miss Heighton, it seems to me in this day there are three sorts of painters. Those who paint what they *want* to see, those who paint what they *feel* they see, and those who paint what they *think* about what they see. Which are you?'

Sylvie spoke while Maud was still considering. 'That is very clever, Madame. Did you read it somewhere?'

'Seems unlikely!' she said cheerfully. 'Unless it was in a Sherlock Holmes novel.'

'I hope I paint what it *feels like* to see,' Maud said at last with some hesitation.

'There! Just when Miss Morel has said I sounded clever, you have invented another category. I cannot allow it. I shall put you in category two, as that seems closest. It is my favourite. The first lot are too pretty, and the last lot think such ugly thoughts. Now what do you make of this?'

She took hold of Maud's arm, walked her into the middle of the drawing room then pointed to a still-life that hung above the fireplace. It was difficult at first to see the painting properly in these surroundings, for it was small for this room – perhaps twenty inches in length and almost square. It showed a rough wooden table with two bowls on it, one containing cherries and the other peaches, on a ruched-up tablecloth. But the perspective was all wrong. The cherries were facing towards the viewer, the peaches turned upwards. Every angle was impossible and clumsy; the brushwork strange, hurried, with variegated hatchings; the colours, other than that of the fruit, oddly muddy; the light source hard to trace. Still it had a mass, a weight that was tangible.

'Cézanne,' Maud said.

'Uh-huh,' the Countess replied, standing by her side and staring with her. 'But what do you think?'

'It seems crude, but I would never stop looking at it if it were mine.'

The Countess clapped her hands. 'Exactly! That's exactly what

I felt! How can something be revolting and so beautiful at the same time?' She stared at it. 'I own a lot of beautiful things, Miss Heighton. I'm as rich as Croesus and I like to spend my money, but if this place was on fire and the people were safe, this funny little painting is what I'd come back for. Isn't that odd? My husband had a huge portrait of his mother here until I bought this. It felt like an act of Yankee rebellion replacing it, but when you really look at it, all this other stuff . . .' she waved her hand at her private palace '. . . just seems to melt away. I think the Count was a little angry with me for a while, but you know what? I now believe it is what he would save too.'

'I'll never paint like that,' Maud said.

'Would you want to, honey?' the Countess asked. Maud thought, and then shook her head.

'Me neither. The world only needs one Cézanne and we've had him. You have to find your own way. Now, I have to run around like a fool getting ready for the train. The servants all know you're here, so you wander about just as you like. The Degas paintings are all in the smoking room. The Count and his male friends think they are connoisseurs, but when it comes down to it, they just like looking at the ballet dancers' legs while they have their cigars. You know I had to chain them to the walls? The first painting of his I bought, he came and took back, saying he wanted to alter something – and I cannot get him to return it! Always, "tomorrow and tomorrow, Madame"!' Maud began to think a little differently about Yvette's story of her raid on the master's studio. 'There's a Fantin-Latour in my dressing room too you shouldn't miss if you want a more classical fruit basket. So do have a good poke around. We can have a proper visit when I come back from the Château of the Dead in a week or so. Nice to meet you, Miss Morel!'

And she was gone.

Maud was intensely happy during the two hours she spent in the Countess's home. There was such a profusion of canvases, and each one offering some fresh revelation. Here were pictures that belonged neither to the violent crudities on display at the Steins' house, nor the polite pastorals of the Salon. And she was alone with the pictures. No matter how early she arrived at the Louvre or how late she stayed, the rooms were always full. The same people she saw in Père Lachaise were there too with their Baedekers and Ward Lock guides, glaring studiously at the paintings, comparing them with the fuzzy reproductions in their guides and reading off, loudly, the appropriate paragraph, before striding onto the next. She tried to ignore it, tried to tell herself it was right that these people too had the chance to look at these great paintings, but they irritated her nevertheless. She wanted to snatch their guidebooks away and stamp on them. 'Just *look*!' she'd complain in her head. 'That's all you need to do. Just stop for a minute *and look*!'

The private galleries kept all their best pictures locked away to titillate their customers with goods unsullied by the inferior eyes of the poor, and the Salons? Packed society occasions that befuddled the eyes. At Madame de Civray's, Maud feasted in solitude. It was indeed an eclectic collection. Impressionists jostled up against Symbolist works, the soft edges of Renoir alongside. There were names she did not know: Rousseau, Utrillo, who painted blank walls and somehow made them live. Some Maud liked, some perplexed her, but each one demanded attention. If the Countess did choose them at random, then her luck was the devil's. Maud wished Tanya was with her. She'd change her mind about the catty gossip surrounding Madame de Civray just as quickly as Maud had.

Sylvie sauntered around with her for a while, but was more interested in the Countess's dressing table than her art. She began picking up the jars of ointment and reading the labels of each one slowly as if committing it to memory. Maud went on and found herself in an upstairs library face to face with a painting of Pissarro's of a meadow in sunlight. A woman, the suggestion of a woman, stood under a group of trees, looking out of the frame. In the distance were the roofs of a small town. It was all so perfectly light and alive; the air moved, the woman would walk away at any moment. Maud closed her eyes and opened them again, trying to fix the image in her mind, trying to see the individual colours and brush-strokes. And all this in peace. No one dragging on her arm. No loud voice behind her, pronouncing. She could reach out and touch it . . .

The door opened and she flinched. It was the Countess.

'Sorry, honey. I won't disturb you but I wanted you to have this.' She handed over a flat black cardboard folder tied with ribbon. Maud took it. 'Open it up.'

She did. It held a slippery mass of photographs of the paintings she had been admiring. 'Oh my goodness!'

'I know, I'm just too kind – don't even say it! Happy Christmas! It was just I thought, Hell, I'm giving that poor girl a couple of hours to take it all in, then throwing her out again. It seemed cruel. We had them done for the insurance in the summer, and I had them make up a few extra sets.'

'Are you quite certain, Madame? I can return them.'

'I'm always sure, honey. It's one of my many virtues – and keep them, for crying out loud. You don't treat me like an idiot and that makes you one of my special friends in Paris. Now, where is that floaty friend of yours?'

Maud laughed. 'I'm afraid she's not as fascinated by these as I am.'

'More fool her. Now I have to go for a fitting, it seems, so stay as long as you like and scoop her up on your way out. Wish me luck in the ghastly Château.'

Maud held the portfolio to her chest. Her heart was lifting and rising; the pictures had made her giddy. 'Good luck, and thank you – thank you so much!'

The Countess sketched a wave as she left the room. 'Pleasure, honey!'

CHAPTER 14

*T*HE VARIOUS STUDIOS OF THE ACADÉMIE LAFOND gave themselves over to pleasure on the morning of Christmas Eve. Lafond himself went from studio to studio drinking a glass of punch at each and giving his blessing to his students. He always came early to the women's ateliers, since a man as careful of his reputation as he was would not visit his young ladies after drinking the punch mixed by his male students. Even at ten in the morning, though, he was jovial and pleasant with them all, released from judging them as they too were released from being judged. He beamed at them all over his fantastic white moustache as he told them it was at this time of year he most enjoyed counting his blessings, to revel in his old age, crowned with friends and prosperity. All his students felt caught up in his pleasure: it was as if Père Noël himself, having swapped his tunic for a tailored suit and high collar, had graced them with his presence.

Maud rather shyly gave her cards to Tanya and Yvette, and was delighted when they both laughed heartily at them.

'You see too much, Maud!' Tanya said. Maud had drawn her in an evening gown and clutching a canvas under her arm, fleeing a Russian Bear who wore a top hat and monocle. 'Oh, I shall keep it forever.'

Yvette's card showed her seated on the edge of the fountain at Place Pigalle with a queue of hopeful artists in front of her. 'I wish it were so!' Yvette groaned when she saw it. 'Still, all the girls with rich friends will be off and holidaying for the next few days so I might have the fountain to myself.'

Mademoiselle Claudette became a little sentimental and handed each of them a little printed card from the studio itself as they left. Classes would begin again on 3 January 1910.

It was all very different from the previous year for Maud. She went to Midnight Mass with the Morels and for the first time since childhood felt moved to prayers of gratitude. After they returned to the apartment, brother and sister fussed over their gifts from her. Morel played cabaret songs on the piano, bashing them out with more enthusiasm than accuracy and making Sylvie and Maud dance around the drawing room behind him. Maud had Morel's gift – a scarf from Worth – tied loosely around her neck and her gift from Sylvie – a brooch in the shape of a butterfly – pinned to her blouse. Sylvie played the coquette with her fan, and Morel wore his new tie over his old one. Maud went to bed at three leaving Morel playing slower songs and Sylvie curled up on the chaise longue watching him. Her bedside-table was a little forest of cards including ones from her brother's family, wishing her luck and success. She felt, falling asleep, she had nothing left to ask for.

After the giddiness of Christmas, the days that followed felt peaceful. Sylvie encouraged her to go out still in the mornings and Maud spent them wandering round the museums, but she left her sketchbook at home and let the works she saw flood over her. She studied individual works, feeling her fingers twitch with the urge to experiment, but avoided her easel. It was a holiday, after all, and should be treated as such. She strolled by the Seine, watching the smoke rise from the barges. It felt as though an early spring had come even as the weather continued cold and damp.

On 30 December Maud spent the morning at the Musée Carnavalet among the histories of Paris and admiring the caricatures of Jean-Pierie Dantan. After lunch she and Sylvie walked together in the gardens watching the students and their models eating pancakes which steamed in the cold air. Sylvie was affectionate, but seemed more subdued than usual. Maud wondered if she was preparing for another attempt to give up the pipe. Later she read contentedly in the flat and was surprised but pleased to hear Morel's voice in the hallway just before the usual hour for supper. She heard the brother and sister speaking but remained in her room until the waiter brought their food. She joined them with the expectation of pleasant conversation, but Morel was quiet and withdrawn. Sylvie was silent too. Maud wondered if they had received bad news from home, or worse, that Morel's business in Paris had suffered some reverse and they would have to leave at once. She was ashamed that her reaction to the idea of their leaving was purely selfish. She would have to find miserable lodgings again while the weather was still bitter, and although the money they had given her already would keep her going through the spring, it would not permit any comfort. She needed another month's wages for that. The way they both piled her plate high and filled her glass made her feel even more sure it was all going to be taken away. She ate and drank hungrily, like a peasant who has sneaked into a feast. When she could eat no more she felt a sudden wave of disgust at herself, the animal which fear of poverty had made her. She was too hot; the rich food had made her sleepy.

'Might we open the window for a moment, Sylvie?' she said at last.

'Not just now, dear,' she said without looking at her.

Morel wiped his mouth and stood up from the table. With a clarity that felt unnatural Maud noticed that his lips were still a little greasy with the sauce. He went to the side dresser and opened it with a key from his waistcoat pocket. Maud watched fascinated as he removed a small striped box and handed it to her.

'Could you tell us about this box, Miss Heighton?'

He looked so grave that she laughed. 'You know I cannot. I have never seen it before.'

He looked away from her, out into the street. 'Open it, please.'

She did so, though it took a slight effort to pull herself up from the table. She set it down, then took off the cardboard lid. 'I don't understand. What is this? Oh, Lord.'

The box contained a blaze of white light. Maud blinked to clear her vision and saw a tiara, made only it seemed of diamonds and air.

'Take it out, please.'

She did. It was far lighter than she had expected. There was one large central stone the size of a pigeon's egg, surrounded by curling fronds of smaller stones. 'I don't understand,' she said again, and reached forward to touch that central stone. It shone like the crystal glasses Morel kept for his whisky. 'Is it yours, Sylvie? Oh, my dear! Please tell me you didn't steal it!'

Sylvie gave a sharp bark of laughter and lit a cigarette. Morel continued to stare out of the window as he spoke.

'My sister found it in your room this morning, Miss Heighton. It belongs to Madame de Civray.'

'How could you, Maud?' Sylvie said.

Maud was confused; the room was so warm she could feel sweat trickling under her hair on the back of her neck. 'How could I what, Sylvie? Stop being so silly. I've never seen it before in my life, and it was most certainly *not* in my room this morning. This is some sort of joke. And it isn't funny.'

Sylvie was watching her with a sad smile. Morel remained at the window with his back turned. 'Some moment of madness, much regretted now I am sure,' he said.

Maud was too surprised to be frightened yet. 'Are you suggesting I stole it? You can't be. I would never do such a thing. Sylvie, you had all those packages with you. You must have picked it up by mistake.'

Sylvie turned to Morel. 'The Countess just leaves her treasures lying around – the temptation must have been too much. Have you not noticed how unhappy Maud has been this week, Christian? How distracted and upset? She has been walking the streets of Paris by herself.'

'The museums, dear,' Maud explained. 'You don't like them.'

Sylvie carried on as if she hadn't spoken. 'Without even taking her sketchbook. I think it began just before Christmas. And you know, Christian, I think she almost wanted me to find it. It was sitting on top of her bed, plain as anything.'

Morel smiled sadly at his sister. 'Perhaps the effects of opium have, as some have suggested, destroyed her moral sense. This cannot be forgiven, Sylvie.'

Maud tried to smile, her eyes going back and forth. 'Sylvie, Mr Morel, do stop. It's not kind. You know I've been happier these last weeks than I think I ever have been before. Do stop.' Her head swam and she put her hand on the table. Her limbs felt alien and unwieldy. She felt she had somehow forgotten the trick of moving them.

Sylvie sighed. 'The papers are full of such things. Poor women, trying to be respectable then falling into temptation. So sad. How long have you been a victim of opium, Maud?'

Maud tried to speak firmly, but her mouth had become dry and her voice came out thicker and lower than usual. 'I have never touched that drug, as you well know.'

'Please don't deny it, Maud. I thought I smelled some strange scent in the air but I had no idea, not until I looked under your bed after finding the tiara.'

'There is nothing there. You are talking nonsense.'

'Oh, but there is!'

Maud would wake up in a moment. Didn't this feel like a dream? Her body so reluctant to obey, her vision blurred. She stood up. There was nothing under the bed. She would show them and that would be an end to it. She had to keep one hand on the wall of the corridor to stop from falling as she went. They followed her and she thought she could hear Sylvie's sympathetic sigh as she stumbled. She shoved open the door to her room and fell to her knees by the bed, then stretched out her arm under it until she touched something. A tray. Her fingers feeling fat and unhelpful, she pulled it towards her. Sylvie must have put it there as a joke. Part of her stupid joke. She was a child at times. She realised she was speaking out loud, but the words were emerging ugly and slurred. She managed to pull the tray out from under the bed. It was not the cloisonné treasure of Sylvie's but a dented metal serving platter like those used in the most down-at-heel restaurants. On it was a cheap-looking brass spirit lamp, a bamboo pipe, a porcelain bowl the shape and size of a door knob. She picked it up, confused and lost in a deep fog that made her arms impossible to lift. The world began to feel very far away. 'That's not mine.'

Sylvie and Christian had come into the room after her and were standing just in front of her window looking serious and sad, and watching Maud as if she were some exotic, but faintly repulsive reptile. An elegant couple visiting the freak show. Maud could see the volume of Ruskin she had been reading lying open on the windowseat.

'Did you see if she was carrying anything when you left Madame de Civray's home, Sylvie?'

Sylvie tilted her weight to one side. 'She *was* carrying a few things, and she seemed very excited.'

'You had boxes – that box. I was carrying some for you but all I took from that house was the portfolio! The photographs!' The words stumbled through her lips and she was no longer sure if she spoke French or English. It seemed suddenly very important that they saw the photographs. If they did, they would understand. They would stop this. She half-crawled towards them, towards the side-table to the left of the door where the portfolio lay, but her hands wouldn't work. She fell towards them, knocking the photographs onto the ground as she went. Neither Sylvie nor Christian made any move to help her.

'Poor Maud!' she heard Sylvie say.

The last thing Maud was aware of was Sylvie stepping over her body to leave the room.

She was wearing her long coat and a hat with a wide brim. Her legs still wouldn't work, but someone was holding her up. The air was freezing cold and she could smell tobacco and brandy. It was a man – a man was holding her. She tried to push at him but her hand hardly moved. She saw it. Why aren't you moving, hand? she thought. It must be part of the same dream. She felt the grip the man had around her body tighten and for a second she was lifted onto her toes, then suddenly set down again. There was the sound of footsteps approaching. They echoed as if they approached down a long stone corridor.

'Everything all right?' said a male voice she did not recognise.

'Yes, all fine. The wife's had a bit too much to drink. Her sister's birthday.' That was Morel's voice, only he was speaking strangely, like a worker rather than a gentleman. Why was she here with Morel? There was another sound too. Water; water moving. No matter, it was just a dream – just a funny dream.

'Well, we'll all be like that tomorrow night with any luck! You need some help getting her home?'

'No, we'll have a little rest here, then it's only round the corner. Marriage, hey?'

'Too right!' the man said and laughed. 'Happy New Year!' Maud heard his footsteps fade.

'OK, my little rabbit? My sweet little cabbage? Oh, you're waking up. Not for long.' Morel was holding her face up towards him, his other arm tight around her waist. His face was so close she could see his eyelashes, delicate as the hair on a sable brush. The light came from above and from far away. She felt a high stone wall at her back and over his head she saw the blank silhouette of the Louvre. The lights on the far embankment were bright as starlight, their aura almost blue. He held her hard against him for what seemed like an age. No man had ever held her so close before. Then he looked to right and left. Such silence. She had no idea Paris could be so quiet and so full of shadows. She could hear someone whistling as they crossed the Pont des Arts above her head. Ah, so that was where she was, on the quayside under that long beautiful bridge, untroubled by horse or motor traffic. She could see the lace patterns of the ironwork. The song faded and the quiet returned; now there was just the lap of the water and the shifting of the boats tied up at the quay. None showed any light.

'Time to go, Miss Heighton.' Morel half-lifted her, half-dragged her a few feet. Her shoes scraped against the cobbles. She could feel the heat from his body. And then her right foot slipped over the edge of the quay and touched nothing. Something in her understood and she felt herself seized with panic. She started to struggle against him but she could feel the weakness flowing through her. He released her suddenly and she felt a sudden blow to her stomach, something between a push and a punch, sending her back into space. Too fast. This couldn't be. Only as she fell did she realise completely that she was awake, that this was in truth happening to her. She struck the water as if falling through glass; the water raged up around her white and freezing, leaping into the air in a shout of spray – then there was nothing but coldness and darkness as the river closed over her.

Part Two

CHAPTER 1

31 December 1909

*H*AVING CONSULTED AT LENGTH AND FOUND OUT who was likely to be where in Paris on New Year's Eve, Tanya's aunts informed her that they had accepted the invitation of the Swedish Ambassador to join his table at the Bal Tabarin in Montmartre. Tanya was surprised until her aunts told her that Perov was a great friend of the Ambassador and instructed her to make herself as pretty as possible. She had a rather sick presentiment that Perov was planning on asking her to marry him tonight. In a slight panic she sent Sasha to the telegram office and snapped at her French maid when she was trying to arrange various items from Lalique's latest collection in her hair.

The streets were full of the signs of festival as they drove through Paris. Music and light pouring out of the cafés, the buildings lit up and the crowds surging back and forth. They stepped out of their car on the stroke of ten. Tanya was nervous of being too early, but there was a steady procession of ladies and gentlemen entering under the canopy and they found the grand ballroom already full and loud with the galloping music of the can-can. The walls, balcony and ceiling were hung with great ropes of flowers, the musicians were sweating over their instruments and the whole hall was brilliant with coloured electric lights. As they made their way over to the long table where the Ambassador was entertaining his party, a group of women in huge picture hats were occupying the centre of the floor, dancing, kicking their legs up in the air to show the snow white petticoats beneath their hooped skirts. Aunt Vera lifted her lorgnette just as one gentleman got a little too close and found his hat knocked into the mocking crowd by one of the dancer's high-heeled shoes. Tanya paused, waiting to see if Vera would be too shocked to stay, but instead she laughed and watched the man struggle to retrieve his hat from beneath the feet of the crowd with apparent pleasure.

Tanya's heart sank a little. She was sure Perov meant to propose now and had told her aunts as much. Ribbons curled down from the balcony in a continuous stream of emerald and scarlet. 'I must ask for time to think,' Tanya said to herself. Above their heads hung large hoops filled with New Year's souvenirs. She could see paper flowers and model aeroplanes, cardboard cigarette-cases and matchbooks marked *1910*. She tried to look further into the crowd, but there was no one she recognised. So taken was she by looking at the faces in the distance, Tanya hardly noticed where she was being seated, but found herself next to a man her own age with an oddly pointed chin. The seat to her left was unoccupied, and for a moment she was afraid Perov would drop into it at any moment – but then she saw him at the far end of the table sitting between her two aunts and looking smug.

The man on her right was thin to the point of emaciation and told her he was a writer. He had a monocle squeezed into his right eye which seemed to require frequent polishing. He peered up the table towards Vera and Lila. They had insisted as always on wearing the styles of their youth in bright silks, and had bullied the weeping fashion gurus of Rue Royale into supplying them with puffed sleeves and pinched waists. Or rather Vera did the bullying. Lila laughed at her for it, then cheerfully wore whatever she was told to. It should have made them ridiculous, but the two women were swiftly surrounded now as ever by a number of young men in tight-fitting dinner jackets who fought for the honour of fetching them champagne and strawberry mousse. Tanya knew they would be trying to make her aunts say something shocking enough to amuse them, and had no doubt they would succeed.

'They are quite the success of the season, these Russian old maids!' remarked the writer. 'It shows how jaded we are become in Paris when our novelties are so . . . *novel* . . .'

Tanya took the flûte of champagne offered by a waiter bending low over her shoulder and looked at him coldly. 'You are speaking of my aunts, sir. Vera Sergeyevna is a widow, not an old maid.'

He seemed quite unabashed. 'Ah, you are the artist we have to thank for bringing them among us! Is it true you labour all morning in an attic and refuse any invitation that might take you away from your work?'

'There are many reasons I might refuse an invitation. I attend the classes of Monsieur Lafond, but that was my whole reason for coming to Paris – so how else should I spend my mornings?'

His expression showed a slight disgust. 'Oh, you will destroy yourself! Leave art and science to the men. It is in our nature to innovate, to adventure into new worlds, while it is woman's duty to support and inspire us. Do not make yourself a half-creature, learning to paint. You are in Paris – it is the place where you should learn to become a woman! To charm and infuriate, to drive us to new heights. *You* are the work of art, my dear. Stop your lessons now before your beauty fades and your charm dulls.'

'And what great heights has my sex inspired *you* to, sir?'

'I have had my successes, though one shouldn't expect the acclamation of the vulgar crowd for works of high art.' The monocle was polished ferociously for a few seconds and replaced.

'You must admire the genius of George Sand,' Tanya said.

'Naturally, but indeed, she proves my point.' He jabbed his long finger towards Tanya with such vigour that his monocle sprang free from his eye and swung on the end of its ribbon; such was his pleasure in the argument he ignored it. 'She was not a woman at all but a half-breed. Her genius *proves* she was not a woman but an hermaphrodite. And look at her! An unfortunate freak. Such intellectual activity crushes feminine charm like your own, the female mind becomes overheated and loses its bloom, its frivolous ability to please.' He smiled kindly. 'Come, Miss Koltsova, I am sure you must agree.'

'I do not. But as you think I am half-witted at best, I am sure that cannot be of the least concern to you.' She was aware as she spoke of a man sliding into the chair on her left.

'Gustave,' he said with an American twang to his French, 'I swear you will turn every woman you speak to into a suffragette. Hell, I listen to you for ten seconds and I want to bop a policeman over the head just to show fellow feeling.'

Tanya turned in his direction, aware that the room had grown suddenly brighter and warmer. 'Mr Allardyce! I did not know you were to be of the Ambassador's party.'

'Neither did I, nor the Ambassador until an hour ago, Miss Koltsova. Then I had a sudden and urgent need to change my plans for the evening. Now, have you had a turn around the room yet? There are lots of shiny lights and rich people in pretty frocks to look at. That should appeal to your feminine fancy, shouldn't it?'

She grinned into her champagne. 'It should.'

'Excellent. Then do stand up with me at once, but be careful not to look back in the direction of your aunts. I am fairly sure they will make it clear they wish you to stay in your seat if you do.'

Tanya got to her feet very gracefully and didn't look round. He led her to the edge of the dance floor to a stop where they could pretend to watch the dancers. 'Well, I am here. What's the emergency?' He spoke in English, his voice dry and tired.

Tanya fixed her eyes on the conductor of the band. He squatted and leaped as he led his musicians, exhorting them to greater efforts with extravagant grimaces. 'There is no emergency. I did not mean you to think such a thing.'

He raised an eyebrow. 'You certainly did. I'm sorry, Miss Koltsova – I've been working hard and that makes me more plain-spoken than usual. What can you want of me? I've chased you round town for a month trying to make myself amusing and dodging your aunts. You know, I don't think in that time I've seen you in the same dress twice?'

'Paul . . .' she whispered. He controlled himself and looked out onto the dance floor again. It was the first time he'd heard her say his first name, but there was such fear in her voice, such sadness. He looked around at all the show and spectacle and felt a black bitterness run through him.

'So it's true, then. Perov is going to ask you to marry him. I've heard the rumour. Have you got me here to make you an alternative offer?' Tanya's eyes felt hot. 'Sorry kid, but I can't make you one – though it's sweet of you to offer me a chance to counter-bid. I've nothing but what I earn, so if you were hoping I've got some railway stocks laid by, you're out of luck.'

The band leader sprang in the air and spun about, aping the movements of the can-can dancers. He looked to Tanya at that moment like a devil.

'You horrible, cruel . . .' She still looked straight ahead, a polite smile on her lips as if she were enjoying some pleasant conversation with an acquaintance. 'If that is what you think of me, why are you here? Even if I were stupid enough to agree to marry you, you would not want me, would you, without all . . . this!' She touched her evening gloves to the diamonds in her ears, the pearls and diamonds at her throat. 'You're just as money-minded as any millionaire in the room. If I didn't change my dress every day you wouldn't chase after me for long.'

'I'd take you in rags,' his teeth were gritted, 'but how could I ever live with myself afterwards, knowing the life you could have had? You'd make me a failure just when I am beginning to get my start in the world. I could never dream of keeping you in the style—'

'Keep me!' She faced him, hissing. 'Am I a horse, a dog? Offer me your arm and smile, you idiot, then take me back to your friend Gustave. At least he is honest about his contempt for women.'

He took her arm and drew her back towards the table, blistered with rage and feeling that though he was greatly injured, he was somehow also in the wrong.

He could not leave, though, but rather sat in heavy misery listening to Tanya sharpening her feminine charms on Gustave for the next hour and sinking every glass of champagne he could get his hands on. Then he noticed that the heavy hoops of souvenirs were being lowered just to within reach of the gentlemen's canes, so some of the souvenirs might be knocked down and claimed. Pushing back his chair with a violent scrape, he set out into the scrum, returning some minutes later rather red in the face and with his blond hair dishevelled.

Tanya looked up at him in surprise. He bowed very formally and presented her with his prize. It was a cheap cardboard cigarette-case printed with one of the advertisements of Bal Tabarin and a border of glass beads, glued not quite straight. She took it from him a little dubiously then laughed; her black eyes lit up and she pressed it to her heart. 'Mr Allardyce, I will treasure it.'

He sat down, feeling a glow of satisfaction that spread painfully from his stomach to his fingertips. She leaned towards him and said softly, 'I will ask for time.' The warm glow became ashy and cold.

'The horse could learn to talk,' he muttered.

'What?' He was about to explain when Tanya straightened and looked across the room like a pointer bitch who had spotted game. 'Oh, is that not Madame de Civray? Are you acquainted with her? A friend has told me about her and I would love to meet her.' She looked so enthused, her fingers were already drumming out a tattoo on the white linen.

'I do know her,' Paul said. 'I write for her father's papers about Paris affairs from time to time, so she invites me to her At Homes. Not that they're very exclusive. Shall I introduce you now?'

'Oh do!' and once again Paul offered his arm. He noticed before she stood up that Tanya slipped his cardboard cigarette-case into her shimmering evening bag and whatever else he felt, he was briefly as happy as he knew how to be. He ushered her through the crowd and subtly made space for them in the circle of the Countess's court, then when she had greeted him with a slight nod of recognition, he bowed and introduced Tanya.

'I am so delighted to meet you,' Tanya said, with a curtsy. 'My friend Maud Heighton told me of your kindness in showing her your collection. She is absolutely thrilled with the photographs and has promised to bring them to the studio in the New Year.'

The effect of this little speech was not what either Paul or Tanya had expected. The Countess's polite smile disappeared and her face became pale. 'You have not heard then,' she said, then looked around the faces of her friends. 'You must excuse me, dears. I have to speak to this young lady.' She took Tanya by the elbow and guided her across the ballroom floor to an alcove behind the band. 'Let us sit down for a moment, honey.'

Paul felt rather aggrieved. He half-followed the women, being discreet but keeping them in sight, watching them through the crowds of dancers. Midnight was coming up fast and the dancing seemed to be getting wilder. There were shrieks of laughter coming from all sides of the room. He could just see them through the bobbing and braying heads of the revellers. Tanya was facing him, and he saw her polite smile vanish, to be replaced by an expression of sudden shock. She had one hand over her mouth and was shaking her head. The Countess de Civray was holding onto her other hand and appeared to be speaking to her urgently. Miss Koltsova wrenched her hand away and bent forward, covering her face. The Countess looked round and caught his eye. Paul forced his way through the crowd towards them. He looked down helplessly on Miss Koltsova's shaking shoulders.

'Allardyce, thank goodness! Could you fetch Miss Koltsova's aunts and explain to them that their niece is unwell? Then speak to Monsieur Guyot at the front desk. Have their car sent to the back entrance at once. Hurry along now, there's a good fellow.'

He went off to do as he was told, leading the aunts to the alcove and arranging for the car. Then he remembered Tanya's evening bag and ran across the room to fetch it. When he returned, Tanya was already getting into the car. She took the bag, and as she thanked him distractedly, he tried to squeeze her fingers with his own. Her eyes were red but before he could ask anything or even tell if the pressure of his fingers was being returned, the more fearsome of the aunts reached across and pulled the car door closed;

he had to move quickly to avoid losing an arm. He slipped back into the ballroom before Guyot closed the door on him too and hurried up to the Countess.

'Madame, what . . . ?' She shook her head and pointed upwards. The apelike band leader was standing on the upper balcony with a pistol in each hand and both arms raised in the air. That instant, the lights went out and in the utter darkness twelve shots exploded, the muzzle flashes singeing the eye. The crowd counted in a great shouted chorus after each shot '. . . *dix, onze, douze!*' The cry of twelve became a general cheer and the electric lights glowed and burst forth again. Strings of them in mauve and yellow were lowered from between the festoons of flowers that canopied the roof. The band let fly with a fanfare on the trumpets and the room erupted into more rolling cheers. As another cascade of ribbons came curling down from the balcony, the back doors opened and a succession of beautiful women, carried on platforms resting on the shoulders of men dressed as Roman slaves, began to parade round the room. Above her head each woman waved a flag sewn with large scarlet letters proclaiming *Love, Beauty, Peace* – and finally and most splendid in her bower, a girl under a stiff arch covered in paper roses and emblazoned *1910*.

Confetti fell over Paul's shoulders. The Countess had disappeared back into the crowd and the dancing had begun again, even less inhibited than before. Paul leaned back against the pillar behind him, exhilarated and confused. A red ribbon fell over his shoulder, and without thinking what he was doing, he curled it and tucked it into his breast-pocket.

CHAPTER 2

1 January 1910

*T*ANYA WOKE SLOWLY, BECOMING AWARE OF LIGHT and movement within the room. Her old maid Sasha was already there, bustling about Tanya's discarded clothes and books. As always, her first thought was, I am in Paris – and for one moment she was happy. Then her memories of the previous evening returned. She saw the Countess's face and heard her saying gently but firmly that Maud was a thief, and dead. Tanya squeezed her eyes shut. Her blood felt suddenly hot and painful in her throat as if she were choking on it. She had managed it all so beautifully; introducing Maud to Miss Harris and seeing her safely established at the Morels' for the winter, and more than that she been sure, *sure* that Maud liked her and that they were friends. She thought of the card Maud had made for her, and the sketch in oil she had done of Maud at work, her suddenly frank and open laugh when she had seen it.

Tanya could never tell if the Frenchwomen she met liked her or not. They treated her like a child, laughed at her for working at Lafond's when she could be sleeping and shopping, writing catty little notes to each other as they did and despaired over her every time she turned down some invitation in order to attend the evening lectures on anatomy. Whenever her aunts dragged her round the fashionable At Homes in the afternoons, their hostesses made sly jokes saying they hoped she would not get paint on their upholstery though she was better dressed than any of them. The aunts would not let her visit her friends from the studios where they lived, nor invite them formally to the house. Even Francesca, though her husband was at the German Embassy, was forbidden to dine with them. Apparently the Ambassador himself, a huge man who looked permanently bored, was a third cousin of theirs, and to invite the wife of one of his juniors to the house when he himself had only dined here twice would be a gross and grievous insult. There were rules about these things. There had been trouble enough when she had only hosted Maud for an afternoon, but as it had not been a formal visit and Maud had seemed perfectly genteel, they had let it slide in the end. Had she been too distracted by her interest in Paul Allardyce, the threatened proposal from Perov, to notice that Maud was still in real danger, in real need? She had seemed so calm and happy. She had not been terribly understanding about the pressure on Tanya to marry wealth. Tanya had thought perhaps that was just the famous English commonsense, something she could learn from that might in time make her stronger. Or perhaps it had only been jealousy, after all.

Tanya loved Paris, but she felt she was kept in a small, rigorously policed corner of it, and had been plotting a means to move the velvet ropes out a little way. She hoped in some part of her soul that if she spent more time among those people who worked for their living – practical men and women who did not devote themselves to fashion and leisure – she might be able to imagine a life among them. She saw Maud as an example. She was so moral, so correct and hardworking, no one could think she was not a suitable companion, but she intended to earn her own living when her training was done. Tanya had been carefully mentioning Maud to her aunts since she began to live in Rue de Seine, repeating the lie about her being the relation of a baronet, only making the relationship a little more vague. Weren't the Morels wise to have a young, respectable companion for Sylvie? Weren't they lucky to be able to practise their English? Wouldn't it be hard for Miss Heighton to go back to an ordinary, albeit respectable boarding house, when the Morels left Paris, having been so comfortable?

Tanya bunched the silk sheets in angry fists. Now Maud had ruined it. She had lost herself in opium. Could she have fallen so far without Tanya even noticing it? She had seen Maud's hunger and her hope that day in Parc Monceau, her longing for the comfort of the apartment in Rue de Seine. She must have been tormented by the idea of losing it again, and then, just at the season of Christmas when all the wealth and light of Paris is on display, so available if you have francs in your pocket, that stupid, stupid American woman had left her diamonds lying about. If Tanya had just told Maud her clever plan, that she should come here when the Morels left Paris, that she would save her from the cats, help her plan an independent life and laugh at the *mesdames* with her; if she had just said to her, 'This is my plan, Maud. Help me,' then the Countess could have left wallets of fresh banknotes around and Maud would never have thought of taking any. But she hadn't said anything, not wanting to disappoint, and now Maud was gone and everything was broken. It was her fault. She drew her knees into her chest and groaned.

'Oh, so you are awake, cabbage? Sit up and drink your tea like a good girl. I've held them off as long as I could but your aunts are pawing at the door. Fainting away in the car might have worked last night, but it ain't going to work this morning.'

Sasha arranged the pillows behind her, then handed the girl her tea. The cup started rattling in the saucer at once. Tanya's shoulders started to shake again and she sobbed. Sasha sat down beside her and lifted her chin in her hand. 'There, there, my little darling! No more crying! Are you sick?' Tanya shook her head. 'No one has been cruel to you?' Another shake. 'Bad news then? I wondered, but who do you know in Paris to cry over so? Not any of those fools who take you dancing when you'd rather be home, I'd lay my savings on it, and I have a few. Did Perov propose? Did he frighten you?'

'No, no . . . not that.'

There was a tapping at the door. 'Is she awake, Sasha?'

'Here we go! Now mind what you say! No scandal, no illness and no nerves! Vera Sergeyevna would have written to your father already this morning, demanding that you be taken home at once – if I hadn't hidden the ink.'

Tanya nodded and prepared herself as well as she could for the onslaught.

'Are you ill?' Vera Sergeyevna said before she even came to a halt by the bed, then without waiting for an answer, she turned to Lila and snapped, 'I knew this was a mistake and I told Sergei so! I did! "She is fragile, my dear brother," I said. "Do not send her to Paris! Her nerves will not take it." And see? I was right!'

Lila Ivanovna placed the back of her hand briefly on Tanya's forehead. 'She has no fever. Some private sadness? Has someone hurt you, Tanya?'

Lila's voice was always softer. She had been the first person to encourage Tanya to hold a pencil. If she had been with Tanya alone she might have soaked all her secrets from her, though what she might have done with those secrets was anyone's guess. Tanya shook her head.

'Poor Mikhail Pavlovich was *so* disappointed when we left,' Vera continued. 'And who could blame him if he decided he did not want a sickly wife, always pulling him away from his pleasure with her fits and fancies.' Tanya gritted her teeth. 'Your father will be extremely disappointed also. Perhaps we should get you back to Saint Petersburg at once. If you drive off the only suitable men in Paris with your fits, then we shall have to find you a husband there.' Tanya kept her head lowered, staring at the folds of her disordered sheets. There was a pause, then Vera said with the air of a visionary pronouncing, 'The Rhum Saint James.'

Tanya was startled enough to look up at her. Vera was standing with her fists on her wide hips. 'I'm sorry, Aunty Vera?'

'You haven't been taking it, have you?' Tanya dropped her eyes. 'You foolish, foolish girl! It was recommended to me by Monsieur Claretie himself. I am only surprised that you are not fainting away every day. I dare say my cousin and I would hardly be standing without its support.'

'I do not doubt it, Vera,' Lila said, and for a second Tanya thought she caught the ghost of a smile on Lila's lips.

Vera tapped her slipper on the floor, frowning, and her eyes fixed on the moulding in the corner of the room. 'Perhaps if Mr Perov is made to understand it was a rare lapse from your usual health . . . The richness of the Christmas diet without taking proper precautions. Men like women with delicate tastes as long as they don't cause too much trouble. Makes them chivalrous.' She sniffed hard. 'You must stay in bed today so I suppose we shall have to do the *whole* round of New Year's Day calls by ourselves. And no doubt every maid will want her tip. You are very thoughtless.'

'I am sorry to have been so foolish,' Tanya whispered. 'And to have ruined your enjoyment of the ball last night.'

'Oh, it is not for *myself*, dear, that I complain.' Vera swept her arm wide with the palm upright. She might have been performing Racine. 'Balls and champagne mean *nothing* to me. But your poor Aunt Lila was not brought up with the same luxury as I was. Your selfishness cost her a *unique* pleasure.' Tanya said nothing but kept her eyes lowered submissively, while Vera Sergeyevna sniffed again. 'I suppose we must go. It will show we are not seriously concerned for your health and we can convey to Perov your apologies for not wishing him a good night and a Happy New Year. If only you had not been talking so much to that American.' Tanya felt her heart clench angrily. 'Allardyce. He has sent you roses this morning. Foolish extravagance! No doubt the servants will talk.'

If Paul had sent her roses yesterday, Vera would have been able to tell what they meant to her, but today in the horror of Maud's death and disgrace, Tanya showed no signs of caring.

Her aunt was reassured. 'Well then. Go to sleep again. And take your tonic. What a *blessing* I never had daughters.' She leaned forward over the bed so that Tanya could kiss her powdery cheek. 'Well. Good girl.' She strode off while Aunt Lila bent for her kiss too.

'I am sorry I spoiled it for you, Aunt Lila.'

'I do not think you can help it. And I do not like the taste of champagne.' She straightened up. 'That young man Allardyce is clever. He wrote a note with his flowers, addressed to us. He was afraid that we would not have had a chance to collect a souvenir because of your falling ill and sent a little box of them; it was prettily done. But Tanya, your father will not support you if you marry him, and you can have no idea of the misery it is to be poor. I escaped it because my sister was beautiful enough to make your father love her and allow her to help her family. I thank her in my prayers every day.'

Tanya had no idea that Lila had seen so much or guessed so

well, but the mention of the misery of poverty made her think of Maud, not Paul, and she felt the useless tears gather in her eyes again. 'Poor treasure,' her aunt said again softly then Lila left the room in the purple wake of her sister.

When they had gone Tanya tried to sleep again but could not. Tried to write in her diary but could not. Sasha brought in Paul's roses and she barely looked at them. She was nothing but miserable. An hour after her aunts had left the house to begin making their calls, Sasha let herself in. She began to tidy up a little, straighten out the silver and pearl hairbrushes on the dressing-table, but all the while she was shooting sidelong glances at Tanya until the girl could ignore them no longer. 'What do you want, Sasha?'

'A little farm, two pigs and some chickens. You?'

Tanya gave a half-laugh, picked up a clean handkerchief from the bedside-table and blew her nose. The first of her angry grief had settled into dull misery, and she gave her answers automatically. 'Paint, canvas and a forest.'

'You can sit on the porch of my farm, if you like.'

'As long as I help feed the pigs.'

'That's right.' It was a ritual exchange and it comforted her. Sasha sat beside her and put her arm around Tanya's shoulders. The young woman leaned into her.

'Maud Heighton is dead, Sasha.'

The servant crossed herself. 'Lord have mercy on her! That nice English girl?'

'Yes.' They sat together in silence for a while and Tanya breathed in the scent of her old nurse's blouse. Sasha received a small bottle of eau de cologne from Tanya's father every year at Christmas and wore it, carefully rationed, every day. It made Tanya think of home. Eventually Sasha shifted.

'Lord, you're getting big. Thanks be to God. There's a letter for you.' She pulled it out of her blouse and handed it to her. It was slightly crumpled. Tanya wiped her eyes and opened it, but as soon as she saw it was addressed from Rue de Seine, she guessed it would be another account of Maud's death and she pushed it back into the envelope. 'And there's a person waiting for you in the kitchen.'

Tanya looked up. 'Who? Why didn't you tell me? Did she bring the letter?'

'A Frenchie. And no, she didn't bring the letter. Says her name is Yvette. Has the manners of a street cat. She can hold on while we have a cuddle, can't she? Anyway, I had to wait until Vera and Lila were well out of the way. Lord, they haven't changed. Those two were just the same twenty years ago.'

Tanya scrambled out of the bed and reached for her dressing-gown. 'Yvette from the studio? The model? Didn't you recognise her?'

Sasha crossed her arms and sank her chin into her chest. 'Models? How should I recognise her? I don't like to look.' But Tanya had already run out of the room.

Yvette was sitting in front of the fire with her feet up when Tanya came dashing into the kitchen. The cook was filling Yvette's coffee bowl for her and the model held a half-devoured meat pie in her other hand. As Tanya came in, she swung her legs to the ground and stood up, swallowing her food and wiping the crumbs from her mouth with the back of her hand.

'At last!' She gulped coffee from the bowl and gave a swift approving nod. 'Have you got any money?'

'What are you doing here? Why?'

'I'm here to get money, because I need it.'

'I'm not going to give you money for no reason!'

'It's not for no reason. I told you, I need it.'

'Why do you need it, Yvette?'

'Because I went on a spree over Christmas and I haven't got any at the moment.' Tanya stamped her foot and the cook found she had pressing business in the far corner of the room. 'All right! Don't fly at me! I can't tell you because if I do, you'll keep me here an hour, and I need to leave right now. But I swear, if you knew why, you'd be glad to give it to me.' She crossed her arms over her chest and looked Tanya straight in the eye.

Tanya drew a deep breath. 'How much do you need?'

'Oh sweetheart, I could kiss you. Twenty francs should do it for now. You got it in silver?'

'In my desk.'

'Then go and fetch it, will you? Come on, get a move on!'

Tanya obeyed in a sort of daze and when she returned she found Yvette pacing in front of the fire. The purse was snatched from her hand.

'Yvette, about Maud – have you heard?'

Yvette looked wary. 'Heard what?'

'That she stole a diamond tiara from Madame de Civray, then when the Morels found it she . . . threw herself into the river.' Tanya's voice broke over the last words.

Yvette looked stunned for a second, then thrust the purse into her pocket and swallowed more of the coffee. She was looking at the broad back of the cook.

'That's bad. Look, can you get away today? I'd like to talk to you.'

Tanya looked towards the cook as well. 'I have to stay at home,' she said clearly, while staring at Yvette with her wide, tear-reddened eyes.

'Shame. If you *could* get away you might look in at the bar next to my office and ask for Daniel. He might give you an address nearby.' Tanya nodded. 'Take heart, princess.' And then she was gone.

Two hours later, Tanya found herself standing on the doorstep of a rather shabby house on Impasse Guelma.

'You brought your maid with you?' Yvette was standing in front of her looking angry and dirty with a dusty apron tied over her dress.

When Tanya looked up from under the brim of her wide hat, Yvette noticed that her eyes and nose were still red. 'I can't go wandering around Paris without Sasha.'

'But you sneaked out of the house!'

'Still, Yvette, there are rules.'

Yvette looked as if she was about to give her opinion of the rules then stopped herself and tapped her foot. 'Can she be trusted?'

'Of course she can. Yvette, what is all this about? I don't like going and asking for waiters by name in bars. If anyone had seen me – particularly when I'm supposed to be sick in bed . . . Is this your house?'

Yvette raised her eyebrows. 'No, it is not my house – and if you don't want to be noticed, have you thought of not wandering about in white satin with a maid, a chauffeur and a hat you could serve a roast boar on?'

Tanya touched the brim; it was loaded with wax cherries and feathers dyed green.

'Oh,' she said, and looked so surprised at the idea that Yvette laughed.

'You are priceless sometimes, princess. Still, I'm glad you are here, maid and all. Get your driver to go and wait in Place Pigalle though before anyone notices, then come on in. But mind your skirts. I've been cleaning for hours and the place is still as filthy as all hell.'

Tanya gave Vladimir his instructions, then Yvette ushered her and Sasha into the hallway and pushed open a door to the right of the uneven staircase. It led to a good-sized room, dim with shadows and dust. Broken bits of furniture were stacked against the walls, old packing cases and general detritus. In the corner, under the single window and next to a cane armchair was a single low bedstead. There was a girl lying on it under thin grey blankets. A wolfhound was stretched alongside her, one forepaw over the sleeping girl's shoulder. Tanya took a step forward and the dog looked up.

'It's all right, Tanya. The dog is friendly. Go and see who it is,' Yvette said softly.

Tanya felt a sudden lurch of hope and ran forward.

'Maud! Oh, *Maud*!'

The sick room oil on canvas 64.8 × 76.3 cm

This beautiful and unusual picture was once thought to be the work of Maurice Utrillo. It shows part of the walls and ceiling of a room as seen, we assume, by a sick person lying in bed. A small window is just in view at the top right of frame, though the sky seen through it is uniform cream white, and at the bottom left, note what appears to be a handful of holly stuck into the top of a bottle. Note also, however, the multitude of colours used to make up the grey of the walls. A picture that seems so empty is, on close examination, shimmering with colour interest.

Extract from the catalogue notes to the exhibition 'The Paris Winter: Anonymous Treasures from the de Civray Collection', Southwark Picture Gallery, London, 2010

CHAPTER 3

*T*ANYA COLLAPSED INTO THE CHAIR BY THE BED AND burst into tears. Every few seconds she would wipe her eyes so she could again convince herself that the girl in the bed was her lost friend, then start to cry again. Yvette put a hand on her shoulder and squeezed, then moved away, biting the side of her thumb.

Sasha had followed them into the room. She closed the door and crossed herself on recognising Maud, then started examining the stove in the centre of the room. After a minute or two she opened it and began to work on the fire. Tanya managed to stop crying. Maud's eyes had not opened and her breathing sounded uncomfortable, viscous. Her skin was bluish-white and her hair was plastered to her forehead with sweat. Tanya touched her brow with the back of her hand and felt the heat of a high fever.

'Oh, Yvette! I think she's very ill.'

'Yup.'

Yvette had settled into a beaten-up armchair at the other end of the bed, her legs hooked over one of the arms and swinging. Her mouth was a thin line and Tanya noticed for the first time how tired she looked. Sasha appeared to have finished work on the stove. It did seem to be giving off a more even heat now. She approached the sickbed as Yvette and the wolfhound both watched her suspiciously, and took Maud's hand. The girl was sleeping very deeply, somewhere beyond sleep. Sasha said something to Tanya without looking at her.

'She wants to know if a doctor's seen her, and if so what he said.'

Yvette shifted in the chair, pulling her legs beneath her. 'That's where half your money went. He gave her a draught of something – laudanum, I think. Though, bless her, she didn't like it much. Ended up with half of it down his shirtfront. He said to keep her warm, and try and get her to eat. Keep her quiet and wait it out. She'll live or she won't.'

Tanya blinked rapidly then spoke briefly in Russian. This provoked an angry-sounding stream of words from the maid. Yvette watched, amused in spite of herself as Tanya tried to interrupt, but she never got further than a syllable. Eventually the maid ran out of breath and put her hand out. Tanya meekly extracted some coins from her purse and handed them over. The maid tied her shawl over her grey hair and stalked out of the room.

'You know, I think I like her,' Yvette said at last. Tanya bent over Maud and brushed a strand of hair from her face.

'Sasha doesn't like doctors a great deal, but she knows how to look after the sick. She'll cook up something foul-smelling on the stove and it'll help. I hope. What happened, Yvette? The Countess told me she'd stolen the tiara . . . How did you find her?'

Yvette watched as Tanya carefully removed her hat and set it, after a microscopic hesitation, on the floor beside her chair. 'I have no idea what happened. One of the river rats turned up at the party last night at the Bâteau-Lavoir looking for me. His father pulled Maud out of the river two nights ago and would have sent for the gendarmes straight away but she bribed them not to. Asked them to let her stay until she recovered.'

'But why did she send for you?'

'Because she didn't recover, you ninny. She gave them the rest of her money to come and fetch me. At least, I suppose she did. I couldn't find another penny on her. Anyway, the kid found me. I guess his people don't like the cops much after all, so that might be another reason they bothered coming to me. So I went and found her.'

'Was she awake?'

Yvette swung forward in her chair and put her head in her hands. 'Not really. She recognised me and said some things, but the only bit I could understand was I must not take her back to Rue de Seine so I thought of this place. I spent all my coin on the cab to get us here. Miserable bastard, that cabbie was. Oh, I hate them, snooty self-satisfied lot.' She stared angrily at the floor. 'If I'd spent a bit less at New Year I could have got a doctor sooner.'

Tanya pulled up the blankets over Maud's shoulder; the dog stirred and then settled again. 'Sasha will help. God would not give her back to us then snatch her away again.' Yvette looked unconvinced. She stood up and began to pace. 'Do you think she did it? Stole that tiara, then threw herself in the river?' Tanya asked. 'The Countess said it was very valuable.'

'I don't know. I'd have laughed in your face if you suggested such a thing last week. I've been thinking about it every second since you told me. She's frightened of something. So maybe she did take it, but . . .'

'But what, Yvette?'

She put her arms out. 'I don't think she's *stupid*, Tanya! If she wanted to steal from the Countess, there must have been a dozen little things lying around. Why take a bloody great tiara? Something impossible to sell, that would be missed? It's the sort of thing a child would take if it wanted to dress up.'

Tanya nodded slowly. Her right hand went up to her earlobe, twisting the pearl she wore there. 'But the temptation . . . being poor is difficult.'

Yvette shifted her weight to one hip and lifted her eyebrows. 'Is it? It's hard, is it?'

'I mean for a girl like Maud . . . Oh, don't look like that at me, Yvette. The Countess said she was a dope fiend.'

'Rubbish. She's been reading too many detective novels.'

'No, she said Morel told her so! He said that Maud was addicted to opium and had been stealing his sister's jewellery and selling it.'

Yvette paused, then shook her head. 'Then I don't believe a word of it. This stinks, Tanya.' She turned on the Russian girl, suddenly triumphant. 'She had money enough on her to bribe the bargemen. The kid said she had coins sewn into her skirt hem. That's not what a dope fiend does. As soon as they have a franc, they spend it on what they need. They don't spend hours at classes, or sketching when there's some spare cash. Anyway, I'd have known if she smoked in any of the Paris dens.' Her voice was bitter and tired.

'How?'

There was a long pause while Yvette pulled at a loose thread on her cuff. 'Because I would have seen her there. There aren't many places to smoke in Paris, but I know them all.'

'Oh, Yvette!' Tanya said.

'Don't "oh Yvette" me. I'm not a fiend. Just sometimes . . . When you have a pipe in your hand you don't have to worry about anything else, about growing old or having no money or a way out. You are just happy. And I don't do it often. And Maud would never . . . I mean, look at her. She's English!'

'You're right,' Tanya said after a pause. 'It does stink.' Then her voice rose a little. 'I just don't understand what's happened.'

'Oh, give me strength! Will you stop saying that, princess? Who does?'

There was a long silence. Tanya blushed and Yvette felt awkward and cruel.

'Where are we?' Tanya said quietly at last. The stove was crackling away now and, looking around, Tanya could see the work Yvette had been trying to do. The floor had been swept, though it was only bare boards and there were still piles of dust in the corners of the room. There were other stools and chairs against the walls. A table, its broken leg tied together with string, stood between the bed and the wall. There was a clean glass and water jug on it and behind them a vase improvised out of an empty wine bottle with sprigs of holly in it.

Yvette pushed the hair off her face. 'A friend's place. Suzanne Valadon has rented it as a bolt-hole now she's left her fancy banker boyfriend for her new lover. I knew she'd never last long as a bourgeoise. She has the studio upstairs, but she'd no use for this room and wanted to sub-let it. That's where the rest of your money has gone. Rent.'

'We are safe here?'

Yvette nodded. Then: 'There's no way to know what happened to her until she wakes up. *If* she wakes up, the poor chicken.'

'You like her, don't you?' Tanya said after a pause.

'I do.' Yvette sat back down again and sighed. 'Most women in Paris seem only to think about being looked at. It makes me sick sometimes. *She* watches.' Yvette stared up at the cracked grey plaster of the ceiling. 'You think she's just all bound up in herself, then she'll say something and you realise she's been listening.'

'It's your job to be looked at, Yvette.'

She yawned. 'It pays. As you so cleverly observed, being poor is difficult. Though when my looks have gone I'll end up scrubbing those rooms I've modelled in for forty centimes an hour. If I'm lucky.' She shrugged and bit her knuckle.

'I told Maud I always sew money into my clothes in case of emergency.'

'She listens, she learns.' Both women were silent for a while, listening to Maud's painful, dragging breaths.

'Oh, Lord,' Tanya said, and began rummaging in her purse.

'What?'

'Blast, I know I have it. Sylvie Morel wrote to me. It arrived this morning. I couldn't bear it, so I just . . .'

Yvette was on her feet at once and almost grabbed the bag out of her hand. 'How the hell could you have forgotten until now!'

Tanya looked up. 'I thought Maud was dead. I brought it to show you, didn't I? Oh, get your hands off, you're not helping.'

Yvette lifted her palms and backed away. At last Tanya pulled out a blue and slightly crumpled envelope. 'Oh, look. She uses the same stationer's as I do.'

'Tanya!'

'All right. You may as well come and read over my shoulder.' Yvette scurried round behind her and leaned on the back of her chair.

'Move your head, will you, and hold it steady.'

Tanya straightened the pages with a vicious snap. 'Better?'

'Much.' For a few minutes they were silent. Tanya turned the page and read on. Four sheets in all. They reached the end and Yvette whistled. Tanya's neck had turned an angry red. 'It is just the same story the Countess told me. But I don't believe it. They are lying.'

'What's their game?' Yvette said. 'Why make her out to be a thief?'

'I don't know. They gave back the tiara, so what could they possibly . . .' Tanya read part of the letter out loud. ' "*My brother and I visited the Countess the same afternoon she returned to Paris, yesterday*" – New Year's Eve, in other words, "*and returned the tiara. She most generously agreed never to repeat the story of the theft publicly in order to safeguard Miss Heighton's reputation. We feel though that you, as a friend of poor, lost Maud, deserve the fullest explanation.*" Well, that's nice of her. Oh, Yvette, what are we going to do? Can't we go to the police?'

Yvette hunched her shoulders. 'And say what? *Someone* took the tiara and the Morels gave it back. Maud's poor. She'd be in prison before she even wakes up. Let's stay out of the way for now until she can tell us what happened. You just look sad and say nothing.'

'What about our host?'

'Valadon? She won't say anything. Too bound up with her lover boy and enjoying her freedom. She's been giving dinner-parties in the suburbs for the last year, so she needs it. Says she can't stop painting.'

Tanya nodded. The door was pushed open and Sasha reappeared with a basket over her arm, uttering a stream of complaints in Russian about the shopkeepers of Paris. Then she began to unpack her cures.

CHAPTER 4

2 January 1910

THE FIRST TIME MAUD WOKE AND WAS SURE IT WAS not a dream, she found herself staring into the eyes of a woman; a square-faced stranger with chestnut curls of fringe hanging over her fierce black eyes. She blew a lungful of smoke out of her nose like a dragon.

'The mermaid wakes!' Her voice was dark and low. 'Got all your senses this morning?' The face did not wait for an answer but retreated, leaving Maud looking up at a low ceiling supported by heavy blackened beams. She could not see properly. Her lips were dry and her throat ached; her head was thick with pain that struck her skull from within with every beat of her pulse. She tried to think. The tiara, the river. Then she had been on a boat with a smoking stove in the corner; there had been scolding and questioning, another ugly and suspicious-looking woman with a baby tied onto her back watching them, then she had been taken somewhere else in noise and darkness. Lights seemed to blister and break in her eyes.

Maud tried to lift herself onto her elbows. The iron springs of the bed groaned and fought against her. She saw a room, the woman standing against the wall with a cigarette. She seemed very far away now. There was a bunch of holly in a bottle near to her. Something warm moved next to her and she started, only to see some huge tawny dog was sharing the bed with her. He stirred as Maud moved and wagged his feathery tail a couple of times before settling against her again. She reached out to touch his warm flanks.

The woman was dressed like a respectable bourgeoise. She wore an apron over her blouse and skirt, and her over-sleeves showed traces of paint. There was a twist to her mouth.

'I think Hugo was a monk in his past life,' she said, indicating the dog. Her voice sounded to Maud as if it were coming from the bottom of a well. 'One of those who used to patch up the knights when they were off crusading. He finds whoever is sick in the house and stays with them while they are in danger.' Maud lay back down again, her belly cramped with nausea. 'There's water there. Can you hold your glass?' Maud turned and saw it and reached over the dog's head to take the glass and drink. It took all her strength. The light fell in through a single smeared window. It was a grey, comfortless sort of room but it was not Rue de Seine and it was not a prison cell and it did not move under her.

'Who are you?' she said. The effort of speaking set off a fresh cascade of pain.

The woman came closer and Maud saw that her long fingers were stained with nicotine.

'I am Suzanne Valadon, Artist. And you are Maud Heighton and either a dull little student of the Académie, a victim of terrible injustice, or a rather pathetic thief. Which is it?'

'I didn't steal anything,' Maud managed to say.

Valadon dropped her cigarette and ground it out on the floor. 'Your friends don't seem to think you're a thief.' She folded her arms in front of her and studied Maud's face. 'The Russian princess, the French model and the English miss. Sounds like the start of a bad joke or a good brothel.' Maud said nothing and Valadon laughed. 'They think your friends in Rue de Seine set you up. Yvette tells me they've been saying you're an opium fiend. Perhaps I am harbouring a dangerous criminal.'

Maud reached for the water glass again and finished what was in it. Criminal. Opium. Thief. 'It doesn't seem to worry you.'

Valadon gave a one-shouldered shrug. 'Why should it? I have nothing to steal.' She walked round the bed and took the glass from her hand before Maud dropped it, then filled it up again from the jug. She was older than Maud had thought at first. There were lines around her eyes.

'Where am I?'

'My house. You're my first lodger. We're in Impasse de Guelma on the Butte.' She gave Maud the glass and this time she drank greedily but the burning pain in her head and throat continued.

'Montmartre?'

'With the drunks, *apaches* and the only artists worth a damn. Thrilling, isn't it?'

Maud felt sick. Her stomach ached and her mouth tasted of riverwater; pain pressed into the side of her head. She handed the glass back to Valadon. 'I didn't steal anything,' she said again.

Valadon replaced the glass on the side-table. 'No. I think if you stole something, you'd hang onto it, wouldn't you? Till they broke your fingers to get it away.' She put her head on one side, watching her. 'I think that they made a mistake, your friends in Rue de Seine.'

Maud lay back on her pillow and turned her face towards the wall. 'You seem to know a lot about it.'

That low gravelly laugh again. 'Oh, I do. It's my job now to watch you while your nursemaids are out pretending to mourn you. It is the second of January, by the way. You missed New Year. Welcome to 1910.' She sat down on the cane chair. 'Did you throw yourself in the river?'

'No. I was thrown in.'

'How calmly you say it. Interesting girl. They didn't know who they were trying to kill, did they? I've seen you sleeping with your jaw clenched so tight the muscles on your neck stand out and your fists pulling the sheets apart. There's a little fighter in there under the English manners. A little demon. Your friends in the Rue de Seine would never have risked throwing you in the water if they'd seen you sleep.'

Maud stared at the plaster on the wall by her head. It was unpainted, but in the pale grey were a hundred points of colour. Mud browns, ochre, yellow, moments of titanium white . . . they shifted and blurred and she closed her eyes.

'What is it like to drown?' Valadon asked.

'I don't remember.'

'Liar.' She stood again and went to the stove. 'The Russian's maid left this soup. I'm to spoon it down your throat whenever you are awake or Yvette will scream at me. Sit up a bit, will you?'

In the early evening Tanya arrived and exclaimed to see Maud open her eyes. Maud managed to squeeze her hand and the Russian burst into tears. She found herself being fed again, this time by the Russian maid. For the next three days her periods of consciousness were still short and painful. She was aware of Yvette from time to time curled at the bottom of the bed, reading. The dog continued to share her bed, leaving only occasionally, and when she woke she was grateful for its animal warmth. Valadon flitted in and out, taking her turn at feeding her when the others were away, and other footsteps hammered up and down the stairs outside her door. There always seemed to be people laughing or arguing in Valadon's studio from late afternoon until dawn. The daylight hours passed in moments, a series of shaking snapshots. The nights were long and suffocating. Then at last the hours began to mean something. The dog returned to Valadon, and Maud realised that this, as much as anything else, meant she would live.

That afternoon, when Yvette and Tanya arrived, she began to ask questions and Yvette told her the story of her rescue, the doctor. Tanya told her about her meeting with the Countess on New Year's Eve.

'Do they not miss me at Lafond's?'

Tanya hesitated and for the first time the name Morel was spoken in the room. He had been to see Lafond with the same story. At first her teacher was sceptical, but he had visited the pawnbroker's office and the shop in Petits Champs, and the Countess herself. After that, he was just amazed. Tanya had suggested they say Maud had been called home over Christmas and Lafond had agreed.

For the first time, Maud told them what she could remember of that last evening in Rue de Seine; the accusation, the strange heaviness in her limbs and her collapse.

'Laudanum, probably,' Yvette said quietly and continued to bite her nails. About those last moments by the river Maud could say nothing, and her friends, watching her carefully, did not press her.

At first Tanya would not read her the letter from Sylvie that described Maud's crime and suicide, but Maud insisted, and Tanya, seeing the fierceness in her eyes, felt afraid and relented. Valadon had drifted in, escaping the chaos of her studio to listen. Her son

Maurice and some of his friends had been drinking since the previous evening and she had grown bored with them and come to look at the women instead. She lounged against the doorframe smoking, her wolfhound at her feet while Tanya read the letter with her rolling Russian accent. Sylvie wrote that a number of small items of jewellery had gone missing in the weeks since Maud had arrived. Her brother had successfully traced them to a pawn shop near Rue Croix des Petits Champs, and the man remembered Maud. She mentioned the sweet, sick smell of opium that they had tasted in the air coming from Maud's room. They said they had tried to speak to her, but she had denied everything. Only when they found the tiara had she become wild, and fled the house in spite of their efforts to restrain her. Christian had gone out in pursuit, only to see her throw herself from the quayside. He had raised the alarm, but the river had already swallowed her. Sylvie concluded by saying that the tiara had been returned and the Countess was deeply sorry that poor Maud had been tempted.

Tanya put her hand on Maud's shoulder. Her body was stiff, rigid.

'Maud? Sweet-one? *Did* you go to the pawn shop?'

She closed her eyes. 'Yes. Sylvie was the opium addict. Morel told me the first day. I went for her, to the pawn shop, to get money to buy the drug.'

'Of course she went there,' said Yvette. She was sitting on the floor with her back to the bed and her knees drawn up. 'They wouldn't write it if they couldn't prove it. "Oh Maudie dear, could you just pop in with this" and little Maud does it because she's so grateful to the nice rich people for feeding her.'

'Sylvie needed it,' Maud said. 'She'd thrown away her supply and was suffering for it. I was trying to help.' She felt her heart clench tight like an angry fist. 'How was I to know?'

'Needed it, did she? Was she throwing up? Doubled over in pain? Cramps in all her bones? Covered in snot and shaking so hard you could hear her teeth rattle?'

'No,' Maud sighed. 'It was not like that.'

The French girl shrugged. 'Then she was faking a nice polite version of needing it for you, Maud, to set you up. If you'd seen what needing it really looks like, you would have run away.'

Tanya gave a little gasp. 'Yvette, you've . . .'

'No, I've never been that way. But I've seen it and it's enough to stop me from visiting those places most days.' She scratched the back of her neck. 'People die.'

'But *why* did they do all that?' Tanya said, still holding the letter in her hand. 'What was the reason? They gave the tiara back. Why go to all this trouble and expense to make Maud look guilty of a crime then give it back?'

Valadon straightened and the dog immediately scrabbled up and yawned. 'Stop asking questions and send that girl home,' she said. 'They wanted her dead. She's alive. She was strong enough to live through the fever and the police aren't looking for her. That means she's winning, as far as I see it. And whatever scheme the Morels had – who cares?'

'But . . . ?' Tanya protested.

'Who cares?' Valadon said again. 'We live, we die. You've got deep pockets, Tanya. Pawn a bracelet yourself and put her on a train tonight. She's got family. Send her back to them and let the rest lie where it lies.'

'They told the Countess I was a thief,' Maud said thickly.

'What? The nice Yankee Countess? Yeah, I know her and I can just imagine.' Valadon bunched her fists and rubbed her eyes. ' "Oh no, that nice English girl was a thief! I am so sad! Now what shall I wear tonight?" And the Académie? The girls are wasting good colour and fat old Lafond is grateful the scandal's not going in the papers to scare away his shit-eating sycophants.' Tanya blushed.

Valadon swept her eyes over them. 'Go home, Maud. You'll never be artists, either of you. Princess, you want everything to be pretty and Maud, you want everyone to think well of you so neither of you will ever tell any truth worth a damn.'

'Leave me alone, Suzanne,' said Maud. 'Madame de Civray was kind to me.'

'Oh, you moth,' Valadon answered, her voice cool. 'Now I shall leave you babies and go back to my work.' She looked at Tanya. 'God, women are stupid sometimes.'

CHAPTER 5

10 January 1910

*I*F IT HAD BEEN A FINE DAY TANYA WOULD HAVE HAD some warning, but the rain had been falling steadily, thin and unbroken all morning, so Passage des Panoramas was unusually full when she left Lafond's at midday. There was a slightly low feeling in the air. The shop windows were offering discounts on Christmas goods and everything seemed a little shabbier, more grey than was usual in Paris, but still the Parisians came out in flocks to shop and crowd into the covered passageways to hunt for pretty bargains out of the rain. At times like these, when the gold and black shop-fronts and the polished mosaic floors were hidden by crowds of silk-lined coats, and the thick low bodies of the men seemed to press near to her, Tanya felt smothered.

Now she was free of the distractions of her work, the image of Perov in evening dress making his proposal returned to her. Thinking of it was like pressing on a bruise. He had come to dinner with her and her aunts as a close family friend, as if the thing were settled already. He had enjoyed his port and cigar, then as soon as he came into the drawing room to join her and her aunts at the tea-table, Vera and Lila had remembered urgent errands in other parts of the house and left them alone. Perov took a seat next to her, made himself comfortable and began to speak as if their marriage were already agreed. He spoke of where in Paris they might live and the size of house he thought suitable; it was some minutes before Tanya could interrupt him.

The memory was strongly tainted by the smell of cigar smoke, the stale sweetness of wine on his breath. Eventually she managed to break in and ask for more time before committing herself to be his wife. He was offended, pursing his lips and blinking rapidly. Only when she forced herself to smile shyly and ask submissively for his patience and understanding did he seem mollified. At no time did he express any sort of feeling for her. He was telling her the result of his negotiations with her family, not asking for her love. Tanya thought of her father and her aunts, the comforts and security of her life. The idea of being without them made her afraid. She had never met a problem before that could not be solved with money. How could she make problems go away without it?

Paul Allardyce she had seen only once since New Year, once again while walking in the Bois and with her aunts on either side of her. She could only thank him for the roses and look at him with a sort of desperate appeal, but he looked at her as if she was something he had already lost. At this thought, she turned her eyes upwards to the glass and ironwork roof of the passage, the light grey and the glass rain-spattered, trying to convince herself there was air here, there was space, but she felt caught in some low deep current.

Some of the men tried to get out of her way, others did not seem to notice her in their hurry to peer in at the shop windows, and her world was crowded with high shoulders in dark cloth. She was starting to pant. It had been useful to her many times in her dealings with her father, her ability to make herself faint when the drama of the moment required it, but it meant she was now liable to faint when she really didn't want to at all. She was just about to break free into the rainswept freedom of Boulevard Montmartre when she felt a touch on her arm and turned to find herself face-to-face with Christian Morel. She stared at him, horrified. His smile became uncertain.

'Dear Miss Koltsova, I am so sorry if I frightened you. I have been waiting here hoping for a moment of your time.'

Her concerns for herself disappeared like smoke in the wind and at once her nervousness in the crowd became simple rage. She wanted to strike him. She wanted to beat him to the ground and shout *murderer*. She had a vision of this pressing crowd closing over him, kicking his worthless body on the slippery stone floor till he was rags and nothingness. He gestured to the little table thrust into the crowd where he had been sitting. There was the half-drunk coffee of the murderer, the folded copy of *Le Matin* the thief had been reading. She wished for a knife, for a gun, for the strength to pick up the table and smash his head in with it while the crowd cheered. 'Might I ask you to join me? Just for one moment?'

She managed to nod and he pulled out the other chair for her. His fingers brushed the back of her coat as he pushed it back in for her and it was all she could do not to turn round and spit in his face. The waiter hovered: no, Miss Koltsova required no refreshment but M. Morel would take another *petit noir*. He watched her while he waited for it to arrive. Tanya looked at the shoes of the men and women passing by. She could not kill him. She must be clever. He thought Maud dead, and he must not suspect otherwise. So Tanya should show not rage, but what? She thought hard of what she should be feeling as the low-laced boots of some idle Parisienne pivoted into the shop opposite. Grief and shame for her friend? With a sickening turn she realised she should be apologising to him, for helping to introduce a drug addict and thief into his home. She was already trembling – well, that would do for grief and shame. So much the better. His coffee arrived and he crossed his legs and sat back while he drank it. She glanced at him. So handsome and so respectable. She pulled a handkerchief from her pocket and touched it to her eyes, preparing her performance.

'I cannot believe this has happened, Monsieur Morel. Poor Maud. I should have answered your sister's letter.' He could take it how he pleased; she could not manage more at first. He set down his coffee cup and nodded. He must be here to see if I believe them, she thought. Why? Because I am the one person who might ask questions, who might have known Maud well enough to see he is a murderous lying thief. *Oh, why haven't you gone away? Why aren't you in hell?* She lowered her face, then lifted it again and looked straight into his deep brown eyes. 'I had no idea her case was so desperate. The mention of opium in your sister's letter was a terrible shock. I am so sorry. I did not know her as well as I thought.' She blinked rapidly.

It was a tiny change in him, a slight relaxation in his shoulders, in the muscles of his face. The smallest disturbance on the surface of a pool fading and leaving it darkly smooth again.

'I hope you do not blame yourself,' he said. Tanya concentrated on her own hands. 'Remember, we lived with Miss Heighton for some weeks and were thoroughly deceived.'

'You are generous,' she breathed, her mouth ashy.

His voice was comfortable now. 'I have sought you out for two reasons. The first is, I know Miss Heighton had relatives in England. She mentioned a brother? I can find no trace of their address in her belongings and Lafond does not have it; his correspondence to her was always addressed to the post office. Hiding her ambitions from the respectable lawyer brother, I suppose. I hoped you might know it. We must write to them, but perhaps it would be kinder to say she met with some accident, rather than reveal the full ugly story.'

'Her family have a right to know the truth,' Tanya replied quickly, then groaned inwardly – too fierce. 'Don't you think, sir?'

'Even in such circumstances as these?' He shook his head slowly, his smile indulgent. 'No, Miss Koltsova, you have the proper convictions of your youth. But I think that at times it is kinder to lie. Why poison whatever memories they have of her?' He sighed and was serious, stroking his black eyebrow with the tip of his index finger. 'Paris, Paris. So beautiful, so full of traps. Even the most virtuous can find themselves . . . lost. Do you have the address?'

'I do not.' She tried to concentrate on the newspaper between them. The wife of a former Governor of the Bank of France had been found dead. MYSTERY OF A TRAGIC DEATH the headline read, then just below it: *Was she assassinated?* Tanya looked away quickly.

'How unfortunate. I have left my address at the Académie, but I think my sister and I will be leaving Paris at the end of January for America. If no one comes in search of her before then . . .'

The thought of Morel pawing his way through Maud's possessions was repulsive. The headline kept pulling her back. *Yes,* she wanted to scream, *yes, she was assassinated!* She moistened her lower lip.

'I have no plans to leave Paris until the summer,' she said slowly. 'If her brother comes, I would be willing to see him, and pass onto him anything you care to leave with me.'

She could feel the gentle smile in his voice as he replied, 'You are too kind.'

'It is the least I could do in the circumstances.' *I want to tear you apart with my teeth. I shall buy a dog the size of a wolf, like Valadon's, only with a warrior soul, and he will hunt you over the city, run after you until you are sweaty and desperate and screaming.*

'There are her painting materials, of course. And her sketchbooks. Her clothes we thought it best to give to the poor.'

'Perhaps you will have the rest sent to me.'

He smiled. 'As it happens . . .' he gestured to the floor under the marble table, and for the first time Tanya noticed a small suitcase sitting there. 'I had hoped you might have the address and I could write my letter here and now. It has been difficult for my sister this last week or so, knowing these things were still there in her room.'

A huge dog, with great powerful jaws to rip your lying throat from your body.

'Naturally that would be uncomfortable for your sister, Monsieur Morel. I shall take them with me at once.' Tanya stood and he did the same before picking up the case and handing it to her. She hesitated. 'Madame de Civray? What did you say to persuade her to keep this affair quiet?'

Morel gave a half-smile. 'Oh, the dear Countess – she is as sentimental as every other American I have met. They are like children.' He stroked his eyebrow again. 'She was distressed indeed to hear of Miss Heighton's fate. I am convinced the tiara means very little to her. She hardly looked at it, and the suggestion that the theft be suppressed was all her own.'

'She is a good woman,' Tanya said fiercely, then afraid she had been too emphatic, managed to smile. 'I shall take proper care of these things, Monsieur Morel. Thank you for letting me take them.'

He bowed and she walked out into the street and out of his sight before stopping on the pavement and lifting her face so the light rain could freshen her skin. Sasha lifted the umbrella over her head and waved to Vladimir.

'Was that the man, pudding? Oh, I knew it! Oh, he looks like my cousin's eldest – and a devil that boy is. Half the bastards in the village are his.'

'What shall I say to Maud, Sasha? He wanted to write to her family, but he hasn't the address.'

'Tell her that then. And be grateful you haven't worse news to share. Now are we going to that old tart's place or not? I've more soup for Miss Maud.'

Maud heard Tanya's voice in the hallway, shouting up a greeting to whoever happened to be in the studio above. One of Valadon's regular visitors was a crazed Italian. He came almost every day and Maud could often hear him, slightly muffled by the floorboards, declaiming Dante as he sat at Valadon's feet while Maud lay drifting in and out of an uneasy sleep below them. The door was pushed open, and there was Tanya as bright as morning with her peasant maid trotting behind her and a fat bundle in her arms.

'Dear! How are you this afternoon?'

The maid began clucking round the stove at once as Tanya trotted up to the bed.

'Better.'

Tanya felt her forehead with the back of her hand and tutted. 'But still not well. Not to worry, Sasha has driven half the French staff out of the house roasting bones and making all sorts of jellies. They taste horrid, but they've cured me every time I've been ill.'

Maud managed to smile, but Tanya became serious. 'Now, my love, I am not sure how to say this to you, so I am just going to talk very fast.' She did, watching Maud's face. Maud made no sound, so Tanya watched the colour in her cheeks, the white of her throat.

Eventually she ran out of words and set the suitcase down on the floor. She could hear Maud's breathing.

'Perhaps I should have kept quiet. Should I put this out of sight?' Maud nodded and Tanya crouched by the bed to slide the case underneath. There was nowhere else to hide it, after all. She remained crouching and put her hand on Maud's arm, trying to read her expression.

'I can't bear that they should go on in the world, Tanya. I know what Valadon said, but I bet if they had done this to her . . . Why? Why should I run away?'

Tanya nodded. 'The whole time I was talking to him I was longing to shoot him through his black heart – if I could find it.' She moved till she was sitting on the floor by the bed, her chin on her arm next to Maud's face. 'Perhaps if you shot him and we explained what happened, they would forgive you.'

'I would like that.' The two women were silent for a while. Sasha turned from the stove and sighed when she saw Tanya curled up on the floor. She decanted her soup and shuffled over with it. Tanya smiled when she saw the bowl. It was one of a grand dining set Vera Sergeyevna had brought from St Petersburg, stuffed in straw and only produced on the most splendid of occasions. Sasha had obviously taken a liking to Maud. Tanya wrinkled her nose when she smelled the soup, but Maud showed no sign of distaste and took the bowl carefully. Thinking about shooting Morel had calmed her a little.

'How do you say thank you in Russian, Tanya?'

'*Spaceeba.*'

'*Spaceeba*, Sasha.' The old maid blushed and she patted Maud on the shoulder before returning to a stool by the stove and rummaging around in her workbag for something to mend.

Maud was just finishing her meal when Yvette came charging

in, her hair and coat damp with rain. She kissed Sasha before dropping the coat over a chair and throwing herself down on the bed. 'Urff, what a day. Rain and rain. And nowhere warm in this whole damn city. Let me share your blanket, Maud, there's a dear. I've spent the morning freezing my tits off for Adler, then when he's done for the day it's all, "Sorry – I'm a bit short at the mo! Come back for the rest on Tuesday when I've sold my canvases!" Arsehole. No one's going to buy his stuff for more than firewood. The canvas was worth more before he started daubing all over it.'

Tanya tutted. 'Why do you have to be so crude, Yvette?'

The French girl shifted round to look at her. 'Why do *you* have to be so prissy? You know I've got tits. Painted them often enough, yourself.'

'It's not ladylike!'

'*Ladylike?* Oh, save it for the ballroom, princess! I thought all you ladies loved my dirty comments. It's as close as you virgins can get to roughing it in Paris, isn't it?'

'I wish you'd stop calling me a princess. I'm not! And even if I were, it's not my fault.'

Maud put the soup bowl carefully aside and lay back down. 'Oh stop it, both of you. Yvette, Tanya saw Morel today.'

Yvette's eyes widened and she gathered the blanket round her and burrowed across the bed so she was closer to Tanya. 'No! Tell at once! That bastard. How did you keep from throttling him?'

Tanya launched into her story at once while Yvette cooed and whistled. 'Thank God he didn't have your address, Maud. You think he was checking whether you believed them, Tanya?'

'I think so.'

Yvette reached forward to stroke Tanya's cheek with her knuckles. 'Clever girl. Oh, by the way, has Perov proposed?'

Tanya picked up the pearls that hung around her neck and

began running them through her fingers like a rosary. 'Yes. On Saturday.' Morel had driven the thoughts of Perov out of her mind. Now they came back, she could almost smell cigar smoke again.

'And?' Yvette said, her eyes wide.

'I asked him to let me finish the spring classes at Lafond's before I gave him an answer.' The pearls were twisted so tightly around her fingers their tips turned pale and bloodless. In the quiet they could hear the rain beating in sudden squalls against the high window. 'My father has written to me. He talks at great length about the advantages of the match.'

'And Paul Allardyce?' Maud said, shifting on her bed so she could see Tanya's face.

'He doesn't ask me to choose. He just stands by and watches. I wish he'd just take me away. I'd go with him if he did, and I think he knows that – but he does nothing.'

Yvette got more comfortable in the bed, making the springs groan. 'How can he? Oh Tanya, we all know you love the poor man and don't like the rich one much. How is waiting until Lafond's spring classes are done supposed to change that?'

Tanya scowled. 'I don't know. But something might happen.'

'The horse might learn to talk . . .'

She looked round at Yvette. 'What does that mean? Paul said it, and I don't know what it means.'

Above them there was a muffled exchange of shouts and the sound of something being thrown across the room. They all looked upwards and waited for the drumroll of footsteps down the stairs and the front door to slam. Another of Valadon's family dramas.

Yvette put her arms over her head, stretching out her shoulders. 'It's a story. A man is about to be executed but he says to the King, "Don't kill me. If you delay chopping my head off for a year, I'll teach your horse to talk." The King says, "Fine, go ahead," and the man's friend says, "What are you doing? What's the point in that?" The man says, "A lot can happen in a year. I might die, the King might die. And who knows – the horse might learn to talk."'

Tanya frowned over this for some moments then said quietly, 'Am I the horse?'

Yvette laughed under her breath, then clambered off the bed and kissed Maud's cheek. 'Come on, Tanya, let's leave Milady here to rest.' Tanya got to her feet, still looking thoughtful, and they left their friend to the sound of the rain and what good sleep could do.

CHAPTER 6

*M*AUD WAS WOKEN BY A PEAL OF LAUGHTER FROM above. It was deep dark outside, and she lay still for a moment, wondering if she could get back to sleep again. Upstairs, someone had begun playing the flute. It was a strange, open song. Almost too subtle, too gentle, flowing on as if the rules of music meant nothing to it. The voices grew quiet. Maud swung her legs out of bed and lit her candle; match after match failed until she managed it. She remembered Sylvie's shaking hands over the opium lamp, the feel of her skin as she took the matches from her. She tried to stand, bent over and still half-leaning on the bed. Her muscles were weak and complaining, as if they had forgotten the way to keep her upright. She waited, then stood straight in the shadows. It was a small victory but it felt like her first in a long time. The wooden floor was cool, almost soft under her bare feet.

She knelt down carefully, leaning on the bed again as she did so, then reached beneath it till she touched the varnished wicker of the suitcase. She pulled it slowly towards her, unbuckled the leather strap and opened it. Her materials were all in their usual places; her sketchbooks just as she had left them. She looked at her hands, spread out the fingers then relaxed them again. It was almost two weeks since she had drawn anything, and her fingers felt stiff and old. It was the longest time she had gone without drawing since she was an infant.

She undid the ribbon that held her palette to the inside of the upper lid; it tilted into her waiting hand and she saw tucked beneath it her oil sketches, one of Tanya and some from the atelier, and the painting of Sylvie, all where she had left them, pressed flat against the lining of the case. She laid them down to one side without looking at them, then pulled at the slippery upper lining of the case with her fingernail until it came loose. There was her collection of fifty-franc notes, her savings from her time with the Morels. She stared at the notes in her hands as she had done on that first night, but rather than feeling rich, looking at them now she felt a tearing darkness in the middle of her chest. This was what she had cost.

She put the money back in its hiding-place and was about to replace the oil sketches, but the portrait of Sylvie stared up at her and she could not put it away with the rest. All the while the flute continued to play, meandering, exploring the air. She placed the painting on the floor while she tucked away the others, then twisted round, her legs folded under her, to look at it properly. The candlelight gave it movement, as if the smoke of the pipe was still moving in the air. She reached forward and touched the line of Sylvie's shoulder, feeling under her fingertips the texture of the paint. How had these things come back to her, found her among the dead?

She closed her eyes and she could see Morel in her room, in black and white like a film, his movements jerky, bundling her few clothes up to send to the poor, burning the cards she'd left by her bed in the fireplace, leafing through the sketchbooks and wondering if they could be turned to his advantage, an opportunity to check that the story had taken.

Maud opened her eyes and let her fingers brush Sylvie's hair, half-pinned up. The interview with Sylvie and Morel on that last evening came back to her in all its details, the injustice of it, the cruelty. She tried to believe she had seen in Sylvie some softening or regret, but she could only think of her casual ease as she stepped over Maud's body after she collapsed. For a moment Maud felt too sick to live. She was nothing, she had meant nothing, and she had not belonged in those comfortable rooms. She belonged nowhere. She bowed her head and listened to the slow flow of the flute then she clenched her fists. A sigh went shuddering through her, then she stood, staggered a little, set her jaw and found her balance. The wall of her cell was covered in drawing pins. Holding her painting by one corner she shuffled across the floor then pinned up the portrait where she could see it from the bed. As she turned away, the strange song of the flute ceased and there was a burst of applause, cheers and whistles. A man was calling for more wine, someone began to scrape at a violin.

Maud stumbled back into her bed and pulled the blankets round her. Her eyes closed, and with terrible familiarity she found herself returning to the scene of her drowning. The waters and darkness surrounded her as soon as she slipped into sleep. The shock of the cold never lessened. Her confusion was as complete as it had been in that first moment. Horrified, betrayed, stupid and trapped in her useless body. '*It will be over soon,*' the dark water said to her. '*Breathe me in and you will never be lost again. Let go, and be with me.*' For a moment in her distress she did let go: warmth, peace soaked through her and pulled her down. Then her self called out to her. Images and sounds. She saw her mother dead, her father drunk. She held her little brother Albert in her arms and whispered him promises, she threw dirt into her father's grave and watched her step-mother ride out of town, blowing kisses and waving like a spring bride. She tried to move in the water, close her mouth to it. The lonely warehouse full of rotting cast-offs. She cheered the flames chewing up the walls, roaring and ripping apart the humiliation of the place with their red and yellow teeth. *Not like this*. She would not die like this.

She pushed against the black waters, broke the surface and sucked in air and water – one breath, two – before the drug and the cold pulled too hard on her and took her down. Once more she fought, once more for the hours spent sketching in the Louvre, for every moment she had been hungry, for the loneliness and the fear; once more for the betrayal, the cruelty, the easy violence. Rage lifted her, the phoenix on the opium box. Another breath, and she was spent and fell again. If she heard the shout from the boatman, the flurry of activity from her rescuers, she did not know it. She drowned; she slept.

When she woke, Valadon was standing by the painting of Sylvie. Maud shifted in her bed and Suzanne looked over her shoulder.

'This yours?' Maud nodded and stretched her fingers. They were sore and stiff every time she woke. 'You're not as shit as I thought you would be.' Valadon whistled and her wolfhound trotted in from the corridor. She crouched to greet him, taking fistfuls of his fur in her hands and shaking him while she shoved her face into his neck. The dog panted and wagged its tail. She looked back at Maud. 'I'm going out. There's coffee there and more of your soup. God, I love that old maid. What a face!' She stood back up and lifted her arms above her head. 'No rain this morning. I shall run up the hill and down again before I pick up a brush today.'

'Suzanne? Thank you.'

The older woman lowered her arms and smiled crookedly. 'Don't think of it. We are at home to every waif and stray here. You're just the latest. When I die I shall go to Saint Peter and he will say, "Suzanne, you've been a very bad woman, but I have to let you into heaven anyway because you are kind to outcasts".'

Maud smiled. Her head felt clearer today. 'And because you are a great artist.'

Valadon lit a cigarette and walked towards the door. 'That should count for something, shouldn't it?'

'Suzanne, I need to write a letter.'

'Can you make it down to *Le Rat Mort* on Place Pigalle? They'll have all you need there.'

Rain oil on board 35 × 25 cm

It would seem from the fountain, just glimpsed in the background, that the painting is seen from the perspective of the interior of *Le Rat Mort* café on Place Pigalle, Montmartre. The café was a favourite for the artists and models of the area during the Belle Époque. Note the strong sense of movement from right to left across the secondary frame of the café window; figures dash past the viewer, sheltering under umbrellas or with their coats pulled over their heads. Note as well the heavy yellow light in the atmosphere and how the rain shows itself in the disturbances in reflections, the thinned and distorted edges of the gutters and figures seen through glass. *Rain* is a tour de force that makes us feel we too have just escaped a cataclysmic storm.

Extract from the catalogue notes to the exhibition 'The

Paris Winter: Anonymous Treasures from the de Civray
Collection', Southwark Picture Gallery, London, 2010

Maud should not have left her bed, let alone the house in Impasse
de Guelma. She paused from time to time as she dressed to sit a
moment and wait for the faintness to pass. She had only the clothes
she'd been drowned in. They had been laundered and pressed, but
she seemed to put the waters on with them and shivered. There
was a broken mirror propped up behind the washstand. She wiped
it on a corner of the bedsheet and looked at herself. Strange, she
looked much as she remembered, only thinner in the face and with
dark circles under her eyes. The good effects on her health of her
stay in Rue de Seine had been wiped out when her hosts tried to
kill her. She almost smiled at the thought then began to pin up her
hair. The movements were familiar and mechanical and she
wondered at them. How could anything be the same? Yet her
fingers twisted her dark hair into the usual neat pile on top of her
head and the pins held.

She pulled out the suitcase from under the bed, took out the
sketchbook and turned to the last empty pages. It was still there,
Madame Prideux's *carte de visite*. She tucked it into her pocket,
along with one of the fifty-franc notes.

On the Boulevard Clichy a man sat on an upturned tea-chest
playing a violin. On his knee perched a little monkey in a red jacket
with its own tiny instrument and bow. A long chain ran from its
neck to the man's waistcoat pocket. It watched him, copying his
movements, checking and chattering. The trams rang their bells all
the way along the road in front of them. The sky was an orange-
grey and Maud was not sure if it was the weather or her own illness,
but the air seemed to press on her. She looked up.

'Find cover, miss,' the violin player said. 'There's a storm not a minute away.' He started to pack up his instrument as he spoke. He stood and the monkey clambered swiftly up from his lap to his shoulder and crouched under the rim of his broad-brimmed hat. The man touched his forefinger to it in salute and sauntered up the road.

Maud crossed the clanging and blaring boulevard in the crowd, protected from the motor-cars by the mass of people around her, and found a place in the interior of *Le Rat Mort* just as the first fat raindrops began to fall. She sat in the warmth and comfort of the interior, listening to the civilised murmuring of the morning customers behind her, the snap of newspapers being opened and the chink of spoons on china cups as the readers stirred sugar into their bitter black coffees. All the surfaces were freshly polished and glowed with reflected electric light. Before the writing materials and her coffee had arrived the street outside was washed with rain, the gutters choked and plashed. The atmosphere outside was strangled with a thick yellow glow and the people fled past as if the thunder had let demons loose on the streets. She looked at the paper in front of her, let her head clear and began to write.

Maud was worse that afternoon, and when Sasha was told her patient had been out wandering the streets in the morning and got caught in a shower on her way home, she let forth a stream of Russian that Tanya refused to translate. Yvette grinned up from the floor. 'I think we get the idea.'

Maud pulled herself up in the bed and drew the blankets around her.

'Tell her I'm sorry, but I had my reasons,' she said. For the first time she told them about the strange visit of Mme Prideux to Rue de Seine, Morel's bloody story of the Commune and Sylvie's casual announcement that the lady had died in a traffic accident.

'Why didn't you tell me then, Maud?' Tanya said. She looked upset. Maud shook her head, not knowing how to answer.

'They had you all tied up, didn't they, sweetie?' Yvette said sadly. ' "Sylvie smokes opium – but don't tell. Here are more of our secrets about the crazy lady because we trust you." You weren't going to gossip once they had you all grateful and helpful. I'd lay money that was why she pretended she'd chucked her supply that day – same day that she told you Prideux was dead. Nothing like making people feel part of your secrets and troubles to keep them quiet and loyal.'

Maud hugged her knees. 'You're probably right. Anyway, I wrote to Prideux's son at the address on the card this morning. I told him I had met Mme Prideux and gave a hint at what Morel said of her. Then I wrote that I was thinking of investing money with Morel, but what she had said before her accident gave me pause. I mentioned that she called him Gravot too.' Tanya had been softly translating for Sasha and the old lady looked startled and afraid, tutting and crossing herself as she listened and worked the stove.

'Could that be done? To kill someone in traffic? Do you think Morel killed her?' Tanya asked.

'Yes,' Maud said, wondering what it felt like to be well, to be free of this creeping sickness in her stomach, the pain in her head. 'Tanya, I wrote the letter in your name. I'm sorry. That means the answer will come to you.'

'Nothing easier than killing someone in traffic,' Yvette put in. 'Friend of mine died like that last year. I always thought her lover pushed her out into the road. He was so jealous and she liked to tease him.'

'You were right to do that, Maud. And I'll bring any reply as soon as it comes. My aunts will think I'm getting love letters, but as long as it's not post-marked Paris, it should be fine.'

'Where do they think you are now, your cats?' Yvette asked.

'At the Louvre. It is one advantage of Perov proposing – they don't want to parade me around so much and it makes my request to stay on at Lafond's seem more sincere if I spend all my free hours in the galleries. I have more time to think now.'

CHAPTER 7

14 January 1910

*Y*VETTE WOKE COLD AND UNCOMFORTABLE, HER head a little thick from the night before. *Tant pis.* She had needed a bit of a spree after spending so much of her time in a sick room, but she had not gone to one of the smoking dens and lost a day. That was good. She could be pleased at that, even if her head was pounding. The damp had got into the blankets and it was like trying to warm yourself with fog. She pulled what she could grab around her and shut her eyes, trying to will herself back to sleep. There was a groan next to her.

'Yvette, you demon! I shall freeze.' An arm snaked round her waist and pulled her back towards the middle of the bed. She could feel the strong lines of his thighs pressing against her own. One hand stroked up from her belly and cupped her breast. She could feel his stubble on her neck. 'You'd better warm me up again.'

She was tempted. Then his other hand pressed on her bladder and she wriggled away from him and out of the bed. The floor was icy under her bare feet.

'Oh, warm yourself up! I'm off.' It was light already. She trotted behind the screen and squatted over the pot while he laughed.

'Why can't you be like little Marie? Stay here and sit by my side and darn my shirts. Play the housewife. I bet Marie keeps her friends warm in the mornings.'

Yvette emerged and started looking for her stockings. 'Why should I care what she does?' Damn, another hole. Still, it wouldn't show. 'Harley? Can I ask you something?' She sat down on the bed beside him as she put on the stockings and pulled the ribbons tight.

'Anything!' He propped himself up then looked more serious. 'My allowance from home doesn't come for another week, but I do have a few francs still. I'll share, even if you don't darn my shirts.'

She grinned and kissed his forehead. 'Save your money for paper and ink, there's a good boy. No one keeps me but me. But I wanted to ask you: why would you steal something, then give it back?'

He yawned. 'Depends what it was.'

Yvette studied him. He was two years younger than her, and at times like these, all tousled and sleep-warm, he looked like a child in a false moustache. He had come to Paris from London to write, but as far as Yvette could tell, whenever he was awake he was in one of the bars that clustered round Place du Tertre, talking and arguing with other young men. When she asked to see what he wrote, he said he was still gathering material. She was always happy to see him and liked talking to him about books. He blushed when he looked at her, which she found more touching than any practised flatteries. When he had money, he was generous and when he was poor, he did not ask her for her cash so sometimes she went home with him even though she knew his room would be cold and there would be nothing to eat.

'Say, like a diamond necklace, something like that,' she went on.

'You planning to rob someone?'

She leaned over him to pick up her skirt and stepped into it.

'Fine, if you can't think of anything. I just thought, you're supposed to be a writer, have some imagination or something . . .'

'No – wait.' He sat upright and rubbed the back of his neck. 'What, give it back straight away?'

She sat back down and leaned against him, facing the other side of the room. 'No, maybe a week later. Say you blame somebody else for it. Say you found it and are now returning it.'

'Like the honest girl you are.'

'Exactly. But you're not honest. You're not very honest at all.'

He put his arm round her waist again; his forearm lay across her narrow belly and she stroked the hairs on it as if he were a pet.

'Maybe you're not giving it back. Maybe you're giving back something that just looks like it.'

Yvette snorted. 'I don't care who she is, a woman will recognise her diamonds.'

'Are you sure?' He sounded enthused, as if the idea had caught him. 'I mean, what if you lever out a few of the stones and replace them with good glass imitations or something? Then the woman gets her necklace back, it looks the same, feels the same. Most of it *is* the same and you get to keep a few diamonds.'

Yvette stopped stroking his arm. 'You could get a lot of money like that, couldn't you?' she said.

He stretched back out in bed again. 'I suppose you could, if you knew what you were doing – thousands and thousands.' He sighed. 'I wouldn't know a diamond if I found one in my glass.'

Yvette sprang up and struggled into her blouse. 'If one turned up in your glass, you'd swallow it before you even saw it. I need my shoes.'

'Over by the door. Are you really rushing off? I hate to see you go. Perhaps I've fallen in love with you.'

'Men fall in love with the woman who is leaving or the one who has just arrived.' She stepped into her shoes and picked up her jacket from the back of the chair. He was looking miserable.

'Do you like me at all?'

'When you say clever things, I do.' She bent over the bed and offered her cheek to be kissed. '*Au revoir*, Harley.'

He took his kiss then rolled on to his side to watch her go. 'What clever thing did I say? I'll say it again.'

Tanya brought the letter to Valadon's that afternoon.

Dear Miss Koltsova,

My thanks for your condolences. As to your questions, I can only say it causes me great pain to reply in detail, but I feel it is my duty both to correct any errors and give you fair warning if possible. I have never heard of anyone named Morel, but the name of Gravot is only too familiar to me. If my mother told you this man you know as Morel is in fact called Christian Gravot, then that is who he is – and a worse scoundrel has never walked the earth. He is a thief and a confidence trickster.

Forgive the vigour of my expressions, but from your letter I must conclude you have been told a number of slanderous lies about my family, and it grieves me excessively. I am therefore willing to lay before you the true facts regarding our dealings with Christian Gravot and his wife Sylvie, which led to my mother's sad derangement.

My father was not a rich man, but he was honest. He worked as a clerk in our town hall from the age of fourteen until his retirement. He was awarded a medal for his distinguished service in 1893 and died in the autumn of 1905. My mother was housekeeper to the Widow Rochoux in our town from her marriage until 1907. She was a loyal servant, and on the death of her mistress she was generously remembered in that lady's will. That same lady also provided for my education and that of my brother: her generosity has allowed us to become professional men. I am now senior partner in our town's law firm. My brother holds a similar position in his wife's native city. As these simple facts must make clear we are a family devoted to respectable service.

It is not the story of my mother and myself you have heard, but that of Madame Claudine Gravot and her son Christian, the snake you know as Morel. He was the child who saw his father's body defiled, not I. You ask yourself perhaps how can I assert this with such confidence? I shall tell you. He and I are of an age and were school fellows in our youth. He told me the story himself, though I knew his mother beat him for doing so. Gravot wished always to be admired, courted and respected, but as he had neither the station, learning nor character likely to inspire such feeling, he instead told and re-told his lurid stories to gain the attention of the weak-minded and lead his more impressionable fellows on tours of petty and spiteful vandalism in our town. I was glad to leave his company. When he heard news of my improved prospects, he made an enemy of me. He was not unintelligent, and I think resented the opportunities offered to me and my brother. I shall not distress you with the details of his campaign against us; let me just say it confirmed him in my mind as a twisted and malicious child.

In 1883 at the age of eighteen he stole a diamond necklace

belonging to one of the rich ladies who come and take the spa waters in our town from time to time. He was transported to Guiana for the crime. His mother owned a grocery store in one of the less pleasant quarters in town and died, bitter and spiteful before the new century began. I sold the business on his behalf and sent him the money when he returned to France at the end of his sentence. What happened to him between that time and his reappearance in our town in early 1908, I cannot say. He returned here with a wife and some appearance of wealth shortly after the death of my mother's patron. He made great show of being a reformed character, and as such was welcomed into our community. His wife, Sylvie, was charming and beautiful though very young, and he himself seemed to have acquired a great deal of polish in his years away.

I am deeply grieved to say I did not realise how intimate this young couple had become with my widowed mother until it was far too late. My only excuse is that I had recently become a father myself for the third time, and had also taken on new responsibilities in my work. I deeply regret I was not more aware, but I was, in truth, as taken in by Gravot's reformation as my mother was. I was simply glad she was not lonely.

The couple left our town in the middle of last year. Shortly afterwards, my mother came to me in some distress. It was only then I learned that she had 'invested' with Gravot all that she had inherited from my father's modest estate as well as from her benefactor. She had also been persuaded to raise money against the value of her small house for the same cause. She believed she had invested in a diamond mine in Angola of all places, but the papers she had from them were worthless. That it was a gross criminal act is without doubt, but Gravot and his wife had so phrased the documents as to make the money appear a gift. My mother was not practised at reading legally phrased documents and had trusted the young couple too much to do more than sign them.

The house my parents had shared through forty years of marriage was sold and my mother joined my own establishment. Her last months with us were not happy. She felt both humiliated and angry, and nothing my wife or I could do would make her accept what had happened or see the impossibility of seeking redress. She would take no ready money from my hand, and sold what trifles she still possessed to fund her trip to Paris. I had hopes that her stated plan – to come to the capital for the sake of a little pleasure – was a sign of her recovery. I suspect now from your letter that my hope was false: she went to Paris in order to search for Gravot and his wife, and it is evident that she found them. She was missing for three weeks. I fear to imagine how she must have spent those days. I brought her body back from the city the week before Christmas and she rests now next to my father.

I close with a word of advice which I hope you will heed, even if it comes from a stranger. If you have not yet handed money to M. Gravot, do not, under any circumstances do so. If you have, consider it lost. I also request that if you have repeated to anyone the slanders of M. Gravot regarding my family, you will correct that error.

Begging you to accept the assurances of my best regard,

Jean Prideux

The women read the letter in turn.

'The poor woman,' Tanya said at last, handing the letter back to Maud.

Maud nodded and wondered about her own behaviour when Mme Prideux had arrived on her doorstep. If only the old lady hadn't been so frightening. She had shut the door on someone who might have saved her – all to protect the peace of the monsters within. The thought made her afternoon black and kept her from sleeping half the long, dreary night.

CHAPTER 8

15 January 1910

HE DAY AFTER THEY RECEIVED THE LETTER FROM Jean Prideux, Maud woke late. She was still weak, and the pain of her continual headache increased once she had hastily dressed and gone outside on the street. The bells of the trams rang and jangled, the horses struck their hooves on the cobbles and the motor-taxis darted among the omnibuses, their iron wheels tearing the road. She crossed Boulevard de Clichy and hugged the west side of Place Pigalle. A huge clock hung above the *épicerie*; it was already a little after twelve, much later than she had thought. She glanced across at the fountain. Only a few women were there, lounging and smoking cigarettes. Other women in their long winter coats and furs shepherded children in sailor hats along the pavements, making for home or the park in hopes the showers would keep off. The two groups were from different worlds and blind to each other.

Maud stumbled against one of the tables set outside *Le Rat Mort*. A waiter, his hair and moustache so slick and oiled they looked freshly painted, started towards her, his look something between concern and suspicion as he tried to decide what world she belonged to. When she straightened up and gave him a slight nod, his face flickered with recognition, and with a cautious bow he let her pass by.

Maud tried to step a little more firmly after that, down the hill along Avenue Frochot, but had to pause and lean against a wall as soon as the bend in the road provided her with a moment of privacy. The people passing might think her drunk, she knew. Her clothes were respectable but she had no hat, no gloves, and in Paris everyone stared. A policeman might pass at any moment. She forced herself to walk on till she found herself in Place St Georges and at the Countess's front door – then before her courage could fail her, she rang the bell.

The butler showed her into the library and took her name. He was English and recognised her accent as that of an educated woman. The library seemed to serve the same purpose in France as it did in England, a place to receive that doubtful class of person one could not introduce immediately into the salon, but whom it might be dangerous to leave waiting in the hall to be gossiped over or noticed by other guests. Maud did not sit down, unsure if she would be able to stand up again if she did. Instead she rested against the window that opened out onto a pretty little garden at the back of the house. It was all in greys and purples at this time of year, sage greens and soil. Earth tones. There was a fountain in the centre of the lawn, silent now; the mermaid pouring nothing into the little pond under the rock on which she sat. A gardener was pulling dead leaves out of her granite hair.

The door was thrown open and Maud turned round to face the Countess. The American cried out and looked behind her as if unsure whether she needed to summon help. Maud felt the familiar nausea and weakness in her limbs. Her head swam and her legs, tired and unwilling, started to give way. I will wake in a prison cell, she thought, and it will be my own fault. The Countess crossed the room and caught her as she fell, lowering her down onto a sofa with an arm around her waist. She was stronger than Maud had expected. Maud didn't quite faint, just breathed steadily till the sensation of falling and spinning began to fade, and opened her eyes.

'You are not a ghost, I think,' the Countess said and released her. Her voice had become calm but her tone was fierce, the words sharply enunciated. 'Has someone been playing a trick on me, Miss Heighton? Is someone laughing at me?'

Maud could only shake her head.

The Countess leaned forward and rang a little bell on the table. Maud stiffened, but when the butler bowed his way in at the door, she only asked him to bring brandy and water. Maud began to speak, but the Countess lifted her hand – no. The brandy arrived on a silver tray with tumblers cut from crystal rather than the great balloons at Hôtel Chopin. They looked as if they'd been blasted from ice. When the Countess filled one and put it into her hand, Maud was surprised the glass was not cold. The Countess then poured herself a generous slug and knocked it back like a worker in a cheap bar. She stared into the empty glass as she spoke.

'That man Morel came to me on New Year's Eve and handed me my tiara. He said you stole it then threw yourself in the river out of guilt, so now I have to ask myself, Miss Heighton, was there some mistake? Or did you steal it, but just not feel that guilty, after all?'

Maud felt the brandy burning her throat and coughed. 'I did not steal it.'

'So you just picked it up and forgot to put it down?'

Maud felt herself being watched now. The Countess was sitting on the edge of the sofa, her empty brandy glass held by its rim with the fingers of her right hand. Her left hand supported her sharp chin. She looked wary now the first shock of seeing the dead girl walking had passed, caught somewhere between suspicious and angry and not sure which way to jump. Her eyes travelled over Maud's face, back and forth.

'I took nothing, and I did not throw myself in the river.'

There was a tap at the door and the butler reappeared. He addressed the air somewhere above their heads.

'Madame, there is a Miss Koltsova demanding to see you. She says she is a friend of Miss Heighton's.'

'I wonder how they found me?' Maud said, amazed.

'Slipped your leash, did you, Miss Heighton? Do you wish to speak to me alone? I can have Arthur stand outside the door with a truncheon to safeguard our privacy.'

Maud swallowed. 'Tanya would not want me to come. But I have nothing to say to you I cannot say in front of her.'

'Then let her come, Arthur!' The Countess's American accent had become a great deal more pronounced since she had entered the room. The butler cleared his throat. 'What is it, Arthur?'

'There is another . . . person with her.'

The Countess looked at Maud, one eyebrow raised.

'Yvette, probably. She is a model.'

'Well, Arthur, bring them all in. And a couple more glasses, I guess.' He bowed and the Countess poured herself another drink. 'Funny thing is, I thought today was going to be a really dull day.'

Yvette and Tanya were both ushered in and Arthur placed glasses for them on the table. He seemed to move with exaggerated slowness. Yvette was flushed and glaring at Maud. Tanya was all but bouncing out of her chair. The moment Arthur withdrew, stately as a swan in a tailcoat, Tanya began speaking in rapid French.

'She is innocent. You cannot arrest her. She did nothing wrong.'

The Countess held up her hand again and the look she directed at Tanya was so fierce that even Yvette shrank away from her a little.

'I wish to hell,' the Countess said very distinctly and in English, 'that people would stop telling me what didn't happen and tell me what *did*. You two shut up and drink the brandy if you have a taste for it. Miss Heighton, explain yourself.'

She did. The words came uneasily at first, but the brandy smoothed her throat, and after the first few sentences, when she began to describe Sylvie taking opium and sending her out for supplies, they came fluently. She told the Countess of Mme Prideux and her accusations. To Maud it seemed that someone else was speaking. She heard her own words, calm, apparently well-chosen, but all she felt was that great black rage that washed over her every night as she slept. Her words floated above the sea of pain in her head. She told the Countess of the night she had been thrown in the river, her illness on waking and the help she had received from her friends, then she explained about writing her own letter to the Prideux family. She then passed the reply from Jean Prideux to the Countess and watched her read it in silence. Madame de Civray then handed the letter back to Maud and set her brandy glass on the table with a click. She proceeded to ask Yvette a question or two about events after Maud was dragged from the water. Tanya, very respectfully, told her of her own meeting with Morel in Passage des Panoramas.

'Interesting. Yet, ladies, I have my tiara.'

'But Madame,' Yvette said – and it was strange to hear her speak English so carefully, her usual profanities and freedom buttoned up by the unfamiliar language – 'are you sure that the *tiare*, it is the same as the one you lost?'

The Countess got up and went to her desk. 'Miss, get this straight. I did not *lose* anything. That is one thing I am sure of.' She picked up pen and paper and wrote something, then rang the bell for Arthur. The butler appeared at once. She met him in the doorway and there was a short conversation of which the girls heard nothing.

'Why are you here, Maud?' Tanya said in a whisper. 'Sasha saw you from the motor as we passed Place Pigalle! Yvette said you'd be here, but I couldn't believe you'd be that stupid.'

The Countess turned back into the room. 'I'm afraid I must ask you to wait a few minutes,' she told them, then closed the door behind her.

'Shit! She's going for the police!' Yvette said, knocking back the last of her brandy like a sailor. 'I say we run.'

'Where?' Tanya hissed back. 'She knows me. And look at the colour of Maud's face. She couldn't escape a tortoise if it really wanted to catch her.'

'What's your idea then, princess?'

'I'm not running,' Maud said simply before Tanya could reply. 'I know I shouldn't have come, but I couldn't do anything else.'

'Yes, you could have done,' Yvette said brutally. 'Look at you! You could have stayed in bed and waited until . . .' She waved her hand in the air.

'Until what, Yvette?'

'Oh, I don't know! Until we'd persuaded you to go home to England.'

Some thirty minutes passed. Maud was not sure if she was calm or simply exhausted. Tanya and Yvette were nervous. Yvette could not stay still and wandered around the room picking up one object then another until Tanya snapped at her. She did not stop, however, just handled the objects she picked up a little more carelessly when she knew Tanya was watching.

When the door finally opened again, the Countess was carrying a dark blue travelling case. Beside her was a thin, elderly man in a high starched collar with a thick white moustache and a slightly apprehensive air. He did not look like a policeman. He stared at the three women, obviously curious. Maud guessed what was in the case and looked away from it.

'Monsieur Beauclerc, these ladies are friends of mine. You may speak frankly in front of them,' the Countess said. M. Beauclerc looked startled at the prospect of speaking frankly in front of anyone. 'Ladies, this is Monsieur Beauclerc from Maison Lacloche in Rue de la Paix.' Her voice was still dry and controlled. She nodded Beauclerc onto the sofa and sat beside him, then placed the travel case in front of him on the veined marble table-top. 'Tell me about this piece, sir.'

Beauclerc looked as if he thought some trick might be played on him, and he glanced hopefully at the Countess in case she might offer some more information, a little guidance. None seemed to be forthcoming, so he gave a tiny sigh, drew the case towards him and opened it. Then, having glanced at it briefly, turned to the Countess. Maud heard Tanya and Yvette inhale sharply. Of course, they had never seen the thing before. The sight of it seemed to pull Maud back into Rue de Seine and she felt thoroughly ill. Beauclerc's voice when he spoke was pitched quite high, and oddly neat and precise for a Frenchman. Each word came out cut and brilliant.

'This is the diamond tiara of Empress Eugénie, Countess. I know it, of course. We cleaned it for your father before he gave it to you as a wedding gift. The piece was designed and created by Bapst Frères in 1819 for Marie-Thérèse. It was made with jewels from the State Treasury so was returned to the State in 1848, then later became a favourite of Empress Eugénie, hence the name.' He blinked owlishly.

Maud heard Yvette whimper. Another day, the sound might have amused her. The diamonds covered the tiara like frost on a winter hedgerow. The larger stones were like light captured and frozen – clarity held.

M. Beauclerc smiled slightly and turned the case towards Tanya and Yvette.

'Is it heavy?' Tanya asked.

He shook his head then looked, questioningly, at the Countess. She nodded and he pushed the case forward so Tanya could pick it up. Yvette crouched by her chair and with one nervous finger touched the glittering stones. M. Beauclerc continued to speak to the Countess.

'After the founding of the Third Republic, many of the French crown jewels were sold at auction.' He was relaxing into his role as narrator now and crossed his ankles. 'The tiara was bought by Asprey in London, I believe, then passed into the hands of Tiffany, from where it was purchased by your father, as I understand it, Countess. The case I made myself, the old one having become really very shabby.' He sounded so distressed at the idea that Tanya looked up briefly and smiled. 'The grand stone is a golconda of the first water, some twenty-two carats in weight. Not the size of the fabled Royal Blue, of course, but some might think it superior, given the clarity and quality . . . of . . . its . . . cut.'

He had glanced towards the tiara that Tanya and Yvette were holding between them as he spoke, and his words slowed down. His face became white, then angry red patches appeared on his cheeks. He clicked his fingers and held out his hand, and Tanya passed the tiara over to him. As the Countess sat back and watched, he began to turn it in his hands, confusion and disgust making his movements brittle; and his shoulders twitched as if he was receiving a series of electric shocks.

'This . . . this was worn by the Queen of France,' he hissed. 'What foul outrage . . .'

The Countess raised her eyebrows, but he was too engaged in staring at the tiara to notice it. 'Explain yourself, sir.'

'These are fakes! The central stone and her larger sisters! The foliage scrolls still hold the original stones, perhaps . . .' He covered his eyes with his hands as if the sight distressed him too much.

'Try and contain your emotion, Monsieur Beauclerc,' the Countess said. Her voice was so tight it sounded like a crack in the air.

'My apologies, Madame. But the shock . . .' He cleared his throat and Maud thought his eyes looked a little damp. 'I would need more time to tell you exactly what has been taken and what remains. Madame, I would be grateful if you could explain—'

'You will have to forgive me, Monsieur,' the Countess interrupted. She stood and walked over to the window, and looked out into the garden at the rear of the house. 'I'm a little short on information at the moment. Let me just say this. Someone took the tiara and a few days later returned it to me in its current condition.'

'Then you have been robbed. We must summon the authorities.'

'I *have* been robbed, sir – but the circumstances are complex. I ask you to keep this visit confidential.'

He looked as if he was about to protest, but after meeting the Countess's eye he dropped his chin.

Yvette had curled up onto the floor where she could keep her eyes level with the shifting lights of the tiara. 'This is good work, isn't it?'

He looked at her with a frown. 'Evrard and Frédéric Bapst were craftsmen of the first rank, miss. It is a classic piece, the symmetry of the foliage—'

'No, not that. The faking, I mean. I know you saw it as soon as you looked *properly*, but you did have to look, didn't you? And you said you're not sure about the smaller stones. To fool a man like you, with all your cleverness, even for a second,' she snapped her fingers and they all jumped, 'that has to be a good fake.'

Beauclerc rubbed the bridge of his nose again. 'If there is such a thing, then yes, they are good imitations. But there are many people in Paris making fake jewels, expert ones. You'll see the signs saying "imitation" hung over half the displays in the boutiques of the Palais Royal.'

'And the settings?' Yvette pressed on. 'I mean, to get the real diamond out and stick in a glass one without it looking wrong? You'd have to know what you were doing, yes?'

Beauclerc looked once more towards the Countess for guidance, but she seemed absorbed in the view of her garden. 'Yes, certainly. But this is Paris – centre of the world for fashion and jewellery. The best craftsmen from all Europe find their way here. I could name a hundred men who could make these fakes, and a hundred others who could set them.'

Now Tanya leaned forward in her chair, her eyes bright. 'But you all know, don't you? All of you jewellers and designers, you all know this tiara and who owns it. It's famous.'

He stroked his chin. 'Yes, of course. I admit that the list of people who, without an express command from the Countess herself, would be willing to do this work and had the capacity *is* rather shorter . . .'

'Well then,' Tanya said, drawing a tiny notebook from her bag and pulling out a pencil thin as a spider's leg from its spine. 'Give us *that* list.'

CHAPTER 9

Caveau des Innocents oil on canvas 64.8 × 76.3 cm

One of the most notorious bars in Paris near Les Halles and known until the First World War as a haunt for the destitute and desperate. Though the patrons are huddled in the rough clothing of the working poor and seen by the light of smoking oil lamps, there is a sense of life and community in the painting. The focus of attention is the singer seated at the back table with her bright red shawl and the violinist who accompanies her, the handkerchief around his neck echoing the same red. The performance seems to transport her listeners, who lean in towards her just as the viewer is drawn towards her – and away from the surrounding shadows.

Extract from the catalogue notes to the exhibition 'The Paris Winter: Anonymous Treasures from the de Civray Collection', Southwark Picture Gallery, London, 2010

When Beauclerc had been hurried, sniffing and unhappy, from the house, Yvette assured the Countess that she could find which of the men on the list had done the work on the tiara if she were given a few days to look for them in the lower haunts of Paris. One of them would have more money than he should, she said, or would have been busy while everyone else was drinking over Christmas and New Year.

Maud lay back on the Countess's settee while they discussed it and let the talk flow over her. She had expected some relief from coming here. She remembered the middle-class living rooms of her mother's friends where she had been petted and praised – the glow of self-worth she had felt. She had felt it again when the Countess gave her the portfolio of photographs during those perfect days before Christmas when she was loved and useful. Now, lying back empty and hollow while the others were so full of purpose, she realised she had been hoping to feel that again, had imagined the Countess tearful and grateful, praising and pitying her back into the world. It had not happened.

'Fine!' the Countess said at last, holding up her hand to stop the talk of the two other women. 'Find who did the work and come and tell me. We shall see about the police after that.'

'You mustn't do anything that puts Maud in danger,' Tanya protested. 'If you do, I shall . . . I shall . . .'

'What? Faint?' Madame de Civray replied sharply. 'Do not fret, Miss Koltsova. I'm sure we can persuade whoever did the work to turn in Morel, or Gravot if that is his real name. Such people do not normally keep their mouths shut for their friends.' She took a breath. 'I'm sorry, girls. Seeing the dead walk and then finding out about that damned tiara has rattled me.'

Yvette looked up at her, eyes slightly narrowed. 'It was brave of Maud to come here, Madame.'

The older woman pursed her lips. 'Yes, it was. I thank her for it and I shan't forget it.' But she did not look at Maud. 'Do you mind if Arthur shows you out of the back door?'

Tanya let them off at Place Pigalle before being carried off to the Louvre to play the part of the devoted student and Yvette supported Maud on her arm back to Valadon's.

'Let me come with you tonight,' Maud said as she sat down on the bed and began to unbutton her boots.

'No. No bloody way,' Yvette said, shocked. 'It is not the place for you and besides, you are not well enough. I can't ask the questions I need to with you hanging over my shoulder. You don't know the language – this is not drawing-room French – and you don't know how to be.'

'And where *is* my place?' Maud's disappointment at the Countess's house was thickening, curdling into something bleak and wretched. 'I will come if I have to follow you through the streets until I fall in the gutter. I want to see. And I cannot sit here quietly while other people plan and do around me. No more.'

Yvette sat down heavily on the bed beside her, making the springs complain. 'Where is your place? Who knows? No one does, Maud.' She pulled her knife from her pocket and flicked it open, then began to pare her short nails. 'Your place is just where you end up, I suppose.'

'Tell everyone I am a new model just turned up with a few francs, and you're using me to buy you drinks.'

Yvette looked at her sideways and spoke softly. 'Why? Why do you want to come? There's nothing to see but misery and stink. A month ago, you would have swooned at the very idea of going somewhere like that. Anyone seeing you go into these places will assume you are a whore or a thief, possibly both.'

'But now I am a ghost, Yvette, I can go anywhere. And I shall. I want to see, and why should I care what strangers think?'

Yvette squeezed the blade shut, slipped the knife back into her pocket then hugged herself. 'Christ, Maud, I hate it when you talk like that. You've always cared what other people think, and you're *not* a ghost.'

'I feel like one. An angry one. I can't carry on thinking the world can be made into what I want it to be, Yvette. That got me killed. I want to see it *as it is*.'

Yvette waited for a while then nodded. 'All right – but say as little as you can. If they think you are not one of them in the Caveau des Innocents, they will kill you. Rest now. I'll come back for you at midnight.'

An arched doorway, an entrance into the cellars of what was once a great house in a dim street a stone's throw from Les Halles. There was a man, hunched against the cold, leaning on the wall outside. His eyes drifted over them and he nodded. Maud wore clothes she'd borrowed from Valadon. A simple skirt and threadbare cotton blouse under a short black coat worn shiny at the elbows. She felt more comfortable than she had in the rose evening gown.

Yvette pushed open the door and led Maud down a narrow stone staircase. The only light was from smoking candles stuck into the tops of bottles on the steps or occasional oil lamps swinging from large metal hooks, and the air was thick with the stench of sweat, sour alcohol and cheap black tobacco. The grey plaster walls were scrawled with names in household paint, a dark vermilion:

Panther, Ugly Henry, Fat Emily. Not decoration, but some sort of declaration of existence.

At the bottom of the stairs, the two women reached the first of a series of low, vaulted rooms. There was a bar of sorts, with smeared glasses and unlabelled bottles. Yvette pointed at one then waited, leaning her folded arms on the bar, for Maud to pay. Against the walls were wooden benches and tables. Yvette picked up the bottle and a pair of glasses and took Maud to a spot in the corner of a second vault that led off from the first, poured the drinks and emptied the first glass immediately down her throat. Maud did the same. The wine scorched her throat, but after the first sting she felt it warm her, drive some of the noxious stink out of her blood.

She began to pick out the details of the room. A man at the far end of the room was playing a violin, and seated at the table next to him, another was singing. The patrons nearest to them swayed with the music and joined in with the chorus. Maud could only make out a few of the words. He was lamenting his girl, shut away in Saint-Lazare, complaining that he had no comfort in life while she was gone. It seemed the song was addressed to the girl's little sister. He was asking her to take up her elder's duties. Each verse seemed to end with a joke or a pun that sent the crowd into fits of laughter before they sang out the chorus.

The bar was beginning to fill and the reek of unwashed bodies, warmed by their closeness, soured the thin air. Yvette held her tumbler close to her face, observing the distorted crowd through the dirty glass. The song ended and another began, a woman singing this time in a low growl. Maud looked at the faces, mournful or intent, the way the men and women watched each other as much with their bodies as their eyes. Yvette slid out of her place and went to lean on the bar again; after a few minutes Maud realised she was talking to the man next to her. Yvette was nodding at him now, her eyes flickering to right and left while he spoke, making sure she was not overheard.

While Maud watched, another man, his hair greased back from his forehead, took Yvette's place beside her and said something to her she didn't understand. She shrugged then felt his arm slide around her waist. His skin smelled of stale bread and onion and she could feel the warmth of his body through her clothes. He was whispering into her ear a mixture of compliments and obscenities, his fingers pressing into the flesh of her hip, his breath on her neck. Suddenly she was yanked to her feet. Yvette had pulled her up and was now leaning into her face in a rage, shaking her arm, talking fast and loud. The man who had been embracing her laughed, said something and grabbed his crotch. The others near to him hooted and applauded. Looking as submissive as she could, Maud took hold of Yvette's hand and kissed her knuckles. She saw the slight flicker of surprise and amusement cross Yvette's face before the girl remembered to be angry again. She delivered one last insult to the man, then wrapped her arm around Maud's waist and carried her off.

Her act of furious indignation lasted until they turned the corner into Rue Berger when she dropped her grip on Maud, leaned against the wall and began to laugh so hard the tears ran down her face. The street was quiet, the shop-fronts and pitches around Les Halles closed away for the night and the doors to the warehouses locked. A dog barked from behind one of the gates and Yvette pulled herself straight.

'Oh Lord, oh I thought I would die when you kissed my hand! Did you understand what I was saying to you?'

Maud put her head on one side. 'Something about being a faithless bitch, I think. What did you find out about the names on the list?'

Yvette waited to see some spark of amusement in Maud's face, some acknowledgement of the adventure, but none came. She wiped her eyes on her cuff.

'According to Freddy, one is dead. Another left Paris last year to try his luck in the provinces. Two of the others have been seen out and drinking most nights since Christmas. But there are two that no one has seen around for a while. The man I spoke to said the bloke who was the pick of Beauclerc's list was Henri Bouchard, and he's one of the ones not seen since before the holidays. Apparently he'd been trying to go straight, working out of a shop in the Palais Royal – but he's not turned up there since then either.'

Maud nodded shortly and Yvette felt a chill in her bones that had nothing to do with the coldness of the evening or damp in the air. 'How did you get him to tell you these things?'

Yvette pulled her shawl over her shoulders and turned north back towards Montmartre, walking briskly. 'I told him I had a fellow interested in getting into the game of swapping real stones for fakes in the shops. Freddy used to do that too – before he got his face cut. Everyone could spot him after that so now he sweats in Les Halles butchering meat.' She could hear Maud following her.

'Are you angry with me, Yvette?' Her voice was calm.

'No,' Yvette took her arm. 'Just a little frightened for you. What would your lawyer brother say if he knew that you had been in that bar? With that man?'

Maud considered it a while and as they passed through the pool of light from a gas-lamp, Yvette saw the suggestion of a smile cross her friend's gaunt face. 'He would have me committed, I think, and what's more, if I had heard the story told about another woman from our town, of our class, I might have agreed with him. Isn't it strange? A place you can go every day if you wish to, yet my brother would probably lock me away forever if he knew I'd let that man put his arm around my waist. Let us go and see the Countess.'

Despite the lateness of the hour, it was still a little while before Madame de Civray returned from her evening engagements. The two women were summoned to her dressing room. The Countess sat in front of the three-part mirror taking the powder from her face with cold cream and brushing out her hair while Yvette told her what she had learned. After consulting her diary, she gave them a date.

CHAPTER 10

19 January 1910

ENRI BOUCHARD WAS DRUNK. HENRI BOUCHARD made a habit of being drunk whenever he had the money and he had money now. It was not half of what he deserved though, not for a job like that. He let out a curse and some tart on the next table looked at him over her shoulder then turned back to her friends. He was a craftsman. They had treated him unfairly. Rushed him through his work and then paid him badly for it. Still, he had enough to get drunk in one of his favourite bars – one with a proper band and lots of girls dancing. Not like in Les Innocents where you had to face nose to nose what a failure you'd become. Only the desperate got drunk in that stink-hole. Here you still got a lively crowd ready to fight and flirt till dawn, but your drinks came in a clean glass.

'What's up, Uncle?'

A young woman slid along the bench towards him. He growled and turned away. 'Oh come on, Uncle, don't be like that! My friends haven't arrived and you look like you could use cheering up. Buy us a drink and I'll sing you a song.'

He half-turned towards her, his eyes narrow. She was pretty

enough. Prettier than the women who normally offered to keep him company these days. Perhaps she could smell the money on him, little enough though it was. Still, what harm could a song do? He nodded to the waiter and the girl put her arm through his. He felt the ease of her warm his flank. A good feeling that, when it was cold in Paris – to feel the heat of a girl next to you, the smoky animal comfort of it. It made it almost a pleasure to remember the hell of the work camps on the shores of Guiana, where you were slick with your own sweat, and hunger clawed every breath, just to feel more sweetly the comfort of this now.

If they'd paid him what the work was worth, he could have lived like this for good, but that Gravot was a swine. He knew too much about the old days – quoted him his own words back from the camp when Henri had liked to boast about the society ladies locking away paste worth five francs in their strong-boxes. And he remembered things – oh, Gravot had a memory on him. That was what had cost Henri his proper fee on this job: Gravot's memory and Henri's boasting. Henri recalled him arriving in the camp. Scrap of a lad; thought he was as like to die in his first week as live, but he held on, the little devil, learning from the old lags around him – sucking it all in with the burning air. And the men liked to talk. There was nothing else to do when they'd done fighting each other for scraps. Then there were his funny turns. They'd caught a wild pig once, and the guards were willing to look the other way for the best cuts of it. Killing it had turned into a bit of a festival and Gravot had seemed as blood-happy as any of them till Vogel had stuck a knife in its belly – and then he'd gone white as paper under his prison tan and started beating him up. Knocked Vogel flying and would have killed him too if they hadn't dragged him off. Such strength he had in his wiry little bones . . .

The band started up with one of the songs he remembered from his youth, and Henri's foot tapped along to it before he even knew he was listening. Gravot was quite the gentleman these days. A fake gentleman, a gentleman of glass and gilt, but a good copy. Henri had been pleased to see him at first. Could hardly hear his 'Good morning' on the street outside the back yard lean-to where he worked for the blare of tropical birdsong Gravot seemed to bring with him. Then when it came to agreeing the price for the job, he showed what sort of 'friend' he was. No wonder he'd got rich while Henri was rotting in the back room of one of the cheapest jewellers in Paris, never allowed to handle anything worth more than a franc and with the steward's eye always on him.

'Uncle, I swear you haven't heard a word I've said.' The girl was filling up his glass and he half-smiled at her. She had pretty hair the colour of sand. Not one of the whores, nicer than that.

'Something about a hat?'

'Oh Uncle, you are funny. No, a skirt I made, and pricked my fingers open to do it and the madame comes in and it's "no, no, not like that" — and I'm to do it all over, and it had taken me hours. Such fine work, and do they understand the quality? Not a chance. If I'd known the price they'd pay me I'd have stitched it so the seams would split on first wearing.' She sighed and put her chin in her hands.

'Now then, flower, I know how that feels.' Poor lass, he thought. 'Same thing happened to me and I thought he was a friend too. But enough of our worries, let's have that song, eh?' She smiled and nodded like a little girl.

Three hours later he was as happy as he had ever been, wandering down the hill past Place Pigalle with this pretty girl chirruping and whistling on his arm. If she wanted his company on the way home it was worth a walk into Rue Laferrière. She actually seemed to like him. He thought so right up to the moment two men stepped out of a doorway and threw a sack over his head. Something struck him and he fell into their waiting arms.

Tanya was seated at dinner between the owner of one of the daily newspapers and Perov, but neither got a great deal of her attention. She tried to talk pleasantly to each of them, but realised she missed their questions and her answers were often vague to the point of rudeness. Perov would probably interpret her distraction as modesty and embarrassment, and draw his own egotistical conclusions. The newspaper-owner probably thought her an imbecile. There was nothing to be done about it, Tanya could not draw herself away from the sight of the Morels seated opposite her. Sylvie was clear-eyed and smiling, and making a conquest of the men who sat either side of her. Tanya occasionally heard her light laugh or her questions. The men were bankers apparently, and both falling over themselves to answer her naive enquiries about their business. They glowed and swelled as Tanya watched.

Further up the table, Morel was talking to the American opposite him, who seemed to have some interests in construction, about his plan to leave France for America, telling him how impressed he was by the buildings of New York he'd seen in photographs. The man, handsome, clean-shaven, in his fifties, was much more taken with Tanya's aunts, who sat either side of him. Their view of America as a land of savages and cowboys obviously amused him. They asked if there were theatres in America and whether they had managed to educate their peasants as yet. Tanya could almost admire the way Morel stuck to it until the man in construction said yes, he would be happy to receive Morel in New York when he happened to be there. Morel smiled around the table as if expecting general applause and, belatedly, tried to charm the very bored woman to his left.

Tanya could not eat. The food was all too rich, and wondering if Yvette had found the man she was looking for and led him to the Countess's house had twisted her stomach into a knot. She wished Allardyce were here. Even if he knew nothing about Maud or the horrors of what had been done to her, she knew that seeing him smile at her across the silverware would have helped her to get through the evening. Being next to Perov was making her skin crawl. His cuff links were diamonds.

She looked again at Sylvie. What had that girl done to surround herself with luxury? Lied and stolen and play-acted, killed and tried to kill, all for money, ordinary boring money. Tanya pushed at a piece of fat white flesh on her plate. The lobsters had come up alive on a special train from Normandy that morning. If she married Perov, perhaps everything would taste this stale – even his proposal seemed to have drained the joy out of Paris – but her father was adamant that this would be a good match.

The newspaper-owner asked her what she was thinking, and before she could stop herself she answered truthfully. 'I was wondering what it might be like to be poor, or at least have very little money compared with what I have now. I'm wondering if I would miss lobster.' She looked round guiltily but Perov was explaining wheat imports to the woman next to him and had not heard her.

The newspaper-man smiled and nodded into his wine. 'My father was a carpenter. A good one, but there were times when he couldn't get enough work to feed us all. I'm one of seven, you know. The little brother!' She looked at his wide belly and the length of his white moustaches and he laughed at her. 'A long time ago, dear child, even old men like me were once boys.'

'Forgive me, I did not mean . . .'

'I can hardly believe it myself. Now I am as rich as any man at this table, I think, and have seen every stage of wealth in between.'

'Being rich is much better, isn't it?' Tanya said sadly, jabbing at her plate again.

'It's a great deal better than being very poor, but I think I was happiest in those early days, when as a young man I set out to do something all fire and fluster! Working next to my wife, wondering if we were going to have enough money to print the next issue, then gradually, gradually watching the circulation rise. Those were the best days.'

'Your wife worked with you?' Tanya said.

'Indeed. She was one of my best writers and still does the odd piece for Marguerite at *La Fronde* – though I can't get her to write for me any more. She says she has too much fun playing with the grandchildren to bleed ink for me.' He raised his glass and Tanya realised he was toasting the woman next to Morel. He was explaining something to her a little loudly; she still looked bored, but when she caught her husband's glance she rolled her eyes and grinned at him. Tanya looked back in time to see the man beside her wink. They were like children, signalling in church. He leaned towards Tanya and said in an undertone, 'You are aware, I am sure, dear child, how many men complain that their wives do not understand them. I always complain that my wife understands me only too well.'

The butler entered and approached the Countess's chair, then bowed low to whisper in her ear. She stood up with a quiet apology to the men next to her and a nod towards her husband. Tanya felt anxiety twist in her chest and fought the impulse to stare at the Morels again, so comfortable and pleased with themselves. She looked instead at the Count at the far end of the table. He was a blandly handsome man who seemed charmed by everything around him and delighted in his ability to pay for it. He had already told those close to him the story of the journey of the lobster, and now he was describing how his wife had bought the plates and bullied the manufacturer for a better price. He noticed he was being observed and raised his glass to Tanya with a smile. She nodded back to him and returned to the glitter of her cutlery, the frosted whiteness of the tablecloth and tried to imagine what was happening elsewhere in the house.

'Happy as a king, isn't he? Happier.' The newspaperman was addressing her again. 'Every time I argue with my wife I tell her I should have married a rich American, but there weren't so many around in my day. She says that none of them would have had me anyway.'

Perov, it seemed, thought it was time to pay a little attention to them. 'An American like that comes at a cost,' he said in his thin pale voice. The newspaperman shrugged. 'I'm deadly serious, sir,' Perov went on. 'Her father made his fortune in oil in the wildest hinterlands of that vast continent, and she, rather than receiving a proper education, used to travel with him. They say she saw three men killed, one by her own father, before she was ten years old. I tell you, *she* runs this house now. Iron hand in a velvet glove, you know. All very comfortable for the Count if he behaves himself, but what civilised man could want a wife such as that?' Tanya felt his gaze slide over her and did not look at him, afraid if she did she would hiss like a cat. 'No, some accomplishments are desirable, certainly, and the taste to create a fashionable and elegant home for her husband, but nothing of the new woman about her, please.'

'Have you ever had your portrait painted, sir?' Tanya asked the newspaperman.

'Indeed, I have, last year. We have hung it in the entrance hall of our building to scare the staff and intimidate the creditors.'

'And how much did you pay for it?'

He laughed. 'A thousand francs, dear.'

'That is very interesting,' Tanya said, and tried to do better justice to her lobster. Perov said nothing, then returned his attentions to the woman on his other side.

Some twenty minutes later, the Countess came back into the room and retook her seat. Tanya looked at her and she gave a quick nod.

CHAPTER 11

WHEN HE WOKE, THE WORLD WAS THE INSIDE OF a flour bag; he could taste the dust on his lips. There was a rag in his mouth; it tasted dry. He was sitting on a chair and with his hands tied behind him. The air was cold and as he shifted his feet he felt his boots drag against stone. Someone must have seen him move. The flour sack was pulled off him and he blinked hard. A cellar. He looked side to side. Wine bottles all round the walls in heavy, expensive ranks. His view forward was blocked by the bodies of two wide gentlemen in long dark coats. They wore round hats. One looked smooth and well-fed. The other had long sloping shoulders, the broken nose and evil eyes of a prize-fighter. The sort that gouges. Henri steadied himself; he knew the signs of a beating coming but he was confused too. He owed no one money. Not today! And if it was just the francs in his boots they were after, why had they bothered to tie him up and bring him down here? The little *grisette* in the bar was cheese on a trap then. He sighed.

The smooth man turned away once he had seen that Henri was awake, and said something in English. A woman's voice replied, and straining in his chair Henri saw between the two men a woman standing further back in the shadows. She was wearing an evening gown and her throat sparkled with sapphires and diamonds. They seemed to gather the light from the oil-lamps and turn it into fireworks. Whatever she had said meant no good for him, for as the woman turned to go, the big man dropped into a fighting stance and drew back his arm. Henri closed his eyes and braced himself. Then another voice, female and rapid. The girl from the bar, but speaking English. Why was she still here? He opened one eye very cautiously. Her words had made the big fella hesitate. It seemed the jewelled lady was in charge, they were all looking at her now. She sighed and nodded to the girl, who then came trotting up to him. She bent down low and spoke in French.

'Henri, I'm going to take that rag out of your mouth. Would you like that?' He nodded. 'But if you say anything foul, I'll shove it right back in your gob. Understand?' He nodded again.

She yanked out the rag and he spat on the ground at her feet, but held his tongue. She waited, but when it became clear he was going to keep quiet she dropped into a crouch next to him, holding on to the back of his chair for balance. He leaned away from her slightly.

'Look, Henri, I'm sorry. These men are Americans. They work for the lady and they think you'll be more likely to talk to us if they beat you up first.' That was probably true. He looked at the prize-fighter again. The man was rolling his shoulders. 'I say you're not that bad a fella. Just made a few mistakes long ago, didn't you?' This whole thing was odd, but by the sound of her voice it was best to agree so he nodded hard. It made the pain in his head wake up and beat on the inside of his skull. 'So will you answer this lady's questions? Then we'll let you go.'

'Without the beating?' She nodded and flashed a grin at him. 'They ain't police?'

'They are Pinkertons.' She breathed the word into his ear and he shivered. 'American thugs for rich people. Clean-shaved, both of them! The gendarmes wouldn't have them even if they could speak French worth a damn.' He shot a quick look at the men. They looked wary, but obviously had not understood her.

'You staying here?'

She put her hand on his shoulder as if he was a schoolboy being presented to the headmaster by his mother, and said, 'He's happy to talk.'

The woman in sapphires stepped towards them. 'Yvette, remember I *can* speak French and I'm not so old I can't hear what you're whispering.'

His champion lost some of her bravery and looked down at the floor. 'Yes, Madame.'

Sparkles looked him up and down for a moment or two. 'You are sure this is the man?'

'Yes, Madame. Henri Bouchard. He's been talking tonight about not getting paid what he's owed, and people taking advantage of his bad luck. I'm sure it's him.'

Had he said that? Probably. Red wine and a big smile like that and he would run on. The tunes the band had been playing had made him mournful too, for his youth when the world seemed like a good place. Then the world took to teaching him the same lesson time and time again. People took advantage. And he'd never found the trick of making a woman like him without making her sorry for him, and he *had* been unlucky! He'd been caught swapping real stones for fakes when cleaning a necklace in 1893 and done five years for it. Now here he was, an artist really stuck making pennies in the back room of a dump that catered to shop girls. And he'd tried to keep his nose clean – at least till that shit Gravot turned up.

Sparkles was staring at him. He found he couldn't look her in the eye so concentrated on the hem of her long dress. It shimmered with all sorts of fancy stuff.

'The tiara, Henri? Who brought it to you?'

That fucking tiara. Of course it was the tiara. He got half – no, half of half – what his work was worth, and now he was in a cellar. 'I'm saying nothing.' Sparkles said something in English to the two men; they started moving towards him. Yvette went pale. Not a good sign.

'They are going to break your fingers, Henri!'

Shit. 'Gravot! Christian Gravot!' Sparkles held up her hand and the prize-fighter looked disappointed. Henri tried to catch his breath. 'He found me. He . . . he knows about a couple of little jobs I did that the cops never caught on to: enough to send me away a good few more years. He said I had to do the job or "the information would get to them". Bastard.'

Sparkles nodded. 'How did you do it so fast, Henri?'

'There are lots of drawings of that tiara. It's famous, isn't it? And they had a good photo of some American chit wearing it, so I had a few weeks to get ready.' He couldn't resist a little smirk. 'Four days was plenty to polish them up nice and swap out the real ones.' Sparkles raised her eyebrows and suddenly she looked sickeningly familiar. Shit again. The smirk disappeared and his shoulders slumped.

'How many stones did you replace?'

'Twenty plus the main stone,' he mumbled miserably to his boots. 'All the big ones. And the great fat cushion I recut. Been working on it since before Christmas.' Sparkles flinched when she heard that. 'Make it easier to sell. Just got the polishing done last night. Been doing nothing else since he brought it to me, but I did it fast even with Gravot breathing down my neck. Had to quit my job to do it. He made me. I just hope they'll take me back. He said he'd give me the rest of the week, but all of a sudden it's hurry hurry, can't stand another stinking evening with me, won't leave me alone for as much as a piss while I'm working.'

'Why hasn't he run, Henri?' Yvette asked. 'Why is he still in Paris?'

Henri looked up at her and shook his head. It made his jowls wobble like a bulldog's. So they knew Gravot. Good. Let *him* sit in a cellar with the big fella then.

'Why should he?' he said. The thought of the prize-fighter catching up with Christian on a dark night and messing up his fancy suit gave him a twinge of pleasure. He could feel it under the pain in his head, his hands. 'He thinks he's in the clear. Good conman never runs. Just ambles off when he feels like it. He's going to sell a few of the little 'uns here, then head off to America. Use the rest to found his business empire.

Henry spat on the ground again, thinking of Gravot sitting behind him while he worked, reading the business pages of the American newspapers, talking about opportunities. How America was the *real* place for a man with ambitions, not France. The country was full of peasants, he'd said while Henri sweated over that great rock for him, hardly losing any of its weight, but disguising it, keeping it just as beautiful, but anonymous. Like dyeing a girl's hair and dressing her in a new frock.

The girl patted him. 'Now Henri, you didn't keep any for yourself, did you? I know you didn't like the price he gave you, so weren't you tempted just to keep one for your trouble?'

Of course he'd been tempted, feeling all that real ice at his fingertips. Such high-grade stones – the clarity, the neatness of the cut. 'That arsehole knows his diamonds and he wouldn't leave me alone with 'em for a second.'

Sparkles was taking the news pretty well, Henri thought. She hadn't set the thugs on him or started crying or yelling yet. Just looked at the wine racks and frowned like she'd seen the Bordeaux sniggering.

'Thank you, Mr Bouchard. Christian Gravot will be arrested and you shall testify that he brought you the tiara and what you did with it.'

Henri jerked up so hard the chair juddered and he almost fell. 'No! No chance! I'm not going back to that hellhole.' They were all looking at him like this was a surprise. 'You don't know what it's like over there.' No one did. The heat and disease, the men dying round you, the ones that lived beating you for rations or for sport even when they knew you had nothing to steal. He blinked hard. 'You can kill me here, but take me to a cop and I'll deny it all. I'll say you lied and I never saw that dog . . . I'm not going back.' He realised it was true as the words were going out of his mouth. 'You can't prove nothing. Only told you to be civil.' He was not a brave man, he knew that, but letting those men kill him here and now with that girl Yvette fresh in his mind and a belly full of red wine would be a fine death compared with what waited in Guiana.

The American men might not understand French, but they knew a refusal when they saw it. The prize-fighter stepped in and swung hard into Henri's kidney. The pain ran through his body like wine spilled on a white cloth and pushed the air out of his lungs. He heard Yvette cry out, and he squeezed his eyes shut, steeling himself for the next strike. Sparkles said a word and no blow came. He opened one eye cautiously.

'You mean that,' Sparkles said. It was a statement not a question, but he nodded anyway. For a long time there was silence then she said, 'How do we know you won't warn Gravot?'

He'd bitten his tongue under the surprise of that last blow. He spat out the blood. 'Because that shit got me here, and I'd love to see him here instead.'

Yvette put her hand on his shoulder again. 'What's he planning, Henri? Tell us something else.' She leaned in very close to him. 'Tell us, and I won't tell them you keep your money in your stocking.' Her breath tickled the inner shell of his ear like the sound of distant water on sand.

'He hasn't sold any yet. Rheims. He had tickets for Rheims in his hand. He's been planning a little jaunt in that direction to sell a few stones and congratulate himself for driving me crazy. He leaves on Friday – back on the Sunday-evening train. He was going to give me till then to finish the polishing, but these last three days he's been at my back every minute chivvying me along.'

'Any more, Henri?'

Ah, fuck him. 'Five of the smaller stones I put in a bracelet for him. Bit of a rush job, but they're easier to smuggle about that way than loose. He wanted the others set too, but I told him he'd had all the work from me I could stomach. Thought he was going to blow, but in the end he just smiled and wandered off like a little king. The sod.'

Sparkles nodded. 'Very well. I must go back to dinner. Boys, clean him up and get him out of here. Don't leave town, Monsieur Bouchard, will you?'

He shrugged as well as his bonds would let him. 'Where would I go?'

She looked into the shadows behind her. 'Come on, my dear.' A figure stood up from the darkness. Another woman, tall and shapely but dressed a little plain and pale in the face. Sparkles took her arm. They began to walk towards the cellar stairs. Sparkles looked over her shoulder. 'Yvette?'

The girl bent down to kiss his forehead. 'Sorry, Henri. You're not a bad old devil.' He looked at his boots and managed another shrug. The place where she'd kissed him glowed in the darkness she left behind.

'Well done, Yvette,' the Countess said. Yvette almost thanked her but bit her tongue. 'So, Miss Heighton, you are vindicated. I believe you, but the law will take us no further. Still, again I thank you for bringing this matter to our attention and I promise it will not be forgotten. You look a little tired still. Go home and rest, honey. I must be getting back to dinner. Arthur will see you out.'

'But what next, Countess?' Yvette said.

'Steps will be taken, dear.'

'What steps?'

'Oh, you'll be informed. Now take that girl home before she falls over.'

'Are *they* here?' Maud said. Her voice sounded heavy and thick. Yvette tightened her grip on Maud's arm and the Countess glanced behind her as if checking that Arthur was still standing at her shoulder.

'They are here,' she said.

Maud took half a step forward and Yvette saw such a look of animal rage on her face that she was afraid. The Countess did not move but the butler stepped closer to her. Yvette kept Maud pinned to her side.

'Maud, you cannot,' she whispered frantically into her ear. 'Please, they will deny everything and accuse you, and nothing will be done but you will go to prison and die there.' Maud was still staring up the hallway towards the receiving rooms of the Countess's home. 'For God's sake, Maud, *come away.*'

'I should not have let you in the house tonight, Miss Heighton. I hoped you would be sensible.' Madame de Civray turned on her heel and crossed the hallway, the train of her gown perfectly pooling and slippering behind her on the polished parquet.

'Maud – please, sweetie – come away,' Yvette said, her voice sounding almost tearful. It was not that Maud was pulling against her, only she could sense the power of her anger ready to burst forward and felt, if it did, she would not be able to restrain her and Maud would be lost.

'His business opportunities,' Maud hissed. 'His trip to America. How lucky that I was there to teach his "sister" better English. Yvette, take me away before I start to scream.' Maud turned back towards the kitchen, and without any more ado let herself be led out of the house, the butler staying two steps behind the women until they were safe in the night and the door was locked and bolted behind them.

When dinner was over and the guests were being ushered back into the drawing room, the Countess claimed Tanya's arm. 'Sweetness, I have a new acquisition to show you, do let me steal you away.' She ushered her into the morning room where they had met M. Beauclerc. There was a man in a grey suit sitting on the sofa, a round hat in his hands. As the ladies entered he got to his feet, but the Countess waved him back.

'Honey, this is Mr Carter of the Pinkerton Agency. We had a very interesting chat with a new friend of Yvette's this evening and the law is a no-go, I'm afraid.'

'She found him? Oh, she is a wonder! But you know Maud is innocent?'

'Oh, as the day is long, dear. But this fellow Henri refuses to say anything to the police.'

'And did you send people to Rue de Seine? Did you find the stones?'

The Countess smiled. 'It was worth a try, but no, they were not there.' She turned towards Carter. 'Your people left no sign the place had been searched?'

'None, ma'am.'

Tanya was confused. They had not found the diamonds and this Henri would not talk to the police – and yet the Countess looked perfectly content.

'We have a chance to play the long game,' the Countess continued. 'It seems Morel is going to deliver himself into our hands.'

'I don't understand.'

'Well then, shush kitten, and we shall explain. Mr Carter? You OK if he goes in English?' Tanya nodded.

'There are limits to what we can do in Europe, ma'am,' Carter said. 'Taking a known criminal like Henri off the street and getting him to talk – well, that's one thing, but it wouldn't do for us to give the same treatment to a fellow like Morel. He hasn't pulled any scams we can pin on him in Paris and he's spent freely enough around town to make some friends. Even this Miss Priddy woman . . .'

'Prideux,' Tanya said.

'Prideux,' he gave a respectful nod. 'From what I hear, her son the solicitor said there was no use chasing the money, and we've asked around about the accident. No one saw anything suspicious, and we can't find anyone who saw her with Morel that night. No surprise there – he's not dumb, but I'm just saying he can't be touched on that.' He cleared his throat and Tanya waited without speaking. 'Now he plans to get a boat over to New York at the end of the month. There our life will be a lot easier. We can reverse-scam him. We've the people for it, the contacts, and we can take him for every penny he's got. Perhaps if we're lucky we'll even get the big stone back. Take it as security on some deal.' Tanya noticed he had a light baritone, the same camel colour as his overcoat. 'There's no way to stop him selling a few stones in Rheims, but we'll get back what's owed to the Countess in the end.'

'That is all?' Tanya said.

The Countess laughed. 'Honey, it's perfect! The fooler fixed. We'll make him good and uncomfortable, and I'll get my money back. Shame about the grand stone, but if Henri is as good as they say he is, and we con Morel out of it in New York, then perhaps I can make something pretty out of it.'

Tanya shook her head. 'And that is all?'

Mr Carter frowned as if she was making a joke he couldn't quite understand. 'The money will be recovered and he'll be sorry he took the stones. That's what we want. Sure, if we took him to the law he might get his neck stretched, but that's not going to happen, like the lady says, and I can't go round assassinating people, Miss Koltsova. Not in Europe at any rate!' The Countess made a little cooing noise between amusement and sympathy.

Tanya spoke quietly, though there was a shimmer of distress in her voice. 'They threw Maud in the river. They told her friends she was a thief then a suicide. I ask you again: *is that all?*'

Mr Carter stroked his smooth chin. 'I suppose, given Miss Heighton's honesty in coming to you, ma'am, and at some risk to herself . . . a reward of some sort perhaps?'

'Of course. I shall arrange something nice,' Madame de Civray said in her usual bright voice. Tanya was disgusted, but the Countess was not even looking at her. 'Oh, and while we are tidying things up . . .' She rang the bell and her butler appeared in the doorway. 'Tell her to come in now, Arthur.'

A maid, certainly less than twenty with thick ankles and apple cheeks, was ushered into the room. She looked very frightened. 'You wished to see me, Madame?'

'I did, dear. I'm afraid you'll have to leave my service at once. You will go tonight, and I will not be giving you a recommendation to future employers.' From her tone of voice you'd have guessed she was sharing plans for some surprise party for her children.

The girl went white and her eyes became watery. 'But, Madame . . . ? If I have not pleased you I will work harder. Please, Madame. My mother, my little brother all rely on my wages here. If you send me away without a reference, what shall I do?'

'You should have thought of that before you entertained gentlemen callers here, shouldn't you?' The girl covered her mouth with her hand and the tears began to run down her face. 'You have my sympathy, honey, but what would it look like if I were to just let you go with a thank you and a recommendation? I would be inviting riot into my home. Mr Carter, would you be so kind as to watch her pack and check her luggage in case she takes any souvenirs?'

Mr Carter stood up and placed his hand on the girl's shoulder. She looked up at him, astonished and afraid.

'Come on, dear,' he said, and steered her out of the room. The girl herself seemed too stunned at the sudden collapse of her world to speak.

The Countess stood and gave herself a little shake. 'There, that is done. Oh, I shall enjoy hearing all about Morel's plans for New York.'

'*She* let Morel into your house?' Tanya said.

The Countess smoothed her gloves up her arm. 'Yes, honey. I

was wondering, you see, taking Maud in like that . . . all the preparation. They knew exactly what they wanted and where it was. The cook wormed the truth out of Odette. That she had been walking out with a gentleman and had brought him here. Not that any of them know about the tiara being plucked, of course.' She took Tanya's arm. 'If they ask you, honey, you can say I was showing you that little Morisot in the corner.'

Tanya pulled away. 'Perhaps you can tell them I am still lost in admiration for a few moments more.'

The Countess shrugged. 'If you wish, dear.' She left the room and the butler slipped in through the door to wait with Tanya. His eyes were fixed straight ahead and his hands clasped behind his back.

'Arthur, are there writing materials I may use in this desk?'

'Yes, miss.'

She opened the drawer and found a plain sheet and envelope and a slim fountain pen. Hoping she would ruin the nib forever, she wrote, *To whomsoever it may concern, I give this gift to* . . . 'What is that girl's name, Arthur?'

'Odette, miss. Odette Suchet.'

. . . *Odette Suchet, to do with as she will.* She unfastened a bracelet at her wrist, fumbling a little with her evening gloves and her indignation, then added to the page, *It is a bracelet of diamonds and sapphires.* She signed the note and added her Paris address below, then put note and bracelet into an envelope and handed it to Arthur.

'See that this reaches her, please, Arthur, and that Mr Carter does not take it back. Have I made myself clear?'

He tucked it into the inside pocket of his coat and bowed to her. 'Perfectly, Miss Koltsova.'

Maud hardly heard Yvette wishing her good night. Every word that Henri had said about Morel burned in her, made her drunk. How pleased he must have been with himself, ready to wander out of town whenever they liked and start their new life in America, stepping over her corpse to do it without a thought. If they thought of her now it was as a nothing, carried away by the river with the rest of the rubbish. They were there now, untouchable in the lamplight, scraping their knives on the Countess's plates and drinking her wine while Maud remained here, neither dead nor alive.

She undressed and slid shivering under the sheets and again dreamed of her drowning. She must have cried out in her sleep because when she woke suddenly, she found one of Suzanne's waifs standing in her doorway. He was a good-looking young man in his twenties, though the flesh on his face looked rather loose and pale, his eyes yellowish. She started.

'Don't be afraid! I heard you shout and I wanted to see you were not needing help. I am Amedeo.' He put out his hand and smiled. His Italian accent was heavy, curling his words and throwing them at odd angles into the air.

'I recognise your voice. You're the Dante scholar?' She sat up in bed and took his hand. It did not seem shocking now, this man wandering into her bedroom in the middle of the night and she found she was not frightened.

'I am!' He stared at her thoughtfully. 'You look ill.'

'So do you.'

'Ha! Perhaps! But I am not really drunk yet. I came looking for Suzanne. When I find her she will give me money to get drunk and I will be well again. You need nothing?'

Maud shook her head and he shrugged and began to saunter back towards the door.

'Amedeo?'

'Yes, young lady?'

'What does Dante say of revenge?'

He turned back. 'That it is a sin. A sin of anger, and those who commit it are surrounded by a rank fog, forever tearing each other apart or gnawing at their own limbs. They are trapped in the marsh.' He sighed. 'I shall not waste the poetry on you if you do not speak Italian. I shall tell you instead what my mother told me when I came home from school covered in bruises from the bullies there.'

'What did she say?'

'To forget a wrong is the best revenge. But she was not right. Some wrong you must get a hot blade into it, take out the poison matter even if it costs you a little flesh. She said I must trust in God – but why should I trust Him to punish my enemies? He let them hurt me in the first place. Good night, young lady.'

CHAPTER 12

20 January 1910

*M*AUD WAS WOKEN BY TANYA, STILL UPSET AND carrying a basket of pastries. The young women ate them sitting on the bed while Sasha made coffee on the stove, Tanya biting down angrily on each one and refusing to talk until Maud said she could eat nothing else. Only then did they exchange their stories of the previous evening. When Maud had heard Tanya spit out the scheme the Countess and the Pinkerton man had dreamed up, she rested her chin on her knees.

'Yvette thought I was going to strike Madame de Civray last night,' she said.

'I wish you had,' Tanya replied. 'It would make me happy. A reward, she says! Like a bone for a dog.'

'The butler would have broken my arm.' Maud put her hand out in front of her and it did not shake. 'You have to go to Lafond's, Tanya. I shall take a trip to Printemps this morning. I need to buy something with a veil.' She saw the question in the tilt of Tanya's chin. 'I don't want anyone from the Académie to see me and ask questions.'

Tanya wiped the flakes of pastry slowly from her dress. 'You are not going home then, Maud? The Countess is a selfish monster, but if there is nothing to be done here . . . I would happily pay your fare if that would be of help.'

'Are you going to tell me to go home and forget it ever happened as well, Tanya?'

'What else can be done?' Maud said nothing. 'It makes me afraid for you, Maud.'

'Why?'

'You are too calm. Too quiet. I feel as if you have made some decision and you are not telling me what it is. Oh Maud, it was such a brief flowering you had. Those few weeks when you were with the Morels, you bloomed. You were easy to be with, less serious, and now there is this . . . I wish to God I had never taken you to Miss Harris.'

'Don't you think in a way it is funny, Tanya? I spent the happiest weeks of my life with people who intended to murder me from the start. I think that's funny.'

'No, it's not,' Tanya whispered fiercely. 'It's tragic. And don't tell me those are different sides of the same coin. I shall shriek here and now if you do.'

Maud shrugged. 'I thought that talking to the Countess, letting her know I was innocent would make me feel easier, but it hasn't. *They* are still out there in the world, and the Countess's answer, the plan of her little men in long coats – it's not enough for me. Morel has to suffer and he has to know why.'

Tanya took her hands between her own. 'You have a life. You have talent. Of course it is wrong, it is unjust, but you know life is not fair. Leave them to God.'

'No. I told you – it's not enough. You know that. And I *don't* have a life, Tanya. I'm still drowned in the river somehow and I need to get out.' She spoke softly and simply as if she were reciting her plans for the day – a walk in the park, a little sketching, revenge.

'And will this . . . punishment – will it help you?'

'I don't know. It cannot make me worse.'

Tanya stood up quickly and a small leather notebook fell from her pocket onto the bed. Maud picked it up ready to hand it to her, but something in Tanya's expression made her curious and she opened the pages. Tanya protested, but seeing it was already too late turned away to pick up her hat from the armchair. Maud looked through the pages and saw neat lists of figures of groceries and rents, the prices of meals in the cheaper restaurants. 'Tanya?'

'Do you remember what Valadon said, that I will never be an artist because I like things to be pretty?'

Maud handed the notebook back to her. 'I do.'

'Well, it's true. But I think wanting things to be pretty might make me some money. Portraits. Ones of wives and children in comfortable homes that might pay five hundred francs a time. I have been about it half the night and it seems to me that five hundred francs can buy a great deal.' She looked both proud and a little ashamed, and frightened too that Maud would laugh at her. 'I know that it is a lot for a portrait, but I think men would rather have me in their home, painting their families, than most other artists.' She looked at the neat lists of figures again, then touched the jewelled pin at her throat. 'Am I being stupid?'

'Five hundred francs does buy a great deal, Tanya. And many husbands might think of hiring you where they would not hire anyone else.' Maud got out of the bed and the world did not spin or lurch. She felt as if she had new black blood in her veins. 'I am going to see Miss Harris later this morning.'

Tanya put the notebook back into her pocket. 'Do you wish me to come with you?'

'No, this I had better do by myself. And in your lists, Tanya, put something aside for sickness or accident.'

Charlotte was with Miss Harris going through the accounts when Maud called, and though she had thought she would speak to Miss Harris alone, she remembered what Charlotte had said about Morel smiling too much and invited her to stay. They had heard nothing from the Morels about her supposed disgrace and so greeted her with pleasure. Miss Harris seemed a little disappointed when Maud lifted her veil and Miss Harris noticed she still looked rather drawn. Then Maud began her story. It felt as if she were relating someone else's history. Once or twice Miss Harris put her hands together, palm to palm, and lifted the fingertips to her lips. It was something between a prayer and an attempt to stifle an exclamation.

When Maud had finished speaking, Miss Harris was silent for some time. Then she reached out to take Maud's hand across the table.

'Oh Miss Heighton! I am so sorry.'

Maud wondered whether, if the Countess had offered that generous sympathy, she might be back in England by now.

'I want justice, Miss Harris,' she said. 'And I would like you to help me.'

Miss Harris still held her hand. 'He is leaving Paris, you say? The Countess intends to reclaim her money from him there before he can do more harm? Well, my dear. Certainly it seems that justice has been denied you in this world, but you shall have it in the next.' Maud tried to pull her hand away, but Miss Harris kept hold of her. 'No, my dear. You shall hear me. There is nothing – *nothing*

– you can do to this man that will compare with the agony he will feel when he finds himself judged before his Creator. His sufferings will be terrible. He will see what he has done in God's Holy Light and you will pity him. Yes, you shall. Pray for him, Miss Heighton. That is my advice. Go home, lead a good and useful life and pray for them both. They have damned themselves. God has saved you for some purpose, I am sure, but I am just as sure it was not to take revenge on the Morels. This is my advice to you, dear Miss Heighton. I shall not help you in any other way.'

Maud's hand was released. She stood and curtsied to Miss Harris with the greatest respect, but left without saying another word.

She walked across Paris. The rain had been steady all day but rather than return to her grey room in Montmartre she walked the length of the Champs Élysées, passing the twin domes of the Grand and Petit Palais and crossing Place de la Concorde. She did not look at the place where Sylvie had shown her the stolen brooch or search for any sign of where Mme Prideux had died. The cars raced by her and the high omnibuses teetered past. When she crossed the river on the Solferino Bridge the embankments became quieter. The rain persisted but the cafés were still full, men and women going about their sanctioned public lives under the striped awnings and behind low, burning braziers. Some of the men stared, tried to speak to her, but she simply looked over the tops of their heads and they melted back into the crowds. She reached the Quai Conti, but only when she was at the bottom of Rue de Seine did she hesitate. Her chest ached again, a dark flowering. She could walk past the door, the windows, and glance up. If, at that moment someone – Miss Harris, Tanya or Yvette – had happened on her and offered her again their comfort and friendship, perhaps she would have left Paris that evening and she would have been saved. But no one came.

She walked down the street looking straight ahead of her, crossed the Boulevard Saint-Germain, then just as she came opposite the house, she looked up and froze. Sylvie was standing in the window with her back to it, facing into the room. She still *is*, Maud thought. She still is when I am not there. How can that be? Knowing that Sylvie was in the Countess's house had been pain enough, but to see her – her white neck with the blond hair gathered on top of her head – it was pain beyond all imagining. Then *he* appeared at her side. Morel. He took her in his arms and held her. Sylvie was laughing, her head thrown back. They are happy because I am dead, Maud thought. The idea seemed to take the air from her. Morel. The man who had thrown her into the water without a qualm, now wrapped around Sylvie and murmuring into her neck, telling her the places they would go with the money they had stolen, the wonderful, delightful life they would have together now Maud was rotting in the Seine and he had his fist full of diamonds.

Morel seemed to feel something – he lifted his head and glanced out of the window, but Maud was already gone, dragging her bitter heart with her. As she walked away, the sellers of the afternoon newspapers began to call out for custom. 'The waters are rising! The river mounts!'

When she returned to the room she was soaked to the skin. At first she didn't see Charlotte sitting by the stove with her legs crossed. She was smoking a cigarette, and on her knee was propped a book; it had the tell-tale thin paper and gilded edges of a Bible. She looked up at Maud's bedraggled form.

'I've lit the stove – I hope that's not a problem. The room was freezing and I wasn't sure how long I'd have to wait.'

'Of course,' Maud said, taking off the veiled hat and putting it on the bed. 'What can I do for you, Miss . . .'

'Just call me Charlotte,' the woman said, waving the cigarette and looking back down to her reading. 'It will wait. Put something dry on before you get sick again.'

Maud did so, glancing at her visitor out of the corner of her eye as she changed out of her wet clothes. Charlotte was dressed, as ever, in black and wore thick-soled shoes. Her forehead was a little lined and Maud wondered if she could be as much as forty. When she had dressed, Maud dragged one of the wicker chairs over so she could sit opposite Charlotte by the fire. Charlotte closed her Bible and reached behind her chair, hauling onto her knee a basket complete with red gingham cover and took out a flask and bread and butter wrapped in greaseproof paper. Without saying anything she poured out milky tea into one of the china cups she had brought with her and handed it to Maud, along with one of the parcels of bread and butter. Then, when she had served herself, she said, 'Miss Heighton, I wish you to know first of all that Miss Harris has done more good in this world than any other individual I have ever met.'

'I understand,' Maud said. She sipped the tea and a wave of nostalgia broke over her so sudden and complete it seemed an outside force. She thought of the tea room in Reeth where her mother had taken her once when she was a child, the charabanc ride up the North Yorkshire Dales and the shifting banks of green on the moor. It lasted only a moment and then she was back in her grey Paris room and listening to Charlotte.

'She has brought more lost souls to God than you can imagine.

Creatures that no one else would think worth a moment of their time have become good and useful members of their community. She has, through nothing but patience and kindness, turned drunks into true believers, whores into nurses. Even those who are still too lost in their own misery to conceive of a God who loves them will follow *her* into church because she believes – and they believe in her. She does not preach. She prays for them and offers them her love, no matter how miserable their condition. I am blessed indeed to see what wonders God can work through her.'

Maud had nothing to say in reply, but continued to drink her tea and watch her. Charlotte leaned forward, lifting her index finger: 'And she is right, absolutely right that you should leave the Morels to God and pray for them, *but* . . .'

Maud looked at her over the edge of her teacup. 'But you are not Miss Harris?'

Charlotte sat back again, her plain face twisted with a half-smile. 'Indeed, I am not.' She put her tea onto the floor and from the basket produced a notebook. 'Explain to me what you have in mind.'

Maud reached for the bread and butter. 'I mean to haunt him.'

When Yvette swung into the room an hour later, Charlotte had finished taking her notes. She smiled with real affection at the model and when Yvette crossed the room to kiss her, lifted up her cheek to receive the salutation with a slight blush.

'There is still a good English community at Rheims,' she said to Maud. 'We have sent a number of girls there who needed to leave Paris and its associations behind them and they will have made friends. Every community relies on shared intelligence.'

'And they will have the necessary authority?'

'Naturally,' Charlotte said, packing her basket again. 'They are trusted. And we shall tell them to make it clear that if anyone buys those diamonds, their names will become mud amongst all of our rich American and English donors. And our Russian ones,' she added with a vague smile. 'It is easy to do the same in Paris. We shall shut all the doors to him and leave him loose on the streets for you to hunt.'

Maud stood to shake her hand and see her to the door. It was strange how these habits of politeness re-emerged in the company of another middle-class Englishwoman.

'Thank you.'

The woman shook her head. 'Do not. I suspect it is weak of me to assist you, but I cannot help myself, and as I have the nature God gave me, I suppose He must have some plan of which I know nothing. Or perhaps He means to test us and we are failing.'

Yvette had thrown herself down on the bed and waved as Charlotte left them. She had snatched up one of the packets of bread and butter and now ate it lying on her back and staring up at the ceiling while Maud told her what Madame de Civray had said to Tanya, and then began to explain her own plans.

'Morel goes to Rheims tomorrow. He returns on the twenty-third. If Charlotte is as successful as she hopes, he won't be able to sell the diamonds. And while the Pinkertons may not be able to do anything illegal in France, I can. I am a ghost, after all.' Perhaps she expected Yvette to protest in some way at this point, but she did not, just waited for Maud to continue. 'I want to hire a pick-pocket to steal them back from him and frighten him at the same time. I want him to wonder if he is being pursued.' She sat down on the bed. 'I saw him this afternoon in the window at Rue de Seine.' And when Yvette turned to stare at her: 'I know I shouldn't have gone. Don't say it. He looked so happy, so pleased with himself.'

'He won't stay like that if the Pinkertons have their way. He'll end up ruined,' Yvette said evenly.

'It's not enough. I want him to be frightened. Scared. And for as long as I can keep him that way.'

Yvette took her hand, wound her fingers around Maud's and unravelled them again as if playing with a toy. 'We want him punished too, Maud. Tanya and I. But we don't want you to put yourself in danger again. You don't care about that though, do you?'

'I'd drag him down to hell myself if I could, even if I had to stay there with him.'

'So you want to find a pick-pocket?'

'Yes.' There was a long pause.

'But you don't ask me for an introduction.'

'I didn't like to assume.'

Yvette groaned and threw herself backwards onto the bed. 'Oh Maud! You've become an avenging angel but kept the manners of an English miss and a proper sense of decorum to your inferiors.'

'You're not my inferior, Yvette. I know that,' Maud said.

'You thought I was when you first saw me. You proper English girls always do. More meat to be put up on the dais and stared at. Don't be sorry. If we worried about the soul of every person we saw on the street, we'd go mad.' Yvette clambered out of the bed and went to the cracked mirror to peer at herself. She saw lines beginning at the corners of her eyes. 'I can help you. I would tell you to stay quiet and let me do the talking, but that's never a problem with you. Are you strong enough for Rue Lepic after all your wanderings?'

'Now?'

'Now. Before I change my mind.'

CHAPTER 13

*R*UE LEPIC WAS THE STEEP NARROW ROAD THAT LED to the summit of Montmartre, kinking and twisting up the hill. It seemed to get poorer and dirtier with every step climbed until suddenly they turned a corner and everything changed. They were surrounded by neat gardens in their winter rest, fruit trees and comfortable freshly painted villas. The street-lamps were being lit, and new patches of light and shadow lifted and glowed along the damp road. A man with long hair and velvet trousers sauntered past and nodded at Yvette. Maud recognised him, his grubby silk scarf. He was one of the men she had seen on the Boulevard Saint-Michel selling his sketches for two francs a time. He looked too old to be a student. Perhaps he was another of these men who had come to Paris in their youth and never escaped it. Maud shivered. To be trapped in Paris seemed no better to her than being trapped in her father's home. As they passed the *Lapin Agile* on Rue Saint-Vincent they heard a great shout of laughter from inside. Someone was singing.

Yvette didn't look round and Maud followed, watching her. The model's usual animation seemed to be draining away. She didn't look at the people passing her and her shoulders were hunched. There had been something of this in her that evening in the bar behind Les Halles, but this was different. She was not playing at anything now; the strain showed on her thin face and made her look older. She turned into Rue des Saules and the respectable country village disappeared like fog. Here the apartment buildings were crushed and dirty, windows broken and boarded up with ragged-edged planks. In the thickening darkness, small groups of men and women watched them from the doorways and steps. The women wore clogs and skirts that showed their ankles, their hair short and framing their faces in straight black lines. The men were young in flat caps and striped shirts, coloured handkerchiefs tied around their throats. The uniform of the *apaches*.

In the first boarding-house Maud had lived in, before she learned the brutal truths of Paris economy and moved somewhere colder and cheaper, there had been a rather silly middle-aged English couple who had invited her on a spree one evening. She had been lonely enough to accept and watched her money disappear in a couple of second-rate hostelries. The couple were determined to see the *real* Paris, and they had taken her to a restaurant where they claimed all the great writers of the city came to dine. Maud thought the clientèle were mostly tourists and the *escargots* were likely made of cat. Their pièce-de-résistance was to take her to an *apache* club. It was an over-priced and soulless little dance hall with rude waiters and a dispirited band, but it delighted them – and when a couple of young men fought on the dance floor for the attentions of a girl, they looked as if they would burst with excitement. The fight appeared unconvincing to Maud, and the gendarmes who arrived to break it up and throw the gawking English out onto the street did not make her think it was any more genuine. Their uniforms didn't fit. Maud had seen a drunk hit a woman; the hissing violence of it, the suddenness of the action, the silence of the blow. These people made too much noise to be in any genuine pain or fear. Her hosts asked if she wished to come out with them again for another evening, and she refused as politely as she could, knowing that they would take it as a sign of her fear and fragility at the wild and debauched life they had shown her, and be rather thrilled at frightening her.

These men here, talking and smoking in the muddy alleyways behind the Rue des Saules were not imitations of outlaws. What Maud had seen in that club was a blurred reproduction and here were the originals in vivid colour. The men and women she had seen at the Caveau des Innocents were older, worn with work and anxious only to distract themselves with drink and song and human warmth. Here the air crackled with calculation and suspicion and suppressed violence. One man stepped forward, his hands in his pockets. His face had a long pink scar that ran from just over his eye down to his jaw. 'Yvette. Haven't seen you in months, little sister.' He looked at Maud, and she felt him weighing her up. She was wearing her veil and gloves. 'Have you brought us a chicken for the pot?'

Yvette took the knife from her pocket and opened it with a click that sounded like a gunshot in the quiet street. She spoke softly. 'I'm here to see Mother, Louis. Touch my friend here and I'll gut you like the pig you are.'

He grinned. 'Oh, Yvette with her little knife! Always ready to defend someone.' He scratched the side of his nose. 'Keep her then. We're off to the Bois to find something fatter anyway. Come with us if you like. You can watch while I throttle some gentleman walking his poodle a little late. Even give you first go of his pockets.'

A young woman appeared beside him and wound her arm through his. Her face looked like an angel's, soft and clear with Prussian-blue eyes. The whites showed round the edge of them, making her face seem oddly bright, attentive. She could not have been more than fifteen. She pressed herself up close to Louis's side. When she spoke, her voice was sharp-edged and her pretty face became older and harder.

'Your real mummy hasn't come to find you yet, Yvette? What was she – a princess? A lady? No sign of her after all these years? Remember the stories you used to tell us – how she was going to take us all away in a white carriage. Poor old Yvette. They never came to look for you, did they?' She gazed up at Louis and whined, 'She was always crazy, Louis. Don't let her come.'

Yvette lifted her chin. 'Don't fret yourself, Nina. I wouldn't go anywhere with *him*.'

He put his arm around the girl's waist and she chirruped with pleasure like a cat grateful for its feed. 'Too right. Leave her to her pipes and books till she has to earn her smoke money on her back. Maybe I'll let you be one of my girls if you're good.'

'Get out of my way, Louis.'

He stood back slowly to let them pass into the yard. 'See you soon, sister. You're starting to look old, you know. Another five years and you'll be selling it for a franc a time with my other pets.' He laughed and returned to the group he'd been standing with at the kerb, taking the girl along with him.

Maud looked sideways at Yvette. Her eyes were bright and her face a little flushed. 'Come on.'

She took her through a dirty yard into a kitchen that opened straight off the cobbles. The table was scrubbed and the floor was being swept by a child about seven years of age dressed in a wool shift but bare-footed despite the season. At the head of the table sat a thin middle-aged female with black buttoned boots and a plum silk dress. It was of an old-fashioned style and for a second Maud was struck by her resemblance to Tanya's aunt Vera. This woman seemed like the dark face of the same coin. She was drinking tea from a delicate service decorated with birds of paradise. She looked up when she heard them approach and smiled. Her lips were dark red, and she spread them to show her yellow teeth.

'Yvette! How nice. And you've brought a friend.'

Yvette clicked the knife shut and slipped it back into her pocket. '*Maman.* I hope you are well.'

Maud did as she was told and took no part in the negotiations other than nod her assent to the price agreed and offer the necessary advance. There was a bitumen delight in offering up her stock of money so easily, without noting each small amount paid and making impossible calculations for her keep in the future. This had to be done and this was the cost. The future would take care of itself.

Much of the discussion between Yvette and the woman in purple she did not understand. They spoke in a French Maud did not recognise – some sort of slang that was slippery and bewildering. The money was folded and placed in an embossed silver purse. The woman nodded to them and returned to sipping her tea with her little finger crooked away from the cup. The streets outside were quiet – the *apaches*, it seemed, had left for the hunt.

Yvette did not speak to her again until they had reached Place du Tertre. She hesitated there, looking at the cafés, the noise and light biting away at the wintry edges of the square, but when Maud asked if she wished to visit one of them, she shook her head. 'I need to breathe.' She took Maud instead to the terrace below the Sacré Coeur, and there they took possession of one of the benches that faced away from the new cathedral, its shocking white and squeezed domes ghostly behind them. Maud opened her umbrella, not a rich silk and tortoiseshell beauty like Tanya's but something more modest from Printemps, and held it over both of them. Their bodies touched shoulder to thigh and warmed each other. Yvette lit a cigarette and folded her arm across her chest. 'Go on then. Ask.'

'Is that your mother?'

She turned away, looking towards the west of the city. 'I don't know. She always said she was, but she takes in babies from time to time for a fee. The little ones always work as pick-pockets for her. I did until I was thirteen.'

'Like Fagin.' Yvette said nothing and Maud glanced at her. 'He's a character in a book, *Oliver Twist*, by Dickens.'

'I know who Fagin is, Maud. The nuns taught us to read. That's where all that . . . what Nina was saying came from. The stories I used to tell of the rich men and women coming to save us from life on the Butte.'

Maud thought of Yvette as a child telling stories about the heroes who were going to rescue her and her playmates, thought how often she had woken in her sickness to see her at the end of her bed with a book in her hands, thought of her attention and mimicry in the studio, of her retreats into the peace and warmth of opium. Maud had hidden from her misery in drawing, in paint; Yvette obviously had her methods of escape too.

'I never thought of you as having family, Yvette.'

'Thought I just sprang up with the weeds from between the cobblestones, did you?'

'I suppose I did in a way.'

Yvette grunted. 'It's not much of a family. *Maman* rules a little shit-heap and sells souls to do it. I thought I was better than that, but who knows. Maybe I will end up back there.' Maud said nothing. 'Thanks for not telling me I'm wrong.'

'I hope you are, but sometimes it takes chance or accident to cut our moorings.'

Yvette glowered out over the city like an angry angel. 'I'm not sure I believe it is ever possible. We are all set on a course the first day we open our eyes. Tanya with her money, you so proper and good. I shall earn what I can and spend it on dope, remembering books and dreaming myself into them. I am only putting off what has to happen by keeping away from the dens now.'

Maud followed her gaze. The city was coming alive with light, its unnatural brilliance affronting the darkness, but the wind and rain still blew across it in waves. 'I have been to the Caveau des Innocents.'

'And within a day you are shaking hands with Charlotte and seeing her out. You can't escape what you are.'

Maud watched her profile, the cigarette smoke tugged away from her lips in the wind and thought of Sylvie in the graveyard, her glamour, her genteelly faked craving for opium that had so convinced Maud. She breathed in deeply as she watched the rain falling through the lamplight, then spoke. 'After my father died and my step-mother left town, I set the fire that burned down the warehouse and our old house.' Yvette turned away from the city and stared at her. Maud blinked rapidly but continued. 'Everyone was telling me to stop putting off the inevitable and join my brother's household. I could not paint well enough to earn my own living and I had no other talents. I should become a wife and mother. But I just couldn't – I couldn't believe that was the only choice. It seemed so wrong. And I hated that house. Then I thought about the fire and it seemed like the only thing to do.'

Yvette put out her cigarette, grinding the butt into the damp ground. It was some time before she spoke and when she did it was almost in a whisper. 'Were you frightened?'

It came back to Maud at once, the smell of burning wood, the sound of her own footsteps hurrying through the empty house once the fire had caught. 'Yes. I had to go back up the stairs after I had set it going and wait for the smoke to reach me. I thought that would make it look more real. And they did believe me, no one thought for a second I could have started it. Poor Maud, running into the street in her dressing-gown and bare feet to escape the flames.'

'But you were free?' Maud nodded. 'I don't think I have anything to burn down.' Yvette turned back towards the city and Maud said nothing. She had always told herself that she set the fire for the insurance, now she wondered if that were true. Someone would have bought the property at some point. She had burned it because she loathed it, because under her mild ways and respectable speech Maud was thwarted, indignant and shimmering with rage. The fire had burned so hot the air seemed to ripple. She remembered what Valadon had said, how her fists were clenched and sore when she woke up in the mornings. Maud thought of herself as a good woman, but now she was beginning to wonder. She wished she still believed in God, believed in Him with all that passionate conviction of Miss Harris or Charlotte. Then she could pray for Yvette and herself and think it would do some good.

'You still want this, Maud? I can call it off if you want.'

She stared out over the soaking city. 'It is what I want. I will not go meekly back to England with him free and happy.'

'Then I had better explain what we agreed.'

CHAPTER 14

CHRISTIAN MOREL LEFT FOR RHEIMS A HAPPY MAN. HE made himself comfortable in the first-class compartment and gazed smugly at his reflection in the polished glass as the train pulled away. He had planned this as a jaunt; a little pleasure trip to ease his mind now the task of keeping a close watch on Henri was done. Still, putting constant pressure on the old codger had done some good. He had done the recutting and polishing faster than Morel could have hoped, and done it well in spite of his indignation. What's more, stealing from the Countess had brought extra benefits. Her gratitude to him for returning the tiara discreetly and with due deference meant he had now made some very valuable contacts with rich Americans. America was the thing. A new, ambitious nation not dead and dried up like France, crisped, its juices all run out and lapped up before Christian had had more than a taste of it. Then he frowned, and still watching himself in the glass, raised one eyebrow. The brilliant man of business considers. Perhaps he should abandon the name Morel in Paris and disappear into that vast new continent as Gravot again. He had heard a couple of men in the club talking about Los Angeles as a place that looked likely to boom. And did he really want to swap Paris for the constrictions of Boston? He and Sylvie would travel quietly to New York, then head out west, sell the great stone in Chicago and arrive on the Pacific Coast like heroes. Yes, let Morel live and die in Paris. He stroked his chin. He was clean-shaven, a modern man. All the ambitious young men in America would recognise him as one of their own.

He went to the best jeweller in Rheims straight from the station with his story ready and waiting on the tip of his smooth tongue. He planned to say he was selling the bracelet on behalf of his sister, a woman of fashion in Paris who had accepted it from an admirer. Now the admirer was replaced by a respectable husband and it would be better if his sister became a wife with an equally respectable bundle of banknotes rather than another man's jewels. They would take it from him with a vague smile, but then seeing the quality and clarity of the stones their hands would twitch to close round it. He would see the gulp of desire in their throats, the sheen in their eyes as they imagined the potential profit.

He took the tram to Place Royale rehearsing these pleasant conversations in his mind. He would seem a little uncertain when the first price was offered. He would say perhaps he should try another of the jewellers in the city, these happy few who supplied the champagne merchants with their diamonds and rubies. The jeweller would begin to sweat and gradually increase his price until he got to a reasonable amount – fifty thousand francs or so. Morel would then agree and everyone would be delighted with their bargain.

He hopped down from the tram and tipped his hat to the statue of the old King watching the square and providing a perch for the pigeons to watch it too, and chose his first target – an elegant little shop tucked into the corner of the square with a discreet window display of luxury and taste. The doorbell rang out and the girl behind the counter smiled at him sweetly as he pushed the door open, wished him good morning and asked if she could show him anything. She had the trace of a foreign accent which reminded him suddenly of Maud, her precise and mannered French. It almost made him stumble, but as soon as he began his story of the sister and the admirer his tongue gained its usual fluency. Her expression did not change, but there was somehow a slight chill in the air. He produced the bracelet, uncoiling it from a velvet pouch he kept in his breast-pocket. She nodded at it, but did not reach out to take it. Instead she rang a tiny brass bell on the counter and an old gentleman with powdery skin and wearing a black suit emerged from a door behind the counter. He had a slight stoop and the flesh hung from his thin face in loose pouches.

The young girl moved away, only very lightly touching his old liver-spotted hand as she passed. The old man glanced at the bracelet and at once came that tell-tale swallow. It was as obvious as licking his lips. He put his hand out and took it, then for fully five minutes examined the stones. Christian began to feel impatient. There could be no doubt about the quality of the stones, and he knew he looked like a respectable man, a man of means – the sort of man who would inspire trust in a well-brought-up Englishwoman, in fact. That he had proved in the last few weeks. The old goat should have named a price already, or at least be making himself friendly.

Christian never thought about his father when he could avoid it, or about his father's death, but sometimes when he was tired or under some sudden strain the images would roll back over him. For a moment, the bracelet in the old man's hands changed, became those half-remembered gleams smeared in his father's blood. He was there again. The crack of gunfire in the distance and the caustic smell of smoke from burning buildings. Petrol thrown onto the barricades and ignited – the stink of it clung to him. He wondered if the old man examining the diamonds could smell it. He felt his mother's hand – he had struggled to hang onto her when she screamed and started running across the square. He would have run the other way, away from the man kneeling over his father's corpse but he had to follow her so he did. He looked away from the man in the shop, tried to concentrate on the mosaic borders in blue and gold that ran around the top of the walls. Instead he saw the woman holding back his mother. She had the build of a peasant and his mother, so thin and uncomfortable to lean against, had not half her strength. He threw himself at the man on the ground. He saw his father's blank and empty face, the bullet-wound in his forehead and the man pawing at his innards. The man struck at him with his elbow and he fell back slightly stunned. Perhaps he could have got up again but he did not, only watched as the man held up one of the stones. He cleared his throat. He was sweating.

The elderly jeweller looked up finally and shook his head. 'I'm sorry, sir. We are not buying today.' *But you want them*, Christian wanted to say. *I know you want them.* And without even making an offer? How could a man have got so old and still be such a fool?

'Very well. Do you recommend any other jeweller in town?'

Did he imagine it, or did the old goat's eyes flicker towards the girl? 'I respect all my colleagues in the city, but I suspect you will not find many willing to buy at this time.' He handed the bracelet back to Christian, and he seemed in the moment the diamonds left his grip, to age a little further. He had the obvious hunger of the connoisseur, but he did not want them?

Christian controlled himself enough to give them a curt nod of farewell and went back out into the square. He had the feeling that the statue of the King was looking at him with a slight sneer. It reminded him a little of Jean Prideux, that self-righteous prig. Well, he had beaten him in the end. He crossed the square and swore violently at the driver of a tiny, ridiculous little motor-car who almost knocked him from his feet, coming out of nowhere and with no regard for the safety of others. Just when he was thinking of Prideux too – it was too much. Morel had to pause for a moment, smooth down his hair and adjust his high collar to reassure himself.

The rival jewellery shop on the square was rather more brash in its display than the first place, and there were two women on the premises already gossiping as the assistant wrapped up their packages. The man behind the counter was younger. He looked prosperous, modern. Christian noticed with approval that the fittings and furnishing of the place made the one opposite look drab and stately. True, this man did not look the type to become emotional about diamonds, and would probably be a greater challenge to bargain with, but surely he could be relied on not to turn down such an excellent offer. And anyway, a little hard bargaining got Christian's blood flowing. However, the jeweller did not even look at the bracelet. As Christian fetched it from his pocket the man was already telling him he had no intention of buying today and with shocking rudeness turned away from his customer. Had a new mine been discovered? Had Rheims suddenly found a river of huge diamonds flowing through their cellars? Had they all become too simple-minded to see the bargain of a lifetime laid out in front of them?

Christian took a room at the Lion d'Or and retreated to it shivering. He had thought his business would be done by now and that he would have the whole of the next day to stretch his legs and buy foolish gifts for his wife. Instead, he ate a poor dinner that cramped his stomach all night and woke to a grey morning with the work still to do. He consulted the directory in the hotel and chose another three places of business that should, by rights, snatch the stones from him in gratitude and delight. All three turned him down.

On the second night in the hotel he tried half-heartedly to seduce a young woman who had travelled from London to see the cathedral, but something in the way she ate her food and mispronounced her French reminded him again of Maud and he lost his appetite for the game. He wondered if he were ill. The lean-to he had rented off Cours du Commerce to house Henri and his equipment had been damp with this continual rain, and he had been bored there, watching, always watching for any tricks from the resentful old devil. Locking him in at night with a bottle of red so he didn't go off on his wanderings, hiding the diamonds in their place. Then that invitation from the Countess and badgering Henri to finish the job, so that the dinner would be a celebration of their cleverness.

He had worked hard for this, Christian thought. The continual restraint, the constant watch he had to keep on his behaviour while the English miss was in their hands. There was that one night after dealing with Prideux when he had drunk whisky late into the night. Sylvie had been angry with him, afraid that drunkenness would scare off their little English bird, but Miss Heighton had slept through his stumblings and he had needed a drink. It was a strain on the nerves to arrange an accident like that, even among the chaos of Paris.

After his story-telling to Maud he had gone in search of Madame Prideux at the raggedy guest-house where she was staying and greeted her like an old friend. He embraced her and insisted on taking her out to dinner, his second that evening, and all the time sympathised, apologised. All a misunderstanding. Letters gone astray. He showed her the stubs in his chequebook to demonstrate the amounts that he had tried to send to her. They had been cashed, he said. So he had assumed all was well. He'd been a little hurt not to receive any letter from her, of course but . . . By saying very little he all but convinced her that her own son was stealing from her. Funny. It seemed she's rather believe that than believe she'd been fooled by him and Sylvie. He praised her brilliance at finding him against all the odds and learned she had seen him crossing Boulevard Saint-Germain but lost him in the crowd again and had spent the next four days asking after him until at last her questions had led her to his house on Rue de Seine.

How glad he was that she had persisted, he said, at which she blushed like a virgin. To explain his use of a new name had been trickier. He told her he associated the name of Gravot with his terrible past so had decided to take his wife's maiden name as his own. He upset himself talking to her about his struggle with those awful memories; real tears trembled on his eyelashes. It was their time in his home town that had done it, he said. He had finally visited his mother's grave and the emotion had been too much. That was why the couple had left so quickly. But he had never, never intended to desert his dear friend Mme Prideux. How could she think it? She could not have lost faith in him? Surely?

The woman was overjoyed to love him again and swallowed his charm like champagne. By the time he led her across the Champs with the promise of one more glass of wine at one of the really good restaurants to celebrate their reunion, she was happy as a child . . . then it was only a matter of waiting till the right moment when the crowd was thick and the traffic was charging by.

Christian took another drink and loosened his tie. He had not wished her to die, though he supposed in the long run, that was easier. A broken leg, the clanging of ambulances, her off her feet and out of the way for a few weeks was all that was necessary, but the car caught her and threw her in the air and into the path of another. He had walked away from the crowd gathering round the accident a little unsteadily. Killing was not easy. Maud too, the way she had tried to cling onto him. Disgusting, but necessary. It would make them rich, but still. Bloody diamonds.

He and Sylvie had arrived in Paris planning another 'investment scheme', called there by all that beautiful American money flowing through the city like the river. One only had to dip in one's hand . . . He had only seduced the maid to gather a little more information about the rich circle Madame de Civray had around her. Then he'd seen the tiara and thirsted for the stones – and the way she just left the tiara in its case in the dressing room! She didn't wear it more than once a year, the girl had said. It was more temptation than he could bear. He came home and told Sylvie. Explained his hunger. She understood and worked out how he could have the diamonds. Dear girl. All her cleverness. The opium had been his suggestion. They both enjoyed a smoke from time to time, and it added just the right thickening to the story of Maud's downfall. It had all gone beautifully. Even Lafond, who seemed sceptical at first, hadn't been able to resist the testimony of the shop girl and clerk at the pawn office. The body hadn't turned up at the morgue, but no doubt it would some day. The Countess had been an angel. Yet after two days of refusals, of seeing the diamonds turned away as if he were trying to sell paste, they began to feel like a curse.

'Hey, fella, you look like I feel.' A man in a brown suit was addressing him. Another American. Why did they always want to talk to everyone? It was as if they were constantly astonished to find other human beings on this side of the Atlantic.

'Can I buy you a drink?' the man went on. 'I've been in this town three days and it's been three days too long. There's no sense of business in this place. No vision. No sense of opportunity. And my Gawd, the food! Still, the champagne is good. I buy for the best hotels in New York, but the way these people are, you'd think they were doing *me* the favour.'

This chimed so neatly with what Morel himself thought about the place that he sat up and began to look more fondly on the man in brown. A drink or two later and he was positively cheerful. Feeling more secure now the drink was in him, he took out the little pouch with the bracelet in and showed it to his new friend.

'What were you asking for them?' Christian told him and the man laughed. 'What, that's about five thousand dollars, yeah? Hell, I know a bargain when I see one. Sure, I'll take them off you for that. We'll go to my bank first thing in the morning.'

The clouds lifted from Christian and in the little bar, the sun began to shine. They ordered another bottle to seal their deal and their new friendship when the maid approached and told the gentleman there was a phone call for him at the booth by the reception desk. He shrugged. 'Only be a minute, friend.'

Time passed. The champagne in the American's glass lost its sparkle. Who spends so long on the telephone? Christian put the bracelet back into his breast-pocket and went out into the lobby where the reception desk stood; the telephone booth behind it was empty. The clerk looked up with a polite smile and a slight gesture of the head that seemed to convey she was at her guest's disposal, of course.

'That American man – came out to take a phone call. We were having a drink together. Where is he?'

The clerk smiled, though something in her eyes was blank and unwelcoming. 'Our only American guest checked out a few minutes ago, sir.'

Morel controlled his temper and went to pay the bar bill. Each note seemed to burn as he passed it over. He hated this town.

CHAPTER 15

23 January 1910

THE TRAIN ROLLED INTO PARIS VERY LATE. MOREL had enjoyed a carriage to himself for most of the journey, but for the last slow part of the trip his privacy had been invaded by a businessman from Éperney who sighed and shook his head over the newspaper. Christian tried to ignore him, staring fixedly out into the darkness and seeing his own handsome face ghostly in the glass. Why had that damned American run off? The diamonds burned next to his heart. Five thousand dollars for the bracelet was a bargain: he would take no less than seventy thousand for the grand jewel when they reached America, yet if he had no buyers they were worth no more than cobblestones. Of all the luck! No doubt the call was from one of the American's contacts in the city and the deals he had thought dead had risen into life again. It was just a coincidence. That and the strange resistance of the diamond dealers in the city to grab a bargain. It meant nothing, it could mean nothing. He and Sylvie had been clever and this strange little trip aside there was nothing to indicate there was any sort of trouble brewing. Miss Koltsova had swallowed the story, so had the Countess and Lafond. He could smell the gunsmoke on the streets of Paris again, see the man, his hands all bloody. He wished Sylvie was with him. If this carried on, he might have one of those moments when he lost himself and came to, not knowing how much time had passed or where he was.

'The waters are rising.'

Christian turned away from his own reflection. 'I'm sorry?'

'The waters, sir. Rising. Such losses in the provinces and now it seems Paris herself is threatened. The river is already higher than it has been for ten years and the waters keep coming.'

'Indeed.'

The man was so determined to talk that even this was taken as an invitation to conversation. 'Our sins will find us out. Be assured, sir.'

'What did you say?'

'Our sins. Look at us with our electric lights and our underground railways. Motor-cars everywhere. The moving walkways at the exhibition in 1900. We rebel against Nature and she will punish us. It is the cutting down of the trees, it makes the wood spirits angry . . .'

The man's first words had sent a tremor of shock through Christian, but as he began to chatter about such nonsense, he relaxed a little. Still, high water in Paris. The river had been full when he left, but floods? Would it affect him, his hiding-place? No, not in a hundred years would the waters reach it. He felt a deep urgency to leave Paris as soon as they could. He would risk selling the bracelet there, after all. The chances of the Countess happening to hear that he had been selling diamonds was infinitesimal, and even if she did, what connection could it have to her with her tiara back in its case and the woman who had stolen it at the bottom of the river?

Finally the train drew into the station in great clouds of hissing steam and Morel descended into the usual maelstrom of porters and guards, stepping round hatboxes and breathing in the cold heavy air of a damp Parisian evening. He walked out into the square in front of the station. After hours penned up in the train his instinct was to walk, but the rain fell steadily, and spiteful gusts of wind threw handfuls of it into his face, where it stung like gravel. He unstrapped his umbrella from the travelling bag and as he stood there he heard a shout in the centre of the square.

'I've been robbed! My wallet!' A tall man in a suit the same cut as his own was turning in circles like a dog chasing its tail. He spotted a gendarme and trotted off towards him, his umbrella raised. Like most of the other gentlemen in the crowd, Christian checked his valuables were still with him, slipping his hand into the breast-pocket of his coat and feeling the diamond bracelet in its little bag.

'Madame Prideux!' A voice shouted the name almost next to his ear. He took a step back and collided with a young man in working clothes. The young man steadied him.

'Careful there, Dad!' Then he disappeared into the crowd. Morel strained to see who had shouted the name and saw another man, older, approaching a young woman on the other side of the crowd and taking her arm. Christian could not see her face, since she was veiled and had her back to him, but there was something familiar about the shape of her. Before the impression could fully form, the man and woman were lost in the crowd.

How common a name was Prideux? He had not met many, but the woman he had killed had two married sons. Had she had brothers? There were probably cousins scattered all over the country. Coincidence. The trip to Rheims, the disappointment was making him nervous and now he was seeing ghosts. The man probably didn't say Prideux at all.

Christian opened his umbrella and bent down to pick up his travelling case. He would walk, rain or no. The exercise would calm his nerves and he would take a glass in Café Procope before returning to the apartment. He did not like Sylvie to see him in this state, it made him feel weak in her eyes and he would wonder why she stayed with him; she with all her cleverness and beauty, she could pick whatever life she wished but she had come along with him, loved him when she said she had loved nothing in her life before. But she had not felt the fabric of those women's clothes, felt their last breath on her cheek.

Enough.

'Disaster approaches!' the newspaper-seller yelled as he crossed the square, pushing through the crowds. 'The water is rising!'

Christian took his time over his walk through the city and across the river. It was high, certainly. The steamers had stopped and the water seemed to be full of wreckage. Wine barrels and timber swirled along, tumbling under the Pont Neuf. It was an impressive sight in the darkness. The lamps shone down on the turbulent black waters, the noise of them had increased to a dark rush, punctuated by occasional muffled blasts as the flotsam and jetsam smashed against the stone piers. He glanced up at the pneumatic clock on the bridge and frowned; seven minutes to eleven. He was sure that he had seen the same time on the clock when he left the station. One of the other gentlemen crossing the bridge noticed his confusion.

'There's water in the works, sir. The clocks have frozen and we are out of time. Still, was there ever a better excuse for coming home a little late?'

Christian managed to smile and nod, and felt for his pocket-watch. The movement shifted his coat against him and he sensed something different about the way the cloth lay against his waistcoat. He reached into his breast-pocket, then with the sweat starting out on his forehead in spite of the chill in the air, he turned out the rest. The diamond bracelet was gone.

He looked up and saw the shape of a woman standing under one of the lamps one hundred yards behind him on the bridge. The waters must have started to disturb the gas supply, as he was sure the shadows were deeper than usual, but something about her, her figure, the way she held herself so straight was familiar – and she was staring at him. He felt a coldness wash over him, a fear that began in his body rather than his brain. Another barrel slammed against the support of the bridge and he turned instinctively towards the sound. When he looked back, the woman was gone but his fear seemed to rise in his throat. He began to walk quickly back the way he had come, examining the pavement and concentrating hard, trying to recall every face in the crowds he had passed through and refusing, refusing to think of that familiar silhouette on the bridge. Just a girl, an ordinary girl. Then he remembered the station, the shouted name, the young man with whom he had collided. His heart seemed to stutter and pound till he could not hear his own thoughts. He felt as if the smooth pavement under his feet was cracking open, showing the corpses and rot below.

When Maud arrived back at Impasse Guelma, Yvette sprang across the room and grabbed her by the shoulders. Maud just had time to notice Charlotte sitting by the stove with her cigarette and her Bible on her knee.

'Maud! You should have been here hours ago. What happened to you? We got the diamonds. Where did you go?'

Maud took off her hat and set it down on the bed and started to pull off her gloves. Her hands were stiff with the cold and the damp. It seemed strange that they were so chilled, given the warmth she had felt spreading through her ever since the moment she had seen Morel's panic.

'Look,' Yvette said, her face flushed. She pulled open the velvet pouch and Maud glanced at the string of fat square diamonds. They were a strange collection of lights. Pure reds, greens and purples flickered along their facets, made little bursts in their hearts.

'They are very pretty. I can see why he was so upset at losing them.'

Yvette looked at her, her mouth slightly open. 'You followed him? That was where you were. You followed him.' She sat down heavily on the bed then reached across and before Maud could resist, grabbed her wrist, squeezing the delicate bones until Maud winced. 'You did not die, Maud. Do not make this your only reason for living.'

She pulled her hand away. '*I* did not make this my only reason for living. *He* did.' The room was very still and the words seemed to hang in the air between them.

'Did it please you to see it? Did you think of us worrying about you at all?' Yvette's voice sounded dull and empty.

'I did not worry,' Charlotte said in English. 'I thought you would want to see him suffer rather than come here and gloat over the diamonds with Yvette.'

'What is "gloat"? I am sure I do not do it. But I wanted you to come back, Maud.'

Maud sat down and tried to put her arm around Yvette's shoulder, but the young woman shook her off and stood again. 'I am not your pet,' she said.

Maud began to undo her hair. 'No. I think more often we are yours, Tanya and I. We're the innocents and you are wise Yvette who knows everything about poverty and opium and sex and crime and laughs at us. Well, I am learning. And Yvette, you do not know what it is like to be alone. You can surround yourself with people who admire you every day. You do not know what it is to be useless and alone and thrown away like rubbish. That man made me worthless. I want to see his mind crack and I want him to think of me as it happens – and I cannot care about anything else until I do see it.' Her voice rose as she spoke until it was almost a shout.

Yvette hesitated, then threw the diamond bracelet on the bed and left the room, slamming the door behind her. Charlotte stood up with a sigh and picked the bracelet up. Maud did not move. 'What shall we do with this then?'

Maud shrugged. 'Keep it.'

Charlotte turned it between her fingers. 'It is the property of the Countess, but I suppose you do not necessarily want her to know what you are doing. Is that so?'

'I suppose not. Her Pinkertons might wish to stop me so that Morel can take his money to America and they can steal it back there. I am like Henri. They would have no scruples about tying me up in a cellar, would they? I am dead already, after all.'

Charlotte nodded, then rolled up her sleeve and fastened the bracelet around her wrist, and smoothed the material back down again to cover it. 'I shall keep it for the time being and we shall see what happens. It is in God's hands.' She reached for her cloak and wrapped it around herself, looking more like a monk than ever.

'Miss Heighton,' she said, 'I understand you feel guilty. Yvette went to a great deal of trouble to save your life, and risking it so blatantly in front of her must stir your conscience, but do not be cruel. I suspect that Yvette would much rather have been brought up in England as a respectable young woman than raised by wolves in the back streets of Paris, don't you? That she manages to make friends with anyone who is willing to speak to her is a sign of her good and generous soul, and you throw it back at her as if it is a sign of *her* lack of worth. She has saved people, Miss Heighton. She has helped Miss Harris take children out of the hands of criminals and she has helped women like you survive where many have starved, sickened and died, or gone mad and destroyed themselves with no one to care. I have to ask, what have *you* done?' She then smiled and picked up her Bible. 'Good night, Miss Heighton.'

CHAPTER 16

Flood oil on canvas 61 × 46 cm

The picture seems to show the famous floods of January 1910 which brought Paris to a standstill for some weeks. It is unusual in that, rather than show us a grand vista of the floods with recognisable landmarks in the distance, the artist concentrates on the waters themselves, looking down into them. At the centre of the frame, the base of a lamp-post stands out at an angle, and though its lamp is beyond the frame, we can see the effect of its light on the water. Here an Impressionist technique is used for a painting of concentrated intensity. The waters are made of thick strokes of pure colour in a dizzying array of tints, circling round the pure black of the base of the street-lamp and almost completely filling the frame.

Extract from the catalogue notes to the exhibition 'The Paris Winter: Anonymous Treasures from the de Civray Collection', Southwark Picture Gallery, London, 2010

24 January 1910

When Tanya arrived at the Académie on Monday morning she found Yvette sitting at the top of the narrow staircase smoking and shifting her weight from hip to hip as if dancing to some tune in her head. As soon as Tanya rounded the curve in the stairs, she jumped to her feet. 'Ah, you're here!'

'Where else should I be?' Tanya said. 'Why is the studio shut?'

Yvette reached behind herself to tap at a piece of paper pinned to the door. 'No school today! Monsieur Lafond encourages all his little students out onto the streets to see Paris face to face with disaster.'

Tanya looked behind her doubtfully. 'But it is raining.'

'Tanya, show a little spirit! Anyway, we can drive around in your car, can't we? They are talking of blowing up the Pont de l'Alma. I was worrying that your aunts wouldn't let you out today. Five minutes more and I'd have been off without you. Aren't they afraid you'll be swept away?'

'Perov has been invited to lunch to tell us all the news, but is it really so bad? I thought there were just a few streets flooded near Rue Felicien David. Lila and Vera went yesterday afternoon to see the people going up and down the streets in boats and came back with postcards. And what of Maud? She was going to meet Miss Harris on Thursday and I haven't seen her since.'

Yvette put out her cigarette and wrapped her arms around her stomach. 'She has had a victory over Morel, but I think she has gone mad. I cannot be with her today.'

Tanya was still on the step below, her eyes wide. 'Oh, you have to tell me everything!'

Yvette raised her arms. 'Oh, I shall, I shall. Only not here. Can we drive out in your little car or not?'

Tanya looked angry, then relented. 'Very well. Come along.'

Yvette ran past her and down the stairs.

Maud had found her in one of the back rooms of the Bâteau-Lavoir almost two hours after she had stormed out of Valadon's place. It was one of the better places to smoke a pipe in Montmartre, and Yvette had gone there to enjoy the utter peace and happiness of the drug, the feeling of floating through one's favourite dreams, recalling them so vividly it was like living them again, but better. No fear, only a sense of wonder and awe at the beauty dancing behind one's half-shut eyes.

She had brought with her the basket of oysters and three bottles of red wine the strange woman who ran the place always charged for entrance, and had intended on indulging herself entirely. Let Maud go mad. It was no business of hers. A day, two days. The hours would have no meaning. She knew she was supposed to model at Passage des Panoramas the next day, and that if she did not go they might not let her work there again, but at that moment she did not care.

She was welcomed in and made her way into the back room where the floor was covered with rush mats and the walls were hung with silks. Men and women reclined on the floor or on benches round the walls, their clothing loosened and their drowsy faces content or thoughtful. She was shown a space at the back wall on one of the raised hard wooden beds and settled herself. The silks were frayed at the edges. She knew that after a few pipes she would think that beautiful.

A few boys and women made their way slowly and carefully among the smokers, preparing the pipes and offering them to the customers. The men and women in the centre of the room – the wealthiest, judging by their clothes – looked quietly ecstatic. They spoke to each other, telling stories in low voices, but Yvette noticed others in the darker shadows of the room, their faces appearing from time to time in the light of the lamps. They were deeper in their affair with the drug and no longer wished to talk. One ran his fingernails through his hair, scratching at his scalp with an expression of complete bliss. Yvette felt a stab of envy and pity. The women who tended the pipes were thin. They did the skilled work of rolling pills in return for the occasional pipe from the customers. The usual rate was one for every five they prepared.

A boy approached her, the tray in his hand, and lit the lamp then picked up the pipe with a smile, offering to ready it for her. It had been a month since she last smoked. She shook her head and sat up, pressing her back to the wall and drawing up her knees, and the boy moved away to look after someone else. When Maud arrived she had still not taken one from him. The English girl took a place beside her and for a long while stared at the other smokers from the shadows just as Yvette was doing.

'I am sorry, Yvette.'

'You should be in bed. You'll get ill again.'

'I'll rest tomorrow.'

Yvette watched for a moment longer. One of the women serving in the centre of the room wasn't much older than her. Thirty, perhaps. She watched her inhale the smoke through the ivory mouthpiece of the pipe while the opium pill vaporised with the smallest hiss. Yvette wondered how long it would be before she herself surrendered and made pipes for strangers. Perhaps a little longer. 'Let's go, Maud.'

They departed with the smell of the smoke on their clothes and the curious stares of the proprietor at their back. Maud left her at the corner of the street where Yvette shared a room with two other girls who used it as a refuge between men, and Yvette watched her start the descent of Rue Lepic, that straight slim back, the falling snow pale yellow in the lamplight.

Tanya directed her patient chauffeur up and down the quayside in increasing excitement. The snow, which had been falling all night and into this morning, added to the sense of a Paris lost in some sort of strange apocalyptic dream. It clung to the bare trees along the river; the pavements had disappeared under the water. Workers were building raised walkways out of narrow planks so the people could get to and fro without a soaking. Here and there, parts of the road were closed off; the water had eaten away the ground beneath, leaving sudden pits and trenches that reached the sewers.

On the Pont de la Tournelle they clambered out of the car and were for a moment silenced by the sight of the river grown so vast and threatening. Notre Dame seemed to have shrunk, cowering from the waters. The Seine surged forward. The public bathhouses moored along the banks were already floating near the level of the embankment. They tugged at their moorings, fighting the speed and strength of the current. Standing in the open, Tanya could see the wreckage in the water – great planks of timber hurtling past them on the river's broad back, heading straight for the six great arches of the bridge. The sightseeing boats passed under this bridge every day, but now there was hardly twenty feet of room between the water and the road where they stood. Another barrel crashed against the stone and the whole structure seemed to shake.

Tanya turned her back on Notre Dame and crossed the bridge to join the crowd on the other side. Yvette took her arm and together they elbowed their way to the front of the throng of whispering sightseers to see what the river was hurling into the city. Furniture, shutters and doors that must have been torn from houses further upstream careered towards them and struck against the stonework. A parade of barrels carried away from the Quai des Vins swam with the current like swans, apparently stately in the distance, till as they approached they seemed to speed up and spin, colliding with the arches or sucked through the diminishing space below them.

For the first time, Tanya found the floods something more than a diverting break from the usual patterns of life: she saw them as a threat. One of the barrels cracked below her and she started. The ground under her feet was being knocked away. Yvette tugged on her arm. 'Look!' There was a group of men hanging over the edge of the Pont de Sully further upstream, trying to catch the barrels out of the water with long poles as they swept by. As they watched, one man, leaning far out over the water, managed to fix his hook into one. For a moment it seemed as if the barrel was going to drag him with it, but one of his companions managed to reach it too and share the strain. They walked it out of the heavy flow of the water to the sound of distant cheers.

The crowd around Yvette and Tanya was mostly quiet; there was only the occasional murmured remark of fear and awe as the waters clambered over all obstructions, tearing at the walls that confined them. 'The river will eat Paris,' a voice behind them said. 'She already has,' another replied. 'The pavements are giving way, the cellars are all flooded. Thousands of homes gone already.' 'When will it end?' 'Not before it gets worse, that's certain.'

There was a loud shout of laughter behind them and Tanya

turned round. At the back of the crowd, someone still wearing evening clothes was climbing up on top of a car. Once established, he helped drag up a friend to sit beside him. 'Ten louis on the dresser beating the table to the bridge,' the man said. He was fat, young, and spoke French with a strong English accent. The friend he was helping scrambled to a sitting position and peered into the river.

'Which table?' he said, his voice high and nasal. Tanya groaned – it was Perov.

'Too late! The dresser has it. You owe me ten. Double or quits if that tree gets to us before I can count to twenty-five.'

'Done! Did we bring anything to drink?'

The Englishman reached down to instruct his chauffeur, realised he had stopped counting and hurried to catch up.

Tanya pushed back into the crowd and was standing directly below them when the tree struck just as the first gentleman reached twenty-three. Perov cheered, then seeming to sense the angry stares from beneath him, looked down.

'Miss Koltsova!'

'Mr Perov,' she said firmly, 'this wreckage did not come from nowhere. You are making asinine bets over the terrible misfortunes of others.'

He went quite red. Tanya was speaking French, and loudly too. There were murmurs of agreement in the crowd. 'The city is under threat and this is all you can do?' she continued, her sense of outrage in no way diminished by her own sightseeing. 'Factories have been destroyed, homes inundated and still it rains. Can you not find useful employment even now?'

He slid back down from his perch on the roof. 'Miss Koltsova, you are too harsh.'

Behind them came another crash against the stonework. The

impact seemed to run through Tanya like an electric shock. She said more softly and in Russian, 'I will not marry you, Mikhail Pavlovich. I do not need any more time to decide. Thank you for your offer and your patience. I shall explain to my aunts why we cannot have the pleasure of your company at lunch today and write to my father myself.'

His mouth hung open. 'Because you see me making bets on the wreckage of some peasant dwelling?' he managed to say at last, his cheeks still red.

'No.' She reached out and patted his arm. 'It is because we are not friends – and no amount of money or family interest can make up for that.' He opened and closed his mouth a couple of times.

His friend also slid down from the roof, nearly tripped then cleared his throat. 'Natives . . . restless. Better view from further upstream.'

Perov took control of himself. 'As you wish it, Tatiana Sergeyevna. Perhaps it would have been more fitting to choose another moment to tell me of your decision.'

Tanya nodded. 'Probably, but I see no reason to keep you in suspense a moment longer than necessary.'

His friend pulled on his sleeve. 'Stop jabbering in that barbaric tongue and come on, will you, Micky?'

Perov said no more, but now rather pale, he made a smart bow and climbed back into the car. The crowd cheered their departure.

Yvette struggled to Tanya's side in time to stare after it. 'Was that . . . ? Did you just . . . ?'

Tanya took a deep breath. 'Yes, it was, and yes, I did. And I am very glad.' Her eyes dropped to the sable muff that had been warming her hands. 'At least I think I am glad. Still, now I will marry Paul so that is good.' She looked up at Yvette, her eyes huge and black and her skin rather pink. 'You don't think Paul will *mind* marrying me, do you?'

Yvette laughed.

Before Tanya returned to her aunts to break the news, she had the story of the weekend from Yvette. She leaned back in the car and blinked rapidly. 'Poor Maud! Do you think she *is* mad?'

Yvette shook her head. 'No – at least not yet. It is this way she has of talking about herself as if she were already dead, yet she is still there somehow. She came looking for me last night, after all.'

Tanya smiled sadly out of the window. 'It gives her licence. Like Akaky in *The Overcoat*, I think. When she is a ghost she can take revenge. She can't as a living breathing English girl. Why are you looking at me like that?'

'I never thought of you as a great reader, Tanya.'

She rolled her eyes. 'All Russians have to read Gogol. It's a rule we have.' Still watching the streets through the window, Tanya rested her delicate pointed chin on her thumb and forefinger. 'I have to tell my aunts about Perov now. Oh, I hope I've done the right thing.' She turned round as she said it, all appeal.

'Of course you have. I saw the man for ten seconds and would rather marry Valadon's dog. Much rather.' Tanya smiled again. 'Do you have time to drop me in Place Pigalle?'

The letter was waiting for her on Maud's bed. Yvette sat down and opened the envelope. It was cold in the room; the stove was unlit and the snow and rain fell in turn outside. She clambered under the blankets and pulled them up around her as she read.

> *Yvette,*
>
> *I know I have not repaid you very well for saving my life. I thought that making the Countess believe I was innocent would make me easy, then that taking something from Morel would do the same. It made me glad to see the fear on his face tonight, but it was a dark, hungry sort of gladness. After we left that place I came home thinking I should rest as I promised you, that just as you could resist that drug, perhaps I could resist haunting Morel any further and leave Paris, but I find I cannot. He will try and convince himself it was all accident. Even if Charlotte's conspiracy of shop girls prevent him from selling any of the other diamonds he has stolen in Paris, I'm sure he and Sylvie will have money enough to get to America by some means – and what if the Countess misses him there? I would disappear from his conscience and he would be happy forever. The idea of that stops me from sleeping.*
>
> *I must be his shadow.*
>
> Maud

'Oh, Maud,' Yvette said and curled the thin blankets more closely around her, letting the note hang from her fingers. Outside the window she could see the snow falling from the clotted skies. Like feathers, that was what they always said of snow in books, wasn't it? That it was like feathers.

When she was a child she used to dance and sing for the gentry as they drank their coffee outside the cafés on the Champs. One of her *maman*'s other little charges would go among the crowd with his cap out collecting coppers and anything that they might have taken their eye off, wallets and trinkets from inside the ladies' handbags, watches and rings.

Once, one of the women had called her over to pet her and stroke her hair and tell her what a pretty child she was. Yvette had submitted happily enough. There was a pigeon feather caught on her blouse. She thought it was dirty and made to brush it away but the woman stopped her and told her it was good luck, a sign that her guardian angel was looking after her. She thought maybe the woman was going to take her home but then the kind lady had released her and turned back to her coffee and her friends. Yvette's companion gave her the signal his work was done and she ran away, disappointed again, but the idea of the guardian angel stayed in her mind. She had thought of it the first time an artist on Montmartre had asked her to model and then paid her, the time she turned down a man as a lover who later turned out to be violent and cruel to his girl. She had thought of it too the second or third time she had smoked opium, the first time the drug had let her fully appreciate its beauty, and thought that in that moment she was finally settling back into her angel's embrace and feeling his wings close over her. That was then. She had not believed in him for a long time. Then in the last year or two, since she could not find him she had tried to become a guardian angel to others, or not an angel, but something hopeful in the world. Imperfect and muddy from the streets, but still . . .

She rested her head on her knee. The whole point of a guardian angel was that they were with you whether you deserved it or not, that they stayed with you, that even if they could not save you, they were there. She threw off the blankets and went in search of Maud.

CHAPTER 17

*S*COLDING, THREATS, LONG LECTURES ON HER LACK of character, her ingratitude, her gross stupidity – all of this Tanya had been expecting, but when her Aunt Vera said nothing at all to the news, only burst into tears and ran out of the room, the girl was shocked. Aunt Lila stayed where she was, her hands folded in her lap and she too said nothing for several minutes. Tanya's bravery began to shiver and retreat.

'Aunty Lila, please say something. I have thought very carefully. I cannot marry someone I do not respect, and Mr Allardyce is a good man.'

Eventually Lila looked up, her features sharp and angry. 'I'm glad you think so, Tanya.' She stood up and smoothed the heavy silk of her dress. 'Do you realise why Vera ran away like that?'

'She wishes me to marry Perov,' Tanya answered a little sulkily. 'I know that.'

Lila shook her head. 'You are a deeply selfish child, Tanya. You always have been, fainting and sighing into getting your way. I never thought you were as delicate as you pretended, but it has suited you, hasn't it, to make your father think you are a weakling in need of constant care? Now you announce to us that you are a modern woman able to make her own way, that you care and think nothing of us and throw all that care back in our faces.'

'Aunt, I do not mean—'

'Do be quiet and listen. You have humiliated Vera. Your father needed someone to look after you and she volunteered. She asked for your father's trust and now he will think that she has failed. You know that neither of us would have a penny if he didn't give it to us. It is easier for me, I have played the shrinking violet for fifty years so no one will blame me, but Vera has actually tried to do something in this world. She tried to help her husband in business but he threw it away at the gambling tables, she has had to beg and flatter to get her son a decent position in the Ministry and hears hardly a word from him. She tried to guide and protect you in a foreign city and you have done nothing but sneer at her and defy her since the moment we arrived. She only wanted to love you, Tanya. She is a busy old woman but she only wanted your love and your father's respect. You never offered her the first and have robbed her of the second. It is very badly done, my girl. Very badly indeed.'

She left Tanya sitting pale and alone. Her first impulse was to cry; first at the injustice and then because she suspected that sweet compliant Lila might be right.

Sylvie wanted to see the floods. Christian had told her about the unsuccessful trip to Rheims and the theft, when he arrived home in the early hours of the morning. After a few moments of stunned silence, she had burst into laughter and kissed him. She would never stop surprising him. It was the gods taking their cut of their good fortune, she said, and now that was done they had nothing left to fear. Now she was in festive mood and wished to be in the open air. He had been worried that in the days he had spent watching Henri work she would have grown bored and begun smoking the drug more than before, but she had not. Her will was iron when it suited her. She showed no sign of missing it and spent her days reading English novels and working on her sketches. Her English and her drawing had improved greatly under Maud's tuition.

Today, Morel's first thought was to collect more of the stones from their hiding-place and sell them in Paris. She dissuaded him. Paris was not herself at the moment, she said. There would be no fun buying or selling while the waters were boiling up through the streets. Much better to have a holiday here until the waters drained away and then they could make the sale and leave the country quickly and quietly as planned.

Morel allowed himself to be convinced. The couple left Rue de Seine after lunch well rested and wrapped in furs and overcoats to see the sight of Paris slowly drowning.

It happened first when they climbed the towers of Notre Dame. It was Sylvie's idea and she was right – it was something to see, with the river swelling and racing under the bridges. The snow had settled on the gargoyles, who stared down on the city with horrified pleasure. It made Sylvie laugh. Occasionally the sky would suddenly, miraculously, clear – and a stream of sunlight would dance over the snow on the roofs, warm the sand-coloured stone and turn the yellow river green and gold. It was at such a moment that he looked down and saw the figure in the middle of the square. You could not pick anyone out at such a distance and name them, of course. The streets were full of people – workers whose factories had been shut down by the water, had brought their wives and children out to see it fighting through the city, but Morel was sure it was *her*, and that her attention was fixed on him.

He called Sylvie, putting out his hand to her and pulling her near to him as soon as her fingers brushed his. He looked down, ready to point her out, confess what he thought he had seen on the bridge the previous night . . . but she was gone. The crowd was one mass again, flowing through the square in waves like the river itself.

'What is it, Christian?'

'Nothing. Nothing, my darling.'

By the time they had reached the Quai de Passy and marvelled at the people punting themselves through the streets in little boats and rafts, he had almost forgotten. Sylvie bought photographs from a street-hawker and clung onto Morel's arm watching the water and the men putting up the wooden walkways along the side of the street.

'I *can* get through there!' Morel turned around. An elderly man, made almost spherical in his greatcoat, was arguing in a good-natured way with one of the policemen on the road just where the waters were lapping up towards them. 'Look, officer, you can see by the tree the water's not more than three foot deep and the cart has a clearance of four – four and a half feet probably! My aunt's just pulled everything she owns out of the basement on Rue des Eaux and I can't leave it sitting on the street for the *apaches* to rifle through.'

'But my friend, the ground is like porridge!' the policeman protested. 'Look, the lamp halfway along is already sinking.'

Morel looked where he was pointing. The street-lamps were still lit and glowing in the afternoon light. No one could get to them to shut off the gas. It did seem to be tilting. The cart-driver waved his hand. 'Pah! I'll trust my horse to know not to step in a sewer.'

A woman stepped out of the crowd, her cheeks pink with the

cold and the same look of glee on her face that Sylvie had. 'Give me a ride, Dad! I want to go through and my husband will help you with the stuff at the other end if you do.' She pulled on the arm of a young man beside her and he touched his cap. If it was to the driver or the policeman wasn't quite clear.

The policeman shrugged. 'Be careful, that's all I'm saying – and don't blame me if you get a soaking.' The mood seemed to have caught him too. He was smiling as he said it.

'All right then,' the carter said, and put his hand down to help the girl up beside him.

Sylvie stepped forward. 'Oh, us too please, my friend!' Morel let himself be led to the cart's side. The older man was looking down at her in the fine furs a little doubtfully. She pulled the butterfly brooch from her lapel. 'I'll give you this.' Morel frowned briefly. It was the brooch she'd given Maud for Christmas and then reclaimed from her little store of possessions after she had gone into the river. Morel felt a creeping sense of cold on the back of his neck, but Sylvie was already scrambling onto the cart and making herself comfortable with the girl and her husband. Before Morel had even managed to take his seat beside her, she had found out he worked in one of the flooded factories in Bercy. She was bright and joking with the young couple. Sylvie always knew how to be with whomever she came across. Never needed a hint. It made him proud.

'All secure?' the carter called out, then urged his horse forward into the water. It was as if they were part of the river. The women linked arms and laughed, half-lifting themselves off the wooden bench-seats to see over the parapet and into the river. The Eiffel Tower stood high and lonely on the other bank. 'It moved,' the girl shrieked suddenly. 'Did you not see it move! Ahh, it will fall at last and crush all the rich in Suffren.' Her eyes were shining. The horse was moving slowly but steadily, and the water was deepening. It was up almost to its chest. The water splashed up and the women squealed. Morel looked back to see if the Tower *was* moving, monstrous thing. He couldn't see any sign of a shift.

Their progress was being watched by the crowd they had left behind. They waved and whistled at each other. Then he saw her. Not ten yards away yet and veiled, the familiar thin shape standing on the very edge of the water. She put up her hands and lifted the black netting that hung in front of her eyes. *Hell and all its devils!*

Morel gave a shout and pushed past Sylvie and the girl, the motion of the cart making him stumble onto his knees. The young man tried to hold onto his arm, but Morel shook him off. He heard Sylvie call to him but looked instead into the crowd. She was still there. The dead woman staring at him. He clambered awkwardly off the back of the cart and fell into the water. The cold seized him as if it had claws and forced the air out of his lungs. The horse whinnied, protesting at the movement, and then surged forward away from him a few paces. The ground felt weak and soft under his feet and some current caught him before he had regained his balance. He fell forward on his hands and was choked by the filthy water. The confusion and sound of it, cold air and freezing water spluttering in his throat. He tried to push himself up but stumbled again. Above the noise of the water he could hear Sylvie shouting his name. An arm suddenly caught him and lifted him clear. Two men, one the policeman who had warned them to be careful and another, a labourer who had been working on the thin wooden walkways, half-dragged him up towards the crowd again. His coat was sodden and pulled him down. The dead woman in the crowd was gone, leaving only these amazed faces – disgusted, frightened or angry. 'Are you mad? Are you mad?' the policeman kept saying.

Morel slid out of their arms onto the cold cobbles. He looked up at them, not understanding what they wanted from him; there was a circle of sky showing between their faces, and the air filled with another of those sudden flurries of snow. Someone was pushing through the crowd. Sylvie. In those few moments she had run all the way back along the walkway. She helped him stand and guided him away from the curious stares. He shivered, and feeling his teeth rattle he clenched his jaw. 'She's coming for me, Sylvie,' he said. 'She hates me and I was kind to her.' It seemed unjust suddenly. He had paid her, fed her and now her ghost felt only rage. He shivered again. The taste of the river was in his mouth, in his hair. If he had been able to use his skinned and stiffened hands properly he would have torn his clothes off right there on the street. He wanted to explain to Sylvie, make her understand – but when he tried to speak again, his throat closed and he retched.

Sylvie waved down a taxicab and after a fierce debate the driver agreed to take them all the way back to Rue de Seine – if he got the fare in advance, plus extra for the wet.

When the Morels arrived back at Rue de Seine, him with his head down and her not letting go of his arm and hurrying him in, Yvette was not sure if she should be proud of Maud or frightened for her. Something had happened – Morel's dishevelled state and wretched stoop told as much – but where was Maud? Taken up by the gendarmes? Murdered? But the couple looked as if their problems were falling over them like the flood, rather than done with, so Yvette let herself hope. She paced back and forth on the Boulevard Saint-Germain, keeping a close eye on the crowds around her. It was not the sort of day when people noticed a girl such as her. The whole city felt strangely tense. She heard snatches of news from the people passing by; of pavements collapsing, more ragged holes appearing in the streets far away from the river. The water was climbing up through the sewers and underground tunnels: all those clever modern tricks of control of which the city was so proud were being turned against her by the river. The level of the water was still rising fast; so much debris collecting against the Pont de l'Alma that engineers were talking of blowing it up before it became a dam. The factories were shutting, the waste-works were closed.

She had been looking for Maud in the crowd for so long, that when she finally saw her, it came as a shock. Maud walked straight past without seeing her, her face a mask. Yvette ran a few paces to catch her up and touched her arm. In the first moment she glanced round, Maud looked irritated, ready to knock away a beggar or a man, then surprised.

'Yvette.' She looked up Rue de Seine towards the Palais du Luxembourg. 'They are at home?'

Yvette was not sure what greeting she had expected, but one with a little more warmth than this. 'Yup,' she replied. 'They rolled up an hour ago and nothing moving since. He looks as sick as a dog. What did you do?'

Maud smiled, cat-like, discreet – but there was such an animal pleasure in it Yvette was shocked. 'I frightened him.'

Again Yvette wondered if Maud was still quite sane. She kept her own voice slow and even. 'You will keep watching him?'

'I shall, as long as I can.'

Yvette had used her time well. 'If you must. There is a woman living in the house opposite with a room on the second floor. We may rent it by the hour if you wish it, though it will be expensive. I shall watch while you rest, if you can.'

Maud looked around her as if noticing for the first time that the sky was growing thick with darkness. 'Good. Why is it darker than normal?'

'Floodwater. In the electricity works, the basements. The lights have failed in places all over the city,' Yvette said. Another scrap of information gathered from the crowds around her. 'Take my arm.'

'I was ready to do this alone,' Maud said. 'Why are you helping me?'

'I don't know – because something tells me I should? For God's sake, the ground is going under our feet. Who knows what is right today?'

CHAPTER 18

*A*UNT VERA WAS IN THE DRAWING ROOM BUT THE lights had not been turned on and the afternoon gloom had silted the room with purple shadows. She did not move when Tanya let herself into the room and settled down beside her. Tanya did not try to touch her.

'Aunty, I think the world is changing and I wish to change too. I love Paul and I think we can be happy together, but I shall have to manage on a great deal less money.' She had her notebook with her. 'I know you only want me to be happy, but I think there are more ways to be happy now for women like us, with an education and some talent, than there were. Don't you think?'

Her aunt still did not move, but Tanya thought she was listening. 'Mr Allardyce once told me he thought you were a remarkable woman. I think so too, and I need your help. With Papa, of course, but also with the other things. Life has been easy for me and I shall have to learn how to manage my money.' Vera was certainly listening now. 'We shall need to entertain, but only in a modest fashion, and I shall need an apartment with three bedchambers at least. Sasha will need one, and I wish to always have a room for you and Aunty Lila, always there when you wish it. Can you help me a little to work it all out?'

Vera sniffed and put out her hand. Tanya meekly handed over the book and heard her aunt beginning to turn the pages. After a few minutes she said, 'You've forgotten you'll need to pay to keep the place warm, Tanya. In these Paris winters . . . Do you wish to have an apartment with an American bath? He will want it, I suppose. Turn that light on so I can see what I am about.' Tanya leaped up to do so, and her aunt stood and carried the notebook over to her writing-table. She carried on studying Tanya's notes then looked round, a spark of interest in her faded blue eyes. 'You think it is likely you will get five hundred for a portrait?'

'I think so. I have asked a few of your friends and they seem to agree it is a reasonable amount. I think I could complete one like that in a week's painting. One needs the commissions, of course.'

Her aunt drew a fresh sheet of writing paper from the desk and put it down in front of her. 'It seems to me you should work to get a portrait in the Salon next year. Something of the style you wish to make a living from.'

Tanya joined her at the writing-table and for a little while as the evening thickened around them they spoke about costs and careers, who they knew who might become a patron, whether Sasha would be willing to learn enough French to become a housekeeper to the young couple.

Vera was writing something down on her growing numbered list when she lifted her head and said: 'Your father must modernise, Tanya. He is too stuck in the old ways of managing a family, his women. Your mother was a good person, but she never thought of anything other than looking pretty and reading novels. He must realise that we new women have our place too.'

'Yes, Aunty.'

'And tell your young man to call on us.'

'He will be reporting on the flood, Aunty. He might not know when he can come, or have the chance to dress.'

'We are not some stuffy household that insists on such things. Tell him to come when he can and covered in mud if need be.'

'Yes, Aunty.'

Tanya excused herself for a few moments and sent a note to Paul's lodgings, then spent another hour with Vera and the figures. It was a little after six when the footman came in to tell them a young girl named Odette wished to speak to Miss Koltsova.

Sylvie would not hear of him leaving the apartment. 'You are still shivering, Christian. I will not let you.' She did not seem to understand the importance of it – that *she* was coming and would creep up with the water into the cellar and snake her way around the diamonds and take them back into the river with her. He could not explain it to Sylvie. She would not believe him. She brought him foul-tasting teas and tried to get him to rest, telling him everything was well and that soon they would be sailing away to America, and that dirty lying Paris, which always looked so fine but was full of holes, torn-up pavements and gunfire, would be behind them. They would be in a country where there were no graves and tunnels.

Again he tried to get up, and again she pushed him down onto the pillows. 'I will go and fetch them, Christian,' she said at last. 'In the morning I will go, but only if you promise to stay still and rest now.' That gave him some measure of peace but when he slept he dreamed he was drowning.

Paul Allardyce arrived at Tanya's house just before nine o'clock that evening and was shown at once into the drawing room where Miss Koltsova was waiting for him alone. He was exhausted, having spent the whole day tracking the floods through the streets, gathering figures and trying to talk to officials whose faces were pale with worry. He had crossed the city half-a-dozen times, guessing the size of the sink-holes and attempting to find words for the strange softness of the ground. He tried to remember what he had heard of the catacombs and quarries, the sewers and underground tunnels, then wrote furiously for an hour before going to the telegraph office and sending his full report, at great expense, to New York. Tanya's message found him at his lodgings where he had gone simply to change his shirt before travelling out once more to watch the river crawling higher and higher.

She was such a beautiful woman, and after the dirt and worry of the day, the poor who had lost everything, the widow of the man who had killed himself rather than leave his home, just looking at her was some sort of relief. She began by saying how glad she was her message had reached him now the *petit bleu* system had failed and half the telephones were not working, that she had been trying to contact her friends with no success . . . He lost track for a minute – she was speaking English but rather fast and low. It took him a few moments to realise the topic of conversation had changed. She was telling him that she had rejected the Russian millionaire and was proposing to marry him; that she was sure she would be able to make money painting, and if her estimate of his income was not wildly inaccurate they should be able to live in Paris quite comfortably and even save against future emergency. He must have been looking at her with a slightly foolish expression because after a minute or two her words trailed away. She stared at the ground in front of her and as ever Paul found himself fascinated by the furious darkness of her thick hair. He took a step forward and tried to find his voice.

'Tanya, I have been awake since dawn. I can hardly think, but are you saying you wish to marry me? Is that what I am to understand?'

She gave a very small nod. 'If you think, that is . . . if you would like me as a wife.' She bent down and picked up a sheaf of papers from the low table in front of her. 'Aunt Vera has been helping me with the sums and says she will teach me to keep an account book.' She thrust the papers out towards him, her black eyes very wide as if she wanted him to examine them. He pushed them out of the way and took her in his arms, kissing her hard. For a moment she was still and frightened in his embrace, then she began to return the kiss with a heat that burned him. He had to pull himself away, breathing hard. She looked at him, her face flushed.

'So you think, Paul, you might love me a little without all the flim-flam?'

He took her hand and thought for a second; his feelings almost choked him. 'Tanya, your smile is one of the great sights of the world to me. The feeling I have when I see it, it's like . . . like seeing a great clipper ship under full sail, or walking through the Alps on a clear day. It stops my heart. I love you very, very much.' He cleared his throat. 'Now let me do this properly. I am only ever going to do it once in my life.' He lowered himself to the ground, supporting himself on the table with his palm until he was on one knee, crumpling some of the sheets of figures in the process, then he reached up for her hand again and with it between both of his own, he began: 'Tatiana Sergeyevna Koltsova, would you do me the honour . . .'

CHAPTER 19

The Reader oil on canvas 56.1 × 33.1 cm

A subject that was a favourite of Edwardian genre painters, this image of a young woman reading by a window is given extra interest by the late-night setting, the treatment of the light falling across the figure, the burning end of her cigarette and the psychological realism of the model's absorption in her book. What can be saccharine in some renderings here becomes an intimate portrait of a state of mind.

Extract from the catalogue notes to the exhibition 'The Paris Winter: Anonymous Treasures from the de Civray Collection', Southwark Picture Gallery, London, 2010

25 January 1910

Maud jerked awake. Yvette was sitting in the chair by the window as she had promised she would. The faint glow of the street-lamps softened the sharp angles of her face and made her look younger again, and gave her enough light to read by. She had borrowed some historical romance from the owner of the house and sat with it now on her knee, a cigarette burning in her other hand and an ashtray improvised from a soapdish sitting on the floor at her feet. The filigree ironwork outside cast vague curling shadows over the folds of her skirt. She heard Maud move but did not look up.

'The rooms are still dark,' she said and turned a page. 'Go back to sleep.'

For a few minutes Maud thought she would, then a sudden explosion shook the room, a great throb of thunder. 'God!' Yvette said, getting to her feet and opening the window as Maud sat upright in the bed, her heart beating wildly. 'They must have blown the Pont de l'Alma after all. Heaven help us.'

Maud slid out of the bed and went to stand next to her. Yvette pointed across the street. A light had come on in the Morels' apartment and one of the shutters was being pulled back. Maud shifted back into the shadows, looking down and sideways as Sylvie appeared in the frame, leaning her small white hand on the ironwork and looking towards the river. The light spilled over her shoulders, the sapphire-blue of her silk dressing-gown, her blond hair loose and long over her shoulders. Other figures appeared on the street, all looking in the same direction. Only Maud was not looking north and west where the sound had come from; she focused instead on the lines of Sylvie's face and her hand on the rail, remembering that head resting on her shoulder, that hand in hers.

Some hours later, Yvette brought coffee, bread and news from the woman on the ground floor. 'The bridge is still there,' she said, handing Maud a sliced and buttered roll. 'It was some factory in

Ivry blew up, but the fire didn't spread. The water is still rising though. Anything from over the way?' Maud shook her head. The shutters to the Morels' drawing room were half-opened but there was no other sign of life. 'Eat something, Maud.' It was the sadness in Yvette's voice that made her try the food, but even so she did not stop looking out of the window. 'I want to get some message to Tanya if I can, to tell her we are well . . .'

The concierge of the Morels' apartment came out into the street pulling her shawl over her head. The snow was falling again and melting onto the soaked pavements as if the ground were drinking it up. Maud sat up in the chair and peered after her. She remained there, her pose one of fixed attention until the woman returned. There was a man with her in a long pearl-grey overcoat and a large leather bag at his side.

'She has been for a doctor,' Maud said and licked her lips. Yvette looked up from the novel she was reading again then set it down and brushed the crumbs of her breakfast from her dress.

'I shall go and see if I can find out what's happening,' she said, and went to the door. Maud did not look round to see her leave.

The concierge was happy to talk. Her older sister had nearly been killed by typhoid and now with her best tenant ill it was all she could think about. 'He came back shivering and soaked last night – fell in the waters, she said – and I don't like the sound of him today. Groaning! There is groaning! And what if the floods come up this far? What are we supposed to do? Leave him to drown or carry him off with us, nasty diseases and all?' Everything she said was in a fierce whisper and spoken out of the corner of her mouth, as if they were at the theatre and speaking at all was bad manners.

'But the water won't come this far. We're safe, surely?' Yvette said, huddling away from the sudden cold wind that ran up the street. She felt it like Maud's impatience, pulling her back to the room to tell her about the fever, the groaning.

'Don't you bet on it, sweetheart! You don't have to walk half so far to see the river today, I tell you. Go and have a look. My Georges has been down there already. He took one look and back he came, emptied out our bit of storage in the cellar and moved it all up to the attic. Now he's a strong man, but a lazy one. There's no way he would have carried my mother's second-best mattress up to the roof if he didn't think it had a good chance of a soaking. That I can tell you for free.'

Yvette ignored the wind tugging at her back and went to look for herself. The shock was sudden and absolute: water everywhere. It rippled along the quays and ate away at the islands; the naked trees, shivering with wet snow, hung at strange angles along the Quai de Conti. The streets were sinking. She turned back up Rue Bonaparte and saw the same fear on each face. The nervous excitement of the previous day had become something darker. Paris was being throttled slowly by her own river, and what had looked like another spectacle laid on by the city for the entertainment of her citizens was twisting into a slow act of violence.

Tanya was certain that Maud or Yvette would call for her early in the morning. The only possible reason why she had not heard from them already was that they had received her messages too late last night to respond – but nothing came. She stared at the clock until she thought it must be broken, and when Sasha came into her room with tea just after ten, she was shaking it vigorously. The old maid took it from her with a frown and set it back on the mantelpiece, then she pulled a telegram form from her apron and handed it to Tanya. She snatched it from her, then a second later crumpled it in her fist and threw it in the general direction of the fire.

'All well? *All well?* That's what they have to say to me?'

Sasha bent down to pick up the note, smoothed it out again then tucked it into her pocket. She thought all such things had value and should be preserved against emergency like short threads and off-cuts of wax paper. 'They think I can have *nothing* important to tell them. That is it. They think all I'm doing is worrying about them and of course I am, but I *do* have something important to tell them.' She turned and pointed an angry finger at Sasha who only stared at it with her eyebrows raised. '*And* I am engaged.'

'I think you mentioned that a time or two last night as I put you to bed, pumpkin,' Sasha said.

'But they don't know that! Yvette only knows I refused Perov . . .'

Sasha yawned and sat on the bed. 'Maybe they can't tell you where they are. Fact they sent this,' she patted her stomach where the pocket of her apron sat, 'means that they *are* thinking of you, so stop wailing. Now I mean to get you out and useful before you tear the house apart. The Red Cross are collecting, and what they are collecting needs sorting.' Tanya started to protest but the look in Sasha's eyes made her stop. 'We shall send a heap of your messages around so they know where to find you and leave word here too. We might as well enjoy having footmen to spare before you make beggars of us, I suppose. Now put something on a sensible woman might wear and let's hurry along, shall we?' She got to her feet again with a grunt and pulled out one of Tanya's more conservative walking dresses from the armoire.

'Sasha, when I marry will you come with me?'

Sasha helped her lift the morning gown she was wearing over her head. 'I'm not sure that's how they manage things here, dear.

Normally you'll just have a girl in to clean and fetch for you by the hour.'

When Tanya's face re-emerged from the white chiffon it was pale and slightly tearful. 'If you wish to go back to Saint Petersburg, of course I shall understand.'

Sasha picked up the walking dress and bent down, fanning out the skirt so that Tanya could step into it. She felt the girl's hand on her shoulder as she steadied herself. 'Don't fret, chicken. I'll help you settle in – you've got some learning to do. Vera and I will teach you.' She stood, pulling the dress up with her and held it so Tanya could slide her long slim arms through the tight sleeves. 'Then I shall open a little restaurant, I think.' Tanya's eyes sprang open and Sasha sniffed. 'There're lots of Russians in Paris might like a taste of proper food from their homeland, and none of these Frenchies can cook a damn. All sauce, sauce, sauce till you don't know what you're eating.'

Tanya turned to let her fasten the dress, thinking the world was a more surprising place than she could have ever imagined.

He kept asking her if she had been to fetch them, though at times he wasn't sure if he had said the words out loud or just dreamed them. She always said, 'In a little while, Christian my love, in a little while. I cannot leave you just now.' He was afraid he had mentioned the ghost of the woman and might have made her angry, but whenever he managed to open his eyes she was smiling at him kindly enough. She knew where they were, she'd take care of it. He sank into a sort of half-dream where he could see nothing, but the air was tainted with corruption and there was a constant sound of trickling water.

Maud watched by the window, eating whatever Yvette handed to her and watching the shutters of the house opposite. The day passed slow as ice. That night she slept a while and let Yvette watch, and for the first time her dreams were not of drowning. She seemed to be again on the terrace outside Sacré Coeur; the rain was falling but it felt warm as a blessing against her skin. She knew Yvette and Tanya were there watching with her as the floodwaters consumed Paris, and below them the lights went out one by one till the city of lights was dark and cold and victory blossomed in her.

CHAPTER 20

26 January 1910

*Y*VETTE BROUGHT HER COFFEE AGAIN IN THE morning and declared her intention to go back to Valadon's place and her own. 'My clothes are stinking,' she said. 'If you insist on staying here until we have not got a franc between us, well and good, but I shall do so in clean clothes.'

Maud only nodded and Yvette began her weary slog across a shattering Paris. The Cours de Rome was becoming a lake fed by the Metro tunnels, and they said part of Place de l'Opéra was collapsing. Back at her room she found four messages from Tanya pinned to her bundle and then another crop at Valadon's. She fished out a length of cord to tie up Maud's clean clothes and cut it to length with her knife. A present from *Maman* the day she had finished her schooling with the nuns. She would rather have had a book as the nuns only handed out Bibles, and Yvette had already decided there was nothing much in those pages for her. She had used the knife to scare other children away from her things and twice used it to protect herself. Once from Louis. After the other men on the hill saw his scar they kept away when she told them to. It was the only gift she remembered being given and she had carved her name into the bone handle and gone out into the world with it. Not gone very far into the world though. She put it back into her pocket and headed to Saint-Sulpice where the latest appeals from Tanya had directed her.

Most of the refugees flooded out of their homes round Paris, Bercy and Javel had been directed here, and Saint-Sulpice had been transformed to receive them. There were cots and mattresses everywhere you looked, and people huddled into little groups round portable heaters. At the back of the church a procession of men and women collected bowls of soup from a trestle table. It was strangely quiet given the number of people there. Even the children were silent. The air smelled slightly rotten. A woman in a Red Cross uniform at the door looked relieved when she realised that Yvette was looking for someone rather than a place to sleep. 'We are nearly full and the waters still rise,' she said. 'On the first night we had only five, now there are five hundred. Oh, it breaks my heart to see them praying. They can only be praying for other people, since they have already lost everything. Miss Koltsova is in the back with a few of the children while their mothers sleep. Take her out for a little while if you can. She was here half the night and from early this morning too.'

When Yvette approached, Tanya saw her through the crowd and put a blonde girl off her knee, kissing her dirty head as she did. Then she flung her arms around Yvette's neck and held her for a moment. 'Oh, you are here! Thank the Lord!' Before Yvette could do anything more than grin at her, Tanya took her by the hand and led her into a quieter corner. 'What I have to tell you seems less important after what I have seen here,' she whispered. 'Oh, it is dreadful. Have you been near the river today?'

Yvette nodded. 'It is higher than the road near Concorde. Only the wall holds it back. And there are crowds everywhere . . . But what is your news, Tanya? Are you engaged to Paul?'

She blushed. 'I am. He is here, talking with the refugees. His paper had already set up an appeal and the American Ambassador has already pledged *such* a sum.' Yvette thought she looked rather proud of this, as if every generous American action reflected rather well on her now. 'But Maud? What news?'

'All my congratulations, sweetheart. There, now you are resolved to work for a living I shall stop calling you Princess.'

Tanya looked pleased. 'Sasha says she will believe I can earn money when I learn to dress myself.' Yvette snorted with laughter and Tanya's eyes danced. 'Yes, I know, but some of these very expensive dresses are terribly complicated. I'm sure it will be much easier with cheaper clothes.' She tried to say it stoutly but Yvette was not convinced. 'But Maud . . . ?'

Yvette told her what she could, murmuring low so that the passing men and women would not hear her, but each seemed so sunk in their own distress and shock she could have sung it. 'Now she watches and waits, for what I do not know. Perhaps if she sees him sick, sees that he believes she is haunting him it will be enough, but she seems . . . not herself. She frightens me.'

Tanya nodded. 'Sasha said she found something dark in the river and brought it back into the air with her.'

'She found the strength to live, that's something. But I must go back to her. Kiss your fiancé for me and tell him he is a lucky man, even if his wife-to-be can't dress herself.'

Tanya put out her hand to stop her. 'Yvette, it wasn't just to tell you I was engaged. That girl, the maid the Countess threw out, came to see me.' Yvette waited, frowning a little. 'She wanted to thank me. She is going to take a stenographer's course, but the thing is, she followed Morel. Yvette, I know where the diamonds are.'

They found Maud still in her place at the window but looking more animated than she had been the previous day. She told them she had seen Morel himself at the window twice since Yvette had left, looking anxiously towards the river then shivering and looking up and down the street, searching the faces of the people coming and going on the pavements, their steps hurried or cautious as if afraid the road was going to give way beneath them. She greeted Tanya with warmth and congratulated her, though even as she did so her eyes flitted towards the window again. When Tanya began to tell them of Odette's visit, however, she became more attentive.

'Morel had taken her to Café Procope in Cour du Commerce once or twice,' Tanya explained. 'Poor thing, she was rather in love with him, I think, and she went back there a few times after he gave her up.' Tanya looked tired; her work at Saint-Sulpice seemed to have drained her, but her eyes were bright. Yvette found it strange to see her in such a plain dress, but she seemed more substantial sitting there than in her usual silks and chiffon. 'She was hoping to see him, and see him she did, going into Cour de Rohan. She followed him whenever she could. Apparently he spent hours a day there, and she said she saw him go into the cellars in the yard a couple of times. The second time she tried to speak to him and he was cruel.' Yvette could imagine. 'Then that very evening the Countess cast her off.' Yvette remembered what Valadon had said about women being fools and wondered if she were right.

'So you think he's keeping the diamonds there?' Maud said. 'In the cellars below Cour de Rohan?'

'What else could it be?' Tanya said, looking up at them with her round dark eyes. 'Close, but not too close. Secluded but somewhere a man like him might easily be dining in the cafés.'

'And you think we should go and search for them?' Maud said, looking back again over her shoulder.

'Of course we should!' Tanya said. 'They can be returned to the Countess and he will have lost what he has worked for so hard. Then Maud, you can be free again. You will have beaten him.'

Yvette watched the Englishwoman's face. There was a moment of light there, like a shifting of the clouds against a stormy sky, as if she had perhaps caught some scent of a future free of this, but then she shook her head. 'I don't care about the diamonds. What is their theft, taking jewels from a woman who has too many already, compared to what he did to me?'

Yvette put out her hand and rested it on Maud's knee. 'It is not what is important that counts, but what is important to *him*, isn't it, Maud?' For herself she thought collecting the diamonds would be by far the best idea. Tanya was right, and for the first time since they had left Henri in the cellar she thought there might be a chance of an ending which Maud might survive. Maud hesitated, then nodded.

'We should go at once,' Tanya said, standing up. 'The waters are reaching higher and higher through the cellars and sewers. If we don't go now it might be weeks before we get another chance, and he might be well enough by then to stop us.'

They hurried Maud up and into her long coat and into the street, but she could not resist looking back towards the apartment. He was there again, looking out of the window towards them, his face grey and his mouth a gape of despair. She turned away and let her friends sweep her along the street.

Still Sylvie would not go. He begged her to but she would not. She tried to dose him with laudanum but he tasted it in the wine and spat it out. He could stand today, and in those moments she left him to himself, he went to the window and strained to see how near the waters were approaching. What if *she* came in the night? If the waters reached to the road under the window, would she be able to leap up to the first floor and throttle him? Would he wake up to find her squatting on his chest, dripping with the foul waters of the Seine? He thought of her face, livid with rot like those of the drowning victims he had seen at the morgue. She would bare her yellow teeth and wring out her sodden clothes so the poisonous damp would trickle into his throat.

His heart thudding, he leaned out again. And he saw her looking up at him from the street below, her eyes a-glimmer with hatred. She was going to take the diamonds, his beautiful diamonds, the emerald-cut great stone five times the size of all the rest that would make him a king in America. She would take it and then force it down his throat with the riverwater and cut it out of his belly again. He saw it in her eyes. He whimpered. Sylvie could come back any moment and she would tell him he was ill, that his imagination was disturbed and his fever high, but she had not seen it, had not felt the hatred of the ghost as he had.

Morel dressed as quickly as he could. The buttons were difficult to fasten with his shaking hands and the sweat on his forehead stung his eyes. He took his coat and waited behind his door for a moment till he was sure the corridor outside was empty then made a dash for the front door, scooping up the large key to the apartment door as he passed the hall-table. His hand caught the flower vase and it went crashing to the floor but he didn't pause until he was outside and had turned the key in the lock. He heard Sylvie call his name and hesitated on the landing; her footsteps came close and then the door handle rattled. He could hear her breathing and put his fingers lightly onto the wood, knowing she was just the other side.

'Christian?' she said softly. 'Christian, my love, I know you are there. Come back and come to bed. Let me look after you, my darling, you know you are not well.'

He felt tears in his eyes; her voice was so soft but she could not protect him from the dead. 'She is coming for the diamonds, Sylvie,' he whispered, pressing his cheek to the wood. 'For *our* diamonds – and we shall not be tricked. No, I will fetch them and then I will come home and you will care for me.' His mind would not work as he wanted it to, his forehead was damp. 'I know I am not well.'

'Christian, unlock the door. We shall go together.'

He smiled, a wave of love for his pretty clever wife lifting his heart as it had lifted the first time he laid eyes on her. 'No, Sylvie. You will stop me. Be patient. I will fetch them and then we will be happy for all times, best beloved.' He let his cheek rest against the wood one moment more then turned and stumbled down the stairs. He could hear her calling his name and the rattle of the door handle as he went.

CHAPTER 21

'WAIT HERE FOR ME,' MAUD SAID AS THEY TURNED into Cour de Rohan.

Yvette frowned. 'No, we go together. I don't think he will have put them in a big barrel marked *Diamonds*. You'll need help to look, Maud.'

'And if someone comes?'

'Everyone is helping their neighbours nearer to the waters,' Yvette said, then looked at Tanya. 'But you stay here anyway, Tanya. Just in case.'

Tanya was busy preparing the lanterns they had brought from the ironmongers. 'Why?' she said indignantly.

'Because! And anyway, Maud and I have spare clothes at Rue de Seine and you do not. It might already be flooding down there, and even if it isn't it will smell and there will be rats.'

'Rats?' Tanya said, taking a slight step backwards.

'Yes,' Yvette said with a certain glee creeping into her voice. 'They panic as the water rises and come swarming out through the tunnels. They will probably try and climb up your dress to escape the flood.'

'Oh, all right! I'll wait.' She sat down on the edge of the water-trough and put her chin in her hand.

The entrance to the cellar was in the corner of the courtyard: a wooden cover set in a stone surround with two large iron rings to lift it, sunk into the wood. Yvette and Maud lifted it off together, the rust flaking off on Maud's pale brown leather gloves like dried blood. Yvette swung herself nimbly down onto the ladder in front of her and when she had reached the bottom, she lit her lantern. From where she watched above, Maud could see nothing but shadows – ghosts of barrels and wooden struts in the ashy Indian Yellow glow.

'Come on down.'

The ground at the bottom of the ladder was dry, but the tunnels smelled of riverwater, and it was clear even in the half-light that the cellar tunnel led quite steeply downwards. The floor was earth, the walls brick. After three or four yards the tunnel ended in a T-junction. In front of them were half-a-dozen arched doorways.

'You start there,' Yvette said, pointing to her left, and with a determined step went right. None of the doors were locked and it seemed that whatever was usually stored in them had already been cleared away. There were wine racks on the walls of the first two rooms that Maud went into, simple shelving in the third.

Yvette suddenly appeared beside her in a blur of diffused light that made her look ghostly, her voice breathy with excitement. 'I've found something.'

'Can you hear water?' Maud said. It was a whispering sound like rain in the trees.

'The sewers will run just underneath here. The ground is still dry. But come on – there's another room leading off this one.'

Maud followed her out through to the T-junction and back into the next store room. At first it looked just like the others, but at the back there was a space of deeper darkness. Yvette lifted her lamp, to reveal a low opening leading back into some older, deeper vault.

Yvette was pushing aside a barrel that blocked the path. Whatever dread Maud felt settling on her shoulders, it seemed as if Yvette felt none of it. Without speaking to Maud she ducked through the opening, and a moment or two later reappeared, grinning. 'It opens out again, Maud. Come through.'

She did. The sound of running water had faded here, but the air seemed heavier; even the flames in their lamps seemed to shrink from it. She straightened up and looked around her. She was in a vault perhaps seven foot at its highest point and all lined with thin and crumbling bricks. It was divided in two by a wall of larger stone blocks that looked as if they could have been pulled from the medieval walls of the city. They did not quite reach the roof. Around the walls, strange shapes gathered – broken furniture and split barrels. It was a dead space, a forgotten dumping ground.

'You go left of the wall,' Yvette said cheerfully. 'Look for something that has been disturbed.'

Morel remembered his gun only when he was out on the street. He could not go back now but the thought of seizing the diamonds back from Maud's ghost frightened him. He felt in the pockets of his coat and found a five-franc piece then half-stumbled across the threshold of the ironmonger's shop on the corner of Saint-Germain and Rue Grégoire de Tours. The old man behind the counter looked up at him in some alarm.

'Are the waters coming?' he said. 'We've emptied the cellars and my son is searching for sandbags. Is it coming up the street yet?'

Christian ignored him, trying to focus on the display of knives hanging on the wall opposite the counter. The reflections of the oil lamps lit about the place confused him and the air was smoky. He made a grab at one almost at random – a hunting knife, its blade four-inches long and curved. Then he put the coin down on the counter and went to leave.

'Sir, are you well, sir?'

He waved his hand as if the man was merely some insect and stumbled out again, shoving the knife into his belt. The crowd seemed to work against him. The street furniture set out to trip him, the men buffeted at him with their shoulders. The crowd became a mass of hostile glances. He leaned against the flaking bark of a plane tree and drew his breath in and out until the world steadied a little and his vision cleared. He thought of her again, the ghost searching for his diamonds. He pushed on and turned onto the cobblestones of Cour du Commerce. It was narrow and ancient here, the old walls of the city cramping towards each other, then the open air of Cour de Rohan. There was the lean-to where he had watched old Henri sweating day after day. He spat on the ground. Then, feeling a hand on his sleeve, he recoiled. A dark young woman was speaking to him. The Russian girl! What was *she* doing here? Could a ghost have human companions? Her voice buzzed into his brain; she was chattering about the floods, asking him for some assistance. He tried to form some reply and free himself from her, but she continued pulling at his arm. His rage, his desperation suddenly broke free and he struck her across the face with all his force. She fell to the ground and did not move. The cover to the cellar steps had been lifted away and he clambered down into the darkness, his hands and feet clumsy on the ladder. There was his candle on the barrel. He took it, lit it and lurched onwards.

The rear cellar extended back a long way. The texture of the ground changed. It felt slippery under Maud's feet. The dividing medieval-looking blocks didn't sit flush with this back wall either. The end wall was made of thin, old-looking bricks; the mortar was crumbling. Lowering her lantern, she saw the earth floor was black and muddy. She heard a dry whisper in the walls and lifted her light again; the mortar between the bricks was trickling out in a thin stream as she watched. She put her hand on the stone and it felt cold. She pressed herself against the wall, listening. It was not the rush of water, but something else. A sense of mass and weight, of pressure. She felt, horribly, the stones shift under her palms and took a step backwards. Her heel caught on the curl of an old piece of railing and she tripped and dropped her lamp. The flame died. Above the wall that almost divided the chamber in two she could see the glimmer of Yvette's light. She pulled herself upright, fighting free of the railings as if she had fallen in a briar patch.

'Yvette, I've lost my light!'

'One moment, I'll come for you. Maud, I think I've found them.' There was the sound of something shifting then a rattle. 'Oh my God. They are beautiful.' Her voice was soft, reverential. 'I am coming now.'

The light shifted and Maud felt her way cautiously along the central wall. In the darkness the pressure of the caged water nearby was palpable in the air. The trickling of mortar seemed louder and there was another noise, a slow scraping of brick. She reached the edge of the dividing wall and saw Yvette stepping towards her over the wreckage, the light in her left hand and a box in her right. Maud recognised it, the phoenix rising on its edge, and she felt her rage lift into her throat.

On Yvette's face was an expression of bliss. She showed Maud the open box. The grand stone cushioned by its smaller fellows. 'We have him now, don't we?' Without waiting for Maud to answer she set it down for a moment to relight Maud's lamp then picked it up again. She was about to speak but before she could, there was a sound in the darkness in the outer cellar and a curse. Someone had missed their footing and knocked into the barrel Yvette had moved.

'Get back, and cover your light,' Yvette said in a harsh whisper and Maud crept back again along the wall, sheltering the reluctant glow of her lantern under her coat. She could hear a heavy laboured breathing. Maud's fingers brushed one of the tangle of short railings again and her hand closed round the free end.

'Mademoiselle?' It was Morel's voice, a little slurred but him, without a doubt. He was on the other side of the partition with Yvette. Maud set down her lamp and pulled the railing free. It was very heavy.

Yvette gave a little shriek. 'Oh! Monsieur, you startled me.'

'What? Why are you here?'

Maud shifted her grip on the iron bar. The water was so close. Even if Morel was ill he might still be strong enough to kill them both, but he was not as strong as the water was, whispering to her on the other side of the thin bricks. It had eaten Paris, it should eat him too. It became her ally. He would not think to harm them if he felt it coming for him – he would run. She moved her palm along the bricks looking for the place where the cold pressure was greatest.

'What are you holding?'

Yvette stood frozen in front of him, the box half-concealed in her right hand, in her left the lantern held high. She put her weight onto one hip and made her eyes wide.

'My aunty swears she left a picture here among the rubbish. A landscape, I think, though she can't like it much, otherwise why would she have left it to rot here for years? But today she must save it from the flood. Will you help me, sir? You've a kind face! Let's have a look around, eh?'

His face was grey and sweating; his eyes darted around the room. He saw the empty place where the little round box had been sitting, its cover clearly lit by her lamp. He dropped the candle into the mud and pulled the knife from his belt. 'Give it to me.' He shuffled forward a step.

Maud closed her eyes and with all her strength swung at the wall. The bricks crumbled under the blow and the water leaped out of its confinement in a joyous blast, taking more of the rotten masonry with it.

The noise made him step back, and at once water gushed in behind Yvette; she could feel its frozen force pushing against her legs. She screamed, and while he was still looking at the sudden rush in horror and confusion, she threw the box towards him. The diamonds cascaded out, striking him in the face, and the great stone fell over his shoulder. He half-turned and dropped to his knees, scrabbling in the rushing filth. Yvette ran past him, but his left arm shot out and caught her round her thigh, tripping her into the roaring waters. The lantern flew from her hands, landing and bouncing against the broken barrels. She fell hard on her hands then twisted round to pull her face from the deepening water. 'Bitch!' he screamed and as the lantern began to splutter and fail she watched, fascinated, as he raised his right arm, the knife hovering in the darkness above her.

'Morel,' Maud said, her voice clear above the sound of the water. She uncovered the lantern so he could see her face. He went absolutely still.

Yvette pulled her own knife from her pocket, struggling to get it free under the water. It rushed up her body, splashing into her mouth and eyes, gushing around Morel's thighs as if he were a stone in a stream. She scrabbled the knife free of her soaked skirts and opened the blade under the flow of dirty water.

'Maud,' Morel said in a whisper. Then Yvette thrust up, her thumb on the blade. She felt a terrible resistance then a release as the knife went deep into his chest. He gasped and toppled forwards. She dropped the knife and scrabbled away from him. Maud pulled her upright. He was floating face down in the water.

'My God!' Yvette screamed and reached towards him as if she thought she might be allowed to change her mind. Maud moved her aside and went to him, pushing his floating body into the wreckage and turning him by his shoulder until she could see his face. The eyes were open and sightless.

'He's dead,' Maud said. The water was nearly at their waist. 'We have to go.'

'Oh Jesus, my knife!' Yvette said, dropping into a crouch, feeling around on the floor and spitting the water out of her mouth as it reached her lips and eyes.

'*Now*, Yvette. Now or we're dead too.' Maud grabbed her and began to drag her towards the opening into the main cellar. Yvette reached out one more time and felt something in the water; she managed to get her fingers around it. Maud pulled harder at her shoulder, helping her to her feet against the force of the river racing ever faster to fill its new space. Together they struggled through towards the storage room, and both had to duck under the slapping water to get through the low opening. Maud let the waters tear the lamp from her hand. There followed moments of death, thunder and darkness with their heads underwater and all the lights gone. *Air*. They stumbled onwards – and ahead of them they heard their names being called – then screamed.

Yvette got her arm under Maud's and they moved forward, their hands pushed against the walls to keep their footing. Rats were swimming alongside them, scrabbling up the walls and along the roof over their heads, falling over themselves in their panic. The track of the cellar began to rise.

'Here!' Maud managed to shout. Tanya came splashing to meet them, her lantern held high, the rats swimming past her and up to her knees in water. She reached for her friends, and pulled them over to the ladder.

'Yvette first,' Maud gasped. Tanya nodded and guided Yvette's shivering hands onto the ladder and went up behind her, pushing her onwards and out, shoving her lantern after her. Then she turned back.

'Now you, Maud.'

Maud hesitated. Around her the waters were still lifting and the rats were screaming and scattering into what escape routes they could find; above her was her friend, framed by the patch of wan Parisian sky. She put out her hand and let Tanya drag her out of the darkness.

CHAPTER 22

*I*T WAS SOME TIME BEFORE TANYA COULD PERSUADE
Yvette to move or speak. Like a mother with a child, she
managed at last to persuade her to come over to the water trough
in the courtyard and clean some of the contaminated waters of the
flood from her with the slightly cleaner water still coming from the
old pump. She put her own coat round Yvette's shoulders then
went to Café Procope to beg towels and a messenger to send to
Paul.

With Maud and Yvette as well protected from the cold as she
could manage, she led them the short distance to Paul's rooms on
Rue Racine. The concierge was a friend of Mr Allardyce's so knew
Tanya's name, and on hearing it, and seeing her and her friends,
she put her usual moral scruples aside and took them in. She
brought hot water, blankets from her own store, and soup. Maud
and Yvette let Tanya attend to them. Maud watched her remove
Yvette's filthy clothes and sponge her pale skin with soap and hot
water, dry her and wrap her in blankets then wash the foul waters
from her hair. Then she settled Yvette on the sofa near the fire and
turned her attention to Maud.

It was when she put her head back to let Tanya pour warm
water from an enamel jug over her hair that Maud saw for the first

time the livid bruise on the Russian girl's cheek. She put up her hand to touch it with her fingertips.

'Tanya?'

The girl smiled and shook her head. 'Don't worry, darling. It left me dizzy for a while, but it was nothing to the sickness I felt when I came to and realised that monster had got past me. Don't fret. Sasha and Paul will be here in a little while, and they will make a great deal more of a fuss over me than I have made over you.' She poured another jug of hot water over Maud's hair, lifting the strands apart with her fingers. 'Can you tell me what happened?'

Maud looked over to the couch where Yvette appeared to have drifted off into an uneasy sleep, wrapped in a mound of blankets. 'He found her with the diamonds. He would have killed her if she hadn't been so quick with her knife.'

Tanya nodded, then took one of her towels from the pile and began to rub Maud's hair dry between her palms.

'What is she holding onto so tight? All the time I have been washing her she's kept her hand clenched over something.'

'Her knife, I think,' Maud said. 'She was searching for it in the water. Tanya, when Paul comes, do you think he might collect our things from the room in Rue de Seine and pay the woman? I have silver enough in my purse, I think.'

'Of course, darling.'

Paul did what he was asked, though it took some time before he was reassured that Tanya was not severely injured. Tanya asked him for his trust and he gave it as easily as he had given his love. Sasha had come with him from the church and now mounted a furious watch over them all, seated on a stool by the stove and working her needles, getting up from time to time to examine them all for signs of fever.

As soon as Paul had delivered their bundles, he left again to continue reporting the water's rise. Maud watched his expression as he exchanged hurried goodbyes with Tanya in the open doorway, and thought her friend had as good a chance as anyone of happiness in marriage.

Maud went behind the screen to dress. She slipped her feet into the cold damp leather of her boots and was catching the last of the buttons together when she heard the sound of something dropping to the floor and a low gasp from the main room. She emerged and saw Tanya kneeling by Yvette. She imagined that the knife had fallen from her hand finally as she slept, and that Tanya's sigh was a sign she had found it with Morel's blood on it . . . but when Tanya turned towards her and opened her palm, she was not holding the knife, but the golconda diamond.

'Maud,' Tanya said, her voice tight, 'the knife is still there. When the waters go down, they will find him and it. She carved her name into it. She must get away.'

Maud stared at the stone. Seeing it in Tanya's palm, the way it shifted the light around it, it seemed ridiculous that even for a moment she could have been fooled by the fake she had seen. The diamond had a power and presence to it that could not be described or captured.

She knelt down and closed Tanya's fingers over it. She never wanted to see it again. 'Do you think Yvette might like to come to England with me? We will need papers perhaps, but there will be some time before the waters go down.'

Tanya touched Yvette's forehead and she murmured something in her sleep. 'Yes, yes I do. Oh Lord, yes, I think that would be best.'

There was a light tap at the door and Sasha went to answer it. Charlotte was there looking weary but otherwise just the same. 'I met Mr Allardyce at Saint-Sulpice,' she said before they had even asked the question. 'And he told me where you were. I thought I'd come along and be warm for an hour before going back to the refugees. It seems everyone knows you are here, by the way. There was a woman waiting in the street and she asked me to give you this, Miss Heighton.' She passed her a piece of notepaper. Maud felt her body shiver as she took it. There was no other woman who might be waiting for them there.

It read: *Pont des Arts, an hour.*

Maud passed it to Tanya. 'From Sylvie.'

Tanya glanced at it then looked back at her. 'Maud, you can't go.'

'Of course I am going, Tanya. You know that.'

Tanya clenched her fists in frustration. 'Then I shall come too. Charlotte, will you watch Yvette with Sasha until we get back?'

Charlotte settled herself into one of the armchairs and glanced at the sleeping girl. 'Of course I shall.'

Maud was shaking her head. 'Tanya, please, you have to take care of Yvette. You are getting married . . .'

Tanya had already put on her long coat and was doing up the buttons angrily. 'No, Maud. Don't worry, I shall not interfere. But whatever happens . . . there should be a witness. You will not disappear into that horrible greedy river again with no one knowing of it. You don't know what it was like, just to be told, to be told something like that by a stranger.'

CHAPTER 23

Pont des Arts oil on panel 29.3 × 23.6 cm

Though this also seems to show the Seine in flood, the focus is on the effect of the lamplight on the snow that has gathered along the railings, and the landmarks of Paris have disappeared into the darkness behind it. The mood of the painting is simultaneously one of calm and threat. We are drawn towards an absence in the centre of the frame.

Extract from the catalogue notes to the exhibition 'The Paris Winter: Anonymous Treasures from the de Civray Collection', Southwark Picture Gallery, London, 2010

'Mademoiselle! By all that's holy!' Maud felt a hand on her shoulder. A policeman in gaiters and a short cape was holding her back. She could see Sylvie on the bridge ahead of her, lit by a gas-light on the centre of the bridge. The river roared around her.

'Let me by, I don't mind getting wet.'

'That's your choice, mademoiselle, but the road is unsafe. It falls away under you, look!' He pointed along the quay, to the men building up the embankment in the sullen yellow glow of oil-lamps. The trees fell sideways like drunks, and the lamp-posts had sunk and tilted to their knees, though some were still lit, struggling to do their duty, to lift their lights above the water.

'That woman on the bridge – I know her.'

He turned round, and seeing Sylvie sitting on the railings of the bridge, he swore and blew his whistle till another policeman some twenty yards along the way signalled that he'd heard and pointed towards the bridge.

'Let me go to her,' Maud said.

'We'll go across together,' the policeman replied. 'If one of us falls in a sink-hole, the other one has to try and drag 'em out. You'll be soaked, you know.'

'I don't care.'

Tanya took Maud in her arms and held her a moment. 'You must come back to us, Maud. All will be well if you come back to us.'

The tenderness in her voice made Maud's throat tighten and she found she couldn't reply.

The officer took her arm and together they battled through the dark waters which showed parchment yellow where the light reached them till they reached the steps up onto the bridge. Maud was soaked to her waist and felt as if she was dragging the river up with her as her heavy wool skirt pulled and coiled around her legs. She looked up. There was someone else on the bridge now with Sylvie. Another policeman was standing some yards from her, to the north. He held his hands wide and low like a man trying to urge a dangerous animal back into its cage. Maud and her guardian approached from the south.

'Good evening, Maud,' Sylvie said lightly, though she was still looking at the other man.

'Sylvie.'

'She has a gun,' the officer to the north said, his voice calm but loud enough for them all to hear.

Sylvie nodded. 'Yes, I do. That is true. I do have a gun.' She held it up into the lamplight to show them, clasping it between her two hands, a finger around the trigger, but somehow relaxed. 'Gentlemen, I wish to have some private conversation with this lady. Would you be so kind as to retreat a little way?'

'I shan't leave you with a gun pointing at you, miss,' the man on Maud's side said. She looked at him. He had a kind face, and was probably not much older than herself. There was no sign of fear on him. Only determination. She had a sudden vision of him walking down the Champs Elysées with his girl on his arm.

'Please do as she says,' she told him, and when he hesitated, 'I promise she can't hurt me. Let me talk to her.'

'I don't like it.'

'I know you don't.'

He looked into her face and she met his gaze steadily, evenly.

'If she aims,' he said, 'don't think, just run.' He nodded to his colleague to the north and they both stepped backwards slowly a yard or two, while Maud advanced until she was in the middle of the bridge and facing Sylvie. Morel's wife looked lovely in the lamplight. She was wearing a dark blue dress, close-fitting, with her fur-lined coat open over it. The snow fell silently onto her hair and shoulders, and along the railings either side of her while the river lunged and roared beneath them.

'Aren't you afraid I'll shoot you?'

Maud realised she had never thought of this moment. She had wanted Morel to suffer, imagined him suffering. When she thought of Sylvie it was only in the past. Sylvie walking in Père Lachaise, Sylvie stretched out reading in the drawing room, Sylvie lighting a cigarette and laughing. Sylvie stepping over her body. She looked just as beautiful as ever, just as graceful, as kind. Maud thought of how it had felt when she had rested her head on Maud's shoulder, rested her light weight on her arm.

'How many times can you kill one person, Sylvie? I think if you are holding the gun, the bullets would pass straight through me.'

'Careful, Maud. You'll make me curious to try. Strange. You were such a slight breath of a girl, tiptoeing about. You seem different.'

'What can I possibly fear now?' Maud asked.

The slightly mocking smile fell from Sylvie's lips and she looked sideways and down into the waters surging just below the bridge, their suck and groan as they pushed through the arches, carrying their loot of debris, planks and barrels with them. 'He's dead, isn't he?'

'Yes.'

She nodded and continued to watch the waters while she spoke. 'He shut me in at Rue de Seine – it took forever for the concierge to hear me. I ran out after him, and all I saw was you and your friends being led away from Cour de Rohen. I followed you to those rooms. I hoped perhaps he'd been arrested, but there were no police. I went back to the cellars and saw they were flooded.' She paused as if trying to work out some impossible puzzle and her voice was wondering when she said, 'I couldn't calm him. I could always calm him – but not today. He thought he had seen your ghost, that you were in league with the river and coming to take him. He didn't say "The river is flooding the cellars"; he said, "*She* is doing it – *She* is coming to take them. To take *us*". Oh, I told him he was wrong, that he was imagining it. But he grew nervous when we couldn't sell the diamonds and you began to appear to him. You never showed yourself to me, did you?'

'No. Only him. It was he who threw me in the river like rubbish.'

'Yes, but the plan was mine.'

The words struck Maud in the centre of her being. It seemed to smash some dam inside her – and her feeling was one of release. Grief flowed from her and the river carried it away.

'Have you ever loved anyone, Maud? Other than me? Someone who might love you back?'

Maud shook her head.

'You cannot know then, what it is like to love someone and not be able to save them. The pain of that! It leaves you breathless.'

'I think I do know what that feels like, Sylvie.'

She looked up at her under her long lashes and smiled suddenly, sadly. 'I understand. Yes, perhaps you do.' She lifted her chin and looked along the river behind Maud. 'Paris is beautiful tonight. All this water, the way the light swims in it. Notre Dame behind you, covered in snow. It looks like a palace. Oh Maud! I loved him so very much, my handsome man. It's strange. I knew he was dead before you told me. The moment I lost sight of him as he ran up the street this afternoon I felt my heart stop, my soul just snap out of existence, like turning off an electric light. I knew I'd never see him again.'

The water from Maud's dress was pooling beneath her like an extra, deeper shadow in the lamplight. Sylvie made a noise halfway between a sob and a laugh. 'Such a little thing. A tiny movement of the wrist. A drop more laudanum and you'd have drowned, just disappeared, and he would be alive and we would be happy. Damn it.' She tilted her head back and blinked rapidly, not letting her tears fall. 'I was such a fool! I was afraid you would taste it in the wine. I should have known I could have added the whole bottle and you'd have drunk it all down like a good girl and thanked me.

Always so grateful! So helpful! It made it so easy. I couldn't believe we had found such a sweet fool. And now here you are to judge me. Perhaps you do look like a ghost, after all. Perhaps you are dead. Surely my dear Maud would be leading me to safety by now? But you just stand there and judge. Not like nice helpful Maud at all. Are you real? I'd like to know.'

Maud looked straight into her blue-grey eyes: they were calm, curious. She took in the curve of her waist, the tight cut of her dress across her shoulders, the lace on her chest, the curls of blond hair over her small ears, the single pearl earrings, caught like globes of smoke. 'I am Maud Heighton. You and your lover tried to kill me, but I lived. I told the Countess what you had done, and we stopped you selling the diamonds. I let Morel see me, hoping it would make him mad. And yes, I do judge you.'

Sylvie swallowed, then licked her lips and took a great shuddering breath. 'What a beautiful night this is.' She looked up into the sky. 'Oh, the glory of it! Very well, Maud. You have that right. Judge away.'

She lifted the gun and placed it between her teeth and pulled the trigger. A mist of red appeared in the air behind her. Maud lurched forward, but while the sound of the shot was still cracking in the air, Sylvie's body crumpled and fell backwards into the black waters. The policemen ran forward from either side of the bridge and Maud collapsed onto her knees. The officer who had helped her across, crouched at her side. 'Are you injured?'

She shook her head and he left her. She couldn't breathe. It was as if the air stuck in her mouth. She put her hands on the ground in front of her and tried desperately to make her lungs open and find air. The world swam and quivered around her; whistles blew and somewhere she could hear Tanya screaming. With an enormous effort, she struggled to her feet and ran from the bridge, lurching through the vile waters, until she felt her friends' arms around her again, gathering her up and pulling her free for the second time.

When Paul Allardyce returned to his rooms that night he found they were filled with sleeping women. They had made nests for themselves on his sofa and chairs. His fiancée was asleep on his second-best greatcoat by the stove and her maid snored next to her on an armchair, using his steamer trunk as a foot stool. He crept through them and collapsed on his bed, where he slept dreamlessly in his dirty clothes.

CHAPTER 24

27 January 1910

THE RIVER HAD ALMOST REACHED BOULEVARD Saint-Germain and the cellars were filling on both sides of the street. It was easy for Sasha to deliver some note of pretended appeal to the concierge which sent her a safe distance into Rue Mazarine. Dawn was still an hour away when Maud walked briskly through the hall and up to the first floor. The door was unlocked, as she had thought it would be. One key was still in the cellar in Morel's coat, the other belonged to the concierge and would never leave the ring on her belt. The image of the moment Sylvie pulled the trigger kept appearing in her mind like the pulse under her skin, the explosion of red under the lamplight.

She let herself into the flat and flicked on the electric light. The smashed vase on the floor reminded her of Mrs Prideux. She walked through the drawing room to Christian's room. It was the part of the apartment she hadn't entered before. The bed was unmade, an angry twist of blankets and sheets. His sickbed. His desk was up against the right-hand wall, cherrywood and roll-topped. She pushed it open and began to make her way carefully through the papers. She looked in herself for grief or doubt, for guilt, but could not find anything so simple. She was bruised, hollowed-out, and her heart seemed to beat slowly – an exhausted animal finally allowed sight of home, but not there yet. Whatever she had to feel about the Morels would come later – slowly, she hoped. Home. Not Alnwick, but Richmond or Darlington perhaps. Somewhere honest with wide landscapes. Countryside you could walk through for days on end where the light changed because of the moods of the sky, not the electric glare of Paris. Peace. There she would be strong enough to feel, let these bruises heal. The Quaker families in Darlington had built libraries large enough to keep Yvette happy for months, and James had mentioned there was a lady doctor in town. He seemed to approve of her. If the town could accept a lady doctor they would probably accept a female painter and a Frenchwoman.

She sighed and went back to her task. There was some correspondence – bills for the most part, but there were also the papers she needed: a birth certificate in the name of Sylvie Morel, born 1 January 1888, in Toulouse. She had lied about her age, just a little. Just as she couldn't stop herself thieving just a little under Maud's nose from the jewellery shop. Maud took it and put it in her handbag, along with any other piece of paper with the name Sylvie Morel on it, and then she made a fire in the grate and burned the rest.

After that she went into Sylvie's room, took a pair of suitcases from under the bed and packed them with the dead woman's clothes – the delicate lace underthings, a pale chemise and long white skirts. A dark blue tea-gown, collars and cuffs. She filled the lacquered jewel-box with the loose trinkets scattered on the table-top, fitted in brushes and combs, stockings and shoes. Everything a respectable Frenchwoman might take with her on a trip to England. She would not ask Yvette to wear them, but they gave the proper impression as they travelled, and selling them in London would give them some money. Might they travel a little around England before deciding where to settle?

She thought of the plans Sylvie had been making with Morel: the vision of her pulling the trigger returned and she felt the soreness in her heart. Regret and hope folded their arms around her like twin angels. She took the two suitcases into the hall and checked that the papers in the grate were fully consumed and the embers dark. Suddenly the lights fizzled and went out. She closed her eyes and waited, a ghost among ghosts, to see who might come for her, but there was no sound apart from the gentle fall of the rain against the glass. The power had finally gone in this building as the water wound its way in, that was all. The ghosts were gone. She went back into the hall, picked up the suitcases and left.

Portrait of Madame de Civray oil on canvas 31.7 × 26.7 cm

The warm earth tones of this portrait give it an unusual intimacy, as does the casual posture of the sitter. Note the reflections of light on her evening clothes and jewels. Uniquely among the anonymous paintings in the de Civray collection, this picture has at some point been clumsily re-touched: you can see with the naked eye the uneven patch of colour on the table in front of the Countess. X-rays suggest that this patching was done to cover an egg-shaped white object that lay there in the original. Some have suggested this was the golconda diamond that Madame de Civray had removed from the Empress Eugénie tiara and converted into a pendant at some time before World War I. Her removal of many of the original stones from the tiara was discovered only after her death, and was greeted with horror in France where the tiara had once formed part of the crown jewels. She left no explanation for what some regarded as an act of vandalism, other than a note in the case itself which said only, *It was a fair trade.* The pendant was eventually bequeathed to the Smithsonian Institute in New York, in spite of protests from some French newspapers.

Extract from the catalogue notes to the exhibition 'The Paris Winter: Anonymous Treasures from the de Civray Collection', Southwark Picture Gallery, London, 2010

'So, Tanya, I have come. What do you want of me? Talk quickly, honey, I'm already late.'

The Countess looked around the drawing room in Rue Chalgrin and seemed to approve. The room was lit only by fire and candles, giving it the feel of an eighteenth-century salon. She dropped the furs from her shoulders and took a seat on the sofa, her arm stretched out along the back. Tanya stood to one side of the fireplace, her hands clasped in front of her as if about to recite or sing to the company.

'I want you to leave Maud Heighton alone, and Yvette. I want you to never mention either of them again. Or the Morels. Please do not employ any of your Pinkertons in France or anywhere else to look for them or enquire after them – and if you ever hear of them again, please do not give any sign you know anything of them.'

The Countess's face had grown serious while Tanya spoke. She raised her eyebrows. 'That is a great deal to ask, Miss Koltsova. In light of what has been taken from me, a very great deal. Why should I do this?'

Tanya stepped away from the fireplace and put the stone she had been holding on top of the table in front of the Countess. The woman looked at it, but did not pick it up. 'That is my diamond, I assume.'

Tanya went back to the fire. 'It is, though I do not think you could ever prove it. Not if Henri has done his work well.'

The Countess looked up again. 'And the rest, Miss Koltsova? The other twenty stones Henri chiselled out and gave to Morel? Where are they?'

Tanya could not meet her eyes; instead she stared into the fire. 'No one will profit by them and the guilty couple are dead.'

'I guess you don't want to tell me any of the particulars?' Tanya shook her head. 'That's a lot of diamonds to lose, Miss Koltsova.' There was a decanter of whisky on the table next to the diamond and a glass. The Countess poured herself a drink and continued to stare past Tanya into the flames as she sipped it. She still did not touch the huge diamond next to her. 'Is she here? Miss Heighton, I mean.' She stabbed a finger suddenly onto the table. 'In this building?'

Tanya hesitated and then nodded. 'Yes, she is.'

'So why am I having this conversation with you, honey?' She was looking at Tanya with fierce concentration.

Tanya remembered the maid, the dismissal, how charming the Countess of Civray could be until she stopped trying. 'Because she doesn't like you much any more, Madame, and thought there was a danger she might spit in your eye if she saw you. So I said I'd return your stupid diamond.'

For a moment the Countess was completely still and then she burst into laughter. 'Oh, you girls! God, you kill me.' She wiped her eyes. 'It won't be the first time I've negotiated with people who want to spit in my eye. Tell her – no, please *ask* her – to come in and bring any work of her own she happens to have with her.'

'This is not a negotiation,' Tanya said stiffly.

'Like hell it isn't,' the Countess said and poured herself another drink. Tanya still hadn't moved. 'Please, Tanya, I'd be very grateful if you could ask Miss Heighton to step in.'

Tanya could not refuse her when she asked that way; all her breeding demanded it. The Countess studied the diamond in front of her, watching its colours dance in the firelight until Tanya returned with Maud beside her. Maud came in and stood in front of her, looking, the Countess thought, very much like the polite, thoughtful young English girl she had welcomed into her house before Christmas. She examined her for a while in silence. She liked it when people came to her house and admired her paintings, admired her – and she realised with a slow smile that she was not so sure she liked it when they did anything else. Well, that was one new thing she had learned – and her father always told her that the best lessons were the ones you paid for. Those you remembered.

Maud put a painting on the table beside the diamond and her whisky glass. It was a portrait of Sylvie Morel with her opium pipe. The Countess considered it for a while, thinking hard, and then looked up at the artist.

'Miss Heighton, I'm going to guess a couple of things and you're going to tell me if I'm right or wrong. You are leaving Paris?'

'I am.'

'And I think that model Yvette I am not allowed to ask about in future is going too?'

'She is.'

The Countess sighed and leaned back again, cradling her whisky. 'My father taught me never to come out of a bargain with what you are first offered, and I take his advice very seriously. Now this diamond is here and I'm told this lady,' she tapped the portrait, 'and her brother or husband or whatever he was are dead, so I think I have an idea of what happened. The guilty will not profit, you say, and I don't think you'd be able to look me in the eye if you were taking the rest of the haul back to England.' She saw Tanya glance at Maud, but the Englishwoman made no sign.

The Countess was impressed. 'No – scratch that. *You* might be able to, Miss Heighton, but Miss Koltsova could not.' She drummed her fingers on the table-top. 'Twenty, five-carat diamonds.' She tapped at the portrait again. 'They are worth a fortune. Not as much as this big one, of course, but still a fortune. I tell you what – I'll sell them to you, Miss Heighton. I'll take this picture, and every year for the next twenty years – if both of us live that long – I want you to send me the best thing you've painted. For that you can have my silence. I'll also pass on any rumours I hear that might disturb your peace, and,' she nodded to Tanya, 'I'll give this girl a commission to paint me, and to paint my children. Then I'll tell everyone in Paris what a clever artist she is. How's that?'

Tanya had blushed a little and was looking at Maud hopefully now, but the Englishwoman's voice was even. 'I'll paint something for you, specifically for you, whenever I wish to. I promise I will never do any less than the best I can for you, and you shall have twenty paintings within twenty years if not before.' She paused. 'But for our safety, in case anyone makes the connection between the pictures, the diamonds and what has happened here, I shall not sign them.'

The Countess considered for a second then knocked back the last of her whisky and stood up.

'Deal. You'll go far, Miss Heighton, and I'm glad you're not dead. The world is more interesting with you in it.' She slung her furs around her shoulders again then picked up the diamond and put it in her pocket as casually as if it had been a cigarette-case.

'Miss Koltsova, have that picture mounted on canvas, framed and sent to me, please. So just nineteen to go now, Miss Heighton. Now if you'll excuse me, the Comédie Française are having a candlelit benefit for the flood victims, and absolutely *everyone* is going to be there. Good night.'

She walked out of the room and left them in the glow of the firelight. As soon as the door shut, Tanya flung herself onto the sofa, filled the whisky glass to the brim and drank.

'Oouf! That woman terrifies me!' She looked at Maud and frowned. 'How is Yvette?'

Maud came and sat down beside her, took the whisky glass from her hand and drank her own share. 'She's nervous, but she is willing to come to England and live under the name of Sylvie Morel. I've told her she could give French lessons to the schoolchildren of Darlington if she promises not to teach them to swear. She says it sounds a better future than the one she thought was waiting for her here.' She handed Tanya the glass back.

Tanya looked a little doubtful. 'Darlington is where your brother lives, is it not? Will he approve? I thought you might go to London or the West Country.'

Maud sighed. 'Oh Tanya, if I know one thing I know I can cope with James now, and I want to see Albert, my little half-brother, grow up. I shall remain Maud Heighton so he can always disown me, and London is too like Paris. No air.' She saw Tanya's confusion and put her arm through hers. 'And I absolutely guarantee there are no opium dens in Darlington. Just a great many Quakers. Yvette is giving your Aunt Vera lessons at the moment on the rates models should be paid, which are the best colour shops, and how to get the best prices.' Tanya laughed. 'Will you come to see us in England? When you are married? You will like the North, and however modestly you dress, the whole county will be amazed at your wonderful sense of style and flock round you like moths.'

Tanya took her hand. 'Then yes, I shall. I will bring my husband and my two – no, my three – children and Sasha, and we will leave all the ghosts behind us.'

Maud laid her head on her shoulder and they were still there when Yvette came to find them a few minutes later. She claimed the whisky glass and sat on the floor between them as they told her of the conversation with the Countess.

'You really won't sign them, Maud? The risk is very small, isn't it?'

'Yes, it is,' Maud replied, taking back the glass. 'But I still don't like her.'

Yvette snorted. 'You're buying those diamonds from her in a way, aren't you? A picture for each one.'

'In a way, yes, I suppose I am,' Maud replied.

Yvette twisted round so she was looking up at them both. 'That must make you one of the most expensive artists in the world.' Maud almost dropped her glass and Tanya put her head back and laughed. 'Oh and Maud, I sold that picture of Tanya you did in class to her Aunt Lila. It should be enough for travelling clothes, if you still have enough for tickets.'

CHAPTER 25

28 January 1910

*T*HE WATERS HAD FINALLY STARTED TO RECEDE. IN Saint-Sulpice the refugees continued to warm themselves under the Delacroix frescos, huddled on mattresses, the women trying to quiet the children and the men staring at their hands as if asking where and how they would find the strength to rebuild. Charlotte was folding blankets and organising into neat baskets the different items of clothing that had been donated. In Paris, for a few days at least, it had become fashionable to be generous. The rich cleaned their closets out and congratulated themselves, knowing that the waters were losing their power and would soon slink back, like the poor, into their proper course and continue to serve them.

Charlotte felt their approach and looked up to see two smart young women dressed for travel with handbags in the crook of their arms and folded umbrellas in their gloved hands. It took her a moment to recognise them. She left her station and embraced Yvette, then shook Maud's hand.

'You know what happened?' Yvette said quietly and the older woman nodded.

'You talked enough in your sleep for me to guess, and there have been rumours about a woman killing herself on Pont des Arts.' Her voice sounded deeply tired. 'I do not know what God means by it all. Perhaps He will forgive them at the last, and you, and me for helping you.' She rolled her sleeve up a little to show the flash of the bracelet with the five fat stones. 'What of this?'

Yvette took Charlotte's arm and pulled the sleeve back over it again. 'The Countess is not looking for them. Make sure you get a good deal from one of your shop girls on Rue Royale and build another home for waifs.'

She nodded. 'An anonymous donation? Well, Miss Harris has been concerned about some of the English dancers who perform in Paris. They get paid late and the accommodation the company provides is wholly unsuitable.'

'Well then,' Yvette said, 'it will do more good sheltering them than decorating the Countess, don't you think?'

Charlotte nodded, her round face thoughtful. She reminded Maud of the Spaniard's portrait of Miss Stein. She had the same uncompromised beauty of intelligence and belief, handsome where so many fashionable women were merely decorative. She realised with a smile that recognising Charlotte's spirit in the painting had made her appreciate it a great deal more. Maud shook hands with her again. 'Give Miss Harris our best love and thanks.'

'She will pray for you.'

'I do not doubt it,' Maud replied, and turned to leave. Tanya was waiting for them.

Yvette did not want to say a formal farewell to Montmartre or anyone on it, but she consented to come close enough to say goodbye to Valadon at Impasse de Guelma. Suzanne's farewell was gruff but heartfelt, and she promised to spread the story on the hill that Yvette had found a rich protector and been swept off to Monte Carlo.

'Good luck out there,' she said, shaking Maud's hand then kissing Yvette's pale cheek. 'I know there is a world beyond Paris, but I can't really understand it myself.' Then she whistled into the cold air for her dog and set off up the hill under a white sun and the cobalt wash of the sky.

Vladimir waited by the car, the engine idling, ready to drive them out of Paris and on to solid ground so they could make their way to the coast. 'You could still call me Yvette, couldn't you, Maud? Even if we say my legal name is Sylvie.' Her voice was soft and cold as the snow.

'I will.'

'Are you ready then?' Yvette's voice was firmer now, more like herself than she had been since that moment in the cellar. 'Show me this England of yours.'

Maud turned and looked down the Boulevard Clichy; the flâneurs and thieves, street-hawkers and shop girls, the philan- thropists, chancers and visionaries, the blandishments of Paris wrapped round its dirty, defiant soul. She put her arm through Yvette's and nodded to the chauffeur. He opened the rear door for them and bowed. 'Yes, I am ready.'

EPILOGUE

'The Paris Winter: Anonymous Treasures from the de Civray Collection', Southwark Picture Gallery, London, 2010

Press Release

Since the opening of the exhibition, the Gallery and the de Civray Foundation have been shown sketchbooks belonging to the family of the artist Maud Heighton which suggest that she is the artist behind this remarkable collection of works. Maud Heighton studied in Paris between 1908 and 1910, and afterwards enjoyed a long career as a portraitist in Darlington and throughout the surrounding area. Her reputation as one of the UK's forgotten female Post-Impressionists has been on the rise for some time, and with the addition of these works to her oeuvre it is set to soar. Heighton was successful in her own lifetime, though it is thought that she and her lifetime companion Sylvie Morel supported their comfortable manner of living largely due to the popularity of the novels written by the latter. These were melodramas of the Parisian underworld, written under the pen name 'Yvette of Montmartre'. Her famous book, *The Death of Cristophe Grimaud*, was filmed in 1932 and starred Claude Rains and Janet Gaynor. The two women owned a large house in Darlington, a cottage in Reeth, a villa in the South of France and toured regularly on the continent. Their work is likely now to reach a much wider audience, and the trustees of the de Civray Foundation are delighted to have contributed to the enhancement of their reputations. By arrangement with their heirs, the works of both women, including Heighton's sketchbooks and the manuscripts of Sylvie Morel, are available to all interested scholars who wish to consult them by appointment and subject to suitable references.

Historical Notes

Académie Lafond and all those who teach or study there are fictional but the school is based on Académie Julian which did have premises in Passage des Panoramas and Rue Vivienne and offered expert training to male and female artists, many of whom are household names today. On the work in the Women's Ateliers I recommend *Overcoming All Obstacles: The Women of the Académie Julian*, ed. Gabriel P. Weisberg and Jane R. Becker.

Suzanne Valadon (1865–1938) was a model and painter, friend and muse to both Toulouse Lautrec and Erik Satie and mother to Maurice Utrillo as well as being a great artist in her own right. For an account of her life I recommend *Mistress of Montmartre: A life of Suzanne Valadon* by June Rose. She was living in Impasse de Guelma at the time *The Paris Winter* is set, but her accommodation was cramped so she probably didn't sub-let. Amedeo Modigliani (1884–1920) was in the habit of reciting Dante to her.

For the description of Gertrude Stein's salon in Rue de Fleurus I've relied on her book, *The Autobiography of Alice B. Toklas*. The paintings that Maud and Tanya notice in particular on the walls are, of course, Picasso's.

Miss Harris is also a fictional character, but inspired by Ada Leigh (1840–1931), a remarkable woman who ran a house for penniless English and American women in Paris during this period in

Avenue de Wagram. I have made great use of her short book *Homeless in Paris: The Founding of the 'Ada Leigh' Homes* published privately under her married name, Mrs Travers Lewis. It gives a rare account of destitute women in Paris during the Belle Époque and many of 'Miss Harris's' anecdotes and victories are in fact Ada Leigh's. Her maid did at times lock her out on the balcony so she could get some fresh air.

For all things opium related I am deeply indebted to *Opium Fiend: A 21ˢᵗ Century Slave to a 19ᵗʰ Century Addiction* by Steven Martin, a gripping historical and personal account of opium smoking and addiction.

The best account in English I have come across about the Siege of Paris and the Commune is *The Fall of Paris* by Alistair Horne.

For a non-fiction English account of the flooding of Paris in 1910 I recommend *Paris Under Water* by Jeffrey H. Jackson. I've also drawn heavily on the reporting of the floods in *The Times* and *Le Matin*, and in *La Vie à Paris 1910* by Jules Arsene Arnaud Claretie, though I've occasionally distorted what was flooded when to suit my own purposes.

I think any twenty-first-century woman might fear for her blood pressure reading *The Modern Parisienne* by Octave Uzanne, but it shed a great deal of light on both the economics of women's lives in the period and the unthinking misogyny dressed up as an 'appreciation of the feminine' current during the period. For other views on women during the Belle Époque I recommend *Feminisms of the Belle Époque* edited by Jennifer Waelti-Walters and Steven C. Hause and *Career Stories: Belle Époque Novels of Professional Development* by Juliette M. Rogers.

Many other books of travel and discovery have been consulted during the writing of this novel, but I'd like to mention two in particular: the charming *Paris Vistas* by Helen Davenport Gibbons which includes a great description of the floods and *Magnetic Paris* by Adelaide Mack which includes an account of the New Year celebrations at Bal Tabarin and some wonderful scenes of life on the Paris streets. I also thoroughly enjoyed *Paris à la carte* by Julian Street and made use of his accounts of the different grades of Parisian bars and cafés. All these are out of print at the moment, but you can read them online at the Internet Archive at www.archive.org. You can read *The Modern Parisienne* there too if you are feeling up to it.

As always all mistakes, misunderstandings and anachronisms are my fault and mine alone.